LIFE AND RECOLLECTIONS OF CALCRAFT THE HAN[GMAN]

CALCRAFT'S FIRST INTERVIEW WITH THE EXECUTIONER.

No. 1

The Life and Recollections of
WILLIAM CALCRAFT, THE HANGMAN.

INTRODUCTION.

In presenting the reader with this, the first and only authentic life of Calcraft ever published, the Editor must disclaim any intention of pandering to a morbid taste for the sensational or horrible. He has no desire to cast any heroic dignity upon the gallows, or to shed the splendours of fascinating romance on the paths that lead to it; but from the large collection of notes and memoranda which have been placed in his hands, he hopes to shed a light upon the dark doings of criminals.

A distinguished writer observes it is a mark of the social and public spirit of this nation that there is scarcely a member of it who does not bestow a very considerable portion of his time and thoughts in studying its political welfare, its interest, and its honour. Calcraft, as public executioner, availed himself of this national privilege, and as he passed from youth to age he gave his opinions, noting and commenting upon the events of each day as they transpired. The author quoted above advises those who would distinguish between social good and evil, to repair to the cells of the convict at the midnight hour, with the murderer who is doomed on the morrow to expiate his crimes on the public scaffold. No one had a better opportunity of studying mankind in this way than William Calcraft.

At the very mention of the name of the hangman most persons give an involuntary shudder. This, however, is but a foolish prejudice, and a popular chimera. He is no more than any other man off the stage—on it indeed he is all-powerful, and much to be dreaded. Calcraft lived in portentous times—in days of great national commotion—at a period when it was thought Church and State were in danger of being wrecked on the rock of sedition, and when the Government considered that they had no alternative but to keep the implement of death in constant exercise before the angry rabble, it was no fault of Calcraft's that so many suffered death for offences which are now visited with what is called secondary punishments.

In addition to the documents placed in the hands of the author of this biography, a vast amount of information has been received orally from Calcraft himself. The work will necessarily be a record of the leading events in the lives of great criminals, and will mainly consist of a narrative of facts. Painful and appalling scenes will have to be described, but these will not be conjured up by the agency of imagination. They are the productions of a pen that describes facts as they are found, and will present pure pictures of guilt and its accompaniments. There will be no artificial colouring. The felon will appear just as he is—as crime makes him, as Newgate receives him. Successful crime may be for a season; but arrested, condemned, scourged by conscience, and cut off from society as unfit for its walks, of all the members of the family of man few have been so rapidly forgotten as those who have been swept from the face of the world by the fiat of the law and the hands of the public executioner. Yet these—the guilty and the unfortunate—have left biographies behind them that speak to future generations in awful and impressive tones. If they were inflictions on the past generation of which they formed a part, they may now be made useful to the present age as beacons to the reckless voyager.

We beg of those who have read the distorted and diseased pictures of the gallows school to read the records of nature—not in health, but disease—and of real but guilty life. The sketches introduced into these "recollections" are not from fancy or fable: they are photographs of prisons and prisoners.

As a public functionary, Calcraft's experience extended over a period of little less than fifty years, during which time he was a keen observer of nature, albeit he was not much accustomed to make known his thoughts to strangers, or, I might add, his intimates. Nevertheless, the fifty years of his working life have not passed over his head without his making memoranda of many leading events which occurred during that period.

He exercised his calling when hanging was in fashion. He carried out the last "dread sentence of the law" through all the eventful and stormy periods of the three royal predecessors of our present Sovereign, when criminals of lesser and greater degrees of guilt were tried and condemned on a Friday and executed from three to six in a row on the following Monday, in the presence of vast surging crowds, which, throughout the "live-long night" had been gathering around the scaffold, and in the avenues leading thereto.

The Royal prerogative, of which so much injudicious use has been made in our time, was seldom exercised to save the condemned at the period when Calcraft first became the hangman of Newgate.

George III., who was reputed to be a kindly-disposed humane man, was under the impression that the punishment of death was absolutely necessary as a safeguard to society. Whether he was right or wrong in such a supposition it is not easy to determine; but be this as it may, he acted according to the dictates of his own judgment and conscience.

It is not necessary in this place to enter into any arguments, pro or con, upon the question of capital punishment. As a deterrent from the commission of crime it will suffice for the present to declare that those who have had better opportunities of judging of its effect than the general public are of opinion that it cannot be abolished with safety.

The subject of this memoir, in common with greater and more distinguished public characters, has had a very considerable share of odium and obloquy cast upon him. He has been reviled by a small section of the community, and has been despised by a still larger portion. This is a subject upon which he was particularly sensitive—and on very many occasions during the visits of the writer of these pages, he spoke with much acerbity and bitterness of those journalists whose business it had been to write from time to time sensational and illogical articles upon the punishment of death, and the odious calling of the hangman.

One fact, however, is patent enough. So long as the death penalty is inflicted in England some one must be engaged to carry out the sentence passed upon convicted murderers, and he who is employed for this purpose is in no way answerable or accountable for the acts of his superiors.

In the year 1039 the executioner was mentioned as a person of exalted rank; and even now the sheriff is nominally the executioner, by virtue of his office. The laws relating to capital punishment have of late years undergone considerable modification. This is clearly evidenced by the following tables:—Harrison's "Description of Great Britain," printed in 1577, states that seventy-two thousand rogues and thieves suffered death in the reign of Henry the Eighth—that is, about two thousand a year. By the 9th of George the Fourth, June 27, 1828, the time for the execution of a murderer was fixed for the next day but one from that on which he received sentence, and hence it was that offenders of this class were tried on a Friday—Sunday being a *dies non* in the eye of the law, the benefit was given them of that additional day. This Act, however, was repealed by the 6th and 7th of William the Fourth, July 14th, 1836. In the ten years between 1820 and 1830, there were executed in England alone 797 criminals, but as our laws became less severe, and the death penalty was abolished for offences now punishable only in a secondary degree, the number of executions decreased. In the three years ending in 1840 they were only 62. The place of execution for London was formerly at Tyburn, and it was customary to take offenders in an open cart through the public streets from Newgate to the fatal spot, where the celebrated "triple tree" stood.

Since 1783 malefactors have suffered death in front of Newgate, and of late years they have expiated their crimes within the walls of the prison. The dissection of the bodies of executed persons was abolished in 1832.

A correct history of crime and criminals has long been a desideratum, because much of the history of the times is ever involved in the prevalence of particular crimes and in the career of criminals.

In every age and country since the foundation of society, events have been occurring, of which, though too minute and fugitive for the vast and rapid page of general history, it must be regretted that no record is preserved.

Few who have written on crime and criminals have kept in their view anything but the crime or criminal; and in the holding up of both to the execration of mankind they have seldom sought for those proximate or remote causes which may have led to the commission of crime by individuals, and created whole classes of criminals. Neither has there been at any time a disposition manifested to scan the criminal's character fairly—that is, by comparison connected with the environment of circumstances. In the course of this work this matter will receive due consideration.

Investigation by comparison is the surest road to knowledge. The whole system of daily intercourse throughout the world is carried on by it.

The passing over all the circumstances connected with the exciting causes to the commission of crime is the result of a notion of very general prevalence. It is thought that in allowing crimes to be palliated by circumstances, we lessen the effects of public examples; but whenever it is proper to publish accounts of persons or events, it is always desirable that the truth should be spoken.

It is pretty generally acknowledged that a very natural and absorbing interest is awakened in the public mind in every minute circumstance connected with the crime of murder.

This absorbing interest is but natural, and arises from natural causes; it is shared by the upper classes in common with those belonging to a lower grade in the social scale.

The subject of this memoir has, from the very nature of his calling, been in a position to become the recipient of many dread secrets, which it will be the business of his biographer to chronicle.

It will be his duty to relate many interesting and touching episodes in the lives of many well-known malefactors, and throw a light on much that heretofore was dark and obscure.

With these few brief introductory remarks we will leave the writer to tell his own story.

CHAPTER I.

MY FIRST INTRODUCTION TO CALCRAFT—THE MEETING IN THE OLD BAILEY.

BEFORE touching on the birth and parentage of my hero, together with the causes which led to his being appointed public executioner, it will be as well to give the reader a succinct account of my first visit to this celebrated functionary.

In April, 1870, a proposal was made to me to write the life of Calcraft. One great difficulty—which appeared at the time to be an insurmountable one—stood in the way. How was the necessary information to be obtained? I was duly impressed with the fact that Calcraft had been importuned by all sorts of people to furnish them with something like a brief chronicle of his life, and that in every instance he had invariably refused to give the smallest scrap of information relative to his private or professional career. He was described to me by those who professed to know him as an obstinate, self-willed old man, who had a great repugnance to being questioned about anything connected with his past experience. The answer the officials at Newgate gave me when I asked for his address, and stated my object in seeking him, was, "that they were quite sure he would not even entertain such a proposition; no golden key would unlock the door that led to the secrets of the prison-house."

I soon found out that the accomplishment of my project was beset with obstacles and difficulties, but despite this I did not despair. I was fortunate enough to obtain the desired address, and lost no time in seeking an interview.

Calcraft resided at the time in Pool-street, Hoxton, in the same house in which he breathed his last a week or two ago. When I waited upon him I was accompanied by a friend. We arrived at a house of no very great pretensions, as far as external appearance was concerned, but it was neat and clean, and, in its general features, was much the same as those occupied by the working class.

The door was opened by a young female, who, we afterwards learnt, was Calcraft's granddaughter, who informed us that he was at home, whereupon we were ushered into the front parlour, a small but neatly furnished comfortable apartment enough.

In a minute or so a stout, burly man, with grey hair and whiskers, entered the room. His manner was by no means conciliatory, and the flash of his dark eyes seemed to indicate that he was in no very agreeable or amiable frame of mind. A few sentences sufficed to explain the object of our visit—whereupon his countenance became still more dark. Without a moment's hesitation he gave a point blank refusal, saying, at the same time, that numbers of persons had asked him to give them the particulars of his life for the purpose of publication. One gentleman in particular—an author of celebrity—expressed his willingness to give any sum he chose to demand for a brief chronicle of his past career, but he would not entertain any such proposition, and declined, in the most positive manner, to give him any information upon the subject; "neither did he intend to do so—not to anybody."

I pointed out to him that his life would certainly be written, that I had received an order to do it, and suggested, at the same time, that it would be much better for him to furnish me with the necessary data and material, to insure something like a faithful chronicle of his professional career.

He hesitated for a few moments, and then said he "was just at that time in the depths of trouble, for his poor wife was dangerously ill—so ill, indeed, that she was not expected to live."

Upon making this declaration he became deeply affected, and shed tears. As the reader will doubtless readily imagine, both myself and friend were quite unprepared for this display of feeling, which was not simulated, but evidently genuine; in fact, he appeared to be completely broken down with grief and sorrow of the most poignant nature, and it seemed at that moment to be hardly right to importune him further.

The conversation, however, was continued, and ultimately Calcraft agreed to meet me on the following morning at a well-known hostelry, which was situated immediately opposite the Sessions House in the Old Bailey.

Having extracted this promise from him I, in company with my friend, took my departure.

At the appointed time, nine o'clock in the morning, I entered the house in question, and inquired of the landlady if she had seen anything of Calcraft. The answer was in the negative. Upon my informing her that he had appointed to meet me, she said—

"Then he is sure to be here. He is a man of his word. He will be here unless his wife is worse—she is very seriously ill."

Shortly after this Calcraft entered with a large bouquet of flowers, gathered from his own garden—so he said—which he presented to the landlady, with whom he was evidently on the most friendly terms. He turned round and addressed himself to me, saying—

"Well, as I have passed my word to you, I won't now go from it—so we had better go into the parlour, and you can take down a few particulars to begin with. As you go on I will give you more."

His tone was cheery, and he appeared to be altogether in better humour than he was on the previous evening. He gave me that morning as much of his history as the time would admit of, and on subsequent interviews further material was furnished, all of which I duly noted down. The facts thus obtained from the lips of Calcraft himself, together with much valuable information from other sources, form the basis of this remarkable biography.

William Calcraft was born at Chelmsford, in the year 1800. He was the eldest of twelve children. His parents were in poor circumstances. His father was proud of him, and his mother made him her darling son, ever watchful, as other tender and loving mothers were then, and are now, over the footsteps of his childhood.

Like many other children of the lower hard-working classes, he was sent to a free Sunday-school, where he received a small modicum of instruction in the first rudiments of the plainest education. He was taught to read and write, and imbibed, at the same time, a little of the Wesleyan principles of religion, and often sang, with the rest of the scholars, Watts's simple hymns.

But beyond what he then acquired, he never afterwards had the opportunities of higher-placed and more fortunate little ones, and the education he received was but a slender and imperfect one.

Like many more, he was too early exposed to the trials and struggles which the poor invariably experience. He came to London while yet a lad. His brother was a ladies' shoemaker, and sometimes he did odd jobs for his brother, but never regularly followed the trade of a shoemaker, although there is a general impression that he was apprenticed to that trade. This is, however, a mistake. At one time he was porter in a large brewery establishment—at another he was a butler to a gentleman at Greenwich.

The first years of his working life were by no means happy ones, and the premature loss of both parents did not in any way tend to forward his onward progress. Nevertheless he struggled on, and when out of regular employment he took anything that offered to obtain a temporary subsistence, being in no way particular as to what he turned his hand to as long as he was able to earn his living honestly.

In those days he is reported to have been a remarkably smart, active young man, full of life and animal spirits; of later years the term morose can with justice be applied to him. This, doubtless, has been occasioned by the obloquy that has been cast upon him by virtuous individuals who think it the correct thing to shudder at the very name of the public executioner.

At the age of five-and-twenty he married—his wife being five years older than himself. His wedded life, from all I can gather, was one of unclouded sunshine. He was a devoted and loving husband for upwards of five-and-forty years. Mrs. Calcraft died between seven and eight years ago.

The loss of his amiable partner seems to have been an inconsolable one. Calcraft was never the same man after her decease. This may appear strange to those persons who have been accustomed to picture to themselves the subject of this memoir as a sort of ogre —a being altogether separate and distinct from the ordinary run of mortals. Such a supposition is, however, erroneous. Calcraft throughout his life was a plain-dealing man enough, with his hopes, fears, feelings, and wants, like most other members of the great human family.

In domestic life he proved himself to be a loving

husband, an indulgent father, and a decent well-conducted citizen.

The odious calling, as it has been termed by sapient critics, chance presented to him in the first instance, and necessity afterwards compelled him to follow throughout the greater part of his life.

How he first became appointed to the office of public executioner will form the subject of the succeeding chapter.

CHAPTER II.
THE EXECUTION OF JOSEPH HUNTON, THE QUAKER, AND THREE OTHERS AT THE OLD BAILEY—CALCRAFT'S INTERVIEW WITH THE HANGMAN.

JOSEPH HUNTON, the Quaker, convicted of uttering forged bills of exchange, was condemned to death. The day appointed for the execution was the 8th of December, 1828.

The unhappy man had moved in a respectable sphere of life. He was a gentle-spoken, quiet, unobtrusive person, but, like Fauntleroy, he, to repair his shattered fortunes, had recourse to forgery—a crime which in those days was punishable by death.

The reader would be surprised to learn the number of malefactors who suffered at one time for this offence.

Previously to the withdrawal from circulation of £1 and £2 Bank of England notes the crime of feloniously passing forged notes of small value was by no means rare throughout this country.

It is calculated that in 1817 the number of forged notes in circulation was 31,180. In 1820 the number of persons arraigned at the Old Bailey alone for this crime was 154, of whom 43 were executed, and in the year preceding the number was more.

By the then existing law all persons to whom forged notes might be traced were liable to be placed on their trial as the actual forgers, unless they could produce indubitable evidence of their innocent possession—that is, of having received the notes through the hands of others, in the legitimate course of business.

The facility with which persons of address and respectable appearance could pass small notes, held out an almost irresistible temptation to the idle, extravagant, and profligate to commit the crime.

There is now little doubt that numbers of young men fell into this crime, to supply the exigencies of the moment, who would not otherwise have appeared in the criminal calendar.

The persons prosecuted for this offence were for the most part young men, of extravagant habits, belonging to the middle class of society.

As the public in general had no test afforded them by which they might distinguish the genuine note from a forged one, it might have been expected that many careless persons would have come under a suspicion of guilt who actually had innocent possession.

Awful as was the period between 1812 to 1820, in reference to the number of lives sacrificed for the commission of this offence, and the vast mass of distress which was in consequence spread through many respectable branches of society, yet there is no reason to suppose, either on the face of the cases themselves, or from anything that has subsequently come to light, that many erroneous or even doubtful convictions occurred; but the law was harsh enough in all conscience at the time to which reference is made.

Hunton's offence, however, was of a grave character, and so from the time of his sentence up to the fatal morning no hopes were entertained of pardon or reprieve.

In those days the exercise of the prerogative of the Crown was rarely carried out.

The ill-fated Quaker, therefore, prepared himself to die.

Three others were to suffer on the same scaffold with him—the names of these being James Abbot, John James, and Joseph Mahony.

Doubtless numbers of persons in the lower walks of life were more or less interested about the three last named, but Hunton was the central point of attraction, and people of all classes debouched from various parts of the metropolis and its environs to see the "Quaker" hung.

Throughout the greater part of Sunday night, and ere the early hours of the fatal morning, groups of persons were to be seen bustling along towards the appointed place. On no previous occasion had a larger multitude assembled to witness a similar spectacle.

Many, as happened at the execution of Fauntleroy and others, took their places at the windows and upon the roofs of the houses opposite the front of Newgate, which they had previously engaged and paid for, whilst the immense space in the Old Bailey, surrounding the scaffold, was crowded to suffocation, the mob extending in a solid mass from the barrier at the end of Fleet-lane, opposite the felons' side, to the end of the Old Bailey in Ludgate-hill.

On the north side of the scaffold the populace was, if possible, more dense, and reached as far as Cock-lane, at the end of Giltspur-street, which was lined on each side with carts and waggons, to which the curious were admitted at a given sum.

Ah! strange love of man for all that pertains to death! Hundreds stood there and gazed on the gallows for hours without turning their eyes away.

It is the night before the execution. There were lanterns placed at intervals of several yards down the whole length of the street. Dark shadows might be seen flitting round these lights; the harsh sound of iron striking against stone rose in the air.

Workmen were busily occupied in fixing the barriers round the scaffold.

At the Ludgate-hill end of the prison there was a yard surrounded by a high wall. The door of this yard was open; lights trembled in its mysterious depths; a group of men and women stood near it; a constable stood at each side of the door.

Occasionally men carrying large wooden bars and posts passed out. These, planted in the ground, were formed into a barrier, that the mob might be kept at a certain distance from the scene of the execution.

Gradually the group in front of the yard increased into a crowd; they clung closer together, and peered over each other's shoulders into that black space, from which indefinite sounds were raised, and which was guarded so vigilantly by its two sentinels.

The curtain of night, which hung like a funeral pall over the scene, soon began to disappear, and the few first shades of dawn were visible in the horizon.

It is morning. The crowd thickens. The salesmen of hot potatoes and coffee take their departure. Their places were supplied by men who offered wares of a different description, vending them with a peculiar cry. These were broadsides and penny sheets, containing the lives and confessions of the notorious offenders who were about to suffer. Some affecting verses, said to have been composed by Hunton, were recited in the usual nasal twang of street-sellers. These were offered at the small price of a penny, and found ready purchasers. They emanated from the prolific press of Catnach, of Seven Dials.

Several peals of laughter were heard, these proceeded from a group of persons at one of the windows of the opposite houses. This unseemly merriment was caused by the contorts of a basket of buns carried by one of the itinerant venders of such dainties being upset, and a scramble taking place for the possession of the same.

Some swells from the West-end, with two or three *femmes galantes* from the Haymarket, had hired the first floor front of one of the houses for the purpose of seeing four men pay the last penalty of the law.

The swells and their female companions had been beguiling the tedious hours of the triple tardy fatal night by sundry p tations; the females are lolling on the shoulders of their male companions, as is the custom with these delicate creatures. The roughs in the street proceed to chaff them most unmercifully.

"Does your mother know you're out?" said one. "Leave us a lock of your hair afore ye go!" observed another.

A number of stereotyped utterances of a similar character follow in quick succession, and the half-inebriated swells retired behind the curtains of their apartment.

"Now, then, missus—where are you shoving to?" said a rough-looking man to a woman who carried a baby in her arms. "Yer ought to be ashamed of yerself to bring a hinfant like that to see four coves turned off."

"You mind your own business, and let the woman alone. She's as much right here as you have," cried a little man by her side.

A wordy warfare ensued, but the woman keeps her position.

A man dressed in a suit of black was busily engaged in distributing tracts, one of which he handed to the costermonger.

"What's this?" says the latter; "an order for the theatre or a ticket for soup?"

This sally evoked roars of laughter from those around.

"Read it, my friend—read it at your leisure," said the tract-distributor.

"My father and mother never taught me to read, you fool," returned the brute.

"I hope Jem 'ell die game," said a burly man, in a hairy cap and fustian jacket, "and not give way at the last moment."

This was in allusion to the condemned man, James Abbott.

"Never fear," whispered a woman, who stood by his side. "He aint one o' yur chicken-hearted ones. Poor boy! and to think he should have to end his life thus —so generous and kind-hearted too."

The speaker began to cry.

"Now, then, don't ye be a fool," said her companion, sharply.

Up to this period, and for some time afterwards, the crowd was of a festive character. Jokes were freely bandied about, and loud laughter was ever and anon heard proceeding from those who were gathered round the grim and solemn apparatus of death.

Some lads were endeavouring to climb up one of the lamp posts, and no doubt one or more of them would have succeeded, had not a rough-looking man pulled them down, much to their discomfort.

"Shame!—let the lads alone!" cried a woman in the throng. "They aint done anything to you."

"You hold your jaw, and mind your own bisness, missus," replied the man. "If you'll take my advice you'll step it."

All sorts of voices issued from the crowd—some condemned the attempt on the part of the lads, some censured their assailant.

"Go it, youngsters," cried a voice from the crowd. "Try again, never mind him—he's nobody."

One boy got on the shoulders of a companion, and by this means reached the top of the lamp post, shouting out triumphantly.

The crowd rewarded him with three cheers.

Another lad, in his attempt to ascend, slipped down, and in his descent knocked off with his foot the hat of a bald-headed old gentleman.

The assembled multitude literally screamed with laughter at the playful little incident. It is most extraordinary what trifles move a London crowd to merriment.

The old gentleman whose hat had been knocked off bore it with the greatest good temper. Perhaps it was fortunate he did, as otherwise a free fight might have followed.

While all these little incidents had been taking place, and a thousand more which it would be tedious to describe, a short active man, with a pair of dark restless eyes, had been threading his way through the crowd, to many of whom he had been selling pies. This man was William Calcraft, who had availed himself of the assembled multitude to earn a few shillings.

Let us enter the prison and see how it fares with the condemned men.

Hunton had composed his mind to meet his fate. He had been visited on the Sunday by several ladies and gentlemen of the Society of Friends, who were accommodated with an apartment in which they remained in their peculiar devotions for several hours. At night he was attended by the elders of the congregation, who sat up with him in the press-room all night.

During that time he composed a long prayer, appropriate to his situation and approaching death. He copied it out and directed it to his dearly beloved wife. At about half-past seven o'clock the two elders left him, after they had "kissed."

About fifteen minutes before the awful hour of eight, Mr. Under-Sheriff Tilson and Mr. Under-Sheriff Richardson arrived at the prison, preceded by their tipstaff and were conducted by Mr. Wontner to the press-room. At the end of this gloomy apartment was seated the ill-fated Hunton, at a long table strewn with papers and books, and immediately opposite sat his "friend," Mr. Sparkes Moline. Hunter, turning his head and observing the group of officers as they entered the room, said, "I pray thee, stop a minute; I'll not be long." He then concluded reading, in a distinct voice, the prayer he had composed in the night. It was couched in the most impressive and devout language that can be imagined.

Mr. Moline, when the unhappy man had done reading, bowed his head and responded "Amen." Hunton then arose, and folding up the piece of paper in a hurried manner, said, "I am quite ready." Mr. Wontner approached him, and said he might remain seated for a short time longer. He thanked the worthy governor, and resumed his seat at the table.

During this time John James, aged only nineteen, who was condemned for a burglary in the house of Mr. Witham, the solicitor, in Boswell-court, was brought into the room, attended by the Rev. Ordinary. He appeared very penitent, and said he sincerely hoped for mercy at the Throne of the Almighty.

The next that entered was Mahony, for a similar crime. This unhappy man also seemed sensible of his awful situation. Abbott was the next led into the room.

James, who had fixed his eyes upon Hunton, left his seat, and, placing himself at the table, looked steadfastly upon Hunton, who, upon observing his vacant stare, said to him—

"Well, friend, hast thou been up all night?"

"No," said James, "I slept a little."

"Ah!" replied Hunton, with a sigh; "I have been up all night. Place thy trust in Christ, and thou wilt be as happy as I am."

"I do, most sincerely," said James; "I hope it is all for the best."

"I hope so," observed Hunton.

Hunton was indulging in a sort of reverie when Mr. Wontner tapped him upon the shoulder. He instantly stood up and deliberately took a white stock from his neck, and approached the officers.

When the officer was in the act of tying his wrists, he said—

"Oh, dear, is there any necessity to tie the cord so fast?"

The officer made no reply, upon which Hunton said—

"Well, thou knowest best."

He again complained of the cord being too tight about his arms, and it was slackened a little. After he had been thus secured, he said—

"Wilt thou allow me to wear my gloves?" and with some difficulty he put them on, and still kept the prayer addressed to his wife in his hand.

The mournful procession began to move on in the following order—the Rev. Dr. Cotton, James, Mahony, Abbott, and, lastly, Hunton.

As the time drew nigh the crowd became a little more orderly. Around the scaffold, and far beyond it, a sea of upturned faces was visible. The sonorous clang of St. Sepulchre's bell tolled, ushering in "thee, thou fell destroyer, Death."

Then, as if by presentiment, the coarse-minded and callous among the throng on the outside of the prison ceased their jests, and then followed one of those mysterious intervals of silence which sometimes fall upon great crowds.

The bell continued to toll. It was the knell of those who were condemned to die.

The prison door opened slowly. One of the gaolers stood in the portal.

Then the people cried with one voice—"Hats off!" and thousands of heads were bared and thousands of faces upturned. One would have believed that it was a performance at the theatre they were witnessing.

The Rev. Dr. Cotton approached with an open prayer-book in his hand, the sheriffs in their robes, the officers of the gaol, the hangman, and the condemned.

A regiment of city officers encircled the gallows with their halberds.

A trembling ran through the crowd, which resembled the waves of the sea beneath the first blast of the north wind; this was followed by a murmur like that of the waves when the wind lashes them into wrath.

The unhappy man, James, was the first to ascend the platform, and, walking to the railings, he then said in a loud voice—

"Good people, I acknowledge what I am brought here to die for. My sentence is just, and may God forgive me. Take warning by my dreadful death in the prime of my life, and may God bless you all—farewell."

He then submitted himself to the hangman.

Mahony next followed, and then Abbott. Hunton was now summoned by the officers. He turned round, and, delivering the prayer to Mr. Moline, each shook each other's hand and kissed lips, the unhappy man observing, "You may say I am quite happy and comfortable. Fare thee well."

He then quickly ascended the steps with the same unbroken firmness and deliberation which marked his conduct throughout the trying period. He took his station under the fatal beam, and requested that a blue handkerchief, to which he seemed fondly attached, might be fastened over his eyes.

The hangman passed a strap round the feet of each of the condemned men, and secured them with horrible deliberation. He tied the handkerchief over the face of Hunton, and drew a white cap over the faces of the others; then he disappeared beneath the gallows.

For an instant Hunton and his companions stood motionless upon their open tomb.

The bolt was withdrawn from below, a black chasm opened beneath their feet, there was a frightful crash, the bodies swung round, and vibrated in the air.

Then commenced those struggles which many assert are merely muscular and involuntary, but which are sickening to behold.

A loud shriek came from some person at the close of the melancholy scene. The sufferings of the unhappy men were but brief. The rope by which Hunton was suspended was longer than the others on account of his remarkably low stature. When it had reached its full tension he appeared to die instantly. Mahony and James struggled a few seconds only.

Throughout this terrible scene the crowd had remained comparatively quiet and orderly. No one attempted to move from his or her position. All present seemed to be wrapt and spell-bound. When, however, the last lingering spark of life had fled from the bodies of the sufferers, those immediately around the scaffold began to converse in hurried whispers, and comment on the day's proceedings.

Calcraft, who had remained motionless and silent during the execution, now began to ply his calling. He threaded his way through the crowd, and began again to sell his pies to those who had appetites to eat them or the pence to buy them. A man with a can of beer, from one of the neighbouring public-houses, was busily occupied in dispensing Barclay and Perkins's entire to the thirsty souls who were craving for that exhilarating fluid. Under ordinary circumstances, the celebrated old Tom Cheshire would have officiated as executioner on this occasion, but for some special reason—illness, it was said—he was not able to attend, and was therefore constrained to find a substitute. The name of this personage, Calcraft informed me, was Foxton, a man unknown to fame.

It will be as well to give the reader an account of Calcraft's interview with the hangman in his own words.

"You want to know how it was that I became engaged in my present occupation," said Calcraft. "Well, I'll tell you. Trade was bad with me—in fact, I could not get anything to do. Being in no way particular what I turned my hand to to earn money, as long as it was honestly got by, I attended the execution of the Quaker, and sold pies to the people round the scaffold. While the four men were hanging lifeless, I saw their executioner come out from beneath the gallows. He appeared to be weak and faint. Poor chap! he wasn't up to his business, and was evidently a good deal flurried, or may be he was a bit frightened, for it was a mob on that morning, and no mistake. I stood within a few yards of him, and heard him call to the beer-man, who did not appear to take much notice; so I made so bold as to go up to him, and said, 'If you want a draught of porter or ale, say the word and you shall soon have it.'"

"Can you get some?' said he.

"Certainly, I can; what's to prevent me? Only say the word—"

"Well, see what you can do; bring it me here."

"Upon this I hastened at once to a house on the opposite side, and got a pint of porter, which I handed to him as he stood underneath the steps of the gallows. He drained off the largest portion, and handed me the remainder, which I refused."

"Ah, that's it—is it?" said he, "too proud, I suppose, to drink with a hangman."

"I aint proud at all," I answered, "but may be you'd like the remainder yourself in a few minutes. I can get what I want—as much as I like over the way —but just to show you that you are mistaken I will drink with you, and so here's better luck to both of us."

"I s'pose you can do with a little?"

"With what?"

"A little better luck!"

"You never spoke a truer word, my friend. Things have gone precious hard with me of late. Had not this been the case you would not see me selling pies on a morning like this."

"Umph! and you are not altogether a bad sort, I should say," returned Foxton.

"I aint afraid of work, and don't much care what sort it is. Now I'll tell you what I'll do, if you've no objection."

"What may that be?"

"Well I'll take to your line of business when you give it up."

"What! turn hangman," asked he, in a tone of surprise.

"That's it."

"Ah, you don't mean what you say."

"Indeed but I do. Never was more serious in my life. I do mean it."

"You haven't any idea what you will have to go through. It's a miserable calling—a wretched, despicable occupation."

"Never mind that. I tell you I'll take to it if I have the chance."

"Well you'll soon have the chance as far as I am concerned, for I tell you I'm sick of it, and mean to turn it up shortly."

"If that be the case speak a good word for me. Will you promise me that?"

The hangman hesitated, and looked hard at me.

"You're a rum un," he said, with a short laugh.

"Am I?"

"Well, I think so, making a bargain with me beneath the scaffold, and wanting to take to my line of business. You are a rum un, but since you seem so anxious, I will pass my word to speak for you if ever an opportunity occurs, but you must give me your name and address."

"All right," says I. "That's soon done," whereupon I pulled out of my pocket one of my business cards.

"In the shoemaking line—eh?" says he.

"I'm in any line, I tell you, so long as it brings in something to support myself and my wife."

"Oh, you are married?"

"Aye, surely, to as good and kind a woman as ever broke the bread of life."

"What will your old woman say? Does she know you want to take my place?"

"How can she? I didn't know myself half an hour ago—never dreamed of such a thing."

"Oh, then it's a sort of sudden fancy come over you all of a minute, I s'pose."

"Well, you see," observed Calcraft, addressing himself to me, "I thought there was a bit of a sneer in Foxton's last observation so I did not make any answer to him. I never for a moment believed he was serious or intended to speak a good word for me to the authorities. It wasn't natural to s'pose so, taking all things into consideration; but to say the truth, matters had run so cross with me at that time that I thought it just as well not to lose such a chance. Any occupation would be a sort of godsend. Foxton was a rough plain-dealing sort of chap, and I thought he had taken a bit of a fancy to me. In this I was not mistaken; leastways if I am to judge by what followed."

"He kept his word then?" said I.

"Aye, he did so, but you shall hear. I didn't part with him immediately. We had a friendly gossip for some little time after this. He told me a goodish bit about the wretched men who had been turned off that morning. He said Hunton was a quiet, mild-spoken, gentlemanly chap, and he seemed to pity him, as did many other persons. It was hard lines for a poor devil to suffer death for putting another man's name to a bit of paper, but it was the law of the land in those days, and there was no getting away from it. When I left Foxton I said, 'Look here, guv'nor, ye won't forget the promise you've made to me this morning.'"

"I will not," he answered, offering me his hand. "I've passed my word, and that's enough. If ever an opportunity should occur of my doing you a good turn, I shan't miss it."

We then parted.

My head was a little in a whirl that morning as I wended my way homewards. The more I thought over the matter the more strange did it appear, and to say the truth, I half regretted having spoken to Floxton upon the subject at all, but it was too late to go back, and I therefore made up my mind to leave the matter to chance, being at that time still under the impression that nothing would come of it. When I got home I said to my wife—"Well, missus, I've had a bit of a game this morning—and I then up and told all that had occurred."

"Law, never! she ejaculated. "You turn hangman! How came you to think of such a thing? Oh, it is not a nice business to say the least of it."

"To say the truth, I don't think it is. But never mind, old girl, it won't come to anything."

"Well, I hope not."

We were, however, both mistaken.

CHAPTER III.
THE MESSAGE FROM NEWGATE—CALCRAFT'S FIRST INSTALLATION.

SOME months passed over, during which period I had not seen or heard anything of my strangely made acquaintance on the morning of Hunton's execution. I had almost forgotten the matter.

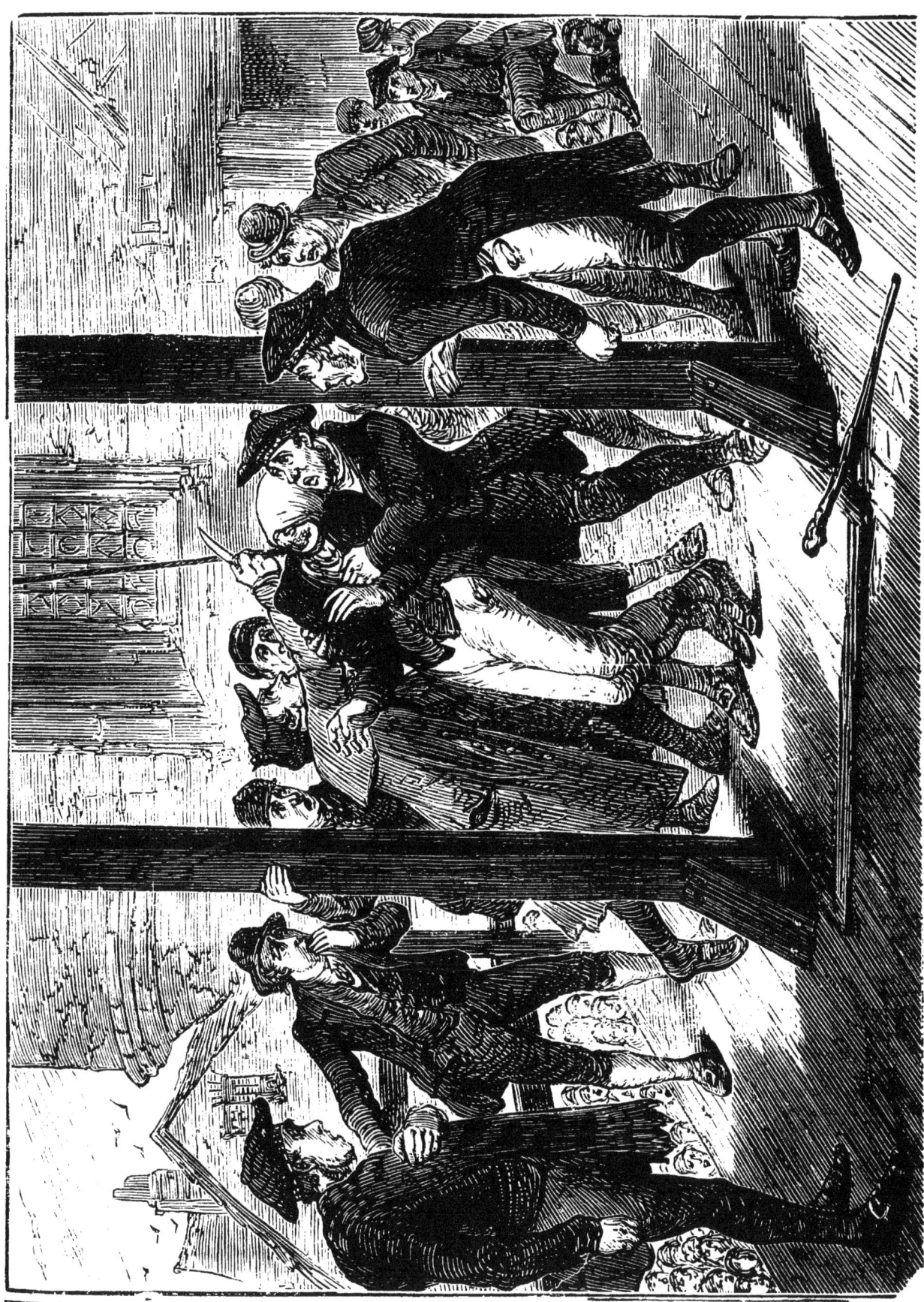

SHOCKING SCENE AT THE EXECUTION OF JOHNSTON.

However, one morning, much to my surprise, a stranger knocked at the door and inquired for me. Upon my asking his business, he said that he had been sent by one of the under sheriffs, with a request that I should present myself at Newgate on the following morning.

I of course promised to be there at the appointed time, ten o'clock, on the morrow.

The missus was in a rare state of mind when she learned who the messenger was, and his object in calling. She was, however, of opinion, as well as myself, that I ought not to go from my word, and so on the morning in question I made as good an appearance as circumstances would admit.

My wardrobe was very limited, and the garments were not by any means of a costly description, but I contrived to be clean and neat, and punctually at ten I presented myself at the little gate, crowned with spikes, which guards the entrance into the prison in whose walls and in the front of which I was destined to play so conspicuous a part in the mournful dramas of criminal life.

Upon my stating my business the gate was slowly opened and I passed into the entrance hall. In a moment or so I was shown into a large gloomy-looking apartment, in which were seated round a table a number of gentlemen. I did not know at the time who they were, but learnt afterwards that they consisted of the governor (Mr. Woutner), one of the under-sheriffs, and several aldermen.

They were all of them pleasant-looking, agreeable persons enough. One of them, who sat at the head of the table, and who appeared to be a sort of top sawyer, addressing me, said—

"Your name has been mentioned to us by—ahem!—by Foxton—the public executioner."

"Yes, sir," I answered; "I'm much obliged to him."

"Well, I suppose you've no objection to make yourself useful? Do you think now that you could flog two or three boys?"

"I don't know, sir, but I will try."

"And do your best?"

"Yes, sir."

There was some little consultation among the gentlemen, after which the first speaker said—

"That will do for the present. Be here at eight o'clock to-morrow morning, when you will receive all the necessary instructions."

I bowed, and retired.

The foregoing account of Calcraft's interview with Foxton, and his first visit to Newgate, I have endeavoured to place before the reader in his own language, much the same as it was detailed to me.

After his interview with the gaol committee, he regretted having been so outspoken to the hangman; but like many other men, both before and since, he was hurried onwards through the force of circumstances.

Whatever faults he may have—and we are none of us without some—he has been throughout his life particular in keeping his word.

A promise once made William Calcraft was not likely to break it, and so, although it was repugnant to his feelings at the time, he presented himself at the Old Bailey on the following morning, for the purpose of receiving instructions in his new calling.

He was informed by one of the warders of the prison that he had to flog four boys.

A few instructions in the flogging-yard sufficed to make him understand the part he was to play, which he did not for a moment shrink from performing.

He proved himself to be so well adapted for the office that, after the punishment had been duly administered, he was engaged by the authorities for that purpose on all future occasions.

The sum he was to receive was ten shillings per week. This was his fixed salary.

Foxton at this time had not resigned the office of public executioner, neither did he retire from his post till some fifteen or eighteen months after Calcraft's engagement.

The latter, however, was present at several executions, and had an opportunity, as assistant to Foxton, of seeing how they were carried out.

During this period he became acquainted with Read, Hancock, Ruthven, Waddington, and other celebrated thief-takers of Hatton-garden Police-office.

He had frequent opportunities of seeing the master hangman on the platform of the gallows, of observing the surrounding crowd with upturned faces watching the proceedings now in breathless silence, so intense that you might hear a pin drop, and now amidst confused murmurs, jibes, and jeers, the hoarse blasphemous murmurings of men, the screams of women, young and old, who have passed so many hours at the barriers below the gibbet that they might not miss one lesson of the dreadful business of strangling a fellow-creature, and feasting their eyes upon the contortions of unfortunate wretches in the agonies of a dreadful and ignominious death.

All these sights he saw, and by degrees he became callous to their awful significance.

During the period of what might be termed his noviciate, he saw enough to fully impress him with the painful and onerous duties of a public executioner.

He had heard much from Floxton of the dreadful scenes that had taken place on the scaffold, one of which, although of minor importance to others which had been made known to him, he himself witnessed while acting as an assistant to Floxton.

CHAPTER IV.

CALCRAFT ENTERS UPON HIS OFFICIAL DUTIES — HIS DESCRIPTION OF THE INTERIOR OF NEWGATE.

As I have already stated (observed Calcraft), I was asked by the civic authorities if I could flog two or three boys. I was, of course, quite a novice at the business; but there is an old saying "that you don't know what you can do till you try," and as I had undertaken the task there was no help for it, but for me to do my best.

When I arrived at the flogging-yard I felt a little nervous, being afraid I might make some mistake; four young ruffians had to undergo the punishment. The mode of operation had been already explained to me by the prison officials, and I got through the task in a way which seemed to be altogether satisfactory to those who were present during the infliction of the punishment, which I have always maintained is both salutary and efficacious when administered judiciously to young ruffians, who, as a rule, dread the lash more than a lengthened term of imprisonment.

I soon found out that it was very rare indeed for a sessions to pass over without a batch of juvenile delinquents having to be flogged. But the days are altered since then, and now other modes of punishment are substituted in lieu of flogging. I am free to confess that I did not like the lash at first, but in a very short time I got used to it, and looked upon flogging as part of my duty.

Foxton had informed me that he would be compelled to resign, as he was in a bad state of health, and would be unable to go through his duties much longer. And it was intimated to me that I was to succeed him as public executioner.

On the following sessions a number of persons were condemned to death, and at Foxton's suggestion it was arranged that I was to be present when the last final act of the law was carried out in front of the gaol of Newgate. By this means it was expected I should be able to learn something about the dreadful business which I was destined to follow for so many years.

One of the convicts who had been sentenced to death conducted himself in such an extraordinary manner that many believed him to be a maniac.

The ordinary, Doctor Cotton, was so anxious about this man that he reported his case, when to his astonishment he was told that it was feigned, in the vain hope of escaping death.

The governor and surgeon were both of this opinion, and observed that such artifices were of frequent occurrence. The ordinary, however, was a dissentient, and he was very uneasy at having such a man to deal with, mixed up as he was with so large a body of doomed malefactors.

Still, notwithstanding this, he continued his visits several times a day till the report came down, when it was his duty to attend at the unlocking of the cells one after the other, with the other functionaries, and to announce to each felon the determination of the council.

The imagination cannot picture to itself the awful gloominess of these passages, visited at such an hour and on such an awful mission.

The condemned yard—or, as it was formally called, the press-yard—was once the "Phoenix Inn," in Newgate-street.

This inn, being near to the Newgate prison, was pulled down for the purpose of enlarging it, and on its site those present tombs of the living were erected. When it was first taken in it was considered as part of the governor's house, who derived a good income by exacting large sums of money for the prisoners he accommodated there.

Those who desired the privilege of a few yards of space to walk two or three abreast were compelled to pay twenty guineas, besides a weekly payment of a pound or more for the accommodation of part of a dirty bed in a place where there were fewer cubic feet of air than of human flesh.

The press-yard took its name from the custom of conveying there such prisoners as refused to plead when placed at the bar, there to be pressed by having a board laid on their bodies with a continual addition of weights till they either consented to plead or died under the insupportable pressure.

The cells of Newgate, when I first made the acquaintance of its interior, comprised three rows of stone building, the front being in the press yard adjoining the chaplain's house in Newgate-street.

The cells were eight feet long by six feet wide, and I was told that formerly it was the custom to lodge three and sometimes four persons in each of these; the accommodation for them being a rope mat, such as is used for wiping the feet on, and one common stable rug, with an iron candlestick for the use of the inmates. This was the mode of treatment in the olden days, but much better and more humane arrangements were made for the accommodation of prisoners in my time.

The walls, floors, and roofs, are all of stone, with a hole through the front wall three feet thick, which hole is barred across, so as to be almost closed, leaving very little space for the admission of light.

In these places the unhappy men used to remain confined from dusk till daylight during winter, and in the summer from dusk till eight o'clock the next morning. At the extremity of these cells were two large rooms, for the use of the prisoners during the day, called wards.

The entrance to these cells was a narrow dark staircase, with darker passages running at the back of each row of cells, into which the strong door of each cell opened. The way to the press-yard from the entrance of the prison was through narrow, devious passages, intersected with and defended by numerous doors of great strength, and an efficient number of turnkeys to open them for ingress and egress.

The only communication prisoners had with their friends was across a narrow passage, terminated by iron bars, between which was a turnkey to see and hear all that passed.

Murderers, women, and very young children were not removed to these cells immediately after a verdict of guilty was pronounced. Murderers were, and are now, confined in a cell set apart for that purpose, and were heretofore executed in a few hours after their sentence —the law said within four and twenty hours, but now it remains with the authorities at the Home Office to fix the day of execution. A separate place is also assigned for women under sentence of death.

Threading their way through the cold and cheerless passages, preceded by two turnkeys, each carrying a lantern and a huge bunch of keys, accompanied also by two sheriffs, the governor of the prison, and four or five strangers, brought by the sheriffs, whose curiosity excited their desire to behold the wretched men receive the messenger of certain death, they all arrived at the outer door of the cell staircase as St. Paul's great bell announced the hour of midnight.

There were seventeen to be informed of their release from the dread of death, and five to hear that the day was fixed for their execution.

Among the latter was the pretended maniac, who had every day since his conviction been gradually getting worse, and exhibiting symptoms that his malady —if malady it was—had increased rather than diminished.

His cell was first opened, the turnkey having the list in his hand, and with the aid of the light in the lantern, called over the names of those who he knew to be in it. Three half-naked, attenuated, pallid figures rose before us.

"Wake up, M——n; he's at his old tricks," called out the senior turnkey.

After some time he was forced from his mat on his knees, in which attitude he began to strike in every direction. The light, however, when thrust into his face, attracted his attention.

He was the only one in the cell unrespited.

As might be expected, every effort was made to impress on his mind the awful communication which was about to be imparted to him; but all was of no avail; he only contorted his countenance and then huzzaed as well as his feeble lungs enabled him.

The other three, at the ordinary's bidding, placed themselves on their knees, and mechanically muttered after him a few words of thanks to the Lord for their deliverance from death.

I may say mechanically, for during this, to them, awful crisis of their fate, one had his tongue thrust in his cheek, while the other winked, and actually punched his companion who was by his side.

Closing the door, they proceeded to the next cell where there were two who were left for execution, and two respited.

One of the latter, when he heard of his escape, exclaimed—

"There, Tom, I've won that wager. I thought the beggars couldn't hang me. Be jiggered if I didn't!"

To this, as is supposed involuntary expression, one of the doomed malefactors answered with an oath—"That 'they,'" meaning the council, "were a set of bloodthirsty murderers," while his companion, who was to suffer with him, muttered as he laid himself down, something about "That it was foolish to wake people up to bring bad news—the morning anyhow would have been time enough for that."

The next cell entered contained a malefactor who had been condemned for forgery, and who had inveighed so loudly against the practice of hanging. He was one of the unhappy number doomed to suffer.

He heard the news with more composure than was expected, while at the same time he bit his lips and clenched his hands, indicating signs of bitter agony of mind.

The usual forms of commending the condemned to prayer and repentance, and the respited to thanksgiving, having been gone through in each cell till the whole number of criminals had been seen, they were again securely locked up and left to their own thoughts.

For all useful purposes for conveying an idea of these scenes (says Calcraft) that were so common at the outset of my career, the above short sketch may suffice.

It made a deep impression on me at the time, but, like all other impressions during my long years of service, it soon wore off, and I afterwards took very little notice of sights which would, in the ordinary course of things, blanch the cheeks of one unaccustomed to deal with criminals.

The feelings of many of my readers would be shocked by my repeating the language or explaining the conduct of prisoners who were ordered for execution, and who are the first to take offence at the anxiety of the chaplain and others to imbue them with religious sentiments.

The law, they think, is their natural enemy as well as every one connected with its administration. After such a visit as I have described passionate joy, wild despair, jealousy, envy, hatred, and the utmost brutal rage all reign at one time in these dreary places.

Although a minister knows that not an instant should be lost in offering counsel to those who are soon to be led to the scaffold, yet the following morning is the most inopportune time to carry such a design into practice. Dr. Cotton, the ordinary, has often made this remark.

At the usual hour in the morning the cells were opened, and the prisoners were all assembled in the yard; and an hour afterwards the doomed men were desired to stand on one side, the others being arranged in a row apart.

Presently a turnkey made his appearnce, calling out—"Respites to the north side" (the transports' yard), and away they were marched through the press-yard gate to their destination, leaving those who were to be executed looking, only at that moment, in consequence of their comparative situations, upon the others as liberated men, and internally cursing and profanely denouncing those who have made the distinction.

Many in the outside world (says Calcraft) who have no experience in matters of this sort have declared that it is a mistake to suppose that the punishment of death has not half the terrors people have been led to believe.

My experience—and it has been a long one—teaches me that it is looked upon with so great a dread that all other punishments are as nothing in comparison to it.

It is not the time for the minister to approach the condemned when they have just been separated from their more fortunate companions.

They have but just been aroused from a broken slumber, in which the hangman, like a huge spider, has been crawling about them.

They stand half awakened out of the hideous sense of what is to come.

They are still dizzy, with a dull head, and heartache. A leaden weight hangs over their eyes—the tongue is feverish and parched. Their frames are overwhelmed with a sickness of soul only known to themselves.

The eye takes a hasty glance at the walls and *cheveux de frise* with which they are surmounted, in a vain resolution of the moment to effect an escape.

The sickness of despair overwhelms them, and their eyes look wistfully on the pavement, as if to implore the earth to open and swallow them up.

Despair and desperation alternately seize the half unconscious minds, rendering them unfit even for the mockery of sympathy.

How shall an honest divine treat such a condition of humanity?

His best course is to appeal to their manhood, and mildly reprove their cowardice. He ought at first only to attempt regularity and decency of behaviour; if he aims at too much at once he will only make hypocrites of them. No one understood this better than the Rev. Dr. Cotton.

It will not be necessary for me to dwell much longer on these particular cases. Three of the malefactors were stolidly ignorant and brutally obstinate, denying the right of the law to deprive them of life—a feeling their more educated companions had been mainly instrumental in bringing about; the other appeared to be insane from the period of his condemnation, and although every attempt was made to bring him to a sense of his situation it proved ineffectual.

The fifth—the forger, as he styled himself by profession—after one of the most heartrending interviews with his wife and three children perhaps ever witnessed, lapsed into something like imbecility of mind, and occasionally sobbed like a child, and again at intervals rallied to an apparent firmness—periods employed in vituperating those whom he considered to be the cause of his death.

There can be no doubt that a long period of agonising suspense destroys more or less the powers of the mind, and hence little reliance can be placed on the accounts given to the world of the condition of the mind in which those who suffer on the scaffold leave their sublunary state of existence.

After much anxious exertion to perform an onerous and sacred duty, the ordinary was called on to officiate at the last scene of this public tragedy.

And as it was my first initiation (says Calcraft) it naturally enough made a great impression on me.

At half-past seven the Irishman was brought forward to be disencumbered of his irons; whilst these were being hammered off a knife was inquired for to cut some part of the cordage which confined the irons on which the wretched man stooped, and with superhuman strength tore them asunder with an effort which nothing but an agony of feeling could have effected. The other three having undergone the same preparation, the man who was said to be a maniac was brought out, when he commenced dancing and calling out "I am Lord Wellington!" clapping his hands, and distorting his features in the most horrible manner. This he continued all the way to the scaffold, and when there, ran up the steps with great rapidity, continuing to dance and kick in a most violent manner, apparently to amuse the spectators.

Two men were engaged in holding him while the remainder of the awful ceremony of adjusting the rope was performed. Scarcely had the platform fallen when, to the astonishment and awe of the people, he rebounded from the rope, and was seen dancing by the side of the ordinary.

The executioner then mounted the scaffold, and pushed him off, and in this manner did he render up his soul.

Since that time I have myself had accidents of similar nature occur while officiating as public executioner (says Calcraft). It is impossible, however careful a man may be, to avoid mishaps.

My experience has taught me, that whenever the law in cases of death is chargeable with cruelty or carelessness in executions the public will invariably sympathise with and decide in favour of the malefactor.

When the condemned themselves see the law about to be executed in the teeth of injustice they triumphantly appeal to the public and screw their resolution up to go to the drop with the courage of martyrs in the cause of a principle of justice.

Although the seventeen evil-doers, loaded with equal or greater weight of guilt than the five ordered for execution, were spared in the name of the prerogative of mercy, it could not but have the effect on the public and the sufferers that an act of injustice in their cases had been perpetrated.

The council in no instance made public the reasons which actuated them in the selection, merely ordering for exection those who were to suffer.

The impression on the public during these times of hanging appeared to be that the Government dared not have the temerity to go beyond taking the life of a certain number of criminals.

It then naturally followed that all who were executed were looked on as sacrificed, while those on whom the letter of the law was not executed felt all the effects of malice defeated.

I may here remark that some malefactors possessed in an extraordinary degree the power of mind, when accumulated adverse circumstances surrounded them, of setting them at defiance, and when inevitable, as in the case of being orde ed for execution under the law, they had even courted them.

Those were brought under the influence of Christianity, when waiting the day of execution, were generally in excellent health compared with the scoffers. The former retained their appetite and slept soundly. On the contrary those who were contending with themselves in a rebellious spirit, generally had a variety of morbid appearances.

It was the ordinary's invariable practice to watch every case of committal for capital offences, and to visit the accused as early as possible after his actual entrance into the prison. His manner of addressing them was peculiarly original. He had always in view the object of leaving no impression that he had paid them a visit intentionally or designedly.

This course he adopted that it might not be thought that he anticipated a judgment of death or appeared to prejudge their case before they came to be as convicted malefactors in the regular way under his religious *surveillance*.

Having read in the police courts of any examination for a heavy crime he usually left word at the office that when the party was brought into prison he should be informed of their arrival, so that on the following morning at prayer, as the prisoners came in or went out of the chapel, he might be made acquainted with his prisoner.

Every day after service it was the ordinary's custom to visit every yard and ward in the prison, so that his appearance on any more extraordinary occasion than usual should not excite any particular notice.

In the course of this work we shall have to give vivid descriptions of criminals of every degree, and it cannot be concealed that from the very nature of the subject scenes on the scaffold must of necessity have a place in its pages, but it is hoped that the reader's attention will be arrested by other and more touching portions of Calcraft's history and experience.

He had now become a noviciate and regular attendant at Newgate, and an attendant also at the executions which took place in front of that prison.

His nerves were a little shaken while witnessing and assisting at the administration of the final act of the law, very shortly after the one he has already so graphically described.

We subjoin a description of the scene.

On Tuesday morning, March 24th, 1829, Thomas Birmingham, twenty-one, Joseph Redgard, twenty-three, and William Kelly, twenty-one, for highway robbery, and Charles Goodlad, twenty-two, for stealing a large quantity of plate in the dwelling-house of his master, were executed in the front of Newgate.

There was a great crowd, one half of which were composed of females. A little before eight o'clock the under-sheriffs arrived, and when the reporters were admitted into the press-room Birmingham and Kelly were already there attended by the Rev. Mr. Rolfe, a Roman Catholic clergyman, to whom they paid great attention.

Birmingham advanced first to lave his arms pinioned, and addressing Mr. Wontner, said—

"Can nothing be done for this poor fellow (Kelly)? He was drawn into it, and should not die."

Mr. Wontner said that no answer had been received from Mr. Peel, and nothing could be done.

"I am sorry for it—very sorry," said Birmingham. Then turning to Kelly, who was quite a youth in appearance, he said, "Don't cry, Bill—be a man."

With the utmost coolness he then held out his arms to be pinioned, and appeared more intent on Kelly than himself.

Kelly was next tied, and then Redgard was brought in by the Rev. Mr. Cotton. He was quite firm, and when the necessary ceremony was performed took a seat by the side of his two companions.

In the pause which occurred before the entrance of Goodlad, Redgard said to the under sheriffs—

"I hope, gentlemen, they will be merciful to poor Crawley (an individual recently committed on a charge of being concerned in the same robbery), and at least spare his life. He did not ill-use the gentleman, nor did he assist in the robbery."

Birmingham directly said, "No, no. He never knocked the man down; it was I threw him down over my legs, and I deserve to be hanged."

Goodlad was then pinioned in silence, and the melancholy procession moved forwards towards the platform, the culprits attended by the Rev. Mr. Cotton, Mr. Baker, and the Rev. Mr. Rolfe.

Birmingham first ascended the platform, and was instantly greeted by a vast number of girls of dissolute character in the mob, who most indecorously called out, repeatedly—

"Good-bye Tom! God bless you, my trump."

By his own request the cap was not pulled over his face till the other three were ready. Kelly was scarcely able to stand, but Redgard and Goodlad were very firm and composed. They all had their neckerchiefs tied over their eyes, and appeared to join fervently in the prayers of the rev. gentlemen who were on the scaffold.

Before the usual signal could be given the drop fell, and at the same instant Birmingham made an attempt apparently to gain the firm part of the platform by throwing himself forward. The rope twisted round and was brought directly under his chin, in which situation he struggled horribly.

The shrieks and groans, intermixed with cries of "Shame," &c., from the crowd were terrific. It was quite impossible to remedy the dreadful occurrence, and for at least three minutes the exertions of the executioner underneath did not appear to have the slightest effect in lessening his sufferings, which must have been horrible.

Several times were his arms raised convulsively, as if with the intention of catching hold of the rope, but the effort was of course futile, and at last all was quiet. The others, with the exception of Goodlad, died without a struggle, but he appeared to suffer slightly.

In the course of Monday Birmingham acknowledged to have been concerned in upwards of thirty robberies. He had lost an eye in a desperate fracas a few months before his conviction.

This case created much excitement at the time, and the subject of our memoir was very seriously concerned at the appalling nature of the proceedings. In conversing with Foxton and others upon the subject he was informed that although the scene was a painful one, it was trivial indeed, compared to many other cases.

The execution of Johnston, the pirate, was of such an appalling nature that it caused a thrill of horror to run through the country, and the memory of accumulated horrors witnessed on that fatal day had not died out even at the time of Calcraft's first introduction to the scaffold.

Foxton would frequently revert to the case, which to say the truth, appeared to have made a deep impression on him.

Johnston's execution took place in Scotland many years before the one described above, but as it possesses a more than usual amount of interest I will relate the leading circumstances.

CHAPTER V.
EXECUTION OF ROBERT JOHNSTON.

THE circumstances with which this execution was attended excited the public mind in a much greater degree than their importance would at first seem to warrant; but on reflection we are forced to admit that everything which is truly and obviously abhorrent to human feeling will make an immediate and strong impression, and that everything which touches the fair administration of the laws ought to make a lasting one.

The temporary interest which has been so strongly felt is thus accounted for, and the proceedings involve so many serious legal principles, and suggest so many lessons of policy and expediency, both to the legislator and the administrator of the laws, that it will not be wonderful if they shall be found to possess an interest of some permanency.

Since they took place we have had account upon account, and pamphlet upon pamphlet, and yet it is by no means certain that the public are satisfied that they have had enough.

The first publication is rash and intemperate, without displaying much talent, but it proceeds evidently from one who had just witnessed the revolting scene, and some allowance must be made for excited feelings, and some credit also given to the writer for possessing them.

The second pamphlet on the same side, if not from the same author, has been written obviously because it was thought it would sell, but without consideration or ability.

The two letters on the other side are as obviously written with the view of giving the discussion a political turn, of which it had nothing in the outset; and for the purpose of creating a diversion in favour of our city executive; but they are both so virulent and so utterly destitute of talent, and one of them in particular of common sense, that they must have injured the cause they were meant to defend.

Into these wretched polemics we have no desire to enter; but we may mention, as a curious circumstance, that the account which has made the greatest noise was written, as we have been informed, by a gentleman who holds political sentiments directly the reverse of those which have been imputed to him, and that his writings on the subject at all arose from the accident of being confined by indisposition to a room which commanded a complete view of the whole unhappy and disgraceful proceedings.

But being thus compelled to be a witness, he found it impossible to resist being also a historian; and it was perfectly natural that anything which he wrote at the moment should be coloured by his lacerated feelings.

The most valuable publication, which has yet appeared on the subject, however, is the letter to the Lord Advocate of Scotland—a tract which is written in a decided tone, certainly, but so far as we can judge in a fair spirit, and which at the same time displays an extensive legal knowledge, and considerable force of reasoning.

But that our remarks may be understood, it is necessary to give some account of the circumstances. In doing which, however, we shall endeavour to separate opinions from facts, assuming those to be correct which have been specially stated by the different eye-witnesses, and not denied in the statement from authority.

Johnston, the miserable culprit, was the son of parents in Edinburgh, who had always preserved a reputable character.

As to himself, it is understood that he became what is known by the term of a low blackguard, occasioning much sorrow to his relations, and at last committing the crime of highway robbery against Mr. Charles, candle-maker and merchant, councillor in Edinburgh.

No great address appears to have been displayed by Johnston and his two accomplices, Galloway and Lee; nor was the crime accompanied either with such aggravated circumstances as could prevent his being a fit object for pardon.

His life, however, was justly forfeited by the laws of Scotland, and there was nothing in his case to excite any unusual degree of attention or commiseration.

The same remark, however, cannot be made as to the place of execution.

Criminals had at one time been executed without the walls of the city, and not far from St. Leonard's, the situation assigned in the "Tales of my Landlord" for the residence of David Deans and his family. At another time the place of execution was on Leith Walk, and for a long time it had been in the Grassmarket, the widest street in Edinburgh, and one which is now least of a thoroughfare.

For some time previously to the removal of the old gaol, the executions took place upon an elevated platform, which communicated with the prison, and which formed the roof of a building connected with it.

No criminal, however, had been executed since the removal of the old Tolbooth and all the buildings connected with it, and as it was rumoured that Johnston was to be executed in front of the library rooms belonging to the Faculty of Advocates and Writers for the Signet, petitions and remonstrances were made against this to the magistrates by the inhabitants of the Lawn-market and by the Society of Writers, and the measure was also previously objected to in the public prints, and other places for execution were suggested.

The gibbet, however, as was originally intended, was fixed in or to the west wall of St. Giles's church, and the scaffold rested on that venerable cathedral.

The apparatus, it is said officially, was prepared by a skilful tradesman, and was inspected and certified to be fit for its purpose by the surveyor of public works.

But, however this may be, the distance between the beam and the scaffold, which has not been positively stated in feet and inches, was supposed by various spectators to be too limited.

To the scaffold, such as it was, Johnston was brought out on the 30th of December, 1818, and placed on a quadrangular table erected upon it, which was intended to answer the purposes of a drop.

He walked from the gaol, and took his station on the table with firmness and composure, paying much attention to a silk handkerchief, which is said to have been the gift of the girl with whom he had lived.

This handkerchief, when removed from his neck, he anxiously secured about his person; he displayed some reluctance to allow the rope to be secured round his neck, and from the changing countenance and the convulsed state of the muscles, it was plain that his courage had given way.

He gave the signal for his fate, however; but through the culpable negligence of those concerned a minute nearly elapsed before the table could be forced down, and even when that was accomplished it was observed that his toes rested on the scaffold.

This was more than human patience could well suffer. It is quite certain, we think, from all accounts and circumstances that there was nothing preconcerted on the part of the multitude, nor even a disposition to commit an outrage.

We have heard it said, indeed, that some sailors and ropemakers had a pique at the hangman from his having been one of their fellow-craftsmen, but this is probably a mere rumour; and all agree in this, that no sympathy beyond what will always be felt for the last throes of a human being was felt for Johnston.

But without speculating further on the causes we shall now give the results, first, from the eye-witness pamphleteer, and secondly, from the eye-witness correspondent of the Scotsman:—

"I turned my back upon the scaffold, and was about to withdraw, when a person who stood next to me exclaimed, 'Good God, the man's feet are not off the scaffold!' I turned round, and it was so! He stood upon the platform; a partial compression of the windpipe occasioned by the sudden jerk, insufficient to cause death, but sufficient to cause exquisite agony, convulsed his whole frame, but did not appear to have destroyed or suspended his mental powers.

"For thrice he bent his legs upwards, evidently on purpose to accelerate the termination of his sufferings. Still he touched the platform; he made several attempts to assist in his own strangulation, but did not succeed.

"During all these efforts at self-destruction, unutterably horrible, you, magistrates of Edinburgh, stood passive.

"Archibald Campbell was the first man to call out for carpenters to try and get the wood below the table cut away. When they came they were at least ten minutes smashing with axes, and could make no impression on the machinery.

"The wretch remained convulsed in very fibre, till the movement of his limbs attracted the attention of the immense crowd assembled. The moment they perceived the awfully protracted tortures of the unhappy man one spontaneous burst of indignation resounded from the Parliament-street to the Castle-hill. Then followed a pause, still as the stillness of death, for a few seconds; but when they saw the protracted sufferings, and did not perceive any attempts to relieve them, another shout arose, but it was accompanied with expressions of indignation, natural to a mob when they imagine themselves neglected, especially if they have been pleading the cause of humanity. A shower of stones aimed at the scaffold accompanied the second expression of popular indignation, and

"What was your conduct, gentlemen?" (addressing those who officiated). "You deserted your posts; you fled for refuge, like convicted criminals, to the church as a sanctuary; instead of doing your duty, you rushed into the Tolbooth Church. You left scaffold, criminal, all to the mercy of the mob. You left your officers without a man to direct them; without counsel, without advice, without a head. When you had fled, when you had deserted your posts, a gentleman, who had observed the ineffectual struggles of the malefactor to rid himself of life, and relieved the generous, though rude, feelings of the spectators, by cutting the man down; and here I desire you to remark (you were too much terrified to observe it, but I insist upon your looking at it) one of the noblest traits of a Scottish mob. When they obtained their end they were satisfied. A cry of 'no rescue' showed the sense the people of this country entertain of the supreme obligation of the law, and there was no mischief done beyond the breaking of a few panes of glass in the church, where you, gentlemen, had taken refuge. Thus far, gentlemen, I saw."

What follows is from the other eye witness mentioned:—

"The populace then took possession of the scaffold, cut down the unhappy man, loosed the rope, and, after some time, succeeded in restoring him to his senses. They then endeavoured to bear him off, and had proceeded some way down the High-street when the officers of police, who had, in the manner above-mentioned, abandoned their posts of duty at the scaffold, proceeded with bludgeons to assail the individuals who were about the half dead man, of whom they at length recovered the possession.

"A spectacle now presented itself which equalled in horror anything ever witnessed in the streets of Paris during the Revolution.

"The unhappy Johnston, half alive, stripped of part of his clothes, and his shirt turned up, so that the whole of his naked back and upper part of his body was exhibited, lay extended on the ground in the middle of the street in the front of the Post-office. At last, after a considerable interval, some of the police officers, laying hold of the unhappy man, dragged him trailing along the ground, for about twenty paces, into their den, which is also in the old cathedral.

"Johnston remained in the police-office about half-an-hour, where he was immediately attended by a surgeon, and bled in both arms, and in the temporal vein by which the half-suspended animation was restored; but the unfortunate man did not utter a word.

"In the meantime a military force arrived from the Castle, under the direction of the magistrate.

"The soldiers, having been *ordered to load with ball*, were drawn up in the street surrounding the Police-office and place of execution.

"It was now within thirteen minutes to four o'clock when the wretched Johnston was carried out of the police-office to the scaffold. His clothes were thrown about him in such a way that he seemed half naked; and while a number of men were about him, holding him up on the table, and fastening the rope again about his neck, his clothes fell down in such a manner that decency would have been shocked had it been a spectacle of entertainment instead of an execution.

"While they were adjusting his clothes the unhappy man was left vibrating, upheld partly by the rope round his neck and partly by his feet on the table. At last the table was removed from beneath him, when, to the indescribable horror of every spectator, he was seen suspended with his face uncovered, and one of his hands broke loose from the cords with which it should have been tied, and with his fingers convulsively twisting in the noose.

Dreadful cries were then heard from every quarter. A chair was brought, and the executioner having mounted upon it, disengaged by force the hand of the dying man from the rope.

"He then descended, leaving the man's face still uncovered, and exhibiting a spectacle which no human eye should ever be compelled to behold.

"It was at length deemed prudent to throw a napkin on the face of the struggling corpse.

"The butchery—for it can be called nothing else—continued until twenty-three minutes past four o'clock, long after the lamps were lighted for the night, and the moon and stars were distinctly visible.

"How far it was consistent with the sentence of the Justiciary Court to prolong the execution after four o'clock is a question which the writer cannot answer, but the fact is certain that it was continued until nearly half an hour after by the magistrates at the head of a military force."

We also subjoin the material part of the official statement:—

"Though from the nature of the crime and the hardened guilt of the criminal there would be no anticipation of any attempt to interfere with the sentence of the law, yet no fewer than one hundred police officers were put upon actual duty, and one hundred and thirty more were kept in reserve.

"Thus every step that human prudence could devise was taken, and the sentence of the law would have been executed in the usual manner, if a lawless mob had not stepped forward to prevent it, under pretence, as is now said, of showing humanity towards the criminal.

"The state of the fact certainly is that, notwithstanding the pains that had been taken to have the apparatus perfect, the rope was found to be too long—a fault alone imputable to the executioner, who has since been dismissed on that account.

"Hence, upon the criminal being thrown off, his toes touched slightly the drop below.

"This, however, was capable of being remedied in a few seconds, and the carpenters in attendance were immediately put upon that duty, and while in the act of removing the drop the mob threw in a shower of stones, and wounded several of them.

"The criminal was also wounded by one of the stones to the effusion of his blood.

"The police officers endeavoured to preserve order, but after several of them had been severely wounded, they were driven in upon the magistrates by the pressure of the very great and unusual crowd that had assembled, and the whole party were then forced into an adjoining church.

"Meantime part of the mob continued to throw stones, and destroyed nearly 200 panes of glass in the church, while another party cut down and carried off the body of the criminal.

"The police officers in reserve now came forward, cleared the streets, and got possession of the body, which was carried into the police-office, where a surgeon, without any order from a magistrate, opened a vein with the view of ascertaining whether the criminal was dead.

"He did not bleed, but shortly afterwards showed signs of life. By this time one of the magistrates had gone to the Castle, and brought down a party of the military, and the apparatus having been put up again, it became the duty of the magistrate to carry the sentence of the law into effect, and accordingly, within the period mentioned in the sentence, the criminal was again suspended, and hung till he was dead."

On the facts contained in these statements various legal objections have been stated to the second suspension of the criminal. He had been out of the custody of the legal authorities; he had been bled or resuscitated; he had suffered a species of torture not contemplated by the law; and, as some writers think (the writer of the letter to the Lord Advocate among the rest), he could not legally be subjected to any new torture, especially as it is understood he was not cut down till after the hour fixed by the sentence of the criminal court.

To that court, however, or at least to the Crown lawyers, it is said the magistrates of Edinburgh ought to have applied after recovering possession of the criminal.

It is a maxim of law, that if death be unlawfully inflicted the consequences are the same, whether the person who suffers it be innocent or criminal, and that the guilt is the same whether it be inflicted by an ordinary subject or a magistrate, unless, in the latter case, it be done in the strict legal execution of his duty.

"Thus," says our ablest writer on criminal law, "if a magistrate shall burn a convict whose sentence is to be hanged upon a gibbet; or, instead of a public execution, if he have him strangled privately in gaol; or if he negligently let the day of execution pass, and think to make amends by executing the convict on some later day, it seems clearly to be such a homicide for which the defender will be answerable with his own life."

THE LIFE OF WILLIAM CALCRAFT, THE HANGMAN. 17

INHUMAN TREATMENT OF A PAUPER CHILD.

The only safe rule for an executor of the law when the act he is going to perform is the taking away of life, is to proceed as far as he can strictly in the term of his warrant; and when any unforeseen event prevents him from so acting, to pause and take the directions of the court from whence his warrant issues.

The worst that can happen under this principle will be the escape of some wretched criminal, and if it be thought that danger would arise from converting any such act into a precedent, it is in the power of the legislature to provide a remedy.

It has been said that a warrant to hang a man till he is dead is not a warrant to hang a man till he is half dead, to reanimate him, or rather to restore him to sensation and feeling, and then to hang and torture him a second time.

No. 3

The case of Margaret Dickson, commonly called half-hangit Maggie Dickson, is told as illustrative of the principle, that a person who has once been suspended and the time elapsed, cannot again be taken hold of for the same crime.

This woman was hanged for child-murder at Edinburgh. While the body was being conveyed in a cart, a motion was felt in the chest in which it was placed. A vein was opened, spirits administered, and animation speedily restored.

Next day she was able to converse with the visitors who poured in to see her, but was never molested again.

In the case of Johnston, however, the case of identity might have been raised.

It might have been possible for the police to have had hold of the wrong man.

A case was on record of a negro who, having committed some horrible crime in the West Indies, was sentenced to be blown from the mouth of a cannon.

While the guard was leading him up to the cannon's mouth through a file of soldiers, he made a sudden bound and made his escape.

In a few minutes a cry was raised that he was at the top of a chimney.

The soldiers were so enraged, that the person thus pointed at was seized and fastened to the cannon's mouth. Just as he was about to be blown into the air the real culprit was discovered.

This was a case in point of what might happen from taking a man from a large crowd and executing him before all these important questions had been decided by a jury empanelled for the purpose.

CHAPTER VI.

A SOCIAL CHAT BETWEEN TWO HANGMEN.

THE misty hours of a dull and cheerless November day were fast verging towards the moonless obscurity of night as a man of no very aristocratic mien wended his way along St. John-street towards Smithfield.

Upon his arriving at the last-named place he passed along till he had reached Giltspur-street. He stood still for a brief space of time, and gazed at the exterior of the prison called the Compter.

After a little reflection he again proceeded along with accelerated speed.

The personage to whom we allude was Foxton, the hangman.

When he arrived at the corner of the street where St. Sepulchre's Church still stands, he hailed a personage who was coming in the opposite direction to himself.

"Hi, there! Hold hard, Bill!" cried Foxton.

"Ah, guv'nor; is it you?" returned Calcraft, "and how goes it with you?"

"It goes anyhow, and I feel as queer as Dick's hatband. I'm as dull and miserable as the d—l."

"What's the matter—any bad news?"

"No, nothing in particular, but I am not up to the mark. Feel bad in every way."

"Sorry to hear that, old man, but you mustn't give way to the miserables. We all have a touch of that complaint at times."

"I'm glad we have met. I know a quiet little drum close at hand. Come along, and we'll have a glass together."

Calcraft was never at any time of his life a man given to drink. As a rule he was abstemious in his habits, and avoided public-houses as much as possible, but he could not very well refuse to accompany his preceptor and patron on an occasion like this.

The two companions walked together in the direction of Newgate-street. At this time there stood a dingy public nearly opposite to the house occupied by the ordinary, or gaol chaplain. A long narrow passage led to a large open bar, and by the side of this was a comfortable, cosy little parlour, which was used in the daytime by the market people; at night it was generally deserted.

Foxton knew the place of old—so he conducted Calcraft into the parlour, and ordered glasses for himself and his friend. They were the only occupants of the room.

"Well, I am sorry to see you so down," said Calcraft, as he seated himself in front of the fire. "But you are not well, I fancy?"

"I'm far from that—I'm very ill," said Foxton, taking a pipe from the tray and filling the bowl with some tobacco, and handing at the same time another pipe to our hero.

"Umph! Let's hope you'll soon get round again," observed the latter, parenthetically.

Foxton shook his head.

"No; I somehow think I shan't. You see, Cal, I've had a pretty goodish run, take it altogether, and the best of my days are over. It ain't of no manner of use a man trying to deceive himself—I aint what I was by a long way."

"Oh, nonsense, you mustn't talk like that—you'll be all right enough after a bit."

"Gammon and all. Something tells me I shan't be right again. I'm as nervous as a cat, and when anything runs cross, which it will do at times with the best on us, I'm knocked silly. Well, it is but natural, we can't always be 'up to the knocker.' A time must come with every man, if he lives long enough, for him to knock under, and I think it's coming pretty fast on me. I shan't be able to carry on much longer, and so you'll have to pull yourself together and go in for the business. 'Cause yer see I'm getting a regular old cripple, and shall soon be of no use at all. You are coming up in the world and I am going down."

Mr. Foxton, after this declaration, laid hold of a spill and lighted his pipe again.

His companion seemed to be lost in reflection—any way he did not make an immediate reply. Presently he said, "Ah, I see how it is, that affair with Birmingham has made you a little nervous."

"Jolly nervous, old man. It was a bad business, and you might have knocked me down with the wind of your fist. But howsomever, that's passed over, let us try and forget it. Mistakes or accidents of that sort will occur, I s'pose."

"Lord bless you, yes—with the best man as ever breathed. Be as careful as you may, accidents like that 'ere will occur—it aint in the nature of things to be otherwise."

"Have you had many such mishaps?"

"Well, I don't say as I had. I've been pretty fortunate, take it altogether. Still I've had my trials and troubles, like the rest of 'em. I got into a bit of a muddle with Corder—him as was turned off for the murder of Maria Martin. You've heard speak of her I s'pose?"

"Oh, yes; she as was hid in the Red Barn."

"That's right. Well, you see, Corder was a fine-made young fellow, but he was a bad un—a rank bad un. He first of all seduced the poor girl, then murdered her, and concealed her body by burying it in the Red Barn. The strangest part of the affair was that it was discovered by a dream. I never knew or heard of a case in all my life with so many extraordinary incidents. Why, Lord bless you, it was more like a romance than a tale of common life. People found it hard to believe it."

"So I have heard."

"Well, you see, my gentleman was bowled out at last, convicted, and sentenced to be hanged, and he deserved scragging if any man ever did.

"I shan't forget in a hurry the morning he was 'turned off.' Although Corder was well aware of the time he was to suffer, he appeared to start when he was told to prepare himself to meet his fate; but he managed to recover himself a bit, and took the arm of one of his attendants, and went down into a room beneath his cell where I pinioned his arms.

"I took the handkerchief from his neck, and put it into his waistcoat, and asked him as I did so if he'd like to have it bound over his eyes at the place of execution. He wouldn't make any answer to this. Everything being ready, several sheriffs' officers attended with their wands to conduct my gentleman to the scaffold, but before doing so he was, at his own request, taken round to the different wards of the prison, at the gates of which the inmates were assembled, all of whom shook him by the hand.

"The unfortunate felons whom he addressed appeared to be much affected while he was bidding them farewell. After a goodish bit of this sort of business he was conducted to the steps which led to the platform. The officers and reporters having taken their places, I stood ready with the rope and cap in my hand.

"Lord, it was a scene, I can tell you! The view from the place where I stood was one of the most beautiful it is possible to imagine.

"In the foreground there were gently rising hills, and in the distance there was jolly big plantations of evergreens, but in course I needn't tell you he did not take much notice of the view before him.

"When he first made his appearance on the scaffold there was a bit of a buzz in the crowd, and all the men took off their hats. Most of the people who came to see him turned off were men, but mind you there were a goodish many females present, and some of them were people of rank, and dressed in the first style of fashion.

"Two women of a common class must have got into the field precious early, as they were close to the barrier, just under the scaffold.

"Well, you must know," observed Foxton, in continuation, "that the scaffold was right enough. It was as simple as possible, and much smaller than the big affair you see at Newgate.

"Instead of being straight the cross beam was a kind of curve with holes in it for the insertion of the rope.

"When Corder saw that I was ready to receive him the sight of the rope did not seem to stagger him, for he turned to one of the bystanders and appeared to be anxious to have the affair over as soon as possible.

"Just as I fixed the rope to the beam, and was busy in tying the knot, I was told by one or two wiseacres that I had left too much for the 'fall.' You know people will take upon themselves to interfere in matters they know nothing about.

"I should like to have given them a piece of my mind, but you know, old man, it won't do to be 'humpy' in cases of this sort, so I had to alter the rope to please them. I felt certain that it was a mistake to do so, but there wasn't no help for it.

"Everything being now in readiness I left the scaffold, and just as the chaplain had commenced the last prayer I cut with a knife the rope which supported the platform and Corder fell, but the fall was a precious awkward one, and it seemed to me that my man would have a bad time of it, so I grasped him round the waist to finish him off.

"In his last struggles he raised his hands several times, but it was however soon all over with him."

"It was fortunate that nothing worse happened," observed Calcraft.

"You are right. As it was, I know it caused me great trouble and anxiety of mind at the time; but it only shows what comes of people meddling in matters they know nothing about."

Foxton's mishap, however, did not escape notice, as the following extract from a paper of the period will prove:—

"A good deal has been said about the awkardness and brutality of the executioner, but we do not consider that he displayed either, although he was certainly disconcerted in consequence of the alteration which he was commanded to make; and it is perhaps owing to this, or a *nervous feeling* which it produced, that he precipitated the felon into eternity before the signal was given.

"This circumstance, however, did not cause any regret on the part of the governor or under-sheriff, for the prisoner was by this time in a fainting state, and it would have been impossible for him to have kept his standing another minute.

"After the execution Foxton expressed his chagrin at having been interrupted in the performance of his professional duty. He said—

"'I never like to be meddled with. I always study the *subjects* which come under my hands, and, according as they are tall or short, heavy or light, *I accommodate them with a fall*. No man in England has had so much experience as me, or knows how to do his duty better.'

"In the afterpart of the day this public functionary visited the corpse in Shire Hall, for the purpose of claiming Corder's trowsers, when he pointed to his handiwork upon the neck of the criminal, and asked, exultingly, whether he had not 'done the job in a masterly manner.'"

A city contractor, who was in the habit of showing Foxton some favours, said to him one day, "Suppose I was to have the misfortune to be condemned to death, could you have the heart to hang me?"

Foxton replied (scratching his head), "You know, master, somebody must do it—why not me? Because I know how to do it more *comfortably* for you than anybody else."

"But you see," said Foxton, knocking the ashes out of his pipe, and addressing himself to our hero, "I'm not so well able to stand trials of this sort as I was a few years ago, and so when I 'chuck it up' you will have to take to the business. We met by chance, you know, and I took a bit of a fancy to you when we first did meet."

"I believe that you did not forget your promise," observed Calcraft.

"Well, old man, the fancy, as one might term it, in a manner of speaking, has grown bigger as we have become better acquainted; and there is no one I should like better to follow me than yourself. 'Cos why? We understand one another."

"You are very kind, I'm sure."

"Not a bit of it; kindness be blowed! I tell you that I can't hold on much longer—it aint in me, Bill. I'm breaking up."

"Oh, get out! Don't be talking like that."

"I—but I must talk like it, because it's as I feel.

Well, what I was agoing to say is just this. I've a lot of papers, and a heap of notes on criminals and such like. When I die, I shall leave 'em all to you."

"Leave them to me?"

"Yes; that's about the size of it. You may make use of them, or you may burn them."

"I shan't do that."

"I shall leave 'em to you. I was never much of a scholar—far from it, but I know my way about, and haven't lived for nothing. Many of the papers are written by clever chaps, such as I'm not fit to hold a candle to. I've kept 'em all, but seldom look at 'em; for, in the first place, some of them are hard to read; besides which, my eyesight aint as good as it was. But such as they are, you are welcome to them. So that matter is settled."

"I don't want to rob you of papers of that sort."

"You won't be robbing me, old man. I give them of my own free will. But we'll say no more about it for the present. I aint come to the end of my tether as yet."

"No; and I hope it will be many years before that time comes," returned Calcraft, with something like commiseration in his tone.

Two persons now entered the little parlour, and the conversation was abruptly brought to a termination.

Neither Foxton nor Calcraft cared much about courting the company of strangers, and in a few minutes after the entrance of the new comers they rose and took their departure.

As our work progresses, some of the documents left by Foxton will be found printed in its pages.

CHAPTER VII.
ESTHER HIBNER'S VISIT TO ST. MARTIN'S WORKHOUSE—PARISH APPRENTICES.

WE stated in a former chapter that, in writing the history of the executioner, William Calcraft, we should have to deal with all sorts of characters, and also portray all sorts of crime.

In a former chapter we took our friends round the interior of Newgate, and having introduced them into the press-room, and explained to them some of the various modes of punishment, in this, the most celebrated prison of England, we will ask our readers now to go with us on a visit to a workhouse.

Workhouses as a rule have been very much alike, so it does not matter much which we go to.

However, we will go to St. Martin's Workhouse, which is one of the most aristocratically situated in the metropolis.

It is near to many a noble mansion, and in close vicinity to the dwellings of many titled ladies, who scarcely know what to do with their money or their time.

One would imagine there were there plenty of district visitors who would look after every interest of the poor.

We shall have a chance, in the course of our rounds, of seeing what they do.

It is now ten o'clock in the morning of the 12th of April, 1828, and as it is the board day and visiting day of the union, we shall have an opportunity of seeing things at their best—that is, as the authorities would wish us to see them.

Most people who read the select literature of official reports have long ago made up their minds that workhouses are very immaculate institutions, where the helpless unfortunate poor are most kindly cared for; where they are comfortably housed, warmly clothed, and well fed, as is instanced by the undeniable fact that on Christmas day every year they have roast beef, plum pudding, and beer.

On the other hand, there are a number of officious, carping, mischief-making people, who believe that workhouses have been places worse than prisons, where all the year round the poor have had little less to live on than their own fat; which having been melted down and absorbed in the usual course, the poor victims were finally ground so small on the treadmill that they at last tumbled to pieces, and were carted away, as described by the poet—

"In a grim one-horse hearse in a jolly round trot,
To the churchyard a pauper is going, I wot;
The road it is rough, and the hearse has no springs,
And hark to the dirge that the sad driver sings:—
'Rattle his bones over the stones;
He's only a pauper, whom nobody owns.'"

The reader perhaps here says, "Oh, but probably these are imaginative, overdrawn, sentimental pictures of workhouse life, drawn from two different standpoints. I should like to see a true scene."

Well, we have arrived at the gate, and we'll get permission to go in.

Having passed the porter's lodge, and obtained a pass from the master, we will now go round some of the wards.

Our readers have asked us for a *true* picture—so let there be no misunderstanding.

We are going to now altogether avoid romance, and it is a strictly true picture of the time and date we are now going to give.

There is the matron of the workhouse there, going on in front.

She has a respectable-looking well-dressed old lady with her, who wants some work girls, and they are going the round of the children's ward, and we'll follow close behind, and listen to their conversation.

"I want," said the old lady to the matron—"I want three or four good strong nice tidy little girls. Have you got any now that you think will suit me?"

"Yes," said the matron, "we have a large number just at the present time, and I have some nice little girls indeed, that I think will just do for you."

"I suppose you give a premium with the girls that are going to learn a trade," said the old lady. "I generally have £5 with each girl that I teach the business to."

"That is a point for the guardians to settle," replied the matron; "but you had better look round, and see which girls will suit you, and then go before the board, and see what the guardians say."

On arriving at the ward, the whole of the girls rose up, and made a low curtsey to the matron, before whose portly presence they seemed to stand with a terribly affrighted awe.

There was scarcely a little child present whose face did not appear to beam with hope, and whose eyes did not seem to speak and say:

"Do please, ma'am, take me, and I'll be such a good little girl."

The old lady went several times up and down the ranks, hesitating which she should choose; for there were there many willing little hearts, and many pretty little faces.

Most of the children were destitute and friendless, and among the four, which she selected for their general tidy and willing appearance, was a little girl named Frances Colpett.

"How old are you, my girl?" said the old lady to her.

"Please, ma'am, I am ten," replied the child.

"And where are your father and mother?" said the old lady.

"They are both dead, ma'am, and I am an orphan," replied the girl.

"And have you no one to look after you?" said the old lady.

"No," replied the child, "I have only got my grandmother, and she is very old."

"Well, would you like to learn a good trade, my girl?" said the old lady.

"Yes, I should very much, ma'am," the little child replied.

"Well, I will take you for one, then, if the guardians will let you go," the old lady then said.

"Thank you, ma'am," the child replied. "I shall be so glad, and so grateful."

The four children having been selected, the master took the old lady before the board to obtain the guardians' permission for the children to be apprenticed to her.

The chairman, addressing the old lady, said: "How many girls do you want?"

"I want four girls, if you please, gentlemen," replied the lady.

"And what are you going to teach them?" said the chairman.

"I am going to teach them spinning and looming, and the making up fancy articles for ladies' dress," she replied.

"I suppose you would do your duty by them?" inquired the chairman.

"Oh, yes, sir," said she. "I shall be as good as a mother to the poor little creatures; they will have a good home, and will learn a good business."

"I suppose you'll have them bound apprentices to you?" inquired the chairman.

"Oh, yes," she replied; "I will take them off your hands entirely, and teach them a good business."

"Couldn't you do with another or two?" inquired some others of the guardians.

"Well, I could after a little while," replied the lady, "when I see I have a few more vacancies."

The matter having been put to the vote the resolution was carried, and it was unanimously resolved —' That the four children be apprenticed to the applicant, on the usual terms of the board;" and the applicant was requested to attend on a future day, appointed for the signing of the indentures.

The four little children, who during the bargaining had stood outside the room, were now ordered in, and informed that they were now going to get a start in life, and that they were going to be sent into the world to do for themselves.

Chairman: You understand now, do you? You are going to be apprenticed. So you must go and do what your mistress tells you, and work for your bread, and don't you become paupers again. And, mind you, if you don't stick to your work, or if there is any complaint against you, we shall send you to gaol.

The poor little friendless children, as they one by one curtsied and left the room, said, "I shall be sure to be good, sir," and so they left the room with no voice in the bargain made.

The clerk was requested to see to the drawing up of the indentures, the fees for which and such like services generally formed a serious item in the public accounts.

The relieving officer was ordered to see that the children were properly delivered up, and the parish was thus rid of further responsibility and care.

On the following Monday the four children were ready for their new situation, and a respectable old woman—a regular inmate of the workhouse—was selected to take them to their new abode.

By nine o'clock in the morning the little adventurers, clean and tidy in their new but scanty outfit, which the parish allowed, were trudging with happy faces and lighter hearts than they had felt for some time by the side of the poor old pauper woman who was to see them safely there.

The old woman had been chosen to take them because she knew Platt's-terrace, the place where the children were going to live, very well.

It was close by Old St. Pancras Church, and very near the house she used to live in when her husband was in business before he died.

It was a fine April morning in the spring-time of the year, and the old woman seemed to freshen up again, and again look bright and cheerful as she for a few hours had left the workhouse walls behind, and was once more breathing the air of freedom, and again looking upon the scenes of her former and happier days.

As the children trotted by her side she pointed out to them the houses of the people she used to know, and she remarked how pretty their gardens and flowers looked—just as they used to do.

Where the gigantic railway stations of the Great Northern and Midland Railways now stand there were beautiful little houses and gardens then, and Platt's-terrace stood among them.

The children were all bright, intelligent children, and they all, as they walked and chatted along, seemed, as the colour of health rose to their cheeks, to enjoy their morning's walk.

Little Frances Colpett, who had been born of rather superior parents, talked of how she should soon now get on in the world, though her poor father and mother were dead, and when the old woman told her they were now getting very near the place her intelligent blue eyes gladdened with delight.

At length the house in Platt's-terrace, St. Pancras, was reached, and the old woman, so well acquainted with the district, goes right to the door at once.

The modest, gentle tap she gave was answered by a rather young-looking woman.

"Is this Mrs. Hibner's, if you please?" said the old woman.

"Yes, it is," replied the young one.

"Will you please to tell her I have brought the four girls from St. Martin's Workhouse," said the old woman.

On this Mrs. Esther Hibner, the girl's new mistress, came downstairs, and coming straight to the door, said, "Oh, it is you, is it? Come in."

On this the old woman and four girls went in, and were shown into a neatly-furnished parlour in front.

"I suppose you would like a little drop of something short now, after your long walk this morning?" said Mrs. Hibner to the old woman.

"Well, thank you, I should," said the woman, "for I haven't tasted a drop this many a long day."

Mrs. Hibner went to a small cheffonier, and unlocking it took out a bottle of gin, and gave the old woman a glass of what she said she could assure her was the real "old Tom."

The old woman on taking the glass said—

"Well, ma'am, here's my best respects, and I hope that you and the childer 'll get on well together, and that they will be a deal of service to you."

"Well, I hope they will," said Mrs. Hibner, and then

turning to the girls, she said—"Come, now, all of you, you had better take your capes and bonnets off."

The children did as they were bid, and carefully folding their capes, laid them down on a chair in the room.

The old woman, having finished her gin, now rose to depart, saying to Mrs. Hibner—

"Well, I must be going now, for the matron told me to get back as soon as I could."

She shook hands with the children, and then wishing them "Good-bye," made a curtsey to their mistress, Mrs. Hibner, and then bidding her good afternoon, left the place, and wended her way back to the workhouse.

The children in the course of the afternoon were duly informed of what their work would be, and having had their usual meals at night, were shown to their room.

We will pass over a few days now, and in the course of a week or so we will for a change go to the East-end, and visit Spitalfields workhouse.

This is a workhouse situated in the very centre of a hard-working and most industrious community. The times with many here have been bad, and this workhouse is filled to overflowing.

We have permission to look round the entrance hall, for it is visiting day here.

We are not allowed to go round the wards, but scattered here and there are groups of people talking.

We can see who they are at the distance—they are the friends and relations of some of the poor inmates, who have come to bring them a little extra tea and sugar in addition to what the house allows.

By a strange coincidence who do we see here, but the very same old lady, Mrs. Hibner, who we saw at St. Martin's Workhouse, selecting some children there?

We wonder how little Frances Colpett and the other young girls are getting on, and we wonder what she wants with so many young girls, for we see she has another batch of five children, which she has selected from the workhouse here.

Evidently from the conversation we overhear they have all been before the board, the consent of the Board of Guardians has been obtained, the usual formalities have only to be gone through, the indentures will have to be signed, and in due course of time the five little children from this place will be bound apprentice to Mrs. Hibner, and duly delivered to her at her establishment, Platt's-terrace, St. Pancras.

We feel that in our tour round the metropolis we would like to visit the place.

It must be very interesting to go round such an establishment, and see the use to which the tiny and nimble fingers of such little girls are put.

We would like to ask her to be kind enough to allow us to go over her establishment, and see the looms at work and the weaving done.

But then we scarcely like. Nobody likes to be intrusive, or to be too inquisitive of strangers, for some people are not very polite, whilst many only insult you if you ask them even a civil question.

Still we feel interested in the little children.

Everyone who has a spark of sympathy or humanity does, especially for an orphan child, and we often wonder how little Frances Colpett is.

Though we do not like to go and ask, we feel we have no doubt in our own minds she is all right, and getting on with her business well.

Besides, it is not our place to go. If we went it would only be looked upon as a piece of impertinence and idle curiosity.

Moreover, it is really no business of ours, or anybody else's.

She has been duly put out apprentice by the guardians, and if it is anybody's place to look after the children it is the relieving officer's business, and nobody else's.

We will, therefore, now leave off visiting workhouses for a time, and comfortable in the general orthodox belief that the children are better out at work than being kept prisoners within the grimy walls of a union workhouse, we will do as the generality of the people of the world do—mind our own business, and let the world and the children take care of themselves.

Still, as the year rolls round, and as the summer comes and goes, and Christmas-tide comes round again, we cannot help now and then wondering how the orphan children are, and whether they at Christmas time have roast beef and plum-pudding, as at the workhouse they used to have.

We again suppose they have, and so the matter ends.

We will now part from our readers for a short period, and we must ask them to meet us again some time in the early part of the following year.

The time soon passes; it is nearly spring again— Feb., 1829. Nearly twelve months have gone by since we visited St. Martin's Workhouse, and saw the old lady, Mrs. Hibner, selecting four children from there as apprentices to her.

We have never been to try and see them yet. It has been winter time, and the weather has been very cold and unpropitious, and we have not been much in the humour for going about on exploring expeditions.

We think, however, we ought to go and see them, and ask how they are. Some people might think us busybodies and officious, but, after all, it would be only an act of charity.

We might, too, take them a few oranges and sweets; perhaps, poor little things, they do not get many of the sweets of this life, and it might encourage them to get on better with their work.

We think we have been remiss in not going before; but if any of our readers wish further to accompany us, we will screw up courage and go to old lady Hibner on Thursday next, and try and see how the girls are.

If our readers, then, will agree to the appointment, we will meet them sharp at ten o'clock very near to the place, Platt's-terrace, by Old St. Pancras Church.

Well, my friends, we have all met according to our appointment; but before we go any further I must ask you whether you have seen this morning's papers. You have not, my friends! Not seen to-day's papers! "No; we generally take in the weekly papers," say you, "and don't see the news till the end of the week." Then, before we go any further, I think I had better take the paper out of my pocket and read the news to you. Here it is. It is to-day's, February 11th, 1829."

SHOCKING TREATMENT OF PARISH APPRENTICES.

Yesterday, at the usual weekly meeting of the St Martin's Board of Guardians, a poor old woman, who seemed so ill with age and infirmity that she could scarcely stand, attended at the workhouse, and begged very hard for permission to go before the board.

On her request being granted she was ushered into the room, and was so much affected she could hardly speak.

When she had recovered self-possession enough to speak, she said—

"Gentlemen, I beg your pardon, but I wish to ask

you if you will please be kind enough to see into the case of my poor little grandchild."

"Who is she?" inquired the chairman.

"Her name is Frances Colpett, gentlemen. If you recollect you bound her apprentice about this time last year to Mrs. Hibner, residing at Platt's-terrace, St. Pancras."

"Yes," said the chairman, "and she was apprenticed to learn a very good trade, too."

"Well, gentlemen," said the old woman, "what I have come to say is that I went to see her yesterday at Mrs. Hibner's house. I had been a great many times since last September to try and see her, but they never would let me. So yesterday when I went I said I was determined to see her if she was in the place at all, and that I would not go away without. They said it was no use me stopping, for I couldn't see her, and shouldn't see her. They ordered me out of the house, and tried to put me out, but I said I wouldn't go away without. 'Well,' they said at last, 'well, you can see her, but you'll see a fine thing when you do.' So at last they let me see the poor child, and I didn't know her, for she was just like a skeleton, and scarcely able to speak to me, and my poor dear little grandchild was all over cuts and wails."

The Chairman: "Do you think they have been ill-treating her then?"

"Oh yes," said the poor old woman, "they have been ill-treating her dreadfully. Besides, when I saw her, poor child, besides being nothing but a skeleton, she was nearly wet through, her hair was sopping wet, she couldn't stand, and she did cry to come away."

Here the old woman burst into tears and almost fainted away.

"Well, we will have the matter inquired into," said the chairman, "and see how the girl has been behaving herself."

"Oh, do please send some one soon," said the old woman. "I am sure she is not a child that would misbehave herself. Her poor mother, when she was alive, always taught her better than that, and I can't bear to think of her being there any longer."

"It would not take one of the officers long to go to Platt's-terrace in a cab," suggested one of the guardians, and if he hastened back we should know what the case is to-day before the business of the board is over, and then we could pass some sort of resolution upon it before we rise to-day. If we defer it till the next weekly meeting of the board, and the child is really being ill treated, we don't know what she may suffer in the meantime."

"Hear, hear," said several of the guardians.

"I think it is a very good suggestion, and we will send some one immediately. Meantime the poor old grandmother can stop in the waiting-room here of the house till the relieving officer comes back; and if it is necessary I think he had better bring the child with him," observed the chairman.

Mr. Blackman, one of the overseers of the parish, happened to be in the room, and it was resolved that he should at once take a cab, and go to Mrs. Hibner's house, and see what was the matter with the child.

"You will make as much haste as you can, Blackman," said the chairman, as the overseer was leaving the room.

"Yes, sir," he replied, and in a few minutes he was on his way to Platt's-terrace in a cab.

After the lapse of a little more than two hours, the cab was driven rapidly up to the board-room door of St. Martin's workhouse, and Mr. Blackman alighting, he at once entered the room.

The guardians were just dealing with the last relief case on the list, and as soon as the applicant had left the room, the chairman, addressing the overseer, said—

"Well, Blackman, what has the girl been up to—misbehaving herself, or something?"

Mr. Blackman, replying, said: "Well, Mr. Chairman and gentlemen, I have been to Hibner's, and I am very sorry to have to inform you that in my opinion it is very likely to be a very serious and awkward piece of business. The girl Frances Colpett is dead. She died last night, and when I got there this morning, they had made an arrangement with the undertaker, and the body was going to be taken away and buried to-day.

"It presented, however, such a fearfully emaciated appearance that I thought I had better warn them, and stop the funeral. I therefore did so. You never saw such a sight in your life. The girl is reduced to a complete skeleton, and though she was a plump little girl when she went from here she does not weigh many pounds now. Her face is dreadfully shrivelled and shrunken, and her body bears the marks of the most terrible ill-usage.

"Her back and thighs are all over livid cuts and weals; some look as though they had been done with a cane, as if she had had fearful canings. Other parts look as though they had been terribly flayed with a rod, whilst other deep bruises appear to have been inflicted with some harder weapon—probably a stick, or something of that kind.

"On going upstairs the most horrible sight I ever saw in my life presented itself. There in the top room I found a number of other girls, perfectly living skeletons. Some of them were sitting crouching on the floor, unable to get up or stand.

"Very few had scarcely a rag to cover them. They were evidently being starved to death.

"I asked some of the girls where their beds were, but they all seemed afraid to speak. They shook and trembled, and evidently dreaded every footstep on the stairs. These girls, too, in other respects, were in a most deplorable condition. Some of them were wealed completely black and blue.

"Several of them had their bones nearly coming through their skins, and they looked as though they wouldn't live many hours. I insisted on knowing where the girls slept, and after a good deal of trouble I ascertained that they all slept on the bare floor without any bed whatever.

"Some of them had got one bit of a rug to cover them, and some had none. They had slept in this manner throughout the winter, bitter as the weather was, and some of the girls had the chilblains so bad that their feet were mortifying.

"On looking again at Frances Colpett's feet I found that her feet had mortified so that most of her toes were gone, they having rotted off.

"I found other girls in other parts of the house, and those who were at work at the looms seemed so weak for want of food they could scarcely stand to their work.

"Altogether, I found no less than thirty parish apprentices in the house. Some had been got from this union, and some from Spitalfields workhouse, and some from others. I thought the case was so serious that I got assistance before I came away.

"I sent off for one of the officers of Spitalfields workhouse, and after getting some of the girls a little food, I left him in charge and came away. I think the watchman ought to be called in at once, the children removed, and the case inquired into directly.

"I should further tell you, gentlemen, that two of the other girls are missing. I cannot get any satisfactory information about them, but I am told that two girls have died from there, and in my opinion they are perhaps made away with."

"This is really a very bad case, and one we shall be bound to take some notice of," said the chairman; "but before we discuss the matter, it would perhaps be as well to call the grandmother in, and inform her that her grandchild is dead, and that we will see to the funeral, and then she can go home, and we can discuss what is best to be done."

"Perhaps it would be as well to break the matter to the old woman as gently as possible, for she was a good deal cut up this morning, or she may take on in the room, and we may have a scene here," suggested several of the guardians.

"Oh, certainly," said the chairman. "I quite agree with you. We ought to inform her of her grandchild's death as gently as possible. I intended to do so."

The master, Mr. Smith, was then ordered to bring the old woman in, and Mrs. Gibbs, the grandmother, at once entered the room.

"Take a seat, Mrs. Gibbs," said the chairman to the old woman, "and compose yourself as much as you can."

"Yes, sir," the old woman replied, and she sat down in a chair, handed to her by the master, at the end of the table.

"Well, Mrs. Gibbs," said the chairman. "I hope you will not distress yourself any more than you can help, but the guardians wish me to inform you as gently as I can that your grandchild is dead."

"Dead—dead! Gone to her poor dead mother! Gone to my own poor dead child!" faintly breathed the poor old aged woman, as her head fell back on her shoulders, and she swooned away quivering in the chair.

"There," said the chairman to the master, "you had better get some assistance, and carry the poor old creature into the next room, and as soon as she comes round let her be seen to, and let somebody see her home in a cab."

The bell was rung. The lodge porter came to the master's assistance, and the poor heart-broken old woman, sitting in her chair, was carried into the adjoining room in a swoon.

The chairman, as soon as the door was closed, addressing the members of the board, said: "Well, gentlemen, I think we may now get to business. I think you will agree with me, gentlemen, that we are all of us very greatly indebted to our overseer, Mr. Blackman, for the timely discovery he has made, and for the promptness and energy he has shown in the discharge of his important duty. I think if it had not been for him this child might have been dead and buried silently in the grave without us being any the wiser. I am quite sure the public will feel that there is great credit due to him for what he has done in discovering this terrible cruelty. I think we ought now ourselves to inquire into the matter, and if any crime has been committed, or cruelty perpetrated, we ought to punish the offender. Our parish has never been backward in doing its duty, and as we ought not to lose any time in investigating the matter, I think some of us ought to go at once."

Several of the guardians were then appointed as a committee to go and inquire into the circumstances, and ascertain what the facts really were.

Four of them then went off in a four-wheeler to Hibner's house at Platt's-terrace, to make further inquiries, and also to decide what course should be pursued.

The committee had not made known their decision when we went to press, but we shall publish further particulars to-morrow.

"Well, that is very dreadful," replied some of our friends. "Perhaps it would be as well to meet again to-morrow at this time and place, and see what course is being pursued."

This course was finally decided upon, and it was resolved that we should meet again next day, and have a walk as far as Platt's-terrace.

CHAPTER VIII.
CRUEL TREATMENT OF SIX CHILDREN — MAGISTERIAL INQUIRY.

IN the interim we anxiously watch the reports of the daily papers, and on perusing the magisterial intelligence we find the following report—

At the Bow-street Police-court, before Sir Richard Birnie, Esther Hibner, aged sixty-one, and also Esther Hibner, aged twenty-seven, daughter of the elder prisoner, and Ann Robinson, twenty-eight, a forewoman in their employ, all of them residing at 13, Platt's-terrace, St. Pancras-road, were charged before the presiding magistrate with having starved and otherwise cruelly ill-used six female children placed as parish apprentices to the elder prisoner.

Four of the children were produced in court, and were in a most deplorable condition, they having been reduced to complete skeletons.

Mr. Blackman, overseer, of St. Martin's parish, gave evidence of the state he found the children in.

An officer from Cripplegate Union stated that the elder prisoner had obtained some children from that parish.

He had missed one of them, named Margaret Howse, and he had been informed that she had been so cruelly treated that she died last week, and was quietly buried without the searchers seeing the body.

Sir Richard Birnie: I think that the body ought to be exhumed and every inquiry made then. It certainly would be a scandalous thing if such things were passed over as a child being perhaps murdered and buried without any inquiry being made in the matter.

The officer said he would be very glad to get the grave opened if it would be of any service, but he thought it would be of no use, as he was afraid the doctors had had the body for dissection.

Sir Richard Birnie: That is just the very reason why you ought to open the grave and see whether the body is there or not; if not, you ought to try and find out what has become of it.

The officer said he would have the grave opened at once.

Evidence having been given by several of the witnesses as to the cruelty of the whole of the prisoners towards the child Frances Colpett they were all committed to take their trial for wilful murder.

THE INQUEST.

Our friends having met us by appointment according to promise by Old St. Pancras Church we proceed in the direction of Platt's-terrace, but as we pass the "Elephant and Castle," St. Pancras, we observe a crowd round, and we turn in, for we hear the inquest on the other child, Margaret Howse, is just about to commence.

The Coroner sits at the end of the table, and around sit the twelve jurymen to hear the evidence.

WILLIAM CALCRAFT, THE HANGMAN.

THE HALF-STARVED CHILDREN IN MRS. HIBNER'S ESTABLISHMENT.

Having been sworn that they will well and truly try, and a true verdict give according to the evidence, they go to view the body exhumed from the grave.

It scarcely looks like a child, for it is nothing but skin and bone, and altogether it presents a shocking appearance. The marks of terrible ill-usage are still visible upon it, for her legs and body are covered with bruises and weals.

Susan Whitby, witness, called, said:—I am twelve years of age, and knew the deceased. She was one of the eight apprentices bound to the elder prisoner. She died last Saturday week. For a great many weeks before her death she scarcely had anything allowed her to eat. All she had allowed her was one slice of bread in a morning, and generally that was all she had till the next morning. We all had to get up at three o'clock in the morning to work. We at half-past eight had a slice of bread, with a little warm water with a tablespoonful of milk in it for breakfast. We had nothing further till the following morning. Sometimes we were not allowed to have any breakfast at all; then we had a little potatoe given us for dinner. Sometimes we were made to work all night long. On one occasion we were made to work the whole of two nights running. The deceased got so ill she could scarcely stand. On the night before the deceased died she and all of us had to work till eleven o'clock. The mistress then gave us a good flogging because she said we had not done work enough, and sent us to bed. At three o'clock the next morning, Ann Robinson, the forewoman, came and made us all get up again to our work. That morning the deceased was so weak and ill she was not able to stand. Ann Robinson then dragged her up-stairs undressed, and gave her a good flogging, and tried to make her stand to her loom to work. She could not stand to her work, and then the mistress came up and flogged her, and as she could not stand kicked her down stairs. At breakfast time, the deceased was not able to stand in the kitchen, and could not get her breakfast. I gave her the slice of bread that was cut for her. She was very hungry, and as she lay on the floor she tried to eat it. She could not eat, and died with the slice of bread between her teeth. I told the mistress I thought she was dying, and she said "Oh, d——n, let her lie and die; it will be a good riddance." She was fastened down in her coffin, and buried in about a week. I am sure she was badly flogged just before she died.

The jury, after hearing further corroborative evidence, and the testimony of the medical men to the effect that the poor child had died for want of food, returned a verdict of wilful murder against the prisoner Hibner.

The hearing of the evidence makes us shudder to think of the cruelties perpetrated upon friendless and helpless children, and we finish our rambles for the day by at last visiting the house.

A great crowd has gathered round; the excitement is intense; people are standing in small groups listening to the statements of some who relate accounts of the dreadful screams and piercing shrieks they have heard in the house as they have passed from time to time.

Strange that no one interfered; but such is life.

The case sent a thrill of horror through the nation, and the interest in it was intense, for it opened the eyes of the country to the dangers and treatment of parish apprentices.

Probably our friends would like to know the result of the trial, and hear for themselves the whole of the evidence. If so, perhaps they will accompany us to that historical place, the Old Bailey.

Friday, April 20th, was the day, and the Old Bailey was crowded to excess, when

Esther Hibner, the elder, and Esther Hibner, the younger, her daughter, and Ann Robinson, were indicted before Mr. Baron Garrow for the wilful murder of Frances Colpett, aged ten, a parish apprentice, bound by the guardians of St. Martin's-in-the-Fields to the elder prisoner, aged 61.

Messrs. Alley and Bolland conducted the prosecution.

Jeremiah Smith said: I am master of St. Martin's workhouse. Frances Colpett, the deceased, was a child in our workhouse. I know the prisoner, Esther Hibner, senior. Colpett was placed with her, on liking, on the 7th of April, 1828, and on the 2nd of April another child was put out from our parish. Colpett was in perfect health. When she went to the prisoner her health was very good. She was afterwards bound to the prisoner.

Cross-examined by Mr. Barry: Was the child subjected to a surgical examination, to your knowledge, before it went?—No.

Mr. Bolland: How long had she been in your workhouse?—About four months. She came from our nursery in the country; she had been under the care of the parish five or six years, and was always in perfect health.

The substance of the indenture was here read, by which Frances Colpett was articled as apprentice to Esther Hibner, sen., of Platt's-terrace, to learn the business of a tambour-worker, she engaging to provide her with board and lodging and all other necessaries.

Joseph Fincham: I live in Westmoreland-street. I saw all the parties execute this indenture; it is dated the 29th of April, 1828.

Frances Gibbs: I am grandmother of Colpett. I saw her several times after she was apprenticed to the prisoner. The last time I saw her was on the 27th of September. I went again on the 30th of November; I did not see my grandchild; I was told Hibner's daughter was dead, and I could not see the child. I did not see either of the prisoners. I called again on the 3rd of January of this year and saw Hibner, jun. I asked her to let me see my grandchild; she said it was not convenient, for it was Saturday night and the children were being washed. I went again on the 8th of February, saw the daughter, and asked to see my grandchild. She (the younger Hibner) then said that she had soiled her work, and I could not see her; on account of the child being so fond of me that was the only punishment she could have. I called again on the 9th of February, and the daughter said she was gone to the Strand. I went again on Wednesday, the 11th of February, and was determined to see her. The children brought her into the parlour where Hibner and her daughter were. I said she looked in a deplorably starved state, and they said she had been ill. Nothing further passed on that occasion, but in consequence of this I gave information to the gentlemen of the parish.

Cross-examined: Do you know of this child being allowed to go to church on Sundays?

She never went to church, for I asked her, and she said she had never been. I do not know of her being sent on errands to the City. They told me that when the child came I should see her in a pretty deplorable state.

John Blackman: I am a cabinet maker and live in Green-street, Leicester-square. In February last I was overseer of St. Martin's parish, in consequence of which I went to Platt's-terrace, to see the children the parish had apprenticed; my first visit was on the 12th of February. I did not see Colpett on that day. I first saw the daughter, and asked her if I might see the children who had been bound from our parish, and without any hesitation she brought five of them in. They went into the parlour with me. Some of them appeared very ill and emaciated extremely. I expressed a desire to both the mother and the daughter to take them away. There was some objection on the part of both of them, and I said I would call the next day, the 13th, accompanied by Mr. Wright, a surgeon. When I got to the house I think the little girl, Harford, opened the door. I saw both the Hibners, and requested to see the children, and we went up into the room in which they were working. Mr. Wright, at my request, asked the children several questions, having first requested the prisoners to leave the room. Several of the children appeared very ill indeed, and we both requested the mother and daughter to allow us to take them away with us. They objected to it very much indeed, but one that was then ill they would have allowed us to have taken. She was not in the room, but in the back parlour; they objected to us removing any of those who were brought into the room. Colpett was not brought into the room. In consequence of what one of the children said we went into the back parlour. Mrs. Hibner accompanied us there. We found Colpett lying on a mattress without any proper covering. There was apparently a dirty shawl or part of a blanket over her; she had a night gown and cap on; she said nothing to my knowledge in Hibner's hearing. Mrs. Hibner endeavoured to find fault with the child, and in doing so turned up her bed in a very rough manner. She almost doubled the child up, ill as she was, and I thought she would hurt her very much. I complained to her of the manner she seemed to act. She appeared to take but little notice of what I said, and we removed six of the children that day, but not at this time. We went afterwards and removed them. Colpett was among them; we took her at once to St. Pancras infirmary, for Mr. Wright considered her in too dangerous a state to be removed further; she appeared very ill, and particularly thin; she appeared merely skin and bone; her lips were contracted a great deal, the teeth much exposed, a redness about the eyes; on one eye I observed a cut, and I think there was a bruise on the forehead, to the best of my recollection.

Cross-examined: Had you any duty at St. Martin's workhouse?—Yes; I had general duty as an overseer. Six children were apprenticed to Mrs. Hibner; I never saw them on Sundays. At the workhouse it is the duty of the master of the house to know who comes; at the second visit they were willing for us to fetch the one away that was ill.

Mr. Bolland: Do you recollect the state of the weather at that time?—I think it was wet—it was cold.

Susan Whitby: I was apprenticed to the elder prisoner. I went to live with her last November twelve months. Colpett came to live there either last Easter or Whitsuntide—I cannot tell which. We had eight apprentices at that time. Colpett used to be called up to work between three and four o'clock in a morning, and continued to work till between ten and eleven at night. From Michaelmas till the time she went away she used to have a slice of dry bread and a cup of milk and water at breakfast time; she had nothing else in the course of the day, and no other meal till the next morning. She had her breakfast at half-past eight o'clock, and was allowed five minutes to eat it in.

Did it ever happen that she had no breakfast at all?—Yes; sometimes they used to say that she had not earned her breakfast, and should not have it, and then they would give her potatoes at one o'clock. There were nine pounds of potatoes between us all, when we had any, including the prisoner's. There were twelve of us in all. When she had potatoes for dinner she had nothing else all day. We went to bed between ten and eleven o'clock at night. We slept upstairs on the floor in the work-room. The mother and daughter had a bed, blanket, counterpane, and sheet; Colpett lay along with eight of us apprentices—we lay together on the floor; we had one blanket under, and one over us, and our clothes on. Colpett's grandmother brought her a frock and petticoat, and she had a green baize of her own; she had no stockings. That was the only accommodation we had during the whole winter from Michaelmas till we were taken away; but we did not lie so before Michaelmas. Once a fortnight, on Sundays, we had meat, and on some Sundays we were downstairs in the kitchen locked in. On other Sundays, when we had meat, we were upstairs in the work-room. Our mistress was at home during those Sundays. The shutters to the kitchen windows were shut on the Sundays when we were down there, and the door locked. Colpett was never allowed to go out; she was in good health when she came to live with us, and continued so till the food was changed, and then she got ill. I first perceived her unwell about a week after the food had been taken off; they made her keep to the frame at her work after the victuals were taken off.

Was she ever found fault with for not doing her work?—Yes; she used to be ill, which prevented her doing it. They all beat her in turns, and sometimes the forewoman beat her. I have seen them beat her. The other prisoner was the forewoman—her name is Robinson. They sometimes beat her with a rod, a cane, or a slipper. The daughter has taken her out of the frame and knocked her on the floor; then taken her up and knocked her down again. I never saw her punish her in any other way.

Do you ever recollect seeing a pail of water in the place?—Yes, it was brought into the bedroom to wash the stairs with, and the daughter took her up by the heels and dipped her head in twice, and then Robinson said, "Take her up, dip her in again, and finish her!" That only happened once. She used to cry and ask mistress for some food, but she didn't get it. Mistress used to say that it was no use for her to cry, for the more she cried the longer she should be without it. Mistress kept a dog, and the food for it was brought from Gray's-inn-lane. The son had some pigs. The man who minded them used to have the wash from the tavern, and when that has been brought for the dog I have seen Colpett, Foster, and Howse take and eat it. There used to be sometimes bits of fish and bits of mutton chops in it, and they used to take it out and eat it. They took Colpett and Proctor to Judd-street one day to a doctor. I never saw a doctor come to the house to them at all.

How often were you washed or cleaned?—We used to sluice our faces in the morning. Our linen was changed sometimes once a fortnight or three weeks. Mary Harford took in the milk that was used in the house; half-a-pint was all that was taken in in the morning, a half-pennyworth was taken out of it for their afternoon tea, and the rest was divided among us.

Cross-examined: Where have you been since you left the prisoner's house?—At Cripplegate. I have not talked this over much there. Mr. Metcalf, the churchwarden, asked me about it, and I spoke to the mistress of the school about it, but to nobody else. The mistress only asked how I lay, and what victuals I had; I did not tell her or the churchwardens the whole story; I told the rest at Hicks-hall.

Have you not stated a great many more things of consequence at Hicks-hall than you told the churchwarden?—Not a great many more. I went to church once when I first went to the prisoner's, and only once. When I first went there I went on a great many errands. I went to the City for cotton—none of the other girls went—sometimes the mistress went herself. We have not had tea since the victuals were taken off. I do not know what month that was in. We have never had tea since that.

Have you not been treated with some kindness by the daughter?—When I first went there they said I should be forewoman over the girls; she did not buy fruit for me. I have had fruit given me by my friends who have come to see us. Nobody came to see me for six months, till a fortnight before I left, when my two sisters came; they are grown up. Colpett's grandmother came to see her; none of the others have got friends except Howse, who has a sister. Nobody has called for a long time, except Colpett's grandmother, to my knowledge. Three of the children have no friends at all. There were eight; four of them came about a month after I got there.

Had you the same number at the time you were removed as before?—No, one was dead. Harris has got a father and mother, and she went to her friends.

Mary Ann Harford, sworn, said: I went to live at Hibner's about a week ago, to do tambour work. There were eight girls in all when I first went, seven besides myself. We used to get up sometimes at three o'clock and sometimes at four o'clock in the morning, and worked sometimes till two o'clock in the night, and sometimes till twelve; if we had not done our work mistress used to keep us without victuals, and she used to give us a good flogging before we went to bed.

Used she to let you go to bed after flogging you?—Yes, sometimes she let us go to bed, and sometimes she kept us up all night; she did so for two nights running. We had breakfast sometimes—I do not know at what particular times—it was a piece of dry bread, and sometimes a drop of milk and water; if we had not done breakfast in ten minutes she would say she would take it away from us; when we had no breakfast we sometimes had potatoes, and sometimes we had none at all. Once we had nothing to eat all day from the time we got up till we went to bed. When we had breakfast in a morning we had no potatoes or anything given us in the day. We sometimes had meat once a fortnight. This short food began about three weeks after we were bound. We had been on liking first, and were fed very well then. I remember Colpett coming. She was in very good health when she first came. She afterwards became sick and ill. That was about five weeks after she first came. She complained of a pain in her side, and sometimes of the headache. She used to tell the prisoner so, and Mrs. Hibner used to say, "Never mind; you must do your work." She did not wear stockings. I knew of her feet being bad, and I told mistress of it. She first told me they were bad in the winter. They were bad a long time before I told mistress of it. When I first told mistress of it, she said, "Never mind; I have not got time to go down to her. You must wait a bit." I complained to her again the same afternoon, and she said, "Never mind; she must lay there." She was lying in the back room then, confined to her bed, and had been so about a week.

Did you speak to your mistress after that about her feet?—Yes, and then she gave me a cup of bread and milk poultice to put to them. She had been unable to do her work for a good while.

Do you remember at any time while she was so ill her being told to clean the stairs?—Yes, the daughter told her (there was a pail of water there. Colpett did her tambour work wrong), and she did them, but could not quite finish them; she fell down on the stairs and said she felt so weak she could not do them. She was then taken upstairs, and flogged well, and then sent down again to do them. The daughter took her upstairs. I went upstairs, for I had to fetch her up. I saw the daughter flog her with a cane, and a rod; she beat her a good bit. She took her clothes up to beat her, and then sent her down to finish the stairs; the daughter then came and rubbed her nose on the stairs. I then saw the daughter take her up by the clothes, and dip her head into the pail of water a good many times; this was just after the flogging. Robinson was there, but mistress had gone out. Colpett's head was dipped into the pail five times. Robinson then said "Blow her, dip her in again, and that will finish her." This was about seven weeks before she was taken away; it was about seven weeks before Christmas.

Have you since October last seen anybody beat Colpett?—Yes, the forewoman did, and sometimes the mother. She was beat very often. They beat her with a slipper. I have seen a slipper, a cane, and a rod, used to beat her, because she did not do her work right, as she complained of a pain in her inside. They beat her sometimes at night, and sometimes in the middle of the day. She was working all day. I sat near her at the frame. She was in the middle of all of us. There were four girls between me and her at the frame. She could not do her work, she was too ill. We all slept on the floor; sometimes in the work-room, and sometimes in the back room. When we slept in the work-room we had nothing but a blanket under us, and one over us. It was very thin, and we were very cold. Colpett was covered the same as we were.

Your mistress kept a dog. Were you the little girl that used to fetch the errands?—Yes; I fetched the victuals for the dog from the place where Hibner's brother kept pigs in Gray's-inn-lane. I used to bring it in a little wooden sieve. It was hog wash, and came out of the tub that hogs feed in; at times there were little bits of fish and bones in it. I used at times to eat some myself, and so did Colpett. We all used to eat it, because we were so hungry. I was the cook, and used to boil the potatoes. I used to get 6 lb., and sometimes 3½ lb. Eight of us and the forewoman ate of them; we had nothing but potatoes. The forewoman used to have a red herring sometimes. Mistress and her daughter dined by themselves.

Cross-examined: The forewoman lived as you did?—Sometimes. I now live at Cripplegate workhouse, and am now very well; all the girls are there now, excepting those who are dead; they are all pretty well now.

Did people frequently come to the house since October?—Not very often; a man came with milk; nobody else brought food to the house. I used to fetch the coals. I used to be put upstairs with the others when the prisoners went out; sometimes when they went out some of us went out, but we dare not go far for fear they should come back. I knew my way to the workhouse. We never went there while we lived at the prisoner's; we went to the church.

How many of the children's friends did you see there? Colpett's grandmother, and sometimes Ellis's father and mother came—that was about five week's ago. The prisoners were there then, and girls at home. We used to eat the dog's victuals every day. It used to be put in two large tubs, but it was brought to our house in a sieve.

Mr. Bolland: What became of you on Sundays?—They used to send us down to bed. We were locked in the room, and could not come out. Eliza Proctor is very poorly still, and has been so ever since.

CHAPTER IX.
CONTINUATION OF ESTHER HIBNER'S TRIAL—SENTENCE OF DEATH.

The evidence of the witness caused great excitement in court, which was crowded to excess, and the interest was intense.

Eliza Norman, who was the next witness called, said: I am eleven years old. I was apprenticed to the elder prisoner from St. Martin's parish. I remember Frances Colpett. I lived at the prisoner's about twelve months. Since Machaelmas last we sometimes used to have about one meal a day. Sometimes we used to get up about three o'clock, and go to work directly. Sometimes we used to work till one o'clock, and sometimes till twelve. We used to have half a slice of dry bread, and sometimes we used to have milk and water, and sometimes none. When we had breakfast we did not have dinner on the same day. When we had dinner, sometimes we used to have potatoes. Colpett was fed in the same way. She used to say she could eat more. She did not get it. When she first came she had good health. She began to get ill after the alteration of our food.

After she became ill was she required to get up and work in the same way as she did before? Sometimes she used, and sometimes she used not, because she was not well. When she did not do her work she was beaten—sometimes by Robinson, sometimes by mistress, and sometimes by the daughter. She was beat with a rod and a cane. I remember her being desired to wash the stairs; she was ill at the time, and was so weak she could not wash them; she was then dipped into the pail of water by the daughter. Robinson was in the room, and said, "Take her up again and finish her." On Sunday we were down in the kitchen locked up. We sometimes at night lay on the floor of the workroom, with a blanket under and a blanket on the top of us. We all eight lay together; we lay in that way all the cold weather.

Cross-examined: What do you mean by saying, "Sometimes we had only one meal a day, and sometimes we had more?"—Yes; when we first entered their service we did, but not very often. We sometimes since October had more than one meal, when we earned it; the second meal was potatoes. We had no tea; we had milk and water in the morning—that was all. We only had milk and water of an evening three times while we were there. The daughter gave me an orange when I was coming to my mother; that was a good while before I was taken away; it was a little after I was bound. I, Colpett, and Proctor had gin and water sometimes, because we were weak; that was not long ago. Robinson took me to the doctor's in Judd-street, and the daughter took me once; Colpett went with me; it was about three months ago. We had no oranges there, they gave us physic. We were left in the house about five o'clock one evening when the prisoners were out; it was not long ago. Robinson's mother was then in care of the house. I do not recollect it being left without her. I do not recollect any of the girls going out while the prisoners were out. I did not know my way to the workhouse. I do not recollect anybody but the milkman calling at the house. I have a mother, and went to see her twice after I was bound.

Mr. Alley: Did Colpett ever go out?—She only went out with a little child in the summer.

Charles James Wright said:—I am a surgeon, and live at Camden-town. I went by direction of the parish officers, in company with Mr. Blackman, to the prisoner's house on the 13th of February, and found Francis Colpett in bed in the back parlour at No. 13, Platt's-terrace, St. Pancras-road. I found her in a very emaciated state indeed, with sores on her toes, which were in a state of mortification. I then requested she might be removed to the St. Pancras infirmary, which was done. When we got her there I examined her minutely. I found the body extremely attenuated. She had a slight cough. The toes were mortified; some of them were about separating at the time; all the toes on the left foot except one partook of mortification, and the right foot was in the same state, but was the worst. I attended her till Sunday, the 15th of March, when she died in St. Pancras infirmary. After her death I examined her body with two other medical gentlemen. There were abscesses on the lungs, with tubercles covering the lungs, a slight inflammation of some of the abdominal viscera, and stone in the left kidney. Her death arose from abscess on the lungs—that was the approximate cause, in conjunction with the mortification of the toes. I have heard two of the children examined, and have no doubt these tubercles might be produced by the treatment described, and want of food. I attribute the mortification of the feet to want of food and necessary exercise; cold and wet would be an exciting cause. The tubercles had been going on for a long time, I have no doubt. She had a bruise on the right eye, and some bruises on the right arm particularly.

Thomas Easling: I am a surgeon, and live in Oxenden-street. I saw this child twice while alive. It was in a dreadfully emaciated state. I examined the body after death; ill-treatment and want of food are very likely to produce the consequences I saw, and which have been described by the last witness.

Cross-examined: You are a member of the Royal College of Surgeons?—I am. I think dipping the child's head two or three times in a pail of water would be very likely to bring the tubercles into action and form abscesses.

Benjamin Bury: I am a surgeon, and live in Brewer-street, St. Pancras. I was called in to see the deceased after she was in the infirmary. I found her in a very emaciated state, and her feet mortified. Dipping the child's head into a pail of water, the want of proper food and clothing, would produce the appearances I saw.

That being the whole of the evidence, the prisoners were called upon by the Court for their defence.

Breathless silence now reigned in the court, every ear being attentive, listening to what the prisoners had to say to the horrible charge.

Esther Hibner, the elder, said: I leave my defence to my daughter.

Esther Hibner, jun., the daughter, was then called upon by the Court for her defence.

When the Court was again hushed in silence she said:—"It is very false what these children have stated. My mother was a very good mistress to them.

They never got up without they pleased. The furniture belonged to me. I lent my mother £200 for those girls. I had nothing to do with the business. When I found the girl was ill I had her put to bed and cleaned. She had clean sheets and clean blankets. I never dipped her in water in my life. I own I beat Mary Harford for not making the bed well. They all frequently went out on errands. Ellis used to go home on Sundays. I took the greatest care of the children. When they complained to me I had them put to bed, and asked them what they would have to eat and drink. I gave them gin and water when they complained of being ill, and gave them oranges, and on Sundays they have gone out to buy oranges. They have met Margaret Howse's sister when they have been out to buy oranges. I beg that Mary Harford should be called up again. I think it shocking for her to say what she has.

Mary Harford was, at the prisoner's request, then called again by the Court.

Prisoner to Mary Harford: Do you know that the stockings of the little girl, Frances Colpett, were changed two or three times a day for her?

Mary Harford: No, they were not; nor were Proctor's changed.

Esther Hibner, junior: Did you not push Frances Colpett down the stairs yourself?—No, I am sure I never did. I was told to do it, but would not.

The Court then called on Ann Robinson for her defence.

Ann Robinson: What I have to say is that I lived with these people four months and three weeks, and never saw any of this treatment to the children. I left at eight o'clock every night, and went again at eight o'clock on the next morning. I slept there four nights during one of the children's illness—there were two good beds and a mattress. I slept on one of them one night with Susan Whitby.

Silence was then proclaimed in Court, and the jury then were asked to consider their verdict.

They wished to retire, and after an absence of one hour and five minutes, during which time the interest and speculation as to the fate of the prisoners was very great, they returned into Court.

As soon as quiet was restored, the foreman, addressing the judge, said, "We find the prisoner, Esther Hibner, the elder, guilty of the murder. We find the other two prisoners, not guilty."

Esther Hibner, the younger, and Ann Robinson were then discharged, and ordered to leave the dock.

Esther Hibner, the elder, was then ordered to stand up for sentence.

The Recorder then assumed the black cap, during which time the prisoner stood with the utmost indifference.

There being now such complete silence in the crowded court, that not a sound was heard during the awful moment, the Recorder said:—Prisoner at the bar, you have been tried by a very attentive, a very intelligent, and a very impartial and humane jury. A sense of the very solemn duty under which the jury felt themselves placed, has compelled them to pronounce you guilty of the wilful and deliberate murder of a fellow-creature. You saw your victim sinking from day to day under the most distressing bodily exertion, and suffering a greater degree of pain and agony of body than a person of a much more advanced age would have been able to endure, and you saw it though you have been the mother of a child—at least one if not more—you saw it without any of that feeling which one would have thought never would for one moment have been absent from your breast. You are now about to receive a sentence (continued the Recorder) which will consign you to that death, to which by your continued cruelty day by day you have consigned an unoffending and a helpless infant. You have had good fortune—I may call it such if you have made good use of it—to have had the time intervening between the last session and the present, to consider the awful situation in which you stand. I hope and pray that you have filled up that interval in reflecting upon the heinous crime that you have committed; that you have not ceased from hour to hour to supplicate from your Creator that mercy which it is impossible for you to hope for from any earthly tribunal. If it should happen that you have suffered that length of time to pass by without reflecting upon your guilt, without praying to the Almighty to forgive you your sins, let not another moment escape, when you shall have been taken from that bar, before you fall on your knees, and from minute to minute, and from hour to hour—so far as human strength can enable you—call upon your God for his forgiveness, for you have but very few hours to live; and if you have not employed that time which has elapsed since your committal to prison as you should employ the short interval that remains between you and eternity, let me pray and entreat you as a fellow creature and a Christian, not to lose one single instant from prayer. The law of the land which condemns you to death has, in the most important task that remains to be fulfilled, while you are permitted to live, given you the assistance of a pious clergyman. He will direct you, as far he is able, how you should best shape your prayers to the Almighty God, and how you should seek that repentance which alone can be of service to you hereafter.

For God's sake, do not neglect his advice (the Recorder said, in conclusion), or reject the assistance he will give you in this great and important object, which is to determine whether you shall hereafter enjoy eternal happiness in heaven through the merits of the Redeemer of mankind, or eternal misery in hell for the crime of which you have been guilty, which is of the deepest dye. Having addressed these observations to you nothing more remains for me to do than to pass on you the awful sentence of the law, and that is that you, Esther Hibner, be taken from this place back to the gaol from whence you came, and that from thence, on Monday morning next, you be taken to a place of execution, there to be hanged by the neck until you are dead, and that afterwards your body be delivered over to the surgeons for dissection; and may the Lord God Almighty have mercy on your soul!

During the address, which was delivered in a manner the most impressive, the prisoner stood at the bar unmoved, and it was not until mention of her body being delivered over to the surgeons for dissection was made that she manifested any symptom of emotion.

No sooner had the Recorder pronounced the words, however, than a slight convulsive tremor agitated her frame; but it was soon over, and she stood as previously, exhibiting, it might almost be said, a species of indifference.

She was then arraigned on a second indictment, charging her with the wilful murder of Margaret Howse, another of her apprentices, and with a cool and collected voice she pleaded not guilty.

There being, however, no necessity now to go on with that case no evidence in it was offered.

CHAPTER X.
ESTHER HIBNER ENTERING THE VALLEY OF THE SHADOW OF DEATH.

As soon as the awful sentence of death was passed, she was seized by two stalwart warders, who took hold of her for the purpose of conducting her to the mouth of the pit, where she would encounter horrors at every step, and be literally forced into the jaws of death.

For a moment the wretched woman clung to the front of the dock with a firm grip, as though buoyed up with the vain hope that some cry for mercy would be raised in her behalf.

But she looked in vain. She had shown no mercy to the poor overworked, cruelly beaten, and famishing orphans, and now none was extended to her.

Not a sigh or expression of regret—not even the faintest murmur at the justness of the sentence could be heard amidst the crowded assemblage. On the contrary there appeared to be a subdued feeling of satisfaction that her crimes were now at an end, and that the earth was to be rid of such a monster in human form.

Her hands were at length broken of their grip, and she walked firmly to the entrance of the pit—that pit so full of horrors which literally leads to the valley of the shadow of death. As she stood at the top of the steps—those steps down which so many have gone, never more to return—her face blanched with terror.

When she got to the bottom, and alighted in the pit, she suddenly said—

"I'll go back, I'll go no further, I haven't had justice. They have all done their best, and they have given me the law, but they haven't given me justice."

She appeared about to make a sudden bolt back up the steps as if she would try and again reach the court and make her escape.

But it was no use. A number of gaol warders blocked up the foot of the steps and prevented such an attempt.

"That is the way you have got to go now," said a most determined and resolute warder as he pointed the way to the entrance of a dark and subterraneous passage, which leads from the pit at the bottom of the dock in the court, a long distance under the yard of the gaol, and right into the condemned cells of the prison.

The way was dark and gloomy, and at the dismal entrance the woman was seized with a horrible fear.

She stood aghast at the entrance, crying out, "I won't go down there—I dare not go down that dark place; you shan't force me down there."

"You must go," said the warders. "That is the way now down to your cell. There is no other way for you now, only through that passage."

As they forced her into the dark entrance of the tunnel, a look of the most indescribable fright came over her face.

Her hair literally stood upon an end, and with her eyes standing half out of their sockets, and staring with a wild glare into the fearful darkness of the subterraneous passage, it appeared as though she could see fiends and goblins in the space before her.

"Loose me, you wretches! Take your hands off me, you —— devils! Let me go, you fiends!" she shrieked out as they pushed her at last, truly, into the valley of the shadow of death, and made her enter into the very portals of the grave.

As they impelled her along she leant backwards, and stood at every step, as though the dark air of the fearful passage was full of hideous forms.

At length the condemned cell was reached, and she entered it, to pass the few remaining hours she had to live.

CHAPTER XI.
OFFICIAL APPOINTMENT OF CALCRAFT.

WHILE the case of the wretched woman was pending, and during the period of its adjournment, the authorities were on the look-out for a good and suitable man whom they could appoint as the fully-recognised common hangman and general official executioner.

We have already stated that the former celebrated executioner, John Foxton, died on the 14th of February, and that for a little time he was succeeded by his assistant, the notorious Jack Cheshire.

This man, however, was also getting advanced in years. He was constantly drinking in the lowest taprooms, and associating with most disreputable characters, or anyone who chose to treat him with drink.

The authorities not wishing, therefore, to run the risk of such another disreputable bungle as occurred in the hanging of Birmingham—one of the ringleaders of the Field-lane gang of thieves—thought it more prudent to endeavour to obtain the services of a more steady and younger man.

It was quietly made known, therefore, in certain circles, after the burial of Foxton, that the office of "Prime Executioner" would be vacant, and that it would be filled up at the earliest opportunity by the election of the most suitable candidate the authorities could get.

There were a good many who no doubt would have aspired to the office had they thought their claims likely to be worth consideration.

Under the circumstances, however, we find there were but two applications—one from a man named Smith, and the other from Calcraft.

The merits of the respective candidates will be best judged of by the qualifications they urged, and by a report of the meeting at which the election took place.

CHAPTER XII.
MEETING OF THE COURT OF ALDERMEN.

YESTERDAY a meeting of the Court of Aldermen took place for the purpose of appointing an executioner in the room of J. Foxton, who a few weeks ago departed this life a short time after he had given two further awful proofs of his skill.

Foxton and Cheshire had been co-partners in the office of Jack Ketch some years; but the latter heard of his old partner's death with the utmost indifference.

When informed that Foxton was dead, Cheshire replied in the most unfeeling and blunt manner—

"Well! How the d——l could I help that?" as though he thought that there was a general opinion that old Foxton's death had been hastened by some neglect of his; or, on the other hand, that there was a general surprise that he had allowed the old man so quietly to die.

The following abstracts of the communications of the respective candidates were then read to the meeting:

Calcraft wrote to the following effect:—

"Hoxton, March 28th, 1829.

"To the Hon. Court of Aldermen for City of London.

"Gentlemen,—Having been informed that the office of executioner is vacant I beg very humbly to offer myself as a candidate. I am twenty-nine years of age, strong and robust, and have had some experience in the office. I am familiar with the mode of operation, having some few months ago been engaged on an emergency to execute two men at Lincoln. I did so, and as the two culprits passed off without a struggle, the execution was performed to the entire satisfaction of the sheriff of the county.

"I am, gentlemen, your very obedient and very humble servant," &c.

The alderman presiding said the second application was as follows from a man named Smith:—

"Westminster, March 27, 1829.

"To the respected Members of the Court of Aldermen of the City of London.

"Gentlemen,—Hearing that you are about to elect another executioner and hangman in the room of John Foxton deceased, I beg to solicit the appointment. I have been for some years in the army, but am now pensioned off. While I was in the army I was always selected to shoot those who by court-martial were deemed deserving of death. During the whole time in the whole number I have shot I have never missed the front of the forehead of the men I shot at at twelve paces distant. Under these circumstances I feel myself fully qualified for the office of hangman, and I hope, therefore, that you will be pleased to give me immediate opportunities for dispatching after another fashion.

"I am, gentlemen, your very humble servant," &c.

The presiding Alderman said he thought that though the qualifications of the last named candidate were very good, yet as the man Calcraft had already had experience as a hangman, he thought he was the most suitable candidate.

It was then unanimously resolved that the applicant, William Calcraft, be appointed the common hangman and executioner for the City of London.

Calcraft, who is described in the report as a strong, robust, good-looking, and very respectable man, was then called in and informed of his election to the office, and on the following Saturday, April 4th, he was duly sworn in.

The reports of the time state that the two candidates, before the election came off, offered to volunteer their services, and made bets with each other as to which could be most successful in any trial of skill the authorities might allow them to make.

Nothing, however, is said in the reports as to whom the experiments were to be performed upon, whether upon each other, any of the unfortunate criminals, or any of the officials.

Calcraft was, however, thus fairly and fully elected to his office, according to the report, on the day named.

There is no doubt old Cheshire soon began to sink into oblivion, and that he some time after was looked upon with considerable odium.

The times were such, and the state of crime so daring and extensive, that Calcraft had no doubt plenty of work in store for him.

It is almost impossible to depict in words the actual state of society—it was simply fearful, but yet in many phases romantic and appalling.

To turn over the long dismal list of the names of those that William Calcraft in the course of forty-five years sent into eternity from the scaffold makes us wonder in amazement at the stupendous amount of crime which has so long existed.

In giving a selection of the various kinds of crime perpetrated we shall endeavour so to set them before the public that they may be aware of the evils that exist, and from the lessons they may see revealed and brought to light in these pages we hope they may be guarded against them, or if they see others in any similar danger it is to be expected that they will try and avert the evil from them.

Many of the facilities which exist for crime exist only because too many people walk heedlessly about with their eyes shut to what is going on, even while they are passing by. Good government and an efficient police system may do much to check crime, but an alert, an intelligent, a well-educated, and a watchful people can do a great deal more.

CHAPTER XIII.

THE NEWLY-APPOINTED EXECUTIONER.

It was a lovely spring morning in April, 1829, when the newly-appointed executioner, William Calcraft, set out for his journey to Bury St. Edmund's to carry out another and final act of the law upon a ruthless murderer at that town.

As I had always been fond of studying the characters and history of men, I thought I would like to see what sort of a man young Calcraft really was.

I reasoned to myself in this manner: "The man who aspires to be the common hangman—the man who, like his predecessor, gets his living by hanging his fellow-creatures by the hundred all over the country—must be a very extraordinary specimen of humanity, and as I want all sorts of specimens for my study, I should like to study him."

In the course of my time I had studied the character of philanthropists, the caprices of all sorts of enthusiasts, the peculiarities of adventurers, the phrenological developments of all the celebrated murderers and criminals of every grade.

I was really well acquainted with the histories of the chief hangman's victims, so now why should I not make my knowledge complete by studying the natural history and instincts of the hangman himself?

A moment's reflection convinced me that it was a capital idea, for I thought also if I outlive the new hangman I'll write his history, and if I do not, well I must do as much as I can, and leave the rest for some one else to finish.

I knew that if I made haste I could overtake the coach at the "Coach and Horses," where it usually stopped a short time to take up other passengers. So away I went, and getting there in good time I saw Calcraft, with a tolerably good-sized bag, sitting up alongside the driver on the off side of the box.

"Is this seat engaged, coachey?" said I to the driver.

"No, sir," he replied; "jump up if you are going, for we are just off."

"Well, I suppose you can do a glass more before you start," I said.

"Thank'ee, ser," said he; "no objection to that, I'm sure."

And so I at once ordered what he asked for—a glass of rum hot.

"Perhaps your friend to the right would like one, too," said I, looking at Calcraft, and wishing, of course, to scrape a friendly acquaintance with him.

"No, I don't want anything," moodily replied the passenger on the off-side, as though he was already suspicious that I wanted to scrape acquaintance with him, and he didn't wish to be known.

"Better take one," says I to him, and then turning to the ostler I said, "Fetch our friend a glass of rum; he's only like the ladies, wants a little pressing, and bring three smokes as well."

One of these I offered the coachman, the other to Calcraft, and the other I kept for myself.

Calcraft, though at first almost doggedly obstinate, however, with the combined aid of my own and the

MRS. HIBNER'S ENTRY INTO THE VALLEY OF THE SHADOW OF DEATH.

coachman's quaint persuasion, at length gave way, and finally accepted the proffered glass and the smoke.

In one more moment we were all lighted up, the whip was unfurled, and we started off with the four horses in front, and the other passengers all apparently in the happiest mood.

Before we had got far on the road, on looking back, we saw a post-boy on horseback, riding full speed after the coach.

As soon as he approached near he shouted at the top of his voice—

"Stop, stop the coach."

The driver pulled up, and the post-boy gave to Calcraft a large official envelope sealed up.

Calcraft asked the driver to stop for a moment while he read it, and after he had perused it he said to the driver—

"I shall not want my seat any farther to-day, for I have a message calling me back."

I guessed in my own mind that it was either a respite or a reprieve for the man Calcraft was then going to hang, and Calcraft then getting down, he walked back to London.

I, seeing that my journey would then be useless, rode as far as the next stoppage, a distance of twelve miles, and then I got down too, at the same time telling the driver I also had altered my mind, and should probably go another day.

By a few inquiries I afterwards made I ascertained that the man at Bury St. Edmunds had been respited for a week, and I then resolved to meet the coach again at the end of that time.

CHAPTER XIV.

ESTHER HIBNER IN THE CONDEMNED CELL.

THOSE of our readers who desire to study real life as it is seen in all phases will now, perhaps, like to accompany us into the condemned cell.

Since the Prisons New Regulation Act has come into operation it is very difficult for a visitor to get an opportunity of seeing the interior of a gaol; but formerly, in the time of Esther Hibner, and even up till recent years, special orders for admission were sometimes obtainable from the sheriffs.

We have frequently obtained the necessary orders, and can, therefore, now take our friends over the mysterious windings of this fearful tomb both of the living and the dead.

Having passed the ponderous door, with its massive locks and keys, and entered the narrow winding passage, we soon come to that part of the interior of Newgate where the condemned cells are situate.

As we stand at a little but respectful distance we see the Rev. Dr. Cotton, the ordinary of the gaol, endeavouring to offer spiritual consolation and advice to Esther Hibner in these her last and trying hours.

"I beseech you now," says he, "to think of eternity. Look the facts now resignedly in the face, and think now no more of the world you have left for ever."

"Don't bother me about religion now," she replied, testily. "It's only a mockery to talk to me of religion and peace, and joy and happiness under the circumstances in which I am placed," said she. "I haven't had a fair trial, I haven't had justice done me, and if you'll go and try to get me out of this you'll be doing me more service than bothering me about another world. What do I want to know about another world? I want to live in this."

"Yes, but it is appointed unto all men once to die, and you are appointed to die on Monday next, and most assuredly will," replied the ordinary; "therefore let me entreat you——"

"And let me entreat you to go, and not bother me," said she snappishly, as she paced the cell in a most frantic and excited state.

"I cannot think of leaving you till I have reconciled you to your awful fate, and seen you at peace with your Maker. Let me therefore entreat you to go down on your knees in prayer."

"Well, if I pray at all it will be to you, and my prayer to you is that you will see me righted, and let Mrs. Johnson and Mr. Lester, and the other witness I wanted, be called, and they could prove that I was always kind to the children. Why am I to be hanged, and my daughter, and Ann Robinson get off? Will you go and see my witnesses for me?" said the wretched culprit.

"I would go and see anyone that I thought would be of service to you, but I am sure it would be no good now," said the ordinary.

"Well, but you can but go and try," said the woman. "The others have been worse than I have been to the children, and I am going to be murdered for what they have done. Why did they not give me a fair trial, and call my witnesses. Then I should have been acquitted, and if anybody had been hung it ought to have been them that did the mischief."

"Well, do go down on your knees with me, and join in prayer for pardon, I solemnly entreat you," said the ordinary.

"I am not going to pray, I'll take care of that," said the woman; "so don't mock me like this, and if you haven't anything better than this to say to me, why you had better go and leave me to myself."

Here she paced the cell backwards and forwards like a fury, using the most terrible blasphemies, and uttering the most fearful imprecations against the churchwardens and other officers who had been instrumental in bringing her to justice.

The reverend ordinary, seeing the excited state she was in, thought it prudent to retire, and also deemed it his duty to go to the governor, Mr. Wontner, and advise with him as to what was best to be done.

As she had expressed a great desire that certain persons she wished to have called as witnesses should be seen for the purpose of a memorial being drawn up to the Government to endeavour to get the clemency of the Crown extended to her, the sheriffs went and had an interview with her, at the urgent request of the ordinary, to get their addresses, and see if anything could be done on her behalf.

She readily gave their addresses, and then seemed a little more grateful to the ordinary for the trouble and interest he had taken.

"Ah," said she, when she heard from the ordinary that the sheriffs had gone to see her witnesses, "that is a step in the right direction, that is something like, there is some sense in that," and she appeared greatly buoyed up with the prospect of hope.

"Now let us kneel down and pray to the Almighty for mercy, and that He will be pleased to overrule all things for good," said the ordinary, thinking to take advantage of the transient ray of sunshine that seemed to beam upon the prisoner's prospects.

"No, I don't want to pray," said the prisoner. "I know as much of religion and the Bible as you do. I used to go to church often enough," said she, "and I want no more religion."

"It grieves me very much to see you in such a state of mind, but let me entreat you not to build too strongly upon a false hope," said the reverend ordinary.

The sheriffs at this point, after the lapse of several hours, returned to the gaol, and informed the culprit that they had seen the persons she wished called as witnesses, and that they had begged them to say anything they could in her behalf, but the reply of one and all of them was that there was nothing they could say, and that their opinion for a long time before matters were found out was that her conduct to the poor little children had been cruel and wicked, but they didn't like to speak about it, lest they should have to lose their time and come up to give evidence.

"The wicked lying wretches," said the culprit; "that is just the way of the world—to kick anybody when they are down. They used to be fond enough of coming to my house to tea when they'd got none of their own, and they used to say 'that if they had to deal with such parish varmints as those parish apprentices were they wouldn't stand half so much as I did from them,' and now they turn round on me like this do they—the sneaking cats?"

Then turning to the rev. ordinary, she said—

"Well, who are you going to see next for me—the judge or the Home Secretary—or who?"

"We have already had an interview with the learned judge for you, to see if anything could be done," said the under-sheriff; "but he deems it a very bad case, and he says he shall not do anything to prevent the law from taking its course, and will not interfere; so you had better now be resigned to your fate, accept of the consolation that the rev. ordinary will give you, and prepare yourself for another world."

At this the culprit broke forth into another frenzied passion, saying, as she again paced her cell—

"You shall never hang me—that you never shall. I am not going to die on the gallows like a dog—mind, if I do."

"Well," replied the sheriffs, "it is time for us to go now; we can but leave the rev. ordinary with you to pray for you; so good-bye for the present, if we do not see you again before Monday morning next; remember, eight o'clock on Monday morning next."

The rev. ordinary was now left with the culprit again, all having retired, with the exception of the warders, who for a time left the interior of the cell, and took up their station outside, so as not to interfere with the spiritual ministrations offered.

"I will now pray for you myself," said the ordinary, kneeling down by the side of the prisoner in the cell.

At this she became vehement and blasphemous, and again wildly pacing the cell, she said, "I'll have no praying here."

The ordinary then rose and said: "Would you like to see your daughter?" thinking that perhaps the daughter might be able to bring the culprit to a sense of duty, and that he might thus be able to make an impression upon her.

"Yes; I think I should like to see her, if you will fetch her."

The ordinary then went and obtained the consent of Mr. Wontner, the governor of the gaol, and they went and asked the daughter, who, along with Ann Robinson, was detained in another part of the gaol to come and see her mother.

On going to her, however, the daughter said, "No, I don't want to see her. I would rather spare myself the scene, and because I couldn't do her any good if I were to see her."

"You had better come and see her," said the ordinary. "It might perhaps soothe her."

"No," said the daughter, "I will not," and she remained obdurate and determined in spite of every persuasion.

The ordinary then, perfectly perplexed, returned to the cell and informed the culprit that her daughter under all the circumstances preferred not to see her again.

"Well," said the culprit, "it doesn't much matter. When you are in trouble even your own children forsake you."

The ordinary, seeing that he could not bring the culprit to any quiet sense of her position, informed her that he would now leave her for a time, and that if she wanted him he would be happy to attend her if she would send for him.

"All right," said the culprit rudely, "but I shall not want you."

The chief warder, as soon as the ordinary had retired, then stepped into the cell and said:—

"Well, Mrs. Hibner, how are you now?"

"Oh, I am pretty well," she replied; "but I should be a great deal better for a good mutton-chop."

"All right," said the warder, "you shall have one;" and as soon as possible he went and got one for her, and in a little time she was sitting down, evidently enjoying her meal much more than anyone under the circumstances could have been expected to do."

After she had had a chop and tea, she again commenced a tirade of abuse against all that had been engaged in her case, and at length worked herself up into such a violent frenzy of rage that the female warder, who had been deputed to watch over her, began to get alarmed for her own safety, and she asked for an extra attendant to be with her in case of necessity.

The ordinary came again later in the evening, and begged her, as the next day, Sunday, was the last day she had to live, to compose herself, and to prepare to employ the whole of Sunday in solemn meditation and earnest prayer.

All his entreaties, however, were of no avail, she only became more violent, and stamped and raged more furiously than ever.

As it was now getting very late he again left her, and retired to rest, asking to be called, should his services be required.

As the solemn hour of midnight drew nigh, the attitude of the frenzied woman became truly appalling.

She walked to and fro in the cell, stamping her feet and gnashing her teeth, while constantly exclaiming—

"I only wish while I was in the dock that I had rushed out to that churchwarden, and ripped his life out. I wish, too, I could just get my hands on some of them now."

Then suddenly turning to the two female warders in charge of her, she said—

"And you, you paid hirelings, don't you think they'll ever get a chance to hang me. I'm not going to be hung—I'll be blessed if I am!"

Then calming a little after some time, she asked the warders to allow her to retire for a few minutes to the private room.

The female warders accompanied her there, and waited for a few minutes outside.

Suddenly one of them heard a strange noise, and on looking on the ground they saw blood trickling from underneath the door.

In the greatest consternation and horror they burst it open, and they found that in spite of all their precautions the wretched woman had secreted a knife, and was in the act of violently cutting at her throat.

Fortunately the knife, though rugged, was blunt, and as no main artery was divided, it was hoped that the wound would not prove fatal.

The female warders quickly snatched the knife from her hand, and then, while one held her, and prevented her from further tearing the wound, or from doing further mischief to herself, the other ran and got the assistance required.

In the course of a little time the governor, Mr. Wontner, and the house surgeon were on the spot, and considerable more aid being procured the culprit was carried to another room, and endeavour was made by the surgeon to sew the wound up she made in her throat.

However, she kicked and plunged so about that it seemed impossible to hold her quiet while the necessary operation was performed.

"We shall have to put a strait jacket on her," said the surgeon. "I see I cannot sew the wound up without she can be kept perfectly still."

"Fetch one of the strongest strait waistcoats you can find, from the cupboard," said Mr. Wontner.

"You shall never put any strait jacket on me, I'm blessed if you do!" said the culprit, plunging and struggling with almost herculean power.

In a few minutes a warder came with a good stout canvas jacket, so constructed that when it was placed upon anyone the patient could not move a hand or arm, and when once strapped down in it was perfectly powerless for further mischief."

The difficulty now was to get it on; but there being plenty of help at hand, though she screamed and hooted, and scratched and tore at the officers like a tigress, it was soon placed on her, and she was at once laid on the table, while the surgeon, with a needle and silk, sewed the wound up which she had made in her throat.

She was then taken back to the condemned cell, laid on her pallet in the strait waistcoat, and so strapped down that she could scarcely move hand or foot, and thus further resistance was useless.

Still, however, as she lay there, with the blood gurgling in her throat, gnashing her teeth with rage, and her eyes flashing fire, she muttered and swore the most dreadful imprecations.

In the course of the night, on many occasions, her eyes appeared to glare with fire, and she seemed at times staring beyond the feeble rays of the small night-light into the darkness beyond as though she was looking with horror upon the forms of skeletons, or of some fearful fiend her own distracted brain had conjured up in fancy, and brought before her vision in terrible reality.

Now and then she shrieked out—

"Get away from me, you fiends! Depart from me, you demons! Jack Ketch shall never have me, for I'll never be hanged!"

At last her bodily as well as mental strength quite failed her, and she eventually fell into a sound and refreshing sleep.

She continued in this during the remaining portion of the night and till late on Sunday morning.

Soon after dinner the Rev. Dr. Cotton, the ordinary, came again to see her, and tried hard to prevail upon her to begin to prepare for death.

She was still lying on her pallet with the strait waistcoat on, but she still as firmly as ever refused any religious advice.

When, however, the ordinary asked her if there was any request she would like to make she said—

"No, unless it was that she would like very well to see her daughter if she chose to come; not that it mattered very much."

Dr. Cotton then went again to the daughter, and informed her of her mother's fearful state, and he then entreated her to make up her mind to come and see her mother once more before it was too late, and also to endeavour to get her to prepare to meet her God.

The daughter positively refused to come, but after many entreaties from the ordinary, who told her that perhaps she might regret not seeing her when she was gone, and when it would then be too late, she consented to go with him and see her.

When she entered the condemned cell she coolly said to her mother—

"Well, how are you?"

"Oh, middling," said the mother; "but I don't like being here. They ought to call my witnesses. I have got you to thank for a good deal of this. Why didn't you speak up a good deal better than you did in the dock? You never said anything hardly."

The two then began to reproach each other in the most fearful manner for the course things had taken, and a shocking scene of recrimination took place.

The governor and the reverend ordinary endeavoured to get the two women to desist from any further display of feelings and to begin at once to finally arrange any little worldly matter, and then to take leave of each other for ever before the mother rose in the morning to be ushered into eternity.

After a little time, and after they appeared to have said to each other all they had to say, the daughter was informed it was nearly time for her to say, "Farewell."

Both of them appeared to take the matter very coolly.

They just shook hands with each other and said, "Good night," as though they had been almost distant strangers instead of mother and daughter.

When, however, the time for taking a final leave did come, the daughter burst into tears. She suddenly appeared to realise her mother's awful situation. She seemed then quite overpowered—shook hands with her warmly, and affectionately wished her "Good bye."

The mother still remained firm and stoical, and her whole thoughts seemed to be upon how she could best escape the gallows, for even just as her daughter was taking her final leave she said—

"They shall never hang me. And I only regret now that when those overseers and churchwardens and officials came to my house that I did not tear them to pieces."

"It is no good you saying that now, mother," said the daughter; "it is no good to put yourself about like that. I know justice hasn't been done, but it can't be helped now; so 'Good bye' once more." And the wretched women parted in this manner.

The Rev. Dr. Cotton, late on Sunday evening, once more visited again the hardened and unrepenting woman, in the hope that before the night was gone he could leave her at peace with her Maker, but she remained as hardened and as callous as before, and once more he bade her "good night."

Soon after that the culprit took a little supper, and directly afterwards, apparently exhausted, went to sleep again for the night—a relief of two more female warders watching over her.

CHAPTER XV.
THE CULPRIT'S LAST SLEEP.

WHILE the doomed woman slept her last sleep there was nothing unusual in her demeanour to be observed.

The two female warders sat near her, nodding and dozing, half asleep and half awake, watching the weary and lonely hours go by.

Now and then they woke with a feeling of cold and chill, and with a strange and uneasy feeling almost akin to a sort of superstitious dread, as they sat in that cell of so many singular associations, where so many hundreds of malefactors have dreamt and slept their last.

Each time they woke they looked nervously round into the darkness that encompassed them, thinking that perhaps they might see the spectres of some of the murderers buried underneath the adjoining stones rise to their view.

They observed nothing, however, but the culprit, breathing her last few hours heavily away, with now and then a violent twitching of her muscles, a distortion of her features, and a nervous quivering of her frame, as though her slumbers were disturbed with fearful visions, and her spirit was not at rest.

A couple more hours had now passed away, and the chill of the cold morning air got more intense, and they anxiously looked for the breaking of the morn.

Presently the grey dawn began to break, the cocks in the vicinity of the Fleet Market began to crow—a babble of human voices, and of a congregating crowd round the walls of Newgate could be distinctly heard. Then as they listened they heard a general shout, and cries of "Here it comes;" then next a rumbling of something heavy on wheels; and they knew full well the ominous sound of the gallows being wheeled round.

Then in a few more minutes there was a heavy vibration against the wall, and then another shout, and they knew the gallows was in its place, outside the debtors' door.

The lumbering of the black, heavy, and fatal machine, the picking and hammering in the streets, and the shouts of the vast increasing mob during the time the barriers were being erected, and the dreadful preparations made, not only awoke the warders but the unhappy culprit too.

"What day is this?" said the miserable woman, as she half-opened her heavy and drowsy eyes, which were blood-shot for want of rest.

"This is Monday morning, and it will soon be time for you to prepare yourself," said one of the warders.

"I won't prepare. They shan't hang me; so you come and unfasten these straps, and take this strait waistcoat off me directly," said the culprit, in as violent a rage as ever; and she again relapsed into her former state of excitement and frenzy.

Meantime, the governor of the gaol was now up and alert.

The Rev. Dr. Cotton, the ordinary, was preparing himself for his last visitation.

The warders were up and busy, and the whole gaol appeared astir.

Foremost among those who were active in the preceding preparations was a short, rather thick-set man, of dark complexion, and rather bushy whiskers, apparently about thirty years of age, and this was William Calcraft.

He had, as has been previously stated, been appointed executioner a week ago, and this was

CALCRAFT'S FIRST OFFICIAL EXECUTION.

He had, according to the requirements of the law, slept in the gaol on the over-night, and had risen early that morning to superintend the arrangements, and see that the necessary apparatus was all in working order.

He had brought with him a good strong, brand-new hempen halter.

He had firmly tied the knot, and seen that the noose would run smooth, safe, and easy, and as he surveyed, with a sort of inward satisfaction and pride, the work of his own hands, he seemed to say to himself—"Well, the shoemaker may say 'there's nothing like leather,' but I think there's nothing like rope; that's as good a halter as ever was made, I'll swear, and there's no fear o' that breaking, or stopping half way either. The bolt works well, too, and I shall turn her off prompt and sharp in a jiffey—see if I don't."

The new executioner was evidently not a nervous man; and as he was not a bad-looking man the warders and gaol officials were friendly towards him, and there seemed a general opinion among them that the authorities had made in him a good choice, and that he was just the man for the work.

While Calcraft was thus busy with his own preparations, and waiting for the victim on which to try his first experiment, a painful and terrible scene was being enacted in the prison.

The condemned woman had taken her last meal; the female warders had held the cup to her mouth whilst she sipped the last little refreshment she was to have.

The church clocks had struck seven, and the rev. ordinary was again in attendance beseeching the unhappy woman to join with him in prayer, and make earnest supplication for mercy, before it was too late, as her time had now nearly come.

It was all no use. Again, and again she kept repeating, "I have not had a fair trial, and I won't be murdered for nothing. Why should you try to hang me any more than the others?"

It was now half-past seven, and the under-sheriffs came into the cell to demand her body from the custody of the gaoler.

She sought to argue with them, saying:—

"It is not me that's guilty—I'm not answerable for what others have done."

"You have had a fair trial," said the sheriff. "It was to your care, you know, that the poor child was entrusted. It was your duty to have seen that it was not ill-used—and because you were the responsible person the jury found you guilty. So do now be quietly resigned to your fate, and walk quietly with us for the law to be carried out."

"I won't go, nor you shan't take me either," said the obstinate woman.

"You must go," said the sheriff, "and you must be dressed immediately."

"I won't," said she; "Jack Ketch shall never lay hold of me."

While this fearful and exciting scene was going on, Mr. Wontner, with his usual feelings of humanity, had carefully and studiously kept Jack Ketch out of her sight, lest even a glimpse of him might excite and terrify her worse than she was.

At last the funeral bell of St. Sepulchre's Church began to toll, and the governor knew, as it was now just a quarter to eight, there must be no more dallying of time.

"Now, then," said the governor to the warders, all of whom were in attendance, "unfasten the straps and get her up from her bed."

The straps were duly undone, and an attempt was made to dress her in a becoming fashion, and also to get her to walk composedly to the gallows.

No sooner, however, was she loosed than she began

to plunge and rave violently again, and all attempts to becomingly dress her were vain.

The funeral knell began to toll more solemnly and oftener still, and it was within a few minutes of the time—eight o'clock.

As nothing else could be got over her, her long white bed-gown was put on her to cover the sight of the strait jacket, and, her hair being pulled up straight and tied in a knot at the top of her head, a man's knitted night-cap was put on her to keep her hair in place, and to prevent it coming down and getting entangled in the halter.

Several good stalwart warders now seized her, and, as she would not stand on her legs, they had to carry her bodily into the room where Calcraft was in readiness to pinion her.

No sooner did he seize her than she set up a most horrid shriek, which was heard through the gaol, and far among the noisy and surging crowd.

The rev. ordinary, dressed in his white surplice and black stole, then appeared on the scene, and took his place at the head of the procession, and commenced the service in a solemn and affecting manner, reading in a distinct and audible voice—

"I am the resurrection and the life, saith the Lord; he that believeth in me though he were dead yet shall he live."

When the procession arrived at the debtors' room at the bottom of the scaffold, the cortège was stopped in order to see if the hardness of the woman's heart would soften, and before it was finally too late to see if she would yet pray to God for mercy.

Once again, however, she finally refused, and the rev. ordinary then proceeded up the gallows steps reading the words:

"We brought nothing into this world, and it is certain we can carry nothing out."

As soon as he appeared on the scaffold there was a general cry of "She's coming now," and shouts of "Hats off in front!" were heard in every direction.

After the ordinary came the warders, carrying in their arms the wretched woman, dressed as before described, she being still determined neither to walk nor stand.

When she came into view she met with the most fearful yells and groans, mingled with every sign of abhorrence and detestation.

The warders placed her under the drop, and in another moment Calcraft emerged through the well-known door, came up the steps, took from his pocket the halter, put the noose over the culprit's head, and then hooking the other end of the rope on to the fatal beam, he finally adjusted the noose.

While these final arrangements were proceeding, Calcraft was loudly cheered again and again, and so repugnant did the crimes of the woman appear that the whole populace seemed to hail the horrid work of the new executioner with delight.

Meantime, as soon as the cheers of the excited crowd had somewhat subsided, the voice of the clergyman could be heard again repeating the solemn words of the service:

"Man that is born of a woman hath but a short time to live, and is full of misery. He cometh up and is cut down like a flower; he fleeth as it were a shadow, and never continueth in one stay."

Jack Ketch having caught her neck properly in the rope, quickly disappeared down the steps below, while the warders stood beside, supporting the unfortunate woman under the fatal beam, the clergyman proceeding with the awful and solemn words:—

"In the midst of life we are in death; of whom may we seek for succour, but of thee, O Lord?"

At these significant words the bolt was promptly drawn; the fatal drop fell; the treacherous floor came down with a crash.

The wretched woman with a heavy thud fell after it into the pit beneath, but the floor was gone from under her, she was caught in the noose prepared for her, which slipped quickly and surely to its place; the rope gave a dreadful jerk; her neck was broken, and she dangled in the air amidst the cheers and joy of the excited crowd.

After hanging an hour Calcraft again appeared on the scaffold, and as he cut the body down he was loudly cheered.

The body of Esther Hibner was then delivered over to the surgeons for dissection, and in the course of another half-hour Calcraft was again on the road to Bury St. Edmunds to perform another execution.

So the work of Calcraft began with a most exciting execution in a most exciting period of English history.

CHAPTER XVI.
CALCRAFT ON HIS WAY TO BURY ST. EDMUNDS.

A FEW days after our previous meeting on the coach I saw Calcraft again on the same box of the same coach, as I had then ascertained that he was off again to Bury St. Edmunds, as the Home Secretary had then finally ordered the execution of Partridge there to be carried out. I did as before, called for glasses and cigars for myself, Calcraft, and the driver, and we were soon on our way as before.

I and the driver got on very well together as we chatted along on the various topics of the day, and when we got past the outskirts of the busy metropolis, I soon found that I had a capital companion in the coachman, who, for a man in his station, was well informed and full of jokes and quaint old saws—in fact, I found that I had got two objects of study instead of one.

On the other hand, I found Calcraft exceedingly reticent, and inclined to be morose when topics of anything like local interest were broached.

It seemed to me as if he was afraid of being known, or else that he inwardly thought he was known, and that he perhaps suspected that I might have been employed on the part of the friends of the culprit whom he was on his way to execute to meet him on the road, perhaps decoy him off his seat at some of the wayside inns, get him into some of the adjoining woods, burke him, and thus, by delaying the arrival of the executioner, prevent it from being carried out.

Greatly as I wanted to put him under the microscope of my examination lenses, I felt almost afraid even to look at him, let alone turn the light on him, and let him know that I knew he was Calcraft, the hangman.

At last I thought to myself well it is no use wasting any more time in beating about the bush, so here goes and I'll launch off with a good broadside on the usefulness, the pluck, the merits, and the patriotism of the executioners of England. I did not say hangman, because I thought executioner would sound better.

I thought I would direct all my observations to the coachman, and then I could by repeated side glances see what effect they would produce on the physiognomy of William on the other side.

So after having touched on a number of extraneous topics I said to the driver—

"What a tremendous number of people there was at that execution of Esther Hibner this morning."

"Yes," replied he, "so I hear."

"They say there were more even than when old Mother Brownrigge was hung."

"Yes," I replied, "and that was a similar case. I hate cruelty, above all things to little helpless children. It is a good thing when such wretches are caught, and the man who is courageous enough to put them out of existence deserves the thanks of his country." Then turning to look towards my second right-hand friend, I thought to myself, "that is pat No. 1 for William."

"I think so, too," said the driver; "there's lots o' that ere cruelty about, and if I know'd the executioner I'll be hanged if I wouldn't drink his health, and have a pot with himself over that."

I then noticed that William raised his eyebrows a little, and as his face became a little more placid, I observed a sort of smile of self-satisfaction evidently shine upon him.

"That will do," thought I to myself, "I am on the right tack; so now for another onslaught."

Then I said: "If it had not been for the executioners what a lot of thieves and murderers there would have been about! Wouldn't there?" said I to the driver.

"Right you are again," said he. "Why they would have multiplied like rats and vermin, and there wouldn't hardly have been an honest person living if they hadn't been worked off. People may say what they like about the executioner, but I say the executioner is a patriot."

"Just what I have advanced," as I looked to my right again to see the effect upon William of pat number two, and I could see that the cold gloom of frigidity of his former demeanour was completely giving way.

I then determined to renew the attack again, for I had yet never met the man that I could not soften and beguile.

In fact I had studied that as an art, and I knew that with proper palaver I should catch William with lime like a bird on a twig. So I next proceeded, again addressing the driver.

"Executioners as a rule have been very loyal men too, for when the regular executioner was called upon to behead King Charles he refused to act," said I.

"Yes," replied the driver, " but I wonder what the present executioner would do under the same circumstances?"

I thought to myself, well that is rather a startling question—quite a poser, and then, turning to look at William, I observed him pull his cap on one side and scratch his head, evidently in his own mind engrossed in the conversation, and at that moment debating a very serious question.

"Oh," I replied, " the days of savage martyrdom and unnecessary bloodshed are over in England, and I think the work of the present executioner will be limited to the proper ridding of the country of mercenary and merciless brutes."

"A very commendable and praiseworthy occupation," rejoined the driver.

And on this I had another side glance at William to observe the effect of pat number three, and I saw that that had the desired effect too.

"They tell me that they have appointed a new executioner in the place of old Foxton; and I saw something about it in the paper myself. I wonder what sort of a man he is?" said the driver.

"Oh, he is a decent-looking man. I saw him very plainly on the scaffold this morning," I replied.

Then I turned to have another look at William, and then I fancied he looked rather uncomfortable, but then I thought it was no use being afraid, so now was the time to try and fetch him out.

Then turning to the driver, I said: "I wonder whether our friend on the off side has ever seen an execution?"

Thinks I that will fetch William out now, and it will be better to say something to set the coachman on to him, than tackle him direct myself.

The bait took, and then the driver, addressing his off-side passenger, said: "Maybe you've seen an execution in yer time, sir?"

"Yes," tartly replied Calcraft, "I have seen a few."

Seeing the game now fairly started, I thought it was time to follow it up, so I said—

"What might be your opinion of executions in general, sir?"

"Oh, I agree with you in what you have said, that under some circumstances they are very necessary operations."

"I am glad you think so, sir," added I. "What do you think of the nature of the crime of that woman Hibner that was hung this morning?"

"Oh, dreadful," replied Calcraft; "there is a great deal more of that starving of little innocent children for the purpose of getting the parish money going on than most people are aware of."

"Then, again," added Calcraft, " there are numberless murders being committed by gangs of cruel villains going about and murdering helpless people for the sake of selling their bodies to the doctors for dissection."

"Is it possible?" said I, "and the country not aware of it."

"Aware of it!" said Calcraft. "People little dream of what is going on."

"Oh," I replied. "Perhaps you are in a position to know something of the under-current of society."

"Yes," he replied. "I have seen a little."

"Did you see the execution this morning?" said I, seeing now my chance for a splendid direct attack on his hitherto reticent demeanour.

"Well, yes," he replied; "I did see it."

"Oh, indeed. Where did you stand—did you get a good place?" said I, looking at him with an affected air of wonder, to notice the effect my closing attack would have upon him.

"Well, yes, I had a good view—I was pretty near," said he.

"Oh, may be you were up at one of the windows opposite, in one of the two guinea seats," said I.

"No," replied he, "I was nearer than that."

"Well," I said, "if I am not too inquisitive, perhaps you got there very early, and had a good stand at the foot of the gallows?"

"No," said he; "If I must tell you I was inside the gaol."

"Indeed," said I, "you rouse my curiosity more than ever. How ever did you manage to get inside the gaol? You are a friend of the governor's, I suppose?"

"No," said he. "I don't know that I am a friend of the governor's, but I was there on business."

"On business," said I. "Well, I never like being impertinently inquisitive, but really you have now so awakened my curiosity, may I ask you what business you were there upon? I hope it is not an impertinent question; but really what a strange coincidence," said I.

"Yes, it is," said the coachman; "to think we have been talking so much about the execution with some one that has been inside and witnessed it all, sitting by our side the whole of the way. Well, I hope none of our observations were personal to the gentleman."

"May be you are one of the sheriffs, sir; if so, allow me to congratulate you, sir, on ridding London of such a monster," said I, and then I took another side look to see how William took that.

"Well," said Calcraft, after a little pause, "it is not always wise nor pleasant to tell everybody who we are; but may I ask who you are? You know what is sauce for the goose is sauce for the gander."

"Oh yes," I said, "I have not the slightest objection in the world to tell you who I am, and what my profession is. I am a 'demonstrator of anatomy, a lecturer on phrenology, and I am the author of several works on Our Criminal and Pauper Population.' That I hope will be a sufficient apology for any close question put to you, which, unexplained, might seem impertinent when I said my curiosity was aroused to know what official engagement you had at the execution this morning."

"Well," said Calcraft, "if you will give me your card, and if you can keep the matter a secret, I don't mind telling you who I am, and perhaps as I shall often have to come this road I don't mind telling the driver too."

"Oh, we will keep the secret," replied both I and the driver. "We should not think of blabbing any gentleman's private business."

"All right, then," replied the outside passenger. "Then, if you must know, I am William Calcraft, the newly-appointed executioner; and it is me, the very identical person that you have both been talking about nearly the whole of the way."

"How very singular!" said I.

"Yes, it is very strange. I hope we have given no offence. I am sure I didn't know who you were," said the coachman.

"Oh, none at all," replied Calcraft. "I've been quietly enjoying the fun, and I am glad to think that real gentlemen know how to value the executioner's calling. Perhaps, sir, in your studies I may be some assistance."

"Thank you, Mr. Calcraft," said I, as I thought to myself how nicely I had hooked him.

Then addressing him again I prepared myself for the grand attempt to get him under my magnifying lenses for the purpose of studying the man's real character, and the real value of the part he had to take in the last execution of the law.

"May I be so bold, Mr. Calcraft, to ask you how it was you first came to take up with such an honourable and useful profession, and how it was you came to be fortunate enough to obtain such a valuable Crown appointment as the sheriff's assistant?"

"Yes," he replied. "I, like yourself, always had a liking for the study of real character, and as my former occupation threw me a great deal into the company of my predecessor in the office I cultivated his acquaintance chiefly for the purpose of seeing as much as I could behind the scenes of life."

"A very interesting study," I observed.

"Well, you must understand that during the last few years I have been a great deal at the old executioner's house, and I have heard him tell many a strange tale of bygone history, and the scenes he has witnessed. Depend upon it, sir, there's a great deal more interest attaching to an execution than the mere hanging of the culprit."

"Ah, that there is," observed the driver.

"You see," proceeded Calcraft, "executions make you acquainted with all sorts of criminals. You have an opportunity of knowing what their dying confessions are—you see the various modes of perpetrating crime—you are led to a knowledge of the motives that propelled the criminal to them, and more than that, you get an opportunity of seeing what is wrong in society, and also of knowing what the remedy for the wrong ought to be. You would scarcely credit the number of murders that are being committed every day at the present time that the country knows nothing at all about, and I can assure you, sir, there is such an organisation for the systematic perpetration of crime that would make you shudder if you knew it."

"I have not the slightest doubt of it," I remarked.

"When I used to be in the itinerant pie trade," said Calcraft, "I had full opportunities of seeing the various tricks of the worst thieves walking, and when I used to visit the old executioner's house I saw such phases of life there that I came to this conclusion, that the various classes of society prey upon one another—literally catch and kill and live upon one another like the bigger animals in nature live upon the smaller. One system that I allude to is the actual killing—really murdering people wholesale for the purpose of selling their bodies to the surgeons for dissection.

"The old executioner, you must know, at one time of his life was a noted resurrectionist.

"He used to make heaps of money by getting the corpses out of their graves, and selling them to the demonstrators at the various anatomical schools. Of course there was not so much harm in stealing bodies from the graves to sell them as there was in murdering people to sell their bodies.

"But, however, my predecessor carried on a large business as a resurrectionist before he was appointed executioner (continued Calcraft), but after he got that office he didn't steal so many bodies, but he dealt largely in them. He used, too, to have a great many of the bodies of those he executed at one time, for very few people who are executed have any friends who afterwards care to come forward and own them, or even interest themselves much about their bodies; many of those therefore which are supposed to be buried, and for which the country is called upon to pay, seldom are honoured with interment, although their coffins may be. If, however, some friend should interfere, the business is of such a melancholy nature that the party uniformly adopts the most ready and private mode of conducting the affair. One undertaker in the vicinity of the prison was recommended on all occasions, who, being in league with the old executioner, used to manage matters so that not one corpse in fifty was actually interred, a substance of equivalent weight always being introduced into the coffin, while the body was reserved for sale.

"My predecessor, who was always called Jack Ketch," Calcraft said, in conclusion, "was very proud of his office, and I used to say to him sometimes, 'Well, Jack, you can look back upon many years now, and I don't suppose any of your predecessors ever had such a long line of business in your particular way as you have had.' With very great emphasis he would then bring his heavy hand down on the table, and say, 'Well, I'm called on to do it. It's been my fate to do what very few men dare do. If it were not for me how would the law be carried out? What are all your thief-takers, magistrates, lawyers, counsellors, judges, lawmakers—aye, even the king upon the throne—but for me, the executor, the finisher of the law.'"

"Very good," said the driver, "where would all that law be if it was not for the executioner, the man that carries the law out?"

WILLIAM CALCRAFT, THE HANGMAN.

MR. KETCH EXPLAINING THE MERITS OF HIS RESPECTIVE ROPES.

"My predecessor," continued Calcraft, "lived, you know, too, in most portentous times, when the Government was afraid of having just as great a revolution break out in this country as broke out in France at the time of Napoleon. The Government thought they would have to take to hanging a great many more here as an example to frighten others when the agitation for Free Trade and Reform was going on all over the country. I recollect him telling me one day that he had been sent for to Downing-street, where there was a council of persons in authority, and before whom he underwent a long examination on the subject of constructing drops upon a larger scale than the one used at the Old Bailey, and that he was particularly asked how many he thought could be strangled in one day, in case the interest of the country required still more desperate measures."

"That was a nice idea, wasn't it?" said the driver. "It's a pity he did not ask them how many there were of them, and have seen what they would have thought of the prospect themselves. I think from what little I know of history, people in office have been too fond of hanging people out."

"Well," said Calcraft, "I was going to tell you my predecessor was a man that grew with the times. He had a strong will, and held strong opinions of his own on many points. Sometimes after an execution he would appear to have a certain uneasiness of mind, and particularly so once after he had executed a young man who had taken upon himself to dispute the justice of the law, and, as a natural consequence, objected to the ceremony. Owing to this the old executioner came to the conclusion that the young man was insane, and that he ought to have been placed in the hands of the mad doctor instead of being sent to him to cure. Having hung for a long time the whole of his thoughts upon this peg, he left no stone unturned to find out facts in support of what he had advanced, and, unfortunately for his peace of mind, the inquiries he set on foot all tended to confirm his impressions of the malefactor's insanity. He collected a number of anecdotes regarding the mad freaks of the young man in early life, and to wind up the whole chain of evidence he at length met with a widow with whom the young man was apprenticed, who informed him that, had she been called on the young man's trial, she should have established his insanity beyond controversy.

"Fully impressed with this idea, he stopped nowhere until he reached the governor's office at Newgate, and delivered himself to the following effect:—

"'I have now held office, sir, nearly forty years, and I believe it is admitted on all hands that I have done the State some service. I have stuck to my post through evil report and good report, and done my duty even in my youngest days like an old general. I have stopped the throats of those who it is well known would have cut the throats of the administration, and who would have overthrown the country. These things have I done, and much more, which I need now not mention; but, sir, I am no murderer, and never will be. You know, sir, it is our duty to put down crime and not to commit it, yet am I a murderer, you are a murderer, the judge is a murderer, the king and council are all murderers. It's a sad business, sir, and what makes the matter still more serious it brings back to my recollection so many like cases that I am struck with horror.'

"'Horror-struck—are you, Mr. Ketch?' said Mr. Wontner, the governor, sarcastically. 'Have you been drinking to-day or are you actually going mad yourself?'

"'No, sir,' rejoined Ketch, 'I have found my senses, not lost them, and have discovered that the last man you brought out to me on the drop was mad, and had been so all his life—think of that—think of that. Then there was poor Bellingham; if I had known that they would not wait for his friends to come up from Liverpool I'd have left him standing there till now (pointing out of the office window to the spot where executions take place) before I would have interfered with the matter. It's a scandalous shame, sir, to conduct the business of the Bailey in this manner. I have depended upon you all, and you have deceived me in this, I can see plainly, as you have done many times before. I must look into these matters for myself in future I can see, but I will now go home and acquit myself, and acquit my conscience, as far as I am able, by marking off in my book all the bad cases I think I have had. I'll expose you, gentlemen, you may depend on it, before I quit the world. It seems to me as though you had put a handkerchief over my eyes all my life, and that it is but this moment taken off.'

"'You know if you don't like the situation, Mr. Ketch,' said the governor, 'you can leave it.'

"'Leave it! aye—no,' continued Ketch, getting into a passion, 'I should like to stay a little longer, and catch hold of some of their sanctified carcases (pointing again out of window). That is the only thing that would make me happy.'

"Now, old Ketch," continued Calcraft, "embodied these cases, which, during his career, greatly troubled his conscience, in his history. I only, therefore, mention this circumstance to show how sudden was his conversion to the cause of mercy and justice. From this period of his life he, till the time of his demise, was a dreadful annoyance to the City authorities, especially to the late doctor of Newgate, whom he would waylay and reproach in the bitterest terms, saying he took pains enough to expose a pretended madman, but never went into the prison to try and find out those who were really insane, but perhaps were not evidently such to every fool, and who, of course, unlike the pretender, wished to make themselves as sane as possible. He never afterwards overcame the compunctions feelings of his conscience, concerning those men whom he supposed had been executed although innocent of the crime for which they suffered, or those who were mad, being frequently heard to mutter to himself even up to the day of his death: 'I was at the top of the law; it was therefore my business to be more particular, and examine into matters before I went so far; people should look into their own business, and not trust to others as I have done.'"

"Well, there was a good deal of reasoning and method in old Ketch's madness," observed the driver.

"Yes," said Calcraft, "he was a shrewd old chap in his way, and it may seem strange in the character of Ketch that he should at one time with such indifference perform his office, and yet show such strong feelings against those who upon many occasions refused to lean to the side of mercy. This apparent incongruity in his conduct will be reconciled when we reflect that although he was proud of being in his office at first, yet he very soon found reason to be disgusted with the great want of justice shown in selecting malefactors, and in deciding after they were all sentenced to death which of them were to be hung, and which of them were to have their sentences commuted and sent into penal servitude for life. No session during his life was he entirely satisfied upon this head, maintaining to the last that he was better qualified to determine which of the prisoners should be spared and which suffer than the Home Secretary himself. Nor was this altogether vanity or a feeling without foundation; it must be remembered that he had a very intimate knowledge of the whole family of delinquents, had played a part a long time behind the wicket, and had means of ascertaining much connected with the metropolitan banditti of thieves, which to all the rest of the world would be a profound secret. His own near prospect of death upon an unfounded charge, and the many fatal mistakes which in his time did really occur, added to many more probably his conceited imagination improperly put down as such, together with the remorse of conscience which overtook him, will fully explain the querulous turn his mind took towards the close. He used to tell many exceedingly interesting stories, some of which if I had time I might relate to you."

By this time the coach had arrived within sight of Bury St. Edmunds. We had had a pleasant ride, some instructive and interesting conversation, and Calcraft promised on our journey home, if we all engaged the same seats, to relate to us some matters of amusing and special interest which had come under his own immediate observation.

We all agreed to come back together, and by this time had arrived at the end of our journey.

CHAPTER XVII.
THE ARRIVAL AT BURY ST. EDMUNDS.

HAVING arrived at Bury St. Edmunds the driver finally pulled up at the "Abbey Arms," and the respective travellers adjourned to some of the various inns for refreshment.

Calcraft, with his ominous-looking bag, which I guessed contained the halter, hastened off in a fly in the direction of the gaol, where, no doubt, some refreshment was provided for him, whilst I ordered a good luncheon at the "Abbey Arms," to which, having done full justice myself, I hurried on to the front of the gaol to witness his second execution.

When I got there many thousands of persons were already in front of the gaol, and the scaffold was full in view.

The funeral bell was already tolling, and a mournful procession was coming down the winding and rural lane.

As it approached I could see the dreadful cortège.

The young man was being brought from the prison in which he had been confined in the district of the crime, to be executed in front of the county gaol.

He was already pinioned, and was sitting in a large open cart, on the top of his coffin.

The sheriffs and governor of the prison rode on horseback in front, and a large number of constabulary of the county rode behind and on each side of the cart.

The awful cavalcade entered the great gate of the gaol, and in a few more minutes the clergyman ascended on to the scaffold with the open book in his hand, reading the burial service for the dead.

Then came the culprit, with his arms firmly pinioned behind.

He was a fine, tall, powerful young man. After him immediately came the sheriffs, and then our fellow-traveller, William Calcraft, stepped upon the scene.

Having properly adjusted the rope, he pulled the white cap over the culprit's eyes, and descended behind the scaffold.

In another moment the culprit suddenly dropped, and was hanging by the neck, showing us that almost instantly the bolt had been drawn the drop had fallen, and the young man had been launched into eternity.

A great shout of exultation was then heard, and from the joy manifested it was evident the crime for which the culprit suffered was considered to be one of the most heinous kind.

After the lapse of a few minutes, when order was restored, Mr. Arridge stepped upon the scaffold, and addressing the assembled crowd, said—

"I have the satisfaction of informing you that the culprit has confessed his crime, and has not only confessed to that, but also to the perpetration of another murder, which has cleared up a terrible mystery which has been hanging over the district now for some time."

After hanging the usual time the body was cut down, and the crowd dispersed.

We then dined and stayed in the town that night, for the purpose of having a look round at the splendid architecture of the historical old place.

Having visited the Abbey of St. Edmund the Martyr, and listened to some of the legends in connection with the monastic orders, we returned again to the "Abbey Arms," and spent a pleasant evening in company with some of the people of the place.

Next morning we set out again on our homeward journey for London. Calcraft occupied his seat on the box along with the driver, and I occupied mine.

He had with him the same bag as before, and now, being on more sociable terms than in the early part of the journey there, I said—

"I suppose that contains the halter with which you did yesterday's work?"

"Yes, it does," he replied; "and a very good one it is, too, for it slipped to its place remarkably well. He was a strong, heavy chap," said he, "and his crimes were as heavy as himself, but he made a good confession at last just before he ascended the scaffold."

"Was he of respectable parents?" said I.

"Yes," replied Calcraft; "he was of very well-brought up people, they tell me. He was the same name as his father, George Partridge, but I pity the father of the murdered little boy more than anybody. Misfortunes, they say, never come alone, and sure he has had enough to break anybody's heart. Twelve months ago the father of the murdered little boy, Mr. Anstey, was a large farmer himself, holding an adjoining farm here. He made some bad debts with his crops through being taken in with a gang of swindlers in London, which entirely broke him up, and he failed, and then he had to go to work as a common day-labourer at ten shillings a week.

"Then he had the misfortune to break his leg. Then last summer a dear little boy of his, Jonas Anstey, six years old, was found dead in an osier bed. As there were no marks of violence, and he was not found for some time, they came to the conclusion at the inquest that he either got lost or died there by accident. Then two or three weeks after his little boy, George Anstey, nine years of age, was found in Mr. Woodgate's field with his throat cut. No motive for such a crime could be thought of, but the guilt of George's murder was brought home to the culprit I hung yesterday, George Partridge, labourer. He was about twenty-one.

"Just before he was going up to the scaffold he said to the chaplain—

"'I acknowledge the justice of my sentence, but I have something more to say yet—I have not told all.'

"He then said—

"'It was I who murdered Mr. Anstey's other little boy that was six years old. It was me also that got that young man off his horse in the dark, and tried to cut his throat, but I could not find my knife quick enough. The reason I did it all was because I have been intimate with all the three young women that live next door to me. These children caught me with them in the field, and the eldest of the sisters always kept saying she was afraid they would tell what they had seen, and she bothered me every day to cut all their throats. She promised me if I would do that she would meet me any time I liked. I then cut their throats to please her, and stop their mouths. Then, after that, she kept saying if I did not bring her money every week she would tell of the murders.' So, you see, the women are at the bottom of everything almost."

"So they are," said the driver.

"I promised on our journey here," said Calcraft, "to relate to you two or three little amusing incidents which came under my own observation, to illustrate to you the character of my former predecessor, old Foxton, or, as he was always called, old Jack Ketch. Besides being very self-opinionated he was a very jealous man, and he was peculiarly tenacious of his claims on society. In the days of the old fighting generals that used to go out to conquer old Bonaparte he used to be constantly pitting his claims against theirs. 'Look,' said he, 'what splendid monuments the Government and the country raise to some of these fellows in St. Paul's Cathedral. What grand pensions too the country provides for them and their families as well. I wonder whether the Government when I get a bit older will provide me with a pension of so many thousand pounds a year, and whether they will ever put up a splendid marble statue for me in St. Paul's Cathedral. I don't expect they will, but they ought. My services to the country have been as good as theirs, and better. What do those generals do? Why they go over and kill a lot of poor helpless foreigners; some of them go and kill thousands of poor harmless innocent negroes, and in killing them cause thousands of the best and most spirited of our own countrymen to fall in doing it, and then for that they come back, receive the royal thanks, and get loaded with honours. Why should they go out into other countries and order the inhabitants to be shot like rabbits—men that never meant any harm to them or us if they had only been left alone? Now, here am I. Haven't I stayed at home, and done the State real good service, by silencing all those fellows as won't work, and only go about plundering other people? Them's the coves I say that wants lifting off. I say it's a piece of rank deception to pretend that these fellows, who go out shooting men like the sportsmen shoot pheasants, do the country or society any service; whilst I, who does the real work, along with the judge and the lawyers and the parsons, only get about thirty bob a week, besides what extras I can make, as perquisites.'"

"Well, that aint much," said the driver—"is it, for strangling people, according to order, considering how fast the gallows is kept going nowadays?"

"No; but you know," continued Calcraft, "I did not altogether like old Jack's talk, because, you see, I always held the notion that if a man is a limb of the law, he ought to be loyal to the body to which he belongs, and not set himself up against it. That argument I can soon explain to you in this way. If your head and eyes saw danger coming to the right, you'd pull the left rein to the left with yer left hand—wouldn't yer?'

"O' course I should," replied the driver.

"Well," said Calcraft, "but suppose yer right hand were to say no, yer shan't pull that way, and were to take hold of the reins and pull to the right, where would yer be then?"

"Well, perhaps, all across the road, and some of us under the coach, for all I know," replied the driver.

"Just so," said Calcraft; "that just illustrates what I mean. If a man belongs to the State he'd no business to meddle with anything only just what concerns him, and that's just the difference between the old Ketch and the young un. Old Jack Ketch, you see, used to have a sort of professional scruple in his last days as to who he ought to turn off. He towards the close of his life wanted to be judge, jury, Home Secretary, and Jack Ketch as well; I only want to be the legal executioner of the law upon everybody the law condemns. I say it is the duty of the judge and jury to try the cases; then to send all them that's guilty to me; and then it's my bounden duty, according to the oath that I have taken, to put the ropes round their necks, pull the bolt at the proper time, and then let them hang till they are dead."

"Just so," said the driver, "it's no business of yours to try people."

"Well, I'll tell you another very good story now," replied Calcraft, "just to show you the lights and shades of human nature:—One foggy day, in the month of November, about two o'clock in the afternoon, I went to Ketch's residence after what he would call a very heavy job at the Bailey. I believe six had been executed that morning. While I was there, a knock came to the door, and as old Ketch never liked people to see who was at his house, or for anybody there to see who came, he hurried me away into a spare adjoining bedroom, and told me to sit down in the corner perfectly quiet, and not to move or make the slightest noise on any account whatever. Having shown me into the room and just pulled the door to, he then walked in a quiet leisurely way, with his pipe still in his mouth, to see who it was at the door on the stairs. The fog had come over so dense that I could scarcely grope my way in the room to try and find a chair. Just, however, as I looked round I saw in the dark dimness of the mist the bed, and on looking towards the head I saw three in bed.

"'Hallo, Jack,' says I, running after him.

"'Do you know you've shown me into the wrong room? I didn't know you kept a lodging-house—and there's three of the lodgers asleep in bed.'

"'Hold your row, you fool,' said he, as he laid hold of me and pushed me forcibly into the room again. 'You won't wake them. Go in there and be quiet, till I see who's at the door—I've got no other room to show you into; and stop there till I call you.'

"Not wishing to offend the old chap I reluctantly again retired into the room, and old Jack pulled-to the door again just as the impatient visitor gave another loud rap-tap at the door.

"Old Jack then went hobbling and muttering along, whilst I again endeavoured to find a quiet and vacant corner. When I had time for a moment's reflection I fancied I smelt a strange unearthly smell in the room, but yet, not wishing to disturb the repose of the sleepers, I thought I would quietly cast a glance at the lodgers in bed to see what sort of lodgers Jack had got in the house.

"As I pulled the drawn curtains of the bedroom window a little on one side, I thought the faces of the sleepers looked greatly puffed; their eyes seemed nearly starting out of their heads, and their necks had a peculiarly swollen and strange appearance. Then I looked round the room, and I thought I saw three other lodgers in sitting positions on the floor, leaning against the wall, and on trying to get a view of them too in the dark foggy light, I thought they had a very strange and quiet appearance. I heard not a sound of breathing, I saw not the slightest movement, and then going closer to the bed, and looking the people in the face I saw that they were dead.

"Presently the thought flashed across my mind that these were all the people that he had executed that morning, and that I was literally in the chamber of the dead. A sort of horror came over me—I cannot describe my feeling. I am not naturally a timid man, but for Jack Ketch to shut me up by myself in a room with six dead people that had been hung was an idea I scarcely liked. I could see no chair to sit down on, and as I was rather tired, and did not want to make any noise by walking about, I resigned myself to my fate, and sat down in one corner of the room as far as I possibly could from the others there who were taking their last long sleep.

"As the door of the room I was in was ajar I could see right into the room where old Jack Ketch and his visitor were, and I could also hear every word of the conversation that passed. The stranger who had knocked at the door had entered the room, and as he stood with his hat off he announced himself as Mr. Figgins, from the provinces."

"Yes," said old Jack Ketch, "you are Mr. Figgins from the provinces," taking the pipe out of his mouth, and puffing forth a volume of smoke. "And what may you please to want?"

Mr. Figgins, who was a very tall, slim, effeminate-looking gentleman, without any whiskers or beard, for a few minutes buried his face in his handkerchief, and seemed quite overpowered.

"Take a seat, Mr. Figgins, and compose yourself a bit," said old Jack, who was well accustomed to see people bury their faces in their hands.

"Sal," said old Jack to his wife, who had now come in, "the gentleman seems poorly, see what you can do for him."

"What is the matter, sir, and what may you want?" said Mrs. Ketch, soothingly, in a sort of motherly old fashion.

"I am given to understand that you are the executioner of Newgate," said Mr. Figgins.

"No; I am not the executioner," said Mrs. Ketch. "My husband there is."

"Oh," said Mr. Figgins, "is that him?"

Ketch then stood forward, still with his pipe in his mouth, and said, "Yes, that's me. I am the person what does the Bailey business. What do you please to want? I am at yer service, sir."

Mr. Figgins, as he looked up in the old hangman's face, evidently started with quite a look of horror, and a sort of involuntary shudder came over him, but in a moment or so, as soon as he had recovered himself, he said: "I must have a little conversation with you, Mr. Ketch."

"Begin, sir; no ceremony. I like to come to business at once. Nothing like business," said Jack.

"Very well, I will come to it at once," said Mr. Figgins. "You must know that I have only this morning arrived from the city of Exeter, having travelled now two days and two nights, which has made me rather nervous and unwell. Oh, dear me, I am so overpowered, do please give me a glass of water."

"Ah," said Mr. Ketch, "I see the old business over again. I suppose then you are the governor of the gaol, or, maybe, you are one of the sheriffs, been trying all over the country to try and get a cheap hand, and yet obliged to come to me at last—eh? That's just like all you country folks, you know. You never will give a man notice beforehand, and if you don't, how can you expect your business done properly? I can't be here and there and everywhere, you know, at the same time, sir. Now, suppose I had another engagement at the same time, what would you do then? Before you fix the day you should always send up to me, and then I could let you know how business runs here at the Bailey and other places. I travel, you know, sir, a great deal, and might have been out on a journey."

"You are mistaken. I am neither a gaoler, nor a sheriff," said Mr. Figgins, "but I am (striking his forehead with his hand), I am the miserable brother of one more miserable. One who is ordered for execution at our county gaol next Wednesday morning; and this is, as you know, Monday, and I have no time to spare."

"What! the brother of the malefactor," said Ketch. "What can you want of me; you had better go to the Secretary of State; it's the Home Secretary you want. I can't grant pardons; unfortunately, I've nothing to do with that; and, therefore, you must go to the Home Secretary; not that I think it will be of much use, for he never pardons—and swears he never will; he says the judges and juries are always right. Mercy on his poor silly soul! I wish I had him for nine or ten days under my keeping; his eyes should be opened on the ninth day like a puppy's, but he's now as blind as a bat, and it's no use going to him; he never can see anything if you put it ever so clear before him; and as to arguments—why, he's as deaf as a post to them. Carry the sun to him if you could, and put it in the office right afore him, and it would not enable him to see a case for mercy, or one of innocence. If you were, I tell you, to stick him atop of the rainbow, he would only see but one colour, and the name of that is obstinacy. But I'll be ——"

"Stop—stop," said Mr. Figgins. "I am not come to consult you on the point of mercy, for we too well know the truth of what you have stated. My feelings will hardly allow me to explain my motives for travelling so far to see you, but they must be overcome. Give me another glass of water, please. You are aware, Mr. Ketch, that when death cannot be avoided, it should be met with fortitude."

"Yes, sir, that's quite true—that's what I always tell my patients, to take it coolly. 'Tis no use making a noise about it, as Captain Thistlewood said to Ings when I had them under hand," said Ketch.

"I have no fear for my brother's fortitude," said Mr. Figgins; "he without doubt will meet his unhappy fate with steadiness, and as much courage as most men show under such melancholy circumstances. But what I want to guard against is any accident occurring if it can possibly be avoided, or that he should be put to any unnecessary pain. We would especially guard against the world having any occasion to remember his untimely end by the recurrence of anything remarkable happening, like that at Lincoln, or at Fowey in Cornwall—circumstances which our family have read with horror. Oh, the very thoughts of those endings make me sick. Goodness! what are our lawmakers made of to tolerate such a perpetuation of such possibilities as those? Give me some more water, please, directly."

"Sal, some more water," said Ketch; "the gentleman seems as though he's going to faint."

Sal now handed Mr. Figgins some more water, at the same time saying—

"Don't make yourself unhappy, sir; you may depend upon my husband. He's the most surest hand as ever is known, and he has the most genteelest way with him, you can't think. You should only see him at his business—he does it reg'lar nate, he does. He's slow, but he's sure."

"Silence, Sal," said Ketch; "don't you see the gentleman's ill?"

"I must go through it! Oh! I must go through it!" cried Mr. Figgins, as he burst forth into a blubbering fit of grief.

"No, my dear soul, you mus'n't go through it—it's your brother what's got to go through it," said Mrs. Ketch, soothingly.

"Hold your tongue, can't you, Sal?" said Ketch to his wife, and then, putting the side of his hand to his wife, he quietly whispered, "Can't you see the poor gentleman's crazy?"

"I really am not crazy," said Mr. Figgins. "Aye, true, my brother must go through it and not me, though I have enough to bear even in the thought of it, but the sudden transition from life to death, the dissolution of the soul from the body, and that by violence the most disgusting and horrible. Who has a right to do this deed?"

"I have the undoubted and undisputed right," said old Ketch, stepping forward in a pompous manner with his pipe in his mouth. "I have the legal right, and am empowered by his Majesty and the Court of Aldermen."

"I dispute that right, and I dispute the authority of any living being to authorise that right," said Mr. Figgins, as he looked up into the face of Ketch. "Man in his formation was endowed with certain rights, with intelligence, and self-independence, and no one has a right to take them from him. No man can give life back, and no one has a right to take it away."

"Oh, I beg your pardon, sir," replied Ketch. "I've got that authority, I have had it many years, and I can show it to you, too."

"No—no thank you, I won't trouble you now," said Mr. Figgins. "Some other time will do—some other time will do very well. You can't show me any real valid authority, I am sure, for no man has a right to take away life, as a man has not even a right to take away his own."

"Ah! I quite agree with you in that latter observation; right you are there. That is about the most sensible observation you have made," said Ketch. "I think you are coming to a bit now. Suicide is a most horrible crime, and I quite agree with you that no matter what are the circumstances, no man, no person whatever, has any right to make an attempt on their own life, especially when they've committed any crime for which they ought to suffer death, for in the first place they cheat the law, they cheat me out of my daily bread, and frequently they do the work in such a bungling manner that they cause themselves double pain to what they would if they'd have patience and let me do the job properly for them, as it ought to be done, in public."

"Well, it's a very complicated question, and very difficult to judge upon rightly," said Mr. Figgins.

"Not at all," replied Ketch. "If the law kills them, right or wrong, let the law answer for it, or those who made it, but I say that malefactors have no right to cheat the law. The murderer of Mar's family committed another murder, and a most revolting crime, when he murdered himself. Montgomery robbed the law when he committed suicide, and so does everybody where they do such desperate deeds as to try and cheat the gallows of its lawful victims."

"Well, well, it's no use arguing about that point any longer," said Mr. Figgins. "We had better get to the business that brought me here. I must go through it, hard as the task is."

"Yes," said Ketch; "we had better get to business—there's nothing like coming to business—there's nothing like coming to the fatherly arms of Ketch at once, as I always say, professionally."

"Well, listen to me then attentively," said Figgins. "Ever since my brother has been under condemnation for the offence of which he has been found guilty, forgery, nothing has run in the heads of my sisters but those shocking affairs which occurred at Lincoln, Cheshire, and Fowey. What works they met with them in I don't know, but they seem to give themselves more concern about the probable recurrence of such another circumstance in the person of our ill-fated brother than the nature of the sentence itself. This may appear odd to you, but so it is. With these notions in their heads my sisters have so wrought on my feelings that I believe they have at length deprived me of them altogether, as well as my senses, or I may ask how I came here; and that question puts me in mind of my business—namely, to try and prevent a similar accident befalling my brother. You are, I suppose, accustomed to these melancholy matters?"

"Well, if you wish to engage me, and I have to do the business, you may depend upon it being all right," said Ketch.

"I wish to goodness you would be quiet till I have done speaking, and pay attention to what I have to say," said Mr. Figgins.

"All right, sir," said Ketch. "Now proceed, and I will sit and listen to you till the bell tolls—I beg your pardon, I mean till the last moment."

"Very well, do," said Mr. Figgins. "Don't interrupt me, and give me another glass of water."

"All right, sir," said Ketch. "Sal, another quart of water for the gentleman. He's so overcome with grief that all the other has run out of his eyes."

"Poor gentleman!" said Sal, as she brought another old brown quart jug from the pump in the court below.

"I am better now I've had a good draught," said Mr. Figgins. "Now I want you to listen. The detestable person who now fills the office of hangman in our city was once servant to my unfortunate brother, and robbed him. My brother, at the instigation of his family, prosecuted this man to conviction, and he was sentenced to death. The sheriffs of the county being in want of a hangman, got this man his respite on condition that he undertook for the future the hangman's office. Well, this he did, and now one of the first persons he has to experiment upon is his old master—my unfortunate brother. These recollections come upon us with strong force, and my sisters will have it that if this man is allowed to officiate malice and revenge will induce him to aggravate his former master's sufferings, even if his want of skill does not cause him to effect it by bungling."

"Of course he would," said Mrs. Ketch. "I know what human nature is, and it's just the very thing he would do."

"Well," continued Mr. Figgins, "these are very unpleasant adjuncts to the case. Since, then, under our hellish laws the business must be performed, we would rather that it were done properly, and now you know the whole purport of my visit. In conclusion, though the sheriffs refuse to remunerate or to have any hand in engaging you, Mr. Ketch, they have consented to your coming down upon the awful occasion if our family will bear the expense. This being now understood, pray what will be your charges? Remember you must without fail go off by this evening's mail."

"What would be my charge?" said Ketch. "Well that depends, you see, upon circumstances."

"What are the circumstances that it depends on?" said Mr. Figgins.

"Well, there are a good many circumstances," replied Mr. Ketch, "and I have to consider them. That makes my charges sometimes more, and sometimes less; but you must own it's much better to have a right bargain before I start, because, you see, when I go into the country and a reprieve comes, I expect my money all the same as though I'd done the job. That's my way of doing business. I only mention this to prevent mistakes; not that there's much of a chance of reprieves coming under a cast-iron Secretary. I should like a surgeon that I know to have him for an anatomy subject. Wouldn't his knives want grinding again directly after cutting a bit about his heart?"

"Keep to the business on hand," said Mr. Figgins. "Don't let us waste time and words. Pray what do you mean by saying that sometimes your charges are more and sometimes less? Pray explain yourself."

"Well," said Ketch, "our profession, like most other professions, depends upon the run of business, upon country assize work, the badness of the times, and affairs in general with the State. When things are going queer at head-quarters they always set the gallows to work to keep the people down, and frighten the ragged rascals, as I heard our Under-Secretary say, after having been to hear a condemned sermon in Newgate. Hard times, you know, sir, fills a prison, and always makes business brisk with me, because the gentlemen at the office, as soon as the prisoners begin to come in fast, always begin hanging two or three to every one they did before. This is their way of doing business, and I know it well."

"You will not come to the point," said Mr. Figgins. "What do you mean by the gentlemen at the office settling the business? I always thought it was the king in person while in council that settled these matters."

"God bless you, no; why how the world is humbugged to be sure," said Ketch. "Why our governor at Newgate, and one of the clerks down at the Transport Office, does more business about hanging men in one year than all the kings that ever reigned in England put together have done. But, as I was saying, business is never quite the same. Those Luddites gave me many a night's journey. I owe Master Lud a glass, if ever I should meet with him, and he shall have it too, for the money he has put into my pocket—there's nothing like country work. Now, my business is very much like that of a Queen's counsel—when I am wanted many ways at once I always take the highest bid, and that I consider all fair. Perhaps you don't know what a lot of money some of them want when there's two or three people after them at the same time; they lay it on then pretty thick, I can assure you, and you know their business is not half so particular as mine. They may make a hundred blunders every day, and nobody be none the wiser. Nobody notices them, and they lose no good name; but if I only makes one mistake I should be sure to lose all my country business, if not that at the Old Bailey too. Now when I have bargained with you, I may, five minutes afterwards, have a better offer to go another road; but then I, like a man of honour, shall not disappoint you; I must take my chance for that; I only mention it just to let you know that it must be considered."

"Well, well—be quick; I am ill and want to go," said Mr. Figgins.

"Well, then, sometimes I have two or three jobs the same road, and then I can offord to abate a little in price," continued Ketch, "because I gets my travelling expenses from all. Then, again, when there's half a dozen to be executed at once, then I make a difference. Besides, there's another thing to be considered: what sort of a rope do you mean to have?"

Here Mr. Figgins suddenly started, respired with great difficulty, and sighed—or rather groaned—with such force that it appeared that his intercostal muscles would be rent asunder. He suddenly started on to his feet, struck his forehead violently with his hand, and then sank back again into his chair.

"Fetch another jug of water, Sal," said Ketch to his wife, "the gentleman's very ill." And this time Ketch poured the remains of the gin bottle into the glass.

He put it to Mr. Figgins's lips, and Mr. Figgins drank a hearty draught, after which he slowly and faintly muttered to himself—

"Oh, what a fool I am to have to undergo all this mental torture through my sisters' folly and foolish misgivings, and to be spell-bound so long as this, and kept waiting here by the—the—the—oh! what shall I call him—the man that is to slay my own brother?"

Then rousing himself again he said, "but I must go through it—I will, however, go through it. Pray Mr. Ketch, what can you possibly mean by asking me what sort of a rope I will have?"

"Ah, I see you don't understand these things," said Ketch, "but as you appear to be a gentleman, I will tell you all about it."

"Good gracious me!" silently muttered Mr. Figgins to himself, "what a monster I am in company with, and what feelings of wretchedness does he not bring upon me. But pray proceed, Mr. Ketch."

At this moment Mr. Figgins's eye caught Ketch drinking some of the gin and water out of the same glass, and then another shudder came over him as he muttered to himself, "and here am I all this time drinking out of the very same glass with the common hangman that is to strangle my brother! What ever would my poor brother and sisters think if they could only see me now?"

Ketch, however, with his usual *sang froid*, continued—

"Here at the Bailey the business is not worth following, if it were not for the pulls it brings besides the reg'lar pay, and the name it gives a man, which brings country practice. It's now all done by contract. The sheriffs only gives me thirty shillings a week, and my man twenty shillings all the year round, whether there be much or little to do, and this is for hanging, catting, and pillorying and all. Besides, I have to find my own cats. Pretty sharp work, I can tell you, for such poor pay. Eight sessions a year you know, sir, and there is a talk of making them twelve. I had need of twenty hands to do justice to all as it should be; and some of the aldermen are not satisfied unless I do all the flogging business myself. Some of them seem to think the culprits never have enough, and that their backs aint flayed properly raw unless I do it all myself. Well, as I was saying, I only gets thirty shillings a week, and curse me if I would do it at all at the Bailey for that price if it were not for the same reason the barristers do it; it gets their name up."

"But you forget I must go," said Mr. Figgins. "Don't talk so much, but tell me about the rope."

"Ah, the line—you want to know about the line. Why, sir, you may have one from two up to five guineas. I have sometimes had ten given me."

"Pray do explain what you mean, Mr. Ketch."

"Well, sir, I'll soon explain what I mean. Here, Sal, open the drawer and show the gentleman the line."

Mrs. Ketch instantly obeyed, and laid on the table a bundle of halters already noosed and fit for use.

At the sight of them Mr. Figgins nearly fainted, but it was very evident he made a desperate effort to go through the painful ordeal.

"This," said Ketch, taking up a rope, "is the country rope; you see, it is a common twist, and the thickest of the lot. Now, the sheriffs will not allow any but this, which makes a man as long again a-dying as such a one as this, for which I only charges two guineas; but if you have one of this kind," showing a very small one, "it's all over in the wink of one of your eyes—this is five guineas."

"But surely this is not strong enough to suspend a man," said Mr. Figgins; "my brother is rather heavy."

"You leave that to me," said Ketch. "So Bellingham said—the man who shot Perceval—when I was going to put his on, although his friend, after he paid for it, told him beforehand that it was all right, he informed him several times that it was to be a patent sash-twist—twice as strong as those which are twice as thick. Now this line, you understand, sir, pinches so tight that it's done almost before a man can feel it. If the sheriffs had any mercy in them they would always use catgut. But then to be sure I should lose my perquisite. Then, again, if this thin one was to make a slip round to the chin, as you was saying your sister read about, it would come so close, and act so sure, that it would not make much difference, although that never happens where I am; it's only your half-and-half workmen that makes all that mess. You spoke about Lincoln; well, that was a bad job, but the thing was so badly done that Atkinson would have hung the whole hour before he was dead, if a soldier of the 69th had not rushed forward, lifted him up, and then hung upon his body. Poor fellow! I was sorry when I heard about it."

"But I always understood it depended upon the dislocation of the neck," said Mr. Figgins.

"Not a bit of it, not a bit of it," replied Ketch, "nothing but a rope to pull well, and come up tight to the neck is wanted. Why if a man's neck was broke, hanging will put it in again. The surgeons will tell you that, but people don't understand it."

"But the ropes cannot cost the price you speak of," said Mr. Figgins.

"Oh, no; they cost a little more to be sure," said Ketch; "but I can use which I like, and those therefore who can afford to pay for the easier-going ones must do so, because those are my perquisites, and I never alters my prices; so say which you will have before she locks them up again in the drawer."

Just at this very moment a very loud and apparently important rap-tap came against the door on the stairs, and Ketch then, with all the alacrity of his youth, catching hold of the lines, pushed them again into the drawer, which he hastily locked; and next putting his hand gently on to Mr. Figgins's shoulder, he said, "I've a gentleman coming to see me now; you won't mind going into the next room for a few minutes—will you?"

"Oh, no; not if you will not be long," said Mr. Figgins; "but it will soon be time for me to go, you know."

"I shall not be long," said Ketch—"go on—there's the room," pointing to the door, and gently pushing Mr. Figgins along behind.

"Oh, but I can't go in there in the dark," said Mr. Figgins. "I never like being in the dark; besides, I might fall over something, or knock something valuable down and break it."

"Get a candle, Sal," said Ketch. "Make haste; don't let's keep gentlemen standing at the door; it may be somebody from the sheriff."

"There is no candle," said Mrs. Ketch. "That's all there is in the house that's in the candlestick now. Oh, go in, sir, for two or three minutes; you won't want a candle, and there's nothing you can hurt, I can assure you."

"Come—go in, there's a good fellow, while I see who's at the door. I don't want 'em kept waiting there," said Ketch.

"No; I would rather go if you haven't time to conclude the business with me now," said Mr. Figgins. "I'm naturally a nervous man, and I don't like going in in the dark. I'll wish you good evening now, and go down the stairs."

"No, you can't go down that way now," said Ketch. "The sheriffs are very particular who I have here, and then they might ask a lot of questions, and you might meet the sheriffs' men on the stairs."

At this point a second loud and impatient knock came to the door, and Ketch was evidently in a great fix.

Sal, in alarm and despair, was about to run and open it, but Ketch ran after her and pulled her back, whispering quietly to her—

"Sal, don't be such a fool as to open the door now, with him in the place. It might be them 'ere chaps with them other bodies what's been hung at Croydon: they are to come to-night. Go and try to get him into the other room."

Sal then ran towards Mr. Figgins, saying, "Do, please go in, there's a good gentleman; there's nothing to hurt you."

"Oh dear no," said Mr. Figgins, "I dare not go in there in the dark by myself after talking upon such a dreadful and melancholy subject."

"Well, I'll go in the room and stop there with you," said Mrs. Ketch.

"No; not if I know it," said Mr. Figgins; "you aint going to catch me in that way; if I am up from the country, you aint going to catch me. No, no, none of your hankey-pankey tricks with me."

At this moment another loud knock came, and a voice was heard on the stairs, through the keyhole, calling out:

"Ketch, what are you about? Why don't you open the door?"

"Wait half a minute," shouted Sal, "I'm only putting my frock on."

"Only putting your frock on!" said Mr. Figgins. "Why you haven't had it off. Oh, dear me, what a den of monsters I'm in, and to think I should have come into such a place as this, and nobody at hand."

WILLIAM CALCRAFT, THE HANGMAN.

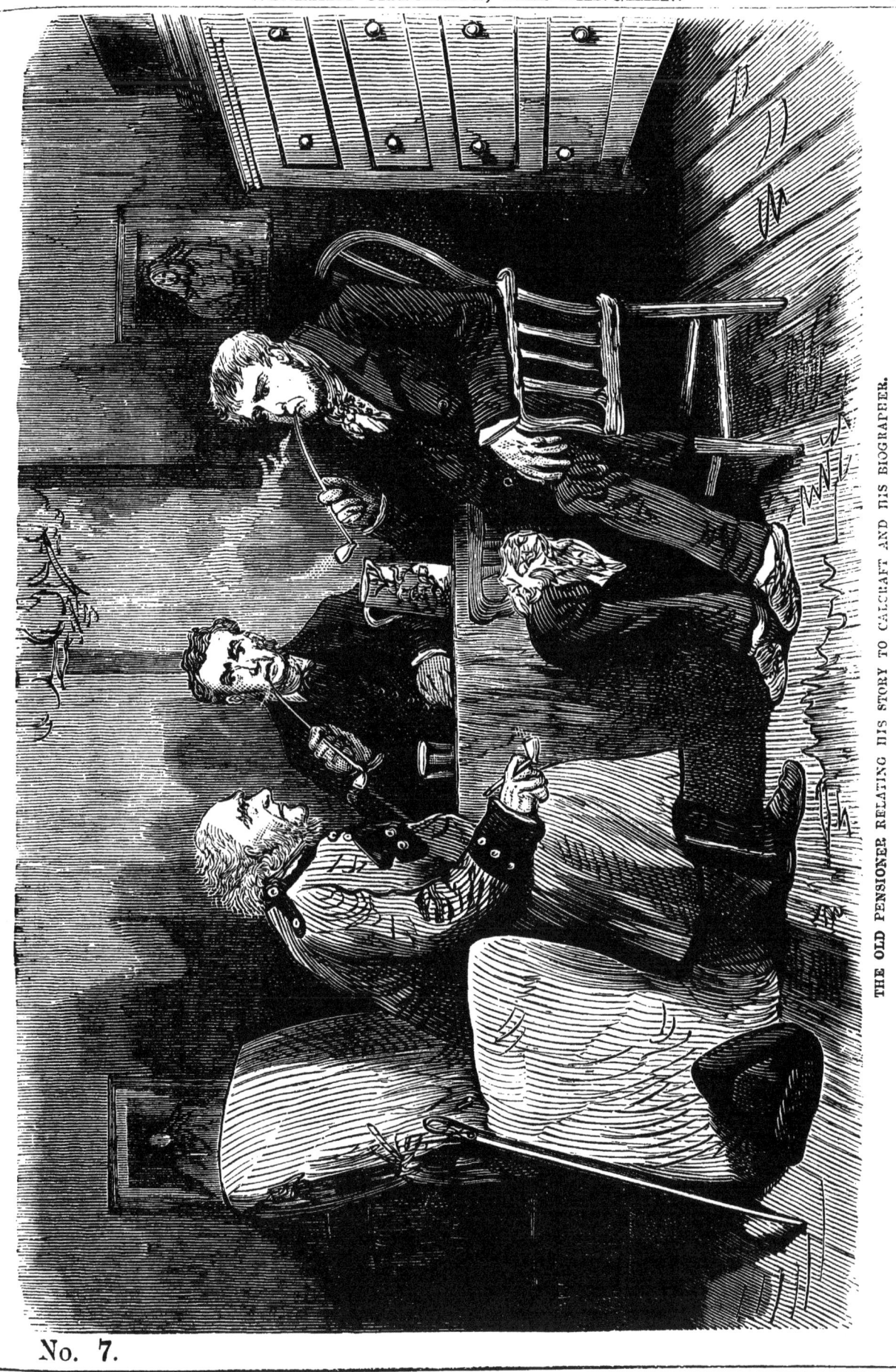

THE OLD PENSIONER RELATING HIS STORY TO CALCRAFT AND HIS BIOGRAPHER.

"I can't stand any more of this," said Ketch, running with all his might against Mr. Figgins, and putting his hands on his shoulders. "You must go in, dark or not dark—so in you go."

With that he gave him a tremendous push; which sent him pale and trembling with fright staggering into the room, and Ketch then immediately pulled-to the door, and, turning the key, locked him in.

Ketch then hastened to the sitting-room door, which opened on to the stairs into the street and, opening it, said—

"Sorry to keep you waiting so long, gentlemen, but we had hardly got the room in a fit state to ask gentlemen in."

"And I was just putting on my frock," said Sal, thinking to make the best excuse she could, also for the unaccountable delay.

"Oh, never mind," said the two visitors, "we have only come on a little private business."

"Sit down," said Ketch, "and make yourselves at home. What is it you please to want?"

During these preliminaries Mr. Figgins was on the other side of the door, peeping anxiously through the key-hole, in a sort of cold perspiration, with his heart nearly in his mouth through fright, and listening with a fearful suspicious horror to the conversation which ensued.

Meantime, said Calcraft, I sat quietly in a dark corner, unobserved, with my pockethandkerchief over my face, still sitting on the floor as has been previously described.

Both of us—both I and Mr. Figgins—could distinctly hear the conversation which took place between Ketch and his visitors.

"Well," said one of the visitors, who certainly had a good commanding voice, and who appeared to act as spokesman for both—"what we have come about, Mr. Ketch, is to tell you that we are medical students; that we want some good subjects very badly. We shan't mind the price so that they are good ones."

"Yes," replied Ketch, "if you don't mind the price and are not at all particular about the figure, I could get you some very good subjects."

"Oh, dear me!" sighed Mr. Figgins, "I wish my sister was here," as his knees fairly knocked together, as though he had been suddenly smitten with St. Vitus's dance.

"What sort of subjects do you want," said Ketch—"male or female?"

"We should like one male and one female," replied the visitors.

"Are you particular as to their ages?" inquired Ketch.

"We should like them to be adults," they answered.

"What age would you like the male to be?" asked Ketch.

"Oh, about 30," they replied.

"Oh, dear," breathed Mr. Figgins; "I'm that age."

"And would you like him tall or short?" said Ketch.

"Well, tall and slim, if we could get one," they replied. "We could see the action of the nerves and muscles well, then."

"Tall and slim," whispered Mr. Figgins, as his teeth chattered together with fear, "that's just me; thirty years old, and tall and slim."

"I suppose you couldn't manage to get us a half-dead one, could you, Ketch?" inquired the visitors. "If we could lay hold of a live one for vivisection we would stand a good round sum."

"Oh, my dear sister," faintly chattered Mr. Figgins. "Here am I, and you don't know it. A live one for vivisection!" he said.

"Well, I might perhaps manage you a half-dead un for vivisection," said Ketch. "I have had them before now."

"A half-dead un," whispered Mr. Figgins, now trembling like an aspen leaf, "I am half-dead, I am! I am sure I am! A half-dead un—that's me! Oh, my poor sister, why did you send me here? But I must go through it. There's the window there, and I'll bolt—I'll bolt!"

At this point Mr. Figgins ran to the window, and, pulling wide aside the curtains, the full moon shone brightly into the room.

"What do I see here?" said Mr. Figgins; "why, here's lodgers in bed. Oh, I will wake them and ask them to have pity on me for the sake of my poor sister."

Here Mr. Figgins went to the side of the bed, and patting one of its inmates on the side of the cheek, he said: "Please wake up—you will protect me, won't you?" As soon, however, as Mr. Figgins placed his hand on the cold, icy, clammy cheek of the occupant of the bed he shrank back, startled with horror, tremblingly whispering to himself, "He feels like dead!" Then, looking over the bed again, he beheld the horrible look of three, all dead.

"Oh, where am I?" said he. "I am in the chamber of death. The room smells of the gallows. I must go through it now, though," said he; "I will look fairly round the room for some means of escape. Oh! here are three more, sitting on the floor against the wall, dead, as though they were alive," said Mr. Figgins. "Oh, my poor sister—I wish I could write and let you know. I would take a leap through the window, but I don't know how deep it is into the yard below; and a leap in the dark, now, would never do. If I try to open the door and run away, perhaps they will knock me down in the attempt, and carry me to the shambles at once. This all comes of me venturing here by myself. I ought to have been more guarded, for I have read all about the Burkers and resurrection people, and I ought to have known better than come like this alone. But I'll hear what they are saying now; I'll just put my ear to the key-hole again and hear what's going on."

"How soon could you let us have one or two?" said one of the visitors.

"Well, I could let you have some to-night," said Ketch.

"Hark at that, some to-night," said Mr. Figgins. "Oh, what shall I do."

"Have you got any near at hand?" said the visitors.

"Yes, pretty near," replied Ketch. "In fact, close at hand."

"Hark at that," said Mr. Figgins, "close at hand. It's me that's close at hand; I'll have a look round the room, and see if there's not some means of escape, for it is evident to me this is a warehouse for the dead."

Mr. Figgins then walked quietly round the room, looking in every corner (said Calcraft), evidently trying to find some means of escape. At last he came close up to the corner where I was in the dark, and in peering about he put his face nearly close to mine. I could not help it; but just at this very moment, unfortunately, I sneezed, and in bobbing my head knocked my forehead on the bridge of his nose, and suddenly I felt something pretty warm spurting all over my face. In an instant he gave one dreadful shriek, and fell back, kicking and plunging on the floor.

I guessed in a moment the surrounding circumstances, and the sudden shock had frightened him nearly out of his senses, and I immediately got up to render him what assistance I could. I went to the room door, and, putting my ear to the keyhole, I heard the two visitors just taking their departure, after bargaining for two of the subjects to be sent that night. Ketch and Sal then came into the room with a light, and, all of us taking hold of Mr. Figgins, we carried him back into the front room again.

We put some smelling-salts to his nose, fanned him, and bathed his forehead with water, and at last he opened his eyes again, saying—

"Oh, my poor sister.! I'm being vivisected now, and cut up bit by bit."

"No, you aint," said Sal.

"Nothing at all of the sort; you are all right, and you'll see your sister soon."

Mr. Figgins gradually came round. Ketch explained to him that there was no room for fear.

"You see," said Ketch, "what you saw in that other room are my perquisites. If it wasn't that I got hold of a good many bodies that aint claimed for burial by their friends, why I couldn't live. But you know I never do any Burking or snatching, or anything of that kind. Not I."

"Oh, dear no," said Sal. "We's too respectable for that."

"Well," said Mr. Figgins, "it's a very dreadful occupation. Show me the lines again, and I'll choose which it is to be, and then I must go."

"Show the gentleman the lines again, Sal," said Ketch, "and if he'll take my advice he'll choose one of them which will do the work the quickest."

Ketch now took the key again from his pocket, and giving it to Sal she unlocked the drawer and pulled the lines out again for Mr. Figgins to choose from.

"What would be the lowest for this one?" said Mr. Figgins.

"For that one—that is one of the best," said Ketch; "the very lowest for that would be five guineas, and I should charge five guineas extra and my expenses for coming down."

"Then I suppose the rope would be our own personal property?" said Mr. Figgins.

"Oh, dear no," replied Ketch—"certainly not. I could not think of leaving such a dangerous piece of machinery in inexperienced hands. It might be a temptation to somebody to commit suicide, you know, and that wouldn't do, for if anyone gets their neck into one of my nooses I don't think they would be able to get it out again."

"But I was thinking we might sell the line to Madame Tussaud or some other exhibitor, to show as a curiosity. You know, five guineas the line, five guineas your fees, and four pounds travelling expenses, makes about fourteen guineas, and that is a good deal to pay to have one's own brother hung."

"Well, them's my prices," said Ketch, "and I couldn't take less any way."

"Well, if I give you fourteen guineas you must be sure and do the work properly," said Mr. Figgins, "and put my poor brother out of his misery as soon as you can."

"All right," said Ketch,; "I'll see that the noose runs extra well, and I'll make a still subject of him in less than a minute. Here, Sal, just smooth all the knots down extra fine for the gentleman."

"Yes," said Sal, "and you may rest assured that it will do its work effectually for the poor gentleman, bless his heart."

Mr. Figgins then having once more impressed on old Ketch the necessity of going by the next coach, then took his leave, saying there was no doubt he would go down by the same conveyance himself.

In the course of a little time Ketch was quite prepared for his journey; and then, putting the selected halter in his bag, after a short rest he started off in time to catch the next coach.

The coach arrived at eleven o'clock the night before the morning appointed for the execution, and Ketch went straight to the gaol.

The next morning the gallows was duly erected in its place, and the selected rope dangled from the beam.

Thousands had assembled to witness the execution, for the culprit was well known, and the family were highly respected.

About ten minutes to eight, however, just before the time appointed, the halter was taken down before the assembled crowd, and the sheriffs announced that a reprieve had just arrived, and that as there were extenuating circumstances in the case, the sentence was commuted.

When old Ketch used to give me what he called lessons in experience, he always reminded me of this incident in order to impress on my mind the necessity of always getting my fees beforehand, lest something should occur to prevent the completion of the work.

"It's very necessary," said the driver, "to do that in a good many businesses. Why, if I were not to do it I should often have gentlemen coming and bespeaking seats for a journey, and then not going at all, and I should be the loser."

I myself felt greatly interested in Calcraft's story of his recollections of the former hangman, especially as he told the tale with great drollery.

By this time we, after talking of other matters, began to get near London again, on our homeward journey, and now having fairly formed Calcraft's acquaintance, I begged him as a favour to allow me to call sometimes upon him for any information I might require in reference to passing events in his peculiar line.

He gave me leave to do so, and said that though he had a great objection to be generally publicly known, and also a repugnance to talking to strangers on the matters of his business, yet as my object was for the legitimate purpose of making people acquainted with some of the strange phases and extraordinary characters of life, he would be always happy to give me any information, and show me any scene he could.

"If you are," said he, "a philanthropist, and feel disposed to turn the information I could give you to good account for the public welfare, I could let you into the light of many abuses that want correcting. Neither you nor the people generally have any idea of a quarter of the things that are going on. We are living in very strange times, and the great wonder to me is, that all these abuses have been allowed to exist so long. Here we are living in what they say is the foremost city of the world, and yet we are in the greatest depths of mental, moral, and physical darkness. The times are so bad, you see, that people all over England are almost in a state of starvation, and the Government don't know what to do."

"Well, what are poor people to do?" said the driver. "I know, as I drive through one town after the other, I see poverty and misery everywhere. If people haven't got work, what are they to do? It is not all of them that will sit down quietly and starve, though a great many of them do it.

The legislators make the workhouses worse than the gaols, so that, between the fears of the workhouse or the gaols, thousands of industrious, virtuous people are being literally done to death. You see these contending factions in Parliament keep the country in such an unsettled state of turmoil that there is no trade to be done; and the land laws are such that they keep the land locked up in the hands of a few private individuals so that the best part of it can't be cultivated—in fact, they keep the millions of working classes that would cultivate it off it, and those that might be prosperous and happy and well to-do if they had the land are obliged to remain idle and die. Can you wonder at society being in the state it is?"

"Well, you see," said Calcraft, "there is some talk of a revolution; in fact, a civil war breaking out, if the Reform Bill don't pass; and it won't do to have a revolution in the country; it won't do to let people have things all their own way, either. So that's one reason why Government's going to be pretty sharp."

"Yes, but that is no reason why the Government should set-to and hang and transport people by wholesale. Before a government does that they ought to try and find the people the means of getting an honest living, and try the effect of that first. They could then punish the incorrigibly bad after."

"Yes, I quite agree with you that there's a great deal of truth in that observation," said Calcraft, "but you must know there are many thousands of people who wouldn't work if they'd got it to do. Thousands live by sharping and by the practice of every kind of vice and infamy, and I maintain that it is to the interest of the country that those people should be worked off as quickly as possible. Why, if I were to take you into some of the infamous dens of vice I have been in, show you the way the gangs of thieves of every kind get their living, it would amaze you; and I maintain that what with one thing and another, the Government has a gigantic work to perform in order to render protection to the people and make the country safer than it is."

We had by this time arrived back in London, and having pulled up at the house from which we started, the passengers alighted, and, we all getting down, I and Calcraft and the coachman had another parting glass.

Calcraft told me that he should be happy to give me any information he could if I would call upon him, and then having wished each other good night, we parted company and retired to our respective homes.

Meantime I determined to accept Calcraft's invitation to go with him to some of the strange haunts of the great criminal classes, and to see for myself life behind the scenes.

I felt even that the visits to the workhouses, the manner in which I had seen helpless children treated, and how easy it was for monsters like the Hibners to live in gross inhumanity, had made me acquainted with one great evil that required immediate alteration.

I had the satisfaction of seeing a few days afterwards that the parish of St. Martin's instituted other proceedings against Esther Hibner the younger, and Ann Robinson, the forewoman, for cruelty to other children.

The case against them was eventually proved, and on their trial at the Middlesex Sessions, Esther Hibner, the younger, was sentenced to twelve months hard labour, and Ann Robinson was sentenced to four months' hard labour, though in my opinion they both deserved hanging.

CHAPTER XVIII.
VISIT TO CALCRAFT'S HOUSE.

As Calcraft had promised to give me all the information he could upon various matters, and as he had invited me to call upon him when I liked, I took an early opportunity of paying him a visit.

The first evening I called upon him I found him at home, contented and happy, in his new avocation, but exceedingly reserved upon the merits of any public business he had to carry out.

He had a particular aversion to disclose any of the details of the duties of his office, and he would frequently exhibit signs of his personal displeasure if he were pressed to divulge any of the secrets of Newgate prison.

"You must be aware," he would say, in reply to any inquiry, "that I have taken a very solemn oath to keep all the duties of my office, and prison matters generally, secret; but I have no objection to give you my experience of the world, and of criminal life apart from any opinion upon the acts I have to perform.

"I can give you many strange romantic stories which come under my immediate notice, which will show you the lights and shades of life without in any way breaking the oath I have sworn.

"As I knew you were coming this evening, I have purposely invited an old pensioner here to-night, for the purpose of giving you a little history which I think you will like to hear."

"I am much obliged to you, Mr. Calcraft," I said. "I shall be glad to hear it, as I have not the slightest doubt it will be interesting and true."

At this point of the conversation someone knocked at the door, and on Mrs. Calcraft opening it a pensioner, who had lost one eye and one arm in his Majesty's service entered the room.

"Sit down, Mr. Donald," said Calcraft. "This is the gentleman I asked to meet you here to-night, and I am sure he will pay great attention to your lady's history."

Some pipes, tobacco, and ale having been sent for, and our glasses having been duly filled, the pensioner began to relate his

INTERESTING ACCOUNT OF THE HONOURABLE MARY ANN ROTHWELL.

The old pensioner then began as follows:—

"You see, sir," said he, "I have lost an eye and one arm in his Majesty's service."

"Some few years ago, before I entered the army, I was in the service of a Scotch nobleman, the proprietor of some large landed estates in Scotland. I had been in the family some years, and was present at my master's marriage to the lady, to whom he was much attached.

"They had one child the issue of their marriage, the Lady Mary Ann Rothwell, who as she grew up a beautiful little girl was the hope and joy of her parents, who seemed to dote upon her.

"She was always a sprightly, vivacious child, and remarkable alike for her beauty and her wit. Many a happy day have I spent coursing upon the moors of Scotland in company with my master and mistress, and my young lady their only child.

"When, however, she was but twelve years old her mother died, and a shade came over her life; her sorrow for her mother's death was bitter indeed.

"There are some people, you know, sir, whose life and destiny is like the flowers. Some persons grow in places where the sun shines on them nearly all the day long from the time it rises in the morning till it sets at night.

"Other flowers are in places where they only get a little sun in the early morning; they are placed under the shade of some great cold wall, and when the sun gets behind that, there's no more sunshine for them, and they, during the rest of the day, are in the coldness of the shade—well, such oftentimes is life.

"When my young mistress's mother died, the brightness of her life appeared to pass away, and the shade of misfortune stole gradually over her. On the death of his wife my master too grew gloomy, haughty, and pensive.

"He was fond of his child, and after her mother's death he appeared to place his hopes upon her. He, however, lost his former love of pleasure, and as he became retiring and thoughtful he became also stern.

"The rigid rules of the house, the change from gay to grave, and the close rules the father laid down, did not suit the vivacious, irrepressible spirit of the child. The young lady, Mary Ann Rothwell, was fast growing into youth, and after a year or two, as soon as the grief consequent on the death of her mother had subsided, she began to show signs that she had a will of her own, which she seemed likely to claim to use as she thought best for her own future welfare.

"During the various times that her father was in his study, evidently brooding and repining over his condition Mary Ann, would steal away for a ramble or a gallop across the moor to gain the full enjoyment of the early morn of her life.

"Like a flower she appeared to rear her head in the bright morning sunshine of her youth. The second gleam of sunshine, however, was but transient, for her father, fearing some evil consequences from the exuberance of her spirits, placed a considerable check upon the freedom of her actions.

"She drooped her head under the coldness of the shade, and under the restrictions of her personal liberty, her health began to give way. Her father, who no doubt was exceedingly fond of her, had in his own mind marked out for her a course of his own.

"He was a man of great influence, and I have heard him say that when his daughter was a little older he would take her to London, and he had no doubt she would eventually be introduced at Court.

"No doubt by the probation of solitude he had chosen he thought so to surround her with his personal watchfulness that her mind would be unsullied, and her affections free and unalloyed with any premature or undesirable attractions.

"But love, like a caged bird, frequently bursts its bonds and flies for liberty to the nearest tree.

"Miss Rothwell seemed to fret and pine under her father's restraint, and at the age of seventeen he brought her to London to see if the change of scene and air would improve the happiness of her mind.

"They resided at the West-end, and Miss Rothwell was frequently out walking or on horseback in the parks, with her father generally at her side.

One day, however, that he was absent, while she was walking and reading a book alone, she was accompanied by a young, gentlemanly-looking man, who was evidently charmed by her personal beauty.

"In Miss Rothwell there was neither pride nor reserve. They both entered freely into conversation together, and were charmed with the society of each other.

"Having spent several hours in company they exchanged names and addresses, and then, finally wishing each other good day, they agreed to meet again by appointment on the earliest opportunity.

"As, however, her father generally accompanied her in her walks or rides for exercise, and as these opportunities for meeting were not very frequent, my young mistress confided to me the secret thoughts of her heart, and begged me to assist her by undertaking the duties of special postman between the two.

"I scarcely liked to do so at first, but when I recollected the ardent and anxious feelings of my own love days, and when I remembered that my young mistress had not much freedom, or many joys of her own, I consented to undertake the punctual delivery of the romantic correspondence.

"I had some doubts at first as to the propriety of keeping the secret, and of becoming the letter-carrier in such an important business as I saw commencing.

"Sometimes I thought I ought to privately acquaint her father, and let him judge of the prudence of the acquaintance; but, on the other hand, I thought—well, he is very strict, and perhaps it is only a little bit of harmless flirtation, and I can keep a good watch over the matter, and see that no harm comes to her so far as giving her good advice goes.

"I dreaded telling her father that she had a clandestine acquaintance, lest he might curtail that liberty she loved so well, and I felt convinced that her own natural quickness would cause her to act on any suggestions I might see necessary for her own protection and welfare.

"I looked upon the whole affair as a young couple's first love, that would take some years to ripen into anything like such a serious affair as marriage.

"After the acquaintance commenced between my young lady and her lover, there was scarcely a day passed but what I had to act as postman, and take a letter from her to Richard Crossley, Esq., and also bring a letter back to Miss Mary Ann Rothwell.

"After the courtship had gone on for about four months, I was greatly surprised one evening, on going up to the house after cleaning the horses in the stable, to find my master almost in a distracted state of mind.

"His daughter had not returned, according to her usual custom, to dinner, and as she had now been out some hours, he was in a state of great alarm for her safety.

"Before evening set in the services of several friends were secured, and they went off in all directions in the park, to see if the young lady could be found.

"Nothing, however, could be seen of her, and as no tidings of her could be got, we all of us had the most terrible misgivings for her safety.

"Her father and his friends were in dreadful fear lest she should have been inveighled into some of the dens of infamy which abounded in almost every quarter of the metropolis at that time, where neither her honour nor her life would be safe.

"As night came on and she did not return, her father became almost frantic with grief and despair, and he went off to the watchmen to give notice of her mysterious disappearance, whilst I was sent to the houses of various friends to ascertain if she had been heard of there.

"The part I had acted in conveying the secret correspondence which had taken place between her and a stranger now struck me forcibly as wrong, and, though I wished, I felt afraid to inform my master of the acquaintance I knew she had formed, lest he might vent his indignation upon me for my secrecy in the matter. I resolved, however, to go quietly up to

Mr. Crossley's address, the young man with whom she had been corresponding, and see if he knew where she was.

"On going to his lodgings, I was informed that he in the morning had left in an unexpected and mysterious manner, taking his boxes with him, and without giving any address where in future he might be found.

"The fear now flashed across my mind that probably they had decamped together, and that very likely a clandestine marriage had taken place.

"Several times during the night I tried to summon up courage to tell my master, but I felt I dared not, because I knew how angry he would be, and I dreaded his stern and resolute disposition.

"During the whole night her father was out searching for her, and when he came in the following morning he was broken-down with grief and fatigue.

"A CLANDESTINE MARRIAGE.

"The first post, however, brought him a letter from her in which she informed him that she was all safe and well, but having formed a strong attachment to her lover, Mr. Richard Crossley, she had yesterday been married to him, and they were now living in apartments together. In her letter she further hoped that her father would forgive her for the independent act she had taken, and that in future he would think of her and her husband as children alike.

"Her father suddenly became furious, and he seemed almost incapable of controlling his anger. The next post brought a letter from her husband, who commenced his communication by addressing him as his dear father.

"This apparently put her father in a greater rage still, for he stamped his foot and swore he would never own either of them, and never more should she be an acknowledged child of his.

"I feared such a vow, because I well knew his dogged and unrelenting disposition. I could not remain silent any longer, because I felt that by my acquiescence in her secret courtship I was greatly to blame if any ill results followed.

"So I said to him, 'Well, Sir Thomas, I am very sorry to hear of such a misfortune as the elopement of your only child.'

"'Ah,' said he, 'it is a dreadful thought for me to see all my hopes blighted by the foolishness of a girl. I thought to have seen her honourably wedded into some noble and distinguished family, with every honour and comfort round her, seeing the education I have given her and the wealth I possess.'

"'Well, never mind, sir,' I said. 'Perhaps the man she has married is honourable, and perhaps possesses rare ability, and he may be a distinguished man, too.'

"'The man she is married to perhaps is honourable, do you say?' said he, in a most furious passion. 'How can he be honourable when he has decoyed my daughter into a clandestine marriage? Is that what you call a specimen of honour?'

"'Well, sir, I said, perhaps under the strong passion of true love that may be pardonable.'

"'Pardonable!' he ejaculated. 'What do you mean by trying to excuse and defend such villainy?'

"'I am not trying to defend it,' I replied; 'but I do hope you will have pity on your poor child, for she was early bereaved of a mother's care.'

"'She knew well enough that it was wrong to get married without my consent, even if she was a motherless girl. I always myself impressed good advice upon her; but, however, she has discarded my counsel, and now, as she has made the bed, so she must lie in it. I wonder what the scoundrel is that she is married to?'

"'I don't know,' I replied, 'but perhaps I might find out.'

"'Well, if you hear,' said her father, 'you can tell me. But, as for me, I shall not trouble any further about her, and if she comes here, mind I shall give a strict injunction to all the servants that she is not again to be admitted to the house.'

"I dared not make any further observation, but I thought her father's conduct, as I expected it would be, was stern in the extreme.

"After a few weeks she sent a number of letters to her father, informing him that the man she had married was a brewer, that he had induced her to the marriage by a variety of misrepresentations, and that as she was thoroughly unhappy, she trusted that her father would forgive her and take her back to his home again.

"Her father, however, remained as obdurate as ever. All affection for his child seemed to have passed away, and he wrote to her one letter stating his final determination not to hold any correspondence with her, or ever again acknowledge her in any way whatever.

"I saw that it was no use for me to speak, for it only made his anger greater, so I determined to quietly watch events, and to personally assist my young mistress if ever it lay in my power.

"About six months after she had left her home I was surprised one evening, after having put the horses up for the night, by hearing some one accost me in a well-known voice, saying: 'Donald, is my father at home?'

"I turned to look, for I knew it was the voice of my young mistress, and there I saw Mrs. Crossley, standing pale and trembling, and evidently in a state of great anxiety. I said, 'Yes, ma'am, he is.'

"She said, 'Do you think he would speak to me or let me into the house if I knocked at the door?' I said, 'I don't know, ma'am. I don't know whether his anger is cooled down or not, but lately I have not heard him mention your name.'

"The tears came into her eyes, and she said, 'Donald, I am in great distress. I want to see my father, for I have married into great poverty, for my husband drinks nearly all he earns, and he ill-treats me so I hardly know what to do. He says he can't afford to keep me, and he expected to have had money with me from my father.'

"'Ah, that is what your father thinks,' I said—'that some one has married you for money.'

"'Will you take this letter to my father,' she said, 'and try to persuade him to see me, and I will wait for an answer.'

"'I will take the note for you,' I said, 'ma'am, and do all I can, but as it is getting late to-night would it not be better to wait till to-morrow before I give it to him, and I will let you know to-morrow what your father's answer is.'

"'Very well,' she said, 'perhaps that would be the better way.'

"I felt grieved to hear the said story of her unhappiness,' and then wishing her good night she promised to come at four the next day to see what her father's answer would be.

"The next morning I gave him the letter, and informing him of her circumstances, I begged of him to allow me, as an old servant of the family, to intercede for her, and to persuade him, if possible, to do something for her by which she could be released from her miserable condition.

"He was still very cross, and looking me full in the face, he said:—'Donald, I should be doing wrong if I were to relent, and furnish that villain with money who has robbed me of my daughter, and of all I held dear. Don't think I do not feel for my daughter in her wretched condition; but, if I were to allow her entreaties to prevail, it would only be a direct encouragement to others to commit similar acts of villainy. No! society must be protected; and if parents would be firm, and cut their children off without a shilling, and stick to their determination, there would not be so many adventurers running after ladies with fortunes as there are. No, no, Donald; I must be firm in my resolution that the scoundrel shall have no money from me. I guessed at first he was a worthless, unprincipled adventurer, and now he has married her he must keep her, for he shall never get a penny of my money; and as for my daughter—or rather she who used to be my daughter—why, if I gave her anything she would only take it direct to him, to go and get drunk at a public tap. No—it's a bad piece of business, but they will get nothing from me.'

"I saw the utter hopelessness of pressing him further—so I retired from the room.

"In the afternoon she came again in great distress to know whether I had been successful in interceding for her. I told her that I had not, and that her father was evidently keeping in the same mind as before.

"She then wished me good afternoon, saying she did not know what to do, for her husband had got into debt, and proceedings were out against him.

"The next day I thought to speak to my master again, and urge upon him with all the power I could his daughter's destitute and unhappy condition.

"He however was taken very ill. Since his daughter's secret marriage his spirits had drooped, and at times he violently trembled as though his nerves were completely shattered.

"A medical man was called in, who, after examining him, said his heart was seriously affected, and that as he was in great danger, anything like a further shock would probably prove immediately fatal to him. As night came on the danger of his symptoms increased, and the doctor informed us that if my master had any business matters to settle it would be well to be prepared and have them arranged at once.

"I felt that a great responsibility rested upon me, and as I had occasion to go upstairs to him I thought I would seek the opportunity to speak to him of his daughter again, lest he might pass away and the time would be too late.

"He, however, seemed in such a serious condition that I feared the result, and I came down again without making the attempt.

"I had occasion to go round to the stables again, and near to the same place as before I saw his daughter waiting again to see me.

"I spoke to her and told her of her father's condition, and she burst into a paroxysm of grief, and for a time was quite overcome with despair. After she had calmed herself a little, she then told me that her husband had run away, and that he had left a note for her stating that he was gone for ever, and that she would never see him again.

"She was now without the means of subsistence, and did not know what to do. During the whole time she kept on expressing the most earnest desire to see her father; but after what had occurred, after she had been forbidden the house, she was afraid to go lest the shock should be fatal at once.

"When I went back to the house the doctor was there again, and knowing in my own mind the seriousness of the case, I asked him how the master was, and what was the real prospect before him.

"I told him I had a particular reason for asking, in consequence of the circumstances of his child.

"The doctor informed me there was not the slightest hope of his recovery, and only a few hours could intervene between him and death.

"I then informed the doctor of the real facts of his daughter's case, and we both agreed that as her husband had deserted her, the matter should be mentioned to him again.

"As I knew who his lawyer was, I took upon myself to send a special messenger for him, and in a very little time he also was at the house.

"The matter was mentioned to him, and he informed us that she was not provided for in her father's will.

"Both the doctor and the lawyer agreed with me that under the special circumstances of the case the father ought to be spoken to again, and entreated to leave her sufficient to keep her at least from the penury of the world.

"We all then went upstairs again, and the doctor, gently speaking to my master, begged him to leave some provision for his child, who he was just informed had been deserted by a worthless husband, and that she was now destitute on the world.

"Her father said, 'I will not leave her worthless husband one penny; neither will I leave her anything by which he can profit. However, fetch the will back, and I will so alter it that she shall have in her own right, and for her own special use, the sum of £2000.'

"The codicil of the will was drawn up just in time and signed, for that night the father died without seeing his child again.

"Early next morning Mrs. Crossley anxiously came to the vicinity of the house, and seeing the blinds drawn she realised at once the dreadful news that her father was now no more.

"She hastily knocked at the door, which was opened by me, and I gently told her of her father's death.

"She rushed up into the room, and, bending over him, cried bitterly, sobbing all the time; for she felt that her foolish and clandestine marriage had hastened his end.

"In the course of the week the funeral obsequies took place. Her father was carried to the grave, and Mrs. Crosswell, deserted by her husband, was apparently lonely in the world.

"A NEW CAREER.

"Had it not been for my promptness, you see," said the old pensioner, "poor thing, she would have been left penniless; and, though £2000 was not much for a lady of her birth, yet it was better than nothing.

"After the death of my master, Sir Thomas, the establishment was broken up, and I had to seek another situation. I obtained one in the service of Captain Smith, an officer in his Majesty's army.

"As I liked my master very well and liked the service too, I regularly entered the army, and agreed to go out with Captain Smith wherever he went.

"Though I saw I had now the world before me, I had one great anxiety on my mind, and that was the thought of the loneliness of my former young mistress, Mrs. Crossley.

"Sometimes when I felt very dull, and no doubt looked thoughtful, Captain Smith would come up to me and say, 'Why, Donald, what is the matter with you? You look all grief—like a cherub on a tombstone.'

"'Well,' I replied, 'captain, I am just thinking of what will become of my former young mistress, who is alone in the world in consequence of her husband deserting her.'

"I then told him the whole of her terrible vicissitudes, and gave him a short account of her early history.

"'I should like to see her,' said the captain; 'perhaps I might be of some slight service to her. You should take an early opportunity of mentioning my name to her, and see if she would like to come out again into society.

"After some few months had passed by I called upon her to see how she was getting on, and also to ascertain whether she had had any further tidings of her husband.

"I found she had not, and then I told her that I had mentioned her case to my new master, Captain Smith, who was anxious to be introduced to her to see if he could be of any service to her.

"She thanked me kindly, and told me she should be glad to accept of the captain's offer to take a drive in the park in company with him and his sister.

"During the next two years the captain and Mrs. Crossley were frequently out together, and they appeared to enjoy greatly the pleasure of each other's society.

"Mrs. Crossley, who was now about twenty years of age, in addition to being a handsome woman well educated, and of brilliant wit, was also a splendid horse-woman, and a dashing equestrian. In fact, she and the captain seemed a capital pair.

"Some time after that the captain said to me—'Donald.'

"I said, 'Yes, captain,' putting my hand flat over my eyebrows, and giving him a regular military salute.

"He then said, 'I have taken quite a fancy to Mrs. Crossley, and should like to marry her. I wonder whether her husband is ever likely to turn up again?'

"I replied, 'I should think not, captain; I think he is clearly gone to avoid his creditors.'

"'Well,' said the captain, 'I think I shall propose to her and see what she says, but the matter must be kept quiet, for some time, at any rate.'

"'All right, captain,' said I, 'don't fear me ever saying anything; I shall keep it quiet.'

"A few more months went by and I could see that they were greatly attached to each other, and that they understood one another perfectly well.

"In the course of a little time, as Mrs. Crossley could hear nothing of her husband, the match was agreed upon, and a marriage took place between her and Captain Smith; and Mrs. Crossley now became Mrs. Smith.

"AN OFFICER'S WIFE.

"The affection between the newly-married couple grew in intensity, and the wife of Captain Smith was frequently seen with him, or near him, even at reviews, parade, or state occasions.

"In fact, so far as circumstances would permit, they appeared inseparable.

"Shortly after their marriage, however, circumstances arose which appeared likely to call Captain Smith away from the company of his wife, and to demand his services in the cause of his king and country.

"Napoleon Bonaparte was at that time overrunning Europe, and a threatened invasion of England was even spoken of.

"The Duke of Wellington was ordered to take the field against him, and the flower of the English army was commanded to prepare for immediate action.

"All over the country recruiting was not only actually going on, but the press-gangs were busy in all directions, pressing men by every possible means into his Majesty's service for the defence of the nation.

"The fame and the daring of the great Napoleon had aroused the martial spirit of the whole world, and the eyes of men in every country were turned to England to see how she would acquit herself in the great and terrible struggle she was about to undertake for the purpose of arresting the power of Bonaparte, and putting an end to the career of the ruthless invader.

"From every part of England troops were marching for embarkation to the coming battles.

"For many weeks scarcely anything was heard in London but the marching of the army, the tramping of the dragoons, the flourishes of trumpets, and the general preparations for the din and excitement of war.

"Among the rest that were ordered out, our regiment with Captain Smith was commanded out too, and I had to take my place in the ranks for battle array.

Captain Smith, whose affection for his newly-married wife was great, wished her to stay at home and abide in safety in the hope of his homeward return.

"But his wife would not for one moment listen to such an arrangement.

"On the contrary, she declared it to be her positive determination to share with him the fortunes of war; to accompany him in all the perils of the field, and to live or die by his side.

"It was in vain for him to expostulate with her or to protest against her exposing her life to the dangers of the fire and the sword. Go, she said she would, wherever his regiment went, and go she did.

"When his regiment mustered for parade at the Horse Guards, she mustered too.

"When it embarked she embarked as well, and she went wherever the regiment went.

"Though Captain Smith did not approve of it at first, I think he sometimes, at the end of a long day's march, felt courage and comfort even in the near presence of his wife.

"As we marched through Brussels, she kept close to the rear-guard of the regiment while passing through the villages, but immediately the lanes were reached she put spurs to her horse and galloped up alongside the captain.

"When I used to see her so devoted to him, I frequently thought so noble and daring a woman deserved the honours of a heroine.

"The forces were now gathering very near, and though it was not expected so soon by the generals, there were many of opinion that a battle was immediately imminent between the British and Prussian forces under the Duke of Wellington and Blucher on the one hand, and the French under Napoleon on the other.

"While we were waiting at Brussels for the French coming up, and thinking that Napoleon's army would not arrive for some days, the Duke of Wellington and his staff officers, with the ladies who accompanied them, were thoroughly enjoying themselves at a ball and soirée that had been provided. Captain Smith and his lady were there also.

"The Duke of Wellington, ill-informed of the rapid movements of Napoleon, was very nearly being suddenly surprised.

THE LIFE OF WILLIAM CALCRAFT, THE HANGMAN. 57

THE MEETING OF WELLINGTON AND BLUCHER AT WATERLOO.

No. 8

"He thought that the Emperor would not attack them there, but that Napoleon would imitate his own tactics by falling back from position to position into the interior of France.

"While this ball given to the English officers by the Duchess of Richmond, however, was going on, on the night of the 14th of June, 1815, Napoleon was crossing the Sambre, driving in the Prussian outposts, and was fast advancing with 108,000 men.

"Whilst the Duke of Wellington was chatting in the recess of a window, amidst the noise and gaiety of the scene, with the Duke of Brunswick, one of his generals, an *aide-de-camp*, approached, and in a low voice communicated to him the contents of a despatch which had just arrived.

"The Duke of Brunswick, who at the time he was chatting was sitting down with a little child asleep on his lap, suddenly rose up in the excitement of the moment, and forgetting the little sleeping child, allowed it to roll from his lap on the floor.

"Wellington turned fearfully pale, but kept buried in his own breast the feelings excited by surprise, and by the imprudence of his own neglect.

"In an instant the news that Bonaparte with his army was suddenly near at hand circulated through the ball-room; the music ceased; the dancers dispersed; the ladies feared and trembled for the safety of those of the officers who were near and dear to them, and having bidden a hasty farewell to each other, they repaired to their various selected places of safety while the Duke of Wellington and his staff held a short consultation as to the best course to pursue, for it was evident the the battle was just about to commence.

"Captain Smith hastily wished his affectionate wife good night, and bid her at once seek the nearest place she could get for safety, whilst he mounted his horse and took his place at the head of his men."

CHAPTER XIX.
PREPARING FOR BATTLE.

"The ladies belonging to the staff officers and others having been sent off to what were considered the surest places for safety in the vicinity, the general body of the officers now took to the field, and anxiously awaited orders.

"The Duke of Wellington having given a few general commands to his staff hastily left the ball-room to send instantly to all the divisions the necessary orders to march.

"One hour after the arrival of the special courier who brought the news that Napoleon was rapidly advancing, Wellington had sent officers flying on the fleetest horses all along the roads of Belgium to call his troops together.

"Along the route, in all directions, as fast as the officers reached them, cavalry, infantry, artillery, field trains, and convoys were careering at full speed, amidst clouds of dust, through the streets of Brussels, to gain the forest of Nivelles, and reach Quatre-Bras.

"Though, however, most of the ladies partook themselves to places of safety there was one lady seated on a fine swift, spirited charger, who was determined to follow her husband, and that was my young mistress, Lady Smith.

"As we all parted with each other, and wished each other God-speed, not knowing whether we should ever see each other again, anxiously did we wish for the day to dawn.

"At length the morning began to break, and Wellington rode up to the summit of a plateau, which slopes from the skirts of the forest towards Quatre Bras, and then dismounting, he placed his powerful telescope to his eye.

"In a few minutes, after carefully surveying the scene around him, he said—

"'I can discern the French, and they are massing together. I know the aspect of their columns well. It is not merely a wing of the army—it is an army commanded by a marshal in person. There is a numerous staff with the chief officer, and I believe it is the Emperor himself. If he attacks us now we are lost; our present force is insufficient against such masses. But this place here is the knot of the war; it is the key of the position, and we must stand or fall here to the last man.'

"Here Wellington pointed to the spot where he stood, and motioning with his hand, indicated that that spot would either be the place upon which he would fall, or the base for the pedestal of his honour.

"Immediately that Wellington was convinced that it was the French army coming, he mounted his horse again, and dispatched courier upon courier to hasten the march of the troops he had sent for during the night.

"There was not one moment to be lost, and every officer present, seeing that his life, the result of the war, and the honour of his country now depended upon one supreme effort, galloped off with almost lightning rapidity to fetch the troops up in time.

"In the excitement of that early morning Lady Smith even outsped her husband, as she dashed along on her steed to aid in bringing up the men.

"As officer after officer departed, Wellington gave each orders of the most stringent character.

"'Tell them that they are not to wait for one another. They must not wait for anything; but come on regiment by regiment; if they cannot come by regiments they must gallop by troops even; battalion by battalion, and company by company if necessary. They must not walk, but run as to a fire.'

"Wellington having despatched his officers, now sat down on the grass of the slope, pensively and anxiously watching the advance of the French, and trembling lest the masses before him should make that movement in advance which would be their victory and his defeat.

"Fortunately for Wellington it was not Napoleon in command of the approaching division of the French army, but Marshal Ney, and he being undecided what course to take now, stopped his course for a time.

"Wellington, in the most desperate and nervous anxiety, still kept his seat on the grass, waiting for his troops to advance.

"Two long hours thus slipped, each minute almost seeming an hour, when at length Wellington's anxiety was somewhat relieved as he espied an advanced picket of his own officers emerge from the forest, and come dashing along the roads at a steaming gallop.

"Following them at an equally rapid rate came a division of the English army, under General Picton.

"Shortly after him came emerging from the forest at a rapid rate the Duke of Brunswick at the head of his auxiliary corps, and next after him came the Duke of Nassau and the men of his division.

"After him officers of every grade, and divisions of the English army began rapidly to arrive.

"Such was the alacrity displayed that day by the English officers that by four o'clock 50,000 chosen men, comprising infantry, cavalry, and artillery, were on the ground covering the position of Quatre Bras.

"Marshal Ney, who had delayed his attack, now

seemed to comprehend the importance of this point, from the number of troops both the English and the Prussians put forth to preserve it.

"Ney now commenced his attack upon us with his 25,000 men, and nothing could withstand the impetuosity of himself and his army.

"After the first charge, in the course of a few moments the troops of the Duke of Nassau were driven back upon the heights, and the French lancers and the French light dragoons charged and scattered the regiments of the Duke of Brunswick.

"The prince himself fell in the charge, he having expressed a belief that he would do so—having had a presentiment that he would—which he told to the Duke of Wellington on the previous evening while chatting with him.

"The battle raged furiously. Marshal Ney, desperate at the fire the English poured upon him, galloped amidst showers of artillery and musket-balls, and urged his forces up to Quatre Bras.

"The heavy cannonade resounded and re-echoed again and again throughout the country round, when, just at a critical moment, two more English divisions, who had heard the firing, came dashing along to Wellington's assistance.

"The Duke of Wellington, now having 60,000 troops under his command, drove back the French regiments to their original position, whilst Marshal Ney stood aghast shaking with rage, and kept incessantly looking towards Frasnes, hoping for the approach of 20,000 men of D'Erlon's division, to whom he had sent special messengers in order to hasten them to his assistance.

"Night, however, was fast approaching.

"For three hours past his infantry and cavalry had been engaged and so decimated that they were incapable of renewing the attack on Wellington, whose forces kept increasing every hour.

"While the batteries hurriedly thrown up by Wellington incessantly vomited forth grape and round-shot on his regiments, Ney galloped up to Kellerman, and entreated him to assist him in making one more desperate effort.

"'Dash forward,' said Ney to him, 'with the two regiments of cuirassiers you have left, right into the heart of the English army, and I will support you. It must be done at any cost.'

"'Charge!' cried Kellerman, without any hesitation to his cuirassiers, and like a thunderbolt they dashed into the centre of the English army.

"The cuirassiers were all clothed in coats of steel, so that scarcely shot or sword could touch them, and they passed through both lines of the English army, sabreing fiercely as they came along, till at last they destroyed some of the English batteries, and penetrated as far as the farm of Quatre Bras.

"When Wellington from the heights above saw the effects of this brilliant engagement he sent a division of the English guards to engage the French cuirassiers, and then after a short but desperate struggle Ney with his forces at length succumbed.

"Though during the engagement the battle raged furiously around me, I believe I thought more of my master's and mistress's safety than my own.

"While various officers kept falling one by one, and the ground was strewn with dead far and near, I was glad to see that my master, throughout the day, like myself, remained unhurt.

"As soon as the engagement was over for the day, the first thought of myself and Captain Smith was to try and find his lady.

"As she did not immediately join him at the head of his regiment, we concluded that as we had galloped a great distance, she had undoubtedly lost sight of us in the smoke and confusion of the fighting, and our anxiety was very great lest she should have fallen among the slain.

"We then retraced our steps along the road we had taken, and after about two hours' searching among the dead, we were glad to find her safe about three miles from the spot of the closing engagement, where she was very busy in staunching and binding up the wounds of some of those who were lying helpless among the wounded.

"It was a great relief to us when we found that we were all spared and safe and unhurt at the close of that eventful day.

"Though, however, we were safe the mistress had had a narrow escape, for her favourite charger was shot under her while she was following the fortune of her husband at the rear of his regiment in the early part of the day.

"Having rendered what assistance we could to the wounded, and as the ambulance waggons were fast coming up with further aid, we returned to headquarters and awaited with patience throughout the night the events of the following day.

"When the news of the defeat of the army under Marshal Ney reached the ears of Napoleon he was greatly chagrined and disappointed, and he complained bitterly of Ney, whom he accused of having dallied with the English in the morning while they were weak.

"Ney, however, explained to Napoleon the circumstances which had caused the failure.

"It appears that Ney, not anticipating the alacrity with which Wellington summoned his troops, had believed himself master of Quatre Bras, and he sent a letter to Napoleon just before his arrival, stating that in a few hours he should be safely master of the place.

"Napoleon, believing in the faith of that letter, sent another letter by Labedoyere to Ney, telling him to fall back upon Ligny, where he intended that the grand army should give battle to the Prussian general, Blucher, on the left, and at the same time also to prevent the junction of the Prussian and English armies.

"Labedoyere, when taking Napoleon's letter, while passing through Frasnes, an intermediate village between the town of Ligny and Ney, met General D'Erlon, with his 20,000 men, on the road to follow Ney to Quatre Bras.

"Laberdoyere showed D'Erlon the letter Napoleon had written to Ney, telling him to fall back on Ligny, and, D'Erlon thinking that Ney would obey that order and go to Ligny, went there himself to meet him instead of at Quatre Bras.

"In consequence of this mistake he failed to render that assistance which he would have done had he gone to Quatre Bras.

"The Emperor Napoleon, exasperated at these mistakes, was for some hours undecided what course to pursue.

"At length he resolved on attacking Wellington himself, and after waiting two days he sent word to Marshal Ney that he would join him at Quatre Bras, and that on the following day Ney was to attack Wellington at daybreak.

"Meanwhile Napoleon divided the men under his own command into two divisions.

"One he kept under his own immediate orders, and the other division he placed under the command of

Marshal Grouchy, whom he ordered to follow the Prussians step by step in their retreat.

"He further ordered Grouchy to keep up with the Prussians, so as to prevent the sudden return of Blucher, and cut him off from rendering any assistance to the English.

"During the whole of that day, the 17th of June, the heavens were overcast with blackness.

"The clouds lowered, and from morning till night, during the past three days, the rain came down in torrents.

"Napoleon hurried his men along through the drenching downpour.

"In vain did Grouchy and Marshal Soult endeavour to bring their men up to Quatre Bras in time.

"The ground was saturated with wet; the fields were sodden, and the artillery got so embedded in the mud of the ruts that the horses were almost unable to pull the cannons along; both men and horses in their march during that unpropitious day were thoroughly exhausted.

"Meantime we kept a sharp look-out on the movements of the French.

"The Duke of Wellington, with his usual sagacity, guessed pretty rightly what the plans of Napoleon were.

"Napoleon had fixed his head-quarters at the village of Planchenoit, in the very centre of his position. This place was like an observatory formed by nature, where he could see all and direct all on the field of battle.

"Every part of the country was overlooked for miles round by this village, and as he stood in this situation he could see every manœuvre of the English army.

"Napoleon, in taking up this position, had calculated that Blucher, pursued by Grouchy, would have retreated; that Wellington, too weak to withstand the French army, would have retired in the course of the night through the forest of Soignies, to receive and strengthen Blucher in the neighbourhood of Brussels; that Marshal Grouchy, being at liberty the next day, would rejoin him on his right; that they would advance together through the forest on the track of the English, and that they would not be able to come to action till one or two days later, when the battle would be fought under the walls of the Belgian capital.

"In this conjecture, however, Napoleon was mistaken. Wellington had no such intention—he changed his position; and Bonaparte was again left to his own resources to find out what move Wellington would make.

"The people of the towns and villages of Belgium were so alarmed at the immediate prospect of a great battle that they fled in consternation, taking with them what property they could, and they generally were so opposed to the ambitious character of Bonaparte that his spies could gain very little information as to the route the English had taken.

"THE NIGHT BEFORE WATERLOO.

"The rain still continued to fall in torrents, and the whole country was enveloped in darkness and mist, whilst the two great armies lay watching for each other.

"Though they were almost close together neither could see each other, and the most supreme silence was maintained around.

"Napoleon had neither slept nor tasted a morsel of food for eighteen hours.

"During the night his troops were drying themselves, and eating and sleeping around their bivouac fires.

"Napoleon, accompanied by only one officer, passed through his line of guards, and he walked a little way on foot into the forest of Soignies.

"Here he suddenly saw on the hills, amidst the forest trees, numbers of bivouac fires of the English troops, and then he knew there was no longer any doubt as to the close proximity of Wellington's army.

"While so walking at half-past two in the morning, he heard the tramping of a few horses.

"He tried hard to make out what the movement was, but the noise of the downpour of rain prevented him.

"He thought for a moment that Wellington was profiting by the noise of the rain and the darkness of the night to raise his camp, but in spite of all his exertions he could not distinctly hear.

"Early on the morning of the 18th of June the rain began to cease, and when the day began to dawn, and the atmosphere began to clear, Napoleon began to see what the tactics of Wellington were.

"THE BATTLE OF WATERLOO.

"Wellington had taken up his position on the eminences of the forest of Soignies.

"Before him lay the plains of Waterloo, where, if possible, he thought, he could gain a victory over Bonaparte, or if not, he knew he could make a secure retreat to the forest, even from tree to tree, where the vast woody space would be inacessible to Napoleon's artillery and troops.

"The selection of such a site showed the genius of Wellington.

"While the troops of Napoleon were worn out with the fatigue of the march, and his artillery and cavalry were bivouacked in the mud, the army of Wellington had had time to rest and recruit.

"On the morning of that day we were all ready, waiting for the action of the enemy.

"Every officer in the English army was at his post at the head of his men, for we all knew that the fortune of the world almost depended on the ensuing battle.

"My master, Captain Smith, as he rode along among the men of his regiment, encouraged them to stand well together, and to especially distinguish themselves in the hour of danger, and at the post of honour.

"My mistress, too, who had borne up bravely, and who had rendered such distinguished services among the poor wounded sufferers, also begged them to show themselves true men, and to help and defend each other.

"Shortly the bugles began to sound, and the drums of the enemy were heard beating in all directions the call to arms.

"Wellington now mounted his steed, and our troops began to get into position, and all now was bustle and anxious excitement.

"My mistress, who each day had mounted her charger, and who had encouraged and accompanied her husband even in the hottest of the battle, now hung upon his neck and kissed him again and again, with the most devoted affection. I could see that she looked pale, haggard, and anxious.

"I too felt that perhaps we were now all going to part, never again to see the dawn of another day.

"While the army was thus standing in position, waiting for orders, my mistress was taken very ill.

"We did not know one moment from another but what the word of command for us to march would be given.

"I knew my mistress was very near her confinement, and I could see that my master was full of anxiety for her.

"Presently I saw the tears roll down her cheeks. She told the captain she was too ill to stand any longer, or to accompany him as before, and in her present pressing condition she must immediately seek the retirement of the most secluded spot she could find.

"The captain immediately called the doctor of the regiment, and begged him to attend her, and my poor mistress, once more kissing her husband, walked as best she could to a small ravine in the wood.

"She had not walked far before she gave birth to a child, and as quickly as possible both mother and her new-born babe were carried upon a litter to a barn on the outskirts of the forest, where, in the pressing emergency of the case they were obliged to be left.

"Meantime Napoleon had taken up a position on a hillock in front of Planchenoit.

"The sun was now shining brightly and his generals were hastening around him announcing the subsiding of the waters, and the hardening of the earth.

"While Napoleon was thus waiting for the sun to make the ground a little passable an officer arrived from his general, Grouchy, informing him that Blucher was wounded in the arm, and that the Prussians were retreating by three different routes to try and join Wellington.

"Marshal Ney now came up to Napoleon for final orders.

"'The English army is superior to ours by more than a third,' said Napoleon, 'but we have ninety chances to ten in our favour, and we shall conquer to-day. It is too late for Wellington to order a retreat: he would expose himself to certain destruction. He has cast his die, and the game is now in our hands!'

"On uttering these words he called at once for his charger, and galloping from position to position he gave the orders he wished carried out.

"In a few more moments the entire French army, under arms and divided into eleven columns, debouched from the hills and dales of Planchenoit, and deployed to take up their ground in front of the forest of Soignies.

"And now began an increased sounding of bugles, the clanging of trumpets, and rolling of drums.

"Napoleon galloped with his staff to the summit of all these triangles of infantry, cavalry, and artillery, and as he dashed along he was received by the whole army with cries of 'Vive l'Empereur.'

"Having now by his presence inspired his army with courage he finally took up his position upon a hill with a gentle slope which jutted out into the plain a little in advance of the wings of his army.

"The name of the hill was Vessemonde, and from this eminence, which had a small farm on each side, he could take in with a single look the whole of the vast scene upon which the booming of the first cannon would call into action 200,000 men.

"The Duke of Wellington, with his principal army, occupied a long terrace bordering on the wood, and directly in front of the village of Waterloo.

"This village contained about thirty farms and cottages enclosed within high hedges, and screened with lofty elms.

"On the right of Wellington was the 1st Regiment of the Guards.

"On his left were the Coldstream Guards, and the 3rd Regiment of the Guards, under General Byng.

"Napoleon waited, contrary to his usual custom, rather late in the day, and then eventually gave the order to attack.

"The Tirailleurs (the French riflemen) then spread themselves in line over the plains of Waterloo, and covered the movements of the army with clouds of smoke.

"General Reillé next pushed forward to try and dislodge Wellington from his position.

"The terrible Battle of Waterloo now commenced in earnest.

"The fire from the French was so hot and incessant upon the chief position of Wellington that he had to reinforce by fresh detachments of his best troops.

"The hills and dales now re-echoed and reverberated with the rapid and crackling firing of the sharpshooters, both on the French and English sides.

"Gradually the riflemen spread far and wide over the plain, crawled and scrambled nearer and nearer to each other, but as yet neither the cavalry nor the artillery had been brought into play.

"Precisely at eleven o'clock, however, the boom of the first cannon was heard, and then in a moment the roar of the artillery came, and the thunder of four hundred cannons in line on both sides of the basin of Waterloo replied simultaneously to the signal, and rent and scattered the clouds, and re-echoed a thousand times among the hills on every side.

"Boom upon boom followed, and the masked batteries kept up continued and unbroken thunder peals.

"Soon the ground was strewn with dead and dying men.

"Wellington galloped to the various scenes of action, to encourage by his voice, his presence, and his gestures, the intrepidity of his men.

"Near to the centre where Wellington took up his position were the remains of the old dismantled castle of Hougemont.

"Large numbers of the English troops were sheltered therein.

"The strong wall of the castle resisted the fire, but the rebounding of the flames and the dense volumes of smoke rendered its further occupation intolerable.

"The French troops stormed the foot of the hill in front of the English troops, and seven different times the French soldiers penetrated through the breach to the courtyard of the castle, but on each occasion they were driven back by the grenadiers of the English guards at the bayonet point.

"At length the shells from the howitzers and numerous mortars set the great barn of the castle on fire, together with all the out-houses, stacks of corn and hay.

"The flames and scorching heat from these forced many of the troops to retire from their positions, and a suffocating blinding smoke enveloped the air.

"To many of the barns numbers of the wounded officers and soldiers had been carried, and deposited there for safety, but they all perished in the flames, for no one could hope to return from them alive.

"While we were thus desperately fighting, and Captain Smith was still heading his men with the utmost bravery, we both often looked towards the little isolated barn at a short distance from here, watching with great anxiety the place to which a little time before his wife with her new-born babe had been carried.

"We often wondered how the poor devoted neglected woman, with her little helpless child, were getting on; without either food, comfort, or necessary attention.

"No man at such a critical period could fall out of his ranks, and none could go to render her help.

"Suddenly while we were hoping that her courage would serve her, and that her strength would last throughout the day, and that the spot where she was lying would be saved from the destruction around, we noticed a missile from the enemy's mortars fly over in the direction of the barn.

"The shell lodged on the thatched roof—a crackly report was heard—a puff of smoke was seen—and in less than three minutes the thatched roof was ablaze.

"I turned my head in terror, for the safety of my heroic mistress, and in another instant I saw the poor woman emerge from the door of the barn, clasping her little babe to her breast, and running for her life as fast as she was able across the plains towards the forest of Soignies to seek another place of shelter from the shots and fire that were falling around.

"Every moment I expected to see her fall, but I watched her as far as I could, till at last she gradually disappeared out of sight, and the smoke of a fresh cannonade cut off all further view.

"I felt the more afraid for her safety, because just at this moment Marshal Ney, with a fresh body of troops, came up.

"The Scotch regiments, dislodged from the castle, formed, and, strengthened by two other English batteries, now threatened to charge the French battalions.

"At this point no less than 400 cannons approached each other at each discharge, and ploughed with their shot and shells the earth, the trees, the crops, and the combatants, and I was greatly afraid lest some of these numerous shots should overtake my mistress, and mow her down in her flight.

"In the midst of this terrible struggle, both Wellington and Napoleon vied with each other, and hoped to win the battle by reinforcement after reinforcement.

"Napoleon saw the desperate character of the situation.

"As he stood on the eminence of his position, he directed his telescope towards St. Lambert.

"He thought he could perceive through it a dark mass on the horizon, but he was uncertain whether it was fixed or moveable.

"Turning towards Marshal Soult, he handed him the telescope, and asked him what he thought it was.

"'I think it is seven or eight thousand men, your majesty,' said Soult; 'probably it is the detachment you demanded from Grouchy.'

"In this state of uncertainty, Napoleon ordered General Subervie to advance with 3000 men to the heights of St. Lambert, to observe and hold himself ready to fight this mysterious stranger if it was a Prussian division, but to precede and guide it to Waterloo if it were French.

"While they were on the road they met a French patrol, who had captured a Prussian prisoner.

"They took him and sent him on before the Emperor, and in reply to Napoleon's question he informed him that the men he saw were 30,000 men of the Prussian army, under General Bulow, whom Blucher had sent forward.

"Bonaparte, astonished at the non-arrival of the division of the French troops under Grouchy, now sent a third despatch after him to hasten him on, for the battle was at this very moment raging along the line of Waterloo.

"The officer who carried this message now galloped off at all hazards in the direction that he thought he would meet with Grouchy.

"Soon after this officers arrvied from Subervie and Dumont, informing the Emperor that the army he saw on the hills was really Prussian, and that the Prussians themselves were sending out detachments to try and find Grouchy, to give him battle.

"Napoleon now became uneasy and anxious, for he thought that by this time Grouchy's cannon ought to be thundering on the rear of Bulow's army.

"Meantime the fight raged desperately round the vicinity of the ruins of the castle of Hougemont.

"The first English line was dispersed, and retreated, whilst General Picton fell dead in the arms of his soldiers, mourned and lost by every English heart.

"So great was the slaughter during those few short hours that over 2500 men were killed in the immediate vicinity of the ruins of the castle of Hougemont, whilst the total loss on both sides in that short conflict amounted to over 6000 troops.

"The scene at the close of this attack was one of the most desperate recorded in history.

"Wellington maintained his position on horseback in the midst of his staff under the shelter of a lofty tree.

"While another fearful struggle was going on he galloped towards two of his regiments of dragoons, and ordered them to the attack.

"They then dashed down the hill like an avalanche upon the French infantry drawn up in squares behind Ney, reached the French batteries drawn up but embedded in the mud, and sabreing the gunners, cut the traces, overturned the cannon, and thus extinguished for the remainder of the day the fire of this artillery.

"Marshal Ney, who had witnessed from a distance this disaster to his artillery, launched against them General Milhaud's regiments of cuirassiers in their armour of steel, and another slaughter ensued.

"Meanwhile Ney was advancing slowly with his columns of attack. He succeeded in reaching, under a heavy cannonade of shell and round shot, the topmost slope which led to the terrace of Mont St. Jean.

"Here, as at the foot of a fortress, French and English officers, soldiers, men, and horses were endeavouring to scramble up, whilst others from the top were dashing them down, till thousands were mingled together under a continuous shower of balls from 200 pieces of English artillery; firing into each other's breasts, sabreing, bayoneting, tearing each other, making of the dead bodies of men and horses, some a rampart, and others bloody steps to defend or to escalade the glorious summit.

"Ney, who saw amidst the smoke the first French uniforms reach the brink of the plateau, rushed forward to seize his victory, sending word at the same time to the Emperor that one last effort of the reserve would win him the battle, and that the English in confusion were already sending off their field equipage to Brussels.

"'I have them then, these English!' shouted the Emperor, with triumphant visage, voice, and gesture in the midst of his staff.

"He remounted his horse, and galloped to the generals of his guard, whom he ordered to form their columns and fly to the support of Ney.

"Behind the English army, on the other side of the forest, everything indicated confusion, and the commencement of a defeat.

"The road to Brussels, and the borders of the fields on each side, were crowded with the wounded, dragging themselves onwards, and sprinkling the road with their blood.

"Mixed among them was a long column of panic-striken peasants—women, old men, and children—driving their flocks before them, or carrying off their furniture and effects in waggons; soldiers, officers, and generals struck by the enemy's balls; horses dying by the sides of the ditches, military servants hurrying to save the equipages of their masters, formed over a space of twelve miles nothing but one mass of fugitives from the field of battle to the gates of the capital.

"The cannon which had been booming since eleven o'clock in the morning, approaching and increasing in volume, had rent the air and dismayed all hearts in the streets of Brussels.

"The entire population had quitted their houses to question each other in the public places.

"The rumour of Napoleon's victory, which should yield Belgium up to his arms, and for the third time turn its flourishing fields into the distracted and sanguinary arena of Europe's contentions, passed from mouth to mouth.

"The people were panic-struck, the princes, nobility, and the wealthy inhabitants dismantled their houses and fled with their families on the road to Antwerp.

"Such, at six o'clock in the evening, was the striking contrast in the aspect of the two different armies.

"Thus, as evening was coming on, Wellington was straitened and almost forced from his final position.

"Eleven of his generals were dead around him, eight of his seventeen aides-de-camp were either killed or wounded, whilst Blucher was wandering at a distance from him in the plains of Namur.

"But in the midst of it all, Wellington remained at the post of duty, with the unshaken resolution of dying or conquering in the cause he had espoused.

"After galloping from brigade to brigade under showers of shot and shell, he would return and take up his post under the lofty oak of Waterloo, that his officers might not have to wander about in search of him when his presence or his orders were required.

"There, under the oak, he remained, anxiously waiting for the arrival of the Prussians, whilst the balls rattled in showers among the branches of the tree.

"While Wellington was thus waiting for the Prussians, Bonaparte was equally anxiously waiting and expecting the other division of his army under Marshal Grouchy.

"Towards the close of evening Bonaparte espied an army approaching. He was the first to see it.

"Slowly and with measured pace they approached behind the summit of the hills of St. Lambert.

"Napoleon for some time could not by any means discern whether they were the Prussians or the French that were thus coming up.

"Meantime Wellington was still anxiously and patiently waiting, for there had been a previous secret agreement between him and Blucher that whichever of the two allied generals should be first attacked by the Emperor should accept the battle and resist him without yielding an inch of ground till the arrival of the other, who was then to advance during the action and attack the army of Napoleon in flank.

"This convention was the secret of the obstinate resolution of Wellington to fight till victory or death should decide the fate of the battle on the narrow borders of the forest.

"Napoleon, on the other hand, was just as resolutely waiting for the arrival of the other division of his troops under Grouchy.

"As he nervously watched over the hills he kept on exclaiming every instant, 'Grouchy—Grouchy! Where is he? What is he doing that he does not come? Send more officers after him, and hasten his march at once.'

"The only sight, however, he saw was the appearance of the long dark columns of the Prussians, 30,000 strong, with the standard of the black eagle visible to his eyes.

"At the sight of these he recalled the order he had given for a general attack, for he now began to fear that Grouchy had been outstripped, and that Bulow, another Prussian general, and Blucher, in full force, were near at hand.

"Meanwhile the French general, Lobau, stationed between Planchenoit and Bulow, fought the Prussian army with intrepid assurance, and delayed its approach on the road for nearly an hour.

"Marshal Ney, relying on the extremity of the moment, now sent order upon order to hasten up all the reserves. The drums beat the charge on every point, and a torrent of troops poured forward on the English troops on Mont St. Jean.

"Wellington, almost immoveable on his wounded horse, was looking with an air of intrepid despair upon this sudden and dashing outburst of the French army, when suddenly Bulow's cannon resounded from under the hills of Planchenoit, and at length just timely brought him that assistance from the Prussians he had so long expected.

"'Now, forward, my lads!' he exclaimed, waving his sword to his troops, 'We have stood to be attacked long enough, it is now our turn.'

"The English now dashed forward with heroic gallantry, and it was man to man—a hand-to-hand fight for life

"Napoleon from his heights viewed the raging conflict with the utmost concern.

"Now 10,000 French horsemen charged at a gallop the English cavalry.

"The ground was immediately strewn with heaps of dead and mutilated men and horses.

"No less than 20,000 horses and men of both armies galloped in turn, like the surging waves, backwards and forwards over the dead and dying, drenched with blood, and as they galloped over them they kneaded them like clay into one vast mass of mutilated flesh.

"Wellington stood at his post under the famous tree, and as he put his telescope to his eyes he could see that the musket balls of the English were deadened and flattened against the steel armour of the French cuirassiers.

"In this extremity Wellington left his post, and passing along the ranks of the Scotch infantry, commanded them to go forward, and allow themselves to be charged by the armoured cavalry of the French, without forming upon them, and then as soon as the cuirassiers came up, the Scotch were to fall down, slip under the horses, and ripping open their bellies with their dirks, cause the cuirassiers to be dismounted, and then fall upon them.

"This mêlée lasted three hours, and 15,000 men of both nations fell in the fight.

"'What brave troops—what brave troops!' said Napoleon to his staff, as he contemplated with admiration this heroism of the Scotch.

"Napoleon, now seeing the desperate character of the situation, immediately sent a column of 6000 grenadiers against Wellington's centre, and they advanced with shouldered arms amidst cries of 'Vive l'Empereur.'

"Wellington contemplated their advance with almost a degree of alarm, but quick to the necessity of the moment he ordered his men to await them with lighted matches in hand, and a battery of forty pieces of cannon.

"As they approached the summit of the hill the artillery fired a volley into their midst.

"The invading mass, thinned now in its ranks for a moment, closed up and approached again, when they were decimated from another volley from the cannons above.

"Column upon column were thus stricken down, and the remainder, dismayed, retired to seek an advance upon other sides of the hill.

"But Wellington covered his army with 200 pieces of cannon, and as the French tried to ascend the hill on the other side, he met them with flames at every point.

"Napoleon turned pale as he watched his fruitless attempt.

"'My horse, my horse!' he exclaimed.

"His favourite white charger, white as a swan, was brought him, and Napoleon mounting him galloped off, surrounded by his staff to encourage his men.

"'Forward, forward!' he cried, animating his battalions with eye and voice and gesture.

"Just at this moment an officer galloped up to him and announced that the Belgians and Germans who formed Wellington's left were falling back in disorder, followed by clouds of smoke.

"''Tis Grouchy—'tis Grouchy—arrived at last to our aid!' cried the emperor. 'The day is ours; go and spread the joyful news. Fly—fly—in all directions.'

"Labedoyere and other officers galloped off to take the gladdening tidings, but the emperor's joy was short and deceitful.

"It was not Grouchy coming to the assistance of Napoleon, but Blucher coming to the aid of Wellington. The conflict was now raging fearfully, and Napoleon quietly surveyed the scene.

"Wellington also stood in the same passive manner. It was raining death around.

"'Have you no orders to give?' said the staff to Wellington.

"'None,' replied the duke.

"'But you may be killed,' said one of his staff.

"'I have no other thought but to stand true to the last man,' replied Wellington.

"On the other side Bonaparte was standing sheltered from that death which so many thousand men were braving for him.

"His brother, Jerome Bonaparte, blushing at Napoleon's safe position, while so many lives were being sacrificed ruthlessly before him, murmured at the immobility of the Emperor, and he said to Labedoyere—

"'Why does he not show himself now? He will never have a nobler opportunity.'

"Soon after Jerome was sent at the head of a column, and he braved fire and death with the devoted gallantry of a simple grenadier.

"Napoleon, now no longer able to withstand this dreadful spectacle, put spurs to his horse, and urged his charger forward to go himself, and support and lead on his guard.

"Bertrand and Dronot, his friends, however, seized his bridle, and held him back into shelter from the balls.

"'What are you going to do, sire?' said they. 'Recollect that the salvation of France and of the army is in you alone!'

"The emperor yielded, and passively remained at his post.

"Blucher, with the Prussian army, now came in sight, and Wellington appeared at the head of his army, and again charged the French.

"It was at this critical moment that he cried out the ever memorable words—'Up, guards, and at them!'

"The brave heroic English soldiers, reanimated once more, now charged again, dashed forward in the most brilliant manner, and overwhelmed, by their impetus, the French cavalry, which was nearly intact.

"The French troops made one more attempt, and in the engagement which then took place I, who had remained unhurt during the day, now lost one eye and one arm in the final struggle which ensued.

"Captain Smith remained with his men, providentially unscathed in the charges we made.

"Just at this moment the French troops were stricken with the instinct of fear.

"A sort of panic came over them as our troops were sabreing them down, and they saw Blucher with his troops arriving.

"'Save a few of us,' some of the French cried, and they began to fly in all directions.

"Napoleon for a moment stood aghast, contemplating the disastrous scene, and then turning pale, he shed tears, and then stammered out—'All is lost.'

"The shades of night gathered round the figure of Napoleon, and concealed him as he turned his back and retraced his steps across the plains of Waterloo.

"As he was leaving the field he saw some cannon overturned by the wayside.

"'Raise them and fire them,' said he to his men.

"They did so, and these were the last French guns that were fired at the great and ever memorable battle of Waterloo by the French against the English.

"Thus did the heroic Duke of Wellington conquer and put to flight Napoleon and his army.

"On the arrival of Blucher at the head of the Prussians, Wellington came down from the height on which he had been standing and, apparently greatly relieved, shook hands with Blucher.

"When Wellington had a little recovered himself he said to Blucher—

"'My brave fellows are exhausted with blood, violence, and fatigue. They have now been fighting incessantly thirteen hours, and I should wish to spare them a little; they are my children and have wrought miracles.'

"Blucher then took hold of Wellington's hands, and pressing them in his own, said with tears of admiration in his eyes—

"'Leave the rest to me, and I will answer for the night, and take the responsibility of the pursuit.'

"Blucher summoned immediately all his commandants of corps, and ordered them to push forward, even to the last man, against the retreating army of Napoleon.

"Wellington shortly addressed his men on the courage and fidelity they had shown, and the army then sent up three tremendous cheers for the noble and complete victory of Waterloo.

"The Prussian bugles now sounded, and their drums beat to arms, and in a very short time Blucher and his men were in full pursuit of Napoleon.

"Bonaparte and his army were dispirited and fatigued with the battle of the day, and they made but slow progress along the narrow and uneven roads.

"As the French army went along, with its ranks broken up in disorder, and the soldiers crowding and jostling to see which could get along first, some of them observed Napoleon, muffled in his coat and partly concealed by the darkness of the night, trying to ride past them and get in front.

"They recognised him by his almost snow-white charger.

CAPTAIN SMITH'S LAST VISIT TO THE GAMBLING TABLE.

"'Oh, he is not dead, then?' said many of the men. 'He is not killed;' but no voice or cheer was heard to escape from the lips of the men.

"While the French army was thus retreating in disorder, a Belgian peasant, who was acting as Napoleon's guide along the road, made an error, and conducted him to a narrow defile leading to a single narrow bridge across the river Dyle, instead of along other broad highways where the bridges were all wide.

"The result was disastrous to Napoleon, and the Prussians coming up with them they opened fire upon them.

"Under the cannon of the Prussians, and the sabres of Blucher's light cavalry, the French again fell in terrible numbers.

"Napoleon was vanquished. That the victory was won, and that we, with the exception of the little one, were all alive—my mistress expressed thankfulness for that, and her spirits gradually, with her strength, began to recover.

"She, however, was very much distressed when she heard that I had the misfortune to lose one eye and one arm in the day's engagement.

"When we arrived in London there were great rejoicings, and our regiment, like all the others that fought in that memorable engagement, received the thanks of the nation."

The old pensioner told the story of the battle of Waterloo in such graphic manner, with such a number of interesting details, that I at once confessed to him that I had not only been highly delighted, but interested and greatly instructed by his recital of the events of that great and memorable day.

"I told you that you would be interested in his story," said Calcraft. "That was just the reason I invited you both here to meet together. I am sure I have felt quite rivetted to the spot while Donald has been telling us about the battle of Waterloo."

"So have I," rejoined I, "and I feel greatly indebted to him, too; but how are Mrs. Smith and Captain Smith getting on? That is what I want to know now."

"Just so," said Calcraft. "I knew you would want to hear the remainder, and Donald, I am sure, will tell us some more."

"Well,'" said the old pensioner, "after the battle was over, my master and mistress settled down comfortably together at the West-end, near to Jermyn-street, and I had a situation as servant in the house. We were going on very comfortably together without anything seeming likely to mar the domestic quiet and happiness of my master's house till such times as he was induced to go to one of those notorious gaming-houses in Jermyn-street, known as the hells. Many of the officers used to meet there, and frequently royal princes would go there too."

"Ah, they may well be termed hells," said Calcraft. "Many a good man has lost his fortune in those places."

"Yes," said Donald, "they have. Well, my unfortunate master, Captain Smith, got so infatuated with these gaming-houses that he got led on from gambling for small sums to large ones. The excitement of sometimes winning and sometimes losing grew upon him and became a curse. He would then frequently stop out till two and three in the morning gambling, sometimes winning and sometimes losing, and then staying later to try and win back his losses till at last his poor wife used to implore him to give it up, and go no more. Sometimes he would listen to her, and say he would not go again. One night, however, he said he would go once more for the last time, for he felt sure he should win a great sum.

"'Don't go, John,' said his wife, 'for you might lose.'

"'No, I shall not,' he said, 'I will only go this once,' and he went.

"The next morning he came back very low-spirited, and my mistress, guessing what was the cause, asked him what was the matter.

"After a little pause he said, 'I have lost all. I have staked my pension and thousands of pounds besides, and I know not what to do.'

"He collected what money he could to pay what gambling debts he could discharge, but he was then thousands of pounds minus the sums he required. The goods were seized, the house broken up, and in a few days Captain Smith came from affluence to the greatest straits."

The old pensioner, continuing, said:—

"Well, after Captain Smith's household furniture was sold up to defray some of his gambling debts they went into private apartments at Westminster. It was a bad turn of fortune this.

"The harpies kept dunning him for money, and his poor wife, in order to try and avert the evil day, let him have the little property that was left to her by her father, for the captain to raise what money he could.

"He sold that, but there were still some thousands owing to the gamesters, and the captain seemed bewildered.

"The people at the lodgings trusted him as long as they could, and when the cupboard began to get bare, we were all badly off.

"One day the master was out very much longer than usual, and my mistress began to get very fidgetty, for she wondered wherever the captain could be so long.

"Towards night a knock came to the door, and on my going to it, I found a man there who had brought a letter for my mistress.

"On reading it she turned suddenly pale, and nearly swooned away.

"She fell back in a chair, and then said—'Donald, read that letter, and see what is to be done.'

"I took the note up, which had fallen on the floor, and then read the letter which the captain had sent to his wife. The letter was to the following effect:—

Tothill Fields Prison.
MY DEAR WIFE,—I just write these few lines to you to inform you that while I was walking along the streets to-day I was arrested by one of the watchmen at Westminster, and charged with forgery. You must not put yourself about or fret over this, but do the best you can for me.—From your affectionate husband,
J. SMITH.

"'Forgery!' cried his poor heart-broken wife. 'Oh, why did he go to that gambling house?—that hell! It is all my fault for letting him go out of the house that night—I ought to have kept him at home by some means or other.'

"'Well,' I said to my mistress—'you must not take on and fret like this. We must do something now to try and get him out of prison. We must raise some money, somehow or another, to-night, to pay a solicitor to defend him in the morning.'

"'Yes,' said my mistress, 'we must raise some money by some means to fetch him out of prison, poor fellow; for it would break his heart to let him lie there.'

"So away we went—she to some acquaintance and I to others to try and borrow what money we could for his defence.

"We managed to get sufficient that night, and the next morning we went and saw him in Tothill Fields Prison, and took a solicitor with us.

"I shall never forget my feelings as we passed along the narrow passages of that old dingy prison, which during so many years had been the scene of confinement for so many criminals of such varied type."

"Poor mistress, I shall ever remember how she started, and how bitterly she wept when she saw the captain there.

"She gave him what consolation she could under the circumstances, and received from him what instructions he had to give her. The captain, however, bore up better than I expected.

"The hour allotted to see him soon passed, and then he had to be taken before the magistrates for his examination.

"The charge against him was that he did wilfully forge and utter a £10 note, knowing at the same time that it was a forgery.

"The evidence against him went to show that on the previous day he entered a haberdasher's shop, kept by a Mrs. Applebee at Westminster, and asked for a pair of gloves. He fitted some on, and then tendered the forged £10 note.

"As she could not cash it herself she sent it out to get it changed, and it was then returned to her as a forgery, and the captain was given into custody.

"The solicitor for his defence made a good appeal on his behalf, but it was useless; the evidence was conclusive, and he was committed to the Old Bailey for trial.

HANGED FOR FORGING A TEN-POUND NOTE.

"When the sessions at the Old Bailey came on he was found guilty, in spite of all that could be done for him, and he was sentenced to death.

"The sentence was passed upon him on the Friday afternoon, and it was ordered to be carried out on the following Monday morning.

"In the meantime my poor mistress on the Saturday and Sunday was engaged going about to all the influential people she could think of to try and get them to use their influence to obtain the royal mercy, and a reprieve for him.

"Unfortunately, while she was travelling in a coach to an influential person in the country, in consequence of her dreadful excitement, another child was born in the coach, and she was laid up dreadfully ill.

"No influence, however, that she could use was able to spare his life. Her husband was not among the number that was put down for a reprieve, and, according to his sentence, he was hung on the following morning in front of Newgate Gaol, without her being able to see him again or wish him farewell.

"Thus, through one of those dreadful gaming houses, Captain Smith, who was one of the heroes of Waterloo—who had stood the brunt of that terrible battle the whole day long—came to his untimely end."

"Ah!" interrupted Calcraft, "I remember Captain Smith being hung very well. What a many I can recollect that have been hung in my time for petty offences—old and young, even mere children; and numbers through those gaming houses."

"Yes," said the old pensioner, "the thousands that have been executed in this country, even for stealing things of small value, is almost incredible when you come to think of it."

"Well," I replied, "I am very much interested in the fate of the captain's widow. I want to know how she got on, and what became of her, poor woman."

"I will tell you," said the old pensioner. "After the death of Captain Smith, and after the loss of her property, she scarcely knew what to do for a living, so she went out and did what little work she could. Then she, in order to obtain a home, married a labouring man; but he left her after living with her a little time. After the lapse of a few years she, several months ago, got married to a physician residing at Hackney."

"Indeed," said I. "Then I hope she is doing well now after her strange and eventful history. I trust that they are now living happy together."

"No, they are not, I am sorry to say," said the old pensioner; "for there is a still stranger sequel to her chequered history."

"Where is she now then?" said I.

"Poor woman," said the old pensioner, almost heart-broken; "she is in Newgate now."

"In Newgate!" said I. "In Newgate!"

"Yes," said Donald; "she is in Newgate now."

"How came she there?" I asked.

"Well," said the old pensioner; "when she got married to this physician at Hackney they didn't agree, and as he was disappointed in not getting any money with her he tried to get rid of her by putting her in Bedlam, and by endeavouring to make out that she was mad. I knew she was not mad, and she soon showed them at the mad-house that she was not mad too. So after they had her there a few days they discharged her at once."

"Well, then," said I, "how did she get to Newgate?"

"Why, after this physician she married saw that he could not get rid of her in that manner, he got evidence together, showing that she had been married before, and that the man to whom she had been married was still alive. He then prosecuted her for bigamy, and, she being convicted, was sentenced to seven years' transportation."

"Yes," said Calcraft, "I saw her yesterday at Newgate. Poor woman, they are going to send her to Botany Bay by the next ship-load of transports that go out to that place."

Calcraft said, turning to me, "I think now, sir, I have been as good as my word when I told you that if you would listen to the old pensioner's story, I would show you a little of the lights and shades of life, and I guess you may read a good deal, and not find such a romantic chequered history as this."

"Well, indeed, it is," said I to Calcraft, "and the information you have afforded me has not only been interesting, but instructive, too."

"I am glad of it," said Calcraft; "and now if you will pay me a visit on another occasion, I will tell you another story, which will show you another phase of the changes of human life."

I thanked him for his kindness, and then wishing him and the old pensioner good night, I retired home, musing on the sufferings so many human creatures are obliged to undergo through the force of circumstances, over which apparently many of them seem to have had little or no control.

SECOND VISIT TO CALCRAFT.

I was so interested in the history of the unfortunate lady doomed to transportation, that I could not rest without going to Calcraft again the very next day to see if something could not be done for her to save her from such an awful fate.

Transportation in those days was a far worse doom than death, and very different at that time to what it became under the judicious and milder regulations of after years.

I found Calcraft at home, and told him that I had

been thinking so much of the dreadful sufferings which seemed to be awaiting the unhappy woman, that I was determined if possible to try and do something in her behalf.

"You can see Donald again, if you like," said Calcraft, "and hear what he will advise; but I don't think it is of any use—for, poor fellow, he has been running about to all the influential people he can think of, and they have been getting up petitions and sending them; but they are of no avail. But, however, you can have a walk as far as Donald's and see."

Calcraft put on his coat and away we went at once. We found the old pensioner at home, and he was glad to see us, for he was very dejected at his unfortunate mistress's fate.

"Well, Donald," I said, "I have come to see if we cannot do something to save your mistress from her terrible sentence."

"Ah, I wish we could," said Donald, "but I am afraid there is no chance, for I have done everything I can think of."

"Are the people that you have been to fully aware of the dreadful horrors of transportation, and of the fearful outrages and atrocities that are carried on?" said I.

"Well, perhaps they are not," said Donald. "But I am afraid there is not much time now, as the ship is going to sail in a few days."

"We should not lose a moment then," I said, "for I have lately been reading the official and other reports of the dreadful barbarities inflicted on the helpless convicts, and I have come to the conclusion that for the sake of humanity the country ought to be aroused to express its indignation, and its determination to put an end to such barbarities."

"I quite agree with you," said Calcraft, "but you know I never can interfere publicly, nor appear to countenance any interference with sentences or the cause of justice, or I might lose my situation."

"True," I said. "We shall not want you to interfere in the matter or to be seen in it. I do not think it would be right to let you. But when we read of such dreadful tortures being applied to transports, and such wholesale murders of helpless convicts, I think that people who are outside the ban of official censure, and who are free and independent, ought to interfere."

"So do I," said Donald; "and I am much indebted to you for the interest you have taken."

"Yes," I continued; "I think it is time the country should be called upon to interfere when we read what we do, that, since the discovery of Botany Bay and the first transporting of convicts there for the purpose of making it a penal settlement, convicts should be so packed together on board the transport ships that nearly half of them die on the road before they get there, whilst others are landed in a dying state from starvation, fever, exhaustion, bad food, and foul air.

"I was reading the other day that some time ago, out of four shiploads that were sent out, no less than 261 had died at sea, whilst nearly all the others were put on shore in an almost dying state.

"To think of crowding so many helpless human beings in the holds of ships, and on the decks all in irons, chained together, with rations not enough to supply half of them, is wicked in the extreme.

"But when we further read that their scanty rations of flour and other miserable dietary has been held back by the overseers for the purpose of selling it, and that the unhappy people have died by thousands of literal starvation, I think it high time the attention of the people should be directed to the perpetrators of such abuses, with the view of their being brought to trial for nothing less than murder.

"But even this is not all. I read of men and women and children, for the most trivial offences—for taking a small bit of food, or for giving a reproachful look to an overseer—being at once tied up to the nearest tree, and from eighty up to 500 lashes inflicted upon them there and then, without trial, till frequently many died under the shocking torture.

"There is no mistaking the truth of these reports, which at this time are reaching England, of the horrors perpetrated in our colonies, and I do not mean to rest till I have done my utmost to prevent this poor woman from being consigned to seven years' transportation, to such a long and awful fate as this for merely consenting to marry a man, who first importuned her to do what she did, and then afterwards actually prosecuted her, and sends her to this fate for doing it."

"I quite agree with you," said Calcraft, "and if anything is to be done it must be done at once."

"Did this physician that prosecuted her knew she had been married before?" said I to Donald.

"He knew that she had to Captain Smith, because she told him; and he also knew that Captain Smith was hung for forgery, but he did not know of her other marriages," said Donald.

As we knew that time was important, we hastened off towards Newgate to see if we could get any information of the time the next transport ship would start.

We all wended our way as far as the Old Bailey, but as Calcraft did not wish to be seen taking any part in interfering with the sentence of a prisoner, we left him at a public-house, known as the sign of the "Old Bell Inn."

I and Donald went across to Newgate and asked the governor whether we could see the convict Mary Ann Smith, and also whether he could tell us when she would be likely to sail to Botany Bay.

"She has already gone from here," replied the governor. "The last batch of convicts left here for the ship this morning."

"I wanted to see whether we could do anything to get her a reprieve," said I, "before she sails. Can you tell us where the ship is lying?"

"Yes," replied the governor, "the ship is lying now in the Thames, moored just below the Execution Dock at Wapping; but I don't think it will be any use your troubling, for some very influential people have tried to get her a reprieve, but they cannot. The judge considers it a very bad case, for she has already had several husbands."

"I suppose we could see her before she starts—could we not?" said Donald.

"You might perhaps," said the governor, "with the special permission of the captain of the ship."

We returned to Calcraft at the "Bell Inn," and then we hired a post-fly at once, and drove down to the docks as soon as we could.

On getting there, and inquiring for the captain, we saw him on shore, superintending the embarkation of the convicts.

We went up to him, and related to him a little of the painful and unfortunate history of the convict we wanted to see; and after telling him of some of the extraordinary vicissitudes she had undergone, we begged of him to allow us to see her before she started.

"Well, he said, it is a painful and extraordinary history, but it is not customary to allow people to come leave-taking on board a ship. However, under the circumstances, you may pass and see her."

THE TRANSPORT SHIP.

Having obtained the necessary order from the captain, we went down alongside the dock, and surveyed the vessel which was to take so many hundreds of unfortunate creatures far away from their own native land, to cast them on shore at the Antipodes, and leave them there miserable slaves at the mercy of a few gangs of mercenary, cruel men, who would yoke them together like oxen in bondage, and who would lash and starve them till many of them fell in death to the earth.

The vessel was a full-masted three-decked ship, for there were no steamboats then, when Calcraft first took office, and the scene on and around the vessel was one full of oppression and bustle on the one hand, and of sullen resignation and terrible suffering on the other.

A double file of marines were drawn up on each side of the gangway of the vessel, with their muskets loaded, and their bayonets fixed lest there should be any attempt at rescue or insubordination.

Passing along between the files of marines, and of the various officers and warders in charge were numerous gangs of the convicts from the different gaols, all heavily ironed, marching up to to their respective holds.

It was something fearful to witness the sorrow that was depicted on every face.

After several gangs had thus gone up, and had been drafted off to their quarters, we passed up, and showed our order to an officer in command, giving us permission to have an interview with the unhappy woman we went to see.

It was a sight never to be forgotten. There on each deck lay hundreds of these unfortunate beings manacled and ironed together in so many groups. One part of the ship was set apart for the men and boys, and one part for the women and girls.

Their clothing was wretched, and they were so closely packed together that they had to lie with the feet of each alternate one towards the face of the other.

Though not more than one half of the number were yet on board, the smell of so many crowded together was sickening.

The most abject squalor, raggedness, and dirt reigned supreme. A large number of those on board seemed to have been born in vice, reared in depravity, educated in wickedness, and they seemed, what they mostly were, a shipload of uneducated unfortunate beings, whose great crime was their poverty, going to be cast adrift on an almost unknown and uncultivated wild, to die and rot, where their sorrows or their death would be neither seen nor heard of.

We were then shown down to the second deck, and there we found the unhappy woman we had come to see. Donald introduced me to her as a friend.

My heart was so full I could not speak at first, for I had such a choking sensation through the grief I felt at her terrible position.

She was a fine handsome-looking woman, with black hair and bright sparkling eyes.

I took her hand, and as soon as I could find words I told her the object of my visit, and that I had come on purpose to see if we could do anything to save her from the fate of transportation.

The tears came into her eyes, and for a time she was quite unable to utter a single word.

I could see she felt acutely the position she was in. There was no chance of us conferring privately, for she was one of six that were ironed together.

Two wretched-looking old women were on each side of her.

Next to one of them was a fat, soddened-looking desperado, who seemed as though she had been the keeper of an infamous house, and as though she was steeped in crime (and, as I was afterwards informed, she had been), and on either side of these were two young girls—one about twelve and the other about thirteen—who, I afterwards learned, were convicted of robbing gentlemen, to which crime they had been instigated and driven to by one of the harridans that infested society at that period of time.

As soon as the unhappy woman had recovered herself sufficiently to speak she said—

"I beg to thank you very much, sir, for your kindness. Do try and save me if you can, if you think there is time."

"Yes," I said, "I will do all that is possible, but I am informed the ship sails in the morning."

"So I believe," she replied. "I am afraid that it is too late, and that nothing more can be done."

"Who have your friends appealed to as yet?" I inquired.

"Oh, they have written to the judge, and to the Secretary of State," she replied.

"And what answer did they get?" I asked.

"Oh, they refused to interfere; and I am afraid there is no hope now. Ah, my poor husband, the captain, when he went out that night so elated, thinking to win a large sum of money, little thought what ruin it would involve him in, and that in the end it would bring him to such a fate, and me to this!"

Here the poor woman burst into a paroxysm of grief, and her whole frame seemed to quiver.

"What are you shaking the irons like that, and making them pinch the flesh like this for, you cowhearted, snivelling cat?" said the fat-looking harridan, to whom she was chained.

"I didn't know I was. I did not mean to inconvenience you," replied the unhappy woman to her fiendish companion, to whom she was manacled.

"Why don't yer lie down and be quiet, or I'll give yer shins a twister, yet puppy-snatching fool," retorted the woman again.

"You should not be disagreeable to one another," said I. "The poor woman, I am sure, would not do anything to annoy you if she could help."

"Ah! it's all very well for the loikes of her to have people running about trying to get her off; but people like us they never takes any notice of. We may go to Botney Bay, or anywhere else, for all they care—mightn't us, old gal?" said she, appealing to the old woman on the other side.

"Aye! right you are," said the old woman, with a sort of demoniacal grin.

"Let us have two or three quiet words with our friend before she sails with you," I said. "I am sure we would do anything to save you all if we possibly could from such a fate."

The women after this seemed a little more quiet, though the jeers and ill-natured observations they every now and then made only showed more strongly the devilish spirits they had within them.

In the course of the other observations which ensued, Mrs. Smith seemed to feel keenly the destiny which had overtaken her.

"My bed is indeed a hard one now," she said. "My father was right when he told me that disobedience and self-will would bring their own punishment, and 'that as I made my bed so I should have to lie upon it.' When, however, I first took that first fatal false step of entering into a clandestine marriage, I was but a thoughtless, motherless girl of seventeen, inexperienced in the ways and treachery and deceit of the world; and now, at thirty, I, who might have been a bright, joyous, useful woman, am a wretched outcast and an unhappy transport."

Then with tears in her eyes and streaming down her cheeks, she took hold of Donald's hand, and said to him—

"Donald, you will do your best to look after my poor orphan boy. Poor fellow, he is only ten; but you will go to the workhouse, and see him sometimes, will you not? And if the guardians, when he gets a little older, apprentice him out, you will then go and visit him, and see that he is not ill-used and starved, won't you?"

"I will do that, mistress. Depend upon it, ma'am, that while I'am alive, I will always look after that boy as though he were my own."

"Thank you, Donald, for that assurance. I know you will keep your promise, and now you have promised me that much, I shall go away more resigned to my fate, and buoyed up with the hope that he will in some way or other be taken care of, though I—I may never see either you or him again."

"Oh, don't think that, mistress. Keep your spirits up, you know, and you will be sure to write and let us know how you are—won't you, when you get the chance?—and always let us have your address wherever you be, and I'll try and keep you well informed how the boy and Old England's getting on," said Donald.

"You may be sure I shall write whenever I get the chance, Donald."

"And may I ask as a favour, madam, that upon every opportunity you will write to me, and give me leave to write to you? I, too, will keep a kindly watch over your poor helpless boy."

"Thank you, sir," said she, "this visit has really done me good. I believe had it not been for these kindly assurances, I should have died on the road from grief and a broken heart."

The officers now came round to say that all strangers must leave the ship.

We then took farewell of the unhappy woman, and bidding her keep her courage up through every hardship and trial, live in the hope that she would come back safe, and that we should yet all meet again.

Early the next morning the ship sailed without our having the slightest possible chance to try and avert the unhappy woman's fate.

As the ship sailed down the Thames the officers in charge paraded the deck with bayonets fixed and their muskets loaded, and so away the vessel went to deposit its living freight of human misery in a land almost unknown.

We returned back to Calcraft's house, and informed him of the departure of the ship, of the interview we had had, and the promise we had made to the unfortunate convict.

The ship with this unfortunate convict sailed for Botany Bay about three months after Calcraft's official appointment.

CHAPTER XX.

IN our last narrative we endeavoured to show the severity with which the law of England was administered when Calcraft first came into office.

The judges sought to repress crime by numerous hangings and wholesale transportations.

When we consider the number of executions which took place, and the many thousands which were sent for life into banishment abroad, it would appear as though they imagined that the only way to defend the country from the viciousness of crime was to extirpate the criminals themselves as fast as they could be secured.

Probably to many at the present time the severities adopted fifty years ago will seem unnecessary and harsh, but the times and circumstances were exceptional, and no doubt the powers that then were thought that the exceptional circumstances required prompt and effective administration.

But a short time before the appointment of Calcraft the laws for the repression of crime were even far more severe than they were when he first took office.

Then men, women, and children used to be hung for minor acts of dishonesty, or publicly whipped along the streets at the tail of a cart, or sent beyond the seas for what to-day they would only get a few weeks' imprisonment.

The life and time of Calcraft then were remarkable, because he lived in two distinct periods of criminal history and criminal legislation.

During the years of his life many changes were made in the law of criminal punishments. In his early life he saw the age of severities, in his later years he saw the law of justice tempered with the law of mercy.

There are, however, other very important changes and improvements which must be taken into account in studying the progress which has been made during Calcraft's long and varied career.

It may sound perhaps strange in the ears of some young people who perhaps personally knew, only several years ago that little active old man with hair and beard almost as white as snow, to be told that he lived in the dark ages.

And yet he really did. This old man, whose face was so familiar to many Londoners, especially at the East-end, lived in the ages of darkness and of light.

When he first used to traverse London streets on his way from that little house of his at Hoxton to his work at Newgate, there was no gas in London then.

After the sun had gone down the streets of this brilliant city, some of which are now illumined with the bright electric light, used at that time to be enveloped in the darkness and blackness of night.

Scarcely anyone dared walk out alone, unprotected or unarmed, after dusk, except in the very frequented streets.

Even the main thoroughfare of Holborn was dangerous for pedestrians at that time, but to venture along any of the back streets was almost a sure certainty of being knocked down and robbed, and in many cases to be either maimed, or in some way terribly assaulted.

It was in short a period of history when the criminal class had by systematic organisation, and by constant acts of violence, nearly got the upper hand of society.

Where the Holborn Viaduct, with its fine ranges of elegant shops, and other proximate buildings, now stands, the ground in Calcraft's early days was covered with slums of the vilest description.

Even at the present time, if a person will take the trouble to walk round the remaining portion of Saffron-hill, and a few old existing alleys near the site of Snow-hill they will see how low the ground was, what a deep valley old Holborn valley once was, and the people and the character of the neighbourhood mostly were as vile as the ground.

At the backs of the few respectable houses that used to be there were low lodging houses, and whole colonies of thieves of the most dangerous and desperate class.

These thieves' colonies were in fact studded nearly all over the metropolis, and their denizens used to sally out at night time to live by wholesale plunder.

Of course it was not much use in calling for the watchmen.

They were very few in number, and many of them were dilapidated old fogies, which, like some of the old dilapidated houses of the present day, ought to have been removed long ago.

If the watchman was particularly wanted when some dreadful melée was going on, it not unfrequently happened that he and his watch-box had been turned over in the mud, and he was found lying on his face, with his temporary station, or box, on his back, like a snail under its shell, and calling out—

"Help, help!" as a sort of chorus to the people who, a few yards off, were singing out, "Watch, watch! Murder! Thieves! and robbery!"

Certainly this was a pretty predicament for a watchman, a guardian of the peace, to be seen in, and a very curious state of safety for the general public too.

THE MURDERERS' DEPOT FOR THE DEAD.

Among some of the audacious acts of several of the London gangs of organised robbers and murderers was that of establishing a general warehouse or depôt for the reception of the murdered bodies of their victims.

This was an old building, which formerly stood near to the side of the Thames, on the Surrey shore, not far from the foot of old Blackfriars-bridge.

When a murder had been committed by any of the dreadful gang who owned this charnel house, the body of the unfortunate victim was first secreted for a time, and then as soon as possible carried to this warehouse, sometimes in a sack, sometimes to allay suspicion in a cart, and at other times by boat, where it was kept for a little time till an opportunity offered to sell it to some of the surgeons at the anatomical schools.

If, however, there were very strong marks of violence on the bodies, then they were sold in limbs at so much per joint.

This place existed when Calcraft first was appointed, and was kept on, both as a human shamble, and frequently used as the actual slaughter-house for some considerable time after Calcraft's election, it being found out that many persons under various pretences were decoyed to the place, and then murdered and robbed therein, and afterwards disposed of in the manner above stated.

The organised murders for robbery and for disposal for dissection then was at its very height when he first entered upon his public career.

How the perpetration of these crimes grew to the alarming extent they did, and how they have since been discouraged and checked, is a matter of interest, and forms an important study in the social government of society.

Doubtless a great deal has been accomplished by the terrible but just repression of the law, and in this active repression no man, during the forty-five years of that period of history, took such a prominent part as William Calcraft.

Few men have put to death more murderers of every grade than he did, and thus it was that so much of the criminal history of that age centred in him; for nearly all the murderers of his time fell into his hands, to end a life they were not worthy to live.

He did much then in his time towards checking one of the great evils of the day which existed when he was elected.

While, therefore, much of the decrease of the terrible crime of murder is due to repression, a great deal, however, must be attributed to better legislation; the greater prosperity of the people, the better facilities for gaining a livelihood by fair and legitimate means, and also by a better system of protection in the establishment of the present large force of police.

These combined have done much to check such fearful outrages, and bring about the comparative safety the community now enjoy. Added to these are the force of education, the growth of civilisation, the love of right, and the thorough detestation of that which is wrong, which is one of the marked characteristics of the present age.

Where formerly we had thieves' kitchens and infamous dens for the study and training of children to vice, we have houses of refuge, working men's clubs, and literary institutions.

Where fifty years ago thousands of youths, owing to the dens in which they were reared and the general depravity of society, prided themselves on belonging to a brotherhood of thieves, and hesitated not to go sneaking about like cowards to violate, rob, and assassinate in the dark, now we have the youth of the present generation enrolled by thousands in volunteer corps, ready to fight to the death if need be for their nation and their homes, and to maintain the honour and the safety of the fairer sex of the community.

All these changes, which have taken place in the life and recollections of Calcraft, have not been brought about suddenly but gradually.

They, too, have been done systematically. The contrast is great, and the means by which it has been brought about is a subject worthy of the gravest study.

It was for the purpose of studying these great social questions, and the problem of how best to continue to carry on the mitigation of the evil, which made us take such an interest in the life and recollections of Calcraft.

There is yet much to be accomplished—many abuses to correct. A great many of the old forms of tyranny and vice are still being carried on, and if by laying these open and exposing them to our readers we can get them to cleave to the good, and eschew the evil—and further, if we can prevail upon them to assist us in denouncing and exposing existing evils wherever they may see them, our work in writing the life and recollections of Calcraft, with all the evil he saw, together with all its ramifications into social abuses and social misery, will not be vain.

THE PASTIMES OF CALCRAFT'S EARLY LIFE.

Throughout the greater part of his life Calcraft was an inveterate lover of fishing.

In fact, if we may judge by the avocation he adopted and the chief diversion he chose, he seems to have always had a great fascination for a line and a hook.

Thus he gained a living by dangling men on the end of a rope, and he found amusement in hooking fishes at the end of a string.

Calcraft, however, in point of intellect, was not wanting, and when he chose he could maintain his opinions with vigorous argument.

For many years he followed his trade as a shoemaker, in conjunction with his office as hangman; and as at one time he had a very good business, a great many people, it may be said, have walked in Calcraft's shoes.

His favourite spot for fishing was at a quiet secluded place, just below the lock at Ponder's-end.

As an invariable rule he used for years to repair to this place in fine weather after his work at the Old Bailey was over.

Sometimes he went alone, but generally in company with one or two of his intimate associates.

It was on some of these occasions that I had an opportunity of hearing

CALCRAFT'S EARLY OPINIONS ON THE STATE OF THE TIMES.

Among the companions of Calcraft who went out with him on his fishing excursions, was one who, for the rotundity of his body, his portly appearance, and the amount of swig he could take, was generally known by the nickname of Falstaff.

While they were sitting by the banks of the river he and Calcraft used to hold many an argument on the various topics of the day, and I have frequently been amused at the opinions the two expressed.

One day when the fish did not appear to take the bait very briskly, Calcraft said to his companion—

"Falstaff, what do you think I have been reading about this morning?"

"I don't know," said Falstaff. "Some criticism on your hangings?"

"No, I have been reading in to-day's paper that some cove down at Birmingham named Watt has invented machines and engines to go by steam, and they say that before long he's likely to bring it to such perfection that carriages 'll go along without horses."

"Carriages go along without horses!" said Falstaff. "Don't believe it. Why if you were to tell some folks that pigs will come to fly yet, I'll be hanged if they wouldn't open their ears and eyes and mouths quite wide, and gulp it all down. Well, well, if that ain't a tale to tell anybody, Cal. Why you must have steam on the brain to believe such foolery as that."

"Well, they say it's true," replied Calcraft, "and they say that one of these newly-invented engines alone will be able to pull ten or a dozen heavy carriages full of people along, and two or three great trucks loaded with coal at the same time, and that one of these engines alone will be able to bring them all the way from Birmingham to London."

"Well, Cal, I'll be darned if you don't amuse me now," said Falstaff. "I always thought you were a sensible man till now. When you got appointed to be the executioner of England, I said to my wife, 'Ah, that man Calcraft, he's a genius and a patriot, too, for he's took office in these wholesale hanging days for the express purpose of working the scum of society off, just to clear away the refuse, and to leave the world with only respectable people in it.' Now I think you must be going off yer chump to believe such a tale as that, that carriages 'll be invented to go along without horses. But, however, that's always the way with clever men of genius. When they get exalted as you have been, somehow or other their brain seems to begin to turn; that's the reason that I myself never wanted to be a genius. Howsomever, I hope you ain't a going to be a candidate for Bedlam or St. Luke's just at present, Cal."

"Well, it may be true," said Calcraft. "You need not be too hard on a feller, for, you know, we've got clocks and watches to go by machinery—and I think they are wonderful inventions—so we can't tell what may be invented yet before we die."

"Ah," replied Falstaff, "they invents these things to go by steam, carriages, and engines of various sorts, as you say; perhaps they'll invent the drop and the gallows to go off by steam, and then the hangman's occupation would be gone, you know."

"Yes, and that would save anybody having the responsibility of taking the culprits' lives; there would be nobody then with the remorse from doubt at the possibility of having taken an innocent person's life, for it could then be truly said that nobody was to blame, excepting the engine, as they'd been executed by steam," said Calcraft.

"Hang me! if I didn't think yer was a studying the question in an interested point of view, as though yer were afraid it might take the work out of yer hands; but what would your case be in comparison with all the thousands of whips, coach drivers, carters, and waggoners that would be thrown out of employment, if such things as these engines and carriages, as you say, were invented. Ah, you may depend upon it, Cal, they'll never come into fashion—why, the country would not allow it. The working classes, too, wouldn't permit such inventions to be brought about to throw them out of employment; and then there's another thing—what would become of all the poor horses, too? Why, there would be no work for them. Ah, Calcraft, don't you believe it. The world aint going to be turned upside down in that way with new-fangled inventions. Depend on't, steam coaches only exist in what's that cove's name—Watt's brain, for the purpose of getting people to subscribe their money in shares for them fellows they call directors to bag; and if anything at all goes off by steam it won't be the coaches—but I'll tell yer what it will be."

"What?" said Calcraft.

"Why the toddy and the whiskey down the directors' throats—that's what'll go down by steam if anything does."

"Perhaps so," said Calcraft, "but however we will wait and see what becomes of the alleged invention."

"All right," said Falstaff, "but in the meantime, Calcraft, what do you think about all this here agitation that's going on in Parliament, and all through the country, about the Catholic Emancipation Act? Do you think if them Roman Catholics get into Parliament, and into power again throughout the country, that it will make it better for you?"

"Well, I don't know," said Calcraft, "some people say it would, as there then would be plenty of extra work for the executioners, as there was in the days of Queen Mary; but I don't think I should accept office under them, not at least to carry out religious executions. However, I don't think we need be afraid, for the days of religious persecution and martyrdom for the sake of religion are all over in England.

"I think so, too," said Falstaff. "Now what's your opinion about this agitation for the Reform Law that's going on and the revolution that is threatened throughout the kingdom?"

"As to them," replied Calcraft, "I think it is all very well for the people to want to have the Parliamentary franchise extended and to get the Reform Bill passed, because the working classes have as much right to be represented as any of the upper classes. I think if the Government would legislate more for the masses of the people, and do something to put work into their hands, and make them more prosperous, that the peace of the nation and the throne of the king would be a great deal safer than they are now. But I don't hold with them being too violent, for if they become too outrageous, you know, I shall have to take them in hand, for they will be sure to catch a lot of the rebels, charge them with high treason, and then send them to me to finish off."

THE LIFE OF WILLIAM CALCRAFT, THE HANGMAN.

AT THAT VERY MOMENT UP JUMPED OLD PROBER, THE SNATCHER, LOOKING A PERFECT FRIGHT.

"Just so," said Falstaff; "but I don't think the generality of the people are very loyal at this particular time. They don't like the dissipation and the expenses of Mr. King George IV. It puts too many taxes on them, and makes against the people in all sorts of ways. Another thing, the spirit of revolution excited by the Cato-street conspirators, and the determination to do away with monarchs, aint died out yet, and if something isn't done to prevent this general starvation of the people I believe there will be a revolution too, and no mistake about it. Then, again, the people don't like King George's treatment of Queen Caroline—they still remember that; and his keeping at Windsor so much, and not coming to London makes very bad for trade."

"I quite agree with you there," said Calcraft, "for royalty has its duties as well as its privileges, and the duty of royalty is to do all it can by legitimate means to promote the prosperity and welfare of the community at large."

"Right you are again," said Falstaff. "Now, Calcraft, what is your opinion of the lower order of society generally?"

"Why," replied Calcraft, "my opinion of them is that they are like weeds that are growing in as fair a garden as ever was seen, and weeds, you know, unchecked, grow apace. There is no country you know that is more beautiful, and none need be more prosperous than this good old England of ours, but you know it is blighted from one end of the land to the other by these hordes of vile characters, and colonies of thieves, which we see almost everywhere, wherever we go. How there came to be so many of them, and such sinks of iniquity as I know, I can't imagine; but, perhaps, on some future occasion I shall be able either to read up or get some important information on the matter, as I have often thought I should like to know how all these great social evils and strange forms of the community first came about. However, as we have not hooked many fish to-day I think it is time to go now, and if you don't mind coming out again next Monday we can have another two or three hours' angling and quiet chat together."

CALCRAFT'S STORY OF A COMIC FRAUD.

On the following Monday we again went out for another day's ramble.

We wended our way through Hoxton-fields, and had a splendid walk through Stoke Newington, over Stamford-hill, through Tottenham and Edmonton, till we came to our fishing place at Ponder's-end again.

Having baited our hooks, thrown in our lines, and sat down on the banks again, we asked Calcraft what was the news of the day.

Calcraft, who always had an eye for the sensational and a zest for a ludicrous practical joke, then related to us the following incident, which he had culled from the newspaper of that day.

Yesterday one of a very crafty gang of resurrection men nearly came to grief under the following circumstances:—

It appears that a party of these fellows being hard up for drink, and desiring to raise some money that night, but not having any dead body to sell, they resolved to cast lots among themselves, which of them should submit to be packed in a hamper, and sold to the first anatomist who would consent to buy him.

There were five of them in the plot, and the lot to be sold fell upon a strong, burly Irishman, named Old Prober.

The other four then went round to some of the well-known anatomists to see if they could find a customer.

They went to Dr. Macdonald, and informed him that they had a fine, healthy, fresh subject, a strong muscular fellow about five-and-forty, whom nobody owned.

The doctor having heard the description of him, and being urgently in need of such a subject for a lecture he in a few days was going to give, consented to purchase the body for ten guineas. The bargain having been struck,

"You wont fail to bring him to-night, will you?" said the doctor.

"No!" replied the snatchers. "You shall have him here sartin, by ten o'clock to-night. Which door shall we bring him to?"

"Take him round to the back door," said the doctor, "and give him to the servant if I am out. Don't tell her what it is though, or she may be frightened, and if I am not in I will leave the money for you."

"You shall have him right enough, master," replied the snatchers, "at ten o'clock sharp."

The snatchers returned to their hovel highly delighted with their bargain, where they duly packed old Prober in a large hamper partly filled with straw, in such a position that he could lie very comfortably during his carriage to the anatomical school.

In the meantime old Prober had been provided with some bread and cheese, a flask of brandy, and a clasp knife in his pocket in case of emergency.

It was guessed by the snatchers that, after they had received their coin, the hamper and body would be taken at once to the dissecting or some other room in the doctor's house, where it would be deposited for the night; and it was then arranged that as soon as old Prober found that the doctor and his family had gone to bed, or that he found himself in a room alone, that he should cut the string of the hamper-lid, pocket anything he could see in the place, and then, bolting through the window, make his escape.

The parties all laughed heartily at what they thought would be a fine practical joke on the doctor, and a capital sell.

When the proper time came the snatchers started off with old Prober in the hamper, and arrived at the doctor's house at the time appointed—precisely ten o'clock.

When they arrived at his house they rang the bell, and on the servant answering they inquired for the doctor, and found him at home.

The doctor, in order to get the girl out of the room while the parcel was brought in, sent her for change, and while she was out the hamper was brought in, and deposited in the servants' kitchen.

The snatchers, in order to counteract any suspicions the doctor might have, unfastened the strings of the lid part of the way round, and, showing him the bushy hair of old Prober's head, assured the doctor he was one of the finest subjects that had ever been seen.

The doctor, who was in a hurry to get off, as he had an engagement out, just took a hasty glance at the top of Prober's head, and the snatchers immediately sewed down the lid with a packing needle and string.

Meanwhile the servant returned with the change. The doctor paid the snatchers the ten guineas, and they immediately left, leaving their confederate sewed down in the hamper, along with the servant in the kitchen.

The doctor, having told the servant to let the hamper remain there untouched for the night, then put on his hat and coat, and went hurriedly off to the engagement at which he was wanted.

In this packed-up condition old Prober, the snatcher,

remained for a considerable period, quite undisturbed, with the exception that he, every now and then, felt the warm breath of the doctor's bloodhound, which frequently came putting his nose to the hamper, and sniffing and smelling around.

As the snatcher lay thus curled up in the hamper he could plainly see through the wicker the form of the fine grown bloodhound pacing to and fro in the kitchen, and he could also see Mary the servant sitting on her chair, busy with her needle on a piece of embroidery.

After the lapse of a little time a gentle tap came against the kitchen window, and Mary rising from her seat at once opened the kitchen door, and let the visitor in.

The visitor on this occasion was one of the cupboard-loving Charleys of the day, who, instead of being out on his beat keeping watch during the night frequently thought it more comfortable to be sitting by the side of Mary, the doctor's maid, whom he professed to love from the bottom of his heart.

"Who's at home, Polly?" said he, buoyantly, as he proceeded to place his staff in one corner, and to deposit his old horn lanthorn in another.

"Oh, there ain't anybody at home to-night, Charley," said Mary, catching hold of his two hands and stretching them as far apart as she could, while she brought her lips in close proximity to his. "I'm so delighted."

"Ain't there nobody at home? Oh, I am so glad!" said he, as he began kissing her first on one cheek and then on another, while he stood before her, with his watchman's rattle hanging half out of his coat-tail behind, like a great rattlesnake salivaing its prey previous to gorging it down.

That's a nice occupation for a Charley, thought the snatcher to himself as he peeped through the wicker of the hamper.

"That's the reason there's none o' them fellows to be seen about while we are snatchin' the bodies. I suppose this is a fair specimen o' the way most o' the Charleys employ their time in the night."

"What have you got in the larder to-night, Poll?" said the Charley, after another very energetic bout of cuddling and kissing.

"Oh, I've the half of a splendid young duck, and some nice cold pudding," said Mary, as she bustled about, and placed the things on a waiter for the Charley's supper.

"Capital," said the Charley. "Them's the things—cold duck to make a feller's affections grow, and cold pudding to settle his love; that's the way to bring about the matrimony day."

While the Charley was thus tucking in the duck, the cold pudding, and stout, the snatcher still lay uncomfortably tucked up in the hamper, getting uncommonly cramped and stiff, and anxiously wishing for some turn of events and change of circumstances which would give him a chance of escaping either out at the door or through the window from his unenviable position, for, what with the fear of detection by the doctor or an attack on him by the dog in the night if he attempted to escape, he began to realise the danger of the situation he was in.

At length the Charley having done ample justice to the flesh of the duck, and left nothing but the bones, he got up to go, and having again armed himself with his staff and lighted his lantern, he bestowed another battery of kisses on Mary's cheeks and lips, and then finally wished her good night, and took his departure, singing out as he got into the street in his usual nasal twang—

"Past twelve, and a starlight morning," as though he had been most assiduously on duty the whole of the night.

Mary now quietly settled herself down again to continue the embroidery she was engaged upon before the Charley came in.

While she was anxiously waiting for her master and mistress coming home, the wind gradually began to rise, the shutters outside to creak, and she fancied she heard other noises about, which she hardly knew were caused by the wind or not.

"Oh, dear, I wish master and missus would come home," said she, as she leant back in her chair, and looked at the clock, with a mouth wide open, and a regular sleepy yawn, as she fancied she saw the table move, then a chair, and then first one thing and then another.

"Time always goes so quick when Charley's here, and I gets so frightened when he's gone—I fancies I hears all sorts of noises, and sees all sorts of things move in the room. If it wasn't for poor old 'Tear 'em,' the master's bloodhound, being here, I am sure I dare not stop at all—no, not for all the world.

"Upon my word, if I don't believe I have seen that hamper move two or three times to-night; but then I suppose it's all my foolish fancy, a hamper couldn't move, and so I must be a silly to think that. I wish master and missus would come; I've got to be up by six in the morning, and now it's nearly one o'clock.

"Upon my honour I believe I saw that hamper move again. What with these creaking noises at the windows, and my fancying I keep seeing that hamper and other things move, it's enough to make anybody believe the house is haunted. But there, I suppose it's all my imagination," said she, rubbing her eyes and giving another wide-mouthed yawn. "I'd go and stand at the door in the street, but I'm afraid of master and missus just coming up and catching me.

"It's a great shame a poor girl can't even stand at the door, nor have anybody in the house to see 'em because masters and missuses nowadays is so pertickler.

"I never see'd such a pertickler man afore anywhere as master is; he won't even let us speak to anybody, if he knows it. Dang me, if I don't believe that hamper moved again.

"Well—well, I suppose it's no good giving way in this world to foolish imaginations, but I could have almost swore I saw it move then.

"Oh, dear me, what a thing it is to be a poor sarvint, to be sitting up by one's self, waiting for master and missus coming home, whilst they goes off to balls and parties, kicking up their heels, whilst if I only had Charley here for half an hour's waltz of a night they'd kick up an infernal row. That's just what masters and missuses do now-a-days, kick heels up when they goes out, and kicks rows up when they comes home.

"I think it's cruel on 'em to keep sarvints up like this half the night, and 'spects us up at six in the mornin' to light fires and get breakfasts.

"Well, people may say what they like, but I could almost take my davy I seed the hamper move then.

"I do wish master would come home, for I feel as though I dare not stop in this kitchen much longer by myself, if I am to be fancying these sort of things."

"Ah, them girls is the best off what's married; there's no sitting up waiting for masters and missuses coming home, with them.

"I wish Charley would make up his mind and take a nice little room. We could be so comfortable. I've got a pair of blankets and sheets, and I'm sure it wouldn't take much to furnish a room to begin with, like.

"I thought Charley really would have took a room before this; he's had all my last quarter's wages to buy the things with.

"Oh, I'm sure I can't stand this. I must go out of here, for I'll swear I saw that hamper move now, unless my eyes deceive me.

"Tear'em fancies he sees something, too, or else he wouldn't be sniffing and smelling round it like this.

"There, there, there! I'll take my oath it moved then! That warn't no fancy—that it warn't; it moved then, anyhow, and Tear'em warn't near it. I shall put my shawl and bonnet on and go to the front door, master or no master.

"I can't stop here to be frightened into highstrikes by myself in a haunted house—so here goes. Oh, lor, a mercy on me! it's all of a wriggle now, as though the hamper is going off into highstrikes, too. This house is haunted, I'll swear."

At this point the girl, who had put on her bonnet and shawl, ran screaming to the door just as a cab drove up, and a knock came which she knew was her master's rat-tat-tat.

The affrighted girl immediately opened the door, and bursting out crying, said—

"Oh, master, do come in, for the house is haunted, and I dare not stop here in any place in the house again by myself. That hamper that you had brought here to-night, it's been dancing all round the kitchen; the chairs have all been scampering round the room; the big dresser table has been hopping about; the rolling-pin and the flat irons have been thrown all about the place, as though there was a reg'lar fight going on in the place with a lot of invisible spirits."

"Make haste in, my dear," said the doctor to his wife. "There is Mary gone clean out of her mind; she has got a sudden fit of madness come on, and I must give her a soothing draught."

"I hope she is not dangerous and furious, darling," said his wife to her husband; "or if so I had better not come in yet till she is safe."

"Oh, I'm not mad, master—I'm not mad, missus. Come in—I shan't hurt you," said the girl, as she stood at the door in a state of terrible excitement, still asserting that the hamper had been dancing about, and that the chairs and tables had been capering after one another as hard as they could.

"Oh, she has gone stark staring mad," said the doctor to his wife. "You had better call the cabby in before you pay him to help me to put the strait-jacket on her, and let him drive her off to Bedlam as fast as he can go."

"You won't put any strait jacket on me, nor send me to Bedlam either," said the girl. "I am no more mad than you are, sir. If you don't believe me, go into the kitchen yourself, and you'll soon see the hamper and things move. I've been nearly frightened out of my li'—I have."

"Have you been drinking, Mary—or what?" said the mistress, who now entered with the cabman, who came into the passage to see if he could be any assistance.

"Drinking! drinking, ma'am!—no, I haven't been drinking either. If you don't believe that the things have been moving about, go into the kitchen, and see for yourself. Why, ma'am, did you never hear tell of haunted houses afore? Besides, there must be something the matter, because the dog has been smelling round the hamper the whole of the night."

Meantime, while this colloquy was going on in the passage, old Prober, the snatcher, had been anxiously looking through the wicker of the hamper to see if any opportunity offered of cutting the string, and making his escape, but during the whole time that Mary had been relating in the passage to her master and mistress the movements she had seen, the bloodhound kept close to the hamper, sniffing with his nose underneath, as though every moment he would turn it over.

"I wish that savage brute would go away," muttered old Prober to himself. "He aint left the kitchen a minute while I've been here, or I would have taken my hook out of this long ago. I don't want to stop here to be worried. If he'd only go out of the kitchen, I'd bolt the door on him, and cut off like a shot."

The doctor now came into the kitchen, and, seeing everything standing exactly as he left them when he went out, he called the servant to come back to the kitchen to convince her that her fright was caused by the fancies of her own imagination.

The mistress also came, and tried to prevail upon the girl to come there, too.

"Come in, you silly thing—do," said the mistress, petulantly. "There's nothing here to hurt you."

"I am sure I dare not come in there again, ma'am," replied the girl. "If them things were to begin their capers again I feel I should lose my senses."

"Come in, wench," said the cabman. "Why you must be a reg'lar born natral to think that 'em 'ere enaminate things could move. You must ha' bin fast aslape, and bin a dramin while the master's bin out—that's about the truth on it."

"Ah! well, you mind your own business," replied the girl. "I aint a coming in there."

"I say, guv'nor, this here bloodhound o' yourn won't bite, will he?" said the cabman to the doctor. "He keeps smellin' and sniffin' round my shins, and payin' his compliments to me, as though he'd half a mind to make a supper off the calves of my legs without my invitin' him."

"I don't think he will hurt you," said the doctor, "if you don't touch him, but you had better not put your hand upon him, or he might spring upon you. He is not over and above particular with strangers."

"Perhaps you had better put him in the stable at once, my dear," said the mistress to the doctor, "for fear of an accident. He might perhaps turn round on the cabman else, especially if he were to put his hand on Mary to hold her while you put the strait-jacket on her."

"You shall not put any strait-jacket on me; that I'll swear," replied the girl again. "I am no more mad than any of you. You wait a bit and see if the hamper or some of the things don't begin to move again, and then you'll see who is right and who is wrong."

"I say, guv'nor, I wish you'd take this dog away," said the cabman, to the doctor again. "I feel quite nervous-like; he keeps on smellin' first one of my shins and then the other like some old woman before a butcher's shop in the New-cut, as keeps on smellin' and smellin' when her don't know which to have. If you don't take him away quick perhaps he'll make his mind up before he's wanted."

"Yes, dear, do lock him up at once in the stable before there's any accident. I can see he has half a mind to bite him."

"Come on, Tear-em," said the doctor to the dog, as he took hold of him by the collar, and led him out into the yard and locked him in the stable, the mistress at the same time following behind, leaving the cabby alone in the kitchen, and Mary standing at the front door of the entrance hall.

"Whatever shall we do, my dear, with Mary, if she

is going out of her mind like this?" said the mistress to the doctor, after they had locked the dog in the stable, and were coming back along the yard.

"I don't know, my darling," he replied. "Perhaps she may be more composed by morning if I give her a sleeping draught, and get her upstairs to bed."

"Do you think there will be any necessity to put a strait-jacket on her, my dear?" said the mistress to the doctor.

"I don't know yet, darling, till I see how she is likely to go on, and whether there is any probability of her becoming violent or not. You know it would not do to run the risk of her jumping through the bedroom window in a fright, or of injuring herself in any other way."

Just at this moment the doctor and his wife were terribly alarmed by hearing the cabby in the kitchen, in an awful fright, roaring out boo—oo—oo.

"Oh, master—oh, oh! come here directly, for this place is haunted."

The doctor ran into the kitchen in haste, while the mistress stood in the yard at the kitchen door in a fright, and then they saw the cabman in a fearful state of alarm, with his eyes nearly starting out of his head, and his hair standing on end as he stood there as though he was rivetted to the spot.

"What's the matter, cabby?" said the doctor. "Surely you are not going off your head, too—are you?"

"Oh, no, guv'nor, I'm not going off my head; but that 'ere hamper—oh, dear me—that 'ere hamper; I seed it move a bit, quietly, as I thought, at first; then I thought I must be mistaken, so I thought I'd watch it carefully, and then while I was a-lookin' at it very carefully, it set to a-rigglin' and a-rollin' and a-shakin' its sides just for all the world like a great waggon horse in harness. Oh, you may depend upon it the wench is right, after all, and this house is haunted right enough, and no mistake about that."

"You must have been mistaken," said the doctor. "Why you are worse than the girl. You have got nervous through being in the kitchen that little time."

"I wasn't mistaken, guv'nor," said the cabman. "I'd rather be paid my fare and go, for there's a hevil spirit in that hamper, I'll swear."

At this the doctor burst into a hearty laugh.

"An evil spirit in that hamper! Well, cabby, that is the richest thing I ever heard in my life. An evil spirit in the hamper! Why, anyone would think that we lived in the dark ages of superstition to hear you talk like that," said the doctor.

"Talk like that!" replied the cabman. "Why, guv'nor, do you think I can't believe my own eyes? I'll take my oath I seed it shake like as though it had got an epileptic fit; and it's my belief that this house is haunted with evil spirits, and that there is one on 'em in that hamper."

"I told yer I was right, sir," said Mary, who by this time had taken courage, and come back to the kitchen door of the passage.

"Why do you not open the hamper, my dear, and convince these two silly creatures there is no such thing," said the mistress, ignorant of the contents. "I suppose it's only a hamper of surgical instruments and bandages—is it?"

"I don't want to unpack it now, darling," replied the doctor. "But just think of the absurdity of two people thinking a hamper could move."

"Ah! you may ridicule me as much as you like, guv'nor, but I tell yer again I seed that hamper go off into a reglar conwulsion, and nothing could cause it to do that but a evil spirit gettin' into it."

"Well, let us try and stick him," said the doctor, laughing, and hastily seizing a sharp three-pronged fork which lay on the table, he began sticking and stabbing at the contents of the hamper in various parts through the wicker work as hard as he could.

"Oh, oh, oh! Stop that game wid yer, will yer?" lustily roared out old Prober, as the doctor kept on digging into him the three-pronged fork.

When cabby, and the servant, and the mistress heard a voice and the terrible roaring in the hamper they were convinced that an evil spirit was, sure enough, there, and they all set up the most hideous and hysterical screaming.

The dog in the stable, hearing the dreadful noise, began to bark and growl and tear at the stable door in the most fearful manner, as though he would break it down in his efforts to come to his master's assistance; and the scene inside the house about three in the morning was one of the most frantic excitement.

The doctor now began to try and discover what were the real facts of the case.

"Don't be alarmed, my darling," said he to his wife. "Stop this noise, and don't let us have the neighbourhood raised like this. I think I can guess what is the secret. Let me open the hamper, and see what is inside."

At that very moment up jumped old Prober, the snatcher, out of the basket, who by this time had cut the strings of the lid, and who now appeared standing bolt upright, trickling in various parts with blood, and looking a perfect fright.

At the sight of him the cabby, the servant, and the mistress set to screaming again, for they then all seemed to think that they saw a real apparition.

"Quiet, quiet, all of you, can't you?" said the doctor. "Let us hear what he has to say before we send for the watchman."

"Well, plaze your honour," said the snatcher, still standing up in the hamper, with his thick hair and whiskers all wet, steaming with perspiration through the cramped-up confinement he had undergone, and with the blood from the prongs of the fork trickling down him.—"Plaze, yer honour, and good luck to yer, I ax yer pardon, but, by the faith of all the powers, there's some awful mistake, and sure I'll jist tell you the truth how it all occurred. Well, yer honour, yer must know as how I come here to do yer honour a very perticklar sarvice. My name is Mike Prober, yer honour, and my muther was a very respectable gentale old 'ooman o' Tipperary county. Yes, yer honour, and indade she was. Well, when I was a comin' over here she says to me—the poor ould craythur did — 'Mike.' 'Yes, muther,' says I. 'Mike,' says she, 'when yer get over there to England, mind yer always do a good turn to anybody when yer gets the chance.' 'Yes, muther,' says I, 'and by the aid o' the powers I will.' So yer must know, yer honour, that when I come to live over her, I got acquainted with Tom O'Leary, Pat Johnson, Dan Mullagan, and Arthur O'Sullivan, and we got to know a lot of the Charleys. Well, yer honour, we got to know as how there was one of these 'ere Charleys that is always a comin' to your house of a night, and stoppin' here when you'd gone out or had gone to bed, yer honour. Yes, we heer'd as how he never could be found on his bate of a night, for he was always a comin' here and stoppin' all night wid Mary."

Here Mary burst out crying, and pulling her apron up to her eyes she screamed out—

"You wicked man, to say such things."

"Just wait a bit, yer honour, while I tell you all about it," said Mike.

"You naughty, wicked man. I'll tear your eyes out, I will, if yer say such things o' me!" shrieked Mary.

"Now be aisy, my darlin', can't yer, while I jist explain it all to his honor," said Mike, as he continued.

"Well, yer honour, we all said what a shame it was for the Charleys to neglect their duties like that, and take the public pay for doing nothing else in the world but going about snakin' into jintlemen's houses, atin' their bread and mate, and desavin' the poor sarvant girls, and perhaps a robbin' the jintleman's houses too.

"So I said to them other chaps, yer honour, says I to 'em, 'Boys, what a raal sarvice it would be to that good kind-hearted jintleman, the docthur that is so very good to the poor, and gives his advice to 'em gratis for nothin' before ten in the mornin',' to catch that Charley for him what goes into his house ov a night, and ates his vittals, and desaves his poor sarvant maid.'

"Wid that, yer 'onour, them other boys said it would be a raal charity to the good-hearted docthur, that is yer honour's own self, and a raal public sarvice too jist to nab the Charley on the bounce, and turn king's ividence again him."

"Says I, 'So it would, boys; but how is it to be done?'

"'Aisy enough,' says they. 'Jist you let us put you into a hamper, and we'll git you into the docthur's kitchen, jist to see what that ere Charley is up to wid that poor sarvant gal.'

"'How will yer get me into the docthur's kitchen, though?' says I.

"'Oh, Mike,' says they, 'be aisy wid yer—we'll find a way o' doin' that. We'll jist pack yer up in a hamper and sell yer jest for a very thrifling sum to the docthur, for a natomy subject. The docthur he'll buy yer, and put yer down in the hamper in the kitchen, and then yer can pape through the holes in the wicker and see what the Charley gets up to wid the gal, and the docthur's vittals while he's out o' the house.'

"So says I, 'all right, boys. I'm a reglar Tipperary boy, an I'll do the docthur the sarvice, for he's a raal good jintleman!'

"Well, yer honour, they packed me up in the hamper, and yer jist gave 'em that thrifle for a dhrop o' beer, and then yer took me in and put me down in the kitchen, and there I lay papin' through the holes in the basket all the while yer honour was out.

"Well, by the honour of my sowl, yer honour hadn't long bin gone out o' the house before one o' them Charleys, who had watched yer goin' out, came tappin' at the window gently like, and faith, by my honour, Mary, poor silly cratur, let him in."

"Oh, you wicked, wicked story-teller," ejaculated Mary. "You shan't tell stories of me, like this, you shan't! I'll have yer locked up, I will, for takin' my character away in this manner!"

"Now, hould yer tongue, my darlin', and be aisy while I explain it to his honour, and tell him all about it."

"You are a wicked man, you—you vile story-teller!" shrieked Mary, in a violent passion; "there's been nobody here, you know there hasn't, you wicked story!"

"Ah, mind now, my honey, and shure don't put yourself into a passion; for it's the thruth I'm spakin' —yer know it is."

"No, it isn't, yer wicked feller!" screamed Mary, in a passion again.

"Now, don't interrupt, darlin'," said Mike. "Shure yer can let me tell his honor about the Charley comin' here and atin' his honour's vittals; and faith yer know very well that if some ov them boys what catches folks and kills 'em for subjects could jist lay hold on the rascal, and burk him, and bring him here for his honour to natomatise, that his honour 'ud find that half duck of his what's gone out of his honour's larder in the Charley's stomach, as well as the remains of his cowld puddin' and six of his bottles of stout. If his honour could jest dissect him now, he could bring all these things as ividence agin him."

"Oh, yer good-for-nothing wicked man," again shrieked Mary, "you know there aint been anybody here at all, and you are only takin' my character away."

"Takin' yer karacther away, is it yer say?" said Mike; "why it's that base Charley that's stolen yer karacther away. What would yer poor ould muther ha' said to both on yer if she'd ha' seen yer?"

"Oh, yer wicked villain, I'll tear both yer eyes out, and pull every bit of hair off yer face, that I will, if the master don't have yer locked up. I won't stand here any longer to have my character injured like this."

"Yer karacther injured like this, is it, yer say, yer dear desateful little injured innocent? Wait a bit now, Mary. Will yer jist tell his honour now what's gone wid that cold half duck ov his out ov the panthry?" said Mike, sarcastically.

"Why I ate it for my supper, yer wicked feller," passionately screamed Mary.

"Yer ate it for yer supper, did yer?" said Mike. "Well, Mary, will yer tell his honour what's gone wid that great piece ov cowld puddin' of his? Now spake the thruth, Mary, mind."

"Why, I ate that for my supper too," screamed Mary, in a still more violent rage.

"Oh, yer ate that too, did yer," said Mike. "Well, what a locker yer must have! Now jist tell his honour, then, what yer did with his six bottles o' stout that ye took out ov his cellar."

"Why, I drank them for my supper!" shrieked Mary, in a greater rage still.

"Oh, yer drank them, did yer, for yer supper? Oh, lor, what a stomach for a little stowaway," said Mike. "Well, then, look here, my darlin' little crathur, jist to be candid wid yer, I'd sooner keep yer one wake than a fortnight."

"You shouldn't have me at all," said Mary. "You are a thief come to rob the house—you know you are."

"A thafe come to rob the house, am I?" said Mike. "Don't be cross, now, but jist tell me wasn't that Charley that yer had 'ere to-night, a thafe to ate this kind gintleman's duck, and his cold puddin', and thrink his stout?"

"No, you wicked man, nobody came," vociferated Mary.

"Be aisy, now, my dear little cherub, but jist tell me, now, in crass-examination who it was that said that cold duck was the stuff to make the affections grow?"

"Why, I said it!" screamed Mary, getting into a still greater fluster.

"And now, my little dear, may be yer'll jist be kind enough to tell us who yer said it to?"

"Why, I said it to myself, yer wicked fellow, I did."

"Now, wasn't it Charley that said it—now?" said Mike. "And didn't he say that cowld puddin' was the stuff to settle a fellow's love, and bring about the matrimony day?"

"No, he didn't, yer bad man—he didn't," said Mary.

"Now, I'll only ask yer one more question, my little

pet. Hasn't that thafe of a Charley had the whole of yer last quarter's wages off yer?"

"I shan't tell yer, yer good-for-nothing man—I won't," said Mary.

"This is really a very strange affair, Mary," said the mistress. "I think this matter must be inquired into. I am afraid there is some truth in what this man says, and that you really have had some one in the house. However, I cannot think of letting the matter remain in this manner; it must be cleared up some way or another—what do you say, dear?"

"Oh, I shall have to inquire into it, my darling, of course," replied the doctor. "I must find out whether she has had anyone here or not; this is the way so many houses get robbed, you know. Meantime, my man, what do you say your name is?" said the doctor to the snatcher.

"My name, yer honour? Why, it's Mike Prober, of Tipperary county."

"Well, Mike," replied the doctor, "as I might want you to give evidence, I think you had better make yourself comfortable a bit, and stop to breakfast here in the kitchen."

"Thanks, yer honour, I'm obliged to yer; for it's some breakfast I want after doin' duty so many hours in such close quarters as that hamper; but, however, it's a good job I seed what that blackguard of a Charley was afther."

The doctor and his wife retired into the breakfast parlour, affecting to be highly pleased with the snatcher's conduct, and also under an obligation to him for his timely discovery.

They then rang the parlour bell, and on Mary attending them there the doctor said that, as it was now very late in the morning, and as a great part of the night had been lost through these strange adventures, Mary had better get breakfast now, and, if she felt tired, go and lie down in the afternoon.

"Meantime," said the doctor, "give that fellow in the kitchen some breakfast, and when it gets later in the day, I shall see what course I shall adopt with him for being found in my house under such extraordinary circumstances; but take no further notice of him, Mary, than that."

The breakfast having been served up in the parlour, and in the kitchen, and the doctor and his wife being now alone in the breakfast room, the doctor said to his wife—

"You know, my darling, discretion is sometimes the better part of valour. I think it is best to keep that fellow here quietly under the belief that he may be wanted as evidence, than to turn round on him and forcibly try to secure him. There is no doubt in my mind that he has been purposely conveyed here by confederates for the express purpose of robbing the house. He is most likely armed, and if we were to try and secure him he might fight for his life, and perhaps use some murderous weapon. If I were to send for any watchman now we should be very unlikely to find one, but if we let him stop quietly to breakfast we shall have plenty of help at hand soon."

"I think it is a very good plan, my dear," said the wife to the doctor, "but I expect there is some truth in what he says about Mary having had a watchman here to supper."

"Oh, I think there is no doubt of that," said the doctor; "but let me secure this fellow first. I shall have plenty of help when the medical students come to the lecture at ten o'clock—it is half-past seven now. Dear me, how the time has gone since we came home."

"I should think you might soon let the cabman go, my dear—may you not? He is still waiting outside, minding his horse."

"I will pay him and let him go after a bit," said the doctor, "but it is best not be without some assistance at hand, especially if that fellow in the kitchen has any of his comrades lurking about. Mary, however, had better take the cabman some breakfast out; he can eat it very well in the cab."

The time soon passed, and shortly after breakfast the class of medical students, twelve in number, began to arrive at the doctor's house to hear the professor's lecture, which that morning was to be "On the Brain and Nervous System; their Physical and Mental Functions."

After all the students had assembled in the theatre of the doctor's anatomical school, the learned professor before commencing his lecture related to his class, amidst great amusement and merriment, the body snatcher's extraordinary adventure and his final capture in the hamper through not being able to escape in consequence of the bloodhound being in the kitchen.

"I have no doubt," said the professor, in conclusion, "that the fellow is one of a desperate and very daring gang of thieves, and had it not been for the dog being in the kitchen, he would have got out of the hamper when we had all been asleep and then have plundered the house."

"Bring him up here," said the students, "bring him up here, doctor, and let us give him lynch law."

"No, we had better not do that," said the doctor. "It will not do to use illegal violence; but, however, as I have bought him for ten sovereigns, and as the fellow no doubt consented to the trick of being sold as a subject for dissection, there will not be any harm in us carrying out the joke."

"Hear, hear," said the students. "If you will fetch him up here, doctor, we will have a regular spree with him."

The doctor then stepped down into the kitchen, and asked the snatcher if he would mind coming up into the theatre of the lecture-hall, for the purpose of relating to a number of gentlemen assembled there his wonderful adventure, and also for the purpose of giving information against the dishonest Charley.

"Not at all," replied Mike, not suspecting the plot; "I shall only be too pleased to be of sarvice to yer honour."

"You have very dirty, thick, hob-nailed boots on," said the doctor. Perhaps you would not mind taking them off and putting on a thin pair of slippers before you come on to the carpet upstairs."

"Oh, I'll take thim off and put some slippers on wid pleasure," said Mike. "It would be a pity to spile any gintleman's carpet."

The snatcher then put on some slippers, and followed the doctor into the anatomical theatre.

Mike made a low bow on entering the room, and seemed taken back with astonishment at seeing so many gentlemen present.

He was then asked to take a chair in the front of the theatre.

The chair he was asked to take was an arm-chair, with brass elbows, a brass seat, and brass at the bottom.

It was connected with a very strong galvanic battery, and he was purposely asked to sit in it in order to play him a practical joke.

Mike accordingly quietly took his seat in the chair, never for one moment suspecting that a galvanic battery was connected with it ' and being entirely ignorant of the powers or properties of such a machine.

He was then requested to narrate his wonderful adventure, and also to state how he had detected the depredations committed by the watchman the night before.

Mike then began to recapitulate his story, and was proceeding to tell how he had consented to be put in the hamper, and sold to the doctor for a "thrifling sum jist for the express purpose of doing the kind-hearted docthur a pertickler sarvice by papin through the wicker of the hamper," and detecting the unprincipled Charley.

"What an infernal lie the feller's tellin'," said one of the students. "I wonder the ground does not open and swallow him up, or the powers of the earth draw him into the vortex below."

Suddenly Mike began to roar at the top of his voice—

"Oh, murther—murther! Docthur—docthur! Save me—save me! By all the powers that be, the earth's drawin' me down. Oh! it's a dhraggin' down all the muscles of my feet and my body, and tearin' all the sinews out of my hands, and the vitals out of my heart!"

Here he began to wriggle and writhe in the most desperate manner, and as he struggled to free himself from his seat his muscles and face assumed the most terrible contortions.

Then he began again. "Oh docthur—docthur, what shall I do to be saved? I can't get up from the chair; I can't lift my arms, nor move my feet; the earth's a drawin' and pullin' me all in!"

"Ah, Mike," said one of the students, "that all comes of yer telling such wicked lies. The earth is drawing you down fast now. Why don't you confess your sins at once and be saved, before it's too late?"

"Oh, I would confess my sins now directly, and spake the thruth if only this dreadful invisible power would let go its grip, but the devil has got fast hold on me now, and he's pulling me down to the bottomless pit."

"Why don't you confess your sins at once, then," said one of the students, "before you are swallowed up and disappear altogether?"

"I will—I will," said Mike, wriggling and writhing again. "It was all a big wicked moighty lie to say I got put in the hamper to sarve the docthur. I did not do it to sarve him at all—at all, but to rob the poor gintleman, and I got sold for anatomy subject, for the purpose of getting into the house."

"Oh, you got sold for an anatomy subject did, you? What! of your own free will?" said one of the students.

"Oh, yes, intirely of my own free will," said the snatcher, "and that is the thruth, the whole truth, and nothin' but the thruth, and the last dyin' speech and confession of poor Mike."

"I think he's told the truth now," said one of the students, "and now I believe he'll find pardon and forgiveness."

At this very moment the chair was disconnected from the battery; the electricity lost its grip, and Mike jumping up exclaimed—"Oh, I'm saved, I'm saved; the ould divil has been obliged to loose his hoult at last."

After Mike had somewhat recovered from his fright, and the strain on his muscles by the galvanic battery and chair, some of the students suddenly seized him, and then pinning his arms and legs, placed him flat down on his back on the dissecting table in the centre of the theatre.

At this he began to plunge, and struggle, and roar tremendously, at the same time crying out "wha are yer arter now?—what are you going to do?"

"Why, going to dissect you now," said the students. "Did not you confess a little time ago that it was voluntarily of your own free will that you were sold for an anatomy subject?"

"Oh! but I didn't mane ralely to be dissected and natomatised," roared Mike. "I don't want to be cut up."

"What did you come for then?" said the doctor; "didn't I give ten sovereigns for you?"

"Ah, yes, shure," cried Mike, "but I didn't dhrame it would come to this—to be cut up alive. Oh, my poor ould muther, if she could only see me now in Tipperary county!"

Here he began to roar and kick and plunge tremendously again, but powerful as he was the students finally succeeded in strapping him down in proper position upon the dissecting table.

They also further fastened him by means of the vivisecting screws, so that he could not move arms, body, head, or limbs.

"Oh, murther, murther! help, help!" roared Mike at the top of his voice.

"It's no use you roaring here," said the students; "nobody can hear you, and if you don't be quiet we shall have to gag you, or dispatch you at once."

Mike, seeing it was no use to roar, as he feared they would either gag or despatch him, now lay perfectly still, while all the students stood round him, some with fine small saws, some with scalpels, whilst others had sharp-bladed scraping knives, and other fine instruments for tracing the muscles.

While Mike looked aghast with fright, and imploringly into the doctor's face, the professor then began his lecture as follows:—

"Gentlemen,—It is not often we can obtain a live subject for vivisection and dissection, but the splendid subject now before you is one of the best developed, and one of the most muscular I have ever seen in my life.

"We are entirely indebted to the liberality of the subject himself for this capital opportunity of study, in consequence of his having come voluntarily forward of his own free will to offer himself up for vivisection on the altar of surgical science, and I cannot help but think that our best thanks are due to him for having come forward in this noble and heroic manner."

"Ah, but I didn't mane it," roared Mike, piteously, as he again looked up imploringly into the doctor's face.

"Be quiet, and hold your tongue, will you," said the students, "and don't interrupt the lecturer?"

The professor then continued.

"Gentlemen, before you each saw off the limbs, arms, head, and other portions of the subject severally allotted to you for study, I wish to call your special attention to the leading points in the patient's anatomical structure.

"I shall commence by taking my knife and cutting open the sterno-hyoidaeus; then I shall lay bare and turn back the mastoidaeus; after which I shall turn over the trapezius, and then strip the pectoralis.

"After that I shall call your attention to the deltoides, and the biceps, and next we will deal with the brachiaeus internus."

"Oh, lor," said Mike, "it's horrible to think of. I'm almost dead now with the fright of it; and, by the powers, I'm shure and sartin I can't stand being vivisected and cut up bit by bit, and muscle by muscle."

The learned professor then explained the uses of the

THE LIFE OF WILLIAM CALCRAFT, THE HANGMAN.

KNOCKING OFF THE IRON MANACLES.

various groups of muscles at considerable length, as seen in the working of the patient's arms.

The hour for the lecture expired, and Mike having during the whole of the time lain strapped on the dissecting table, the doctor and students thinking he had undergone fright sufficient, now privately arranged to leave his cords so slack that he could easily work out of them while they went to lunch.

This they did, and the snatcher, becoming aware of the fact, bolted through the window, greatly frightened, but not much hurt.

The professor and students thoroughly enjoyed the practical joke, and they had reason to hope the snatcher was so frightened that he made his escape a wiser and more truthful and honest man.

The doctor afterwards reprimanded the girl Mary for her thoughtless conduct in allowing a stranger in the house during his absence, and he having also found out the Charley, reprimanded and cautioned him for the future too.

Calcraft told the story with such dramatic effect that we were highly amused, and thus after another day's fair sport, having hooked pretty well of fish, we returned home by the same route we went, and finally, on parting, wished each other good night, promising soon to meet again.

CHAPTER XXI.
THE STATE OF SOCIETY IN CALCRAFT'S EARLY DAYS.

THE next time I and Calcraft met again was about three months after his official appointment.

It was a fine bright day in the month of May, 1829, and London was at the very height of its busiest season.

He had had rather a busy time during his first quarter's engagement, and had drawn pretty well of money from the Corporation of London, and from the various counties he had attended in carrying out the duties of his office.

He was dressed in a new suit of clothes, and had made several new additions to the furniture of his neat little parlour.

Calcraft at this time resided at Mount-place, in the East-road, nearly opposite to the end of Great Chart-street, and it was here that we frequently met and started on our first rambles together.

We got on very sociably, for while he could give me a vast amount of information in reference to the undercurrent of society, and the manners and customs, and the tricks and haunts of thieves and criminals, I frequently could entertain him with the historical origin of the different places we visited, and the origin of the various classes we met.

Calcraft's favourite pastimes in his early days were rambling and shooting in Epping Forest, or fishing, either at Temple-mills, Snaresbrook, or Ponder's-end.

On the day in question we started for a ramble to Lea Bridge, through Epping Forest, past Queen Elizabeth's lodge, and right to High Beech.

Our former jovial friend Falstaff was again with us, and we had a fine day's enjoyment.

The conversation upon this occasion turned upon—
THE DEPRAVITY AND SADNESS OF LONDON LIFE.

"What is your opinion, Calcraft," said I, "of the present depravity and sadness of London life?"

"Oh, it is just dreadful at this particular time," said he; "I think things are getting worse and worse. If Government doesn't soon do something to stop this tutoring of the young to vice and crime they will want ten times the number of gaols and workhouses yet than what they've got, and the poor taxpayers won't be able to support 'em. Why, what with the number of thieves' dens, training schools for teaching little children to pick pockets, and the enormous number of infamous houses kept by these wicked French, Irish, and Jewish harridans for the systematic procuring of young girls from all parts of the country for prostitution, it seems to me that half the population is being reared for transportation and the gallows by a set of aliens, who are permitted to live in the country and carry on their base, nefarious traffic entirely unchecked."

"I think so, too," said I, "and I quite agree with you that the Government ought to pass some very stringent laws against these people. It is a very dreadful thing that the lives of so many young English children should be blasted for ever by the mercenary traffic of these cruel unscrupulous wretches."

"I think it ought to be known for the sake of the character of this country that by far the greater part of this vice, and the worst of the most dreadful crimes we hear of are perpetrated by people not of English blood. I think this is an important fact in the history of crime which ought to be generally known, and which the English race ought to vindicate," said Falstaff.

"Yes," said Calcraft; "what a shocking sight it is to see in this year, 1829, with all the talent there is in Parliament, so many young girls of such tender years driven along the Strand, and round Charing-cross, and the Haymarket, and other populous thoroughfares, by these gin-sodden, bloated harlots, who walk behind the poor girls, and make them accost and try to entice every likely-looking gentleman they meet into the dreadful houses in which these poor children are kept.

"Talk of Turkish harems—why the system of inveigling English girls into these infamous houses at the present time is every bit as bad; and those in authority, instead of checking the evil, seem to close their eyes to it.

"The robberies and murders that go on in the thousands of these houses all over London are something shocking, and this infamous vice is going on almost every hour of the day and night.

"You should only get the chance of hearing the history of some of these poor little children when they are caught and brought to Newgate, like I do.

"They are really to be pitied, I can tell you. When I hear the history of some of them from the Ordinary of the gaol—how some of them have been kidnapped, or entrapped away from respectable homes and affectionate fathers and mothers, and then forced into a life of prostitution at night, and made to go about picking ladies' and gentlemen's pockets in the day, I sometimes don't like flogging 'em, as I have to do, let alone hang some of them, or see them sent to the hulks, or into transportation.

"I say that a good deal of the fault of all this is owing to the Government in not putting a stop to such traffic, and in not breaking up these dens of thieves.

"The audacity, too, with which these people act is something startling. Why, when a child is caught picking pockets, these harridans actually have the impudence to come forward before the magistrates and claim the children's clothes.

"Lots of them come forward and say that they rigged the children out, and that they must either have their clothes back, or else have compensation for them.

"There was a case the other day where the magistrate refused to make an order for the children's clothes to be given up, and the keepers of the house really had the assurance to threaten the magistrate with an action for the recovery of the value if the clothes were detained by his order.

"What do you think of that? Don't you think that looks as though these vile brutes were getting the upper hand? Why, some of these atrocious wretches have as many as thirty young girls in one house."

"We want a lot of these old rookeries, too, pulled down that are about London," said Falstaff. "Things will never be any better till the poor are better housed, and till they have more decent sleeping accommodation provided. What a disgraceful thing it is that the industrious poor should have to pay such exorbitant rents for houses or lodgings!

"The rents are so high that whole families, and oftentimes lodgers, with boys and girls just growing up into youth, have all to be crowded together into one room, where they all live and sleep together, without the slightest chance of decency.

"What I say is, that Government ought to acquire sufficient land and accommodation in London and all large towns, and be obliged by Act of Parliament to provide the people with good homes and the means of decent living at a moderate rental.

"Where the health of the industrious poor is so largely at stake we want to do away with that class of middle-men, property-holders, who run the rents up to such extortionate charges.

"Look at the number of vile ruinous old houses there are about, with neither water nor decent accommodation, and families crowded into every room.

"These vile slums and alleys all around us in every part are nothing but vile sewers of filth, and horrible sinks of iniquity.

"They ought to be condemned by the Legislature, and the people who own them and keep them in such a filthy condition, while they are making immense fortunes out of them, ought to be prosecuted."

"You'd see a good many big-wigs in the dock then," said Calcraft, "if all the people that own these slums and alleys were to be prosecuted. Why it would utterly astonish you if you knew who some of them belong to.

"Would you credit it that a lot of them belong to aldermen, vestry men, poor-law guardians, and all sorts of official people with interest?

"Ah, if you knew who own many of these places you wouldn't be surprised that none of them come down till there's some great public improvement going to be made with the public money; that's the way some of them bags their thousands of pounds at a time, and goes off and lives in their fine houses on their big estates, and drives up to London in their carriages; and there's a few dukes among them, too, what owns a lot of the vile slums. Look at the scarlet fever there is about now, and I wonder we don't get the cholera breaking out again."

"Well," said Falstaff, "I should like to see the Government rout all these wicked harridans and the thief-trainers out of the country, and also level these nasty vile rookeries to the ground. Aint it a very singular thing, when you come to think of it, that so many of these thieves of various kinds and sharpers and murderers live together in colonies."

"Yes, it is," replied Calcraft. "I have often wondered at that in my own mind, and thought it strange that so many of these people should come to live together. It seems like as though there are two distinct species of people in the world; some naturally good, and others naturally bad, and that the bad have all gravitated together."

"And don't the thieves all hold together, too," said Falstaff. "I should like to know how all these thieves' colonies came to be first founded."

"So should I," said Calcraft. "It must be very interesting."

"I can tell you," I said, "what was the origin of most of these places."

THE FIRST ORIGIN OF THIEVES' COLONIES, AND DENS OF INFAMY.

"Most of these places, Calcraft," said I, "have existed as colonies for thieves and vagabonds of every kind for many years.

"Some of the old historians give us a very lucid account of their early history, and it is indeed very interesting to study how London has gradually grown from the time of its early foundation up to the present time, till now it is one of the most crowded, as well as one of the most ancient and historical cities in the world.

"In order to comprehend the rise and growth of these colonies of thieves and vagabonds we must go back to London's early religious history.

"In fact, to thoroughly understand the growth of London life we should go back to the third century, when London was first walled round by Constantine the Great.

"Passing, however, rapidly on through the period of its commercial growth to the time when, in the Roman Catholic history of the city, numerous monasteries, convents, and other religious houses were erected, we find that in connection with most of these establishments there were sanctuaries or holy places attached.

"These sanctuaries or holy places, founded by the Christian Church, were set apart and sanctified as places of refuge to which, by the laws of the Church any criminal might fly for safety and demand protection, no matter how great his crime might be.

"In fact they were the literal continuation of the cities of refuge established by the Mosaic law in the days of the early Israelites.

"Among the most notable of these places of refuge or sanctuaries was the well-known Broad Sanctuary of Westminster.

"Stow, the historian, in treating upon the subject, says that 'the church at Westminster hath had great privilege of sanctuary within the precinct thereof; from whence it hath not been lawful for any prince or other to take any person that fled thither for any cause.'

"Under the dominion of the Normans there appears to have been two kinds of sanctuaries, or places of refuge, both for criminals and debtors, from arrest— one general, which belonged to every church, the other which seems to have originated in a grant by a charter from the king.

"The general sanctuary of the church afforded a refuge only to those who had been guilty of murder or other capital felonies.

"By the common law of England, if a person guilty of felony, excepting sacrilege, fled to a parish church, or churchyard for sanctuary and refuge, he might, within forty days afterwards, go clothed in sackcloth before the coroner, confess the full particulars of his guilt, and take an oath to abjure the kingdom for ever, swearing not to return unless the king's licence were granted him so to do.

"Upon making his confession and taking his oath, he became attainted of the felony; he had forty days, from the day of his appearance before the coroner, allowed him to prepare for his departure, and the coroner assigned him such port as he chose for his embarkation, whither the felon was bound to repair immediately, with a cross in his hand, and to embark with all convenient speed.

"Stow, in reference to the sanctuary at Westminster, gives the wording of the charter granted to it by Edward the Confessor, of which the following is an extract:—'I order and establish for ever, that what person, of what condition or estate soever he shall be, from whence soever he come, or for what offence or cause it be, whether for his refuge unto the said holy church (of the blessed apostle of St. Peter at Westminster), he be assured of his life, liberty, and limbs . . . and whosoever presume or doth contrary to this, my grant, I will he lose his name, worship, dignity, and power, and that with the great traytor Judas that betraied our Saviour, he be in the everlasting fire of hell.'

"The privilege, however, of refuge in any sanctuary doesnot, meanwhile, seem to have been allowed to those who escaped from the sheriff after having been delivered to him for execution, and even if a person who had the privilege of sanctuary did not go out of the kingdom at his appointed time, he was condemned to be hanged, unless he was a priest, in which case he was allowed the benefit of clergy.

"There, however,'seems also to have been some sanctuaries with a peculiar special privilege, to which a person might flee if he had committed high or petty treason; and where; if he chose; he could remain undisturbed for life.

"In the Westminster Sanctuary were two cruciform churches, built one above the other—the lower one in the form of a cross; the upper one is supposed to have been for debtors, and the inhabitants of the Broad and Little Sanctuaries, whilst the lower one is supposed to have been appropriated to criminals.

"This privileged haunt of refuge from the punishment of crime caused the houses within the precincts to let for very high rents; but the privilege of sanctuary in Westminster was totally abolished by James I. in 1623, though the greater part of the houses composing the precinct of that sanctuary were not taken down till 1750.

"These places of refuge, then, originally built and instituted by pious persons for the most benevolent purposes, degenerated in times of corruption to be places for the refuge and dwelling of criminals of the very worst type.

"As at one time the metropolis was studded over with abbeys and monasteries of various orders of friars, and as there were connected with most of these places sanctuaries and refuges for criminals, so in course of time the whole of London came to abound with these haunts of villainy and wretchedness.

"They, in fact, became nothing less than colonies of murderers and thieves.

"The dissolution of the monasteries and abbeys by Henry VIII. also cast upon the country whole hordes of mendicants, formerly the idle inmates of the monasteries and abbeys, and many of these, like a great pauper population thrown suddenly adrift, went to swell the ranks of criminals, vagrants, and religious and other impostors.

"The sanctuaries of refuge became thronged with the most desperate criminals, who, living in thorough protection from the punishment of the law when they escaped to these places, constantly committed the most horrible atrocities.

"Among the worst of these sanctuaries were the Minories, Fleet-street, Whitefriars, Ram-alley, Mitre-court, Fulwood's Rents, Holborn; Baldwin's Gardens, Gray's-inn-lane, the Savoy, St. Katherine's Hospital, and the precincts of the docks; Montague-close, Deadman's place, the Clink, and, as has been before stated, the Broad Sanctuary at Westminster.

"There are hosts of romantic and touching histories in connection with the flights of various persons to the Westminster Sanctuary.

"Whilst many who sought its refuge have been criminals and murderers, others have fled there from the oppression of the persecutor. Among the many of this unfortunate class was Elizabeth Woodville, widow of Sir John Grey, who was slain in the battle of Bernard's Heath.

"Edward IV., King of England, afterwards fell in love with her and married her. When, however, he lost his throne, he and his queen were committed to the Tower. King Edward made his escape, and fled the kingdom.

"His wife, too, Elizabeth Woodville, made her escape from the Tower, and fled to the Westminster Sanctuary, where she registered herself and her family as Sanctuary women.

"Here she gave birth to her child, Edward V., who, though the legitimate child of a king and queen, was born in sorrow, baptized in his exile among the criminals of the Sanctuary like an outcast's child, and thus commenced his short and unhappy career.

"He ascended the throne of England at twelve years of age, as is well known. However, he together with his brother, Richard Duke of York, were afterwards murdered in the Tower at the instigation of their uncle, Richard Duke of Gloucester, who having had them smothered under two pillows caused himself to be proclaimed King of England by the title of Richard III.

"Among the very worst and most notorious of all the London places of refuge, however, was the Southwark Mint.

"This precinct became very early a refuge for debtors, coiners, and vagabonds, as well as for traitors, felons, fugitives, and outlaws of every description.

"This place was one of the haunts of Jack Sheppard, and Jonathan Wild at one time kept his horses at the "Duke's Head," in Red Cross-street.

"As time, however, rolled on these places became a still greater pest to society, till at length they became such an intolerable nuisance that the privilege of sanctuary was at length totally abolished by an Act of James I., in 1623."

SPITALS, LOKES, AND MODERN ROOKERIES.

"In addition to the sanctuaries or places of refuge which formerly existed, there were also established lokes or leper hospitals, as well as spitals or almshouses, and infirmaries for those afflicted with contagious diseases.

"There were numbers of them over the metropolis, but one of the most famous lokes was in Kent-street, in the Borough, whilst the other large hospital for lepers was at St. James's, Westminster, and the other at St. Giles's-in-the-Fields, whilst Spitalfields also was formerly the site of an ancient almshouse.

"In connection with all these places were special churches for the exclusive use of those affected with leprous and other contagious diseases, from which other persons wisely kept away, it not being safe for any healthy person to attend the churches these infected people attended.

"St. Giles's hospital for lepers was afterwards converted into a parish church, now St. Giles's-in-the-Fields.

"Hence we see that the precincts of the old sanctuaries and places of refuge have continued to be, up to the present time, the principal nests where London thieves, prostitutes, and beggars, and vagabonds and murderers of every description, have been born, bred, and reared.

"Many of these rookeries and infamous dens have been swept away, and their sites are fast being covered with the houses of honest labourers, and the habitations of some of the cleverest artisans the world has ever produced.

"Many more of those dilapidated old tenements in those vile old districts are already condemned, and no doubt in some few years to come they will be covered over with noble warehouses, and the splendid depots of the merchant princes of the world."

STEWES, OR BORDELLOS, AND A BISHOP OF WINCHESTER'S GEESE.

"Next to the old places of refuge, in furthering the spread of crime were the old stewes or bordellos—the regularly-licensed houses of ill-fame—for the reception and harbouring of lewd women, and the repairing thither of incontinent men.

"There were about twelve of these licensed houses at first.

"They were situated at Bankside, Southwark, and the fronts of the houses faced the Thames.

"They were, in fact, on the water side, and the stew houses themselves belonged to William Walworth, then Lord Mayor of London.

"They, however, were farmed out by settlers from Flanders for this infamous purpose; and they were not only the resort of the licentious, but of many of the criminal class.

"They had sign-boards on their fronts, painted on the walls, the principal of which were the 'Castle,' the 'Gun,' the 'Boar's Head,' the 'Cross Keys,' the 'Crane,' the 'Cardinal's Hat,' the 'Bell,' and the 'Swan.'

"The disreputable loose women who inhabited them were under the jurisdiction of one of the old Bishops of Winchester, and hence in former times they were always known by the title of the Bishop of Winchester's geese.

"They were forbidden the rites of the Church as long as they continued their sinful life, and unless they repented before their death, and were reconciled to the Church, they were forbidden Christian burial.

"As great numbers of them died in their wretched immorality it was found necessary to set apart a special plot of ground for their burial far apart from the churchyards, and known by the name of the Single Women's Burial-Ground.

"The women of these places communicated the most terrible and loathsome diseases, and as they spread in number the contamination was engendered far and wide.

"The number of bordellos increased, and at length recognised houses of ill-fame were opened by thousands in every district of the metropolis.

"From time to time throughout the various reigns they have been the places where the young and unsuspecting have been entrapped to for purposes of infamy; they have robbed parents of their favourite children, and they have disseminated disease and desolation broadcast into millions of families throughout the land.

"They have frequently been the scenes of the most cruel robberies and horrible murders, and the great wonder has been that the Legislature has not adopted more strenuous measures for the suppression of the fearful traffic, which for so many generations has been a scourge to society and a disgrace to the land.

"Since the growth of various sanctuaries into colonies of thieves, and the establishment of so many other places of vice, the denizens of both have mingled together and inter-bred till we have had produced that miserable, mongrel, wretched race of low, cowardly, dastardly thieves, born in vice, trained and matured in infamy, and whose blood is so corrupted with the loathsome diseases of their class that they have become just what we see them at the present time—so mentally, morally, and physically corrupt as to be a curse to themselves and the society amidst which they have been permitted to live.

"Many writers are agreed that these mendicant criminal classes are peculiarly constituted, and that they are, both mentally and physically, a different race of people to the industrious classes.

"They argue that as by the ordinary laws of human life hereditary insanity is engendered from generation to generation, so that the moral taint of idleness, natural dishonesty, and general tendency to the committal of brutal crimes, is in like manner also engendered, and a distinct race of beings, human in form but brutish by nature, are thus begotten, and numerously spread in those districts so long peculiar to them."

ANCIENT AND MODERN PUNISHMENTS.

"Thus it will be seen that the better class of society have had to deal with a sort of criminal plague. These hordes of sturdy beggars, thieves, and impostors, have, almost from time immemorial, sought to foster themselves upon the industrial portions of the community. When they could not live well by begging then they stole—sometimes by open violence, and at others by the sly, sneaking, cowardly methods adopted by the burglar and the highwayman.

"Hence various statutes have in different reigns been passed against them. The 27th Act of Henry VIII. enacted that a sturdy beggar detected begging was to be whipped for the first offence, that for his second offence he was to have his right ear cropped, and then if found begging again he was to be indicted for wandering, loitering, and idleness, and then to suffer the execution of death as an enemy to the commonwealth.

"This Act from its over severity sent many to death, and thus, in the reign of Edward VI., another Act, considered more lenient, was passed in 1547.

"This ordered that every able-bodied person who did not apply himself to some honest labour should be taken for a vagabond, branded on the shoulder, and sent into slavery for two years to anyone who chose to demand him. If not demanded by anyone as a slave, he was to be kept to hard labour on the highway in chains.

"During this period he was to be fed on bread and water, and refuse meat, and made to work by being beaten.

"If he ran away in the course of his two years' slavery he was to be branded on the cheek, and adjudged a slave for life; and if he ran away a second time he was to suffer death as a felon.

"This statute, however, did not have the desired effect, and in the reign of Queen Elizabeth another Act was passed in 1572, wherein it was declared 'that all persons able to labour, and who should refuse to work, should for the first offence be grievously whipped and burned through the gristle of the right ear with a hot iron of the compass of about an inch; for the second offence such persons should be deemed felons, and for the third offence they should suffer death without the benefit of clergy.'

"About twenty-five years afterwards this law was amended, and by the 39th of Elizabeth, caps. 3 and 4, it was enacted 'that every able-bodied person that refused to work for ordinary wages was to be openly whipped until his body was bloody, and forthwith sent from parish to parish the most direct way to the parish where he was born, there to put himself to work as a true subject ought to do.'

"Three years later on these fearful laws were repealed, and by the 43rd of Elizabeth there was commenced for the first time—

"THE ESTABLISHMENT OF WORKHOUSES.

"These huge buildings, intended for the housing and maintenance of the poor, soon began to rise in numbers, and now we have these gigantic establishments erected in every union of the land.

"Almost everyone is familiar with their prison-like exterior, and there are very few persons who pay taxes who do not feel the heavy burthen of the poor's-rates.

"The community who contribute to the rate would doubtless do so more willingly if they could but feel that it was more usefully and charitably applied.

"But there is a widespread and well-founded opinion that the whole poor law system is a gigantic blunder, and the remnant of a barbarous and merciless law.

"The policy of the poor-law system has been one of an indiscriminate cruel repression.

"It has been equally applied in all its brutal rigour to the unfortunate, the helpless, and the aged poor, as well as to the designing sturdy mendicant, who occasionally in the inclemency of seasons has accepted its miserable dole.

"By the cruel tortures of its treadmills, its stone-breaking yards, its oakum-picking sheds, and other kinds of prison labour, combined with its miserable scale of starvation dietary, it has for centuries shattered the constitutions of countless millions; it has starved and then sold into bondage worse than African slavery, millions of orphan children, and has sent thousands of unhappy beings whose only crime was their helpless poverty into premature graves.

"No wonder, then, that we find so many of the really respectable poor dying of absolute starvation, either in the streets or their own comfortless empty homes, rather than enter these worse than prison institutions.

"Instead of providing a timely shelter or some little auxiliary help to the overworked and down-stricken poor in the shape of out relief, the unfortunate poor in the days of misfortune are forced to sell the furniture of their humble but treasured homes, and thus, being compelled to enter the workhouse, are made paupers for life, and become a burthen to the ratepayers, till at last they gradually die, oftentimes of want and despair.

"The evil of the poor-law system, from its very commencement, has been that the rigours of its statutes of repression have come down upon the wrong class.

"In most instances the helpless poor have been the victims upon whom the lashes of its punishments have fallen, while the numerous hordes of the various kinds of idle and crafty vagabonds have managed to avoid the repressions of a workhouse life, by the adoption of all sorts of chicanery, whereby they have preyed upon society, or failing that they have resorted to murder, open violence, and robbery.

"These latter have been the people who have constituted that numerous class who have from time immemorial been the denizens of the sanctuaries, the inhabitants of the alleys and slums, the dens of robbers, and the vast colonies of thieves with which the public and the Legislature have so long had to deal.

"They have formed themselves into fraternities, and there are as many different classes of thieves as there are breeds of dogs.

"Each class has its own peculiar mode of attack, and they have frequently inhabited houses for periods of years which they had so constructed with secret closets, trap-doors, and subterranean passages, for the better carrying on their fearful work, that it has been almost impossible to discover them, for their escape was easy and their detection difficult.

"Very few people have the slightest idea of the number of the various classes of thieves, and the systematic manner in which they carry on their nefarious proceedings, and unless a person has some special facility there is very little chance of anyone having any opportunity of either studying them or their ways."

CALCRAFT'S DESCRIPTION OF THE VARIETIES OF THIEVES.

"I can tell you all about the variety of thieves, though," said Calcraft.

"There's very few men what has had such an opportunity of going into their dens and seeing their ways as I have had.

"When I used to go into their kitchens with my pies why I sold baskets full in no time.

"If any of the prigs had had a good haul they would stand a treat to some of the rest, and since I have been executioner at Newgate, why I have recognised lots of their old faces, and I have had to score a few of their backs, too.

"You would really be surprised to hear what a many kinds of thieves and murderers there are.

"Of the different class of murderers at the present time there are the wholesale systematic murderers, who burke and murder people by the score, like Burke and Hare, who have just been executed at Edinburgh for murdering persons for the sake of their teeth, or selling their bodies to the surgeons at the anatomical school for dissection.

"Then there are the various keepers of lodging-houses, who decoy people with money there for the express purpose of murdering and robbing them.

"Another class of people obtain victims for their lustful passions, and then murder them to hide their shame and guilt.

"The different varieties of thieves may be divided principally into the following classes:—

"1st. The 'Rampsman,' or 'Cracksman.' This class of thief is perhaps the most adventurous and daring of all. They do not hesitate to rob by force.

"Among them are the burglars or housebreakers, who generally enter houses at night by scaling walls, and effecting an entrance by forcing a window sash, and decamping with what booty they can find.

"The highwaymen used to be mounted on horseback, and would demand your money or your life at the pistol point.

"The footpads generally go in gangs, and assail their victims with brutal violence in the highroad, and then having knocked them down, rifle their pockets of their valuables, their money, and their watch.

"The 'Drummers,' or 'hocussers,' entrap their victims into houses of ill-fame, or other places, where they stupify them with drugs, and then plunder their pockets.

"The 'Mobsman,' or 'swell pickpocket,' generally adopts a fashionable style of dress and a respectable exterior, and gains his or her booty by mixing in respectable society, or in large crowds, and adroitly picking the pockets of any likely game.

"The 'Sneaksman' is of a lower class still. He

plunders by stealth and commits various kinds of petty larcenies, such as shoplifting or pocket-handkerchief snatching.

"The 'Shofulman' gains his living by purchasing and passing counterfeit coin. His method is to purchase some trivial article, or call for drink at a taproom, and then by passing a counterfeit coin, receive good money in change.

"Coiners plunder by making base imitation money, and then selling it at so much per dozen to the shofulmen, who pass it.

"The 'Flat Catchers' live by a regular system of artful cunning, by swindling and obtaining goods by false pretences, dropping worthless rings in the street, and then picking them up again in the sight of some respectable passer-by, pretend that the ring is gold, and the setting a diamond, and finally frequently obtain a half sovereign, or a sovereign, from some flat, who, believing the story, parts with good money for trash.

"The 'Hunters' and 'Charley Pitchers' generally gain their living by attending race-courses, or other assemblies, and there rob and cheat by low gaming and thimblerigging.

"The 'Bouncers' exist by frequently making, against respectable innocent persons, fearful charges, and then intimidating them by threats of exposure, obtain large sums of money by extortion.

"The 'Cadgers' are a class who go about with all sorts of false devices, such as pretending to be paralysed or crippled, and thus they obtain a livelihood by exciting sympathy for their assumed misfortunes, whilst the other large class,

"The 'Vagrants,' gain their living by begging in the daytime, and wandering from parish to parish, and after begging all the day they spend their nights in the casual ward of the workhouse."

CALCRAFT'S DESCRIPTION OF THIEVES' DENS.

"And now, having explained to you the various classes of thieves," said Calcraft, "I must tell you something about those houses which are generally known as the regular thieves' dens. There are a great number of them about the metropolis, and there is scarcely one of the old privileged districts but what has some dozens of these houses in them.

"Many of the thieves' kitchens are long secret rooms, built at the back of some of the low ale-houses, and the only entrance to them is by means of a secret door opened from the inside.

"One of the most notorious of these places, at which about thirty of the most desperate footpads meet every night, is nearly opposite Shoreditch Church; another organised gang have a regular kitchen at Bethnal-green.

"There has always been a large number of meeting houses and other dens, the abode of thieves in the Borough and other parts of Southwark, especially in the vicinities of London-bridge, the "Elephant and Castle," and the Victoria Theatre.

"Others, too, of a very dangerous class, exist at Ratcliff Highway.

"At these houses thieves and prostitutes of the worst type congregate at a number of gaffs, where dancing in wild Indian fashion is actually carried on, and the nightly orgies are of the most repulsive character.

"Sailors as fast as they land from aboard a ship are nightly enticed to these places and robbed, and after that are frequently turned with scarcely any clothes into the streets.

"The gangs of thieves which infest Holborn, Fleet-street, and Ludgate-hill come from Field-lane. This Field-lane gang has long been notorious as being composed of some of the most desperate characters in London.

"Murders have been committed by them, and even the watchmen fear to enter their places.

"Another fearful place I know of is in Whitechapel, which, if a stranger were to enter, he would not come out alive, and I am glad to hear that all these places will soon be stopped and shut up."

After a long day's ramble on that occasion we returned home, and having again wished each other good night we parted company.

CALCRAFT'S DESCRIPTION OF THE HORRORS OF GAOL LIFE.

Some little time afterwards I called upon Calcraft again to see if he would go out for another day's stroll, but he informed me he at this particular time was very busy, and had received repeated applications to go into the country to carry out executions there.

He, however, had had to attend at Newgate so much to carry out the floggings that he could not undertake all the executions he might have.

"You would be surprised," he said to me on the occasion of this visit, "if you could only see the unjust effects of an incomplete law. Would you credit it that there are numbers of innocent people in gaols?"

He then called my attention to a case which appeared in the *Morning Herald* of that year, 1829, in which it was stated that a person of the name of Starkie had been confined in Newgate on a charge affecting his life.

When the time for the trial came the prosecutrix never made her appearance. It was well known that the woman who had made the charge against him was a most abandoned character.

The man applied to a magistrate for redress, but was told that he must go to an attorney.

The attorney told him that he could not obtain redress unless he was prepared to spend £100.

That man had been thrown amongst the vilest thieves, and he thought that magistrates under such circumstances ought to bind people over to prosecute, and then if it were shown that the charge made was false and malicious, the prisoner ought to have some redress.

"I don't like," he said, "to give my opinion upon the justice or the non-justice of any sentence, but there are a great many, not only in Newgate, but in the other gaols that assert that they are there on unfounded charges, and they seem to have such an air of truth about them that you cannot help but believe some.

"I have just received an order from the sheriff to carry out the execution on three men next Monday. I have been round to the gaol to-day, and some people were making great efforts to get one lad, named James Butler, off.

"It appears that he was tried at the last sessions before Mr. Baron Hullock. He was indicted for that he on the 17th of May, at St. Luke's, Chelsea, did unlawfully, maliciously, and feloniously set fire to the Floor Cloth Manufactory of Mr. Thomas Downing.

"The prisoner had worked for Mr. Downing from 1824 to 1828, at which time he was discharged. On the Sunday morning in question the premises were all on fire, and damage to the amount of £13,000 was done.

"In the prosecution against him it was alleged that on the Saturday night the premises were locked up safe, and on Sunday morning they were visited, and then no fire was seen, but later on in the morning the prisoner was noticed to be coming away from the building.

"It was alleged that, though there was a large ferocious dog there, yet it would not have barked or bitten the prisoner as he was well accustomed to it. A box of matches was also found upon the place that did not belong there.

"It was also shown that two little girls had that day bought a similar box of matches, and one of them was the prisoner's sister.

"The groom to Mr. Downing deposed that on the Friday evening before the fire, while he was watering the garden, the prisoner came to him and said 'Graham, you beggar, water away,' and then looking at the factory he said—'You'll want plenty of water soon.'

"William Poole, a constable of St. Luke's, Chelsea, deposed that when he arrested the prisoner and told him that he had instructions from Mr. Downing to apprehend him, the prisoner, said—'Blowed if I didn't think so.'

"The prisoner's brother and also his brother-in-law were called to prove an alibi, and deposed that the prisoner had been with them all the morning round St. James's Park.

"Other members of the family were also called, who deposed that just previous to the commencement of the fire the prisoner was at home to dinner.

"The jury found the prisoner guilty, and he was sentenced to death.

"The evidence against him was purely circumstantial; but though the alibi was very positively spoken to, the evidence was weakened by the fact that it was mainly supported by the prisoner's relatives.

"The culprit, on hearing the verdict, in the most cool and solemn manner protested his innocence; and when he was taken to the condemned cell he as positively maintained his assertion."

PREACHERS IN THE CONDEMNED CELLS.

"At this early period of my induction into my new office," said Calcraft, "it was customary to admit preachers, city missionaries, and others, whom the culprits desired to have with them, into the condemned cells, for the purpose of exhorting the unhappy prisoners to repentance, and also to pray with them and give them religious consolation.

"On such occasions, when executions are about to take place, the governor is besieged with applications for admission by all sorts of people.

"If there was general good taste and discretion always shown by those who volunteer to converse with condemned criminals, perhaps there would not be much objection to such a privilege.

"This, however, is not always the case, and it sometimes happens that there is a kind of indecent scramble even nearly up till night-time, for permission to watch by the prisoner.

"It is to be feared, too, that a great many half-educated ranting fanatics sometimes push themselves forward as spiritual guides for the mere sake of making capital out of the poor dying criminal, wherewith to stud their sensational and ill-advised religious harangues with scenes from the condemned cells, whilst others get admission under that pretence from mere prurient motives and morbid curiosity.

"As I have said before, it would be very well if the admission of none but discreet persons could be ensured, but when you come to hear the ravings of some of them, and see their violent gestures and excited contortions, I question whether they do the prisoners that real service that the regular ordinary does by his quiet, calm, and feeling exhortations.

"The Rev. Mr. Cotton, the appointed ordinary, is much respected, and generally bears the character of being most kind to the unfortunate prisoners; but he sometimes has to protest against the extravagances and denunciations of the volunteer preachers.

"I think some of them do more to frighten and unsettle the unhappy people than they do to comfort and console them.

"Some of the better class of Dissenting ministers no doubt are more useful, and are both zealous and sincere.

"This young man, Butler, has been visited all along by a Methodist minister.

"The Rev. Mr. Cotton, however, did not altogether approve of his visits, and there has been some misunderstanding between them.

"The minister, I think, firmly believes in the lad's protestations of innocence, and there is a very strong effort being made to get him a reprieve.

"No doubt there is a general hope that he will be among the number whose sentences of death will be commuted to transportation for life.

"In fact, it is astonishing how strong some people feel for him, and maintain his innocence of the charge."

THE ALLEGED HANGING OF AN INNOCENT MAN.

At the last session of the Old Bailey, a considerable number had been sentenced to death for various offences, and it was with very great anxiety that the final order was waited for.

When the recorder's report of those who were to be respited, and of those whose sentences of death were to be carried out, great disappointment was felt that young Butler was left for death.

Besides him two others were also left for execution—namely, Edward Martelly, aged twenty-five, and Henry Jubilee Conway, aged twenty, for forgery.

All three men after their condemnation behaved with great circumspection, and paid great attention to the religious instruction and consolation given to them.

The morning of the execution, namely, the 27th of July, 1829, was ushered in with all the usual ribaldry during the erection of the gallows in front of the debtors' door.

At an early hour great crowds assembled, and impatiently awaited the fatal moment. The scene inside the press-room, however, was of the most painful character.

A very graphic account is given in a book published by an eye-witness of the scene.

He says that the three unfortunate men were brought from the condemned cells into the press-room heavily manacled and ironed.

There was something awful and startling in the noise of their clanking chains as they came along the cold dismal narrow passage of stone.

When they entered the press-room they were received by the governor, Mr. Wontner, the sheriffs, and the warders in attendance, together with some yeomen of the county.

The work of knocking off with the hammer their heavy irons then began.

Martelly was the first to submit himself to this painful and jarring operation.

As soon as the irons were knocked off him he ran forward and shook hands with the governor, and thanked him for his kindness.

When asked if he was at peace in his mind, he replied, "Oh, yes, I am happy now. Talk of happiness, I never knew what it was till since I have been in Newgate and found peace with Jesus."

Conway was the next to have his irons knocked off, and during the operation he underwent considerable pain.

THE MURDER OF HANNAH DAVIES, THE WELSH GIRL.

In reply to the question put to him, he said he was satisfied with the justice of his sentence, and felt prepared to die.

He, too, was then pinioned, and took his seat on the bench by the side of Martelly.

Butler was the next to have his chains knocked off, and when asked whether he was resigned he simply said "Yes, but I am entirely innocent. I, however, forgive everyone for what they have done and said against me."

Calcraft in the meantime had been kept out of their sight.

The mournful procession then began.

The governor ascended on to the scaffold followed by the sheriffs. Cries of "Hats off!" rang through the assembled crowd, and in another moment Martelly, who was the first to emerge through the debtors' door, appeared on the scaffold. Conway came next, and Butler last.

Calcraft immediately followed behind, and having adjusted the rope round each man's neck finally pulled the white caps over their eyes and then disappeared quickly down the steps.

In another moment the drop fell, and the three men quivered as they hung in the morning air.

Martelly and Conway, who struggled but little, were soon dead, but Butler died hard, and struggled rather long.

After the bodies had hung the usual time Calcraft ascended the scaffold again and cut them down.

The execution of Butler caused considerable excitement, and gave rise to an amount of correspondence.

CHAPTER XXII.
ANOTHER INTERVIEW WITH CALCRAFT.

WHEN next I called on Calcraft he greatly surprised me by showing me a communication he had received from Ireland, asking him if he could carry out some executions in that country, as an emergency had arisen there.

The request had arisen in consequence of the death of the celebrated Tom Galvin, the Irish executioner.

It appears that this man had been the public executioner for Ireland during many years, and was as notorious in that country as common hangman as old Foxton had been in this.

Tom Galvin, in the course of a long service, had hung all the remarkable criminals that had been condemned in his time in the southern and western districts of Ireland.

It was rather a remarkable coincidence that he died in Ireland nearly on the same day as old Foxton died in England, and the deaths of both men were recorded in the same week.

A FEMALE EXECUTIONER.

Shortly afterwards, as Calcraft could not undertake the hanging of two men named Reilly and Macdermott, at Kilmainham, the hangman for the northern counties of Ireland had to be engaged to perform the operation.

This man, too, was also very notorious in his district for the number of persons he had put to death in a comparatively short career.

Formerly he had been a ploughman in the employ of the governor of the goal of Carrickfergus, and once on an emergency when a man in that gaol had to be flogged, he was deputed to perform the flogging.

It appears that he used the cat-o'-nine-tails so dexterously that the governor afterwards frequently employed him, and some time after that he was engaged to carry out an execution.

Having satisfactorily shown his ability to become hangman, he was then regularly appointed as the executioner for that circuit.

His engagements, however, were so numerous that he could not personally fulfil them all.

Some short time after his official appointment he married a girl of sixteen years of age, and as in course of time his work became still more pressing that it was obvious he would either have to appoint a deputy or another hangman would have to be engaged, he met the difficulty by dressing his young wife up in man's clothes, and having so disguised her by also dressing her hair in man's fashion he initiated her into the mysteries of the gallows, and invariably sent her to perform any simultaneous executions to those he was undertaking himself.

She became quite an adept at the horrible work, and for some years she and her husband carried out between them all the executions in their part of the country.

This man at one time hung thirteen persons at once for burning Wildgoose Lodge.

After about twelve years' joint service the scandal of a female executioner being thus employed came to the ears of the authorities, and a protest was made against such an unseemly arrangement.

"Only think of a young woman being employed," said Calcraft, "in such work as that! Why, it is bad enough for a man to do it, let alone a woman. However, I can't go to Ireland, and do the work here; so I have had to decline the job."

CHAPTER XXIII.
DESPERATE ENCOUNTER OF SOME OF THE OLD CHARLEYS IN A THIEVES' DEN.

"SOME little time after I was first appointed," said Calcraft, "I recollect a most desperate encounter taking place at a secret thieves' den in Shoreditch, in which some of the old Charleys nearly lost their lives.

"It appears that a gentleman named Whitehead, residing in Saville-place, had lost a very beautiful little King Charles spaniel. He put an advertisement in the papers, offering two guineas' reward for the recovery of the dog.

"A man named Sergeant then called upon him and informed him that he knew where the dog was, and that if he would give him something extra beyond the two guineas he would say where it could be found, but the two guineas would have to be given to the man who had it.

"Mr. Whitehead asked the man how he came to know where the dog was, and he replied, 'To tell the truth, I saw the dog stolen.'

"Mr. Whitehead, on hearing this, said, 'You are then a *particeps criminis* in the act, and unless you produce it I shall give you into custody.' He refused to say where it was, and Mr. Whitehead then sent for the watchman and charged the man with the robbery.

"He was taken to Marlborough-street and brought up before Sir G. Farrant and Mr. Roe.

"He still refused to say where it was, and was then remanded for further inquiries.

"After being locked up some time he sent for Plank, the officer, and told him if the two guineas were forthcoming he would take the watchmen to where the dog was.

"The magistrate directed two watchmen, named Goddard and Clements, to accompany the prisoner in a hackney coach, and he then took them to a most notorious house opposite to Shoreditch Church.

"The front part was a noted public-house, but at

the back of it was a large den of thieves of a most fearful character.

"The two officers had no idea of the dangerous gang they were going among, or they would have been better prepared and gone in greater numbers.

"When the man, Sergeant, arrived with the officers at the house, he first stipulated that the two guineas should be handed to the landlord to hold while the dog was fetched.

"The money was accordingly given up to him. Sergeant then sent a message to bring the dog. When it was brought the officers requested to be informed who they had to give the money up to.

"There were several in the gang, and they said that the money was to be left with the landlord, and they would divide it among the proper parties.

"The watchmen replied, 'No; we must give it to the right man that took the dog, and that therefore those who claimed to own the dog would have the two guineas for giving it up.'

"None of them, however, would personally claim the responsibility.

"The officers said, 'they must take the dog, then, and the two guineas back.' The little dog during this time had been fondling and playing, and seemed quite delighted at seeing his master, a servant-man, there, as though glad at the prospect of getting home again.

"As none in the gang would personally claim it, the landlord gave the two guineas back to the watchman, and they were about to leave with the dog.

"Upon this a great row ensued between the watchmen and the thieves, and a struggle for the possession of the dog ensued.

"A whistle was now blown, and a door at the end of a passage was opened by some robbers concealed in a secret room. This was a regular robbers' den.

"At the signal given, thirty of the most desperate cut-throats came running out, all armed with long-bladed knives, swearing with the most horrible imprecations to murder anyone that interfered with any of their body. In the terrible struggle which ensued, they tried to cut off the head of the poor terrified little animal, as they declared that unless the money was left the dog should not go out of the place alive.

"The landlord, seeing the serious nature of the conflict going on, at once jumped over the bar, and opening a side door that was generally kept locked, stood between the exasperated thieves and Mr. Whitehead's servant, whom he let out with the dog under his arm.

"Having got into the street safely with the dog, which was considered exceedingly valuable, he at once made his escape with it to his master's house.

"The whole gang of the thieves, however, commenced to set upon the watchmen in the most brutal manner. They knocked them down and trampled upon them, and, with the most horrid curses, threatened to stab them with their knives.

"The watchmen were knocked down and kicked, and would no doubt, have been trodden to death, but the landlord interfered, and other aid from outside being obtained, the officers were got away from the murderous gang.

"Further assistance now arrived, and Sergeant was taken back to Marlborough-street, to be charged with being an accessory in the stealing of the dog, and in the assaults on the watchmen.

"The desperate encounter was next morning reported to the magistrates, and a warrant was issued against a man named John Plomer, who was the recognised leader of the gang of thieves that were there discovered.

"Both he and the man, Sergeant, were afterwards brought up and charged, and fined £10 each and costs. As the money was not forthcoming they were then sent to four months' imprisonment.

"The arrest of only two men out of such a desperate gang was not a very grand display of the majesty of the law. But it seems to have been all the old watchmen, or, as they used to be called, the 'Charleys,' of that day, could accomplish.

"There is no doubt, however, that the old watchmen were inefficient both in numbers and in training. Whilst some of them were in league with the numerous thieves that existed, others were terrified at their audacity and daring.

"Even magistrates in some cases seemed almost afraid to act, for there are many instances on record where gangs of thieves had retaliated with terrible revenge on some of the officers who had signalised themselves in bringing any of their number to justice.

"In some of the old papers there are cases recorded where the thieves have frequently broken into the houses of the watchmen, and also into the houses of other officials, and carried them off to the robbers' dens, in the old privileged districts of the Mint, at Southwark, where they have fastened them up with ropes, stripped them to the waist, and nearly flogged them to death.

"Other atrocities could be cited from the various records, showing that the state of the times, and the brutally fearless character of the gangs of desperadoes which existed, demanded that the legislature should take the matter up, and deal with a strong hand with the ruffians of that age.

"Accordingly, about this time, numerous representations were made to Parliament on the insecurity of life and property, and a number of anonymous letters were received by Sir Richard Birnie and other magistrates, informing them that there was every reason to believe that there was a system of wholesale murder going on in London for the purpose of getting bodies to sell to the surgeons of the anatomical schools.

"The magistrates, in reply to the letters they received, publicly stated that if any persons really had cause to think that such a system was carried on in London it was their duty to come forward and give the requisite information so that crime could be stopped and the offenders punished.

"The various representations made had the desired effect.

"Sir Robert Peel in this year (1829) brought in his bill for the establishment of a police force.

"The old watchmen were abolished, with all their old-fashioned quaintness, and the new police came into service."

THE LAST OF THE CHARLEYS.

The following lines appeared on the subject:—

The last of the Charleys came down from Guildhall,
And he fretted and fumed like a wolf in its stall;
And his coat was as rough and as shaggy to see
As a bear in the Exeter menagerie.

Like a whist-player's face when a game has been won,
Those features at Easter with happiness shone;
Like a whist-player's face when the rubber is lost
His features at Christmas look whiter than frost.

For the renegade Peel showed his bill to the House,
And stole on the guardians of night like a mouse.
And the eyes of that Charley waxed deadly and chill—
He had told his last hour, and for ever grown still.

And there lay his pipe, but no baccy was there,
And through it there rolled not the sweet-scented air,
And the ashes which filled it lay white by its side,
And cold as the spray on the rock-beating tide.

And there stood poor Charley, with a cold in his throat,
With a pain in his head, and a hole in his coat;
The gin-shop no longer rebounds with his wit,
His watch-box is empty, his lantern unlit.

And the wives of the Charleys are loud in their wail,
For each rattle is broke, and each pot without ale,
And the staves which so oft have fought for our weal,
Have vanished like snow at the humbug of Peel.

THE FIRST ESTABLISHMENT OF THE NEW POLICE.

The first parade of the new police took place on the 25th of September, 1829, when they mustered 800 strong in front of the Foundling Hospital.

There was great opposition to them at first, and the men had to show great forbearance in bearing up against the attacks made upon them.

The newspapers of the period described their first appearance as ludicrous. Their clothes did not fit, and some small men were put in such large suits that they could scarcely move freely about.

They were assailed with many gibes and jeers, but eventually they were put through their drill and then dispersed, and finally assembled at the stations of their divisions.

A code of rules was drawn up and distributed at every station, and the promise of promotion held out to the men of good behaviour.

There were many delinquents among them. A great many showed a decided preference for the company of the servant maids in their masters' kitchens than they did for their duty among the thieves and vagrants of the streets.

Others committed gross outrages and unwarrantable assaults on many unoffending inhabitants, and the ratepayers were not long in discovering that to a great extent an uneducated, undisciplined, armed and brutal mob had been let loose upon them.

There were, consequently, numerous complaints against them, and eventually a stronger supervision was kept over them.

The force, however, got weeded of many of the roughs that had gained admission to it.

Many of them were discharged for impropriety and brutality, and when only the better class of men were retained the police force grew in favour with the ratepayers and the public.

Of course they have had enemies, but they have been largely of that class of persons whose interests were in the demoralisation of the people, and who generally were opposed to all respect for law, order, and morality.

Their early efforts were directed to clearing the streets of disorderly characters, and afterwards to the detection of some of the numerous gangs of murderers and robbers which existed at that time.

The fights between them and the street roughs were numerous, and broken and bandaged heads were generally in fashion.

As time, however, went on, the police force was greatly extended, and many other improvements took place.

There was amongst these the extension of gas, which some few years before had been partially introduced into London.

This was found to be so useful, and such a protection against thieves, that there were numerous petitions for its extension generally to the various parts of the metropolis, and in accordance with the requests made the general lighting of the principal streets took place.

Shortly afterwards there was the introduction of the railways, consequent upon the inventions of steam power application, and the arts, science, education, and general good order of the people seemed to rapidly increase.

PARTIAL FALL OF THE GALLOWS—A HALF-HANGED MAN.

Among the many notable incidents which took place in the first year of Calcraft's appointment was that of the partial falling of the gallows at Carmarthen gaol.

The event was one of the most painful on record. It appears that a young Welshman, named David Evans, had been keeping company with a young woman named Hannah Davies, residing at Tyrcwmn.

He was acknowledged as her regular suitor, and the two lovers used frequently to go long rambles together along the various winding paths of the mountains of that lovely district.

One night in the month of June, 1829, she called at Evans's house, and, after staying a little time, she asked him to come for a walk, and accompany her part of the road home.

According to the evidence he at first refused to go, but eventually consented to accompany her, though very reluctant.

After having been out for some time he returned home in the evening, and commenced putting up some palings in his father's garden.

Nothing further was thought of the circumstance, till some time afterwards the body of the young woman was found at the bottom of a deep ravine, with about twelve wounds about her head and neck.

The wounds were of a most fearful character, as though they had been inflicted with a sharp instrument.

An inquest was held, and the evidence tended to show that the wounds might have been produced by a bill-hook, which was found in the prisoner's possession; and as he was the last person seen with her alive, suspicion fell upon him.

In making the post-mortem examination, it was found that she was enceinte, and as he gave a very unsatisfactory account of where he last saw her that evening, a verdict of wilful murder was returned against him, and he was committed for trial.

The case came on at the Carmarthen Great Assizes, and after a long and patient investigation a verdict of guilty was returned against him, and he was sentenced to death.

The judge, in passing the sentence, commented strongly on the enormity of the crime, and gave him no hope of mercy.

The barbarous murder created such a sensation throughout the country, that when the morning of execution came there were at least 10,000 persons gathered together to witness the execution.

The gallows was erected in front of the gaol, well in view of the enormous crowd.

At the time appointed, the mournful procession came on the scaffold. A roar of voices and signs of general indignation were heard on every side as soon as the culprit came in view.

The unhappy man stood firm, but ghastly pale, while the noose was being adjusted round his neck, and the end of the halter attached to the beam overhead.

As the storm of yells and hisses came from the angry and excited multitude, he looked piteously towards the people as though about to address to them some few short observations, but nothing could be heard excepting the din and the growling of the mob.

There is no public record as to who the executioner was, but as soon as the preliminaries were ready he stepped down behind the scaffold, and drew the bolt.

The drop, however, through some oversight, caught a chain that was intended to fasten a portion of the gallows, and the weight of it breaking the rope, the unfortunate man fell down on his face, greatly shocked and shaken, but not otherwise seriously injured.

Another horrible yell now came from the vast multitude of spectators, and mingled cries of "Shame—Shame! let him go!" and "No—no; hang him—hang him!" filled the air.

The wretched man having regained his feet, now came to the front of the scaffold, and said—

"I now claim my liberty."

"Oh, no!" said the sheriffs, "the law must be carried out."

"No, no!" said the prisoner; "you have hung me once, and you have no power or authority to hang me twice."

A scene of great excitement and confusion now ensued. The culprit, with his arms still pinioned, struggled violently to get down from the scaffold and make his escape among the crowd.

While this dreadful scene was being enacted it was discovered that the gallows was shaking and vibrating as though it would come down, and the beam at the top was nearly coming off its uprights.

On examining the gallows further it was then discovered that the carpenter who had been employed by the county to put it together had forgotten to put in the coupling pins, and thus the beam at the top was very nearly coming down on the heads of the governor, the chaplain, and all engaged on the drop.

In the course of a little time the gallows was got ready again; and everything being once more prepared the culprit was the second time brought up.

He was now deadly pale with fear. It seemed as though the shock had so shaken his nerves that he could scarcely stand. Further, he was under a strong conviction that, having been hung once, he had complied with the requirements of the law, and they had no legal right to hang him again.

So strong was this conviction settled in his mind that he refused to ascend the ladder again, and they had to compel him to go up by force.

He spoke in Welsh, and also in broken English, saying, 'The gentlemen in London do not hang anyone twice. It is against the law. I have read it. You will be committing murder if you hang me now."

Upon this the executioner again stepped forward and said, "You are greatly mistaken. There is no such law as that to let a man go if there's an accident, and he's not properly hung. My warrant and my order is to hang you till you are dead—so up you go, and hang you must till you are dead."

"No, no, gentlemen," said the culprit, turning and appealing to the sheriffs. "Give me time, and inquire what the law is. I am certain you have no authority to hang me now."

The hangman now began to exhibit signs of violence and impatience, and, seizing the culprit again, he forcibly pushed him under the beam, and with some extra assistance they got the rope round his neck again.

During the whole of this time the wretched culprit, with a ghastly pallor on his face, and apparently terrified by the suffering he had just undergone, continued to entreat them to spare his life till the Government could be communicated with.

The crowd all the while were surging and raging to and fro, and uttering the most horrible imprecations against the principal actors in the awful scene.

The hangman, with the assistance he obtained, having succeeded in again getting the noose round the culprit's neck, and, fastening the halter to the fatal beam again, once more descended down the steps behind the scaffold, and withdrew the bolt.

The drop now fairly fell, and the unfortunate man came down with a heavy thud.

The executioner seized his legs, and after the body had vibrated a little all signs of life were over, and thus ended one of the most disgraceful spectacles which have ever taken place through the carelessness of the gallows officials, or that has ever been placed on record.

THE CONFESSION.

After hanging an hour the executioner cut the body down, whilst the vast concourse was still surging in front.

The excitement around the scaffold was very great, and there were frequent threats of violence. Though the hangman's name is not mentioned, it is not unreasonable to suppose that Calcraft was the executioner.

Old Tom Cheshire, who, when Foxton died, was getting advanced in years, used to have occasional jobs, and at the death of Foxton was looked upon as the one who by right, having been assistant executioner some time, should have succeeded him in his office.

Calcraft, however, who was in the full vigour of life, and who bore the character of being a very determined man, of strong nerve, and of great physical power, used at first to be frequently called on to carry out the provincial executions.

As all England and Wales, with the exception of Yorkshire, was then generally considered within the province of the London hangman's duties, there is little doubt of Calcraft being the hangman who attended on this fearful occasion.

The circumstance of the culprit having denied the right of the hangman to suspend him a second time caused considerable discussion, but it seemed to settle the point and prove that the law requires that the hangman shall hang a culprit till he is dead.

After the terrible excitement had subsided, it was made known that the culprit, just prior to his execution, left behind him a full confession of his guilt.

He stated that on the night of the murder the unfortunate girl called upon him to get him to go home with her, and make some arrangements. He had previously seduced her, and she then being in the family-way by him, wanted him to make some sort of settlement.

Not feeling disposed to do this, he armed himself with the bill-hook before starting, and when in a lonely part of the pathway by the mountain side, he attacked her with the bill-hook, and after nearly severing her head from her body, he pushed her down the deep ravine, where she was ultimately found.

CHAPTER XXIV.
DEATH OF TOM CHESHIRE.

HAVING in previous chapters shown the state of the times when Calcraft obtained his probationary appointment as assistant to old Tom Cheshire, who immediately succeeded old Foxton, we may mention that the Corporation not liking to finally throw the old man, Cheshire, out of his office, nominally retained him in their service till his last illness and death.

He lingered on some time however, unable to personally perform the work of his office, and when Cheshire, who till the time of his death was nominally the chief executioner, died, Calcraft, his assistant, then succeeded him in his full office, and was finally appointed the executioner for England and Wales.

It was not at all generally known at the time who the executioner really was on particular occasions, for very frequently the hangman wore a mask, so that his features might not be recognised.

In fact, this precaution seemed almost necessary, as there was, among the lower classes, a very vindictive feeling against all executioners.

Calcraft knew this, and for a time endeavoured to keep his appointment a secret. To such an extent did he maintain this reticence that if it were not that the brutal, violent character of the mob must be taken into consideration, Calcraft might be thought to have been a timid and nervous man.

After his appointment began to be whispered about it was currently reported and believed that he was one of the assistants at the execution of Thistlewood and his confederates for the Cato-street conspiracy.

Calcraft, however, in his early days always denied it, and there is no reason to doubt the truth of his statement, for when he first applied for the office of assistant hangman he stated that the two men he hung at Lincoln were the first he ever executed.

CHAPTER XXV.

CALCRAFT TAKING THE SOLEMN OATH OF THE EXECUTIONER, AND RECEIVING THE AXE, THE HALTER, AND THE KNIFE—THE ANCIENT CEREMONY—AT THE DREAD HOUR OF MIDNIGHT.

AMONG the quaint old customs of England probably there is none more curious than that of taking the fearful oath to carry out in its full entirety the awful work the executioner is sometimes called upon to perform.

Nothing could possibly be more repugnant to any person of sympathy or feeling than the words of the ancient oath.

It will be seen that the law had no regard for age or sex, but it was supposed to be administered to all duly convicted, without fear or favour, or any respect whatever to kindred or station.

The swearing in of the public executioner has, from time almost immemorial, been considered a frightful and awful ceremony, and it was always carried out in the most imposing and solemn manner.

It was in the council chamber of the Guildhall that the ceremony took place.

When, therefore, a vacancy occurred in the office of hangman there used to assemble together with great pomp the Recorder of London and his secretary, the Clerk of Arraigns, the Lord Mayor and his head clerk, the Sheriffs and the City Marshal, the Governors of Newgate and Horsemonger-lane Gaol, one of the Crown Judges, with the Town Crier and officers of the peace, javelin men and other officers.

After due proclamation, and some days had elapsed to permit of the receipt of applications, and the proper filling up of a list containing the Christian and surname of the candidates, to which sometimes the names of noted criminals (guilty of any crime except murder) would be admitted; then at a appointed time after the dread hour of midnight, they would gather themselves together in secret conclave; the Crown and City Judges before mentioned being seated at a bench mounted high, covered with black cloth and having dark caps on their heads trimmed with red, and underneath a very large scroll, inscribed with the words— "Whoso sheddeth man's blood by man also shall his blood be shed."

All the other officials, too, were dressed in their full civic costumes—scarlet robes, wigs, and gowns, some holding in their hands their wands; others their respective batons of authority, and various insignia of office.

The Recorder now proceeded to announce in solemn voice that the court for the choosing and swearing in of an executioner of felons and traitors was now sitting according to the laws and statutes of this ancient realm, and that it was the pleasure of his most gracious majesty the king to have chosen a fitting instrument for such lawful purposes—namely, to hang, behead, draw, and quarter the aforesaid felons and traitors when sentenced after conviction to die.

The crier of the court then in solemn, stern voice, amidst the breathless silence which now reigned in the imposing scene, cried out "God save the king," to which the whole assembly responded "Amen."

A bell now began to toll in the most solemn manner the regular funeral knell, and as this was done soon after midnight it had a dread effect.

After a few silent impressive moments the judge asked for the name of the selected candidate to fill the solemn office of the executioner of England.

The sheriff then in a strong voice said—

"The man we have chosen to be his most gracious majesty the king's executioner, my lord, is William Calcraft."

"Bring in a well-sharpened axe," said the sheriff.

The proper keeper of the axe then brought in a very wide-bladed axe, sharpened to a keen edge, and laid it on the table before the judge. This axe was the same that had been long used for the beheading of traitors.

The sheriff now said, "Bring in the usual leg-irons, handcuffs, and other fetters."

The keeper of the irons now brought in the leg-irons, handcuffs, and other manacles, and laid them on the table.

During this time the bell was at intervals kept solemnly tolling the usual death-knell.

"Now bring in the halter and a pair of white caps," said the sheriff, "and the beheading knife, well sharpened."

The keeper of the halter, straps, caps, and knife then brought them in and laid them on the table.

"Bring in the candidate now," said the sheriff.

The doorkeeper then threw wide open the door, and called William Calcraft.

In another moment William Calcraft walked in. He was dressed in his best suit, and wore a high-collared coat, which were fashionable at that time, with a light waistcoat, and coloured necktie. He was rather a short thick-set man, slightly pock-marked, with large mouth, rather thick lips, and very thick, short, curly, black hair, and when first appointed was clean shaved.

He was then ordered to kneel and take the usual oath of secrecy in his office, which he did.

The sheriff then said—

"Let him now be sworn, and take in the most solemn manner the solemn oath of his most gracious majesty the king's executioner."

Calcraft, still kneeling on the floor, then took the oath.

The ancient form prescribed was, that the candidate then laid his left hand on the axe, and his right hand on the Bible, and then, in the most solemn manner, repeated after the clerk of the arraigns the following solemn oath:—

"I do hereby most solemnly swear to hang or behead, or to draw and quarter, or otherwise destroy, all felons and enemies of the peace of our lord the king and of his subjects, duly sentenced according to law, and that I will do the like unto father, mother, sister, or brother, and all other kindred whatsoever, without favour or hindrance, irrespective of sex or age. So help me God."

During the whole of this time the judge held over his head the great sword of justice. The axe, the halter, and the knife and manacles were then given into his hands, and it is stated on record that he snatched at them with marked delight at his full installation into his dreadful office.

Upon the conclusion of the oath and his receiving the terrible weapons of justice, the executioner, according to the ancient laws in olden time, was then commanded to rise.

A thick black veil was then thrown over his head at his rising, so that his face could not be seen, and he was led out of court amid the horrid groaning of the assemblage, the tolling of the death-bell, and the execrating words of the judge, "Get thee hence, wretch," ringing in his ears.

If we could ourselves fully picture that terrible scene and duly feel the awful and horrible duty the executioner takes upon himself—namely, to hang, draw, or quarter, or behead, or otherwise destroy, any fellow-creature by law condemned to die, no matter how near or dear, it is not surprising that the whole assembly, gathered according to ancient custom, shuddered at the thought of such an oath, that they all looked with some curiosity on the man who, for the small pittance of twenty-five shillings per week, could be found to swear that oath and be willing literally to perform it, and that after he had sworn to do so they should all show their utter detestation of his office as to send him from their presence by a storm of execration and the most horrid yells, the effect of which should be still further increased by the judge ordering him from his presence with the words of "Get thee hence, wretch."

No doubt the executioners expected a very different reception, and a very different ending to the cremony.

In all probability they had cherished the belief that they would be welcomed and looked upon by the representatives of the majesty of the law as heroes and patriots, and, in fact, the only truly brave men that could be found with courage sufficient to enable them to be willing to strangle any the law might condemn, or otherwise put to death all doomed to suffer.

No wonder that it is said that they appeared to shrink from being publicly known as the common hangmen—the men who had undertaken such a fearful responsibility.

It is said that many of Calcraft's former associates, when they heard of his appointment, shrank from him, and no longer cared for his company.

On the other hand, it is said that when he sought and undertook the office he, like many thousands of industrious men at that time, was in great poverty.

He had tried for work and could not get it, and he was thus glad to accept the appointment as offering him the certainty of a living, though the duty would be painful, and the work terrible to contemplate.

Still, though the calling to which Calcraft had devoted himself was an unenviable one, and though the work itself was odious, Calcraft has been frequently spoken of by those who personally knew him as a good neighbour, a jovial companion (unless you broached the subject of hanging), a good husband, and a good father to his children.

These, it will be admitted, were traits of character which would go to show that he was not altogether that callous, cold, unfeeling being that many would surmise him to have been from the nature of his business.

After his appointment, it appears that he greatly desired to do what nearly all his predecessors had been allowed to do—namely, to appoint a deputy as assistant hangman.

This, however, the sheriffs would not consent to, and Calcraft was greatly disappointed.

When he asked them for a reason for their objection, and for an explanation of their determination to depart from the old custom, they replied that it was contemplated by the legislature shortly to abolish the penalty of hanging for stealing, coining, forgery—in short, all other crimes except murder, and this would greatly lessen the work he would have to perform, and therefore no assistant would be required in future.

It is, of course, impossible to tell what were the private feelings of Calcraft on this point, for, though he had a regular salary for his work, whether the executions were few or many, there is no doubt he would be a loser in the number of perquisites.

These, at one time, were numerous, and on some occasions have been valuable.

For many years the hangmen had been allowed to have the clothes of the criminal, and all property found upon them at the time of their death.

These they had frequently sold to various exhibitors, and at one time they could always ensure a good sum from Madame Tussaud for the clothes of any notorious criminal with which to dress the wax models of the culprit.

There used also to exist among the people of some classes a morbid desire to possess some relic of a terrible crime or criminal, and hence it has been known that even the rope with which they have been hung has been sold by the hangman at prices varying from one shilling to five shillings per inch.

It not, however, unfrequently happened that while the hangman was selling the real identical halter at this price around the foot of the gallows, fellows at the end of the Old Bailey were gulling the public by selling as portions of the halter pieces of any old rope at from 3d. to 6d. per inch, which had never hung anyone at all.

Calcraft, in addition to his salary of 25s. per week from the City authorities, and his perquisites from the dead men's clothes, had also £5 per quarter allowed him from the county of Surrey for the executions he would be required to perform at Horsemonger-lane Gaol; and, in addition to these sources of income, he also had the fees he received from his provincial engagements.

Besides the money he made by hangings, he also made a considerable amount by the floggings he performed at the gaols.

By some of the early receipts we have seen signed by his own hand, it appears he had 5s. for every person he flogged.

One of the receipts runs as follows:—

"Received from the sheriffs of Middlesex ten shillings for flogging two boys at Newgate.
"WILLIAM CALCRAFT."

Though in some respects he was a rough man, and inclined to be uncouth, yet he was of a stamp superior to some of his predecessors.

The drinking propensities of his chief, old Tom Cheshire, and of his principal companion, Long Tom Coffin, together with the drunken habits of Tom Cheshire's wife, added to the odious character of the hangman's duty, made the whole surroundings of Tom Cheshire look low and despicable.

Their constant drunken orgies and general levity

caused them to be looked upon as people almost devoid of feeling.

The former Mrs. Ketch, too, was not much better than her husband, which will be seen from the following case which took place shortly after Calcraft's appointment as Tom Cheshire's assistant.

The case ran as follows:—

MRS. JACK KETCH IN COURT—SHOCKING BRUTALITY.

Ann Cheshire, an old woman, the wife of old Tom Cheshire, alias Jack Ketch, the common hangman, was summoned for a shocking assault on four young children.

The case came on at the Guildhall, and the evidence showed that as Mrs. Ketch was coming towards her home she was noticed by a number of children to be in a dreadful state of intoxication.

She lived in a court in Giltspur-street, not far from Newgate Gaol, and she was approaching the court, reeling drunk, when a crowd of children gathered round her, and commenced shouting various gibes and jeers, "There goes old Mrs. Jack Ketch!"

Enraged at this, she suddenly turned round, and seizing four of the most helpless little ones, who could not run fast away, she threw them one after the other down the flap of an open cellar-window into a cellar beneath, ten feet deep.

The children were dreadfully shaken and bruised, and the outrage created quite a sensation against her.

The little ones belonged to a poor woman named Cahill, who lodged in the same house with her.

So great was the indignation, that for a time the people were inclined to give her lynch law.

Better counsel, however, prevailed, and a summons being taken out against her, she had to appear before the magistrate in the city.

After hearing the evidence the magistrate expressed his opinion that it was a very serious case, and he ordered her to remain in custody one day.

CHAPTER XXVI.
THE BAND OF THE FORTY THIEVES.

IN a previous chapter we have shown the origin of several forms of evil and vice which existed in Calcraft's early days, and it will now be our duty to expose others, and also to see to what extent the new police have helped to the detection and the putting down of crime.

In the first year of their office they discovered a large number of houses for the regular training of young thieves.

Among some of the worst was a house in the Lambeth-road, situated immediately behind the old Scotch Kirk, which existed at that time.

This house was a perfect den of thieves of the worst description.

It was, in fact, a secret society of thieves and murderers, bound together under the most solemn oaths and imprecations to rob and murder, and to assist and protect each other even unto death.

The accounts given of this fearful gang state that they had secret signs and passwords, and that none were admitted to the house, or as members of the community, but those who were well known and properly introduced, and who were willing to become sworn members of the association.

The community consisted of forty in number, and was known by the name of "The Band of the Forty Thieves."

The organisation consisted of several orders, each being trained to their various pursuits, and the ages of the members ranged from ten years up to all ages, but the greater number being from eighteen to twenty years of age.

None were admitted as candidates but those who could show that they had committed a certain number of robberies, and had either totally escaped detection, or if they had been before the magistrates, had so managed matters that a conviction was impossible.

If they could prove their capability to the satisfaction of the captain and other officers of the band, then they were duly proposed, and if elected were initiated into the secrets, mysteries, and the confidence of the society.

Having been received into the association, it is said that they were made to swear by the most fearful oath that they would be true and loyal to the band; that they would obey the commands of the captain or their regular officer; and that if they did anything to betray any of their confederates, or either "peached" upon them if ever they got into gaol, or before the judge, or upon the gallows, they hoped the most awful curses would come upon them.

They were then sworn to serve the captain and his band for a certain term of years, and then sent forth to commit the robberies or other crimes allotted to them.

The younger members were chiefly employed in picking pockets, or were taken by the experienced burglars to be put through windows into houses in the dead of the night, when they would unbolt the doors from the inside, and let their older comrades in.

The booty they obtained was all brought home to the captain, and shared by the whole body in certain proportions.

The depredations committed by this fearful and organised gang were so numerous, and the frightful outrages and highway robberies they committed near the "Elephant and Castle," and along the Kennington-park-road, the Walworth-road, and southern suburbs, attracted so much attention, and created such a widespread fear, that special efforts were directed to the association, and eventually a large number were caught.

Some of them received sharp castigation from the cat, at the hands of Calcraft; some were imprisoned, and others sent into transportation, and eventually the whole gang was broken up.

The dispersion of this gang, which had so long been such a fear and scourge to the south of London, was one of the first achievements of the new police.

CHAPTER XXVII.
THE SOCIAL EVIL.

ANOTHER dreadful phase of evil with which society was at that time cursed, was the unchecked facility for prostitution, and the enormous number of houses of ill-fame which then existed.

Never, perhaps, was there such a period of English history, when the honour of even children was so little thought of.

Everywhere houses existed, where fiends in human form made large sums of money by entrapping thoughtless, innocent children into their vile dens for the most dreadful infamy.

The shocking trade of procuration was carried on in the most systematic and unblushing manner, and scarcely anything was done in the way of legislation to check the evil.

The children of thousands of families were ruined in their childhood, and it was not till some few of the more respectable people came courageously and fear-

BELL, THE BOY MURDERER, CUTTING YOUNG TAYLOR'S THROAT IN DULCE WOOD.

lessly forward to demand that something should be done to check the frightful increase of prostitution with all its social and physical horrors that the police were instructed to do what they could in the suppression of disorderly houses.

Among the first that were brought under the notice of the public in the early days of Calcraft, and in the first year of the establishment of the new police, was a house kept by a man named Brookes and his wife at No. 8, Monmouth-court.

It was shown in evidence that these wretches had for a very long time been in the habit of respectably dressing up their own daughter, a girl about nine years of age, and sending her out of an afternoon to get into the company of any decent-looking little girls about her own age she could, and to invite them to come home with her.

Sometimes she would meet a party of girls from nine to thirteen years of age, all of whom were welcomed by her mother, and enticed to remain to tea in the house.

This woman was in league with another woman, the keeper of a regular place of ill-fame, who kept paying constant visits to her to see what likely girls she had.

By these means a regular supply of fresh girls was kept up, and their virtue sold to some of the worst debauchees of London. The evidence showed that from six to seven girls were fetched away on an average every night from this place to various houses of infamy.

The horrors that ensued, and the gigantic manner in which this evil grew, by means of this and similar places, was the means of calling public attention to the matter, and also of bringing into action public protest against such a scandal.

CHAPTER XXVIII.
SCENES OF LIFE FIFTY YEARS AGO.

In some of the previous chapters we have endeavoured to show some of the hardships the poor have had to undergo.

We have hastily glanced at the rise and progress of the Poor Law, and have shown some of the barbarous cruelties practised on starving people under the pretence of making them find work when really there was none to do.

The history of our social and criminal laws exhibited many strange phases of inequality and injustice.

No doubt much of this has arisen from the evils arising from class legislation, and in no class or profession has there been so much as in that of the law.

Though there has been a great opposition to the establishment of trades unions among the working classes it cannot be denied that the trades unions existing among the lawyers and law-makers are the greatest trades unions of all.

One of the first principles of good government is that there should be equal rights, equal laws, and equal justice for every citizen.

If there were these then the breakers of the law could be justly, and should be summarily, punished.

In every community there has been, and always will be, a large number of persons who, for selfish purposes, will break through every principle of equity and right.

Against such the law-abiding well-conducted people have no remedy, unless the redress, which the laws would give, is available, and within their means.

Those, however, who have had anything to do with law know what an expensive thing it is, and how it is encompassed round with cumbrous, old, antiquated, and perplexing statutes, and almost endless expenses.

No matter how rich a man may be, even if he be at the very summit of prosperity, and the height of fortune, if he once puts his foot over the precipice, and stands on the slippery steeps of the law, he very soon gets eased of his money, and slides down into the low lands of trouble below.

The reason of this is because the complexity of the law has been perpetuated in the interests of the profession.

Thus, though the rich man can always get plenty of law, yet his obtaining equity and justice is oftentimes very uncertain, whilst if a wrong is done to a poor man, he is obliged to put up with the loss, and go without either law or justice at all.

But there is another feature in the injustice, of class legislation and the abuses of the law to which we desire to call special attention, and that is the exorbitant scale of fees which have been fixed for the purpose of putting large sums of money into officials' pockets.

Society would scarcely credit the gigantic and brutal frauds which have been perpetrated in the name and under the sanction of the law.

Whilst war has killed its thousands, the cruelty of the law has broken the hearts of millions of fathers, and sent its tens of millions of mothers and fatherless children into starvation, prostitution, and infamy.

The past history of our civil and criminal administration would form one long terrible indictment against unjust judges, corrupt magistrates, extortionate clerks, unscrupulous informers, and brutal gaolers, who one and all have systematically been in league to draw their fellow-creatures into misfortune, purposely dragging men into the meshes of the law, as spiders do flies into their webs, for the purpose of living upon the blood and vitals of their victims. We all know how heavily the fines in some of our present courts press upon many unfortunate families.

Many of us are aware of the petty system of espionage carried on by some of our country police, to get some little trifling charge against a poor peasant, for the purpose of mulcting him in fines, and of swelling the amount of the fees, which go partly into the pocket of the informer, but more largely into the pockets of the magisterial clerks.

But to be a magistrate in the olden time was to have the power to employ mercenary spies to seek out unfortunate people, who in times of depression had no labour to perform, and concoct against them tales of idleness and vagabondage or crime, so that they could be imprisoned, involved in hopeless penalties they could not pay, and failing that they became the property of the magistrate, and were sold by him into the most horrible colonial slavery at so many hundred pounds per head.

It is a recorded fact that magistrates looked with especial favour on those informers who brought them the greatest number of culprits, that the magistrates used to quarrel fearfully among themselves as to the number of victims they claimed, and that the early fortunes of many were made by this frightful traffic.

The present principle which exists in many places of paying magistrates' clerks by the fees taken in court is but a remnant of the old barbarous custom.

It is a direct incentive to the bringing to the police-court poor hard-working labourers on the most frivolous charges, the costs of which involve them in total ruin, necessitate their selling the little furniture they possess in order to provide the court fees, and save themselves from being committed to gaol.

We have constantly seen this gross abuse repeated.

Take one of many instances which frequently occur to agricultural labourers.

Everyone knows how many long weary hours they have to work—frequently from three in the morning till six or seven at night. In addition to this they are sent with waggon-loads of produce to the London and other markets, which necessitates them travelling for miles by the sides of their horses the whole of the night.

Sometimes, after being up two whole nights, on their return journey into the country, when they get into the lanes they ride in the waggons; and while the horses are quietly going along the poor men, worn out with fatigue, fall asleep.

Can it be wondered at, after so many hours of toil? It cannot.

But as they go along there is always, in many districts, some county constable who, purposely feed by a magistrate's clerk, is ever on the watch to catch these hard-worked, ill-paid, unfortunate men napping while riding in their waggons. Forthwith the name and address are taken.

It is, perhaps, a hot summer's morning, or, on the other hand, a bitterly cold winter one, and the man so overtaxed could not keep awake.

But against him a summons is issued, and he has to appear at the magistrate's court for the offence.

On the petty sessions day we have seen the magistrate's clerk in high glee drive to the court, and in his over-anxiety to calculate the amount of fees he is going to take home, ask with the most greedy haste, the number of summonses issued.

For this offence of not being able to keep open the weary eyes, we have seen the unfortunate father of a large family, struggling hard to maintain his children, cast in penalties and fines, ranging from twenty to forty shillings.

Sometimes we have seen the little home and its treasured bit of furniture entirely sold up to provide for these extortionate penalties.

At other times we have seen the men sent to gaol for three weeks or a month's hard labour for the offence, because of their total inability to pay the monstrous fines.

But the evil arises entirely because of the officers of the law being in great part paid by the penalties and hearing fees obtained.

If it were not for this infamous system, the paid practice of such espionage would be dropped; such miserable cases would never be brought, and we should not have the scandal which we constantly see of our county constabulary and various police employed in hunting up trivial matters, whilst the more serious cases of gigantic frauds, impudent and audacious swindles, and cold-blooded murders, and deep-designed robberies go almost neglected, or if inquired into at all they are inquired into in such a bungling incapable manner as to leave wide open the way of escape, and to close for ever the chance of justice and proper retribution.

But, unfortunately, corruption, extortion, and cruelty have long been the marked characteristics of the limbs of the law.

Formerly it used to be that the most exacting extortion was practised whenever a man got within its clutches.

As soon as the sheriff's officer made his appearance, the expenses began, which generally finally ended in a man's hopeless incarceration in gaol.

Then when fairly caged, all hope seemed to fly.

Thanks, however, to the efforts of philanthropists, and the various reforms which have been carried, many of the old abuses have been swept away, but many still exist, and it will still require great and united labour to accomplish the good work begun, and complete the reform of our laws.

We have to a great extent done away with the tyrannical severities of judges, the corruption of magistrates, and many of the old forms of gaol oppressions, and there is still hope for the future.

It is, however, wise sometimes to take a retrospective view, and look back and see what has been done in the past—and thus by seeing what cruelties men have been capable of perpetrating, we may form an opinion of what some might still commit if they are not properly watched and checked.

It will be well, then, to see what prison life was fifty years ago, and as few men had better opportunities of observing the abuses which existed than William Calcraft, we may introduce here some of his recollections of the scenes of many of the old London prisons.

CHAPTER XIX.
CALCRAFT'S RECOLLECTIONS OF OLD PRISONS AND PRISON LIFE FIFTY YEARS AGO.

WHAT an amount of misery and human suffering used to exist in those old debtors' prisons when I first came into office (said Calcraft one day, when he was giving us an account of his early recollections). It used to appear to me (said he) that half the people spent the best part of their life in gaol.

If a poor man or woman owed a few shillings which they could not pay at the time, the expenses soon were ran up to many pounds, which they never could pay, and thus generally they were hopelessly in debt, and, as a rule, hopelessly in gaol for life.

Everyone of these prisons (said Calcraft) is or was a little town in itself, crowded with unfortunate beings who seemed to have no hope of release from a long and weary imprisonment.

In many cases the original debt was but one or two shillings, but the costs run up to pounds; and there they lay in starvation and misery, whilst their wives and children were wandering about begging a little bread from whom they could.

There were here in these places the high-born and the humble, frequently mixing together, and wearing away lives in confinement that otherwise might have been valuably employed.

I once knew many of the inmates of these places (said Calcraft), and among them was an old clergyman, who having got into debt, spent a great part of his life as a debtor, first in one prison and then in another.

He used to relate some strange stories of the scenes he had witnessed, and frequently made me wish, as many others did who have seen what I have, that the law of imprisonment for debt would soon be abolished.

The law of arrest for debt, he used to say, was a permission to commit greater acts of oppression and inhumanity than are to be met with in the annals of slavery itself.

If a poor man or woman only owed a trifling sum the law gave authority to the creditor to tear the father from his weeping child, the husband from the distracted wife, and to hurry him to a dungeon to linger out a life of pain and wretchedness.

In order to understand some of the abuses of the old laws and the old prisons, we will first begin with an account of the various sweating stages, and give an insight into

THE SPONGING-HOUSE.

The old clergyman (continued Calcraft) once related to me a true story of a young gentleman named Montford.

One day Charles Montford stood at the window of his lodgings in Bury-street, St. James's, while the servant was laying his breakfast-cloth.

The boy was summoned from his occupation by the postman's knock. In two minutes he returned with a letter directed to "Mr. Charles Montford."

"Mister Charles Montford. Who the devil writes me 'Mister,' I wonder?" And the young man broke the wafer.

Few attorneys are sufficiently acquainted with the etiquette of good society. Those among the fraternity are very rare who venture on the word "esquire," or afford sealing-wax. Hence, there was usually a characteristic vulgarity about a lawyer's letter which identified it at once.

We now give a cheaper copy of a letter than ever was made by an attorney of the epistle to Mr. Montford :—

"Clement's-inn, Nov. 10th, 1832.

"Sir,—Your acceptance of £142 12s. in favour of Lieut. Strong, due yesterday, having been dishonoured, I am instructed by Messrs. Wing & Co. to take proceedings without delay unless the same, together with 3s. 6d. noting, and 5s. the costs of this application, be paid to me before twelve o'clock to-morrow.—Your obedient servant, W. DUNMORE."

"To Mister Charles Montford."

"Ah," said Montford, putting the letter behind the fire, and sitting down to his breakfast, "the debt is due."

There was another knock at the door. The boy again left the room, and the legs that mounted the stairs on his return were more than two.

There were three slight knocks—one came in from the interior, and then an unceremonious opening of the door, and entry of a short red-haired, pock-marked, ferret-eyed person, who immediately took off his hat, and did not bow.

"Can I speak with Mr. Montford?" said the man.

"Certainly! I am Mr. Montford. What is your business?" asked our youth.

"It is Mr. Charles Montford I want," returned the man, doubtingly.

"My name is Charles," was the response.

"Then, sir, I have a writ against you."

"The devil you have!" And the bailiff, handing him a slip of paper, signed to his partner, who had hitherto stood outside, to come into the room.

The second man was the perfect cut of a thorough ruffian—ten shades worse in dress, manners, and respectability than his red-haired companion, of whom, in the slang of his profession, he was called the follower.

"Surely there is some mistake," said Charles, as he glanced at the writ. "This is for a debt due but yesterday, and I have only just received notice from the attorney of the bill being dishonoured."

"Haven't you indeed, sir? Ahem!—that's strange, but you see our orders, sir. You must come with us, and then you had better send for your lawyer. Shall my man call a coach?"

"Yes, certainly," said Charles.

"Go for a coach, John," said the officer.

"But you are not going to take me to prison—are you?"

"No, sir—not unless you wish."

Our hero did not wish any such indulgence, and accordingly he suffered the men to take him to Chancery-lane, and deposit him in the sponging-house of Philip Selby, Esq., officer to the sheriffs, and duly instructed in the art of captioning the image of his Maker.

A sponging-house was, we believe, originally intended as a house for the accommodation of prisoners when first arrested, where they might, if they had a chance of arranging their affairs, do so without going to prison, and where, to say the least, it would be a great convenience to remain until they could send for their professional advisers or their bail.

Every man had a right to go to one of these houses for twenty hours before going to prison, or he could, when first arrested, repair at once to Whitecross-street, if he preferred the alternative.

A small charge was fixed by law for the convenience of lodging at these places, and there can be no question that they were meant as public benefits for debtors. How far they fulfilled the purpose for which they were designed will be more than proved in the experience of these pages.

For ourselves, in digressing as we are bound to do, and leaving Charles Montford time to send for his solicitor in his new dilemma, in order to describe what a sponging-house has been, after having told what it was intended to be, we declare in the outset that the convenience it affords is not in any degree proportionate to the price paid for it, inasmuch as the man with little money is sure not to be allowed to stay one moment after his shattered finances are exhausted; while he who has plenty is equally sure if he remained of spending in driblets, and almost imperceptibly, as much as would, if collected, in all probability have paid his debt.

But the greater evil was to come. No sooner does a man entrust himself within the bars of these demi-prisons—these anticipations of the positive gaol—as mild aperients are given to prepare the frame for the most powerful physic—than he discovers he is a sacrifice to combination, that he is merely one out of the world of victims, to a succession of plots, a routine of discounted bills, actions, and auctions. A complicated maze of accommodation, usury, and law, all cunningly concocted, cleverly managed, and adroitly concluded, by which purses, pockets, we had nearly said banks, are emptied, in order to secure the fortunes of some three or four or more persons, the *dramatis personæ* of the combination itself, the *disjecta membra*, the scattered relations of a family, which, like the Plunketts, modern Hannibals, are to be provided for, or, like the more ancient Carthaginians, seem to have sworn as great an enmity to honesty as the general himself once adjured against haughty Rome. To these family combinations all debtors who go to sponging-houses are more or less victims, because sponging-houses are their gaol.

Take one, for instance, which used to be well known.

The person who kept it was a Jew. His family were Jews. His banker was a Jew, and kept what we believe is an accommodation bank or loan office.

The sheriff's officer has several sons—one a bailiff, one a wine merchant, one or two sons attorneys, and one an auctioneer. The banker has made—or, at all events, his father before him has made—a fortune of usury by discounting bills at a high premium.

We will give a case in point of the progress of one bill which he discounted through the combination of the sponging-house.

The amount was £60. The banker discounted it, and gave a £50 note. It was at three months; it had three names on the back, and when it became due the acceptor was out of town, having previously let the banker know that he could not take it up until two or three days had passed over, and he should return.

The bill was made payable by the Jew banker, at the Jew sheriff's office, where, as soon as it was dishonoured, he sent to his son, the Jew attorney, who, as there were three names on it, immediately issued three writs without notice, and despatched them to his brother, the Jew wine merchant and bailiff, and this person at once let the parties know of the writs, in order to be recompensed by each of them with the usual fees.

The bill was paid two days after it was due, with nine guineas costs; but had the persons whose names were on the bill been arrested by the son they would have been taken to the sponging-house of the father, and the expenses would not have fallen far short of the bill itself.

As it was the Jew banker made ten guineas, the Jew attorney nine, and perhaps the bailiffs two or three more.

Such was the influence of combination, and such the means by which debts and liabilities were thrust into law, and law itself into a spoliation, which only differs from larceny in this—that it is not a petty theft.

Now, if either of the three actions commenced on the one bill had gone on to execution, in all probability the sale of one of the indorser's effects would have been awarded to the Jew auctioneer; but, of course, in all matters of actual arrest the sponging-house itself was the scene of plunder.

The lawyer arrests; he has interest in keeping up dilly-dallying in the sponging-house; he does not wish to send you to prison, because you are spending your money in his father's house; you are paying a guinea a day for his father's drawing-room; you are devouring his father's food, and drinking his father's wine, and your purse empties in proportion as your belly fills.

The wine his brother got for almost nothing; his father, the officer, sells to you at 200 per cent. profit, and the same wine merchant does not mind cashing you a bill at 30 per cent. to get you out; because he knows that his brother, the lawyer, will have the costs of his writ, if you do not pay it; and his father, the officer, will have the pleasure of locking you up again.

Such is the system upon which half of the young men in London were drawn into liabilities, such the combination which took them—like our young friend, Charles Montford—in the first instance, to the sponging-house.

When this young gentleman first entered the domain of Mr. Selby he was asked the question—

"Do you want a private room?" and, having decided affirmatively, he was shown into the drawing-room.

Selby's drawing-room is worth describing. There was a fireplace surmounted by a mirror at one end, portraits of Mr. and Mrs. Selby and a sofa at the other, with a couple of card-tables and a musical clock, which the moment you entered was set working by the servants, and played in its chimes with most provoking accuracy—

> Home, sweet home—
> Be it ever so humble
> There's no place like home.

In addition there were a few sporting pictures, a loo table in the middle of the room, and a proper quantity of iron bars securing the curtainless windows, fill up the interior furniture of the room, which was never deemed completely furnished unless some miserable and dejected being was caged therein, dispirited by the load of his difficulties—the apparent helplessness of his situation, or perhaps the heartrending thought of a mother, a sister, and a wife in tears, and heartbroken at the thought of his terrible captivity.

What, however, preyed as much as anything on the young heart of Charles Montford was being separated from the amiable young lady to whom he was so much attached, and to whom he was shortly to have been married.

Charles Montford's solicitor arrived a few hours after his incarceration, and he had honesty and respectability plainly marked on his brow. He was a very different man to the firm of swindling Jews into whose trammels Charles Montford had fallen, and, besides being an honest lawyer, he was an old friend of the family.

Mr. Dovon, his solicitor, however, could not give Charles any advice till he had made him master of the circumstances even to the very letter.

Charles Montford was the son of a valued officer, who having by family interest procured him a situation in the Post-office, with a salary of £100 a year, and being able to add to it a private income of another £150, thought he had left his promising young heir well off in the world when he shook hands with him, and took an affectionate farewell of him on his departure for foreign service.

But Charles's mother and sister thought otherwise. They dreaded lest his generous disposition, and his love of life and gaiety might lead him into extravagance, and lest his associates should involve him in recklessness and liability.

When, therefore, he accompanied his father and mother and sister to the ship that was to bear them far away, he remained on board until the heavy cable rose and the grasping anchor had lost all hold of the sand and weed and shells that held it in its watery bed. He saw the cords drop from the yards, the white canvas gradually unfurled and filled, and then giving a few more hurried kisses to those who fain would have kept him for a thousand, he dropped into the small boat at the side of the ship, that had not one more moment to wait.

In a few more minutes he saw the "Bride of the Waters" preparing for full sail, his fond mother, sister, and father bending over the vessel's stern with tears in their eyes, as they waved their white signals of adieu.

As the vessel sailed on and on, with the eyes of all straining to catch the last glimpse of each other, he heard borne on the wings his mother's last words, "God bless you, my boy," as she fell fainting and senseless on the deck in her agony of grief in that last parting scene.

The constant prayer of the loving mother every night was for the welfare of her darling boy, and in that prayer his father and sister always joined.

Six months, however, had only waned away, and the son for whom that prayer was offered was passing the ordeal of the sponging-house, and was becoming a prisoner in a debtors' goal.

CHAPTER XXI.

CHARLES MONTFORD had no one bad trait in his disposition, but he had some dangerous associates, and an inherent wildness as well as warmth of heart that carried him where pleasures wooed him and temptation called him away.

During the six months subsequent to his mother's departure he did not neglect the business of his office, but he passed expensively the hours of interval between its duties.

He had a clique of friends—a coterie of young companions more rich in wit than wealth, blessed with more mirth than money; and while they led him from party to party, from theatre to theatre, and saloon to saloon, they dined often at his hotel, supped at his expense, and partook, when time trod upon the heels of necessity, of the contents of his purse.

They all acquired habits of luxury in his society, upon his credit and with his cash. When the funds failed then bills! bills! bills were the first expedient, and they rushed at once to gather the easy fruits of those hotbeds of luxury, where money is forced upon them in the first instance, but assuredly from them in the last.

Charles Montford had been early led into this system—a system more intimately connected with the debtors' prisons, and with the means as well as the persons who take men there, than any of the positive acts of the swindlers, or any regular course of any insolvencies or bankruptices in trade.

Montford had accepted right and left for his friends, and to do them justice they had done the same for him.

He had paid the bills, while he could, when they became due, and when he could not they were dishonoured; but what with the liabilities they had involved, and the expense of renewing again and again; he at last found himself at Selby's, in the drawing-room described, with £10 only in his pocket, but the much larger sum of £600 in debt.

"And now, my dear sir," said he to his solicitor, when he had told him really how he stood, "What must I do?"

"Go to prison," was the pithy reply.

"Go to prison!—impossible."

"Not at all; you must stay here to-day, and in the morning I will take out a habeas to remove you to the Fleet. Once there, I will get up a letter of license—we must wait a little while to see whether your creditors will sign it, and if they will not you must take the benefit of the Act."

"No, by Heaven!—not for a fortune!" exclaimed Charles.

"Well," said his solicitor, "we will try the letter of license first; at all events, go to the Fleet, and try that."

Mr. Dovon, the solicitor, was a respectable man. He urged this course upon Montford, because he knew it was the right one to pursue.

Montford took a few turns up and down his room, and then, with an air of decision, he turned round, walked to his writing-desk, wrote a letter, and presented it to his solicitor, saying it was an application to the principals of his office for leave of absence, and intimating that he had made up his mind to the course which Mr. Dovon advised.

His solicitor congratulated him on his good sense, shook him warmly by the hand, and telling him he would be there by three o'clock on the following day with his habeas, left him once more alone in the sponging-house.

Charles Montford was not one of those who like to be left alone at any time, and therefore he did not at all approve of that loneliness which left him no other companions but a prayer-book and a musical clock that played one eternal tune—

"Home sweet home."

Charles called the servant to ask what he could have to eat.

"They are just going to dine in the coffee-room," said the servant, and they have got a piece of roast beef. Perhaps you would like some of that?"

"By all means—just the thing." I should like some very much—bring me some at once."

"Would you mind taking it with them, sir?" meaning the inmates of the coffee-room. "They won't let me cut it, and if you wait till they have done, sir, it will be very cold."

"Are there any gentlemen among them?" inquired Charles.

"Oh yes, sir, several; there are three or four gentlemen and one lady."

"A lady, eh?—well, if they will not think I intrude, I will go."

"Not at all, sir—pray come in," said a tall white-haired gentleman, who had opened the coffee-room door, and had heard the last of the conversation, and Montford walked in accordingly.

Montford sat down at the table of the smoking joint, which was immediately carved by the tall white-haired major—the military president of the mess.

The gentlemen each ordered a pint of wine, ale, or porter, as their finances would allow, and the waiter, with becoming caution duly abstained from fetching the beverage till his fingers had felt the weight and value of the money that was to pay for it.

There was not much conversation at the table during the dinner. The only observations made were that one remarked that the spoons, which were of pewter, were common things to put on a table; another noticed that the beef was tough, and a third was of opinion that the ale brought was not of the best quality as ordered.

The waiter, at each observation, gave a contemptuous smile, as much as to say, "I question whether any of you have got much better at home," to all of which the company remarked, "What better can you expect in a sponging-house?"

Charles Montford was not long in discovering that most of those who had dined at the table, and who still sat round it over their grog, were however old subjects of the law.

The white-haired major had served a long apprenticeship in the Bench and Fleet, and the others were not unaccustomed to similar institutions.

All present were full of anecdote, and they told marvellous and ludicrous stories of how officers had been cheated by experienced roués, how many had their moods of kindness and brutality, how one would take the civil fee not to arrest a man, and how another would break into a lady's bedroom without giving her time to dress.

We will leave Montford for a little time (said Calcraft) now, and postpone his experience in the sponging-house, together with all the curious revelations of the law, while I relate to you the story of another very painful duty I had to perform.

We will before long return to some of the curious scenes of prison life again, for in the old time they were very interesting, but in the meantime I will relate to you one of my remarkable executions, and that was

THE HANGING OF A BOY.

It was a lovely summer's day in June, 1831, when I received an order from the sheriff of the county of Kent to attend and carry out an execution at Maidstone gaol.

The circumstances at first were involved in great mystery, and for some time no one could conjecture how the murder occurred.

It appears that on the 4th of March, 1831, a labouring man, named Taylor, who resided near Rochester, sent his son, Richard Falkland Taylor, a boy thirteen years of age, to Aylesford, for the purpose of fetching him nine shillings, the weekly sum allowed him as parish relief.

The boy did not return at his usual time at night, and as the walk from Rochester to Aylesford was a long and lonely one, his parents began in the evening to manifest great anxiety for his safety.

When, however, the night passed and morning came and he did not return, his father and mother were in a terrible state of grief and distraction.

The following day they went to Aylesford, and having ascertained that the boy had been there and received the nine shillings all right, the frightful apprehension came over them that perhaps he had been robbed and probably murdered.

Nothing, however, could be heard of him further than that he was seen on his return journey home somewhere about three miles from his father's house, but there all trace was lost of him.

Day by day went on and afterwards even weeks passed away, while the sorrowing parents were searching and inquiring for him almost everywhere.

One day, after he had been missing about two months, as a man named Isard was going through a very lonely blind path of Great Delce Wood he saw the body of a boy, about thirteen years of age, lying among the grass.

His throat was cut from ear to ear, and so far was the decomposition advanced that his face was nearly eaten away with worms, and his features were totally unrecognisable.

The man immediately communicated with the constabulary, and they informed the parents of the lost boy of the discovery made. They directly went to the wood, and there, to their great horror, they identified the body of their lost and murdered child.

His hand, which appeared to have held the money, was still clenched, as though he had kept firm hold to the last, even in his death grasp, of the treasure he was taking home from the parish for the family support.

On a further examination of the body being made, and an inquest held, it was found that the throat was very jaggedly cut, and there were three different wounds.

There appeared to be no motive for the terrible crime, excepting robbery, but by whom it was perpetrated was a perfect mystery, as there was not the slightest clue to lead to the detection of the murderer.

At length some suspicion fell upon a labouring man named James Lingard, who lived in the village, and he was arrested, and remanded from time to time.

There was, however, no real evidence against him, and various circumstances tended to show that he was entirely innocent of the matter, and he was discharged.

After the lapse of some little time, two boys, named John Any Bell, aged fourteen, and James Bell, aged eleven, were questioned to see if they knew anything of the matter.

They said they did not, and that the last time they saw the deceased was about two or three months ago; they eventually admitted that they saw him on the day he was missed.

Subsequently, the elder boy, John Any Bell, voluntarily made the following confession. He said—

"I met the deceased boy, Taylor, on the afternoon of the 4th of March. I knew that he had been to Aylesford to get their money from the parish.

"I met him on purpose to kill him. I had thought of doing it for two or three weeks. I was about doing it the week before.

"I and my brother Jem met him, and we first asked him to go with us into a turnip field, to get some turnips. I thought of killing him there and burying him, but one or two men kept coming up, and I could not get the chance.

"I and my brother then enticed him into Great Delce wood.

"We kept telling him that through the wood was the nearest way home, and that if he would come with us we would show him the way.

"He at first refused, but afterwards came along with us. The wood is about two miles from Rochester. When I got him a good way into the wood I pretended that I had lost my way, and that I did not know the way out.

"The little boy Taylor then began to cry, and he lay down crying when he thought we were all lost in the wood.

"While he was lying down crying I then sprang on him and cut his throat with a pocket-knife. My brother James stood away some distance off.

"While I was cutting at his throat he cried and said—

"'Oh, please don't kill me—don't kill me, and if you will only let me go I'll never hurt you, and I'll love you all my life.'

"I did not care for what he said, but kept cutting him all the more. While I was doing it he squeaked, just as a rabbit would squeak.

"I saw him put his knife in one of his gloves and put it in his pocket.

"While I was cutting his throat more he then said—

"'Oh, pray don't hurt me any more; my father knows your father; let me go. Spare my life, and I will be so good to you.'

"I, however, kept on cutting his throat deeper. He clenched his money very tight, but at last I forced it out of his hand. The money was inside a bag inside his glove.

"When I told my brother I was going to kill Richard Taylor and get his money, my brother said that 2s. would be enough for him. I, however, only gave him eighteenpence, and kept seven shillings and sixpence for myself.

"After that I went to a pond and washed all the blood off the knife I did the murder with."

The two boys, John Any Bird Bell and James Bell, were then taken into custody, and charged before the magistrates with the murder.

On their way to the station John Bell showed the policeman who had charge of him the pond where he washed his hands and the knife. A little further on he said—

"That is the road which leads to the place where I killed the poor boy. Don't you think he is better off than me, sir?"

He then said—

"Torment will come upon me for this—I know it will; I know I shall be hanged for it, sir."

It was very evident to all who saw and heard the boy that he was truly sorry and contrite for what he had done.

In fact he looked penitent, and seemed greatly grieved. In appearance he was of very diminutive stature, very strongly built, and muscular. His complexion was fair, and he had all the appearance of a wild peasant boy.

The father of the two boys was also apprehended, but as there was nothing to show that he had any knowledge of the murder, or participation in any of the proceeds of the robbery, he and the younger boy were discharged.

The elder boy was then committed by the magistrates to take his trial at the ensuing assizes.

After the boy was fully committed to take his trial the Rev. Mr. Butler, one of the magistrates, asked the mother of the prisoner to stand forward.

He then addressed her on the manner in which she had allowed the boy to grow up.

In the course of his observations he said, "Mrs. Bell, we are sorry to have to commit your boy for such a crime as murder, but the magistrates believe that you are greatly to blame for the manner in which you have allowed your children to grow up.

"From our knowledge we know that you have brought them up in ignorance and in idleness. You have even permitted and encouraged them at various times to be dishonest.

"More than this, you have opposed your husband as the father of those boys in his own house, and when he has been trying to reform them you have prevented him from correcting them. At one time your husband was a singer in the church, and used to read his Bible.

"He used to read it on a Sunday evening to you and his boys, but that was not according to your inclination.

"There is no doubt you have greatly hindered the father's control over his children, and thus instead of being properly controlled and rightly instructed, they have grown up lovers of Sunday pitch-and-toss, and various kinds of gambling.

"This has created in the eldest boy a sordid craving for gain, and a species of covetousness and love of pleasure which you appear now unable to check.

"This was the mainspring which first led him to covet that money the deceased had, and the coveting of that led him to perpetrate this hideous murder.

"We look upon it that, morally speaking, you are the one that is culpable, morally, of that murder.

"You have stood in the way of the boy's education, and now at this very young age he is charged with this dreadful crime.

"Whatever now may be your own thoughts on the matter, we are of opinion that the boys have come to this greatly through your evil influence, and we hope that these dreadful circumstances will be a warning to you."

The woman listened to the magistrate's observations apparently unmoved, and then, without any reply, turned round, when he had concluded, and went suddenly away.

The prisoner was then tried for the murder at the following summer assizes before Mr. Justice Gaselee.

Mr. Walsh and Mr. Brett appeared for the prosecution.

Mr. Clarkson, at the request of the court, took chage of the defence.

In the interim between the committal and the trial there were great efforts made to get some sort of influence to bear to prevent him from being tried for the murder, owing to his youth, the bad example of his mother, and his gross ignorance.

This, however, was of no avail—a true bill was found, and the trial proceeded.

The case created so much interest that very early in the morning there were crowds in waiting, anxious to obtain admission to the court, and the trial.

The boy was placed in the dock, wearing a sort of short blue gaberdine smock frock, with blue waistcoat and coloured necktie.

On coming into the dock he looked wildly round the court, as though he scarcely comprehended the proceedings.

The charge having been duly read over, the trial proceeded, and at the close the jury found the prisoner guilty of wilful murder.

The judge then asked the prisoner if he had anything to say.

The boy said he had not, and the judge, then assuming the black cap, said, "John Any Bell, though only a boy, you have been found guilty, on the most conclusive evidence, as well as upon your own confession, of the murder of this poor unoffending boy, whom you enticed into that wood for the purpose of wilfully murdering and robbing him. It was a most cruel and deliberate murder.

"You own in your confession that you had planned it some time before, but you were thwarted in carrying it out.

"You, however, succeeded in meeting him at last, and also in decoying him away into that lonely wood.

"Then, in spite of the poor boy's entreaties—in spite of all his pathetic appeals to you for mercy, you persistently carried out your cruel determination, and unmoved by his cries and his tears, you wickedly murdered him.

"You showed him no mercy, and I can hold out no hope of mercy for you in this world.

"The sentence of the court is that you be taken hence from here to the gaol from whence you came, and that afterwards you be taken to the place of execution in front of the gaol, and there hanged till you are dead, and may the Lord have mercy on your soul.

"I also order that, after you have hung for one hour, your body be cut down, and handed over to the anatomical schools for dissection."

The boy heard his sentence almost unmoved, and then at the conclusion he looked round the court in the most piteous manner, as if about to implore for mercy.

He, however, said nothing; and the warders of the gaol then taking hold of him, they conducted him back to his cell.

On the morning of execution the gallows was erected on the top of Maidstone gaol.

This was the first execution there on the new drop. I arrived at the gaol on the over night, and people then were beginning to assemble.

They kept gathering the whole night long, and carts and vehicles were arriving from all parts of the country.

I slept in the gaol that night, and when I awoke in the morning there could not have been less than 40,000 people present.

I went up and examined the drop, and found it all right as I thought, and then waited about till I was wanted.

The minister got up early and had some more talk with the boy, and then they were praying and reading a good bit together.

Though the lad was so ignorant, when he went into the gaol, that he did not know a single letter, yet, on the morning of his execution, he was able to read short words.

Just before the arrival of the sheriffs the chaplain read the 51st Psalm, and then he made him pray with him again when he came to the verse—

"Deliver me from bloodguiltiness, oh Lord, and have mercy upon me."

The sheriffs then arrived and had an interview with the boy. He sadly wanted to see his father and mother again, and cried bitterly.

They, however, had taken their leave of him two or three days before. Some of the warders said it was a very affecting sight to see the parting between him and his mother.

THE LIFE OF WILLIAM CALCRAFT, THE HANGMAN.

THE RESURRECTIONISTS RAISING A BODY OUT OF THE GRAVE.

She called him her dear, tender-hearted boy, and then he fell to crying bitterly again, and begging his father and mother to take him away out of that place, and get the prison people to let him go home, and he would never do such a thing again.

The execution was very late on the morning appointed, for the sheriffs did not get there till two or three hours after the usual time, and an announcement had to be put up at the gate that the time was postponed.

When all the sheriffs arrived then they sent for me to go in to pinion him, and I went into the room for that purpose.

The boy then began to cry dreadfully, and fell down on his knees and prayed for mercy.

When, however, I told him I must carry out my orders, and that he must submit, then he stood still while I put the straps on him.

He then walked very quietly and firmly to the scaffold.

The excitement was very intense, for he was but a very little fellow, and there seemed a great deal of pity and sympathy for him.

When he got on to the drop there was a very dreadful scene. He fell down on his knees before the crowd crying out—

"Oh, pity a poor boy—pray for a poor boy, so that I don't go to torments. All you people take warning by me."

Lots of people cried out, "What a shame to hang a boy like that," and the uproar was getting very great.

I then put the rope round his neck and adjusted the noose.

Then when he had done praying I told him to get up and I put the cap over his face, and pulled the bolt and he fell directly. The drop, however, being a new one, did not act very well, and he lingered some little time.

After he had hung an hour I cut his body down, and it was afterwards brought up to London, and taken to St. Thomas's Hospital for dissection.

The crime caused so much interest through the country that the case was talked of almost everywhere, but the hanging of him caused a general horror throughout the country.

A great many phrenologists went and saw the head, and they were all agreed that it was a very bad one, and this no doubt would lead him to be predisposed to crime.

Most people, however, concurred in the observations made by one of the magistrates that his mother was very much to blame, for she was a woman that seemed to have little care for right or wrong, and added to this she always showed a tendency to spoil her children by letting them have their own way, and also in encouraging them to set their father at defiance.

I myself during the time of my painful duty came in for a very great share of opprobrium, but of course I had to do my work in accordance with my oath—namely, to hang or to destroy anyone I was ordered to kill.

I always consider, as my predecessor used to say, that the hangman is only the finisher of the law.

CHAPTER XXII.
DESCRIPTION OF THE OLD SPONGING HOUSES AND DEBTORS' PRISONS.

I PROMISED (said Calcraft) on a former occasion to continue my description of the old sponging houses, and the history of Charles Montford in a debtor's prison.

Nothing could be more iniquitous than the systematic running up of monstrous costs in these dens of wretchedness.

Once fairly within their grip, a man was almost sure to be hopelessly in debt for life.

The consequence was that people settled down in them in a sort of helpless resignation, and they made themselves as contented as they could in their wearisome captivity.

Sometimes they would try and beguile the time away with anecdotes of their adventures, and at others by cards and other games.

Among the anecdotes told at the dinner-table that day was that of the adventure of Bob Slaney and the bailiff, and the relation of it seemed to cause considerable amusement to the lodgers in the sponging house.

Bob Slaney was a jovial young Irishman, who would do almost everything but pay his debts.

He had, however, a "letter of recommendation to the mimbers of parlyment for his counthy," and when he came to London he was determined to make the best of his opportunities.

Owing to that system which the Irish have of helping each other Bob had not been long in London before he by some means or another got a commission in a regiment quartered at Knightsbridge.

He there attended the levees, and very shortly made the discovery that as a lieutenant in his Majesty's army his credit was much longer than his purse.

He, however, got quite used to being in debt, and therefore if any attorney's letter came he generally found it dry enough to burn, and even if he was served with a writ he never noticed it till it amounted to a declaration.

Lieutenant Robert Slaney was not at all particular where, or how, or how much he got into debt, especially as his regiment was ordered to embark for Egypt.

His creditors, however, happened to hear of his probable departure, and proceedings were at once issued against him.

It was a fine bright morning for catching a gentleman on the eve of making his exit abroad, and so cutting off his hopes of escape, when Mr. Lawyer deposited in the hands of his trusty friend Joe a square piece of paper which instrument in law is called a *ca. sa.*, and at the same time told him to go forthwith, and take Robert Slaney in execution.

Joe departed. Our hero on this occasion was not at Long's Hotel as usual; he had been busy beating up recruits, and was now in full preparation for his journey to Egypt.

But Joe went his way, and tracked him like a bloodhound, as if guided by the smell of the guinea Bob had promised him in Newman-street, when he once arrested him, and let him go again on a previous occasion, and which guinea he had not yet had.

Slaney was full of his occupation. His captain was ill, and the duties of the company had fallen on his own important shoulders.

He was longing to be off, too; anxious for a battle, and most proud of his men. As we said before, it was a bright morning.

Bob was in the barrack-yard, superintending the drilling of some of his new recruits; the barracks and the canteen were close by, and here and there a non-commissioned officer was seen passing to and fro in the yard.

Slaney, who had been observing his sergeant as he put the awkward squad into one position of their drill, was about to try their proficiency by giving the word of command for changing it, when a gentle tap on the shoulder, and the words "I want to speak to you, sir," apprised him of the presence of Joe.

He knew the voice and the countenance of the intruder, changed his own and then stepped on one side with the bailiff.

We give the rest in a dialogue—

"I've got a writ against you, sir," said Joe.

"Blood and 'ounds; a capias is it?" said Slaney.

"No, sir, an execution," said Joe.

"An execution! Och, divil burn the bad luck o' me! An execution, och, Jasus, and I going to Egypt," said Slaney.

"Well sir, never mind—you must try and pay it. It's a bad business, certainly, but you know I can't help it," said Joe.

"Well, Joe, that's thrue enough for ye; but I say ould boy, you know it's I that'll do what's right wid the mopasses; and ye won't expose me here, right in the teeth of my own men," said Slaney.

"But, sir, what am I to do. You know I dare not leave you, or let you out of my sight," said Joe.

"Lave me—out of yer sight! Oh, by the powers not you; but Joe, I'll tell ye what ye'll do," said Slaney.

"What?" said Joe.

"Ye see that white place there wid the door open?" said Slaney.

"Yes," said Joe.

"Well, that's the canteen. Do you take this shilling, and go in there and get some dhrink; and you may just keep me in your eye while I put the men through drill, and then I'll go wid you quietly. Sure I can't run away from ye here," said Slaney.

Joe was not afraid of that—so he took the shilling and walked towards the canteen. He had got his man safe, and there was no fear of his running loose out of a barrack-yard.

Lieutenant Robert Slaney now called out "Corporal!" at the top of his voice, and a corporal came.

"D'ye see that ruffian there—there, that fellow by the canteen, going in now—him that was spakin' to me a while ago? Take a couple o' men of the guard and lay hold of him. Put a ribbon in his cap to show that he has taken the king's money. I just gave him a shillin' of it, and turn him out here in the awkward squad," said Slaney.

The corporal touched his hat, and the first part of the order was executed without delay, but the second was fiercely resisted.

Joe demanded what they meant—what right they had to touch him. He was, in fact, bounceable at what he called the liberty of their joke; but when the old Irish corporal told the men to do their duty, and they led him out of the canteen, Joe vociferated against their impudence, and swore that he came with a warrant to take Lieutenant Slaney.

"And by the powers it's Liftinant Slaney that mane's to return the compliment, and take you," said the corporal.

"Take me, take me—how, take me? Where, I should like to know? You said 'take me,' didn't you?"

"Och, murder! Where is it, ye want to know? Why, to Egypt, to fight for the Pyramids—a pleasant occupation ye'll find it, my honey," said the corporal.

"To Egypt! To Egypt! I defy him," said Joe. "I tell you I'm a king's officer."

"A king's officer! Tundher and turf! Why man, it's only a private ye are. May be, my honey, ye'd be a king's soldier by the time you have drilled a bit in the squad. That sargeant there is a divil for rapping the knuckles," said the corporal.

Joe could contain himself no longer. He swore lustily, and pulled out his *ca. sa.* "I tell you, sirrah, that I am an officer, and there's my warrant."

"Your warrant," said the corporal.

"Yes, my warrant—my commission," said Joe.

"Your commission! Och, blazes, what a booby! Sure, ye thief of the world ye, haven't I been fightin' these five and twinty years in his Majesty's army, and haven't got a commission yit? Stop a bit till ye gis battling for the mummies on the banks of the Nile there, and then by the time you've lost a leg, and had a riddle or two in your body, you will be proud of being non-commissioned, ye bumbailiff, ye will," said the corporal.

The corporal was right; Joe was captioned, Bob Slaney revenged. The shilling had been regularly taken; the recruit regularly enlisted.

The bailiff was treated to a stiff stock round his neck, a ribbon in his cap, a regular drilling by the rap-knuckle sergeant, and a journey to Egypt.

The company were greatly amused at the outwitting of the bailiff, and most of them seemed as though they thought they would like to get a similar chance of besting their own custodians.

Charles Montford retired to his own private room, and we may here remark that nowhere is the distinction between the moneyed and the penniless, or even between the gentleman and the tradesman, more strongly marked than in the sponging house.

The inmate of the private room gets in that room thrice the civility which the very persons who pay it to him would deny him in the public one.

In one room he could get a messenger in a moment; in the other he must bide the waiter's time.

In one almost any bail would be taken, in the other the strictest inquiry would be made.

The same principle applied to the sleeping arrangement of the house; the gentleman in the drawing-room may get a private bedroom, the people in the coffee-room must sleep together in a many-bedded apartment, where one guest may be noisy, another diseased, and a third (as was the case in an instance we shall mention) afflicted with madness that always attacked him in his dreams.

Of course money—the great god of our country—may get over this inconvenience; but then we speak of a custom, not of the exception by which it can be occasionally overcome.

Most of these sponging houses were kept by Jews, and in them was collected such a mass of valuables that would scarcely be seen in any other establishment.

There were generally large quantities of plate, cut glass, splendid mirrors, fine pictures, many of them by the old masters, and very valuable, all sorts of curiosities; everything, in short, that fixes the stamp and character of wealth, and all so crammed, as though every inch of room in the place was worth a diamond.

All these expensive valuables were the unredeemed pledges of men who had given bills and securities to the bailiff, and lost the security when they dishonoured the bill; they were, in fact, the remnants of executions put into the debtor's house, where an auctioneer son has sold the article, and a sheriff officer father has bought it in.

How many a man has gone—in the second or third stage of an unlucky or dissipated life—into a Jew sponging house and been warned of the flight of time by a clock which formerly told the dinner hour in his own dining-room, or seen a massive chain, a bright tiara, or an enamelled gold ring glittering upon the finger of a girl who answered his wine summons, too well remembering that in a moment of extravagance he had once bought it for his daughter or his wife. Before that day wore out the company in the sponging house had considerably increased by the arrival of new visitors.

One or two fellows had been brought in quite drunk, four residents in the dwelling were playing a game of whist, two or three wives of persons, for the first time involved in difficulty, were bidding their husbands "good-bye" for the evening, and one or two attorneys were promising their credulous clients to call the first thing in the morning.

A French Jew, with madame and a lively little girl, was loudly declaring that he was ruined by the man who had destroyed his mercantile credit by arresting him; and, amid general sobs, tears, laughter, madness, drunkenness, dreadful oaths, blasphemy, and distress amongst the motley assembly, the servant of the sponging house entered to tell the inmates that their friends must leave.

Accordingly there was a clearance of visitors, and these had scarcely retired when the clock struck eleven, and this being the sponging house bed-time, the inmates of the dwelling were ordered to their beds.

There was a general bidding of "Good night," a general shaking of hands among people who had never seen each other before, a rush to the staircase, and an ascent; some staggered up, holding by the bannisters, others moved as though they had walked all day, whilst the one lone abandoned woman trod the stairs mechanically as though they had been a treadmill, heedless of remarks that would have shocked her in the happier days of girlhood.

Charles Montford, in the midst of the bustle, disgusted with the language and ribaldry, drew back for a moment into his own room.

Just as he was going in, the waiter, with his hat in his hand, followed him to the door, and, addressing him, said—

"Here is a gentleman here, sir, that wants to speak to you."

Montford stood for a moment at his door, when a young man, apparently in great distress, stepped up to him, saying—

"Forgive me, sir, for being so bold, and for disturbing you at this hour, but I heard that you are a gentleman, and that you have money. Alas! I have none—nothing at all, not a penny."

Montford put his hand into his pocket and took out his purse, but the young man stopping him said—

"Oh, no sir; it is not money I care so much for, as a little timely service. I have been staying here some days, and, as yet, have had no money come to pay my account. I have plenty of money coming to me, and though I have now signed a bill for double the amount I owe them here, they are going to send me to Whitecross-street."

"Well, perhaps they will take my surety also for the amount," said Charles Montford.

"Oh, no, it is too late now," said the young man; "besides, that is not what I want; but you might be of great service to me if you will take a little trouble."

"Name it—name it," said Charles Montford, "and if I can be of any service to you I will."

"The coach is waiting to take you to Whitecross-street, sir," said the servant; "we can't wait for anything."

"Mr. Denton is wanted," shouted a voice below, "the coach is come from Whitecross-street."

"Come, sir, come," said the servant again, in a very impatient manner, "you can't keep the coach standing."

"Yes, yes; I am coming in a minute," said the young man as he covered his face with his hands, struggled for a moment, and his features were convulsed with the agony of his mind.

"Mr. Denton must come immediately," shouted the voice from down stairs again. "We can't keep the horses standing like this."

"Forgive me, sir—forgive me, sir," said Mr. Denton to Charles Montford; "but my wife has just written a letter to me to say——"

"Indeed you must go down the stairs, and get into the coach directly, sir," again interrupted the servant. "We never keep the coach waiting like this here."

"Give him time to tell me what is the matter, and what he wants, can you not?" said Charles Montford. Then turning to Mr. Denton, he said, "What were you going to say?"

"My wife has just written a letter to me, sir, to say that my child is dying—is dying, sir," added the captive, with convulsive agony. "This letter is to tell my young wife how to act, what physicians to send for to try and save his life. They might perhaps even save him now; but, sir," and here the poor fellow became quite choked with grief, "they will not even send this letter to her without the whole of the money I owe is paid first."

"Will Mr. Denton come down directly?" again shouted the bailiff from below, and then the servant led him by the arm down the stairs with his voice choked, and his breath as though almost taken away by a stifling guttural sound.

Charles Montford had only just time to say the letter should go at once, when the young man was pushed into the coach, and the door being most unceremoniously slammed upon him, the rickety vehicle was driven slowly away.

There was no means of sending the letter that night; so Charles Montford retired to his solitary room, to muse over the hard-heartedness and harshness of some forms of human nature.

This one unvarnished scene of a sponging house shows how foolish and how inhuman it is for one man to seize on the person of another for debts he may be willing but unable at the time to pay, and thus involve him, his wife, and children, as has been too often the case, in starvation, ruin, and death.

It frequently happened that, when a man was once entrapped into a sponging house, he had to spend £100 in driblets, when perhaps his debt was not £50, but that £50 he could not obtain at once.

Charles Montford slept but little that night. His sheets felt damp, and his bed uncomfortable, and next morning he rose but little refreshed.

Mr. Dovon, his lawyer, came early the next day, and informed him that it would be to his interest to leave that place as quickly as possible, and that for that purpose he had procured a habeas.

Charles Montford inquired what that was, and his lawyer informed him it was a process to remove him from there to the Fleet.

"To the Fleet!" said Charles. "Surely you are not going to take me to the Fleet prison!"

"That is the best course I can take for you," said his lawyer, "and you had better act on my advice."

Charles Montford, with great reluctance, assented. The coach was at the door; he stepped into the coffee-room and wished good-bye to the rest of his companions in quod, and then stepping into the coach he was driven off to the Fleet prison, where we must now leave him for the present, to pine for a time in that old London gaol, the former scene of so many strange histories and curious adventures.

CHAPTER XXIII.

CALCRAFT'S RECOLLECTIONS OF THE LONDON BURKERS.

NOTHING in the whole of my recollections, said Calcraft, has ever caused so much widespread fear in the metropolis as the atrocities of the London Burkers, and the horrible acts of the various notorious resurrectionists.

Soon after the execution of the Irishman, Burke, for his many barbarous murders in Edinburgh in conjunction with Hare, their example seemed to be largely copied throughout the United Kingdom.

In fact there was scarcely a town or village in England where there were not rumours of persons missing, of graves being robbed of their dead, or of corpses being stolen from the houses of their friends, and in many instances of their bodies having been sold for dissection to the surgeons of the anatomical school.

Depots for the sale of dead bodies had been opened in Scotland, another large place existed at Dublin, near to the quay, and another place was discovered at Bankside, near to the Thames at London.

Burke before his execution confessed to having committed nineteen murders for the sake of selling the bodies of his victims for dissection, whilst the graves of the Scottish churchyards were being nightly ransacked for subjects.

In reference to the depot near to the Dublin quay it was shown that a number of dead bodies were stopped whilst being shipped on board the steamers for transit to Scotland.

Some of them were packed in piano cases to avoid suspicion, and marked "pianos with care."

It was believed that some of them had been murdered, and there were many circumstances to justify the assertion that doubtless a large number of persons had been decoyed into the building under various pretences, and murdered there and then by the murderous ruffians in waiting.

About eighteen months after these discoveries the London magistrates received from time to time a number of anonymous letters informing them that to the writers' knowledge there was a system of wholesale murder being carried on in London, for the purpose of obtaining bodies for dissection.

The magistrates publicly asked for further information, but what the replies were was not publicly made known.

It was thus seen, to the horror of every respectable person, that murder was reduced to a system, and that there were in the midst of society a class who, like the most ferocious wild beasts, preyed the one upon the other.

The country was horrified from end to end, for there was no safety, either for the living or the dead, from the attacks of these murderous villains.

The system of body-snatching extended to the provinces, and at length the country was aroused into horror and indignation.

Some of the surgeons made up their minds to assist the ends of justice in the matter, and the honour of bringing some of the murderers to justice fell upon Dr. Partridge, of Lancaster-place, Demonstrator of Anatomy at King's College, London.

CHAPTER XXIV.

THE CAPTURE OF THE NOTED MURDERERS AND RESURRECTIONISTS, BISHOP, WILLIAMS, AND MAY.

IT was on Guy Fawkes night, the 5th of November, 1831, when London was gratified with the information that at least three burkers had been caught.

The information rapidly spread, and people even left their bonfires, and squibs, and guys, in order to have the latest information of this important capture.

Throngs of people congregated round Bow-street Police-court to try and get the latest information in reference to the crime, and the description of the men brought in.

Meanwhile, another large concourse of persons had assembled round King's College, to hear the news there.

From what could be gathered on the spot it seemed that between two and three o'clock that afternoon four men went to King's College Hospital, one of whom carried a hamper on his head, and they offered a body for sale.

They had been to the hospital between eleven and twelve in the morning, and inquired if a body was wanted, and when asked their charge they replied that twelve guineas was the price.

"It's a fine healthy boy," said the men, "and a capital subject."

"I do not particularly want one to-day," said Mr. Partridge, the surgeon, "but if you like to take nine guineas for him, and he is fresh, you can bring him."

"You shall have him," said the men, "and if you'll leave the money we'll bring him for you this afternoon."

The bargain was struck, and the arrangement made.

At the time appointed the body was brought. Shields, a noted resurrectionist, carried the hamper on his head as easily as though it had been a hamper of game, whilst Bishop, Williams, and May walked close behind.

Shields placed the hamper on the floor of the college, and gave it up to Hill, the hospital porter, while Bishop and May assisted in unpacking it.

When the lid was unfastened they took the body out of the basket, and it appeared to be the body of a boy about fourteen years of age.

The circumstances of the case show with what brazen and fearless audacity these miscreants carried on their frightful traffic.

"Hullo," said Hill, the porter, "why what did this boy die of?"

"I don't know, nor I don't care," replied May.

"I don't think the doctor will like the look of that," said Hill; "it seems too fresh to be come by honestly, and I don't think he will like the look of that cut on the forehead."

"Oh, that has been done now in getting him out of the hamper," said Bishop.

"I shall have to call the doctor to look at him before I give you the money," said Hill, and he went and fetched Dr. Partridge.

When the doctor came at the request of the porter he looked at the body, but made no observation.

"You had better come into my room, Hill," said the doctor, "and go and get me change for a note, and then I can pay them; meantime the men must wait a few minutes."

Hill followed the doctor into the room, and Dr. Partridge then said to him "Hill, that poor boy has undoubtedly been murdered. You must pretend to be going to get change for the note, but instead of doing that you must hasten as quickly as you can to the police station and bring a sufficient number of police here directly."

Hill, on going out, showed the men the note, and they, thinking it was all right, quietly sat down on the bench waiting his return with the change.

In the course of about twenty minutes Superintendent Thomas, with about a dozen policemen, walked into the hospital, and the four men appeared terribly surprised.

The poor boy lay on the floor of the hospital, and the doctors that had been called in now began, along with Dr. Partridge, to make a careful examination.

"Why the blood has actually been forced through the lips and eyes. How do you account for that?" said Dr. Partridge.

"I don't know how it came there," said May.

"And here is the breast-bone, all driven in, too," said the doctor.

"I don't know anything about that either," said May.

"Everyone of the teeth are actually extracted," remarked the doctor.

"Perhaps that is the reason of all this blood coming from his mouth," said Bishop.

"But that cut on the forehead appears as though it has been recently inflicted," observed Superintendent Thomas.

"No, it aint," replied Bishop. "It wasn't done afore death, that I can swear, for it was done in getting him out of the hamper."

"Well, the case looks to me very suspicious," said Superintendent Thomas. "Here you are in possession of a body which, to all appearances, has been murdered, and you are not able to give any satisfactory account as to how it came into your possession."

The superintendent then ordered his men to arrest all four of the resurrectionists, and take them at once to Bow-street under good escort.

It was useless for them to try and resist.

The police put the handcuffs on them, and, having made their prisoners secure, marched them off to Bow-street station.

It was quite evident that a most barbarous murder had been committed, but as to who the poor ill-fated boy was there was as yet no clue.

CHAPTER XXV.
THE MYSTERY.

WHEN it became known that the murdered body of a boy had been thus timely discovered the public excitement became very great, but the mystery deepened because as yet there was no clue as to who he was.

There were at that time a number of persons, both old and young, missing, and the uncertainty as to their fate was painful in the extreme.

Among those who sought for a boy about that age was a Mr. Hart, a respectable tradesman, of Oxford-street.

His boy, he said, had leave on the previous Tuesday to go out for a time for a walk.

He did so, but had not since returned, and the whole family were in a state of the greatest anxiety for his safety.

The poor man wept bitterly, and said that though he had advertised for his son in the newspapers, and that he had used every possible means for his recovery, he could gain no tidings of him.

He had therefore come to the conclusion that his son, like many others, had been made away with by some abominable means, and disposed of to the surgeons—a circumstance which he considered as not at all unlikely from the facility with which bodies appeared to be disposed of at dissecting rooms.

The unhappy man was permitted to see the body of the murdered boy at the hospital, but it was not his son, and other parents who had also lost their children were allowed to see him, but he remained for a time unknown without the mystery being solved; but the inquiries made showed the vast number of persons missing from their friends.

CHAPTER XXVI.
THE HISTORY OF THE NOTED RESURRECTIONISTS—BISHOP, WILLIAMS, MAY, AND SHIELDS.
Bow-street Police-court, November 7th, 1829. Before Mr. Minshull.

THE four noted resurrectionists, James May, Michael Shields, Thomas Williams, and John Bishop, were duly brought up on Monday before Mr. Minshull at Bow-street, charged with the murder of a boy about fourteen years of age, whose name was unknown.

The court and precincts were crowded, and the greatest excitement prevailed.

As the trial proceeded numbers came from all parts to try and catch a glimpse of some of those inhuman monsters whose dreadful acts had for some time terrified the metropolis.

Though the poor unfortunate boy was unknown, there was evidently a strenuous determination on the part of the people generally to aid the ends of justice, by giving all the assistance they could in trying to get him identified, the murderers brought to justice, and his untimely death avenged.

Superintendent Thomas, on the opening of the case, said he had not yet been able to gain any satisfactory information as to who the boy was, especially as there were several different beliefs as to his identity.

The case is about one of the most remarkable on record, inasmuch as the evidence tendered at the examination of the prisoners, as to the mode and causes of his death, and also as to the later alleged identity of the body, were at direct variance with the voluntary statements of the prisoners.

The relative worth and reliability of the two theories form a very curious, interesting, and important study for those who take an interest in criminal jurisprudence.

As the case is a very celebrated one, we shall give it at rather greater length than we otherwise should in a work of this kind.

Mr. Hill, the porter at King's College, was the first witness called, and proved seeing a cut on the deceased's forehead when the body was taken out of the hamper.

Superintendent Thomas: As the blood came from that wound in streams it appeared to me that the wound had only been recently inflicted.

Prisoner May: Did not that blood that you saw proceed from the mouth, and was it not caused by the teeth having been drawn out?

The witness Hill replied that very likely the greater part of the blood might have come from the mouth.

May: Oh, it might have come—might it?

The magistrate here asked the superintendent whether the prisoners had in any way accounted for the manner in which they came into possession of the body.

The superintendent replied that the prisoner Bishop told him that he got the body at Guy's Hospital, and employed the prisoner Shields to carry it from thence to the King's College.

As this declaration on the part of Bishop appeared to be very important, a messenger was sent to Guy's Hospital to request to know whether a boy answering the description of the deceased had died there lately.

An answer was received on a slip of paper stating that since the 28th ult. three persons had died there; that one was a woman, and the other two were males, aged thirty-three and thirty-seven, so that the statement of Bishop as to where he obtained the body could not be true.

Mr. Minshull, the magistrate, then asked if any person had been to claim the body.

Superintendent Thomas said that a gentleman named Hart was present whose son, aged fourteen, was missing since Tuesday; he had been to see the body, but found it was not his son.

Mr. Hart, a respectable tradesman, of 356, Oxford-street, then came forward, evidently in great distress of mind, weeping bitterly.

He said he had lost a son of the same age, and he feared he had been made away with and sold to the surgeons through this abominable practice, but the boy he had seen was not his son.

The magistrate told the prisoners he was ready to hear anything they had to say in their defence—if they had anything to say—but what they said would be taken down in writing, and might be used as evidence against them.

The prisoner Bishop said that he had nothing to add to what he had already stated.

He got a body at Guy's Hospital, and employed Shields to convey it to King's College.

The prisoners, Williams and Shields, declared their innocence, and the latter said he merely acted in the matter as porter to Bishop.

The prisoner, May, who was dressed in a countryman's frock, and who appeared perfectly careless during the examination, in answer to the question if he wished to say anything, replied that he knew nothing at all about the matter, and said that he merely came to the college to get some money that was due to him.

"It was not my subject," he added. "I know nothing about it."

Here two or three constables who were in the body of the office exclaimed that they knew May to be a noted resurrectionist, and one of them said he had had him in custody at Worship-street office for stealing a dead body.

The prisoner, May, here turned furiously round to the quarter from which the voice proceeded, and dared the constable to produce his proof.

Superintendent Thomas said that May's left hand was tied up, and it might be of importance to know whether it was owing to a cut.

Mr. Partridge, surgeon, examined the wound, and he said the end of one finger was injured, either with a cut or a bite; it had been poulticed, and the injury might have been done two or three days ago.

The prisoners were then remanded for further inquiries, and for the obtaining of further evidence.

Superintendent Thomas said it would be very necessary to have the prisoners extra watched, as they were all very violent characters, and made a desperate resistance before they were secured.

The prisoners were then removed to the cells at the back of the office.

After their removal Mr. Berconi, an Italian image maker, residing in Great Russell-street, came to the office just as the prisoners were removed, and said that he had seen the body of the boy, and from what he could judge of its appearance he was induced to believe that the deceased was a Genoese by birth, and had obtained his livelihood by selling images in the streets.

The sequel led to an opinion that Mr. Berconi was in an error, for other persons came forward and expressed a contrary opinion.

The report having got abroad that the murdered boy was a foreigner, caused other foreigners to come forward and view the body.

Some of them then expressed their conviction that the deceased was one of those itinerant Italian boys who perambulate our streets with their monkeys, and as one of them had been lately missing it was immediately concluded that the deceased was the missing boy.

It is not the least remarkable part of this extraordinary case that the body of the deceased was never fully identified.

On the contrary, a man named Berini, the person who brought the boy from his native country, when called upon to identify the body as being that of Carlo Ferrari, unequivocally declared that he could not positively speak to the identity of it, on account of the change which the countenance exhibited arising from the violence which had been used.

Mrs. Paragalli, it is true, swore to the body as being that of the Italian boy, whose name she did not know, but whom she remembered perambulating the streets with a tortoise and some white mice.

One of the strange features in this case, however, is that, according to the statement afterwards made by the murderers themselves, the deceased was not an Italian at all, but a boy who had come from Lincolnshire with a drove of cattle.

If the statements of the prisoners were true, then three persons were indicted and tried for the murder of a boy of the name of Carlo Ferrari, when the murdered boy was not Carlo Ferrari at all.

Our readers must judge of the truth of the case for themselves according as the evidence stands.

Two or three persons who saw the body expressed their belief that it was the body of the poor little fellow who used to go about the streets hugging a live tortoise, and soliciting, with a smiling countenance, in broken English and Italian, a few coppers for the support of himself and his dumb friend.

The error into which persons sometimes fall in such cases ought to act as a salutary warning against persons expressing their opinion dogmatically and decisively unless they are fully certain in their own minds of the truth of their depositions.

Caution should also be used in attributing every loss or every crime to any suspected person. As an instance the boy of Mr. Hart, who was supposed to have been burked, was afterwards found drowned in the Regent's Canal.

THE INQUEST.

The inquest was opened on Tuesday, the 8th of Nov., at the "Unicorn" public-house, corner of Henrietta-street, Covent-garden, before Mr. Gell, coroner.

The evidence as to the offering of the body for sale having been taken—

Mr. George Beaman, of 28, James-street, Covent-garden was next examined. He said: I am a surgeon, and inspected the body of the deceased on Saturday night at the request of the superintendent of police. He was about four feet six inches high, and had light hair and grey eyes.

The witness then gave his evidence as follows:—

The body appeared to me to have very recently died, and I should think had not been dead more than from twenty-four to thirty-six hours.

The body was stiff, the face appeared swollen, the eyes full, prominent, and very fresh. The external coat of the eyes was much blood-shot, and there was a wound in the forehead over the left brow nearly an inch in length, and of the depth of about one-eighth of an inch. Blood was flowing from this wound, and on my using pressure to detect invisible fracture a small additional quantity of blood then oozed out.

All the front teeth had been drawn, the tongue was swollen, but I did not then perceive any more marks of violence on the body.

I examined the neck, throat, and chest very particularly; there were no marks of pressure on these parts, and I was induced to examine them, more particularly the face and tongue, and the eyes being so full and blood-shot.

On the following evening, with the assistance of Mr. May, Mr. Partridge, and others, I commenced the dissection of the body.

I then very particularly observed the external appearance of the neck, throat, and chest, and I used a sponge and warm water to cleanse them thoroughly.

There were not the slightest marks of violence. I then examined the head, and upon turning back the skin which covers the upper part of the skull, I detected a patch of extravasated blood directly beneath the skin.

This patch must have been the effect of accident or violence. The bone underneath was not injured.

The membrane investing the brain seemed rather more florid than usual.

The spine was next examined, and on the skin being removed from the lower part extending to the shoulders below, a good deal of blood was extravasated.

This, I have no doubt, was the effect of great violence. There was no fracture of the spine, but on removing the arch, with the view of observing the spinal marrow, a quantity of coagulated blood was found within the spinal canal pressing upon the marrow, and I have no doubt in the present instance that what I have just described was the cause of death—namely, the extravasation of blood into the upper part of the spinal canal.

Coroner: Do you suppose that the death of the deceased could have been occasioned by the appearances you have described without producing any external wound?

Witness: I do. The wound on the forehead could not of itself produce death.

The witness then proceeded to state that in his opinion some blows must have been given to the deceased with a blunt stick or bludgeon, or other blunt instrument, or even by the fist of a strong man. The whole of the viscera were perfectly healthy. He didn't believe the body had ever been interred. The stomach contained a tolerably full meal, and smelt slightly of rum. Unquestionably the deceased did not die from suffocation or strangulation.

Superintendent Thomas here intimated to the coroner that the Rev. Mr. Bernasconi had just seen the body, and recognised the boy as one of his flock, but could not tell his name.

Mr. Richard Partridge was the next witness. He said I am demonstrator of anatomy at King's College. The prisoners asked me to purchase a subject from them. I agreed to do so, but not liking the look of it, I kept them waiting for the money, in order to detain them while I sent for the police. I agree with the evidence of Mr. Beaman, and think that probably death was caused by the injuries at the back of the neck.

A porter from Guy's Hospital was next examined. He said my name is Thomas Davis, and I am a porter at the dissecting-room of Guy's Hospital. On Friday evening last the two prisoners, May and Bishop, came to the hospital with a sack containing, as they said, a dead body, which they offered to sell.

I told them there was none wanted, as the gentlemen were already supplied. They then asked permission to leave it that night in the hospital, and I allowed them to do so.

The next morning, Saturday, between eleven and twelve o'clock, I saw May and Bishop about the hospital. I went out, and on my return found that the body had been taken away, and that it had been removed at half-past twelve or one o'clock.

My assistant, James Wix, delivered the sack containing the body to some person, but to whom I cannot say. I am persuaded the body was never taken out of the sack while at the hospital.

Mr. Charles Starbuck, stock-broker, of No. 10, Broad-street-buildings, City, one of the Society of Friends, on his solemn affirmation deposed as follows:— In consequence of the reports I read in the papers I went to see the body of the deceased, and have no doubt it is the body of an Italian boy whom I have frequently seen at the Bank.

On Thursday evening last, the 3rd inst., between half-past six and eight, I saw an Italian lad, whom I suppose to have been the deceased, sitting near to the Bank with his face almost in his lap. He attracted attention by his position, having a mouse-trap under his arm. I remarked that he seemed unwell. There were several men and women round him. I have little doubt that the body I saw yesterday was that of the same boy. I have not seen the Italian boy alive since.

Margaret Paragalli, of No. 11, Parker-street, Drury-lane, sworn. On Sunday morning last I saw the body of the deceased. I do not know the name of the boy. He was an Italian. I have known him during the whole of last summer, and I am quite certain the body is that of the boy I have known so long. On Tuesday, the 1st inst., I saw him alive in Oxford-street, carrying a mouse-trap.

Mr. George Duchoy, surgeon, of 34, Golden-square, was then sworn and examined. I attended the post-mortem examination of the boy on Sunday evening last. My opinion is that he died suddenly from external violence, and that the injuries at the back of the neck were quite sufficient to have caused death. I observed a mark on the right wrist, apparently produced by pressure. My firm opinion is that the boy had first been stunned by a blow on the head, and after that his neck had been dislocated in the same manner as it was usual to wring the neck of a duck.

Superintendent Thomas said that since the opening of the inquiry he had had eight applications from parents who had lost boys of a similar age.

After an adjournment the jury re-assembled on the 10th of November.

After the jury had been sworn, Mr. Cribb, the foreman, produced a letter, which he said he had received from Mr. Starbuck, the stock-broker in the City. The letter was handed to the coroner, who read it to the jury. It stated that Mr. Starbuck had been mistaken with regard to the identity of the boy, whom he supposed to have been an Italian lad, and whom he had seen near the Bank on the night of Thursday. He had now, he stated since, seen that boy alive.

Joseph Higgins, constable of the F Division, sworn: I live at No. 8, Newton-street, Holborn. Yesterday, about four o'clock, I went to a public-house in Giltspur-street, called the "Fortune of War." I there saw Mrs. Bishop and Mrs. Williams, her daughter, coming out. I told them I must take them to the station-house. Mrs. Bishop begged of me to let her go home for her child, which I consented to do, but I said I must go with her. I then went with them to No. 3, Nova

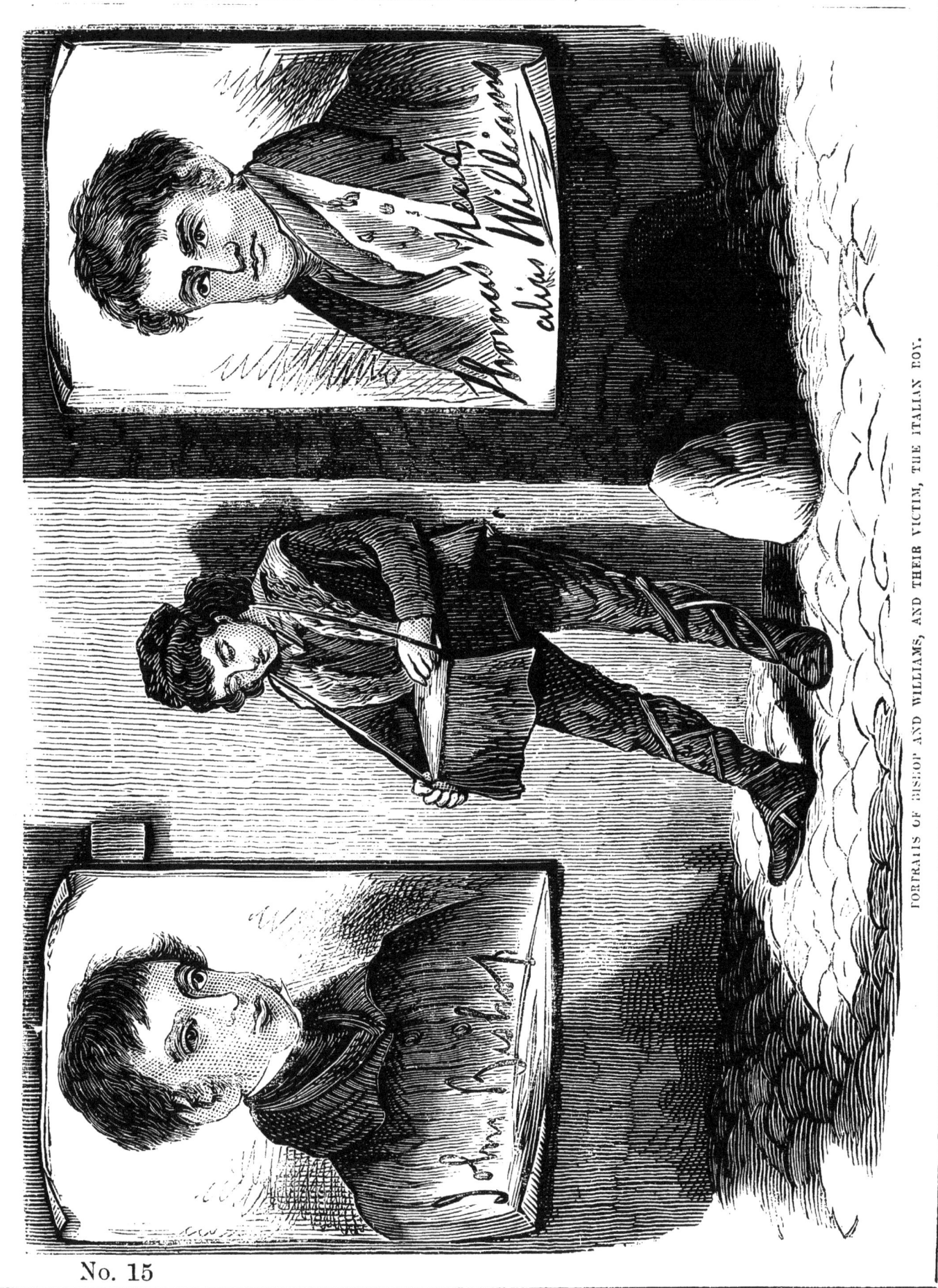

PORTRAITS OF BISHOP AND WILLIAMS, AND THEIR VICTIM, THE ITALIAN BOY.

Scotia-gardens, Crabtree-row, Hackney-road. I proceeded to search the house, and found the implements I now produce. I said I know what these are for, and she replied "I dare say you do, but do not speak before the children." I found two crooked chisels, which Mrs. Bishop admitted were for opening coffins. I also found a brad-awl, with dry blood upon it. I said "This is for punching out teeth." She replied that her husband had used it for mending shoes. I also found a file. I then searched Mrs. Bishop and found upon her the petition which I now produce. She told me that it was from her husband and three other persons for pecuniary assistance, saying that they were resurrectionists, and they had no means of defending themselves from the offence of which they were charged. The petition, which was as follows, was then read:—

PETITION.

The humble petition of John Bishop and three others,

SHEWETH—That your petitioners have supplied many subjects on various occasions to the several hospitals, and being now in custody they are conscious in their own minds that they have done nothing more than they have been in the constant habit of doing as resurrectionists; but being unable to prove their innocence without professional advice they humbly crave the commiseration of gentlemen who may feel inclined to give some trifling assistance, in order to afford them the opportunity of clearing away the imputation alleged against them. The most trifling sum will be gratefully acknowledged; and your petitioners, as in duty bound, will ever pray.

The petition was not signed. She admitted that Williams was not her son-in-law's right name; but she said he did not wish his right name to be known, as he had not been out with her husband for more than two or three times. She added, that her husband went out the night before he was taken into custody accompanied by her son-in-law, Williams, and that he came home the next morning and washed his hands in a basin, at the bottom of which she saw a great deal of mud.

James Weeks examined: I am assistant to Mr. Davis, porter at the dissecting room, Guy's Hospital. I know May and Bishop. On Friday, the 4th instant, about five minutes past seven, I went to the hospital. They left a sack at the hospital, containing something, and I saw projecting through a hole in the sack a portion of a knee of a human being. I heard May say to Mr. Davis, "the fact is, the subject don't belong to me, but to Bishop." Mr. Davis, on their request, allowed them to leave the sack with its contents in the hospital. They then went away and came to the hospital the next morning about one o'clock with two other persons, and I delivered the sack with its contents to May and Bishop.

One of the jury here stated that he had heard that the name of the murdered boy was Giovanni Montero, and that he was brought from Italy to this country about a year ago by a native of that country, named Masea.

Joseph Parragalli said he had inquired at the Alien Office, and, from the description, he did not think he could be the same boy, whose death was now the subject of inquiry.

It was here determined by the jury to have the prisoner before them.

The prisoner, Michael Shields, was then brought in, strongly guarded.

The Coroner, addressing him, said: You are not obliged to answer anything unless you please, but I tell you fairly that we have before us sufficient evidence to prove that the deceased boy came to his death by unfair means; and having traced the body into your custody, we wish to know whether you are inclined to give any explanation touching your possession of the body in question.

The prisoner, in reply, said he was willing to speak the whole truth, and having been sworn he deposed as follows: My name is Michael Shields. I live at No. 6, Eagle-street, Red Lion-square. I am a porter, and on the morning of the 5th inst., about ten in the morning, I was hired by Bishop, whom I met in Covent-garden. I went with him, together with May and Williams, to Guy's Hospital, and they gave me a hamper directed to Mr. Hill, of King's College, which they said I was to take, and I did so. In reply to the coroner witness said I some times assist the grave-digger at St. Giles's parish church in digging graves. I have known Bishop about eight or nine months. I have often met Bishop and May at the "Fortune of War" public-house, which is a noted house for resurrection men, and I have often carried hampers and boxes to the dissecting rooms for them, but I never knew for certain how Bishop, Williams, and May got their living.

The Foreman: Do you know how this boy came to his death?

Prisoner: Bishop, while coming to Bow-street in the van, said the body was got from the ground, and that he knew where it was got from.

The prisoner Bishop was next brought in and questioned, after receiving the usual caution as to whether he had any explanation to give.

Bishop: I dug the body out of the grave. The reason why I decline to say the grave I took it from is because two watchmen were on the ground, and they allowed me to do it, and, as they are of good family, I don't wish to betray them. I shall certainly keep it a secret as to the grave I got the body from. I know nothing as to how it died.

Bishop was then removed, and the prisoner May was next brought in, and cautioned in the same manner. He was told that the result of the inquiry might affect his life, and if he said anything it might be taken down in writing and produced in evidence against him.

Prisoner: My name is James May, and I live at Dorset-street, Newington. I took two subjects to Mr. Grainger's, in Webb-street, on Wednesday, and on the next morning I removed them to Mr. Davis's, at Guy's Hospital. After getting the money for them I went drinking at the "Fortune of War," in Smithfield. Bishop and Williams then came there. Bishop then asked me where the best place was to get a good price for—for—things. I told him I had just sold two for a good price at Guy's. Bishop then said he had got a very good subject, and had been offered eight guineas for it. I told him I could get more than that for it, and Bishop then said that all over nine guineas I could have for myself. I then agreed to get what I could, and we called a chariot off the stand, and then drove to Bishop's house, where he showed me the lad in a box or trunk, and I put him into a sack, and then put it into the chariot, and drove off with it to Mr. Davis's, at Guy's. Mr. Davis said: You know, John, I can't take it because I took two off you yesterday, and I've not got names enough down for another, or I would take it. I then asked him if I could leave the body there that night, and he said I might. Bishop was with me and he then told Mr. Davis that it was his subject, and that he was not to give it up to anybody in the morning but to him.

Thomas Head, alias John Williams, was next brought

in, and being cautioned not to say anything to criminate himself, he stated that he met Bishop on Saturday morning in Long-lane, Smithfield. They then went to the "Fortune of War" public-house, and then, in company with May and Shields, they went to Guy's Hospital, and fetched the body and took it to King's College.

James Seagrove, a cabdriver, sworn, stated that at a quarter to six o'clock on the Friday evening, while he was sitting in a public-house in the Old Bailey, two men came in. Their names were May and Bishop. May asked him if he would do a job for him. Witness asked him what job it was, and May replied that it was to carry a "stiff 'un," and that he would give him a guinea for it. Witness declined, and then he saw them trying to make a bargain with another cabman.

William Hill, the porter at King's College dissecting-room, said that he had forgotten to state that when there was a delay in paying Bishop and May for the body, Bishop said to Mr. Partridge, "Give me what money you have got in your purse now, and I will call for the remainder on Monday." That was a very unusual thing for persons selling dead bodies to do, especially when all was right. They were people who generally waited for their money.

The room was then cleared, and the jury then came to the following verdict:—

"We find a verdict of wilful murder against some person or persons unknown; and the jury beg to add to the above verdict that the evidence produced before them has excited very strong suspicion in their minds against the prisoners, Bishop and Williams, and they trust that a strict inquiry will be made into the case by the police magistrates."

The prisoners, however, remained in custody on the suspicion of having committed the murder, and Mr. Minshull, the magistrate, expressed his full determination to pursue the inquiry to the utmost.

The evidence brought out at this preliminary inquiry showed the tacit encouragement which was given to the horrid vocation of the resurrectionists, and which seemed to have become a settled system, so that not only the sanctuary of the grave was violated, but human life even was sported with, as if the laws had no restraining hand upon the criminals, and they were to be allowed to carry on their murderous trade in defiance of humanity, religion, and law. To such an extent did this system prevail, that it is no wonder the people were thoroughly aroused, and the land shocked from one end to the other.

CHAPTER XXVII.
THE NOTED RESURRECTIONISTS, BISHOP, WILLIAMS, AND MAY.

NOTHING could exceed the public excitement (said Calcraft) which was manifested between the time of the adjournment of the hearings, and especially between the close of the coroner's inquest and the further examination before the magistrates.

The anxiety to know who the poor boy was, and how far each particular prisoner was implicated, I have never known exceeded in any other case.

THE ADJOURNED MAGISTERIAL INQUIRY.

The magisterial inquiry was again resumed on the 18th of November, when Mr. Corder appeared on behalf of the parish of St. Paul's, Covent-garden.

In doing so, he said he wished to call the magistrate's attention to a very important point, and that was that he should be able to show that the prisoners had not met in the manner they had described before the coroner. With this view he should call—

Henry Locker, who, being sworn, said that on the 4th of November instant he was waiter at the "Fortune of War" public-house, in Giltspur-street. Bishop, May, and Williams called in between eleven and twelve o'clock on Friday morning, and had something to drink. They went out about twelve and returned about three o'clock, and remained until it was dusk, when they went away again and came back at eight o'clock or past. They had with them a strange man, who appeared to be a hackney coachman. They went into the tap-room and had something to drink, and then May came out of the tap-room and went to the bar. He had a handkerchief in his hand, which seemed to contain something. He poured some hot water on the handkerchief and began to wipe its contents, which proved to be human teeth.

Witness remarked that they appeared to be the teeth of a young person, and were worth something. May answered that they were as good to him as two pounds.

On the following morning (Saturday) Bishop, Williams, and Shields called again. Bishop asked what they should do for a hamper, and Williams said there was one inside the railings of St. Bartholomew's Hospital. The prisoner Shields went and fetched it, and then all three went away.

The witness, in reply to the magistrate, said that when May was engaged in washing the teeth he had on a dark-coloured smock frock.

Mr. Corder said that it was not intended on this examination to offer any evidence with respect to the exchange of clothes in Field-lane, but evidence would be produced on a future occasion.

George Gissing, fifteen, the son of a publican, who lived in Birdcage-walk, Bethnal-green, sworn, said that on Friday evening, between six and seven o'clock, he was standing at his father's shop door, when he saw a yellow-bodied chariot stop at the corner of Nova Scotia-gardens. The prisoners, Bishop, May, and Williams jumped out of it, and the two former went up Nova Scotia-gardens; they were dressed in smock frocks, and May had a pipe in his mouth. Williams stopped, leaning against the fore wheel of the chariot, in conversation with the coachman. Bishop and May returned in a short time carrying something heavy. May had the sack on his back, and Bishop was holding it up behind. The sack was placed in the chariot, and after the prisoners had taken their places it drove off through Crab tree-row in the direction of Shoreditch Church.

Thomas Trader, another boy about the same age as the last witness, gave evidence corroborative of that of the boy Gissing. He added that Mrs. Cannell called his attention to the prisoners, and asked him to follow them down by their houses, and see what they were after, as she thought there was something wrong.

Ann Cannell corroborated the previous witness, and added that when she asked him to follow the men he said he would not, for they would not mind giving him a topper. The coachman did not get off the box till the men returned, and that excited her suspicion.

James Chapman stated that he was a porter at Guy's Hospital. About seven o'clock on Friday evening, the 4th inst., the two prisoners Bishop and May drove to the hospital. They brought with them a sack containing something heavy, which Bishop carried towards the dissecting-room.

Bishop: Are you certain that it was I who carried the sack?

Witness: Yes.

May: Why, it was I who carried it, and not Bishop.

Some evidence was next elicited, showing that it was customary for the porters at the hospitals to receive considerable amounts in fees from men who brought subjects.

The next evidence turned on the question as to whether or not the body had been buried.

It was shown that there was some dirt or clay about it, but the evidence went to show that it had been smeared on purposely to make it appear that the body had been buried. Other evidence was given tending to show that in all probability the body had not been laid out.

It was further proved that when the body was taken out of the sack the left arm was doubled up, and the fingers clenched.

A police constable named Higgins, of the F division, produced a heavy iron instrument, one end of which was bent and nearly as sharp as a chisel, and the other thick and round. He also produced a bradawl clotted with blood.

Some discussion took place as to what the bradawl might have been used for.

May: Oh, I took the teeth out with the bradawl.

The other instrument was then handed to Mr. Partridge, who gave it as his opinion that the sharp end might have inflicted the wound on the forehead of the deceased, and that the thick rounded end was likely to have inflicted the blow on the back of the neck, which, in his opinion, was the immediate cause of death.

The policeman Higgins further stated that when he went to the house he found the instrument produced, together with a rope with a noose at the end of it, which he produced. He also found the breeches now produced belonging to the prisoner, and he discovered the marks of blood upon them. He saw some fresh blood on the floor of the room where he found the breeches.

May: The blood on the breeches is that of a jackdaw, which cut its leg and afterwards hopped upon them.

Superintendent Thomas said that in fairness he must say that as the breeches were not found until a week after the prisoner was taken into custody he thought that the blood was entirely too fresh to connect it with the murder.

A police-constable named Kirkman deposed that while he was in plain clothes in the station-house at Covent-garden on the evening of the 10th inst. the prisoners were there to be in readiness to appear at the inquest. A bill was posted on the wall announcing that a boy had been murdered, and was then lying for examination at the bone house. Bishop read the bill, and as soon as he had done so, he said to May, in a low tone of voice: "It was the blood that sold us." He then got up and read the bill again, repeating the words, "Marks of violence on the body!" Then turning to May again, he said: "There were no marks of violence on the body, but only a few breaks on skin," and as he said so he sat down, smiling.

The prisoner Bishop admitted that he had read the bill over, but denied the expression imputed to him.

Margaret King, a respectable-looking woman, stated that on Thursday afternoon, the 4th of November, one day before the body was offered for sale, she was standing with her children in Birdcage-walk, near Nova Scotia Gardens, when she saw an Italian boy, whom she had frequently seen before in the neighbourhood of Bethnal-green, standing at the corner of Nova Scotia Gardens, with a little box slung before him. He stood about thirty yards from where she was standing. She never saw that boy since. He had either a box or a cage with him.

Mrs. Parragalli was recalled, and stated that on the 1st inst. she saw the deceased, whom she knew. He was then in Oxford-street, and had a cage with white mice in it.

Bishop: Are you quite certain that the boy you saw in Oxford-street was the same boy whose body you saw at the station-house?

Witness: I have no doubt of it. He used to carry about his little cage, suspended in front by strings across his shoulders. At a distance the cage might appear like a box.

The prisoners were then remanded for further evidence.

The wife of Bishop, and also Rhoda Head, alias Williams, wife of the prisoner Williams, were then brought up before the magistrates and remanded.

Mrs. Bishop had been the wife of Bishop's father by a second marriage, so that his wife was also his mother-in-law. Rhoda Head, alias Williams, was Bishop's sister.

On the evening of the same day that the prisoners had been examined at Bow-street, an Italian named Agostino Bruni, the master of the ill-fated boy, arrived in London from Birmingham, with the view of identifying the body. For this purpose the body was disinterred on Saturday morning, the 19th of November.

He seemed to entertain no doubt of the body being that of a boy he had brought from Sardinia, and whose name was Carlo Ferrari.

He spoke positively to the colour of the hair and of the eyes, and also as to the height, which particulars corresponded with the description of the boy he had in his service, but who had left him a year previously, and who had since been wandering about town, exhibiting his cage of white mice.

It was understood that this man Bruni was the master of a juvenile crew of poor, ragged, half-starved little urchins who were brought to this country on speculation.

The following curious particulars connected with this tribe of travelling mendicants to which Carlo Ferrari belonged, will be interesting as showing the profit made by these unfortunate children.

The principal haunts of these miserable children were Vine-street Saffron-hill, Bleeding-heart-yard, on Holborn-hill, Coal-yard, in Drury-lane, and in the purlieus of Shoreditch, whose houses are occupied by these wretched children who sleep eight or nine in a bed.

Each boy's monkey is chained near him every night on going to rest, and the other curiosities are placed in situations appointed to the owners; so that on starting out in the morning each boy takes his own companion.

On the ground floor reside the men to whom the monkeys and other things belong.

They provide each boy with a lodging, and basin of gruel in the morning, for which they charge him fourpence per night.

They make the further charges also for the curiosities they let out.

For a porcupine and an organ, 4s. per day—being 2s. 6d. for the porcupine and 1s. 6d. for the organ; for a monkey undressed, 2s. per day; for a monkey in uniform, 3s. per day; for a box of white mice, 1s. 6d. per day; for a tortoise, 1s. 6d. per day; for dog and a monkey, 3s. per day; for an organ with figures waltzing, 3s. 6d. per day.

FURTHER EVIDENCE.

To return to the evidence of this barbarous murder. The police next made a further search of the premises occupied by the prisoner Bishop in Nova Scotia-gardens.

In digging up the ground several pieces of human flesh were raised from the soil, and also the scalp of a head, which was evidently that of a female, from the profusion of dark brown hair which was attached to it.

In another part of the garden a child's blue jacket was dug up, and a pair of black cloth trousers, corresponding in size, was next discovered.

Next a small shirt for a child about the same age was found.

On digging further a coarse blue coat was next discovered, and also a pair of trousers made of coarse grey cloth, together with a striped waistcoat and an old shirt. These articles were apparently made to fit a boy of about fourteen or fifteen years of age.

The trousers were patched on the knees, and stains of blood were discovered on the waistcoat.

The coat was of a peculiar cut, and resembled those worn by charity-school boys.

The clothes found agreed with those described by Mrs. King as having been worn by the Italian boy.

Mr. Thomas Mills, a dentist, residing in Newington-causeway, having been sworn, stated that on Saturday morning, the 5th of November, the prisoner May came to his shop, and offered him a set of teeth for sale, for which he asked a guinea.

Witness observed that one of the front teeth was chipped, and said that it did not belong to the set, upon which May said, "Upon my soul to God they all belonged to one head, and that not long since, and that the body had never been buried." He ultimately agreed to take twelve shillings for the teeth.

Mr. Corder asked witness whether he had observed anything peculiar about the teeth.

Witness: Yes, portions of the gums were adhering to them, and part of the jaw-bone. There could be no doubt, but that the teeth had been forcibly removed immediately after death. I said to May that from appearance the teeth belonged to a female. May's reply was, that they belonged to a lad about fourteen or fifteen years of age.

While this witness was giving his evidence the prisoner May appeared for the first time to change countenance and lose that hardness of nerve which distinguished him throughout the whole of the proceedings.

May: Did I tell you the body had not been buried?

Witness: Yes.

After another adjournment the examination was resumed on the 21st of November.

When the prisoners were again placed at the bar at Bow-street, Bishop appeared to be considerably depressed in spirits, and as new facts came out against him his countenance fell, and his eyes which were full and prominent assumed a glassy appearance as he listened apparently with great anxiety to the witnesses.

May also appeared to pay particular attention to the evidence, and also to lose that levity of manner which marked his conduct on previous occasions.

Williams, who had evidently less nerve than either of his companions, betrayed a restless anxiety, and on several occasions his colour changed, and his lips grew white and dry.

As to the old man, Shields, he stood upright in the dock in a sort of stupor, without once changing his position.

John King, son of a previous witness, called, stated that he remembered his mother's washing day in the first week of November; it was on a Thursday. He then saw an Italian boy standing at the corner of Nova Scotia-gardens. He asked his mother to let him go and see what the boy had got in his cage or box, but she refused to let him go. The boy wore a brown hairy cap, and stood with his right foot turned out, and his arms resting on the cage or box. He believed he had seen the same boy before, conveying a box with a wax doll in it with two heads. He had not seen the boy since the Thursday in the first week of November; he was then standing to see if any one would come and see what he had to show; he did not see him go away.

Margaret King, sister of the last witness, gave corroborative evidence.

Joseph Higgins, a police-constable, was then sworn, and he stated that in accordance with instructions he had received from his superintendent he had dug up certain parts of Bishop's garden. They first tried the ground with an iron spit, which struck against some spongy substance in the earth. They dug up the earth and found a jacket, a pair of trousers, and a little boy's shirt. About a yard further the iron rod again struck against something soft, which proved to be a blue jacket, or short coat, a pair of trousers, and a striped waistcoat.

Mr. Corder: Did you perceive anything particular on the waistcoat?

Witness: I perceived marks of blood on the collar, both inside and out. I found in the pocket of the waistcoat a piece of a comb, and I also found a piece of an old shirt, which was torn down the centre.

The magistrate: Look at the waistcoat again, and say whether those marks, like blood, were on the neck part when you took it from the ground?

Witness: They were. They had more the appearance of blood when I took the waistcoat from the ground than they have now—they appeared to be deeper and fresher.

The waistcoat was then further examined, and it was then observed by the magistrate that the waistcoat appeared to have been made for a grown-up person, and taken in at the back in order to make it fit to whosoever it last belonged.

Superintendent Thomas observed that it had been taken in with coarse worsted, and in a very rough manner.

The magistrate said he considered those important points, as it might be the means of bringing forward the person to whom it originally belonged.

Superintendent Thomas, examined, stated that he had the previous day made a further search of Bishop's house, and on examining the front parlour he found, among a heap of old clothes and dirty linen, the cap which he now produced.

Mrs. King was then recalled, and, in reply to the magistrate, stated that the blue coat last found resembled in colour, size, and shape the coat worn by the Italian boy she saw in Nova Scotia gardens on the day named.

John King and Margaret King, children of the previous witness, said that the fur cap produced was exactly like that worn by the Italian boy.

Agostino Bruni was then called forward, and Joseph Paragalli was then sworn to interpret his evidence truly. He stated that he knew a boy named Carlo Ferrari, and that he brought him two years ago to this country from Piedmont. He was a Savoyard. Witness took him from his parents. His father's name was Joseph Ferrari. Witness had the boy for nine or ten months, and then bound him over to another person for two years and one month. The last time the witness saw the boy alive was about fifteen months ago. This was after he had been bound, and he then went with his new master towards Bristol, and witness left town in another direction. The boy, who was about fifteen, lodged about that time at the house of Mr. Elliot, No. 2, Charles-street, Drury-lane. Witness saw the dead body of a boy on Saturday, but he could not identify the face. The hair, colour of the eyes, and also the size of the body corresponded with the description of the boy whom he had named.

Joseph Paragalli, the interpreter, was then sworn, and stated that he remembered a boy named Carlo Ferrari, who lived with his master about eighteen months ago at No. 2, Charles-street, Drury-lane. Witness examined the body of the deceased before the inquest took place, and was quite positive that it was the boy, Carlo Ferrari, whom he had known. Witness saw him alive in the Quadrant, about twenty yards from the County Fire Office, about a month or five weeks ago. It was a very wet day, and the poor boy looked cold and miserable. He had his cage suspended from his neck. He was present when the boy was bound over by the last witness to his new master.

The evidence having arrived at this stage, Mr. Corder said it was not intended to proceed further with the case that day.

The prisoners, in reply to the usual questions, said they had nothing to say.

They were then about to be removed, when

Superintendent Thomas, before the prisoners were remanded, said he had now to request that Bishop and Williams might be placed at the bar alone, as he had now to charge them with

ANOTHER MURDER.

The Magistrate: Is it your wish that the other two prisoners should be removed from the bar before you make the charge?

Superintendent Thomas: I am willing to make the charge in presence of all four, but I have no wish that May and Shields should remain.

The magistrate then directed Dodd, the gaoler, to remove May and Shields, and leave Bishop and Williams at the bar.

Superintendent Thomas was then sworn and stated that he felt it his duty, as a public officer, to charge John Bishop and James Williams, alias Head, with the murder of another boy, whose name for the present was unknown. He was in possession of some evidence at present, but he expected much more.

The prisoners were then formally charged, but no evidence was offered on that occasion, and the whole of the prisoners were then remanded till the following Friday.

The wives of Bishop and Williams were then brought up, charged with being accessory to the murder of the Italian boy after the fact, and again remanded.

Two of Bishop's children were taken from the workhouse where they had been placed on the apprehension of their mother, and lodged in the station-house at Covent-garden, with a view to their giving evidence in the case, one of them, a little boy, having told another boy, before the murder was discovered, that he had some nice little white mice at home, and that his father had broken up their cage to light the fire.

From the tender age of the children, however, it was determined not to make witnesses of them, and they were accordingly sent back to the workhouse, Bethnal-green.

When Higgins, the police-constable, was engaged in digging up the garden ground on the previous Saturday, Bishop's eldest son, a boy about twelve years, was present, and when the officer looked suspiciously towards the raised pathway, beneath which it will be remembered the clothes were discovered, the boy told him to be cautious how he dug there, as the cesspool was under that part of the ground, and if he (Higgins) attempted to remove the earth he would be sure to fall into it.

This fact, which was stated by the constable, led to the belief that the child was aware of the clothes having been buried where they were subsequently found. It is not improbable that the concealment of the articles took place immediately after Bishop and his associates were taken into custody.

It now became a subject of serious deliberation whether the case as it now stood against the prisoners, with whatever evidence might arise in the interim, should be sent to the ensuing Old Bailey Sessions, commencing the 1st of December, or whether it might not be advisable to await the issue of the second charge of murder, which Superintendent Thomas preferred against the prisoners Bishop and Williams.

The magistrate, Mr. Minshull, was in favour of keeping the case open for the reception of fresh evidence, and the Recorder of London waited upon Mr. Minshull to request that a case of such public importance might not be sent to the Old Bailey unless the evidence was as complete as circumstances would allow.

The same anxiety was also expressed at the Home Office.

SUPPOSED THIRD MURDER.

The exertions of the police officers were now leading them to the discovery of another murder, committed by the horrid wretches, Bishop and Williams, and which perhaps would never have been discovered but for the detection of the murder of the Italian boy.

It will be remembered that in consequence of the strict search which Superintendent Thomas caused to be made at the residence of Bishop a quantity of human flesh, together with the scalp of a woman's head, to which a considerable portion of long brown hair was attached, were found at the back of Bishop's house.

It was at first conjectured that these were portions of a subject which Bishop had procured from a churchyard, and that the limbs had been sold to the surgeons separately—a practice by no means uncommon. Events, however, had raised a strong suspicion that the residence of Bishop had been the scene of more than one murder.

Superintendent Thomas, acting on that impression, went on the previous day to Bishop's house, with the view of making a still further search, and he appeared before Mr. Hales the same day, at Bow-street, to communicate the result. He was accompanied by two females, mother and daughter, who lived in the neighbourhood of Bishop's house. The mother had stated to him that about three weeks ago a daughter of hers had disappeared in the most sudden and mysterious manner, and under circumstances altogether unaccountable. She had taken tea with her mother and sister on the evening of her disappearance, and went out to execute some trifling errand. Her return was therefore expected every minute; but from then to the present she had neither been seen nor heard of. There had been no previous quarrel to account for her absence, and her relatives were under the dreadful impression that she had been waylaid and murdered.

Superintendent Thomas stated that in consequence of his having made further discoveries that morning in the house adjoining to Bishop's residence the mother and sister of the missing young woman, who were now present, called upon him at the station-house, and upon showing them the hair which was found at the back of Bishop's house they both of them declared it to be similar to that of the young woman whose absence had given rise to such dreadful apprehensions.

The mother and daughter were then called forward before the magistrate, and the daughter was asked to describe her sister's hair. She replied that it was of a dark brown colour, very long, and that it closely resembled her mother's hair.

Superintendent Thomas then drew the attention of the magistrate to the mother's hair, and said that it was exactly like the hair which had been found in the manner before described. He then added that from inquiries he had previously made he was enabled to prove that, about the time when the young woman was first missed from her home, Bishop had sold two subjects—one of them, the body of a young female—at Guy's Hospital. Having been engaged, however, at the time he ascertained this fact, in the case of the Italian boy, he did not feel it necessary to make any particular inquiries respecting the two bodies he had mentioned, but he should now feel it his duty to cause such inquiries to be made.

The magistrate observed that the circumstance stated by Superintendent Thomas had certainly a very suspicious appearance, and he told both mother and daughter that they might rest assured that every means would be taken by the superintendent to sift the matter to the utmost.

CHAPTER XXVIII.

SUPERINTENDENT THOMAS said it was not without good good reason he had asked for the detention of Bishop's wife and sister, for he considered it quite impossible that they could have been ignorant of what was passing in the house.

He had that morning examined the house next to that in which Bishop lived, and which, till within a week of Bishop's apprehension, had been empty for a considerable time.

The result was that he had found a woman's gown, shawl, a pair of stays, chemise, and a pair of stockings hidden away at the back.

Bishop's house was situated in rather a lonely place. It formed one of what he might almost call a colony of cottages, which, although placed in the immediate vicinity of each other, were divided by a low wooden paling enclosing a small space of garden ground attached to the separate dwellings.

Bishop and Williams resided together in the same house for the last eighteen months, and as the house contained but three rooms altogether, and those were very small, he was quite convinced that all who were inmates in the house must have been aware of what was passing in it.

Bishop and Williams had the use of the adjoining cottage, and the discovery he had made that morning showed, he thought, that they had taken advantage of the circumstance in order more effectually to carry on that abominable traffic. As the palings of all the cottages were very low they had by stepping over the palings access to about fifty gardens.

After another remand the prisoners were again brought up before the magistrates.

Sarah, the wife of John Trueby, sworn, stated that she was landlady of the cottage which Bishop had lately occupied. The houses No. 1, 2, and 3, Nova Scotia-gardens belonged to her husband. In the month of July, 1830, she let the house No. 3 to Bishop's wife. Bishop lived there until the 5th of Nov., 1831. About four months since she let the house No. 2 to the prisoner Williams, alias Head, and he lived there about two months. The house stood empty some time, but it was now in the occupation of a man named Woodcock; she believed that Williams had lately been residing at Bishop's house.

William Woodcock, sworn, said: I am a brassfounder, and occupy the house No. 2, Nova Scotia-gardens, adjoining Bishop's cottage. I went to live there on the 7th of October last. I remember the night of Thursday, the 3rd of November. On that night I went to bed about half-past nine o'clock, and about three or four hours afterwards I was awakened by a noise in Bishop's house. I got up, and heard a scuffling or struggling.

The Magistrate: Describe particularly the noise you heard.

Witness: It was like men's feet; I could swear to three men. I account for the number by first hearing a scuffling in the house; then I heard two men run away through the gate from Bishop's house, and while they were away I heard the heavy tread of one man in Bishop's house. The two men came back again almost immediately. I also heard the voices of men—I can positively speak to two voices, but cannot speak as to the third. I got up to listen but I thought it was only a family quarrel. I believe I can speak positively to the voice of Williams as being one of the men. The scuffling took place in Bishop's front parlour.

The prisoner Williams here observed that the noise witness heard was a row in consequence of Bishop breaking his (Williams's) things.

Witness: Why the row of which you speak took place on the Sunday night.

Williams: No, it was on the Thursday, and I went for the policeman, who came with me to the palings, about two o'clock in the morning, but refused to go any further.

The Magistrate: The explanation, prisoner, which you give, is that the row, as you call it, took place on Thursday night, and not on Sunday night.

Williams: It was either Thursday night or Friday night. The woman can say which night it was. Here Bishop whispered something to Williams and the latter said no more.

Thomas Wigley, of 17, Cock-lane, Smithfield, was then sworn, and stated that the night of the 4th of November he went into the taproom of the "Fortune of War." Bishop and May came into the room, and Bishop said to May, "What do you think of our new one? Didn't he go up to him well? I told you he was a staunch one. Don't you think he is a staunch one now?" Bishop then further said to May: "You stick to me and I will stick to you. I know the other is all right."

This concluded the evidence before the magistrates, and the prisoners were then asked in the usual way whether they had anything to say.

Mr. Corder said it was not intended to offer any evidence against the old man Shields.

The magistrate then told Shields that he was discharged, but that he meant to swear him as a witness, and Shields was then put in the witness-box.

The oath having been administered to him he went into a long statement as to the manner in which he first met Bishop.

The statement was different from the one he made before the coroner, and he concluded by saying he did not know what the hamper contained.

Mr. Burnaby, the clerk: You know, Shields, that you have frequently carried bodies to the hospital for dissection. You should remember you are on your oath now.

The magistrate said it was quite evident that the man could not be believed on his oath.

There was a general conviction that the witness was endeavouring to baffle the ends of justice by keeping back all he knew, and the magistrate then ordered his rearrest, as there might be a charge of another description against him.

Bishop, in reply to the usual questions as to whether he had anything to say, said "Nothing."

Williams: I have nothing to say.

May: I have nothing more to say than that this man, Bishop, can clear me of everything if he likes to speak the truth. He knows I am innocent of the charge. The man says he got the body from the ground, but he doesn't like to say where because of injuring the watchmen who were left to guard it. Things, however, are come to such a crisis now that he ought to speak the truth, and I wish him to speak the truth, for I defy him to say anything to implicate me. I knew nothing of the body till I went to take it from Bishop's house.

The witness then looked Bishop full in the face.

Bishop, in a low tone said, "I have nothing to say against you. You knew nothing of it till then."

May: I did not—that is the truth.

The Magistrate: Prisoners, you will all be committed to Newgate to take your trial at the ensuing sessions of the Old Bailey, commencing on the 1st of December next, for the wilful murder of Carlo Ferrari; and there will be another count in the indictment charging you with the wilful murder of a person unknown.

The prisoners were then removed to Newgate, strongly guarded.

When Calcraft had finished reading the account of the magisterial examination of the prisoners he called my attention to the fact that many crimes were allowed to go unpunished because there was no public prosecutor, and the expenses of a prosecution frequently fell upon the parties commencing it.

APATHY OF THE HOME-OFFICE OFFICIALS.

Just listen to this, said Calcraft.

At the close of the magisterial inquiry Mr. Corder, addressing the magistrate, said that he had done all he could to assist the prosecution, and on the part of the parish which he represented, he should of course proceed. He was, however, instructed to say that the expenses of prosecuting this case fell rather hard upon the parish, inasmuch as the body was not found in it; neither had the boy come by his death in the parish. He was aware that it was necessary that the body should have been removed for safe custody to the station-house, and, therefore, that so far the thing was unavoidable. The parish, however, was not in a very prosperous state, and he was fearful, from an interview that he had had with a member of the Government at the Home Office, that no pecuniary assistance was to be looked for from that quarter.

So you see by this (said Calcraft) that murder might be committed wholesale, and the Treasury would not do anything to prosecute in the matter.

In fact there are many cases of dreadful murder they know of, but they don't do much towards bringing some of them to light. Look at the numbers of mysterious cases that have taken place in which the murderers have never been brought to justice.

Why, many of them entirely escape for that one reason—that one stereotyped phrase, because there's not much assistance to be hoped for from the Home Office.

They won't spend much money in getting up facts, but there's lots of it goes into some of the lawyers pockets for doing little or nothing.

After the prisoners had been removed from the bar, the wives of Bishop and Williams were brought up and discharged.

When the prisoners were removed in the van from Bow-street to Newgate, they were followed by some hundreds of people, hooting and yelling, and had it not been for a strong body of police, it was feared that they would have been dragged from the van by the mob, and lynched there and then.

The old man Shields, who carried the hamper, was also discharged.

SUPPOSED MURDER OF A WOMAN.

It will be remembered that Superintendent Thomas stated that at the back of the house adjoining Bishop's house he had found the entire dress of a woman. The clothes had since been identified as having belonged to a poor woman named Frances Pigburne, who had suddenly disappeared about six weeks previously.

Michael Shields, the porter who was discharged, now came back to the police-station, and told Superintendent Thomas he wished to make a statement. He said he was now anxious to do all in his power to further the ends of justice.

He then made a long statement, in which he admitted that early on Sunday morning, the 9th of Oct., he was employed by Bishop and Williams to carry a trunk from Bishop's house to St. Thomas's Hospital.

Bishop and Williams walked on one side of the road, while he walked on the other with the trunk on his head.

Mrs. Williams also walked by the side of him, carrying a band-box tied up in a handkerchief for the purpose of making it appear, as he thought, that she was a servant going to a place, and that the box he was carrying was hers.

As Bishop was not able to sell the body at St. Thomas's Hospital, he had to carry the trunk to Mr. Grainger's dissecting rooms.

On arriving there Bishop took a body from the trunk for Mr. Appleton's, the porter's, inspection. The body was that of a middle-aged female, it was a particularly fresh subject, and had not the appearance of a body taken from the grave.

There was no dirt upon it, and the witness observed that the hair of the corpse was dark and short, and that the subject was altogether thin and light in weight. Mrs. Williams was not present then, but remained in a public-house.

Bishop sold the body at Mr. Grainger's dissecting rooms, and Appleton paid Bishop the money, and then Bishop sent for some gin, of which they, including Appleton, all drank.

Superintendent Thomas, perceiving that the statement of Shields corresponded with the time of the disappearance of Fanny Pigburn, she having been last seen alive on the night of the 8th of October, and as Shields dated the carrying of the trunk as the morning of the 9th, and as the personal description of her age, size, and appearance, corresponded in every particular, and as the whole of her clothing was found at the back of Williams's house, he felt that the information was sufficiently important to justify him in re-arresting Mrs. Williams as an accessory after the fact in the murder of Frances Pigburn.

THE LIFE OF WILLIAM CALCRAFT, THE HANGMAN.

THE MURDER OF FANNY PIGBOURNE.

He, therefore, took her into custody, and entered the charge against her.

She was then charged before the magistrate at Bow-street. In reply to the charge she admitted that, at the request of Bishop, she had carried the bandbox, as described by Shields.

The prisoner was then remanded.

PUBLIC EXCITEMENT.

In the interval which elapsed the public alarm was increasing in every direction.

A terrible and general indignation broke out against the medical profession, as it was believed to be the secret encourager of a system by which human life was very greatly sacrificed with the most heartless indifference.

The medical profession in turn were very indignant at the imputations cast upon them, but in their defence they threw the blame on the then existing laws.

Some of them agitated for a repeal or alteration of the law, and about one of the best arguments issued at the time was one by Dr. Southwood Smith, who in one of his reported speeches, said:—

The medical profession dare not practise without a knowledge of anatomy; you cannot prescribe for a patient, you cannot undertake the management of any surgical or medical case without a direct violation of the law until you have adduced before legally-appointed authorities evidence that you have studied anatomy with such an effect as to be able to stand a searching examination.

For the same law that makes it imperative on you to study anatomy in order to acquire a legal right to practise your profession renders the possession of the means of pursuing the study illegal.

Human anatomy cannot be known without the dissection of the human body, yet the possession of a body that has been exhumed for the purpose of dissection (no body except that of the murderer being obtainable in any other mode) is penal.

So that you are to be punished for not conforming to a law which you cannot qualify yourself for obeying without breaking.

Did any civilised country ever witness such a situation as that in which the law has placed you and the public?

It has been contrived to raise the price of a dead body to such a height as absolutely and appallingly to endanger the safety of the living.

Of this danger both the public and the Legislature have been long and earnestly warned.

Several years ago, before any instance of actual perpetration of the crime had been discovered, the temptation and the consequent danger was fully brought to view in a pamphlet entitled "The Use of the Dead to the Living."

Investigation was set on foot—a Parliamentary inquiry was obtained; the medical profession performed its duty in the fullest manner, and stated without reserve all the odiousness and all the danger of exhumation.

It laid open the true character of the hardened and desperate men engaged in this employment.

It had not yet occurred to those men that it might be more easy to murder the living than disturb the dead, but the possibility of the occurrence of such a thought, and the probability of their acting upon it, was distinctly foretold.

Over and over again it was stated that the price always to be obtained for a subject—from ten to fifteen guineas was a temptation to murder not likely to be resisted, and with an earnest voice the profession implored that this risk might be no longer incurred.

The Administration was impressed; the public was excited; something was promised; a little was attempted, but nothing was done.

Then came on the Edinburgh horrors, committed by Burke and Hare; and now we are thrown into a state of intense alarm lest the same horrors should be perpetrated—and now are perpetrating—at our own doors; and knowing this it is said it behoves the teacher and the medical profession in general to be extremely cautious to examine with the utmost vigilance whether anything suspicious appeared, and if it do to investigate it to the bottom.

If, however, it is made worth while to pursue murder as a trade, it can be carried on to a prodigious extent without detection.

The only effectual remedy is the removal of the temptation—the taking away of the motive, by rendering the dead body so cheap as to be in fact without value as an article of sale; and the mode of doing this is simple.

All that is necessary is to repeal the existing law, which renders it illegal to possess a dead body for the purpose of dissection; and to enact a law rendering the possession of a body for the purpose legal.

Mr. Brodie, another authority on the subject, wrote:—

Such is the importance of anatomy that those who are engaged in the study of medicine and surgery will always endeavour to learn it as far as lies in their power to do so, but the present system of procuring them by robbing churchyards is attended with very great mischief in various ways.

Some are rendered miserable because they know that the bodies of their friends have been stolen from the grave, and carried to the dissecting room; and others, because they are apprehensive that the bodies of their friends may be served in the same way.

The men who are employed to exhume bodies are of the very worst description. They are outcasts of society, who, being pointed at as resurrection men, are unable to maintain themselves by any honest employment, and are thus driven to become thieves, housebreakers, because, when not actually employed in stealing bodies, they can do nothing better.

The commission of murder for the purpose of obtaining subjects for the anatomical schools is now found to be no imaginary evil, but the public need not be surprised that it has occurred.

It has been foreseen by medical men who had attended to these inquiries for some years, and the danger has been long ago pointed out to many members of the legislature, nor can all the activity of the police, nor all the watchfulness of the teachers of anatomy prevent it from recurring some time or the other, if there be no easier method of supplying subjects for dissection than that which is now resorted to, and if they continue in consequence to produce the enormous sum which they produce at present.

CHAPTER XXIX.
THE TRIAL OF THE PRISONERS.

THE trial of these extraordinary criminals took place on the 2nd of December, 1831, and as early as eight o'clock in the morning the court at the Old Bailey was crowded to excess in every part.

Among those on the Bench were H.R.H. the Duke of Sussex, and at ten o'clock Lord Chief Justice Tindal, Mr. Baron Vaughan, and Mr. Justice Littledale entered the court with the Lord Mayor and Sheriffs.

The prisoners, John Bishop, Thomas Williams, alias Head, and James May, were then placed at the bar, and were then indicted for the wilful murder of Carlo Ferrari, otherwise Charles Ferrier, and in another count with the wilful murder of a male person whose name was unknown.

They all severally pleaded "not guilty."

They seemed but little moved by the awful situation in which they were placed, and they encountered the inquisitive glances of the assembled crowd with a careless air.

Their appearance rather indicated low cunning than hardened ferocity.

In the countenance of Williams there was something unusually repellent, and on the Duke of Sussex taking his seat and applying his glass to his face, Williams appeared to direct his stare full upon his royal highness with all imaginable impudence, as if he were almost determined to stare him out of countenance.

Mr. Bodkin having opened the case,

Mr. Adolphus proceeded to state the leading facts of it to the jury on the part of the prosecution.

In the course of an able address he said that the murder did not appear to have been committed through any of those motives that have ordinarily occasioned the committal of such a crime in this country.

It was not to gratify revenge for a wrong done that the unfortunate victim in this case had been deprived of existence.

The minds of his murderers had not been stimulated by any passions of that description to the commission of the dreadful deed.

Neither wealth nor the other common allurements, which influenced the action of wicked men under such circumstances, had impelled them to perpetrate this crime.

Nothing but the sordid and base desire to possess themselves of a dead body, in order to sell it for dissection, had induced the prisoners at the bar to commit the crime for which they were now about to answer before a jury of their countrymen.

The learned gentleman then proceeded to detail the facts of the case as they were stated in the evidence.

The evidence which has already been given was recapitulated, and did not differ from that given before the magistrates, and which our readers have already before them.

The witnesses were cross-examined by Mr. Curwood, on behalf of the prisoners, but nothing material in their favour was elicited.

One of the chief points, however, more strongly brought out against the prisoners was, that they stated that the body they were offering for sale, on the day in question, was that of a boy about fourteen or fifteen years of age.

Various witnesses spoke positively to the fact that the prisoners used the words in reference to the age of the subject, as being that of a boy about fourteen or fifteen.

There was, however, some little discrepancy between two witnesses as to the colour of the Italian boy's coat, who was seen near to Nova Scotia-gardens.

Whilst various witnesses stated that the colour of it was blue, a Mrs. Rebecca Baylis said she could not say positively, but she was inclined to the belief that it was more of a green than blue.

John Randall, labourer, residing in Bethnal-green, sworn, spoke positively to having seen, on the evening of the 3rd of November, an Italian boy standing under the window of the "Bird Cage" public-house in Nova Scotia-gardens—a boy who had a cage with two white mice in his arms.

The cage had a box in one part and the other part went round like a squirrel cage. The boy had a brown fur cap on him like the one produced.

Edward Ward, a child six and a half years of age, was next called. He was, previously to being sworn, examined as to the nature of an oath. The child, with infantine simplicity, said that he knew it to be a very bad thing to tell a lie; that it was a great sin, and that he who would swear falsely would go to——, and be burnt up with brimstone and sulphur. He was then sworn, and stated that he lived with his father near to Nova Scotia cottages, and that a few days before Guy Fawkes-day he went to Bishop's cottage to play with Bishop's children, three in number—one a boy older than himself, a little girl, and a boy about his own age. Bishop's children then showed him a cage which went round, and contained two white mice. He never saw either a cage or white mice before with Bishop's children. On his return home he told his brother, who was much older than himself, all the circumstances.

John Ward, brother of the last witness, corroborated the latter part of his little brother's statement.

The clothes which had been dug up, and which were believed to be those belonging to the Italian boy, were then shown to the jury.

That being the case for the prosecution,

The court then informed the prisoners, if they wished to address any observations to the jury on the evidence given against them, that the present was the time.

Three written defences were then read by the officer of the court.

The prisoner Bishop in his defence stated that he was thirty-three years of age, and had followed the occupation of a carrier till within the last five years, during which he had occasionally obtained a livelihood by supplying surgeons with subjects.

He most solemnly declared that he had never disposed of any body that had not died a natural death. He had been in the habit of obtaining bodies from workhouses with their clothes on, so that he could not have any difficulty in procuring them after a natural death.

The statement then went on to describe the localities of the prisoner's residence in order to show that they admitted of great facilities of ingress and egress to all persons resident in the neighbourhood. His garden and premises were open to them and theirs to him.

With respect to the clothes found in his garden he knew nothing. As to the cap he should be able to prove that it was bought by his wife from a woman named Dodswell who resided in Hoxton Old Town. The green cape he sewed on himself.

The prisoner called upon the jury to divest their minds of all undue prejudices, and to judge his case by the evidence alone.

By so doing they would be discharging their duty, and would acquit him of the crime charged against him.

In conclusion, the prisoner Bishop declared that neither Williams nor May knew how he procured the body.

The prisoner Williams's defence stated that he had never been engaged in the calling of a resurrectionist, and that he had only by accident accompanied Bishop on the occasion of the sale of the Italian boy's body.

May, in his defence, admitted that he had for the

last six years followed the occupation of supplying the medical schools with anatomical subjects, but he disclaimed ever having anything to do with the sale of bodies which had not died a natural death.

The remainder of his defence was a recapitulation of his declaration at the coroner's inquest, to the effect that he had accidentally met with Bishop at the "Fortune of War" public-house on the Friday on which the body was taken for sale to Guy's Hospital.

Rosina Carpenter, on behalf of the prisoner May, deposed that she lived at Macbeth-court, Golden-lane, that she was acquainted with May for the previous fourteen or fifteen years; that May came to her between four and five o'clock on the afternoon of Thursday, the 3rd of November, and stayed with her till twelve o'clock the next day. On cross-examination, however, she admitted that no one saw them together on that occasion.

Mrs. Sarah Trueby was recalled, and swore that she had not seen any white mice at Bishop's house during all the time she used to call for the rents.

Bishop: What! Why don't you recollect your cat having killed some in my garden?

Witness: No—never.

Mrs. Mary Dodswell, residing at No. 26, Hoxton Old Town, said she kept a second-hand clothes shop, and knew the prisoner Bishop's wife. She sold her a boy's cap about two years ago, which was a cloth one, with a black leather peak. She never sold her any other.

CHAPTER XXX.

Two witnesses, named Mary Ann Hall and Jane Lewis, were called on behalf of the prisoner May, and whose evidence went to show that in consequence of an accident to a jackdaw some blood got upon May's clothes.

The Chief Justice then proceeded to sum up the case. In the course of a long and elaborate charge he said:—

The indictment contained two counts: the one charging the prisoners at the bar with the murder of Carlo Ferrari, an Italian boy; the other count charged them with the murder of a boy whose name was unknown.

The jury would learn from this circumstance that it was by no means necessary that the name of the murdered party should be known, and that all that they need have to decide was the fact itself.

They accordingly would first direct their attention to determining the fact whether the body which the prisoners had proffered for sale had come by a natural death or not; and next, whether if they were of opinion that the prisoners were the murderers, and to what degree they were implicated.

With respect to the first point he thought they would experience but little trouble, after the explicit evidence of the medical gentlemen who had been examined, and whose conduct it was but justice to say was an honourable rebuke to any calumnious imputations on the medical profession to which the present case may have given birth.

The jury had heard evidence which traced the Italian boy close to the premises of Bishop at twelve o'clock on the 3rd of November, on the night of which it was probable the murder was committed.

They had evidence also to show that on the night a scuffle took place in Bishop's cottage, in which Bishop's voice was discernible.

The evidence, however, to show that May was present or participated in the actual offence was by no means decisive, so that the jury would have to determine how far he was or was not a principal, or an accessory.

It might be that they would arrive at the conclusion that Bishop alone, or that Bishop and Williams were the criminals, and in such case they would find a verdict of acquittal for May, or it might be that they would find that all three were equally guilty, or that they were guilty, but not in an equal degree.

Their verdict would be according to their decision on this point, rendering it incumbent on them to cautiously weigh those parts of the evidence which bore particularly on Bishop and Williams and on the other prisoner.

He left it to their unbiassed judgment to find according to the evidence which had been submitted to them.

At eight o'clock the jury retired to consider their verdict, and the prisoners were removed from the bar and taken out of court.

After an absence of half an hour the jury returned into court at half-past eight o'clock.

The most death-like silence now prevailed through the court, interrupted only by a slight buzz on the re-introduction of the prisoners.

Every eye was now fixed upon them, but though their appearance and manner had undergone a considerable change from what they exhibited on being first placed at the bar, and during the greater part of the trial, they did not seem conscious of the additional interest that was centred in them.

They scarcely raised their eyes as they entered, beyond a glance or two on the jury-box.

Bishop advanced to the bar with a heavy step, and with rather a slight bend of the body. His arms hung closely down, and it seemed a kind of relief to him when he took his place to rest his hands on the board before him.

His appearance when he got in front was that of a man who had been for some time labouring under the most intense mental agony, which had brought on a kind of lethargic stupor.

Bishop's eyes were sunk and glassy, his nose drawn and pinched, the jaw fallen, and of course the mouth open, but occasionally the mouth closed, the lips became compressed, and the shoulders and chest raised as if he was struggling to repress some violent emotion.

After a few efforts of this kind he became apparently calm, and frequently glanced his eyes towards the bench and the jury-box, but this was done without once raising his head.

His face had that pallid blueish appearance which so often accompanies and betokens great mental sufferings.

Williams came forward with a short quick step, and his whole manner, we should say, was the reverse of that of his companion in guilt.

His face had undergone very little change, but in his eyes and his manner there was a feverish anxiety which was not observed during the trial.

When he came in front and laid his hand on the bar the rapid movements of his fingers on the board, the frequent shifting of the hand, sometimes letting it hang down for an instant by his side, then replacing it on the board and resting his side against the front of the dock showed the perturbed state of his feelings.

Once or twice he gave a glance round at the bench and the bar, but after that he seldom took his eyes from the jury-box.

May came forward with a more firm step than either of his fellow-prisoners, but his look was that of a man who thought that all chance of life was lost.

He seemed desponding, but there appeared that in his despondency which gave an air of ———; we could not call it daring or even confidence, but we should say it was a greater physical endurance which imparted to his whole manner a more firm bearing than that of the other prisoners.

He was very pale, but his eyes had not relapsed from that firmness which was observable in his glance throughout the whole of his trial.

Ordinary physiognomists who, without having seen the prisoners, had read the accounts of their horrible atrocities, would have been greatly disappointed in the appearance of all of them as they stood at the bar.

There was nothing in the aspect or manner of any of them which betokened a predisposition to anything like the outrage on humanity of which they stood convicted.

There was something of heaviness in the countenance of Bishop, but altogether his countenance was mild.

Williams had an aspect of sharpness and cunning and something of mischief, but nothing of the appearance of a villain.

May, who was the best looking of the three, had a countenance which most persons would consider open and manly.

When the three prisoners were placed at the bar the jury, on their return, said they had found all three prisoners guilty of wilful murder.

The verdict was received in court with becoming silence, but in a moment it was conveyed to the immense multitude assembled, who evinced their satisfaction at the result by continued cheering and clapping of hands.

The prisoners were then severally called upon to say why sentence of death should not be passed upon them, but none of them availed themselves of this opportunity of saying anything.

The learned judge then assumed the black cap, and, amidst the most breathless excitement in court, he said—

Prisoners at the bar,—After a very patient and diligent attention on the part of the jury, you are all found guilty of the crime of wilful murder. With that verdict I fully concur, for it has been supported by the most conclusive evidence.

Bishop : By false evidence, my lord.

The Judge: I will not encroach by any lengthy remarks on the very short time that will elapse between now and the time you will have to appear in the presence of your Creator.

A month has now elapsed since you were first committed for this crime, and I hope that that time has been spent in looking back on your past lives, on the horrible agony which you have inflicted on some of your fellow-creatures, and on the dreadful outrage on human nature of which you are now convicted.

I hope that the few hours you have now to live will be spent in prayers to the Almighty for pardon. It now only remains for me to pass upon you the last dread sentence of the law, and that is that you be taken from hence to the place from which you came, and that from there on Monday morning next you be brought to the front of this gaol, and there be hanged by the neck till you are dead, and that your bodies be then delivered over for dissection and anatomization, and may the Lord have mercy on your souls!

The prisoners heard their sentence as they had heard the verdict, without any visible impression. When ordered to be removed May raised his voice, and in a firm tone said—

"I am a murdered man, gentlemen, and that man (pointing to Bishop) knows it, and could clear me if he chose."

Williams : "We are all murdered men, gentlemen."

Then turning to the Paragallis, and other witnesses who had identified the deceased's body as being that of the Italian boy, he said, "and before three months you will suffer for the false evidence you have given against us."

Bishop made no observation, but retired from the bar, apparently more absorbed by his awful situation than he had appeared before.

CHAPTER XXXI.
THE PRISONERS IN THE CONDEMNED CELLS.

WHEN the prisoners were put into the condemned cells—those cells which have been the last habitation on earth, from which so many hundreds of criminals have gone to that last stage in their mortal existence—the gallows—the shadow of desponding gloom seemed to settle over them.

Watchers were with them night and day, and the last hours glided uneasily but rapidly by.

A kind of feverish excitement stole over them in the day-time, and at night their hours of sleep were broken by fitful starts.

Sometimes they would open their eyes, and look round the blank walls of the dismal cell; till at last they, having assured themselves they could see nothing but the gaoler's eyes upon them, turned round to sleep again.

On Saturday night the gaoler who was placed over Williams saw him grow anxious and uneasy—towards midnight his agitation increased, which greatly attracted the attention of his keeper.

Williams observed it, and said, " Don't be frightened, sir ; I am not going to do anything wrong, but I wish to ease my mind. Let me see the governor."

Mr. Wontner was then called from his bed, and the Rev. Mr. Cotton, the ordinary, was also in attendance in a few minutes.

When these gentlemen came into the cell, Williams, looking at them steadfastly for a moment or two, burst into tears, and said, " Gentlemen, I wish to unburthen my mind. I know I am guilty, and I ought to suffer the utmost punishment of the law. I am a murderer—I confess it ; but the witnesses were all mistaken as to its being the Italian boy."

He was then urged to relieve his mind as calmly and as coolly as possible, and after some effort during which the mental agony which he endured was dreadful, he made a statement of which the following is the substance.

On Thursday the 3rd of November he was in the neighbourhood of Smithfield when he saw a boy whom he had often observed before assisting in driving cattle to the market.

This boy was about fourteen or fifteen years of age, and exactly corresponded with the description of the Italian boy.

He enticed him from the cattle and took him to the "Fortune of War" public-house, and sent for Bishop, who was waiting at another public-house in the neighbourhood for the purpose of receiving communications from him (Williams) as to anything he might do.

Bishop came and they took the boy away to Nova Scotia-gardens, giving him some soup and potatoes by the way.

When they got him there they set him to play with Bishop's children until near dusk when they gave him some rum and he became stupefied.

They (Bishop and Williams) then took him into the garden and on the way threw him down, and pushing his head into the water barrel, as already described, held him until he was suffocated.

They then conveyed the body back to the house, kept it snug till the next day, when May was applied to to assist in disposing of it.

May had nothing to do with the murder of that boy. Here the statement concluded.

Williams seemed greatly relieved after making this confession, and went to bed and slept soundly.

CHAPTER XXXII.
BISHOP'S STATEMENT TO A WESLEYAN MINISTER.

AFTER the trial of the prisoner a great deal of doubt was created in the public mind as to whether the body sworn to was really that of the Italian boy or not.

The prisoners Bishop and Williams asserted that it was not. A great discussion was then created as to the value to be set upon their statements, and the most intense interest was awakened as to which was the most credible—the evidence given at the trial, or the solemn assertions of the convicted men.

On one side it was argued that if it was not the body of the Italian boy then the men were condemned for a murder that had perhaps not taken place, and which certainly they had not committed.

On the other side it was maintained that the weight of the evidence was in support of the case that the body was that of the Italian boy; that he had undoubtedly been murdered, and that the prisoners were properly convicted, and ought to be executed.

In a paragraph which appeared in the *Times* newspaper there is great complaint made of what was considered an improper withholding of reliable official information to the public, in the officials refusing to give the necessary information to the reporters of the press.

It will be seen from the following copies of documents that conflicting statements were made, and thus the public were left in that uncertainty and doubt which probably would not have occurred had the reporters been given all the necessary information without reserve.

It was stated that more than one statement was made, and when the reporters asked for explanations on this point, there seems to have been in this case, as in many others, an attempt made by officials in authority to baffle public judgment.

There is no doubt that cases of apparent injustice have occurred through this frequent course of official arrogance and assumption.

Public officials, whether high or low, are the servants and not the masters of the public.

They are paid from the purse of the public, and to the public they ought to be amenable.

As a rule many of them are subservient till they get into authority, and then when they have filled their own purse at the nation's expense, the authority they arrogate is almost intolerable.

In these days of national enlightenment and national advancement the sooner a public check is placed on high-handed officialism wherever found, the better it will be for the general welfare of the State.

The conflicting statements seem to have been made under the following circumstances, and our readers must endeavour to solve the problem for themselves.

One of Bishop's statements was made to the Rev. Mr. Williams, a Wesleyan minister, who, according to the privilege of those times, was permitted to pray with him.

According to some accounts, Mr. Williams endeavoured to work upon the prisoner's fears by holding out to him little or no hope of mercy in a future state unless he was thoroughly truthful and repentant before death.

Two other ministers were also in the cells with the other prisoners, talking to them upon doctrinal points, and there seemed to be some jealousy in the mind of the regular Ordinary on account of the interference of other ministers with the prisoners.

In the course of his interview with the Wesleyan minister, Bishop observed that as he had no hopes of mercy here, he did not wish an innocent man to suffer for his crimes, and he declared that May was not concerned in the murder of which he had been convicted.

He said he was ready to make a confession of the murders in which he had participated.

According to the Wesleyan minister's statement, Bishop then admitted that he had been concerned in the commission of three murders—namely, that of the Italian boy, the murder of Frances Pigburne, and of a drover—a boy who had come to London with cattle from Lincolnshire, which boy the witnesses on the trial had sworn was the Italian boy, to the best of their belief, though he had disposed of that body before.

Bishop then entered into a minute description, most horrible in its details, of the mode by which he had perpetrated the inhuman murders.

CHAPTER XXXIII.
BISHOP'S CONTRADICTORY STATEMENT TO THE UNDER-SHERIFFS.

WE now come to a very contradictory statement made by Bishop to the under-sheriffs. Our readers must judge of their respective veracity, and the relative value of each.

Newgate, December 4, 1831.

I, John Bishop, do hereby declare and confess that the boy supposed to be the Italian boy was a Lincolnshire boy.

I and Williams took him to my house on the Thursday night, the 3rd of November, at half-past ten o'clock from the "Bell Inn," Smithfield. He walked home with us. Williams promised to give him some work.

We got to our house in Nova Scotia-gardens about eleven o'clock. My wife and children and Mrs. Williams had not gone to bed, so Williams went in to the house and sent them to bed while I and the boy stopped in the garden.

We then took him for a little walk about ten minutes while the family went to bed, and then when all was quiet we took the boy into the house.

We then lighted a candle, and gave him some bread and cheese; and after he had eaten it we gave him a cupful of rum, with some laudanum in it.

The boy drank it in two draughts, and then afterwards a little beer.

In about ten minutes he fell asleep on the chair on which he sat, and I removed him from the chair to the floor, and laid him on his side.

We then went out and left him there while we had a quartern of gin and a pint of beer at the "Feathers," near Shoreditch Church.

On our return in twenty minutes we found him asleep as we had left him.

We then took him into the garden, tied a cord to his feet, to enable us to pull him up by, and I then took him in my arms and let him slide from them headlong into the well in the garden, whilst Williams held the cord to prevent the body going altogether too low in the well.

He was nearly wholly in the water of the well, his feet just above the surface.

Williams fastened the other end of the cord round

the palings, to prevent the body getting beyond our reach.

The boy struggled with his arms and legs in the water, and the water bubbled for a minute. We waited till these symptons were past, and then went indoors, and afterwards, I think, we went out, and walked down Shoreditch to occupy the time.

Then in about three-quarters of an hour we returned and took him out of the well by pulling him by the cord attached to his feet.

We undressed him in the paved yard, rolled his clothes up and buried them, where they were found by the witness who produced them.

We carried the boy into the wash-house, laid him on the floor, and covered him over with a bag.

We left him there, and went and had some coffee in the Old-street-road, and then, a little before two o'clock on the morning of Friday, went back to my house.

We immediately doubled the body up and put it into a box, which we corded so that no one might open it to see what was in it, and then we went out again and had some more coffee at the same place in the Old-street-road, where we stayed a little while, and then went home to bed, both in the same house, and to our own beds as usual.

We slept till about ten o'clock on Friday morning; took breakfast together with the family, and then both of us went to Smithfield to the "Fortune of War," where we met May.

The witness then described at length how they got into conversation with May, and the various places they went to to try and sell the body, till at last they took it to King's College Hospital, as shown in the evidence. He then stated the manner of their arrest, when they were taken into custody, and signed his name to the document containing his confession.

JOHN BISHOP.

Witness, ROBERT ELLIS, Under-Sheriff.

BISHOP'S SECOND CONFESSION OF OTHER MURDERS.

I declare that this statement is all true, and contains all the facts as far as I can recollect.

May knew nothing of the murder, and I do not believe he suspected that I had got the body, except in the usual way, and after the death of it.

I always told him that I got it from the ground, and he never knew to the contrary, until I confessed it to Mr. Williams, since this trial.

I have known May as a body-snatcher four or five years, but I do not believe he ever obtained a body except in the common course of men in that calling, by stealing from the graves.

I also confess that I and Williams were concerned in the murder of a female, whom I believe to have been since discovered to be Fanny Pigburn, on or about the 9th of October last.

I and Williams saw her sitting, about eleven or twelve o'clock at night, on the step of a door in Shoreditch, near the church. She had a child four or five years old with her, upon her lap.

I asked why she was sitting there. She said she had no home to go to, for her landlord had turned her out into the street. I told her that she might go with us and sit by the fire all night. She said she would go with us.

She walked with us to my house in Nova Scotia-gardens, carrying her child with her.

When we got there we found the family in bed, and we took the woman in and lighted the fire, by which we all sat down together.

I went out for beer, and we all partook of beer and rum. I brought the rum from Smithfield in my pocket.

The woman and the child lay down on some dirty linen on the floor, and I and Williams went to bed.

About six o'clock next morning I and Williams told her to go away, and meet us at the "London Apprentice" in the Old Street-road.

She met us again at the "London Apprentice," without her child, at one o'clock. We gave her some halfpence and beer, and desired her to meet us again at ten o'clock at night.

After this we bought rum and laudanum, and at ten o'clock we met the woman again at the "London Apprentice." She had no child with her.

We drank three pints of beer between us and stayed about an hour. We should have stayed there longer, but an old man came in whom the woman said she knew, and she said she did not like him to see her there with anybody.

We therefore all went out. It rained hard, and we took shelter under a doorway in the Hackney-road for about half an hour.

Then we walked to Nova Scotia-gardens, and Williams and I led her into No. 2, an empty house.

We had no light. Williams stepped out into the garden with the rum and laudanum, which I had handed to him.

He then mixed them together in a half-pint bottle, and came into the house to me and the woman, and gave her the bottle to drink from. She drank the whole at two or three draughts.

There was a quartern of rum and about half a phial of laudanum.

She sat down on a step between two rooms in the house, and went off to sleep in about ten minutes. She was falling back; I caught her, to save her fall, and she lay with her back on the floor. Then Williams and I went to a public-house, got something to drink, and in about half an hour we came back to the woman.

We took her cloak off, tied a cord round her feet, carried her to the well in the garden, and thrust her into it headlong. She struggled very little afterwards, and the water bubbled very little at the top.

We fastened the cord to the palings to prevent her going down beyond our reach, and left her, and took a walk to Shoreditch; came back in about half an hour. We left the woman in the well for that length of time that the rum and laudanum might run out of the body at the mouth.

On our return we took her out of the well, cut her clothes off; hid them away at the back; carried the body into the washhouse of my own house, where we doubled it up, and put it into a hair-box, which we corded, and then left it there.

We did not go to bed, but went to Shields' house in Eagle-street, Red Lion-square, and called him up; this was between four and five o'clock in the morning.

We then got him to go to my house, where we stayed a little while to await the change of police. I then told Shields that he was to carry that trunk to St. Thomas's Hospital.

He asked me if there was a woman in the house that could walk alongside of him, so that people might not take any notice.

Williams called his wife up, and asked her to walk with Shields, and to carry the hat-box which he gave her to carry.

We then put the box with the body in it on Shields' head, and went to the hospital.

As Mr. South at St. Thomas's Hospital could not look at it till the next day, I went and sold it to Mr.

Appleton, at Mr. Grainger's dissecting rooms, for eight guineas.

Mr. Appleton gave me £5 then on account, and the remainder of the eight guineas on the following Monday.

I never saw the woman's child after the first day before mentioned.

She said that she had taken the child and left it with the person she had taken some of the things to, before the landlord took her goods.

The woman we murdered did not tell us her name; she said her age was thirty-five, and, I think, she said that her husband before he died was a cabinet-maker.

She was thin, and rather tall. I also confess the murder of a boy, who told us his name was Cunningham. It was a fortnight after the murder of the woman.

I and Williams found him sleeping about eleven or twelve o'clock at night, on Friday, the 21st of October, as I think, under the pig-boards in the pig-market, at Smithfield.

Williams woke him, and asked him to come along with him; and the boy then walked with Williams and me to my house in Nova Scotia-gardens.

We took him to my house and gave him some warm beer sweetened with sugar, with rum and laudanum in it.

He drank two or three cupfuls, and then fell asleep in a little chair belonging to one of my children.

We laid him on the floor, and went out for a little while and got something to drink, and then returned, carried the boy to the well, and threw him into it, in the same way as we had served the other boy and woman.

He died instantly in the well, and we left him there a little while, to give time for the mixtures we had given him to run out of the body. We then took the body from the well, took off the clothes in the garden, and buried them there.

The body was carried into the washhouse, and put into the same box, and left there till next evening, when we got a porter to carry it with us to St. Bartholomew's Hospital, where I sold it to Mr. Smith for eight guineas.

This boy, who was about ten or eleven years old, said his mother lived in Kent-street, and that he had not been at home for a twelvemonth and better.

I solemnly declare that these are all the murders in which I have been concerned, or that I know anything of; that I and Williams were alone concerned in these, and that no other person whatever knew anything about either of them, and that I do not know whether there are others who practise the same mode of obtaining bodies for sale.

I know nothing of any Italian boy, and was never concerned in or knew of the murder of such a boy. There have been no white mice about my house for the last six months.

My son, about eight months ago, bought two white mice, and I made him a cage for them. It was flat, with wires at the top.

They lived about two months, and were killed, I think, by a cat in the garden, where they got out of the cage.

Until the transactions before set forth, I never was concerned in obtaining a subject by the destruction of the living.

I have followed the course of obtaining a livelihood as a body-snatcher for twelve years, and have obtained and sold, I think, from five hundred to one thousand bodies; but I declare, before God, that they were all obtained after death, and that, with the above exceptions, I am ignorant of any murder for that or any other purpose. JOHN BISHOP.

Witness, ROBERT ELLIS, Under-Sheriff.

These statements appear to have been very unwisely allowed to be made in the presence of the prisoner Williams, alias Head, and thus all chance of getting an independent confession from both men entirely frustrated.

Under these circumstances it is not at all surprising that the conduct of the authorities has left the whole matter still in great doubt.

The following was therefore just the short statement purporting to be the confession of Williams, alias Head:—

Newgate.

I, Thomas Head, alias Williams, now under sentence of death in Newgate, do solemnly confess and declare the foregoing statement and confession of John Bishop, which has been made in my presence, and since read over to me distinctly, is altogether true, so far as the same relate to me.

I declare that I was never concerned in, or privy to, any other transaction of the like nature; that I never knew anything of the murder of any other person whatever; that I was never a body-snatcher, or concerned in the sale of any other body than the three murdered by Bishop and myself; that May was a stranger to me, and I had never seen him more than once or twice before Friday, November 4th last, and that May was wholly innocent, and ignorant of any of those murders in which I was concerned, and for one of which I am about to suffer death.

Witness, R. ELLIS, Newgate, December 4th, 1831.

The above confessions taken literally from the prisoner in our presence.

T. WOOD, }
R. ELLIS, } Under-Sheriffs.

It seems a very curious anomaly of the English law that so much trouble taken is to close the mouths of prisoners, and prevent them from saying anything at all in the course of their trial.

There is no doubt that frequently the ends of justice are by these means defeated by the practice of the law itself, whereas as a rule prisoners would frequently, by their own bungling attempts to blind and baffle inquiry, not only fail to do so, but would themselves throw the light on the real facts of the case.

In proof of this we may state one case among others —namely, that of the Stauntons, who actually convicted themselves out of their own mouths by the untruthful statements they made and swore to before the coroner, which ultimately greatly led to their own condemnation.

Many cases might be cited, but in the case of Bishop and Williams it will be seen they eventually denied the murder of the Italian boy and all knowledge of him—though his fur cap, his clothes, his cage that had contained his white mice, and other corroborative circumstances were spoken to.

The real probability is, that the Italian boy was murdered, and that the pretended sincere confession of Bishop was only made in order to try and escape from the capital sentence.

The object most likely to be aimed at was a respite from the execution of the capital sentence, combined with the hope that it would afterwards be commuted to transportation.

The confession of Bishop made a very great impression on the public mind, and also on the minds of some of the ministers engaged.

THE LIFE OF WILLIAM CALCRAFT, THE HANGMAN.

THE FIRST MURDER OF A LONDON POLICEMAN.

One of the effects of it was, that there was an immediate movement to get a commutation, at least, of the sentence of May, and for this purpose the Rev. Mr. Williams and Mr. Wontner, the governor of the gaol, waited upon Mr. Justice Tindal at his residence, and they also waited upon Mr. Justice Littledale and Baron Vaughan, who undertook to see the Home Secretary on the subject.

The sheriffs, under-sheriffs, and other officials, however, were decidedly opposed to any mitigation of the sentence on May, or to the slightest delay in the execution of the law.

In this conflict of opinion the sheriffs and under-sheriffs were asked to have another interview with the prisoners, the result of which was that they too changed their former opinion, and ultimately declared themselves in favour of a commutation of May's sentence.

The result of all these investigations was that on Sunday afternoon, at half-past four o'clock, a respite, during his Majesty's pleasure, arrived at Newgate for May, and his sentence was commuted to transportation for life.

STRANGE EFFECT OF THE RESPITE UPON MAY.

Shortly after the arrival of the respite at Newgate, Dr. Cotton, and Mr. Wontner went to the room in which the three prisoners were confined.

The reverend gentleman opened the paper, and began to read it aloud.

The most anxious attention was paid to its contents by all the prisoners; but the interest manifested by May was quite painful to witness.

His agitation was dreadful; but no sooner had Dr. Cotton repeated the words, "that the execution of the sentence upon John May shall be respited during his Majesty's pleasure," than he fell to the earth as though struck by lightning.

His arms worked with violence, and his face assumed the most convulsive contortions, and four of the officers of the prison only could hold him with difficulty.

His countenance assumed a livid paleness, the blood forsook his lips, his eyes appeared set, and pulsation at the heart could not be distinguished.

All persons present thought that he could not possibly survive. It was, indeed, believed that the warrant for mercy would prove his death-blow.

At last, when recollection returned, he attempted to clasp his hands in the attitude of thanksgiving, but his limbs shook so violently that he found even that was impossible.

His lips moved, but nothing but inarticulate sounds came from his tongue.

When restored to something like composure he poured forth his gratitude for the pardon extended to him.

Meantime Bishop and Williams looked upon this awful scene with an indifference amounting to the utmost unconcern, though it was generally remarked that the fearful contortions of May's face must have brought to their minds the recollections of some of the struggles of their murdered victims.

STRANGE ALLEGATIONS.

In reference to the truth of Bishop's confession a great variety of opinion existed, and the doubt was greatly increased by the strange allegations made by the Rev. Mr. Williams as to further confessions having been commenced to him.

It appears that whilst the culprit Williams was making a further confession to the Wesleyan minister, the Rev. Mr. Williams, of Hendon, the ordinary of the gaol, the Rev. Mr. Cotton, stepped in, and put an end to all further disclosures, by calling out to Mr. Williams, "Come—come, Mr. Williams, what is all this about? I suppose you want to extract a confession from the criminal with a view to get them for publication. Let me converse with the criminals."

Upon this interruption the Rev. Mr. Williams then left the criminal, and went to another part of the room.

The Rev. Mr. Williams considered he was very improperly interfered with, and stated that the other culprit, Bishop, during his interview with him (the Rev. Mr. Williams), had confessed to the commission of three murders, and he was proceeding to detail the particulars of a fourth, in which a black man, a negro, was the victim, and he was proceeding to give the name of other parties who were implicated with him, when he was stopped, as before mentioned, by the ordinary, and Bishop would not again resume his narrative.

THE DAY BEFORE THE EXECUTION.

The conduct of both Bishop and Williams, throughout the whole of Sunday and Sunday night, was one of recklessness, varied at times with hardened indifference.

They were conversed with by several ministers up till a late hour.

The culprits then retired to rest, and both of them slept during the night, but awoke at intervals, and conversed with the officers of the gaol appointed to watch over them.

When one of the warders began to talk to Williams of the time approaching, Williams told him that it was not till his wedding night that he had any idea as to the mode in which Bishop got his living.

His wife, as soon as they were married, begged him not to have anything to do with the snatchers.

This led him to ask his wife what she meant, and at last she told him fully how Bishop got his living.

It afterwards happened that Williams was thrown out of work, and Bishop then informed him how he got a living, and asked him to go in partnership with him.

He (Williams) then assented, and became a regular resurrection man.

Williams then stated (according to this information) that he grew tired of the difficulties and dangers of the trade of stealing bodies, and he then proposed to Bishop that instead of being at the trouble of disinterring them they should murder subjects.

Williams was then asked what made him think of such an idea? and he replied that it came into his head through reading of what Burke and Hare used to do in Edinburgh.

After some other facts tallying with those in Bishop's account, he stated that on the Sunday after the murder of the woman Pigburn, they attempted to burke a man whom they actually allured into their power.

The laudanum, however, which they had mixed with his liquor was not strong enough, as Bishop said, to stupefy him, and he was therefore allowed to escape, partly from a fear of his struggles, and partly from Bishop's arm becoming quite palsied by a feeling that the man he was about to despatch resembled *his* father as he slept.

On the following Tuesday, however—still bent on their murderous trade—they endeavoured to get another subject by the same means, but the laudanum again did not act, and the victim in this case was allowed to escape through a fear coming over them.

THE MORNING OF EXECUTION.

During Sunday afternoon crowds began to assemble round the front of Newgate.

Nearly all the houses opposite had bills in their windows—"Seats to Let." The usual price asked was one guinea per seat, but in some instances the whole window was let for ten guineas.

During Sunday every window along the whole street was let, and in many instances the persons took up their abode in the houses over night.

On Sunday evening the crowd was immense, and it was evident many intended to take up their position on the over night.

The crowds became so enormous, that, though a number of barriers had been set up on the Saturday, many others were put up on the Sunday and Monday morning.

In addition to the usual force of the city police, a large number of special constables were sworn in, and a number of officers of the various wards were ordered to attend.

Shortly after midnight the gallows was wheeled round from the yard amidst cheers of the assembled crowd.

The workmen then proceeded to erect it in its usual place opposite the debtors' door of Newgate. A large space around it was barricaded to keep off the crowd, and the inside of the space was subsequently nearly filled by constables and marshalmen.

The work of putting the gallows together several times awoke the culprits, who frequently during the night opened their eyes, and looked round their cell, and then turning round they endeavoured to fall to sleep again.

By five o'clock in the morning nearly two-thirds of the Old Bailey was filled with a dense mass of people.

The buzz of the surging multitude, the glare of light from the torches that were used for the purpose of enabling the workmen to proceed with their labours, and the terrific struggles among the crowd, presented a scene never to be forgotten by those who witnessed it.

When the fatal drop was stationed in its usual place, it was observed that three chains were suspended from it.

As soon as Mr. Wontner heard of this mistake, he ordered one of them to be removed, and though it was then dark, a shout was raised: "May is respited—one of the chains is taken down!"

The announcement did not seem to create much surprise, although some expressed their disapprobation by yelling and hooting.

So great was the concourse round the barriers adjacent to the gallows that when the last contingent of 200 police came up to be stationed there, they could not make their way through the crowd, and they had to be taken through the gate, and let out at the debtors' door.

INSIDE THE PRESS-ROOM.

At half-past seven o'clock, the sheriffs, under sheriffs, and several gentlemen, to whom they had given permission to be present, entered the prison.

The sheriffs immediately proceeded to the condemned cells, where they found Mr. Wontner with the convicts.

The sheriffs then formally demanded the men for execution, and the governor then immediately gave Bishop and Williams up to them.

The two culprits now shook hands with the warders, who had been sitting and watching over them during the night, and then they obeyed the request of the sheriffs, and followed them to the press-room.

Calcraft was here in waiting in readiness to receive them, and without any further ceremony he at once approached Bishop with the straps, for the purpose of pinioning him.

When he first came into the press-room there was a kind of melancholy settled stupor plainly depicted upon his face.

He advanced into the room in rather a drooping manner, with his eyes looking upon the ground.

His step was slow and uniform, and his whole bearing was that of a man partly unconscious through excessive terror.

When he got half way into the long room he looked round, and then gave a half-suppressed sigh, and then he relapsed into his former stupor.

He moved, as it were, mechanically up to Calcraft, whom he seemed to recognise, and who stood ready to tie his hands.

When his two hands were firmly tied together, then he turned round for Calcraft to pinion his arms, and when that was done he took his seat at a side bench without uttering a single word.

His eye was now sunk and heavy, and seemed to shrink from the gaze of those around him.

One of the under-sheriffs took a seat by his side, and in a low tone said to him—

Bishop, you have now not many more minutes to live. Have you anything more to say, or to confess?

Bishop: No, sir. I have told all.

The Under-sheriff: If you have anything now more on your conscience speak in time, before it is too late.

Bishop: No, sir. I have nothing at all more to say.

Williams was next brought into the press-room, accompanied by two warders.

He came in with a short hasty step. His whole frame seemed to have undergone a terrible alteration.

The cunning flippant sinister look which he had during the whole of his examination had entirely left him, and his eyes seemed fixed with a wild frenzied vacant stare of horror.

The natural hue of the countenances of both men had also left them, and they seemed tallowy and ghastly pale, as though the very shadow of death was already literally upon them.

When Williams got to about the middle of the press-room he appeared to be suddenly seized with downright horror.

His hair fairly stood on end as Calcraft approached him, and as he stood before him Williams's mouth opened; his features were drawn up with the shock of horror, and then with his eyes partly standing out of his head, he looked aghast at Calcraft.

As soon, however, as Calcraft put his hand upon him his whole frame shook and trembled, so that Calcraft found it inconvenient to tie his hands alone, for Williams shook so he could not hold them steady.

Calcraft then called to some of the officers to come and assist him by holding up Williams's hands, while he bound his wrists together.

As soon as this was done Calcraft then began to pinion his arms, and while he was doing it Williams kept exclaiming—

Oh, I have deserved all this and more. Oh, I have deserved all I am about to suffer.

One of the under-sheriffs now said to him, "Williams, have you anything more to say, or have you any further disclosure to make?"

Williams: Oh, no, sir; I have told all. I hope I am now at peace with God. What I have told is the truth.

Neither Bishop nor Williams took any notice of each other in the press-room; in fact, so absorbed did each appear that neither appeared conscious of the presence of the other.

It was now within a few minutes of eight o'clock,

and the sheriffs told the convicts it was time for them to go up to the scaffold.

The procession was formed, and the sheriffs, accompanied by their officers, now left the press-room, and proceeded along the narrow corridor, with the ordinary preceding them in front, reading the selected portions of the burial service.

Both culprits came along in the same gloomy manner, with their hands firmly tied, and their arms pinioned.

THE EXECUTION.

It was now within a moment or so of eight o'clock, and considerable surprise was manifested among the crowd that the usual funeral bell had not yet begun to toll.

For some reason or another it seems that it had been decided that no bell should be tolled.

It appeared as though the omission was purposely made to mark the universal contempt and abhorrence with which these two vile miscreant wretches were to be sent out of the world.

When the executioner appeared in sight a loud cheer was raised.

Bishop appeared on the platform, and then one long loud yell was raised, followed by the most fearful hissing and other signs of dreadful execration.

Calcraft at once placed the rope round Bishop's neck, and at the same moment the governor and the ordinary appeared on the scene.

A little time elapsed before Williams came up, and there was some considerable speculation as to what caused the delay.

It appears, from what was afterwards made known, that on arriving at the foot of the gallows, Williams was again suddenly seized with agitation and trembling, and he begged to be allowed once more to speak to the Rev. Dr. Russell, who was accompanying him.

His request was granted, and Mr. Russell at once came forward and seated himself near to Williams.

Williams said something to him in under-tone, which was not distinctly heard, and Mr. Russell then said to him:—Now, Williams, you have but another moment intervening between you and death, and, as a dying man, I implore you to tell the truth. Have you told me the whole truth?

Williams: All I have told you is true.

Mr. Russell: "But Williams, have you told me all?"

Williams (still evasive): All I have told you is quite true.

This was the last remark he made, and in a few moments he ascended to the gallows.

His appearance on the drop was now the cause of another horrible burst of indignation from the assembled crowd, and he was also greeted with the most fearful yells.

Meanwhile Bishop had stood quite firm, unmoved, with the halter round his neck.

Calcraft then put the halter round Williams's neck, whilst the two clergymen, the governor, sheriffs, and warders stood around the drop.

During this time it was fearful to witness and hear the surging and roaring of the crowd.

So great was the feeling of disgust and indignation felt towards the two heartless wretches now on the gallows with the two halters round their necks, that the sheriffs, officials, and even the hangman departed from the usual custom of shaking hands with the criminals, and wishing them farewell.

They seemed destined to go out of the world without the slightest mark of sympathy or compassion from the crowd.

The white caps were now drawn over their faces by Calcraft, and the ordinary now having come to the fatal words in the burial service—

"In the midst of life we are in death. Of whom may we seek for succour but of Thee, O Lord, who for our sins art justly displeased?"

Calcraft stepped down behind the gallows, and drawing the bolt the drop fell, and the bodies of these two diabolical murderers writhed and wriggled in the air before the eyes of the vast and exulting crowd.

Bishop soon died, but Williams struggled and vibrated for several minutes.

Just at this moment the surging and struggling of the people was most appalling.

FEARFUL ACCIDENTS.

Shrieks of people being trampled upon, and of others being robbed in the crowd, came from all directions.

Notwithstanding the many precautions taken by the City authorities to prevent accidents some very serious ones occurred.

At the end of Giltspur-street, nearly opposite the old Compter, a large heavy barrier gave way with the pressure of the crowd, and a large number of persons were at once forced down on the ground, with the barrier falling upon them.

The screams and shrieks of the injured were dreadful.

Among those who were under the barrier was a City policeman. A cry of "Stand back, stand back!" was raised, but the surging crowd came trampling on, impelled by those from behind.

The sufferers were at length extricated and carried to St. Bartholomew's Hospital, and before nine o'clock every bed in the Colston ward was filled with the injured.

CUTTING DOWN THE BODIES.

After the bodies had been suspended the usual time, Calcraft again appeared on the gallows—precisely at nine o'clock—and the bodies of the miscreants were cut down in the sight of the vast and lingering crowd.

After the concourse had been partly dispersed a cart drove up to the platform, and the bodies of the two culprits were placed in it, covered with sacks.

The cart then moved off at a slow pace, followed by the sheriffs and City Marshal, and a large body of constables, to the house of Mr. Stone, No. 33, Hosier-lane, Smithfield, followed by many of the crowd, hooting and yelling.

On reaching Mr. Stone's house, it was with difficulty the bodies could be removed from the cart, the crowd appearing anxious to get possession of the bodies.

At the house of Mr. Stone, the bodies were placed upon a table, and in the presence of the sheriffs (in conformity with the law) an incision was made in their chests, preparatory to dissection, and the sheriffs then withdrew.

STARTLING STATEMENT.

After the execution of the culprits, Sir. J. Sewell, one of the magistrates, wrote a letter to the *Times* newspaper, in which he said:

"Sir,—Having dined yesterday with some of my brother magistrates, I learned, upon information which I have no reason to distrust, that besides the confessions published, another was made on Sunday, the 4th, which comprehended a catalogue of about sixty murders, and would probably have gone on to a much greater extent, but for the interference of the ordinary. When to this is added the large supply which, by the public confessions of Bishop, appears to have been furnished for dissection, the great number of persons employed in the same way, there is certainly but too much reason to believe that this system of murder which Bishop said he resorted to, as both less expensive and less hazardous than collecting from cemeteries, is become extremely common, and is in a state of progression."

He then submitted a plan for the amendment of the law. Combined with the unsatisfactory character of the culprits' depositions, and the lethargic action of the legislature, the public mind was at length aroused to demand from the Government what they had a right to have expected long before, namely greater protection from the villainies of such miscreants.

Notwithstanding the prevalence of these fearful atrocities the Government were some time before they took action, and this is but one case in point of the length of time known abuses are allowed to exist before the very eyes of the legislature, without the slightest thing being done to remedy a frightful evil.

As regards the probable truth or falsehood of the confessions made, they afford some curious points for study.

The case is a celebrated one, and having placed all the material points before our readers we must allow them to form their own conclusions upon the facts adduced.

CHAPTER XXXIV.
THE FREQUENCY OF CAPITAL PUNISHMENT.

There were many other cases of burkings (said Calcraft) that I could tell you about, but I think I have told you enough to show you what a frightful pitch crime and deeds of violence of every kind had got to.

It certainly does seem very strange that matters like these should have been permitted to go on so long, but it used to seem to me that there was more notice taken of trivial crimes and more severe punishment for petty offences than there were for the most terrible outrages against the person and against life.

Why I can recollect the time (said Calcraft) when the judges would sentence even young boys and girls to death for robbery, and send them into transportation for very long terms for committing some little theft to get something to eat to keep body and soul together.

What I have always maintained is that there should have been more employment found for the poor, and they should have had better opportunities of doing well and living by honest industry than they have had.

It is all very right and proper to punish the idle and vicious and those who would rather live by violence and murder, but there are, and always have been, people who would only be too glad to live by downright hard work if they could get it to do than they would by stealing from any one.

There is no doubt Calcraft was perfectly right in this view he took of the state of society, for though there have been millions of money spent by religious societies in religious tracts and literature to disseminate among the poor, there has been very little practical effort made to benefit their unhappy condition.

In looking back over the various movements that have been made to remedy the existing evils during the last three hundred years, we find no end of benevolent societies started to ameliorate the condition of the helpless poor, and with a few exceptions the greater part of the money subscribed by benevolent persons has been squandered away in printing waggon-loads of religious leaflets, which tender-hearted ladies and tender-hearted gentlemen give away to all classes, indiscriminately, under the false hope that they are doing a very great deal towards the conversion of the world.

Far better would it have been if a large proportion of this money, so uselessly wasted, had been spent in acquiring land for the necessitous poor to cultivate, whereby they might have found food for themselves and their starving children, rather than push into the hands of a famishing man a piece of paper threatening his soul with future torments in the world to come in addition to those he already endures here, unless he " hungers and thirsts after righteousness," instead of hungering and thirsting after meat and drink and other natural food, the lack of which those who present him with tracts never knew the want of.

We have looked through many of the philanthropic movements for the last three centuries, and we do not hesitate to say that, throughout the various times of trouble the poor have had to undergo, that there have been thousands of persons who would give a hungry man a tract who would not give him a crust, for fear they should by chance be encouraging a worthless individual in deception and fraud.

The greater number of cases of distress, however, doubtless arise from sheer helpless poverty, and it is better to err on the side of charity than callous indifference, for there cannot be a greater religious mockery, or a greater religious sham, than to give a hungry man a paper with a text and a cross on it, instead of a bun or a penny to buy one with.

It is an undeniable fact, proved by criminal history, that all great outbursts of crime—long-continued series of crimes—have followed long periods of national distress, and these periods have been followed by the establishment of societies for the reformation of the people.

HUMAN SLAUGHTER-HOUSES IN THE FIFTEENTH CENTURY.

In the fifteenth century, according to a curious old tract, published in 1614, we find that there existed in London regular houses where murders were systematically perpetrated for the purposes of robbery.

One of these wholesale slaughter-houses was in Rosemary-lane, near East Smithfield, and another was in the hamlet of Wappen-Stepney.

It would be foreign to our purpose to go into any of the crimes committed in these infamous dens; but suffice it to say it called into existence a society for the reformation of the manners and customs of the people; and the doings of the society, as related, are not a little curious.

The society procured the prosecution of a very large number of persons, and at its instigation many thousands of men, women, boys, and girls were imprisoned, and publicly whipped at the tail of a cart. Crime, however, and vice went on increasing, and then the religious societies were numerously started.

As we have before stated, little was done by practical effort and well-directed means to find work for the people, unless it was the useless work of the treadmill in the workhouse; and so society went on till the country was on the very verge of a revolution in the early days of Calcraft.

The state of the times, owing to universal distress and general excitement, was desperate; and in crime some of the most fearful desperadoes existed at that time.

DESPERATE ATTEMPT TO BLOW UP NEWGATE—EXECUTION OF FOUR MEN.

Among the many daring things which I recollect in my early days (said Calcraft) was an attempt by some condemned prisoners to blow the gaol of Newgate up with gunpowder, and thus effect their escape.

In the early part of 1830 four men were ordered for execution.

These were Thomas Maynard, thirty-six, for forgery on the customs; William Newitt, thirty-six, for sheep-stealing; William Leslie, thirty-one, and Stephen Sandford, twenty-four, for burglary.

During their incarceration, however, it appears two of them, in conjunction with another convict named Lindsay, came to the determination to try and effect their escape, either by blasting the prison wall, or failing that, to take poison, and thus prevent the punishment of the law.

It appears that shortly before their execution a bottle containing poison was found hidden between a crevice in the stone wall of the press yard, which it was supposed had been placed there by some of the culprits' friends whilst on a visit to the gaol.

The bottle, however, was discovered, the poison taken out, and a harmless liquid put in its place, and the bottle was again restored to the crevice, in the hope of detecting the prisoner intending to take it.

The plan, however, failed, as none of the culprits appeared to notice the bottle planted there.

As this plan was frustrated another plot was attempted. A halfpenny was thrown over the wall as a signal, and after this two packets of gunpowder were also thrown over.

It transpired that it was the intention of Sandford and Lindsay to place the powder in the crevices of some stones of the wall of the gaol, and then at a given time to fire it, and for the prisoners in the secret to effect their escape in the confusion expected to ensue.

The whole plot was, however, discovered; the prisoners were stripped and searched, and then put in heavy irons, and a strong watch for the remainder of their time kept over them.

The morning of the execution arrived, and the execution itself is said to have been one of the most painful ever witnessed.

Before the day came the wife of Newitt, almost frantic, appeared at the gate, imploring the warder to allow her to see her husband once more, but he was obliged to refuse, and her piercing cries were most painful to witness.

The gallows was brought out at the usual time, and great crowds assembled. The cries of the men on the drop were heart-rending.

Both Tom Cheshire and Calcraft acted as executioners on this occasion, but in consequence of some mismanagement, all the men struggled a long time after the drop fell, all dying exceedingly hard.

EXECUTION OF WILLIAM BANKS.

Shortly after this execution, said Calcraft, I had to attend at Horsemonger-lane gaol, to carry out the last dread sentence of the law on William Banks.

He was a very powerful, athletic man, standing 5 ft. 10 in. high.

Owing to his muscular strength and daring, he was the regularly recognised captain of a desperate gang of thieves.

Some of the gang broke into the premises of the Rev. Mr. Warrington, of West Moulsey.

Having broken into his house they fastened the reverend gentleman, together with his wife, by ropes in the coal cellar, threatening to take their lives if they raised any alarm.

They then rifled the house of the whole of the valuables, and drove off with their booty, taking the minister's own horse and gig.

The culprit remained hardened and callous almost up to the last moment, but just as the drop was about to fall, he cried out, "Lord, have mercy upon me!" and the bolt then being withdrawn, he was launched into eternity.

DEATH OF GEORGE IV.

I recollect that the year 1830 (said Calcraft) was a very eventful and exciting year.

As I have already told you, the whole kingdom was agitated from end to end with political excitement and the badness of trade.

Then, on the 26th of June, came the news of the death of the king.

In his early days George IV. had been extravagant and licentious, and during the ten years he acted as regent, during the malady of his father, he had contracted enormous debts.

King William IV. was proclaimed on the 28th of June, and all parties then became more vigorously still astir in the hope of obtaining an extended bill of reform, and an amelioration in the condition of the people.

Referring, however, to matters of crime, and events with which I had to deal, I recollect that shortly after the proclamation of the new king there was great rejoicing among some of the tradespeople, owing to the recapture and trial of

THE NOTORIOUS ISAAC ALIAS IKEY SOLOMONS.

This man for many years had been one of the most expert thieves and receivers of stolen property who had existed in London since the days of Jonathan Wild.

He was caught in 1827, for extensive robberies, but on being taken to the Court of Queen's Bench on Holy Thursday in that year he treated one of the warders, named Richard Smart, and before giving the man the drink he managed to drug it, and the warder becoming stupid and helpless, Ikey took the opportunity of bolting.

He managed to get clear off to America, where, hearing that his wife had been convicted and transported to New South Wales, he went there to try and find her.

As, however, there were a great many of his pals there he thought it was not safe to stop; so he tried to leave.

He, however, was recognised, re-taken, and brought back for trial, as I tell you, in June, 1830.

He was then tried at the Old Bailey on eight different indictments.

The first was for stealing drapery to the amount of £500, but he got off that.

Then he was charged with burglary and stealing property to the amount of £220, but the jury found him not guilty of that.

Next he was charged with another burglary, and stealing property to the extent of £10, but the prosecution failed in that case.

He was next indicted for another burglary and stealing silk goods to the amount of £200, but he was acquitted also on that charge.

He was then tried for burglariously breaking into a City warehouse and stealing goods to the value of £479, but he also got acquitted on that.

He was then charged with receiving a large number of watch movements to the value of £100, knowing them to have been stolen, and on this, and also on another charge of receiving, the jury at last found him guilty, and he was sentenced to transportation.

DESPERATE ESCAPE FROM NEWGATE.

Talking about prisoners escaping, I recollect, some time before this, a great commotion being caused by the escape of some prisoners from Newgate.

You would hardly think people could escape from such a place as that, but there is no knowing what some of these fellows could do.

This affair I am speaking of now took place before I was sworn in as executioner.

I made a note of a good many of these things and I find it was on the 19th of July, 1827, when Mr. Lynch Cotton, son of the ordinary, the Rev. Dr. Cotton, who slept in a back attic at the back of Newgate, was awakened by a noise overhead on the roof.

He listened for a moment, and then he distinctly heard some footsteps, and then someone say, "This is the way, Charles." He then heard them attempt to force the trap-door, but it was securely bolted from inside.

He immediately suspected that some of the prisoners had contrived to escape from their cells, and he roused his father, and they went and woke up the governor.

The governor got up, and the officers and turnkeys were immediately aroused and armed, and as it was thought that the prisoners had not yet succeeded in getting down into the street, the gaol and houses in the vicinity were surrounded.

Mr. Cotton took his station at the north side of Newgate-street, and kept a sharp look-out between that of his father and Warwick-lane.

He had not been long there before he saw the door of an empty house open, and two young men came out.

The next moment four more came out, and then a general alarm was raised. There was now great excitement; the warders and turnkeys dashed after them as the men rushed towards Cheapside, and a terrible struggle ensued.

The men were all, however, secured and brought back, when it was found that George Plummer, convicted of burglary; John Petre and George Williams, stealing in a dwelling-house; John Haines, burglary; John White, stealing in a dwelling-house, had made their escape from their cells.

It appeared from the inquiry which took place, that they had possessed themselves of an iron spike, on which mats used to hang, with which they picked the stones out of their cells.

Through the aperture thus made, they got to the next ward, where they tore up a ward form, which they reared first against one window and then another, till they reached the top of the wall, and thus made good their escape on to the tops of the roofs, on which they were heard by Mr. Cotton.

They were afterwards put in irons, and made to undergo their sentence.

DEATH OF JACK KETCH, ALIAS JACK CHESHIRE, ALIAS OLD TOM CHESHIRE.

It was on the 10th of July, 1830, when I heard of the death of old Jack Cheshire, the hangman, who for so short a time outlived old Foxton, and who up till the time of his death had been his assistant.

The death of old Jack was not unexpected, as he had been ailing for some considerable time.

The old man in his lifetime had seen so much of the body snatchers, and of their acts of daring, not only in taking the bodies from the graves, but also from the houses of their friends, that he always dreaded in the latest years of his life lest the snatchers should have his body too.

He died at his house in Bell-court, Giltspur-street, about the 9th of July, 1830, having occupied the post of "assistant finisher of the law" for many years.

The resurrection men used to plague him a good deal by telling him that "on their oath they would be sure to have him" as soon as he was dead.

A short time before he died he therefore sent to Mr. Wontner to beg of him to let him be brought to Newgate as soon as he expired and allow him to be buried in Newgate.

But the governor had no power to do that, so it was arranged that he should be buried in St. Sepulchre's churchyard.

Before he died he begged of his wife to be sure and not let the snatchers have him, and she promised him she would not.

On the night he died she actually lay by his side and slept with his dead arm under her head; but she was awoke at two o'clock in the morning by two resurrection men getting in at the window of the third floor, where they thought the corpse was shut up alone, to try and steal it.

The noise awoke her, and they had to make their escape over the roof of the house.

He was eventually buried in St. Sepulchre's churchyard, but whether the resurrectionists ever got him or not it is impossible to say.

He had assisted at a great many executions of some of the most notorious criminals, and he had also hanged a very great number of persons for what would now be considered merely petty robberies.

He virtually held the office of hangman till he died, but upon his death I then became the chief executioner of England, and was formally officially appointed.

PROPOSED AMENDMENT OF THE CRIMINAL LAW.

About a week after old Jack died, Mr. Ewart gave notice in the House of Commons of his intention in the next session of Parliament to move for leave to bring in a bill to abolish the punishment by death for stealing cattle, and for stealing in dwelling-houses, and this was soon followed by a general movement to abolish the punishment of death for all crimes except that of murder.

EXECUTION OF CAPTAIN MOIR AT CHELMSFORD.

Captain Moir was among the early persons I executed after I was made chief executioner.

The execution of Captain William Moir caused a great deal of excitement throughout the country, as he was so well known and generally respected.

It appeared that he committed a murder in the heat of passion, under the following circumstances—

He found a man named William Malcolm, fishing with a net from the side of his farm at Stanford-le-Hope.

He ordered the man off, and threatened to cut his net. The man became abusive, and Captain Moir threatened him.

The man then went away, but Captain Moir followed him as far as Shelhaven Creek.

Here Captain Moir ordered him off again, and as the man said he had a right to net there, Captain Moir pulled a pistol out of his pocket and shot him in the arm.

The man went to a surgeon and had the wound dressed, but eventually dying of lock-jaw Captain Moir was arrested and tried for the murder.

He was tried in July, 1830, at Chelmsford before Lord Tenterden. Mr. Brodrick and Mr. Round conducted the prosecution; Mr. Gurney, Mr. Clarkson, and Mr. Dowling were for the defence.

The jury found him guilty, and he was sentenced to death. There was great hope that he would have been acquitted. His wife was waiting at the nearest hotel buoyed up with the hope, and the assurances of her friends.

When the news of the verdict reached her she became almost delirious, so great was her grief.

She was only twenty-four years of age, and deeply attached to him. After she had recovered she gave expresssion to her feelings in the following words:—

"Deeply overwhelmed as I am," said she. "with grief and horror, I would not change situations with the most happy wife. The recollection of the few years I have spent with Captain Moir, and the happiness I have enjoyed in the love of the most affectionate of husbands, and the best hearted of men, is such that I would not exchange that recollection for the reality possessed by any other woman."

A petition signed by over 1000 persons was immediately got up and sent off, with a deputation by post-horses, to the Home Secretary, praying for a reprieve.

The appeal, however, was ineffectual, as Lord Tenterden refused to interfere. In addition to the general respect felt for the culprit, there were many who pitied his wife and children still more.

Captain Moir, before execution, said he did not fear death, but it was the thought of leaving the stigma upon his three poor fatherless boys—the eldest not fourteen, and the youngest not yet seven.

He was a native of Forfarshire, North Britain, where he was highly connected by birth and marriage. He was the brother-in-law of Sir James Gardiner Baird, Bart., and he was also the first cousin to Sir William Rae, the Lord Advocate of Scotland.

THE EXECUTION.

When he was given up by the Under Sheriff, Mr. Gepp, to the executioner, there was not the slightest fear or trepidation in his manner.

When Calcraft put the halter round his neck, he said:—

"I bear no animosity to anyone; I die in peace with God and man. I hope God will have mercy on me, and sustain my poor sister and my poor wife and children."

Calcraft then withdrew the bolt, and the unfortunate man was launched into eternity.

MURDER OF A NEW POLICEMAN.

Among the varieties of crimes which took place in 1830 was the murder of the policeman Long, which took place in August, near to the Gray's Inn-road.

He was the first man among the new police who fell a martyr in the force, whilst in the just execution of his duty.

He had for some time one night been watching three men lurking about in the Gray's Inn-road, who he believed were attempting a burglary.

Finding themselves disturbed they ran away, and the policeman, John Long, pursued them.

After they had turned a corner he ran after one man who was running, and captured him, and a struggle ensued.

The man then drew a shoemaker's knife, and, stabbing the unfortunate policeman to the heart, killed him.

An inquest was held, and several witnesses swore to a man who was afterwards captured as being the one whom they saw stab the officer.

He most positively refused to give his name, but after a great deal of trouble, he said his name was John Smith.

Two others were also afterwards arrested, named Henry Summers and Charles Baldwin.

The man who gave the name of John Smith, but who would not give his address, was, however, committed to take his trial for the murder.

Throughout a very long investigation he most positively asserted his innocence of the charge, asserting in his defence that, hearing the cry of stop thief, he ran to see what was the matter, when the deceased constable arrested him.

When laid hold of by the policeman he said to him, "Why don't you let me go, and run off after the right man. There he is on in front." He also denied committing the murder.

All the witnesses, however, maintained their testimony that the prisoner was the man who murdered the officer. The jury found him guilty and he was sentenced to death.

During nearly the whole time he refused to say who he was or where he came from.

When asked whether John Smith was his real name he most positively averred it was.

In the course of his trial, however, he was recognised by a young man, who swore the prisoner's real name was William Sapwell, and that some time previously he had undergone a term of imprisonment for keeping a disorderly house.

It was strange that none of the police or prison warders had recognised him before, but there was little doubt but that his name was Sapwell, and the fact of his former conviction was one reason for trying to keep his name a secret.

After his conviction, however, he protested his innocence of the crime as strongly as he did before.

The gallows was erected as usual in front of the debtors' door at Newgate, and a large concourse of persons assembled in the course of the night to witness the execution.

STRANGE SPEECH TO THE SHERIFF.

When he was brought from the cell to the press-room Calcraft stepped up to him and commenced to pinion him.

The prisoner then, in the meantime, turned to the sheriff, and, looking him full in the face, said—

"You are going to send me before the Almighty, and when I get to Heaven God will say to me, 'Who sent you here?' What answer shall I make Him?"

The sheriff replied, "You can make him what answer you like, but if I were you I should say, 'Lord, I have been tried by a righteous judge, and a patient jury, and they have found me guilty of an enormous crime, and they have sent me here.'"

The prisoner replied, "No, I shan't say that. I shall say, 'I have been tried by a judge and jury of a crime I know nothing at all about, and the sheriff sent me.' Then the Almighty will say, 'Well you have committed a great many sins, but you have been unjustly accused of this, and have no business here; but, however, walk in.'"

He was now ordered to move on to the scaffold, and the funeral procession at once commenced.

When he arrived under the fatal beam Calcraft placed the noose round his neck, withdrew the bolt, and the prisoner died in the course of a very short time.

After hanging the usual time the body was cut down, and given over for dissection.

This case, like many others, had various points of interest to those who study the value to be placed on evidence, and the merits of a criminal's protestation of innocence.

THE LIFE OF WILLIAM CALCRAFT, THE HANGMAN. 137

THE MYSTERIOUS MURDER OF MRS. WILLIAM.

CHAPTER XXXV.
MYSTERIOUS MURDER OF MRS. WITHAM.

On the 19th of August, 1830, the metropolis was shocked by the account of another murder.

The victim, in this case, was Jane Witham, an elderly female, fifty-eight years of age, who resided at No. 30, Princes-street, Lambeth, a narrow thoroughfare, leading from Lambeth Church towards Vauxhall.

As it was generally reputed that, though living in this small house, she was possessed of considerable means, it was at first conjectured that the motive of the murder was robbery.

On searching, however, upstairs forty-eight sovereigns, besides other money, were found beneath the bed and the mattresses.

Several watches and other things not hidden, however, were left untouched.

The unfortunate woman was found in a back washhouse, with her head beaten in.

A bar of iron was discovered near, one end of which was smothered with blood.

This was the instrument, it was thought, the murder was perpetrated with.

She married when young a man named Whinnet, a tailor, with whom she lived at Mortlake for some time.

In the year 1802 they removed to the house where the murder was committed.

She adopted a youth, and put him out as an apprentice to the business of a barge-builder.

After she became a widow, and then opened a shop as a marine store dealer.

In course of time, she clandestinely married the youth she had adopted, whose name was Thomas Witham, and who was twenty-eight years younger than herself.

They had been living together about eight years when the murder was committed, but none of her children or relations were aware of the marriage.

It appears that she had made a will dividing her property equally between her two children, in which Thomas Witham, as an adopted child or husband, was not included.

When she was found two coats, one of which was his, was found over the body.

There was blood on the coat usually worn by Witham, and as he had been home to tea about half-past four in the afternoon the murder was committed, he was taken into custody on suspicion.

The body was discovered in the evening, and when Witham was questioned, he said he left the deceased all right doing some washing when he went back to his work.

The old woman had resident with her a son, called Samuel, a daughter, and her husband, named Norris, and the young man Thomas Witham, formerly an adopted child, but at the time of her death in reality her husband.

As there were two very ferocious dogs in the house at the time of the murder it was thought they would have barked had the crime been perpetrated by a stranger.

During the afternoon it was stated that the son, Samuel, was absent.

Norris and his wife had gone to Camberwell fair.

After coming home to tea Witham, it was said in evidence, went back to work, and stayed till seven.

Then he went to a public-house till nine, and then met Samuel Whinnet, the old woman's son.

On going to the house they said they found the door fastened, and on getting admission to the house they found her weltering in her blood.

A man named Gough, who was said to have been seen near the house, was also arrested, but a witness swore he had not been out of his house during the time of the murder.

The cause of suspicion against Whitham was increased by the supposition that he might have wanted to have got rid of an old wife, and that, as husband of the deceased, the will made by her would have been useless, and the property have come to him.

It was, however, stated in evidence that he and the deceased appeared to live happily together.

The inquest was held before Mr. Carttar, coroner, but the jury returned a verdict of wilful murder against some person or persons unknown, and the vestry afterwards offered a reward of £100 for the discovery of the murderer.

This is one of the earliest of the numerous mysterious murders that occurred in his time.

MYSTERIOUS MURDER OF CHARLOTTE BILLMORE.

One of the most barbarous and mysterious murders which occurred a very short time after I was appointed chief executioner (said Calcraft) was that of Charlotte Billmore. Poor little child, she lost her father and mother at a very early age.

As she was an orphan without friends, and as she was born of very respectable parents, the clergyman of the parish put her under the charge and care of some labouring cottagers named Ford, residing at Mortimer West End, a place about nine miles from Reading.

She was a bright, happy intelligent little girl, eight years of age, and she used regularly to attend the village school of that place.

On the afternoon of November 20, 1830, she went to school as usual, and returned part of the way home in company with two other little girls.

She, however, did not come home at her usual time to tea, and as night came on and she did not arrive, considerable anxiety was manifested for her safety.

Nothing was heard of her during the night, but a day or two after her disappearance she was found in an adjoining wood most fearfully mutilated.

The clothes were torn off her body. Her head was cut open, and the scalp of her head turned completely back.

The face was skinned in a similar manner. Her throat was cut from ear to ear. Her body was cut open from her neck to her thighs. Her bowels, and the whole of the viscera were taken out and laid by her side, and her legs were shockingly bruised, and one thigh broken.

It was evident that the poor little sufferer had been subjected to the most horrible diabolical cruelty, and the news created quite a sensation throughout the metropolis.

A verdict of wilful murder was returned against some person or persons unknown, but so great was the indignation caused in the metropolis that several societies and other bodies offered large rewards, amounting altogether to £1,100, for the discovery and apprehension of the murderer.

CALCRAFT AT THE EXECUTION DOCK AT WAPPING.

During Calcraft's first year of office a number of men were tried for various offences on the sea. Some of them were for slave-dealing, and others for piracy and other illegal acts upon the ocean.

Two of them, named George Huntley and William Watts, charged with piracy, were found guilty, and condemned to death.

They were tried at the Admiralty Court, as was usual in those cases, and sentenced to be executed at Execution Dock at Dockhead, Wapping.

On Thursday, the 16th of December, 1830, they were brought out of Newgate, and placed in an open cart with their coffins.

There was a strong escort of police, and in the procession were the sheriffs and other officers in their carriages.

Besides the police there was also a strong body of javelin men.

A large concourse of persons assembled along the line of route, to see the prisoners on their way to execution, and also, if possible, to catch a sight of the new hangman.

When the culprits arrived at the place of execution a large number of persons had assembled in boats in front of the gallows dock.

As soon as the men came on the scaffold they were met with yelling and other signs of indignation.

Calcraft speedily put the halters round their necks, and in a very short space of time the men were suspended in the air as a warning to men of their craft.

RIOTS AND NATIONAL DISTRESS.

During the year 1830 the general distress among the artisan and labouring classes went on increasing, and in many instances the populace resorted to the destruction of machinery, incendiarism, and other acts of violence.

In Ireland there were records of the most brutal revenge—murder, mutilation, and the cutting out of the tongues of men against whom malice was entertained.

In England and the metropolis the people were agitating for reform, and not only publicly denouncing the abuses that existed at large meetings held for the special purpose, but they even went so far as to threaten to destroy by fire some of the mansions of the rulers.

THE NEW POLICE CALLED OUT.

During the month of November, 1830, the streets of the metropolis were unusually crowded, and great excitement prevailed.

While the city was preparing for the annual festivities of the usual Lord Mayor's Show Day, a great meeting was being held at the Rotunda, Blackfriars-road.

The meeting, which was in support of reform and the amelioration of the distressed state of the people did not terminate till half-past eleven at night, and then a tri-coloured flag was raised with "Reform" painted upon it, and a cry of "Now for the West-end!" immediately went forth.

This seemed to act as a preconcerted signal, for the individuals comprising the meeting assented, and sallied forth with the flag unfurled.

They then proceeded over the bridges by thousands; shouting as they passed along, "Reform; down with the police!" "No Wellington—no Peel!"

In their route they were joined by others, and in this manner they proceeded through Fleet-street and the Strand to Downing-street.

The theatres were obliged to be closed, and some of the members of various aristocratic families had to be carefully guarded to their homes.

The long pent-up distress, dissatisfaction, and indignation of the people appeared to have broken out at last, and as great meetings were also being held all over the country the nation seemed on the very verge of a terrible revolution—like that which France had experienced only a few months before.

When a portion of the mob had got to Downing-street, they drew themselves up in front of Earl Bathurst's house, and a gentleman then presented himself at the balcony armed with a brace of pistols, and declared that he would fire upon the first man that attempted to enter the house.

Yells and groans followed this declaration, and a cry of "Go it, go it," was raised by the mob. At this moment another gentleman came out of the window, and took the pistols from the hands of the other, which seemed to appease the people, and they then gave hearty cheers.

A strong body of the new police arrived, and formed themselves into line, to prevent the people from going to the House of Commons, where they intended to proceed.

A general fight now ensued, in which the police were assisted by a number of persons who had volunteered to aid them.

Reinforcements of the police began to come up fast, and a detachment of the Royal Horse Guards Blue were at once mounted and called out.

They did great service in clearing the streets for the night, but at an early hour on the following morning the police were called out again and drawn up on duty.

This was not without just reason, for it was found necessary to protect the gas ornaments that were in course of erection for the general illumination.

During that day the metropolis was again in a fearful state of excitement, and many thousands of rioters assembled along the principal streets.

Towards five o'clock another immense crowd assembled and paraded the Strand, and other fights took place.

Several arrests were made, but as the parties arrested expressed their regret at what had occurred, and as there was but little damage done, there were only slight convictions.

RIOTING AND DESTRUCTION OF MACHINERY.

The disturbances, however, in the counties among the agricultural population, in consequence of the depressed condition of the labourers, was of a much more serious character.

Many of the men attributed much of the suffering they had to endure to the general application of machinery for agricultural purposes, which was then being largely introduced.

Great meetings were held, and men went about in gangs of from forty to 500, breaking the new machinery, firing the farms, and striking terror wherever they went.

The chief disturbances at first were in Sussex, Hampshire, Wiltshire, Kent, Berkshire, and Essex, which spread to other places.

A special commission was opened at Winchester on the 18th of December to try the rioters.

The number to be tried amounted to about 270 at the commencement of this commission alone, and Calcraft looked forward to a very bountiful supply of work.

In fact, it seemed as though he had before him a rich harvest of death.

The Judges appointed to try the rioters were Mr. Baron Vaughan, Mr. Justice James Parke, and Mr. Justice Alderson. Sir Henry Joseph Tichborne, Bart., and many influential noblemen, were on the jury. The Attorney-General prosecuted.

The evidence showed that in many cases the rioters had gone about armed with bludgeons, headed by leaders, some of whom were on horseback, and their followers, amounting to five hundred at a time in number, went from farmhouse to farmhouse, levying money under the most terrible threats.

In many cases large sums of money were given them,

but even then they persisted in destroying the machinery.

The Home Secretary had been appealed to for advice as to what course was best to pursue, and he had urged that there should be no parleying with the rioters, nor any quarter shown them.

In some districts the military and the yeomanry had been called out, and engagements with the rioters had ensued.

At Pyt House, the seat of Mr. Benett, M.P. for Wiltshire, a desperate encounter took place.

The cavalry came up, and charged a mob of five hundred rioters.

First they fired blank cartridges over their heads, but as this had not the desired effect, the rioters only pelting them with stones, the cavalry charged, and one man was killed, and many wounded.

Many rioters were that night taken prisoners, and twenty-five were lodged in Pinkerton gaol.

At the first sitting of the commission many were sentenced to transportation for life; others were transported for various shorter terms, and some were sentenced to death.

During the sitting of the commission, however, a great many more were brought in for trial, making the total number about 600.

The judges then had to go to Hampshire, Salisbury, and other places, and then to return to Wiltshire, to try the remaining prisoners.

NUMEROUS EXECUTIONS.

Many of those condemned to death for rioting and incendiarism were young men about twenty years of age.

One young man, named Goodman, who was sentenced to death at Lewes for an incendiary fire at Battle, confessed shortly before Calcraft pinioned him, that he had been moved to commit this crime, and also others by hearing the speeches of Cobbett, who in his political lectures had used the words that unless the farmers of this county mended, and listened to the wants of the people, the fires would be lit in this county as they were in others.

EXECUTION OF JAMES EWEN AT CHELMSFORD, ALLEGED TO BE INNOCENT.

This man was executed at Chelmsford, charged with setting fire to the barn of Mr. Sach, a farmer, at Rayleigh, in Essex.

The principal witness and evidence against him was a man named Richardson, a notorious bad character.

Ewen, to the last—though he acknowledged he had been guilty of many crimes—declared his innocence of this.

The prisoner, in company with another man, named Thomas Bateman, who was sentenced to death for highway robbery, was executed in front of Chelmsford gaol in December, 1830.

A shocking scene took place on the scaffold.

When Calcraft had placed the halter round Ewen's neck, Ewen said—"This is very tight."

Calcraft then for the first time noticed that the rope was not long enough.

The prisoners then had to stand on the gallows waiting, while Calcraft spliced another rope.

After this was done, Calcraft then adjusted the nooses again, and then, withdrawing the bolt, the men swung in the air, struggling and writhing in a fearful manner.

It is alleged that while Ewen was waiting during the time Calcraft was lengthening the rope, he complained very much of the cold.

The unfortunate man, it appears, trembled violently, and after the bolt was drawn both men struggled hard for some time.

The general impression afterwards was, that Ewen was innocent.

EXECUTION OF THREE PERSONS ON PENENDEN HEATH.

Calcraft was exceedingly busy during the month of December, 1830.

In addition to the executions he had to carry out at other places he had to hang some boys for setting fire to a stack on Penenden Heath.

As a caution to some of the other labourers it was resolved that the execution should take place on the heath.

Accordingly the gallows was erected as nearly as possible on the very spot where the stack stood.

Two of the culprits were brothers named Henry Packman and William Packman, aged respectively eighteen and nineteen.

They did not deny setting fire to it, but asserted they had been instigated to it by the promise of a reward of £1000 by an accomplice named Goodman.

Another man named J. Dyke was also condemned to suffer with them for a similar offence.

The latter prisoner throughout protested his innocence. The three prisoners were brought from Maidstone gaol in a cart, under a strong escort.

They sat upon their coffins as they came along, and there appeared a great amount of commiseration manifested for them as they passed through the respective villages. On their arrival at the heath, the two Packmans caught sight of the gallows already put up. One of them then said, "That gallows looks an awful thing."

When they came underneath the fatal beam, Calcraft first put the rope round the neck of Dyke.

The two Packmans looked on, perfectly appalled, with a look of horror fearfully depicted upon their faces.

Whilst Calcraft was putting the ropes round the necks of the two boys, the chaplain asked Dyke if he had anything further to say, to which Dyke replied, "No, I am pefectly innocent."

"You have but another moment to live," said the chaplain, "and I do entreat you to tell the truth."

Dyke then again replied, "I am perfectly innocent."

When everything was at last ready, Henry Packman said, "Brother, let us shake hands before we die."

His younger brother then shook hands with him, and then Calcraft whipped the horses away.

The cart was drawn from underneath the unfortunate youths, and they hung on the heath in the air.

They struggled hard for a time, but after life was extinct they were left to hang an hour in the sight of the crowd, and eventually cut down.

THE HORRORS OF TRANSPORTATION.

Many more were executed in various parts of the country for outrages in connection with the distressed condition of the people, and the political excitement of the times.

The prisons were filled to overflowing; the hulks at Woolwich were crowded to excess, and the scenes perpetrated on the hulks and other convict ships almost baffle description.

There was scarcely a prison in England which was not in the most filthy and lax condition.

They were hotbeds of vice, and the scenes of the most horrible indecency.

At this particular time men, women, and children were lying both in the criminal and debtors' prisons, dying of starvation, being eaten up with vermin, and literally rotting in filth.

The most flagrant acts of injustice, cruelty, and indecency were perpetrated by governors and warders, and the whole system and régime in which prisoners were kept was nothing short of a national disgrace.

Everything around told of extravagance in high places, of class legislation, and of the total neglect and indifference with which the wants of the famishing poor were treated.

The people, however, were becoming desperate: they were dying by thousands of starvation in their homes.

The workhouses could offer little or no assistance, for the middle classes were over-burthened with taxation, and there was nothing but starvation and death in the workhouse, too.

It was in these times of depression and social depravity that the cry for Reform came, and that cry was taken up by the people from one end of the kingdom to the other. There was no mistaking it—the people were in earnest.

Squalor and hunger were rampant in the land, but from the middle classes there came forth a few brave earnest men who raised their voices against the oppression and the indifference of the upper ten thousand, and their voices and their appeals galvanised the dying multitude into renewed life, and a vigorous, fearless, and unflinching struggle for the rectifying of abuses, and for those reforms some of which the people now possess.

But the engines of repression for years were kept fast at work, and the horrors of transportation, the treadmill, the lash, and the gallows were constantly before the eyes of the people.

Still, however, the agitation went on, and men were found who, in spite of public obloquy, advocated the rights of humanity and denounced the oppressive tendencies of the landed classes.

Though doubtless the fear of a general revolution tended to the reforms being obtained, yet it is to be regretted that so many misguided men were led into acts of lawlessness and crime.

Their zeal, in some cases, and their lack of discrimination and justice excited them into those acts of violence, which sent so many hundreds of young men into transportation for life, and thus brought upon them greater horrors than they could have experienced at home.

The accounts of the suffering which men and women in those days endured while in transportation were truly appalling.

They showed to what depths of inhumanity and barbarism men could descend, and how utterly callous they could become to the sufferings of their fellow-creatures.

In the early days of our colonisation the Governors of Botany Bay, and other settlements to which convicts were sent, were little better than despots.

The greatest ruffians became overseers, and occupied places of trust, and the most terrible cruelties were practised.

It is recorded that powers equal to those held by the first Governor of New South Wales, if held, had never been exercised by any other official in the British dominions.

He could sentence to 500 lashes, fine £500, regulate customs and trade, fix prices and wages, remit capital as well as other sentences, bestow grants of land, and create a monopoly of any article of necessity.

All the labour in the colony was at his disposal: all the land, all the stores, all the places of honour and profit, and virtually all the justice, were in his despotic keeping. The long voyage of the transports, too, was a bad preparation for useful labour.

The convicts were heaped on board ship without preparation or selection.

Boys and girls, men and women, who had only been guilty of even trivial offences, were chained to the most hardened criminals, and jostled against each other as the convict ship heaved and tossed on the turbid sea.

In some cases the prisoners died in their irons in the holds of the ship; and so short was the scanty allowance of food allotted, that their fellow-captives concealed the fact of their deaths, so that they might share between them the rations the dead at their side would want no more.

In such state did the ship proceed on its way, tossing and rolling from side to side, while the overseers paraded the decks with lash in hand, till at last the smell of the putrefying corpses told its own horrible tale of death, and the decomposed bodies had to be thrown overboard, lest plague and pestilence should add their horrors to those already afloat.

Then, as has been too often the case where selected officials, without ordinary ability, without judgment or foresight have been put in command, there were constant cases of bungling and injustice through oversight and neglect.

In many instances men were sent over without any accompanying documents to state whether they were sent for life or only for shorter terms.

Oftentimes after a lapse of time convicts asserted that their sentences had expired, and that they claimed their liberty.

Then it was found that the documents of their committal were in England, and the answer generally was that they would have to serve another two or three years.

Some of the prisoners expressed dissatisfaction at this delay.

Thereupon they were at once seized, tried by a criminal court, and sentenced to be immediately tied up, to receive 600 lashes from the cat, and to wear irons for the next six months.

In the evidence given as to the state of the colony one man says:—

I have often taken grass and pounded it, and made soup from a native dog. For seventeen weeks I had only five ounces of flour per day. The motto of the overseers was, "Kill them or work them—their provision will be in store."

About 800 died in six months from over-work and starvation at Toongabbie. I knew a man who, because he was weak, was thrown alive into a grave.

He begged not to be covered over. "Don't cover me up," he said; "don't cover me up."

The overseer replied—"—— your eyes, you'll die to-night, and we shall only have to come back to bury you."

The man was allowed to get out of the grave, and lived for some time after.

The governor would order the lash at the rate of 500, 600, or 800, and if the men could have stood more they would have had it. Men have been hung there for nothing else but stealing a few biscuits.

Such is but a mild picture of the fearful enormities practised and cruelties perpetrated in convict life in Calcraft's early years.

The question may very properly be asked, whether there has been such a supervision and improvement since that time as civilised society ought to expect and demand.

During the year 1831 the cry for reform and the redressing of the wrongs of the people still went on.

In February Lord John Russell was entrusted to introduce a Reform Bill into the House of Commons.

In support of the measure meetings were held all over the country, and everywhere great interest prevailed. In connection with the bill there was also a proposition for the disfranchisement of a number of boroughs with small populations.

In addition to the cry for parliamentary reform the opposition to the introduction of machinery still proceeded, and the number of riots and outrages increased in every county.

It was a dark sorrowful year for many poor families who had to part from friends for ever.

DESTROYING THE WORKHOUSES AND BREAKING MACHINERY.
WINCHESTER.

In the first week of January a special commission sat at Winchester to try a large numbers of rioters and incendiaries.

Some were committed to prisons, others sent into transportation, whilst three men, J. T. Cooper, thirty-three, H. Eldridge, twenty-three, and J. Gilmour, twenty-five, were capitally convicted.

Mr. Baron Vaughan, in addressing the prisoner Cooper said:—The most painful duty of a judge is to select for capital punishment those whose fate may serve as the most warning example of the danger and wickedness of violating the law.

The law delights not in punishments—its object is the prevention rather than the punishment of crime; and we have passed many an anxious, and I may say sleepless, hour in the endeavour to discriminate between the various degrees of guilt.

Those who are the first and foremost in aggression ought to be the first to suffer and the foremost in punishment; and therefore it is that, with respect to you, James Thomas Cooper, we have come to the conclusion that it is not consistent with public safety to spare your life.

He then addressed himself in like manner to Eldridge and to Gilmore, and concluded by saying: The days of all of you are numbered—the gates of mercy on this side of the grave are closed against you for ever. It now only remains for me to pass upon you the last sentence of the law, and that is, that you be taken from hence to the place from whence you came, and from there to a place of execution, and then hanged by the neck till you are dead.

The prisoners were then all removed, evidently in great distress.

ANOTHER SENTENCE OF DEATH.

Robert Holdaway, thirty-eight; James Arnalls, nineteen; and Henry Cooke, nineteen, were then brought up into the same dock.

Baron Vaughan then addressed them in a similar manner, saying: I must now exhort you all to prepare in the most solemn manner for the great change which awaits you.

All interest and care in the pursuits of life must vanish, for you will soon have to appear at the bar of that heavenly judge, before whom all hearts are open, and from whom no secrets are hid; there to render an account of the transactions which you have participated in in this world of sorrow.

He then sentenced them to death in the usual form, and they were removed for execution.

Sentence of death was then recorded against a very large number of prisoners for various acts of incendiarism, but it was afterwards commuted to transportation for life.

KINGSTON ASSIZES.

Immediately following the condemnation of the before-mentioned prisoners, James Warner, aged thirty, was also sentenced to death for setting fire to a flour mill at Aldbury.

This man also, on receiving his sentence, was greatly affected.

EXECUTION AT HORSHAM.

Calcraft next proceeded to Horsham, and executed Edward Bushby, twenty-six, for setting fire to a stack of wheat.

When Calcraft was pinioning his arms, the unhappy man said: "I hope to the Lord I am going to a better and a happier world," and the drop immediately fell.

The unfortunate man died with scarcely a struggle.

THE RIOTS IN WILTSHIRE.

The judges next proceeded to Salisbury, to try the rioters for the various outrages in Wiltshire.

At the special commission opened for this county there were over 300 prisoners for trial.

The evidence showed that in this county, as in others, the rioters had gone about in armed gangs, demanding money, breaking machinery, setting fire to farms, and doing every kind of wanton and irreparable damage.

The yeomanry and special constables were called out, and wholesale arrests were made day and night. The number of men sentenced to transportation in this, as well as in the counties of Hampshire, Dorset, and other places was so great, that various movements were commenced by some of the ratepayers to get a remission of some of the sentences, or, if that could not be done, to obtain leave for the wives and families of the convicts to go out with them to the colonies to which they were to be sent.

It was argued that by this wholesale system of transportation which the judges were pursuing, that the workhouses, which were already full, would be overcrowded by the helpless wives and children left behind. Further, that they would come as extra burthens on the already overburthened ratepayers.

It was, however, on the other hand, contended that such a proposition was impracticable; the judges were inexorable, and the unfortunate men were shipped away, many of them never more to return.

CONVICTS WITNESSING THE EXECUTIONS.

In most of the counties where the special commissions were held a certain number of men were left for execution, and in some instances it was arranged that the convicts sentenced to death should be executed before the eyes of those sentenced to transportation.

Accordingly, when Calcraft arrived at the various gaols, he found at some places from 300 to 400 of the sentenced convicts all in irons, paraded and drawn up in the yard to witness the execution of some of those who had been deemed ringleaders in the riots.

Of the six men ordered for execution at the fine old historical city of Winchester, four were respited, and only James Thomas Cooper and Henry Cooke were left for death.

Calcraft, in this instance, pinioned them at the foot of the gallows, and also placed the ropes round their necks, and the caps on their heads before they ascended the scaffold.

Cooper came up first, and when he appeared with the halter round his neck, and the white cap on his head, there were loud cries of "Shame," "Murder," and other marks of disapprobation.

As he stood on the scaffold waiting for the other unfortunate man coming up, he kept repeating the prayers, "Lord have mercy upon me! Christ have mercy upon me!"

Calcraft then came up with the other culprit, and fastened the ropes to the beam.

Then going down behind the drop he withdrew the bolt, and the unhappy men swung and vibrated before the eyes of the assembled crowd.

CONVICTION OF AN INNOCENT MAN.

It is to be feared that in some instances innocent men were convicted, some through mistake, some through the mercenary motives of unscrupulous informers, and others by the infamous practice of wilfully giving false evidence, either from motives of malice or for the sake of reward.

There are many cases on record where men have not only been sent into transportation, but even to the scaffold, through that terrible sin of giving false or flippant evidence.

If those called upon to give evidence would only reflect upon what they are doing there would be less of this cruel crime.

We have had instances of it even in recent times, but were all these cases put together they would form a long and fearful catalogue of crimes amounting to positive murder.

There is no character more sublime than that of the man who has a strict and sacred reverence for the truth. On the other hand, there can be nothing more contemptible, nothing more abominably wicked than to bring punishment upon an innocent person by lying and wicked evidence.

"Thou shalt not bear false witness," is one of the oldest as well as one of the most important commandments; but unfortunately in our courts of law it is a commandment constantly broken.

There has been too great a tendency on the part of some magistrates, and on the part of some judges, to give too much credence to the evidence of policemen and informers as against the evidence of independent witnesses.

Juries sometimes err through this and give erroneous verdicts. We give the following case as a remarkable one in point:

At the trial of the rioters before the judges at the special commission at Salisbury, just alluded to, a very respectable man, named Isaac Looker, the father of a grown-up family, was indicted for sending a threatening letter to a man named John Rowland.

The letter was as follows:—"Hif you goes to sware against or a man in prisson you have here farm burnt down to ground, and thy head chopt off."

The prisoner pleaded "Not Guilty."

The first witness called was Philip Watts, who said he had seen the writing on the paper produced, and he had no doubt it was in the handwriting of the prisoner at the bar.

Evidence was then given that the letter was picked up near the prosecutor's house.

The witness Watts was cross-examined, and he admitted that though he had sworn that the letter was in the prisoner's handwriting yet he had not seen him write for three or four years.

William Woodman was called and he swore that the writing was that of the prisoner.

Edward Vaisey was the next witness called, and he swore it was in the prisoner's handwriting.

But, cross-examined, this witness also admitted he had not seen the prisoner write since 1824, a period of seven years back.

A Mr. Smith was then called, who stated he had no doubt the letter was in the handwriting of the prisoner.

Witness was a special detective constable employed to detect the writer of the letter.

In company with Taunton, an officer from Bow-street, he went to the prisoner's house and there searched the prisoner's bureau.

In that bureau he found three pieces of paper, which were torn, and the marks of the tearing all corresponded to the torn paper on which the letter in question was written, and to the marks of the tearing of two other pieces of paper on which a similar epistle was written to two other persons.

The quality of the paper on which the threatening words were written was of the same as the remaining portion found in the prisoner's bureau, and the water mark was the same; in fact, every part of the letters fitted with the remains of the paper found in the prisoner's bureau.

He also produced the prisoner's account-books, but it was not shown that the writing corresponded.

For the defence a number of witnesses were called.

William Sulley said he had known the prisoner twenty-five years as a respectable man, and had often, recently, seen him write, and was quite sure the handwriting was not that of the prisoner.

George Edwards said he was a vestry clerk, and he had also been a schoolmaster. He had frequently seen the prisoner write, and he was quite sure that letter was not in his handwriting.

The prisoner always wrote a systematic round hand. The letters were written in an angular and pointed hand.

John Bristowe White was the next witness. He knew the prisoner's handwriting well, and was quite sure the letter was not in his handwriting.

The jury considered that the manner in which the torn edges of the letters corresponded with the remainder of the paper found in the prisoner's bureau was conclusive proof, and they brought in a verdict of guilty against the prisoner.

The unfortunate man seemed almost staggered by the verdict recorded against him.

Baron Alderson then proceeded to pass sentence upon him in the following terms:—Prisoner at the bar, you have been found guilty on evidence which must satisfy every reasonable man.

Prisoner: My lord, I am innocent. I never touched the paper; I never wrote a line of it; I am innocent.

The Judge: You have been found guilty of a crime which is certainly not mitigated by denying it after the evidence given. That is a crime which strikes at the very root of society by tending to try and obstruct the due administration of justice.

Prisoner: I am innocent, my lord. I declare I am innocent; I never wrote the paper; I never put my hand to it. The desk in which the pieces of blank paper were found was always open to six or seven persons in the house as well as myself. My lord, the law may find me guilty, but it cannot make me so. I now declare solemnly that I am innocent.

The Judge: I cannot attend to these asseverations, for we all know that a man who has been guilty of such an offence as you have been convicted of will not hesitate to deny it now. I would rather trust to such evidence as has been given in your case than to the most solemn declarations even on the scaffold. Sitting here to administer justice I must not be deterred from doing my duty in passing sentence upon you. The sentence of the law is that you be transported for life.

The jury then retired for refreshment.

It is impossible to fully realise what must have been the feelings of the unfortunate man.

There was not really one tittle of evidence against him.

He was convicted against the weight of evidence for the more respectable witnesses, and the greater number swore that the letter was not in his handwriting.

On the other hand, there was every probability that he wrote a different hand.

There was nothing to show that the pieces of blank paper were there at all before the special constables went to the bureau, and therefore there was no positive proof that they had not been maliciously and purposely placed there, perhaps through bribery, as an evidence of guilt.

Such instances of placing things, as likely evidences of guilt, have been known, and in all cases strict precautions ought to be taken against the possibility of such an injustice.

But the great mistake of the case lay in the fact that it does not seem to have occurred to the minds of either the judge or jury that those letters might have been written by some one else in the house; neither do they appear to have even asked whether in the house there was anyone else who could have written the letters and placed the remnants of the paper there.

THE FATHER SAVED BY HIS SON.

When the court re-assembled, a boy about seventeen years of age, the son of the prisoner, stepped to the front of the court, and stated that he had written the letters.

He had obtained the paper at his uncle's, and, thinking to prevent the witnesses from appearing against two of his cousins (arrested for machine-breaking), he had written the letters, and, after tearing the leaves off, he had placed the remainder of the paper in his father's bureau.

His father was out when he wrote the letters, and never saw them, nor did he know anything at all about them.

He was then asked if he could repeat the wording of the letters, and he did so.

Next he was asked to write copies of what he sent, and he did so from memory.

The specimens he wrote were then compared with the threatening letters, and the handwriting corresponded in every particular—in fact, they seemed exact duplicates.

The judge took time to consider, and the next morning he intimated that he was now convinced the letters were in the handwriting of the boy. He then ordered a case to be drawn up against the boy on his own confession.

The father was then acquitted, and the boy transported for seven years in his father's stead.

At the conclusion of these special commissions the gaols were so full that the prisoners had to be huddled together without regard either to decency, morality, or health.

The hulks already burthened could receive no more. The "Warrior," the "Defence," "The Unité," and other floating prisons were nothing less than nests of pestilence.

Some of the officers stated in after reports that the crimes, filth, disease, and mortality on board, were both frightful and dangerous.

Some few of the convicts on board were under ten years of age, a greater proportion still were under fifteen, whilst a still larger number were under twenty.

Officers in giving evidence said that "The Justitia" alone contained no less than 700 convicts, and at night these men were fastened, numbers together, in their dens.

In the hospital ship the "Unité" the great majority of the patients were infested with vermin, and their persons, especially their feet, were begrimed with dirt.

No regular supply of body linen had been issued, so much so that many men had been five weeks without a change, and all record had been lost of the time when the blankets had been washed, and the number of sheets was so insufficient that only one could be allowed to each bed.

At last, when it was imperative that the convicts must have a change of shirts, they were black with vermin, as though they had been sprinkled all over with pepper as they hung upon the rigging.

In this fearful state of things the cholera broke out to such an alarming extent on board the convict hulks that the chaplain refused to accompany the dead for burial.

The corpses were taken to the marshes in numbers at a time, and cast into common graves, whilst the clergyman stood a mile away reading the burial service, and dropping a white handkerchief when he came to the words, "Dust to dust, and ashes to ashes," as the signal for the lowering of the bodies.

RIOTERS TAKING LEAVE OF FRIENDS.

Meantime the work of transportation proceeded slowly, negligently, and cruelly.

The same reckless carelessness marked every stage of shipment, and showed official incapacity and blundering at every point.

Before the rioters doomed to transportation were embarked, however, their friends were allowed to take a final farewell of them before they left their prisons.

The roads and lanes throughout the various counties were sometimes filled with fathers and mothers and brothers and sisters and friends going to wish the unfortunate people a long last "adieu," and the last partings of so many friends at the gaols were in many instances truly heartrending.

As soon as Calcraft had completed the hanging of the rioters condemned by the special commissions, above alluded to, he was required at various other places to execute criminals who had been condemned to death for murder and other crimes in various counties of the kingdom.

It would take too long to even enumerate the names of those he put to death during his long career of office, and now having glanced at the exciting state of the times when he was first appointed, we shall pass on to a review of the most celebrated cases of romance and crime which occurred in his time, and give some of the remarkable executions in which he was concerned.

A TERRIBLE TRAGEDY AT COVENTRY.

In the renowned city of Coventry, so famous for the traditional history of Lady Godiva and Peeping Tom, there resided in 1831, in a small homely cottage, a charitable old man, and a young girl, whose clean genteel appearance and rosy complexion had attracted the attention of many a young swain, who fain would have courted her affections, and in time made her his own.

The young girl, whose name was Mary Ann Higgins, was an orphan child, the daughter of the old man's brother.

In her early years she had lost her parents, and when she was thus left alone in the world her uncle, William Higgins, rather than allow her to be cast upon the cold charity of the parish, found her a home, and brought her up as though she was a child of his own.

THE LIFE OF WILLIAM CALCRAFT, THE HANGMAN. 145

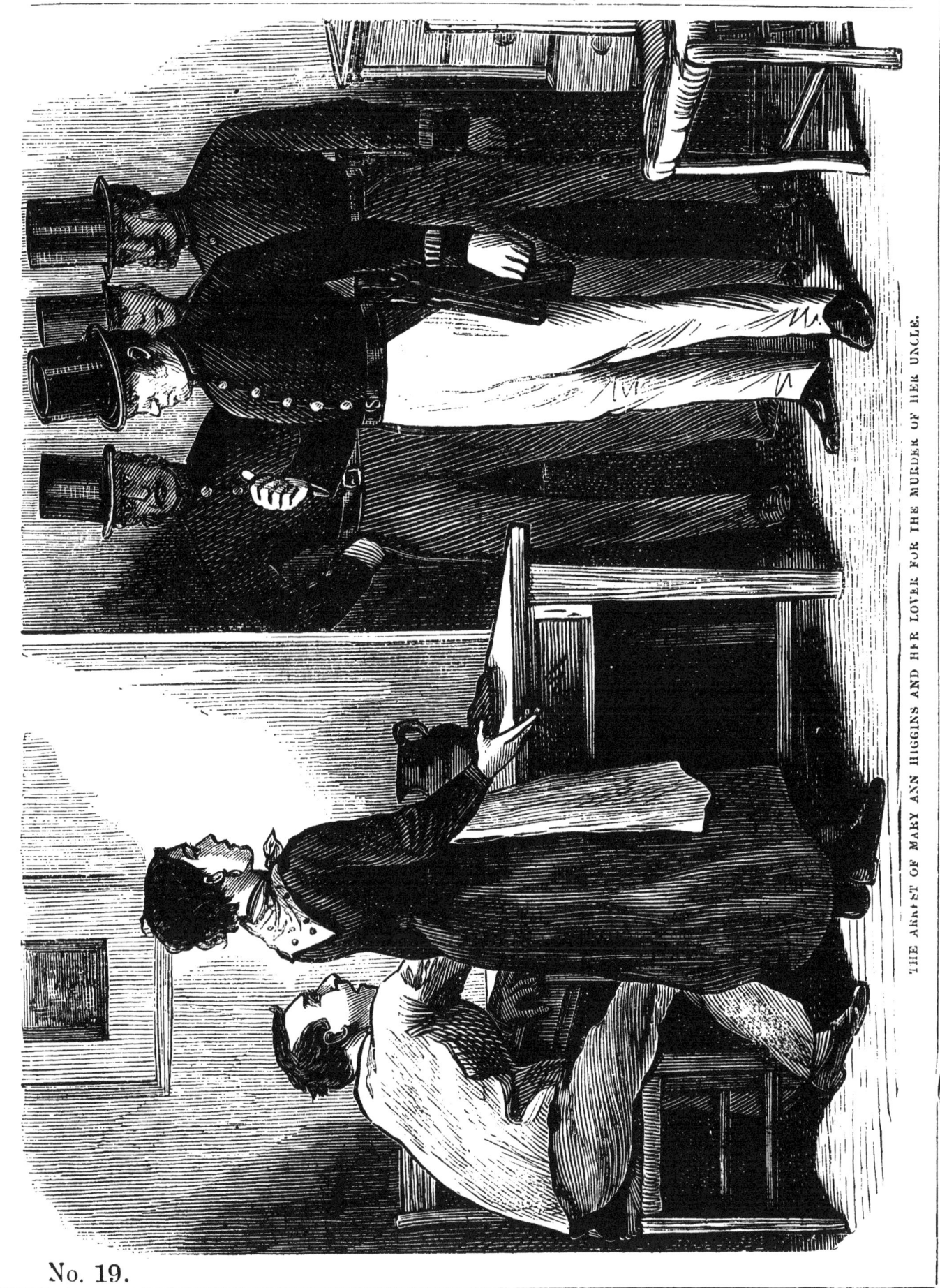

THE ARREST OF MARY ANN HIGGINS AND HER LOVER FOR THE MURDER OF HER UNCLE.

No. 19.

As she grew up in years she became useful in his house, for when he returned from his daily labour he found his home clean and tidy, and his meals always prepared with punctuality and care.

There was but one fear the old man had, and that was lest, among the many admirers Mary Ann had, she should take up with one who would take her from her present abode, and leave him in his declining years once more solitary and alone.

Still he did not wish to unduly influence her in her attachments, for he always said he wished her to be happy, and the way for people to be happy was to have if possible those they truly love.

Of the many suitors who proffered themselves there were two to whom Mary Ann seemed more partial than to any of the rest.

One was Henry Neville, a young industrious farmer, the other was Edward Clarke, a young man twenty-one years of age, who had just completed his apprenticeship at the watchmaking trade.

Both young men were jealous of each other, and both urged their respective suits with all the eloquence they could command.

As to prospects Henry Neville urged that farming was far better than being a mechanic, for Mary Ann would have a farm of her own and a pony and chaise to ride in.

Edward Clarke, in support of his claim, said he should soon be able to get a shop, and in course of time a manufactory of his own, and then Mary Ann could go with him to London, and about with him when he travelled for his orders.

Sometimes Mary Ann thought she would have one, and sometimes she thought she would have the other; but at last she promised Edward Clarke that she would have him, and nobody else but him.

The old uncle, too, seemed to rather favour Edward Clarke, for he seemed rather inclined to make the cottage his home; and the old uncle, who really did not want to part with Mary Ann, thought they might, for all he could see, live very happily together.

He had saved a little money, which he had no doubt would be useful to him in his old age, and, as he still worked, he hoped to save considerably more.

The period to which we refer was the fourth Sunday in Lent, and the clergyman at the old parish church, after the reciting of the Creed, stood in front of the altar, and in a clear and distinct voice said—

"I publish the banns of marriage between Mary Ann Higgins, spinster, and Edward Clarke, bachelor, both of this parish. If any of you know any just cause or impediment why these two persons should not be joined together in holy matrimony, ye are to declare it. This is the first time of asking."

Henry Neville was in church, and, on hearing the banns published, the colour flushed in his cheeks as a pang darted through his heart, when he heard it publicly announced that the young girl whom he so dearly loved was really about to give her heart and hand to another.

After church was over many a young girl hastened home to her mother with the news that Mary Ann Higgins was going to be married to Edward Clarke, and that Henry Neville was in church and heard the banns published for the first time, and that he looked so cross.

The banns were published in the usual way again on the following Sunday, and in the course of the following week everything was being prepared for the wedding-day.

One evening, however, during the following week, the poor old uncle who had watched over Mary Ann from a child, was found ill in bed, and Mary Ann ran to a neighbour's house, screaming and crying, "Oh, do come directly, for my poor uncle is dying!"

The neighbours came in directly, and they found the poor old man rolling on the bed apparently in the greatest agony, and retching and vomiting in the most violent manner.

Two of the neighbours, Mrs. Green and Mrs. Moore, did what they could for the suffering man, and whilst Mary Ann appeared overcome with grief, they sent off for medical assistance to come directly.

In the meantime the old man vomited, and one of the women then remarked that there seemed something peculiar in his sickness, as though it was caused by poison.

"What has your uncle had to eat, Mary Ann?" said one of the neighbours.

"Nothing that I know of," replied the girl, "but a little pea-soup for his dinner when he came home."

"Did you have any of it?" said the woman.

"Yes," said Mary Ann, "I had a basin as well; and it has not hurt me."

"Is there any left?" said one of the women.

"Yes," said Mary Ann. "There is some in the pot."

In the space of a little time the poor old man expired before medical assistance arrived, and Mary Ann, retiring into another room, flung herself upon a bed sobbing and crying, "Oh, my poor uncle—he's dead—he's dead."

Edward Clarke, who was in the house at the time, endeavoured to calm the girl as much as he could, and he followed her to the room to which she had retired from the dreadful scene of death—the death of her only friend in life; the one who had been to her her guardian, her protector, and her friend.

In the meantime the two women had found two basins with the remains of soup in them.

They noticed that the soup in one looked nice and clear, whilst the soup in the other appeared to have in it a sediment, and whitish-brown powder.

They saw also that there appeared a whitish-brown powder in the vomit which lay in the room.

As they suspected that the poor old man had been poisoned, they locked the two basins up in the cupboard.

Some time afterwards the doctor arrived, and on looking at the unfortunate man he at once expressed his belief that he had died of poison.

He, however, could not say for certain till the time of the inquest, and after a post-mortem examination had been made.

The news of the unfortunate man's untimely end rapidly spread, for he was much respected by all who knew him.

Pending the inquest there was considerable excitement and interest manifested as to how he came by his death.

He was generally of a mild, happy, and peaceable disposition, and as he was thought not to be a man who would be at all likely to commit suicide, there was a strong impression among the neighbours that he had been wilfully poisoned, but by whom the deadly ingredient had been administered it was yet difficult to say.

When Mary Ann Higgins was shown the two basins of soup, and asked whether she could account for the difference in the appearance she said:—

"Oh, yes, one was made on the Saturday and

the other on the Monday, and one I thickened with flour, and the other with oatmeal."

"You have lost your best friend now, Mary Ann," said Mrs. Green, a neighbour, who was in the house with her."

"Yes," said the girl, "he's been a good friend to me, and I don't know how I should have got on if I had not been going to be married. The wedding is fixed for next week—so I shall have to go into black, and then take the black off for the day, and then put the black on again after the wedding is over. I could not be married in black, for they say it's bad luck."

"But I should think you would put the wedding off now for a time. I should," said Mrs. Green.

"Oh no, I couldn't do that," said Mary Ann. "It wouldn't do to put it off, because you know how I am by Edward."

"Ah, well, you shouldn't have been in that way till after you were married," said Mrs. Green. "I am sure I should never go and be married the day after the funeral—that will look bad; but, however, you had better come with me, and let us put his room straight a bit."

"Oh, no," said Mary Ann, "I could not bear to look at him again, and see my best friend dead; and I am sure I can't sleep in the house again. I must go out somewhere to sleep."

The neighbours began to be suspicious of foul play, and by this time the police had arrived, and they gave strict orders that nothing should be touched, and they also expressed their opinion that Mary Ann had better not leave the house, as they might wish to put some questions to her.

Meantime the question as to how the supposed poison could have got into the old man's stomach was fully discussed, and the belief that some one had wilfully poisoned him was broadly and more fearlessly hinted at as every little bit of new information came to light.

"I told you how it would end," said one of the neighbours. "Mary Ann ain't been like the same girl since her's picked up with that fellow, Edward Clarke. That fellow has allers bin a talking about how much money the old man had got, and I expect that either the one or the other have finished him just on purpose to get hold of the poor fellow's savings."

"Well, it is very hard to judge," said another, "but perhaps he had nothing at all to do with it. You know there's no knowing what some women will do; especially when they get man-mad; they'll steal or murder, or do any mortal thing o' purpose to find a chap money and get him to have 'em. But, howsomever, it's a very mysterious case, and perhaps neither of 'em murdered him arter all—so the best way will be to wait for the inquest, and pass no opinion on the case till then."

During the day the doctors came, and, having opened the body, they made a post-mortem examination and took away with them the stomach and its contents for analysis.

While these inquiries were going on Mary Ann kept importuning Edward to fulfil his promise and marry her on the day appointed.

"No," said Edward Clarke, "I should rather put it off now till the funeral is over and the things are settled."

"Oh, the wedding can't be put off," said Mary Ann. "You know how I am—my wedding-dress and everything is made, and we can just go to the church and be quietly married, and then see to the funeral afterwards; I could easily take my wedding things off and then go into black."

"No," said Edward, "I shan't do that; I'm sure I aint a going to the church first."

At this Mary Ann began to get quite indignant, and again told him that it was his bounden duty to take her to the church as he had promised to do, and then they could see about the other arrangements afterwards.

Just at this moment four policemen entered the house, and told both Edward and Mary Ann that they would be required to go to the police-station at once.

"What for?" inquired Edward.

"What do you want us to go to the station for? Can't you ask us anything you want to know here?" said Mary Ann.

"No," replied the police; "you will both have to go to the station."

"Well, but surely you will let us get married first," said Mary Ann, "and then in a day or two we will come up and answer you anything you like."

"Oh, that won't do," replied one of the officers. "I have got orders from our superintendent to take you to the station at once. From information which has come to our knowledge you will both be charged with being concerned with the murder of the deceased."

"Humph," said Mary Ann, "that's a very fine thing to have to go to the station and be charged with murder, instead of going to the church to be married. However, if that's it, I'll go." So she put on her shawl and bonnet, and accompanied the officer along the street.

"How came you to be so silly as to let anybody persuade you to do such a thing as that, as poison the poor old man?" said the policeman as he was taking her along, thinking to trap her into a confession.

"I was not persuaded by anybody to do it," said the girl, in an angry manner.

"Well, you had better tell the truth, and say who it was that told you to do it," replied the constable, again thinking to catch her in another way.

"Nobody told me to do it," again said the girl, more angry still at being thus pressed and drawn into making some sort of answer that might entrap her into a criminal admission.

At length they reached the station, and Mary Ann having been duly charged with having administered poison to her uncle, she was locked up in the cell.

Shortly afterwards Edward Clarke was brought in also, and after having been duly charged with having been an accessory to the murder, he was locked up in another cell in the same station.

THE INQUEST.

Shortly afterwards the inquest was opened at the "King William the Fourth" beer-house, Spon-street, before the coroner and a jury of the neighbourhood.

The witnesses called proved the following facts:—

James Jenson, a youth, employed in a neighbouring chemist's shop, stated that a few days previously a young woman, whom he knew as Mary Ann Higgins, came to the shop and asked him to serve her with a pennyworth of arsensic to poison rats with. He told her that he could not make less than two pennyworth, and then that he could not serve her unless a witness was with her who knew her.

John Wyley, an apprentice to Messrs. Stott and Wyley, chemists, of Coventry, deposed that the female prisoner, Mary Ann Higgins, came to their shop a few days back and asked for a pennyworth of arsenic, which she said she wanted to kill mice with. He told her he could not serve her unless she brought some one with her who knew her. She then went out of the shop, and in some little time afterwards returned with another girl named Elizabeth Russell, and then he sold the arsenic to her.

Elizabeth Russell, a young woman, stated that on the day in question Mary Ann Higgins stopped her in the street, and asked her if she would mind going with her as far as the druggist's. She did so, and they went to Messrs. Stott and Wyley's, where Mary Ann Higgins bought some arsenic. On their way along the street the prisoner looked at the label, which was marked "Poison," and she tore it off, and threw it away, saying, "I wonder what he's put that on for; I don't want that on."

Mary Ann Southam, residing in Spon-street, said that on the evening the deceased died Mary Ann Higgins met her and asked her if she had seen Edward Clarke, as she was looking for him. She was going into the various public-houses to see if she could find him. She told witness that she wanted him to come and sit up with her, as her uncle was taken very ill.

Mrs. Southam deposed that on the night the deceased died she went along with other neighbours to see if she could be any assistance, and while there they found in the pantry two basins partly full of soup. They showed them to the female prisoner, and asked her whether that was what she and her uncle had had for supper. Mary Ann said, "Yes; one was her basin and the other was her uncle's." They asked her which was hers, and she showed them the lightest. Then they pointed out to her that one seemed to have a sort of powder in it, and she said "Yes; it was made on two different days. One she made on the Saturday, and the other on the Monday, and one lot she thickened with flour and the other with oatmeal. The darkest was what her uncle had left."

The medical evidence was then taken, and showed that on making the post-mortem examination the stomach and intestines of the deceased were found to be greatly inflamed, and that on analysing the contents of the stomach a large quantity of arsenic was found.

The remains of the pea soup which the deceased had had for his supper also contained a considerable amount of arsenic.

Benjamin Hulme, called, said he knew the prisoner, Edward Clarke. He had seen him several times during the last several weeks. Formerly Clarke used to be very short of money, but lately he had had a good bit. He had seen him change a guinea, and some silver. He had also bought himself a watch and some trousers. Clarke had also recently told him he had been asked in church, and was going to be married to Mary Ann Higgins.

Mr. Wilson, a beer-house keeper, said that Clarke had been in the habit of coming to his house. Mary Ann Higgins had also been in the habit of coming for beer. She had several times lately changed gold at his place, as well as several guineas. On one occasion he lately said to her, "Why, you will change all your fortune away." She laughed, and said she was engaged to Edward Clarke, and was going soon to be married to him. The witness very strongly advised her against the connection, as he did not think he would be any good to her.

John Gavey, who said he worked in the same factory with the male prisoner, Clarke, stated on the morning after the old man died that he was going up to Higgins's house to see whether he was alive or dead, as Higgins had been taken very ill on the previous night after taking his supper, and he wanted to know how he was.

Several witnesses were then called, who depose that during the last several months they had seen Clarke with a great deal more money than he used to have.

Other evidence was then given showing that Clarke had stated that he was in Higgins's house when the old man had his supper, and then went to bed about eight o'clock at night sick and ill.

He had told them also that he had been asked at church with the girl, and that the old man had got some money in the house, and more out at interest.

Mrs. Ruth Clarke said she was the mother of the prisoner, Edward Clarke. Her son worked for Messrs. Vale and Robinson, watch manufacturers. On the night in question her son came home some time about midnight, and said that the poor old man Higgins was very sick and ill, and that he had gone to bed very bad. He then went to bed, and when he got up at a quarter to six he said he should go round and see how the poor old man was.

William Crofts said he had lately seen Clarke with a good deal of money, and the other day he said to him "You seem pretty flush of money?" and Clarke then replied, "Yes, fairly." Witness then said to him, "How do you manage it?" Clarke replied, "Why, I ask my girl for it, and if she don't give it to me I then say 'Well I'll be hanged if I'll come again,' and then she goes and fetches it."

Thomas Gardner said he was one of the watchmen, and he said to the girl "What a pity it is you have been persuaded to do this by anybody!" She then said "I did it myself, because my uncle had some words with me, as at last he was against me marrying Clarke." The old man had told her that she was to have all he had when he died, and as she wanted to get married she got the arsenic and put two teaspoonfuls into his basin, and then poured the soup on to it. All the money that Clarke had had from her was three shillings, one half-sovereign, and one guinea.

The jury then returned a verdict of wilful murder against Mary Ann Higgins, and also a verdict against Clarke of being an accessory before and after the fact.

The case created intense excitement, and the two prisoners were then conveyed to Warwick Gaol to await their trial at the ensuing Assizes.

THE ASSIZES.

In the following August the two prisoners were tried before Mr. Justice Littledale, and the proceedings created greater interest in the county than had been known for many years.

The whole of the evidence, as given before the coroner, was laid before the jury, and at the close the prisoners were asked whether they had anything to say.

The female prisoner said she had not.

The prisoner Edward Clarke said he was not able to address the jury as he would wish, but he had instead prepared a written defence, which he hoped he would be allowed to read.

He then read a very long, elaborate, and able statement, in which he begged to assure the jury on his most solemn oath that he was perfectly innocent of the crime imputed to him.

He had, he said, not only no hand in the poisoning, but he had no knowledge, either before or after the old man's death, that poison had been given to him, till he heard it hinted at by the neighbours, and afterwards in the statements made before the coroner.

He admitted that he was in the house during the time the old man was taking his supper, and also during a part of the time he was ill, but he neither saw nor knew anything of poison either having been intended or given to him.

As to the allegations by some of the witnesses that he had been flush of money, they were great exaggerations, for the money that he had had from the girl was but very trifling indeed.

There was nothing inconsistent, he said, in his having a little money to spend, seeing that he worked at a trade, and as for him saying that he could always get money by threatening to stop away from the girl, that was an untruth.

He asked the jury to remember that it had been sworn on oath that the girl had got a stranger to go with her for poison, and even the girl herself had stated that no one had persuaded her to the act.

He concluded by reminding the jury that his life was now in their hands, and as there had not been one single fact proved against him, he felt certain that, in justice to him, the jury would say he was not guilty.

The jury then, after a short consultation, said they found the prisoner, Mary Ann Higgins, guilty of wilful murder, and that as they considered that she committed the act deliberately and alone, they found the prisoner, Edward Clarke, not guilty.

The prisoner, Clarke, was then discharged, and at once left the dock, leaving his intended bride standing there alone.

The judge then, assuming the black cap, said, Mary Ann Higgins, you have been found guilty upon the most clear and conclusive evidence of the terrible crime of wilful murder.

In the most deliberate way you purchased poison, and in the most systematic and wicked manner you mixed that poison up, and with it took away the life of your uncle—the man who had been your guardian, your protector, and your friend.

It is indeed a sad sight to see one so young—a girl just growing up into womanhood—capable of such a wicked design and cruel murder.

I can most solemnly assure you that you have not long to live in this world, for you will soon have to appear before the bar of your Maker, there to answer for the deeds done in the body.

Let me, therefore, urge upon you not to lose one moment of the time allotted to you here, which will be very short, but use every moment of it to entreat God, whom you have so greatly offended, for mercy and forgiveness.

I can hold out no hope of mercy to you here, and it now only remains for me to pass upon you the just sentence of the law, and that is that you be taken from hence to the gaol from whence you came, and from thence to a place of execution, and that you be there hanged by the neck till you are dead, and that after that your body be given to the surgeons for dissection, and "may the Lord have mercy on your soul!"

A number of persons in the court responded "Amen."

The girl, who heard the sentence without the slightest emotion, then left the dock, and was conveyed to the condemned cell of the gaol.

"Ah!" said some of the neighbours, when they heard of the sentence; "you don't know what some people are capable of. Whoever would have thought that the poor old man would have been brought to such an end as this by one that he had sheltered since she has been a child? But, howsomever, she hasn't got long to live now, and there's no doubt there'll be lots go to see her hung."

THE EXECUTION.

The crime created such a thrill of horror throughout the Midland counties, and so many people it was expected would flock to witness the execution, that it was determined to erect the gallows on a large open space called Whitley Common, and a gallows, with a temporary drop, was accordingly erected there.

STATEMENT IN THE CONDEMNED CELL.

When the wretched girl was conveyed back to the gaol she was visited in the condemned cell by the Rev. S. Paris, jun., and the Rev. F. Franklin. Both of them exhorted her to repentance, and earnestly entreated her to pray for pardon and mercy.

Like many other criminals she was inclined to attribute blame to an over ruling power, and to charge the fault upon the circumstances by which she was surrounded.

She seemed to fall into the common error of overlooking the fact that she had been endowed with intelligence and a knowledge of good and evil, and the power to discriminate between right and wrong.

She had been kindly brought up and taken care of till such time as she was able to take care of herself, and was on the very eve of obtaining, what most women seem to pride themselves upon obtaining, a husband, and a home of her own.

She, however, did not resist temptation to evil, even when the goal of her anticipated happiness was actually within her grasp, but she allowed herself to be influenced by that strange, subtle spirit, which working secretly upon the heart has brought so many millions to destruction.

While in the condemned cell she told the clergyman that it was not true that she had not been instigated to commit the terrible deed. On the contrary, she had been urged to do it.

She further stated that the man who urged her to do it refused to get the poison himself, and also refused to go with her to the shop as a witness.

She also further said that the man who instigated her to do it went out for a quarter of an hour whilst she mixed the poison with the soup and gave it to her uncle, and, finally, after seeing that it did not kill the old man quite quick enough, he said, "Why, hang you, you have not given him enough."

She, however, fully acknowledged her crime, and the justness of her sentence.

The case as it stood, with the statement during the trial that no one prompted her, and then a contradiction just before death, is but one more instance of the many on record showing the little value that must be placed upon the statements of criminals, and it is but another illustration of the positive necessity of judging a case by the facts proved and the positive evidence given.

It is evident that no reliance could be placed upon her last statement, which was probably made, as many others have been made, for the sole purpose of endeavouring to obtain an extension of time, and perhaps a reprieve, when she began to realise the fact that her last hours were approaching.

THE PROCESSION TO THE GALLOWS.

Calcraft arrived in Coventry the night before the day appointed for the execution.

His appearance as the new executioner awakened considerable interest.

When the morning for execution arrived, the whole line of route was thronged with the thousands that had assembled from all parts of the district.

The girl had been brought from Warwick gaol, and had been lodged during the night in the city gaol of Coventry, and thus the whole road from the gaol to the gallows on Whitley Common was thronged with carts, vehicles, and spectators of every grade.

Shortly after eleven o'clock the sheriff's carriages drew up in front of the gaol door, and the sheriffs then emerged from the prison and took their seats.

Next another carriage came up, into which stepped the governor and assistant-governor of the gaol.

In front of the carriages were a large number of the mounted yeomanry and county constabulary.

After these had moved on a little distance, an open cart with a coffin in it was driven up to the door, which was at once opened, and then the girl came out, and walking up some steps into the cart she took her seat upon the top of the coffin, which was so raised that she could be seen by the whole assembly.

After her came the two clergymen, who also stepped into the cart, and took their seats upon two chairs provided for them.

Two warders then came out, and also took their seats in the cart.

Next Calcraft came, and carrying the halter in his hand.

A great shout at once arose of "There's the hangman. There's Jack Ketch, with the rope!" And then it appeared as if the whole of the crowd were standing on their tip-toes to catch a sight of the new executioner.

Calcraft did not get into the cart, but walked behind all the way on foot. A number of javelin-men now took their places on each side of the cart, and two walked on each side of Calcraft.

The procession then moved on, a large number of constables and watchmen bringing up the rear.

As they proceeded on their way to the fatal spot it was evident that the girl recognised many of her old playmates, companions, and friends, for her eyes every now and then were suffused with tears.

There seemed, however, very little sympathy for her in the crowd, and it was evident that the only two who could give her consolation or hope were the two clergymen in attendance upon her.

As soon as the procession had started they again sought to impress upon her mind the necessity of earnest sincere prayer for mercy.

This towards the last she did, and joined with them in repeating a few passages of Scripture, such as, "Lord, make me to know my end, and the measure of my days, what it is, that I may know how frail I am. Behold, Thou hast made my days as an handbreath, and my age is as nothing before Thee."

She then offered up one or two fervent prayers on the road for mercy.

When the procession arrived at the borders of the common she caught sight of the gallows in the distance, and her eyes and face were suddenly seized with a fearful expression of dismay.

When they came to the foot of the gallows, all hats were taken off, and the officiating clergyman, in his robe, then at once commenced the reading of the burial service, commencing with the solemn words, "Man that is born of a woman hath but a short time to live, and is full of misery. He cometh up, and is cut down like a flower; he fleeth as it were a shadow, and never continueth in one stay."

The two clergymen then ascended on to the scaffold. The girl next followed up, and at once placed herself beneath the beam.

Then some of the warders came up, and afterwards the sheriffs, and then the governor of the gaol.

Calcraft now came up, and put the noose of the halter round the girl's neck, and fastened the other end of the rope to the beam above.

Next he pinioned her arms and legs, the girl standing the whole time perfectly firm and unmoved.

Then he untied her bonnet, and taking it off, he put it down on the drop, and finally shook hands with her. The girl then shook hands with both clergymen, and her last words were, "God bless you—God bless you."

Calcraft then put a white cap on her head, and pulled it down over her face, and the clergymen proceeded with the burial service, taking up the words, "In the midst of life we are in death. Of whom may we seek for succour, but of thee, O Lord?"

At this moment the drop fell. Calcraft had slipped underneath, and drawn the fatal bolt, and the girl bounded and plunged and struggled fearfully in the air.

As she was dying very hard and struggling for some minutes, Calcraft jumped up, and catching hold of her legs, swung with his full weight upon her, to try and dislocate her neck, or otherwise end her sufferings.

She was several minutes dying, and the scene was painful to witness.

After hanging the usual time the body was cut down, and given over to the surgeons for dissection.

Such was the terrible end of this young girl, who, had she chosen to have acted with prudence, with gratitude and respect, seemed as though she had every opportunity of life and happiness before her.

She was blessed with good health, considerable personal attractions, and a robust constitution.

She had passed the dangers of bereavement and orphan childhood, and she was at the age when she perfectly knew right from wrong, and she had full facility and encouragement to choose the better path.

She, however, chose the evil way, which led her, not as she thought it would, to the church and the altar of God, but to the gallows and the halter of the hangman instead.

CHAPTER XXXVI.
THE MURDER OF CELIA HOLLOWAY—CASE OF SHOCKING MUTILATION.

It was a bright summer day in August, 1831, when a farm labourer, named David Mascall, who was passing through a thickly wooded plantation in Preston, Sussex, had his attention attracted by part of a woman's garment sticking out from beneath the mould, some distance in the wood.

A strange unaccountable feeling seemed to come over him, and a sort of involuntary shudder appeared for a moment to vibrate within him, as he stood for a moment looking at the piece of cotton gown, part in and part out of the ground.

"I don't like to meddle with that," muttered he to himself, "for if that's part of the proceeds of a robbery, or the remains of some terrible crime, and I should happen to be seen interfering with it I might get into trouble—so for the present I shall leave it alone."

He went on his way to his cottage, and on arriving home said nothing of the circumstance as to what he had seen.

But during the night he felt that he could not rest, for the sight of the rag sticking out of the ground appeared still to keep before his eyes, and the same kind of thrill and shudder every now and then came over him, as before.

During the whole of the following day, also, he felt uneasy, and a sort of curiosity kept stealing over his conscience which made him feel that he ought to tell someone and that they ought to go and see whether there was anything there besides the gown or not.

So on the following evening, the 12th of August, he told another labourer, Abraham Gilham, what he had seen, and asked him to go along with him to see what it was.

Gilham scarcely liked to go at first, but after a little hesitation, with a certain amount of nervous fear, they both went.

When they got near to the spot in the path that led to the place, Mascall hurriedly and nervously said, "There it is; there, look—it's still there!"

They proceeded to the spot, when Gilham said, "Yes, that's part of a woman's frock, sure enough."

"What shall we do?" said Mascall.

"Oh, let us pull it out and see whether it is a whole frock or not," said Gilham, and the two men pulled at the gown, but they could not get it out on account of the weight of mould upon it.

Then they set to work scraping and scooping the mould away with their hands, but the gown went deep down, and at last Gilham said, "It appears to me, David, that this is a newly-made grave."

"So it does to me, Abraham," said Mascall, "and it seems to me as though it smells dreadful."

"I don't like interfering with it further," said Gilham, "so I think we had better let it alone and go home."

"All right," said Mascall, and so they both returned home for the night.

When they got to their cottages they told Gilham's wife and mother, and the women's curiosity being excited, and they also thinking that, perhaps, they would get some reward if it was anything, they told a neighbour, Mrs. Sherlock, and they all agreed to get up early in the morning and go and see really what it was.

At six o'clock in the morning the whole party set out, the men taking with them a spade and a garden fork for the purpose, this time, of digging the ground.

As soon as the women got there they expressed their conviction that something was dreadfully wrong there by the smell, and the men at once began digging round the outskirts of what appeared to be a grave.

Gilham first pulled out a portion of a gown.

Then on digging down a little deeper he dug up one thigh, evidently belonging to a woman.

"Oh, there's been a murder committed," said the women as they began to shriek and tremble, and almost go into hysterics.

"Why can't you keep quiet, now you are come?" said the men, and then they proceeded digging again, and in a few minutes more they dug up another thigh.

"Oh, dear me," said the women, "just look at that!"

The men then dug a little deeper, and they next came upon something which looked like a bundle.

It was heavy, but on getting it out of the grave they found it was the whole trunk of a woman with the stays and clothes on.

They then searched about to see if they could discover the legs, arms, and head, but they could not find them.

They then returned home and communicated with Mr. Stanford, the owner of the plantation and adjoining farm, and also with the constable of the village of Preston, near where the discovery was made.

A special messenger was at once sent off to the High Constable of Brighton, and he and some of the constabulary under his charge in a few hours were on the spot.

The shocking discovery was quickly made known throughout the district, and an inquiry was set on foot to see if anyone was missing.

In addition a full description of the clothing, the material of the gown, and the pattern of the stuff, was published for the purpose of seeing if anyone could give information of any person who had been in the habit of wearing a gown of such a pattern.

In a little time the pattern of the gown was recognised as one which used to be worn by a young woman named Celia Holloway, who formerly lived in Brighton, but was now missing.

Information was given to the effect that deceased had lived very unhappily with her husband, John Holloway, who had been known many times to have ill-used her, and who some time ago had left her, and had gone to live with another young woman, named Ann Kennet.

Search was then made, and the police discovered that Holloway had been living with Ann Kennet at some lodgings in Brighton.

On proceeding there they found Ann Kennet there, but not John Holloway.

In reply to the police, the woman Kennet said she could not give them any information, as she knew nothing at all of the matter.

The officers then proceeded to a house in Margaret-street, where John Holloway had been living, and they proceeded to search the premises, and on emptying a privy at the back they drew out something tied up in some bed ticking, and on opening it they found it to contain the head of the unfortunate wife, Celia Holloway.

They also discovered the legs with the stockings on, and also the arms with the clothing on.

The various parts having been washed and laid together, the body was fully identified, and as John Holloway could not be found, the woman, Ann Kennet, was taken into custody.

In the course of a few hours John Holloway came voluntarily to the watch-house at Brighton, and surrendered himself to James Feldwicke, a constable on duty there, at the same time declaring himself innocent of the charge.

THE CORONER'S INQUEST.

The inquest on the mutilated remains of the unfortunate woman was held at the "Crown and Anchor Tavern," Preston, when the body was fully identified as being that of Celia Holloway, and other evidence having been given as to the finding of the remains, the two prisoners were fully committed to take their trial at the ensuing assizes at Lewes.

THE TRIAL.

The trial came on at Lewes Assizes, Sussex, on December 14, 1831, before Mr. Justice Patteson, and a respectable jury.

The prisoner, John Holloway, aged twenty-five, was indicted for the wilful murder of his wife, Celia Holloway, on or about the 16th of July, the deceased woman at that time being about thirty-one years of age.

Ann Kennet was also charged with being an accessory.

The first witnesses called were David Mascall, and Abraham Gillham, who proved the finding of the trunk and thighs of the deceased buried in a copse at Preston, adjoining the farm of Mr. Stanford on the 14th of August.

The next witness was Mr. W. Muil, who stated that on examining a privy at Mrs. Lewes's house in Margaret-street, Brighton, he found beneath the night soil two arms, two legs, and the head of a human being.

Police-constable W. Pilbean deposed that he recognised the head found as being that of the missing woman, Celia Holloway.

Mr. John Hardgrave, surgeon, and Mr. Richardson, surgeon, stated that they had made a post-mortem examination of the remains found, and they had come to the conclusion that they were the remains of a female about thirty-one years of age, who had died from suffocation, probably through strangulation.

Several witnesses then deposed to finding a box in the copse, with other portions of the remains in it.

Mrs. Amelia Symmonds stated that the deceased resided at her house for a time previous to her death. On the 14th of July the prisoner also came there, and afterwards they both went out of the house together.

Frances Symmonds, a little girl nine years of age, was next called, and stated that she saw the prisoner, John Holloway, come to her house about the 14th of July and fetch a box away.

James Symmonds, and also Frances Hawkins, deposed that on various occasions they had seen John Holloway strike and ill-use his wife, and that they had also heard him say to her, "that she should suffer."

Another witness, a boy named J. Marchant, stated that he remembered Holloway bringing a box to another house he had taken, at No. 11, Donkey-row, Brighton.

On seeing him take the box into the house, he looked in, and the prisoner Holloway then said, "You be off—will you?"

Mr. D. Folkard, the High-Constable of Brighton, deposed that he had examined the house, No. 11, Donkey-row, which the prisoner Holloway had last taken.

He found the stairs all covered with blood, and there was also a quantity of blood in the closet under the stairs.

Mrs. Brown deposed that she resided in the next house to the one in Donkey-row which the prisoner Holloway had taken.

One day in July she saw him bring a sack with something in it into his house, and in three days afterwards she saw him carry a box out, tied up in a dirty handkerchief.

He went down the yard with it, and away into the street.

The jury then found Ann Kennet not guilty, and she was discharged.

Robert Salvage, a warder of Lewes gaol, was next called, and deposed that Holloway while in prison had made two different confessions, which he (witness) had taken down in writing and now produced.

The following were

THE CONFESSIONS.

Lewes Gaol.

I became acquainted with the deceased about eight years ago. She was with child by me soon after our intimacy began.

About seven years ago, in 1825, when I was about nineteen years of age, the overseers compelled me to marry her. We lived pretty happily together at first, until my wife's relations took from us some furniture which they had given us to induce me to marry her.

After that they did all they could to make us wretched, and my wife did all she could to destroy my peace of mind.

Whereupon I left her, and went to live with Ann Kennet, and we passed as man and wife.

For some time before I committed the deed I had resolved to destroy my wife, and for that purpose I several times tried to induce her to accompany me to some retired spot, so that I might dispatch her, but finding that of no avail I took a house in Donkey-row, near Brighton, under the pretence of again living with her.

She then accompanied me there, and when I got her into the house I seized her by the throat unawares, and she fell to the ground.

I then threw her under a chest of drawers, and continued pressing on her throat with all the force I could until I strangled her.

When she had ceased struggling, I took out my knife and cut her throat.

I did not strip the body, but finding I could not carry off the corpse whole I cut off the head, and then divided the limbs with my knife; and then I cut her in the manner in which she had been found.

I put the trunk and thighs into a box and carried them to the place where they were found in the copse.

Then I dug a hole and buried them there. I was the only person in the house when the murder was committed.—Signed. JOHN HOLLOWAY.

After making this declaration and signing it before the magistrates, the prisoner then told the magistrates that his mind was greatly relieved.

SECOND CONFESSION.

A few days after making this confession Holloway made a different one. He said:—

After I had got my wife to the house in Donkey-row she sat down on the stairs.

I then approached her as if I was going to kiss her, but instead of that I suddenly tied the cord round her neck, threw myself upon her body, and exerted all my force to strangle her.

She fell from the stairs and struggled a good deal, and then I took hold of one end of the cord in each hand, and continued stretching it till I had extinguished life.

I then dragged the body to the closet underneath the stairs, where I hung it up for the night.

The next day I went and took the body down, and cut it up as before described.

I then emptied the chaff out of the bed ticking, and putting the head, arms, and legs into it I formed a bag, which, with the assistance of Kennet, I conveyed to Margaret-street, and threw down the privy.—Signed JOHN HOLLOWAY.

The prisoner was then called on for his defence.

Prisoner: My lord, some time ago a man named Winter committed a shocking murder—he was pardoned, therefore why should I be hanged? I don't wish to live—a man who commits murder ought to die, but I have the same right to be sent out of the country that Winter had. I know I committed the murder, but it is not plain or clear in evidence. The woman might have made away with herself, and out of fear I might have concealed it. I don't say that that is the case. Whether Cecilly was murdered or not I don't wish to live; but let me only say this—Ann Kennet is innocent. I have no witnesses to call. I don't want witnesses to save my life.

The learned judge then summed up the evidence. He commented on the fact that the prisoner seemed to have premeditated the murder, for he had actually taken a house in Donkey-row, not apparently for the purpose of living in it, for he was living somewhere else, but evidently for the special purpose of committing a murder in it. After calling attention to the other facts of the case his lordship left it with the jury to say whether the prisoner was guilty or not.

JAMES COOK DEALING THE FATAL BLOW WITH THE PRESS PIN.

The jury after a short consultation found the prisoner guilty.

The judge then, assuming the black cap, said:—Prisoner at the bar, you have been found guilty, after a most patient hearing, of the crime of wilful murder, and the unfortunate victim was the wife you had promised to cherish and support. The circumstances of the case are about the most barbarous and appalling that have ever come under my notice, and it now only remains for me to exhort you to make the best use of the short time you have to live, for I can hold out no hope of mercy or pardon here. The sentence I have now to pass upon you is that you be taken from this place to the place from whence you came, and from thence to a place of execution, and there hanged by the neck till you are dead, and may the Lord have mercy on your soul.

FINAL CONFESSION.

After the prisoner's removal to Lewes gaol, after his condemnation, he expressed a wish to see the Rev Mr. Wetherby, and accordingly that gentleman and the Rev. Mr. Abbott had a long interview with him in his cell.

He then made a further confession of his wicked career.

He stated that the reason he had said that Ann Kennet was innocent was because he wished to save her life.

There was nothing, however, to show that she had any hand in the murder, or that she was an accessory to it.

Some further information obtained of the life and antecedents of the prisoner prove him to have been naturally of a bad disposition.

It was known that he had on one or two occasions induced girls to go with him in a boat upon the sea, and that when they were out of sight of land that he had threatened to drown them unless they submitted to his violation.

In one instance one girl struggled with him to such an extent that she threatened to drown him unless he at once desisted from his purpose, and he had to row her back in safety to the land.

While in the gaol he also became the leader of a most desperate gang of prisoners, and he proposed a conspiracy to them to assassinate the turnkeys and governor, and make their escape.

The plan, however, failed, and he was safely kept in irons till the morning of the execution.

CALCRAFT ON THE GALLOWS ATTEMPTING A MIRACULOUS CURE.

Two days after his condemnation the prisoner was removed from Lewes gaol in a cart to Horsham for execution, where the gallows was erected.

Both he and the deceased were well known in that part of the country. The deceased, Celia Holloway, was born of poor parents at Ardingley, in Sussex, her maiden name being Celia Bashford.

Her husband, the prisoner, was born at Littleton.

He had been employed in various ways, first as a butcher's boy, a bricklayer's labourer, a blockade man, and last of all he obtained subsistence by working on Brighton pier, where he was last employed on the day he surrendered.

A great number of persons assembled to witness the execution, and as he appeared on the scaffold he was received with loud groans and yells.

Calcraft then came up, and adjusted the rope round his neck.

The rope was not very long, and the culprit, who died rather hard, swung fully in view of the immense multitude gathered together.

A sickening spectacle then ensued, which caused Calcraft to be hissed and hooted from the scaffold, and brought him into considerable disfavour with the sheriffs and other officials engaged.

It appears that a man who throughout his lifetime had been afflicted with a very large unsightly excrescence—a wen upon the neck—had prevailed upon Calcraft to allow him to come upon the scaffold for the purpose of trying the old superstitious method of endeavouring to cure the wen by stroking it with the hand of a hanged man.

As soon, therefore, as Calcraft saw that the culprit's life was extinct he unfastened his hands, and unpinioned his arms, and then, taking hold of one of the dead man's hands, he commenced stroking with it the wen on the other man's neck.

The vast crowd looked and wondered for a time at what was going on, and not being able to comprehend the meaning of it, they came to the conclusion that Calcraft and the man were having a lark, and carrying on a sort of senseless pantomime, just to please the people, and thus setting aside all decorum, they were endeavouring to show their indignation at the character and acts of the deceased culprit.

The people began, however, to hiss, hoot, and yell, but the man stood quietly still, while Calcraft kept on stroking and rubbing, endeavouring to charm the wen away with the dead man's hand.

"What are they doing of?" cried the people. "What does this mean?"

While Calcraft was thus busily employed, quite intent on working and completing the miraculous cure, the sheriffs ran upon the scaffold, and demanded an explanation of the ludicrous and sickening performance.

Calcraft and the man then informed the sheriffs that they were adopting the charm which often used to be performed, and which was stated in some very old books of the middle ages to be the best and only cure for a wen on a person's neck.

The sheriffs immediately ordered Calcraft to desist from his magical operation, as his duty was to kill and not to cure.

THE REFORM BILL RIOTS—THE GAOLS ON FIRE—HUNDREDS KILLED AND WOUNDED.

In consequence of the House of Lords having rejected the new Reform Bill, brought into the House of Commons in 1831 by Lord John Russell, the whole country was indignant, and great excitement prevailed from one end of the kingdom to the other.

In fact, as has been recently said by one of the Cabinet ministers, England was at that time within twenty-four hours of a disastrous revolution.

There was scarcely a town where great meetings were not held.

The demonstrations, headed by Mr. Thomas Attwood, of Birmingham, on New Hall-hill and other places; the disturbances at Manchester and other cities filled the Government with alarm, and truly showed them that the temper and spirit of the people must no longer be trifled with, but that reforms must be granted in accordance with the advancing education, enlightenment, and requirements of the age.

It was at Bristol, however, where some of the greatest excesses took place, and as a single spark will sometimes cause the greatest conflagration, so oftentimes a single unwise action will lead to terrible results.

It appears that Sir Charles Wetherell, the then

Recorder of Bristol, had taken active measures with the Tory party in opposing the proposed bill of reform.

When, therefore, on the 31st of October, 1831, he came to Bristol to sit at the assizes, it was determined by the people to mark their disapprobation of his conduct by an open demonstration.

He, on his part, was determined to make a public display by entering the city in a carriage drawn by four greys, a strong escort, and a guard of 400 policemen.

The Government, too, on their part, had also advised magistrates and sheriffs to take every precaution against being overawed or intimidated by the people of the reform party, and thus it was that throughout the whole country the two parties were almost on the verge of civil war.

When Sir Charles Wetherell arrived in Bristol the streets through which he had to pass were lined with thousands of people.

As soon as the procession came in sight he was hissed and hooted, and followed with every discordant yell.

Great fears were at one time entertained lest an attempt might be made to drag him from his carriage, and thus subject him to personal violence.

On his arrival, however, at the Guildhall, there were fully ten thousand people congregated, and a cry was raised, "To the back, to the back!"

It was now evident that violence was intended, and there was a general rush made to the back yard of the Guildhall.

In this yard there happened to be at the time huge piles of faggots and sticks, and the people, having broken into the yard, armed themselves with the thickest of them, which they used as staves to fight with.

The next cry that was raised was, "To the Mansion House, some of you off to the Mansion House."

Hereupon thousands rushed frantically off to the Mansion House and made an attack, while others were engaged in rioting round the Guildhall.

When the rioters got to the Mansion House they tore up the iron palisades, and armed themselves with them as pikes.

Next they battered down the shutters which had been put up, and broke the windows, and began to otherwise demolish the building, doing immense damage.

The trumpets were now heard sounding at the barracks, and the bugles through various parts of the city calling the soldiers together, and in the course of about an hour a body of cavalry came dashing along the streets.

As they were coming, riding nearly over the crowded masses, one man struck one of the soldiers, and the soldier immediately turned round and shot him dead upon the spot.

The attacking party of the rioters having by this time forced the doors of the Mansion House, had it completely in possession.

The inmates had been obliged to fly, and the rioters now seized every valuable in the place.

Some thousands of them went into the extensive wine cellars of the Mansion House, where there were large stores of fine choice old wines and spirits.

The rioters in one cellar found 3600 bottles of old port, besides sherry, and other liquors, of which they drank as much as they could themselves, and then distributed the rest among the people in the street.

In the course of three or four hours thousands of men, women, and children were lying helplessly drunk about the roads, like so many intoxicated flies.

Numbers of special constables were sworn in, and the police and soldiers went about the streets picking up the senselessly drunken people, and carrying them off wholesale to the cells of the various neighbouring gaols to await their trials on the charges to be brought against them. Meantime, while all these scenes were being enacted, large reinforcements of rioters, with flags, and red caps of liberty on poles, came up in all directions.

As they marched through the various districts, they gathered fresh strength in every street.

Some hours passed away in this manner, with the people increasing their forces as they paraded the city, evidently intent on putting the magistrates, the police, and the military at open defiance.

The cavalry at length charged, and some serious conflicts took place, but the populace, pressed from one street, only rushed to another, smashing the windows, and otherwise destroying the dwellings of those prominently opposed to reform.

The ranks of the rioters were now again greatly reinforced by a number of women, and a cry of "To the Bridewell, to the Bridewell," was next raised, and numbers of the rioters rushed off to that prison.

On their way they seized a number of heavy hammers from blacksmiths' shops, and with these they proceeded in the direction of the Bridewell.

They completely overpowered the police drawn up there, cut through their ranks and got up to the Bridewell gates.

Here they at once commenced hammering away at the massive iron doors and windows with the heavy sledge hammers which they had brought, and the doors and windows falling before the weight of the ponderous sledge irons so vigorously applied, the rioters broke in with a rush, and hundreds entering the prison they set to work inside—battered down the doors of the cells, and liberated every prisoner within.

The prisoners now being set free, tremendous shouts of triumph echoed through the corridors, and "Hurrah—hurrah," rang again and again upon the air from within the battered walls.

In the midst of these shouts of joy the rioters knocked off the shackles of the prisoners, and the prisoners—men, women, and children—determined not to be captured in the streets in their prison clothes, threw them off and ran home completely naked through the streets, whilst the rioters stayed behind, and setting the prison on fire, burnt it to the ground.

While these lawless proceedings were being carried on at the "Bridewell," another cry, "To the gaol—the new gaol," was next raised, and immediately a strong contingent of the rioters, followed by thousands of persons, proceeded there.

On their way, they broke into the ship-yards, and, having stolen a large number of heavy hammers from there, they at once attacked the new gaol, by battering the doors, windows, and walls with the hammers.

In the space of a short time they effected an entrance there also, and, bursting open the cells, they knocked the irons from the prisoners there, and set everyone free, amounting to over one hundred in number.

The prisoners here then took off their clothes, and ran into a field naked, and then home nearly naked through the streets, having obtained a few rags just to cover them.

As soon as they had cleared the gaol, they then set fire to the treadmill, and then to the building, and in less than an hour the governor's house was also in flames.

In addition to the other regiment of cavalry that had been charging through the streets, the 3rd Dragoon Guards were called out, and they came up at full gallop, to endeavour to prevent the destruction of the gaol.

The next cry that was raised was, "to Gloucester gaol—off with you lads to Gloucester gaol."

The ringleaders led the way, and thousands following them; they went next and attacked the county gaol of Gloucester.

They battered the doors of that prison open too, and after knocking the shackles from the prisoners there, they set them free as well.

Having cleared that gaol they set that on fire, and as the fires were not extinguished at the other places, there were three prisons blazing at one time.

Whilst the destruction of the gaols was going on, another contingent of the rioters had gone off to the bishop's palace, and commenced the work of destruction there.

At the same time another body marched off and attacked the Mansion-house and set that on fire, and fifty houses besides, whilst another gang went to the Custom-house, which they first plundered, and then fired in the same way.

In the various skirmishes which took place, chiefly between the police and the people, many persons were killed, about 100 were seriously wounded, whilst about 300 received minor injuries.

During three whole days the rioters were complete masters of both cities.

This was, however, owing in great measure to the moderation shown by the officers of the military, and the reluctance they exhibited either to charge or fire upon the people.

Considering the temper and the spirit of the populace, it is well that it was so.

Had the dragoons and other cavalry regiments fired down the crowded streets the slaughter of the excited but comparatively unarmed people must have been terrible.

It is true that a great deal of valuable property was destroyed, that the prisons being broken open, and the prisoners being released showed that the Government was utterly put at defiance, but what was that in comparison with the greater excesses which would most certainly have followed had the sabres of the soldiery been drawn and the people mowed down like grass.?

Had such been the case civil war would undoubtedly have spread.

The people would have seized arms, and in most towns they would have risen *en masse*, and the fearful retribution of a general revolution would have followed, in which, undoubtedly, nobles, artisans, and peasants would have fallen alike, which probably would have shaken Royalty from its throne and would have raised another form of government in its place, as France already had done.

THE SUPREME MOMENT OF REVOLUTION AND THE CRISIS.

It was at this critical moment, at this crisis when the rioters were exasperated and excited, that orders came from the Government to the sheriffs, mayors, and magistrates in a general proclamation commanding them to use the most strenuous exertions for repressing the rioters.

The mayor and the magistrates of Bristol first appealed to the commanding officers of the soldiers to assist in quelling the riot.

As they did not respond in that prompt manner, by at once coming and charging the people, the mayor then gave peremptory orders to the officers to come to the assistance of the civil authorities at once.

But the officers, undoubtedly reluctant to undertake the responsibility of shedding so much blood considerably delayed the time in coming.

When they eventually did turn out some of the officers appealed to the people, and endeavoured to persuade them to desist from lawless acts of violence, and many appreciating the moderation shown returned to their homes, and the riots gradually subsided.

It will thus be seen that for the time the military officers were wiser than the civil authorities, for the moderation shown prevented the extension of the flames.

ARRESTS OF THE RIOTERS.

Several hundreds of the ringleaders of the rioters were, however, afterwards arrested and charged with rioting, murder, and the wilful destruction of property.

Of these, 180 at Bristol were committed for trial, and when the special commission opened they were nearly all convicted, and a large number of them were sentenced to transportation for life.

No less, however, than fifty were found guilty upon the capital charge and sentence of death was recorded against them.

Petitions, however, were prepared and sent to the king, explanatory of the manner the riots had commenced, and setting forth the excited state of public feeling owing to the rejection of the Reform Bill, and also praying for a commutation of the sentences in the lesser serious cases.

The capital sentences were all, however, commuted into transportation for life, with the exception of four cases, in which the men were left for execution as a warning to others:

THE EXECUTION.

It was in January, 1832, that Calcraft had to go to Bristol to execute the four unfortunate men who had been left for death.

Their names were Christopher Davis, William Clarke, Joseph Kayes, and Thomas Gregory.

Owing to the many violent and daring speeches which had been made of a very threatening character, it was anticipated that probably a rescue would be attempted.

At one meeting in which the petitions to the king were being discussed, one speaker argued that the open exasperating display Sir Charles Wetherell had made had been the chief cause of the riots, and he maintained that it was Sir Charles Wetherell, if anyone, who ought to be hung.

Another speaker said that, unless the king at once acted and prevented these threatened wholesale executions, the people must act for themselves.

The Government, however, were quite determined to show that they would not be intimidated by the populace, and in spite of all the threatening proceedings they ordered the executions to be proceeded with.

When the morning for execution came a very large contingent of constables and other officials kept the ground, and a large force of artillery, cavalry, and infantry were in reserve, and at the time appointed the four unfortunate men appeared on the scaffold.

With as little delay as possible Calcraft came up and put the ropes round their necks, and after placing each man in his proper position under the beam, he shook hands with him, and then hastened down behind the scaffold, and the drop immediately fell.

COURT-MARTIAL ON THE MILITARY OFFICERS.

The authorities being very indignant at what they

considered the supineness of Colonel Brereton, who had command of the soldiery at Bristol, and also displeased with the alleged dilatoriness of Captain Warrington, of the 3rd Dragoon Guards, the Government ordered them both to be tried by court-martial.

A great deal of evidence was adduced against them, charging them with neglect of duty, and also throwing upon them the blame of all the loss that occurred through their refusal and negligence to act.

SUICIDE OF COLONEL BRERETON.

The charges brought against Colonel Brereton, and the general displeasure which his conduct brought upon him, so preyed upon his mind that on the fourth day of the trial he shot himself with a pistol, and immediately upon his death becoming known the evidence as concerned him was brought to a sudden termination.

The evidence, however, against Captain Warrington was proceeded with, and he was found guilty. The sentence upon him was that he should be cashiered, and dismissed the regiment.

TRIAL OF THE MAYOR OF BRISTOL BEFORE THE KING'S BENCH.

A charge of neglect of duty was also preferred by the Government against Mr. Pinney, the Mayor of Bristol, for not having taken prompt measures at first to quell the riot, and prevent the destruction of property which ensued.

He explained to the jury, in defence, that he had done all he possibly could.

He had called on the military, who neglected to obey his orders, and he could do no more, as he was comparatively powerless against so many thousands of lawless excited people.

The jury acquitted him of the charge, and found that he had done all he was able in the trying circumstances in which he was placed.

EXECUTIONS AT NOTTINGHAM.

About the same time that the riots were taking place at Bristol, similar disturbances broke out at Bath, Coventry, Worcester, Derby, Manchester, and Nottingham; partly in consequence of the rejection of the Reform Bill, and partly through the introduction of machinery into various manufactories.

At Nottingham the rioters set fire to a silk mill, and they also caused great destruction to property by setting fire to Nottingham Castle.

Many of the rioters were arrested at these places, and at Nottingham five men were left for death, whilst a number of those convicted were sent into transportation.

Two of those, however, left for execution, had their sentences commuted just before the time fixed for their death.

Calcraft therefore proceeded to Nottingham on the 1st of February to carry the sentence out on the three men ordered to be hung on the 2nd.

When the time for the execution arrived, as it was feared that a rescue would have been attempted here, the ground for a considerable distance round the gallows was kept by a large body of the 15th Hussars, and a strong contingent of the 18th Infantry, besides a large body of the town watchmen.

The three men who suffered death at Nottingham on this occasion were George Beck, George Hearson, and John Armstrong.

Calcraft on this occasion also adjusted the ropes as speedily as he could, but Hearson danced on the scaffold, and called to various people he recognised.

Calcraft then running quietly down behind the gallows the three men paid the penalty of the law.

SPREAD OF THE CHOLERA.

While the excitement, in reference to the Reform Bill was at its highest the cholera broke out with alarming virulence, and many persons were carried away with the dreadful pestilence.

The physicians throughout the kingdom in the most patriotic and fearless manner tendered their services publicly to all affected, and by combined attention to sanitary improvement the fearful scourge was at last stamped out.

PASSING OF THE REFORM BILL.

No sooner had Parliament opened in 1832 than numerous addresses were sent in to the Crown demanding immediate reform.

These addresses were in no way distinguished by moderation of tone or language; the Chartist associations were spreading fast throughout the kingdom, and at length a new Reform Bill, under the Administration of Earl Grey, was rapidly hurried through the House, and having been allowed to pass the House of Lords on the condition that no new peers should be created, it received the royal assent on the 7th of June.

A better Parliamentary representation having thus been obtained, a greater amount of contentment was secured, and the people looked forward with hope to the remedying of many existing abuses and to increased prosperity.

DEATH OF SIR RICHARD BIRNIE.

The chief magistrate of Bow-street Police-court, who had risen by his own industry in a remarkable manner, and before whom many notorious prisoners had been charged, died in April of 1832.

SHOCKING CASE OF MURDER AND BURNING AT LEICESTER.
EXCITING CHASE AFTER THE MURDERER.

One of the most shocking cases of murder, mutilation, and burning, which disgrace the annals of crime, also took place this year.

The crime took place at Leicester, in the month of May 1832, and the discovery of the crime was made in the following manner:—

A working man, who resided in a back house up a court in Wellington-street, Leicester, late one evening noticed a bright light in a workshop at the top end of the court, which was occupied by a young man named James Cook, a bookbinder by trade.

The workshop was over some cow-sheds, and as it was an unusual thing to see a light in it that time of night, the man concluded that a fire was just breaking out.

Thinking to stop the further progress of what he considered a fire, he ran up the yard and burst open the workshop door for the purpose of rendering what assistance he could.

On entering the shop he was astonished to find that the light only proceeded from a large fire in the grate, but his attention was attracted by a terrible smell, as of the burning of flesh.

He noticed that some was burning on the fire, whilst several other large pieces were lying near. He went downstairs, and communicated with the watchman of the district, who came and made a cursory view of the place, and he finding a good deal of flesh about went to young Cook's house to inform him of what had taken place.

Young Cook, who was twenty-two years of age, resided with his father in New Milk-street, Leicester, and on proceeding to the house they found him there.

On telling him that they had been into his shop, as they thought there was a fire there, and had found some flesh burning, he replied—"Yes—oh yes, I had a large dog promised me, and I bought a lot of flesh for it, but as I was disappointed in not getting the dog, I thought I had better burn the meat, as it began to smell so bad."

The watchman, however, afterwards called in a medical man, and after examining some of the various portions left, he gave it as his opinion that they were the remains of a human being.

They went back to the house, but young Cook maintained they were not. They, however, were about taking him to the lock-up on suspicion, but as his father assured the officers that he would be answerable for his son appearing to answer any charge that might be made against him in the morning, if they would allow him to sleep at home during the night, they consented to let him remain, and they went away.

The next morning they made a further search, and then they found other pieces, which were unmistakeably parts of a human body.

They found also a chopper, and a large bar of iron with blood upon them, and in raking the embers, they found a small pencil case with a "P." upon it.

Afterwards they discovered the remains of some clothing, portions of the legs of a gentleman's trousers with blood upon them.

Meantime, the news of a suspected murder spread through the town, and inquiries were then instituted for the purpose of ascertaining whether anyone was known to be missing.

In the course of a few hours they received information that a commercial gentleman, Mr. Paas, brass ornament manufacturer, and maker of book-binders tools, of No. 44, High Holborn, London, was missing from the "Stag and Pheasant," of Leicester.

It was stated that he had come there on the 27th of May, on his usual business to the town; that he went out to call upon his customers, leaving his portmanteau and some of his boxes of patterns still at the hotel.

The suspicion then at once gained ground that the remains found were those of the unfortunate gentleman, and his friends in London were communicated with.

Some of them immediately went down to Leicester, and recognised several trinkets, and other things found in Cook's shop, as having belonged to the deceased gentleman.

The following day after the murder was discovered the watchmen went again to Cook's house to arrest him, but in the meantime he had decamped, and was no more to be found. They now regretted having left him at home through trusting in his father's word.

The father was then arrested, and the inquest was opened, but there being nothing against the father he was discharged.

THE INQUEST.

It was shown in evidence that an elderly gentleman with rather gray whiskers had been seen by some witnesses to go up the yard to Cook's shop, and he was not seen to return.

A boy who worked for Cook deposed that a week or two ago Cook purchased a saw and a chopper, and that he had the chopper ground very sharp.

When it was ground Cook hung it up on the wall, and told him not to touch it for anything.

After that Cook sent him for a quantity of straw, which he kept tied up in bundles in a corner of the shop.

He had bought Cook a quantity of laudanum from different places, which Cook kept in a phial bottle.

He also recollected seeing Mr. Paas come for his account, and for some more orders on the afternoon of the 28th of May.

When Mr. Paas came into the shop, Cook came to him (witness) and told him that he could go home then, and stop away four or five days, as he would not want him again for about a week.

He then went home, leaving Mr. Paas with Cook in the workshop.

Several witnesses stated that they had for a day or more noticed a dreadful smell of burning, like the burning of flesh.

It was further shown in evidence that a night or two after the murder had been committed, Cook went to a neighbouring public-house to play at bowls, a thing he was rather unaccustomed to do, and that he appeared rather flush of money.

Other witnesses proved that he had been trying to dispose of some jewellery, which he said he did not want, and which he would sell very cheap. One article was a mourning pin of a peculiar manufacture, which from the description left very little doubt that they had belonged to Mr. Paas.

The jury returned a verdict of wilful murder against James Cook, and the coroner issued a warrant for his apprehension, which was at once put into the hands of the police.

The police having obtained information which led them to believe that Cook had left the town, and that he had an uncle and aunt who kept an eating and boarding-house in Liverpool, they thought it probable that he might make for there, and that he very likely would endeavour from there to get to America.

Accordingly, some of the officers started off on their way for Liverpool, and they had not long been on the road, before they ascertained that a man, answering Cook's description, had been seen to go in that direction by a previous coach.

At every stage of the coach's stoppage they made inquiries, and heard tidings of a man having several days before gone on the road.

At length they arrived in Liverpool, and proceeding at once to the house of the aunt of the prisoner, they kept observation a little time, but not seeing anything of him, they went in and showed the landlord a handbill containing an account of the murder.

"Good heavens!" said the landlord; "why that is a description of my nephew." The uncle and aunt then assured the police he had not been there, but that if he should come they would detain him.

Next the officers communicated with the chiefs of the Liverpool police, and they promised every assistance.

In fact the public feeling was everywhere so aroused at the atrocity of the crime, that there was a general manifestation of feeling to bring the murderer to justice.

The police now inquired at all the shipping agents' offices, to ascertain if any vessels had lately left the port, and having ascertained that none had left Liverpool for America since the commission of the murder, they felt cheered with the hope that their man was still hiding somewhere in the neighbourhood.

In the course of their inquiries, however, they learnt that a vessel bound for America was going to sail that very morning, and that she was then lying off the Mersey, just getting up her sail.

The officers now promised all the water and lightermen a handsome reward for any information they could bring that would lead to the murderer's arrest.

In the course of a little time some of the watermen went off in various directions with their boats, and of them shortly came back with the information that a man on the over night had made an engagement with a waterman, from the Cheshire side of the Mersey, to row him to the ship about the middle of the day.

"Now then, lads, said the superintendent, "there's no time to be lost. Here's two sovereigns for the best boat and best crew that you can get together to take us to the ship and back, and £5 to be divided among you if you put us on board before the ship starts."

"All right, captain," said the watermen to the superintendent. "The tide's coming in strong, and she'll soon be off; but never mind, jump in here, you and your men, and we'll try and get you there."

The superintendent and two of his officers got into the boat, and as they were preparing to be off the superintendent said to some of the other constables—

"Look here, two or three of you had better be off in another boat, and keep observation on the Cheshire shore."

The watermen now dipped their oars in the water, and pulled away with firm, regular strokes, and soon the boat, with the superintendent and his men, were out of sight on their way to the vessel lying at sea outside the river.

In a few more minutes another boat was manned, and two officers from Leicester, Halwell and Cummins, jumped in, with some picked watermen, to go down beyond Seacombe, and keep observation on the Cheshire coast.

These men now pulled away with all their might, and as they too glided out of sight on the tide, which was now coming in very fast, great excitement prevailed.

Great numbers of persons were on the quay, and also on the banks of the river, and many followed miles down by the shore, anxious to watch the pursuing boats as far as their eyes could reach.

Some even went out with telescopes to some of the hills and neighbouring rocks, where a good view of the sea and shipping could be obtained.

The ship, as it lay out at anchor at sea, by the aid of a powerful telescope could be distinctly seen. The sailors were running up and down the rigging, busily engaged in unfurling every sail.

Now there was a movement round the ropes of the anchor, and it was evident they were getting the ship under weigh.

Presently the boom of the first cannon was heard as a signal that the ship would soon be off.

"The boats won't be up in time now, if they don't make haste," said some of the spectators.

"Yes they will, I think," said some of the others. "There are two more guns to be fired yet before she's off, and the superintendent's boat is not far off now."

Meantime the other boat, with the other two officers in it, was cruising away some distance past Seacombe on the Cheshire coast.

All of a sudden a third boat was seen to emerge from some place beyond the Black Rock, and to be pulling hard towards the ship.

"What's that third boat I wonder?" said some of the spectators, who had telescopes. "It's pulling hard towards the ship as though some one is nearly left behind."

"By George, Halwell and Cummins's boat is rowing after it as though they see something," said others of the spectators.

"There's something up. They are chasing it," said others.

The excitement now on the hills and on the rocks became intense, and the eagerness of the people to try and make out what was going on knew no bounds.

"Allow me to have a look through your glass," said first one and then the other, and "What are they doing now?" and such like requests and questions showed the exciting interest taken.

All interest seemed to have been taken from the superintendent's boat to watch the chase that Halwell and Cummins were making in the other.

It appears, from what was afterwards given in evidence, that as soon as Halwell and Cummins saw the strange boat come from behind the Black Rock their suspicions were aroused, and they were determined to try and come up with it if they could.

"Now, my lads, pull away," said Halwell to the watermen, "and here's three sovereigns for you if you come up with the boat, and five—I'll make it five—sovereigns if the fellow is there and we apprehend him."

The watermen now redoubled their vigour, and pulled even harder than they had pulled before.

In fact, the perspiration fairly rolled down them.

Meanwhile, the men in the strange boat pulled equally hard towards the ship, and as they appeared to be almost rowing for their lives, it was evident they were stimulated by some handsome reward too.

In the course of a little time the officers' boat gained sufficiently upon the other, and brought them near enough to see the figure of a man sitting in the middle of the boat.

"Pull away, boys; I'll lay a wager that's him," said the officers again, and in a moment the officers' boat put on another spurt.

Suddenly the strange boat, instead of continuing its course towards the ship, turned round as if it would again make for the Black Rock.

"What does that mean, I wonder?" said the officers. "That looks like him, I believe; and I think he recognises us, and he's off."

"Ah, then, he means escaping again to the shore," said the watermen.

"Pull away, my lads; mustn't lose him now," said the officers, and the men again renewed their efforts.

The strange boat now seemed to have all power put on, and the men in that were fast pulling down the Mersey by the side of the Black Rock, still pursued by the constables' boat.

The two boats were now dodging each other with all the ability and strength that could be commanded, and the chase became more and more exciting.

In a little more time the constables' boat got near enough to the other to see distinctly, for certain, that it was Cook that was in the boat.

He was evidently bribing and cheering his men on to get well ahead, and land him somewhere in safety.

The constables called loudly to the men in the boat to stop, but the men heeded not, and strongly pulled away. The officers' boat, however, followed in hot pursuit, and very nearly came up with the other underneath the Black Rock.

Cook, now seeing that he was nearly being captured, put his hand into his pocket, and gave his boatmen some sovereigns, and then, standing up in the boat, he at once jumped overboard into the sea, and sank out of sight.

"Pull away after him, my boys," said the officer. In another moment Cook appeared again upon the surface of the waves, a short distance from the boat, for the purpose of getting breath.

As soon as he appeared in sight this time Halwell jumped into the sea after him, but Cook, seeing the constable also take to the water, now took another header underneath, and having dived a considerable distance, he appeared again upon the surface some distance below both the constable and the boat.

The constable and the boat pursued him again, and then Cook, having taken breath again, took another dive.

"Take the boat a good way down this time," said Halwell, and the constable then took a dive, and swam some distance under the waves.

The next time both Cook and the constable came up to the surface again for breath, they were almost close to each other, and very near to the officers' boat.

Halwell now made a desperate spring, and nearly touched Cook, but he, like lightning, took underneath the water again.

Halwell dived after him, but Cook, becoming exhausted, soon came to the surface again.

Halwell also floated to the surface, and as he rose he came up close against Cook, and this time succeeded in laying hold of him.

Cook tried hard to beat him off, and shook him like a dog, evidently determined, if he could, to make his escape to the rocks, and if not, then to drown himself.

The officer, however, held him fast, and dragged him to the boat, and he was at once pulled in.

As soon, however, as they had got him into the boat Cook put his hand into his pocket, and taking from it a small bottle of poison put it to his lips and began to drink the contents.

As soon as the officers saw what he was doing they knocked it from his lips saying "What are you doing now, you scoundrel?" And they at once took possession of the poison bottle.

The chase and the fearful struggle in the sea were watched with the most breathless anxiety by those on the rocks, who had their glasses with them, and who could discern what was going on, and the information they every moment gave to the by-standers around increased tenfold the intense excitement.

At length the boat was rowed back towards the quay, and as it passed the crowds of spectators the officers were loudly cheered.

When the boat got up to the quay, and the prisoner was landed, thousands rushed round in the effort to catch a glimpse of such a brutal criminal as the man who could be guilty of such an atrocious act as the burning of the flesh bit by bit of his unoffending and unfortunate victim.

The officers first took their prisoner to the Liverpool lock-up, where he was safely put in irons, and then duly brought under a good strong guard back to Leicester.

The news of his capture was received with intense satisfaction both in Leicester and in London, and when the officers arrived with him in the town, thousands lined the road to see him arrive.

As he passed, he was hissed along the whole route, and it was evident he was held in the most utter abhorrence.

He was taken to the Bridewell, and the following morning brought up

BEFORE THE MAGISTRATES.

The court was densely crowded, and when Cook was brought in he appeared quite firm.

He seemed to be about twenty-two years of age, about the middle height, with sallow, characteristic, strongly-marked features, rather inclining to sharpness, dark brown hair, without any whiskers, which had been shaven off.

He wore the gaol dress, and when spoken to his answers were direct and respectful.

Mr. George Welborn Owston, the chief constable of Leicester, was the first witness called.

He stated that on the 1st of June he set off by the "Red Rover" coach to Liverpool, in company with William Cummins, one of the borough constables, with a warrant for the prisoner's apprehension.

A reward of £200 had been offered, and he obtained the assistance of the Liverpool and Manchester police, and also of some watermen, as he thought it likely the prisoner might make for America.

The witness then described the chase they had had after the prisoner, and stated that on arresting him they found on him the deceased's purse, forty-one sovereigns, seven half-sovereigns, and a guinea.

Other evidence was also given, showing that certain other property found on the prisoner had belonged to the deceased.

The officer Halwell also gave evidence of the terrific struggle which took place between himself and the prisoner, and also as to how the prisoner was secured by some sailors coming into the water to his aid.

THE PRISONER'S FIRST CONFESSION.

On the following Thursday the prisoner was brought before the magistrates again, for the purpose of affording him an opportunity of saying anything, or giving any explanation he thought proper in reference to the terrible crime.

He was then very heavily ironed, and wearing the prison dress, but even though he was in the presence of many gentlemen he had often met with under better circumstances, he did not show the slightest emotion.

Mr. Burbidge, the town clerk, then addressing him, told him he was not bound to say anything to criminate himself, but if he desired to say anything the magistrates would hear it.

The prisoner then said: I am innocent of wilful murder, and my conscience is not burthened in the manner that you gentlemen seem to suppose.

Mr. Paas called on me in the morning, but what morning I cannot exactly say, my agitation of mind has been so great ever since, and I paid him a bill of 12s.

There were two bills due; one was for a larger sum. Mr. Paas wrote "settled" on the 12s. bill, and I told him I would strive to pay part of the other if he called again in the evening.

Mr. Paas did call again, but I was not able to give him anything.

He was angry and I was angry, and disagreeable words took place and a scuffle ensued, and in this manner I was brought to this shameful and disgraceful end.

Mr. Burbidge, again addressing the prisoner, told him that they had reason to suppose, from the examination made, that the upper part of the body had been moved from the premises and probably buried, and they understood that he had admitted as much to one of the constables.

He wished to know on the part of the relatives what he had really done with the body as it would be a relief to their anxiety, and as he had admitted he had committed the murder that could not prejudice his case.

The prisoner, after hesitating a short time, said he would take time to consider what answer he would give.

It also further transpired that one of the constables had said that the prisoner had informed him that during the scuffle Mr. Paas had thrown the great hammer at his head, and that it hit his shoulder, and he, the prisoner, had picked up the press pin, and hit him with it on the back of the neck.

THE LIFE OF WILLIAM CALCRAFT, THE HANGMAN.

THE TRIAL OF SARAH SMITH.

No. 21.

As the prisoner did not then seem inclined to say any more he was removed back to his cell.

During the evening, as the friends and relatives were very anxious to recover for decent Christian burial any portions of the body that might be hidden away, Mr. Owston, the governor of the prison, visited Cook in his cell, and asked him whether he had thought over what Mr. Burbidge had asked him, and whether he would now say what he had done with the whole of the body.

Cook then in reply said he would tell him in the morning.

At ten o'clock the following morning the governor visited him again in his cell, and asked him if he would then fulfil his promise.

Cook then said: "I know I shall have to suffer for the foul offence, as I believe there is a just God in heaven, and therefore what I tell you shall be true, so help me God."

Cook then went on to say that no time could give any opportunity for finding the body or any portion of it excepting what was found, even if it went on for a thousand years, as he had burnt the whole of it.

Mr. Owston: Say truly how it was all disposed of.

Prisoner: I burnt the whole of it except the part found.

Mr. Owston then expressed his astonishment, and left to inform the magistrates of what the prisoner had stated, and that he had expressed his surprise that it could have been done in so short a time.

It was then arranged that Mr. Burbidge, the town clerk, Mr. Owston, the governor of the gaol, and his son should have another interview with the prisoner, to try and persuade him to state truly in detail what he had done with all the portions of the body, and accordingly the same afternoon the prisoner was visited in his cell.

Mr. Burbidge commenced the conversation by asking the prisoner how he felt.

The prisoner replied that he was now more comfortable in his mind since he had made the confession than he had been since the commission of the crime.

Mr. Burbidge then asked him if he would now state what he had done with the trunk of the body.

The prisoner again replied: I know that I shall suffer as there is a just God; I burnt the whole of it. It is true I am about to suffer, and it is no use telling stories. I have entirely destroyed the body, but how I can hardly tell—it was all burnt.

Mr. Burbidge: When did you do it?

Prisoner: In the course of Wednesday night.

Mr. Burbidge: How did you do it?

Prisoner: I decline to state.

Mr. Burbidge then told the prisoner that he had been informed by surgeons, that it would be totally impossible for him to destroy certain parts of the body, and he once more begged the prisoner for the sake of the friends, to tell them exactly how he had disposed of it.

The prisoner again in reply stated that he had burnt all the parts excepting the one found.

Mr. Burbidge: But how did you prevent the great flow of blood?

The prisoner then detailed the precautions he took, and again asserted that the whole of the body was burnt.

Mr. Burbidge then expressed his astonishment that a greater smell had not been noticed during the night.

Prisoner: Ah, sir, it was a terrific stormy night, and that may have had something to do with it.

The prisoner then in the most positive manner asserted that no one but himself either had anything to do with the murder or knew anything at all of it. Everyone else was as innocent as a lamb.

The magistrates, in the course of the afternoon, assembled and discharged from prison the sister and one of the brothers of Cook, as well as his father, but Michael, his brother, from Queensborough, who had also been arrested on suspicion, they still detained in custody.

The Town Clerk, Mr. Owston, and the Governor then left the prisoner in his cell, and he occupied his time chiefly in reading very popular religious works—namely Baxter's "Saint's Everlasting Rest," and "Call to the Unconverted."

On the following day, Sunday, the chaplain from Fancourt preached a special sermon from the 102nd Psalm, 20th and 21st verses—"To hear the groanings of the prisoner, to loose those that are appointed to death, to declare the name of the Lord in Zion, and his praise in Jerusalem," to which the prisoner paid great attention.

FUNERAL OF MR. PAAS.

The remains of the unfortunate gentleman were buried on the following Monday afternoon—as far as they could be collected—in the burial ground of old Paddington Church, Paddington-green.

The funeral had been purposely postponed to see if the prisoner would give any information as to any other remains being in existence, but he did not do so.

THE TRIAL.

The prisoner was brought up for trial at the assizes before Mr. Justice Park, on the 8th of August.

The court was densely crowded.

There were several counts in the indictment.

One charged the prisoner with having murdered Mr. Paas, on the 30th of May, by striking him on the head with a press pin.

The second count charged the prisoner with murdering him by throwing him on the fire, and keeping him there till he was burnt to death.

The third, with striking him heavy blows on the back of the head, then cutting him up, and then burning him.

The fourth count averred that he had, by divers ways and means, and by instruments unknown to the Crown, destroyed, and afterwards burnt the body in a way counsel were unable to set out.

In several other counts not stating the instrument or manner of the murder, the prisoner was charged with having cut, and destroyed, and consumed by fire, the body of the said Mr. Paas so as to make it impossible to set forth the instrument of death.

During the reading of the indictment he drew a small volume from his pocket, which he seemed to read with much attention.

The learned judge, addressing him, told him to close the book and pay attention, for though he was himself anxious that he should prepare his mind for his situation, yet at the present time his attention was otherwise required.

He then closed the volume, and the clerk addressing him, asked him whether he pleaded guilty or not guilty?

Prisoner: Guilty!

Judge: I suppose you are aware of the inevitable consequence of so pleading?

Prisoner: Yes.

Judge: And you do so deliberately and decidedly?

Prisoner: Yes.

Judge: And you mean to adhere to the course on which you have determined?

Prisoner: Yes.

The officer of the court then said: James Cook, you stand convicted, on your own confession, of wilful murder; have you anything to say why the court should not pass on you sentence of death?

The prisoner made no reply, but seemed to be engaged in prayer—his eyes being closed, but his lips moving.

Proclamation for silence having been made, a solemn silence ensued.

The judge then assumed the black cap, and said:—

James Cook, you have by your own confession, been convicted of wilful murder—a crime of so deep a dye that it is impossible for an earthly judge to consign you to any other fate than that which the law of God decrees—when it says : " Whoso sheddeth man's blood, by man also shall his blood be shed ;" and also, " The land cannot be cleansed of the blood that is shed therein but by the blood of him that shed it."

Had you pleaded otherwise than you have done, there can be no doubt that you would have had a full, fair, and impartial trial; yet having read the deposition as I am bound to do, I am convinced that no other result could have followed than that which must now ensue.

If at all times murder must be shocking, ten times is it more so in this dreadful act of yours. Though I am conversant with the records of crime I have never heard or read of a deed so deep in its atrocity as this; so horrible in its circumstances, and so calculated to make the thoughts of every decent man recoil.

No man of feeling can learn unmoved, that in cold blood—when your innocent victim was guilty of no other offence than seeking the trifling sum which was rightly his due—you knocked him to the earth with a mortal blow, and then with the view to prevent the discovery of your crime—which never can be done while a God of retribution rules above—that you (oh! most miserable act of all) barbarously cut the unfortunate gentleman in pieces, and on a consuming fire strove to destroy his body limb by limb.

For a deed so foul it is impossible any mercy can be shown. Truly does the indictment speak when it says you were instigated by the devil. He who would show mercy then would be almost as guilty as yourself.

Let me then beseech you to let your sincerity be in proportion to the magnitude of your offence, and oh! may you cast yourself upon that blessed Redeemer who came to save us all! Little time now remains to you here, and there is still a great deal to be done.

Think of nothing but of another world.

Seek diligently and you may yet find mercy; knock and it may yet be opened unto you.

The sentence of the court upon you is, that on Friday next, the 10th of August, you be taken to the place of execution, there to be hanged by the neck till you are dead, and that afterwards, pursuant to a recent enactment, your body be hung in chains, and may God in his infinite mercy have compassion on your guilty soul!

The prisoner, who was dressed in a blue coat, dark waistcoat, white trousers, and who also wore white gloves, betrayed no emotion, was then removed from the bar.

THE CONDEMNED CELL.

The culprit was placed in the condemned cell in irons. A great number of religious ladies took special interest in him, as his expression of religious repentance attracted considerable favour towards him.

He had a quantity of religious books sent him, and there was a feeling manifested among some that before his end he had been purified of his sins, and that he went to his death almost as a saint.

Others thought that the ordering of special new clothes for his last appearance in public—only about an hour—and his general demeanour were evidences of affectation and pride.

It is probable that there was a mixture of both, but his final confession showed the falsity of his first statement, as many other cases show great disparity in a similar manner.

FINAL CONFESSION.

The day before his execution he asked that Miss Ann Owston might be sent for, as he wished to make a full disclosure, and that he would make it to her.

He was also willing for one of his attendants named Richards, and Mr. Burbidge to be present.

Cook then stated that he was willing to confess all, and he then contradicted a great portion of his first statement.

He said that the murder did not originate in a quarrel, but that he had premeditated and prepared for it some time previously.

The thought first came into his mind when he received Mr. Paas's invoice and letter informing him when he should call upon him. He then thought he would commit the murder, and possess himself of Mr. Paas's money, as he knew that he frequently carried large sums about with him.

He believed that Mr. Paas had as much as between £500 and £600 sometimes with him, and he thought he would be able to get a good sum of money in that way.

He had no doubt that his crime really at first originated in pride, for he often used to think what he would do if he had more money.

Then when he had made up his mind to commit the crime, he began to make preparations.

He bought a chopper and had it ground and sharpened and hung up in readiness.

He also bought the saw for the purpose of sawing the bones.

He purchased the hay and straw, and had it in readiness to spread on the floor that there should be no blood seen.

He had besides laid in a stock of coal for burning the body.

Mr. Burbidge: If you had found more money on him—say £500 or £600—was it your intention then to have gone to America or somewhere?

Prisoner: No; I had made up my mind to remain in the same shop, even if I had had £500 or a £1000. I meant to destroy the body—and should have destroyed every trace of it, but for the drink. I stood the sight as long as I could, and then I felt as though I must go and get something to drink before I could finish destroying the remainder, so I made up a good fire while I went to get some drink, thinking to come back shortly to finish burning everything up; but in the meantime they thought the shop was on fire through the glare they saw, and then, bursting open the door, they discovered the crime. Oh, how horrible it is to have to recall to the mind's eye all that dreadful sight, and the fearful doings of that night!

Mr. Burbidge: When did you give the deceased the first blow? When he was writing the receipt?

Prisoner: No, I was going to do it then, but my courage failed me. In fact, I had a great mind to let him go without doing it, but Satan prompted me.

He seemed to be at my elbow prompting me, and saying—" Now hit him." I kept wishing something would occur to prevent me, but Mr. Paas turned to look at some book binding I had been doing, and as he turned round I had the press pin—a large iron bar—in my hand, and Satan then prompted me again, and seemed to say—" There now hit him—now's the time." I then struck him a fearful blow.

He did not fall, but took up a large heavy hammer, and cried out "Murder—murder!" and ran towards the door, and opened it, and nearly got part outside.

Just then he dropped the hammer, and Satan seemed to say—"Pull him in and hit him again." I did so, and then struck him three times with the iron bar.

He then fell down and did not move again.

Gentlemen, it is painful to recall the sight I had in my eyes then; I cannot fully describe it.

You cannot fully realise it, and what my feelings were. I then all at once realised what I had been prompted to do. There lay the body.

Gentlemen, what was I to do with it? Satan had prompted me thus far, and then he seemed to be my accuser.

He seemed to whisper—"You must get rid of the body now." Then it was that I had to commence the work which appears so revolting to you all. Something seemed to be saying to me:—

"You must go through it now—you must dispose of the body or you'll be found out."

I felt then as though I wished that somebody or something would cause me to be detected then; but Satan still appeared to be behind me prompting me to go on and cut it up and burn it, and I commenced.

I found £55 upon him in gold and notes, and then I began to cut him up, and then to burn him bit by bit.

Oh, that dreadful work! that dreadful sight I cannot and have not been able to get it from my eyes.

When I had nearly done the dreadful work, something seemed to say, "Have a drop of drink, and then you'll be able to finish."

I felt I could not finish it without. I was prompted to go and get drink, and was thus snared into leaving behind me full evidence of my guilt, even after I had adopted such revolting means to try and hide my crime.

Satan then seemed to say to me: "You are a murderer, and the most atrocious of criminals."

I feel much better gentlemen since I have made a full confession of my guilt, and I hope I shall find mercy before the Throne of God.

This final confession made a great impression on those who heard it, and created quite a sensation among many religious people of the town.

Many ladies who took an interest in him expressed their full conviction that he was a thoroughly penitent and converted man.

He spent his last hours in prayer, reading religious tracts, and singing hymns.

SINGULAR REQUEST.

As his end drew near he told the chaplain he should esteem it a favour if he would preach the condemned sermon from the 19th chapter of Judges, the 29th and 30th verses: "And when he was come into his house he took a knife and laid hold of his concubine, and divided her, together with her bones, into twelve pieces, and sent her into all the coasts of Israel, and it was so that all that saw it said: 'There was no such deed done nor seen from the day that the children of Israel came up out of the land of Egypt unto this day; consider of it, take advice and speak your minds.'"

It is not stated in the public accounts, whether the chaplain complied with this singular request, and preached from a narrative which the culprit, no doubt, thought equalled in atrocity his own crime.

Certainly there had not been any for some time which equalled it in terrible details, and the culprit, in fully realising the magnitude of his wickedness, thought that the chaplain would, if he preached upon the subject, forcibly bring out the latter words of the text: "Consider of it, take advice"—that ye are not beguiled and led into the first temptation.

THE EXECUTION.

When the morning of execution arrived the culprit rose early and carefully prepared himself for his appearance on the scaffold.

He spent the last two or three hours in thoughtful meditation and earnest prayer.

Shortly after half-past eleven on the 10th of August, he was brought into the press-room where Calcraft was in waiting.

Calcraft at once advanced, and the sheriffs introduced him to the culprit.

The prisoner then said, "I am quite ready," and Calcraft began to pinion his arms.

The two clergymen, the Rev. Dr. Fancourt, and the Rev. Dr. Barnaby, stood near, giving him words of consolation and hope in the last few moments.

It was now within a few minutes of twelve o'clock, and the sheriffs, governor, and officers all being ready, the procession formed and proceeded on its way.

People had come from all parts to witness the execution, and there was over 30,000 people congregated round the gaol within view of the scaffold.

Though the murder was so atrocious, yet it was generally known and believed that the prisoner repented himself of his crime, and the multitude, though so vast, was so orderly and silent, that not only could the solemn tolling of the funeral bell be distinctly heard throughout the vast assembly, but also the solemn words of the chaplain as the procession appeared. As soon as the culprit appeared upon the scaffold, he stepped quickly underneath the fatal beam, as though anxious to pay the debt the law demanded.

While Calcraft was adjusting the rope the voice of the chaplain could be distinctly heard repeating the impressive words, "I said I will take heed to my ways that I sin not with my tongue. I will keep my mouth as it were with a bridle."

Then, while Calcraft was strapping his legs, the words were heard, "O spare me a little that I may recover my strength before I go hence and be no more seen."

Calcraft then drew the white cap over the culprit's face, whose lips seemed to be moving, and repeating after the clergyman the solemn words "Man that is born of a woman hath but a short time to live, and is full of misery. He cometh up and is cut down like a flower; he fleeth as it were a shadow, and never continueth in one stay."

Calcraft now stealthily stole away behind the drop, leaving the culprit standing alone, underneath the fatal beam, while the clergyman was repeating the words—

"In the midst of life we are in death; of whom may we seek for succour but of thee, O Lord, who for our sins art justly displeased?"

There was some little delay in the action of the drop, and the clergyman proceeded—

"Yet, O Lord God most holy, O Lord most mighty, O holy and most merciful Saviour, deliver us not into the bitter pains of eternal death."

At this moment the culprit, who held a white handkerchief in his hand, gave the signal that he was ready by dropping it, and the drop at once fell, and he hung, convulsively vibrating, and heaving, and struggling, before the assembled crowd, for several minutes.

He at length died, but exceedingly hard, and apparently in great agony.

The body after hanging the usual time was taken down, and conveyed to the gaol infirmary.

Here it was laid on a plank, the head shaved, and the face and head covered with a plaster of pitch.

HANGING THE BODY ON A GIBBET IN CHAINS.

The body thus prepared was then encased in chains, with side irons for the legs, and iron girders under the feet.

On the following Saturday morning it was taken and hung on a gibbet, thirty feet high, which had been erected in Saffron-lane, on the road to Aylestone, about a quarter of a mile distant from where the terrible crime was perpetrated.

Large numbers of persons assembled to witness the gibbeting of the body, but shortly afterwards the Home Secretary sent an order for the body to be taken down.

Such was the end of a man who, through not having wisdom enough to resist the first temptation, was led on, in fact forced on step by step, after he had struck the first blow, to pursue his horrid work to the end, with the most fiendish atrocity, till such time as he developed into about the most infamous monster of his time.

He was young, with a good business and fair prospects in life, till he was vain, and then foolish enough to think he could better his position by the shedding of blood.

Every record of crime, however, shows us that the various allurements and instigations to murder are but the baits with which the trap of death is set, and all history proves incontestably this one fact, that when a person once commits murder there is a sudden end to all prospects of their prosperity and happiness; their peace of mind flies from them for ever—the terror of their crime haunts them day and night, and however they may think they will hide the dreadful deed yet that some strange, unaccountable, unlooked-for chance interposition steps in to bring their fearful work to light and themselves to justice; and thus they generally end their lives on the gallows; or, if for the time they manage to elude the vigilance of justice, they wander as outcasts and vagabonds in society, fugitives from the terrors of the law, with the canker-worm of remorse and guilt gnawing at their heart, thus making them suffer through life a punishment even worse than the gallows itself.

This case is full of incident, and it should make all who read it make one firm resolve, and that is always to at once shun the first temptation to evil, and above all things never to lift the hand to murder, but to follow on in the paths of truth, honesty, and justice, and then happiness and gradual prosperity are always before a man till the natural end of life.

After Cook had been gibbeted there were various pieces of poetry written, from which we give the following:—

THE CONDEMNED CELL.

The judgment was sealed, and the sentence was passed,
The prisoner removed to his dungeon at last—
That dungeon whose walls he had gazed on before,*
Which soon he must quit to behold them no more.

The crime of his guilt was thrown open anew,
And the sentence of death flashed full in his view;
He passed to his cell where the darkness and gloom
Were rendered more dark by the thoughts of his doom.

That night his eyes flash, and fearfully roll;
How dark is the gloom that hangs over his soul,
As frantic she raves in her dwelling of clay,
And fears for the doom that must take her away.

Distracted, his thoughts turn to happier years,
Those emotions of memory which childhood endears,
Like floods they roll on him, and mark his dread fate,
While from his soul's anguish he cries—"It's too late."

* As a friend and visitor of the officials.

Those days that are vanished—those stings of the brain,
Like spectres of time, now haunt me again,
Oh, leave me, ye phantom-fiends, all I now crave,
Is to let me sink peacefully into the grave.

The grave! Oh, there's no grave for the murderer found—
His crime has a shelter denied in the ground;
Oh, why am I living?—beating heart burst?
My body unburied, my bones are accursed.

THE MURDERER.

'Tis well the future scenes are veil'd from sight,
Or how could parents bear the dreadful thought,
While watching o'er their youth with fond delight,
That soon to a shameful end they may be brought?

Ill-fated youth! thy mother little thought,
When, with the care a mother only knows,
She screen'd thy tender frame from fear, and fraught
With tenderness lull'd thee to soft repose.

That in a few short years thy little hand,
Now soft with innocence, should dare to raise
The murderous bar, should o'er thy victim stand,
And, fiend-like, watch it midst the horrid blaze.

The latter verses show the necessity of checking in time the terrible tendency to passion.

CHAPTER XXXVII.

PROGRESS OF THE AGITATION FOR SOCIAL AND POLITICAL REFORM.

IN the midst of the general excitement consequent on the agitation throughout the country, which still continued, cholera and fever began to increase, and inspectors from the various boards of health also began to send in reports that the sanitary condition of the houses of the poor was all throughout the country such that nothing but the promulgation of disease could be expected to a most alarming extent.

It was not from London, but throughout the provinces that these fearful reports came.

We just select one instance from the *Observer* of April 22, 1832, headed "Revolting Condition of Manchester Operatives:"—

"The inspectors report that they have examined 687 streets, and have inspected 69,591 houses—2221 were entirely without necessary accommodation.

"The inhabitants were mostly Irish, and the houses cannot be said to be furnished.

"They contain one or two chairs, a mean table, the most scanty culinary apparatus, and one or two beds loathsome with filth.

"A whole family is often accommodated on a single bed, and sometimes a heap of filthy straw and a covering of old sacking hides them in one undistinguished heap, debased alike by penury, want of economy, and dissolute habits.

"Frequently the inspectors found two or more families crowded into one small house containing only two apartments—one in which they slept, and another in which they ate; and often more than one family lived in a damp cellar containing only one room, in whose pestilential atmosphere from twelve to sixteen persons were crowded.

"To these fertile sources of disease were sometimes added the keeping of pigs and other animals in the house, with other nuisances of a most revolting character.

"Some of these districts have frequently been the haunt of hordes of thieves and desperadoes who defied the law, and they are always inhabited by a class resembling savages in their appetites and habits."

We give this extract verbatim, lest it may be said that the picture of the social state of the lower orders has been overdrawn.

The people, as a natural result, were dying by

thousands of plague, pestilence, and famine; the poor were literally perishing for want of bread.

Of course, something had to be done; so the Government recommended a special day of humiliation, and a national fast to be strictly observed, to which the Bishops and House of Lords at once gave their approval, and a proclamation was at once issued ordering it.

The people refused to obey it. They looked upon it as the old remedy of seeking to do by prayer what ought to have been more efficaciously done by legislative enactments against sordid gain, in the ordering of the destruction of the miserable dilapidated dwellings by which the rich got richer, and revelled in luxury, but in which millions of the people starved, rotted, and died.

When, therefore, the day for fasting came the people met again in thousands and clamoured for more practical measures for the relief of the poor, and the alleviation of the national distress.

They looked upon it as nothing less than cruel mockery to order famishing men to fast still more, and the cruelty of the order was, no doubt, greatly increased by the fact that in that time of sore distress it deprived the families of one whole day's work and one day's wages by the closing of business places.

The people, therefore, in meeting and protesting against the order denounced the legislature for its long inattention to the existing hardships, and the want of proper laws and facilities for opening up labour for those industriously inclined.

The Government, however, in spite of the agitation carried on by the leaders of the people still adopted the repressive measures, and various of the speakers and ringleaders were tried.

TRIAL OF WILLIAM COBBETT FOR SEDITION.

Among those who were early brought to trial the case of William Cobbett who was indicted for sedition excited, perhaps, the greatest interest.

He was tried at the Guildhall in July, 1831. He had in the most fearless manner denounced the Government for its inattention to the requirements of the times.

When he came into court he was greeted by clapping of hands and loud huzzas,

Then turning round he said to the people "If truth prevails we shall beat them yet."

The Attorney-General stated the case for the Crown, adverting to the system of riot, fire-raising, and breaking of machinery, which had spread destruction through so many counties.

He then quoted, among many others, the following extract from Mr. Cobbett's writings—

"At last it will come to a question of actual starvation, or fighting for food; and when it comes to that point, I know that Englishmen will never lie down and die by the wayside."

In another passage he said that the criminals ought not to be made to suffer for anything they had done in the riots.

The trial excited great interest, but the jury, after being locked up all night, could not agree, and Lord Tenterden discharged them.

The hanging and transporting of the people still continued, as though the judges were determined to try and stamp poverty out by stamping out the lives of the people, as in the time of Henry VIII., when, according to Stow, it is related that 72,000 persons were hung in his reign of thirty-eight years, being on an average upwards of 2000 a year.

Some of the convicts who were sent away were lost on the voyage, and the following poem which appeared gives a graphic account of

THE WRECK OF A FEMALE CONVICT SHIP.

Yes! women throng that vessel's deck,
  The haggard and the fair;
The young in guilt, and the depraved,
  Are intermingled there.
The girl who from her mother's arms
  Was early lured away;
The hardened hag, whose trade hath been
  To lead the pure astray.

A young and sickly mother kneels,
  Apart from all the rest;
And with a song of home she lulls
  The babe upon her breast.
She falters, for her tears must flow,
  She cannot end the verse,
And nought is heard among the crowd,
  But laughter, shout, or curse.

'Tis sunset. Hark! the signal gun,
  All from the deck are sent—
The young, the old, the best, the worst,
  In one dark dungeon pent!
Their wailings and their horrid mirth
  Alike are hushed in sleep,
And now the female convict ship
  In silence ploughs the deep.

But long the lurid tempest-cloud
  Hath brooded o'er the waves,
And suddenly the winds are roused,
  And leave their secret caves;
And up aloft the ship is borne,
  And down again as fast,
And every mighty billow seems
  More dreadful than the last.

Oh, who shall tell the agony
  Of those confined beneath,
Who in the darkness dread to die—
  How unprepared for death?
Who, loathing, to each other cling,
  When every other hope hath ceased,
And beat against their prison-door,
  And shriek to be released!

Three times the ship hath struck! Again
  She never more will float—
Oh! wait not for the rising tide,
  Be steady—man the boat!
And see assembled on the shore,
  The merciful, the brave;
Quick, set the female convicts free,
  There still is time to save!

It is in vain! What demon blinds
  The captain and the crew?
The rapid rising of the tide
  With mad delight they view.
They hope the coming waves will waft
  The convict ship away;
The foaming monster hurries on,
  Impatient for his prey.

And he is come—the rushing flood
  In thunder sweeps the deck;
The groaning timbers fly apart,
  The vessel is a wreck.
One moment from the female crowd
  There comes a fearful cry—
The next they're hurled into the deep,
  To struggle and to die.

Their corses strew a foreign shore,
  Left by the ebbing tide,
And sixty in a ghastly row
  Lie numbered side by side.
The lifeless mother's bleeding form
  Comes floating from the wreck,
And lifeless is the babe she bound
  So fondly round her neck.

'Tis morn—the anxious eye can trace
  No vessel on the deep
But gathered timber on the shore
  Lies in a gloomy heap.
In winter time those brands will blaze
  Our tranquil homes to warm,
Though torn from that poor convict ship
  That perished in the storm.

The above poem, together with the account of the frightful shipwreck on which it was based, created a vast amount of sensation at the cruel manner in which the convicts on various vessels were put on board and cruelly treated.

The following is a short account of the terrible wreck:—

The "Amphitrite" convict ship sailed for New South Wales from Woolwich on the 25th of August, 1833.

Captain Hunter was the commander.

There were on board 108 female convicts, some of them very young, twelve children, and a crew of sixteen persons.

When the ship arrived off Dungeness a gale arose, and the ship was too heavy for sail.

She was in sight of Boulogne; the sea was heavy, and the wind exceedingly strong.

Three men were saved out of the crew, and it appeared from their statements that all the rest had perished. As soon as she had struck, a pilot boat, commanded by Francois Heuret, was dispatched, and came under her bows.

The captain, however, refused assistance. The crew said they could get to shore in the boats, and save the women and children.

The long boat was got out when the ship appeared to be going down, and the captain and surgeon consulted together.

The crew again wanted to be allowed to take the women and children to the shore in boats, as there was still plenty of time, but the captain again refused, saying he had no authority to liberate anyone committed to his keeping.

The terrified women and children who were battened down under the hatches, on the vessel running aground, now became desperate for their lives.

As the ship nearly split in two the convicts broke the aft deck hatch away, and frantically rushed on deck.

They entreated the captain to let them go on shore—they implored him, and promised him they would not run away, but the captain was a red tape man.

He had, he said, no "authority" to liberate them, and so the convict ship, with its women and children, went down in the dashing and surging waves.

The captain, like a great many more Government officials, was a poor, miserable, short-sighted man of but one idea.

He could only remember that he had no authority to set them free, but the wretched embodiment of Government stringency seemed incapable of realising the fact that he certainly had no "authority" to drown them in the sea.

THE CONTINUED HORRORS OF TRANSPORTATION.

About this time reports and evidence reached the country of the continuation of the most horrible, revolting cruelties practised on the unhappy transports.

In some cases they were sentenced to extra work, to wear extra heavy irons round their necks and waists, and to receive 600 lashes—100 being inflicted each day for a week—till many succumbed and died under the dreadful treatment.

DEATH OF OLD TOWNSEND, THE BOW-STREET RUNNER.

Another celebrated character who, I recollect, died soon after I was appointed (said Calcraft), was old Townsend, the Bow-street runner.

He had been engaged in all the great cases for the previous fifty years. He used to tell many stories of the romantic and exciting cases he had been in which occurred during the stormy period in which he lived.

He died at his lodgings in Eccleston-street, Pimlico, in the 80th year of his age, on the 10th of July, 1832.

Some of the newspaper proprietors tried very hard to get him to write a biography of his life, but I don't think they could ever get the old man to do it.

ROBBERY AND MURDER ON THE THAMES.

After Calcraft had executed other people in the provinces for various crimes, he executed two youths, named William Kennedy and William Brown, on the 10th of September, 1832, for a robbery and murder on the Thames.

The two culprits belonged to a gang of young river-thieves, who used to go up and down the Thames in boats for the special purpose of robbery.

At that time, as now, many young people used to enjoy a row on the river, but they were never safe from the attacks of ruffians in boats, who used to row up against them purposely, and nearly upset them. During the panic which ensued among the people in the smaller boats, who were afraid of being drowned, the thieves would steal their clothes, or watches, or anything else they could get.

In the month of July they attacked a party of young men, among whom was a young gentleman named William Wilkinson, aged twenty-four.

After robbing him, they were rowing away, but he sprang after them, but fell into the water. The evidence went to show that the prisoners then struck him on the head with their oars, and killed him.

The prisoners, in defence, denied having given him the fatal blow, and said that it was done by one of his party, who struck him in mistake.

They protested their innocence up to the last, even to just before Calcraft drew the fatal bolt.

JONATHAN SMITHERS.

Calcraft executed this notorious culprit in July, 1832. He was by business a tobacconist, having a retail shop at, then, 398, Oxford-street.

At six o'clock on the morning of the 28th of May a fearful fire broke out on his premises, which spread with alarming rapidity.

Smithers suddenly came running out, with his face blackened, and considerably burned.

The upper portion of the house was let out to families in apartments, and as soon as the fire began to spread the unfortunate inmates appeared at the windows in their night-dresses, imploring for assistance.

Their cries were heartrending.

The neighbours brought out blankets, and called to the people to jump down.

Sarah Smith, a young girl, a servant, ventured, and was caught, but was greatly bruised in the fall.

At the windows on one floor Miss Caroline Twamley appeared, carrying in her arms her mother, seventy years of age, who had been bedridden for some time.

She was told to throw her mother through the window into the blanket, and then jump down herself. Just as she was about to do so, however, the flames reached her, and both fell, scorched and senseless, on to the leads below. They died in terrible agony.

At another window appeared Miss Eliza Twamley, a young lady well known as a dancer at Covent-garden Theatre.

She was carrying a little nephew in her arms, named Charles Richard Feango.

She threw him out, and he was caught in the blanket, but dreadfully scorched. He recovered.

The unfortunate young lady, however, who had so heroically borne him to the window was immediately afterwards suffocated by the flames, and falling inside the room was literally burnt alive.

The shocking and terrible scene caused deep commiseration throughout the metropolis, but this gave place to terrible indignation when the real cause of the fire came to be known.

It appears, upon the firemen searching the premises, that they discovered a large quantity of salt petre, and various combustible materials stowed away underneath the shop.

There was also a quantity of oiled shavings and other rubbish saturated with turpentine.

In addition there was a long train of gunpowder with fusees in various directions, all planned for setting the premises on fire.

The servant girl, Sarah Smith, gave evidence, showing that on the Sunday night she saw Smithers carrying the shavings to where they were found.

He had also procured the turpentine and other inflammable things that were found, and up till a late hour he was very busy with them.

It was also shown that he had procured the gunpowder, and it was further proved in evidence that five weeks before the fire he had insured his stock with an insurance company for £600. He was tried for the offence,

The jury found that he wilfully set fire to the premises for the purpose of obtaining the insurance money, and that by his act three persons lost their lives, and that he was guilty of murder in every case.

He was tried before Mr. Justice Gazelee, who condemned him to death.

The prisoner, who treated the matter very indifferently, then gathered up his papers and walked from the dock.

He was visited in his cell by his wife, with whom he had lived on very bad terms, and she was accompanied by her only child.

The last parting was a very cold and formal one. There did not appear much feeling between them.

She kissed him on leaving, and said, "Good-bye, Smithers," and then came out, both parting without any display.

He was known to be a very violent man, and the sheriffs gave Calcraft orders to pinion him tight, and take care that he did not attempt any violence on the scaffold.

When, therefore, Calcraft was pinioning him, he complained very much of the straps being too tight. He was told he would die all the easier, and then he said "Very well. All right."

Up to the last he protested his innocence of the crime of murder. He would not make any confession, but he did not really deny setting the place on fire.

When the drop fell he struggled hard for several minutes.

There is reason to suppose that he recklessly set the place on fire, without thinking or caring of the disastrous consequences which might ensue.

EXECUTION OF SARAH SMITH FOR POISONING AT LEICESTER.

Sarah Smith, aged twenty-eight, a woman of very forbidding appearance, was indicted in March, 1832, at the assizes at Leicester, before Mr. Justice Bayley, for the wilful murder of Elizabeth Wood, at Montsorrel, on the 15th of the previous December, by administering poison to her.

The prisoner lived with her husband at Montsorrel, and she invited the deceased, a young woman, sixteen or seventeen years of age, to leave her place of service, and come and live with her.

The deceased did so, and took her clothes. On the 8th or 9th the prisoner purchased an ounce of laudanum at the shop of a person to whom she represented that a young woman at her house was suffering from a complaint like the cholera morbus, and she wished to give her some laudanum and brandy.

On the 9th she called in a young man who had formerly been apprenticed to a surgeon, and he proposed to give her an emetic, but the prisoner to that said the deceased had a great objection.

He then prescribed a powder for her, and the following day found her better, but on the 11th she was worse.

On that day the prisoner sent for the girl's sister—a girl about twelve years of age—to come and attend her sister.

This girl observed that the prisoner gave the deceased no food of any kind either on Sunday or on Monday, and that from that day till the following Thursday all the food she gave her was a small piece of bread and two small biscuits.

On Wednesday, the 14th, she (the prisoner) purchased another ounce of laudanum, and made the same representation as she had made before.

On Thursday, the 15th, she purchased six pennyworth of laudanum, saying it was for a person up the yard, and she also purchased one pennyworth of arsenic, which she said she wanted to destroy mice.

On the night preceding the deceased's death she put some dark liquid in a cup, and told the deceased's sister, Mary Ann, who slept with her, to give her three spoonfuls five times in the course of the night, and to be sure and shake it well first.

On the 15th, when the young doctor called again, after telling him he might wait and see the deceased take the broth, she showed him the paper of arsenic, which she said she had bought to destroy the mice with, and requested him to mix some for her, as she did not like to meddle with it.

He accordingly took out a small pinch and mixed it up for her in some crumbs.

During the afternoon the girl got worse, and asked to be allowed to have some one to pray with her.

The prisoner then sent the deceased a little broth up stairs by her sister.

In the course of the evening she complained of hot burning sensations. The prisoner then sent for a jug of water, and as the deceased was complaining of great thirst and agony the prisoner went up to her.

As the prisoner had no one to defend her, the learned judge questioned all the witnesses at great length in her favour.

The evidence throughout was very remarkable. The prisoner, it was shown, had endeavoured in one instance to get the deceased's sister to say that she saw the young doctor with the paper of arsenic, and that she saw him take some out, and that she was to tell the court that the prisoner had scolded her for not mentioning it to her before.

The prisoner, at the close of the case, read a long document which she had prepared, in which she said that her husband's brother was courting the deceased, but after he had got what money he could from the girl to buy some furniture with he refused to have her. She then, at the close of her paper, made a most fearful charge against her own husband of wilfully poisoning the girl.

She stated that as soon as her husband heard that an inquest was going to be held he said to her, "I am afraid they will find arsenic in her."

She said to her husband "Why?"

He then said, "Why don't you recollect me mixing a powder on Thursday night?"

I replied "Yes. You said it was from the young doctor, Hamlet Vernon."

TAKING THE TRADES' UNION OATH.

I then asked him the reason why he gave it to her, and he said, "Don't you recollect my brother bringing home six stone of flour one night?"

I said "Yes."

He then said that his brother had stolen that flour, and the deceased, Elizabeth Wood, knew it, and that she had told him that if he did not marry her she knew what would transport him. He also said his brother had had £4 off Elizabeth Wood on the Tuesday night before she was taken ill. When my husband told me all about this, he said his brother d——d him for doing so. But my husband then said that he told his brother he always had trusted me, and if he could not trust me with this it was a pity.

This statement was so plausibly made that the judge ordered a number of witnesses to be recalled.

The venerable judge, who was very advanced in years, then summed up the case, commenting on the fact that the prisoner had openly bought the poison, and had made no concealment of its possession.

She had also procured a sister of the deceased to attend her at her bedside, and she had also apprised other members of the family of the girl's illness.

The learned judge left it with the jury to say whether that did not look like the act of a perfectly innocent woman, or whether that she, being guilty, had resorted to these open appearances for the purpose of throwing suspicion from her guilt.

The case had assumed a certain amount of complication. There were some who had up to the time of the woman's statement thought her guilty; now they seemed to believe that she might be innocent.

The jury evidently paid great attention to the evidence, and in the end brought in a verdict of guilty.

The judge, now assuming the black cap, said:—

Prisoner at the bar, after a most patient and dispassionate attention to this mysterious case, the jury have decided upon your guilt, and that it was by your guilty hand by which the unfortunate young woman died is clear to me beyond all doubt.

The defence which you have set up is only an aggravation of your crime, for that a husband should make his wife's bosom the depository of the commission of so foul a deed is too improbable for belief.

The defence set up by you is very extraordinary—so unnatural, charging your partner in life as the perpetrator of the foul murder of the poor young woman—that I hardly know in what terms to express my abhorrence of such unfeeling conduct.

In a few short hours you must stand before the bar of your Maker.

The sentence of the Court is that you be hanged by the neck till you are dead, and may the Lord have mercy on your soul. Your body will be given over for dissection.

THE CONFESSION.

There were many who had their doubts as to the justness of the verdict, as her statement in court seemed to make an impression upon the minds of some.

They were at a loss to see any object or motive she could have for the murder.

On the following day, however, she made a full confession of her guilt.

She stated that on the night deceased died she gave her a teaspoonful of arsenic in a cup of water, and that the deceased died in one hour and forty minutes.

She then stated that her reason for doing so was because she knew that the deceased was aware that the flour was stolen, and that, had she chosen, she could have transported the whole lot of them.

She then determined to get the girl to leave her situation, and induce her to come and live at their house for the purpose of putting her out of the way of getting them into trouble.

THE EXECUTION.

After her condemnation she got so unnerved and weak that she was quite unable to stand.

The following day she had to be carried in a chair into the yard for a little airing, and also to be supported with stimulants during the time. At one period it was feared that she would not live till the morning of execution.

When, therefore, Calcraft was introduced to her on the morning of the 26th of March he found her quite unable to stand to be pinioned.

She seemed almost unconscious. When the time arrived she was supported up to the drop, before which more than 25,000 people had assembled.

While Calcraft was adjusting the noose round her neck, and fixing the other end to the fatal beam, she had to be held up by the warders.

When all was in readiness Calcraft then withdrew the bolt, and the drop fell.

Being a very small light-made woman her weight did not seem enough to cause the rope either to strangle her or dislocate her neck, for she plunged and struggled and heaved and vibrated a long time.

The scene is described by those who witnessed it as one of a very appalling character, and it called forth strong condemnation.

The case may be considered a very remarkable one, as showing the real value of disinterested evidence, and the little importance to be attached to the unsupported statements of accused persons, who, as in this instance, sometimes do not scruple to endeavour to fix the crime upon innocent persons, not even hesitating to accuse those nearest to them.

EXAMINATION OF WILLIAM JOHNSON FOR ROBBERY AND MURDER AT ENFIELD CHASE.

At the Old Bailey Sessions of December, 1832, William Johnson, twenty-nine, a gardener, and Samuel Fare, were indicted for the murder of Mr. Benjamin Crouch Danby, at Enfield Chase, on the night of the 19th of December.

The deceased, who, it was supposed, had a little money, having returned from India, on the night in question was drinking at the house of Mr. Perry, of the "Crown and Horse Shoe," Enfield Chase.

He left the House at eleven at night slightly intoxicated, and four men, Richard Wagstaffe, a baker, John Cooper, eighteen, William Johnson, and Samuel Fare, who had been playing at dominoes, went out about the same time.

The deceased the following morning was found dead lying on his face in a ditch at the bottom of Holt White's-lane with his throat cut.

The four men who were last seen in his company were then questioned, but they denied all knowledge of anything having occurred.

Circumstances, however, showed that the deceased had been robbed and murdered, and on the watchmen looking at Johnson's clothes they found blood on his trousers, and he was taken into custody.

It was also shown that Samuel Fare had more money on the day following the murder than he had had before, and he also was arrested.

Richard Wagstaff, who was one of the men who left the public-house when the deceased did, stated that he saw Johnson and Fare leading the deceased down the lane in which he was found, and that John Cooper was walking behind.

As the case proceeded John Cooper said he would become approver, and give King's evidence.

He then stated that he saw the prisoners, Johnson and Samuel Fare, leading the deceased gentleman down the lane under the pretence of seeing him safe home.

When they got part of the way down the lane Fare let go of the deceased and said he should not go any further and went away.

Johnson then asked him (witness) to help him with the deceased, and he then took hold of him.

When they got to the bottom of the lane Johnson said "I'll be d—— if Sam Fare hasn't robbed him (the gentleman), and gone."

Upon that Johnson put his foot out, and threw the deceased down, and he (witness), not knowing what he was going to do, fell into the ditch.

When he got out of the ditch he heard the deceased crying out, "Don't hurt me—don't hurt me!" and Johnson at this time was kneeling with his knees on the deceased's breast.

He then said to Johnson, "Don't hurt him—don't hurt him," and then he heard the deceased make a gurgling noise in his throat.

Johnson said to the deceased, "What will you give?"

The deceased replied, "Anything."

When he (witness) got into the middle of the road, Johnson showed him an open knife, and said, "There, you go and finish him, for I have begun him."

Witness refused to take the knife and said, "No, I won't."

Johnson then said, "Well, don't say anything to anybody."

The prisoner Fare was acquitted of the charge of murder, and the jury finding Johnson guilty, he was sentenced to death.

After his condemnation he made a long confession, in which he gave a number of details, but declared, on his most solemn oath, that it was Cooper, the approver, who first threw the deceased down, and commenced cutting his throat in the ditch.

He (the culprit) then finished him.

He maintained this assertion to the last.

Calcraft executed him on the 7th of January, 1833.

CHAPTER XXXVIII.
ANOTHER MYSTERIOUS MURDER.

ANOTHER of those mysterious murders which have from time to time shocked the metropolis, without the perpetrator being brought to justice, occurred in December, 1832.

This case is very remarkable, as showing the superficial manner and carelessness with which dead bodies are examined when they are first found under circumstances of great suspicion.

The deceased gentleman, Mr. Henry Camp Sheppard, was the head clerk of Messrs. Williams and Sons, soap-makers, of Compton-street, Goswell-road.

He was sixty years of age, and on Sunday morning, the 16th of December, 1832, he was found lying dead in his employer's counting-house in a pool of blood.

A surgeon was called, who made a superficial examination, and finding a very large fracture at the back of the skull, and a chair not far from the deceased, came to the opinion that the deceased had probably been standing on the chair, had fallen backwards after putting up his ledgers, stunned himself, and died.

Three men who were present concurred in this random speculative opinion, and supported the theory by adding that, no doubt in coming down he struck the back of his head by falling against the iron safe.

But after some little time, when the place came to be further examined, a poker was found in the room, the end of which was covered over with congealed blood, and the weapon itself was bent almost double from the violence with which it had been used.

Then another surgeon was sent for—Mr. Whittall, of 77, Myddelton-street—and in company with the other surgeon, who said it had not first occurred to him that the deceased was murdered, they found that his head was terribly beaten in, his right arm was fractured above the elbow—probably done in endeavouring to ward off the blows of his assailant—and in addition there were several other cuts on the skull crossing each other.

Altogether the unfortunate gentleman must have received no less than two dozen blows on his head and body, which was most fearfully bruised.

The doctors said the attack upon him must have been ferocious, and must have lasted full five minutes.

The deceased gentleman only resided next door to the counting house, and a small terrier dog used to run about the yard.

There were some suspicious circumstances in the case, which probably might have been followed up.

The Coroner, however, told the jury, which they too often do before they have fully exhausted the evidence they might have before them, that if they brought in a verdict probably the Government would offer a reward.

The jury returned a verdict of "Wilful murder against some person or persons unknown."

It is somewhat strange that no one in the house where he resided seems to have missed the old gentleman or sought after him, and the *Observer*, commenting on the case, said it was strange that not a single question was asked at the inquest as to whether anything was missing or in any way to elicit some motive for the murder.

It appeared from other information, however, that the deceased probably was robbed, as his watch was gone.

The cases on record which have failed in justice through the want of proper systematic inquiry are very numerous. There were many others about this period.

CHAPTER XXXIX.
MYSTERIOUS MURDER OF A BOY, ROBERT PAVIOR.

ON the evening of the 26th February, 1833, a fine intelligent boy, named Robert Pavior, aged thirteen, was suddenly missed from the door of his father's house, a respectable carman, who resided at 26, John-street, Tottenham-court-road.

A Mrs. Crawley, who rented one of the parlours, stated that she knew the boy was standing at the front door about seven o'clock, and directly afterwards she heard a scuffling.

Thinking it was some drunken men going by, she got up and shut the door, as the sound seemed to her that they were almost going to fall into the hall.

There seemed little doubt from the evidence afterwards given that in so doing she at that time unfortunately shut the door on the poor boy, who at that time was being dragged away by his murderers.

The boy was not seen again alive, and his father and mother, who were very fond of him, sought London over.

His father then had bills printed, and offered a reward of £5 for his recovery.

In the course of some time a man named Marshall who said he had seen the bills of the description of the boy came to the mother and told her that he had seen a boy answering that description in company with some marine boys by St. Katherine's Docks, and he had not the slightest doubt the boy was going to run away, and go to sea in a ship that was lying there named the "Hereford."

The mother took a cab, but could not find any tidings of her son, or hear of any marine boys having been there, or of a ship called the "Hereford."

When this man, Marshall, gave her this information he was in company with a man named Taylor, who lived next door to her.

These two men were also seen afterwards by different people in company with another man named Evans.

There were various persons who believed that the three men knew something of the boy, and a great deal of important information tending to cast suspicion upon them was given at the inquest.

On one occasion the mother overheard Marshall say to Taylor, "Shall I take him to Portsmouth, and make a pound or two more of him?"

Taylor then replied, "You'll go too far."

It was further shown that at another time Marshall had said to a young man named Elm that unless the mother would give £10 for his recovery, there would not be much use in looking for him, and that, for anything he knew now the boy might be either gone to Hell or Halifax, either dead or alive.

Another witness name William Higgins gave very positive evidence that he heard Marshall say he knew where the boy was.

During the whole of this time the unhappy parents were in a state of the greatest distress, but it seemed very difficult to understand whether Marshall was trifling and jesting with the wounded feelings of the parents, or whether he and the other two men really knew something of him.

The mother of the boy gave further evidence, and stated that while she was up at her window Evans, who was a French polisher, shook his fist at her, and said something, but what it was she could not tell.

Mrs. Sarah Smith deposed that she had seen Evans shake his fist at the boy's mother, and say, "I'll be d——d if you shan't be plagued a bit longer yet."

Some evidence was then given by neighbours of the terrible bad character of Taylor's house. which was next door to where the boy's parents lived.

Other witnesses were called, who swore that they had heard Marshall say that he knew places in the City where boys were taken, and the treatment they were subjected to.

It was also shown that Marshall kept asking people whether they thought, if he produced the boy, the money for him would really be forthcoming, and they replied "Yes."

There were so many suspicious circumstances against the men, but especially against Marshall, that the father, on his own responsibility, gave Marshall into custody.

He was brought up at Marlborough-street Police-court, but there being no direct evidence against him he was discharged.

On the 11th of March, three weeks after he had been missing, the body was discovered floating in the Regent's Canal by David Williams, a lock-keeper.

The medical evidence showed that the poor boy had been subjected to the most shocking treatment, exactly corresponding with what Marshall had intimated.

There were dreadful wounds on the head, and both his arms were broken, besides other injuries.

George Bundey and Sarah, his wife, proved that on Saturday evening, the 23rd of February, they had occasion to pass over the Regent's Canal-bridge, when near the "York and Albany Tavern" they observed three men; two were leaning over the parapet, and had a large parcel, which they appeared desirous of concealing.

When they got a short distance from the bridge they heard a splash in the water.

They thought Marshall and Taylor were like two of the men, but they could not swear to them.

On the witnesses coming near the bridge one of the men said, "There's some one coming."

Phœbe Palmer said she resided opposite the boy's father's house, and on the evening that he was missed she heard a child crying out, "Oh, no—don't you—don't you!" The sound seemed to come from the door of Pavior's house.

William Somerville, a boy, stated that on the night the deceased was missed he was playing in John-street, and saw the boy Pavior there. He saw a man like the prisoner, Taylor, speak to him, but he could not be sure he was the man; the man came out of Taylor's house; he saw the deceased also go to Taylor's house and peep through the keyhole; he saw a gentleman come out of Taylor's house and speak to the deceased.

For the defence Mary Ann Kent was called, who said that Marshall lodged with her at 5, Warren-street, Fitzroy-square, and on the evening of the 19th of February he was at home between six and seven in the evening, and did not go out afterwards.

The officer Keys, who arrested Marshall, in contradiction to the evidence of the last witness, said that before he arrested Marshall he asked the woman if she could say where Marshall was that night, and she repeatedly said she could not.

The case was tried before the Lord Chief Justice at the April Sessions of the Old Bailey.

In summing up he bore particularly upon that part of the evidence in which it was said that Marshall in course of conversation had said that he knew Captain Beauclerc, who had recently committed suicide in Hersemonger-lane Gaol, and that he also knew other rich men, and that unless the reward offered by his parents was increased from £5 to £10, the boy might be found in the water subjected to the exact violence in which it had been found.

Though the judge, however, strongly summed up against the prisoners, the jury returned a verdict of not guilty.

MISSING BOYS.

Previous to the trial of the three prisoners for the murder of the unfortunate boy, Robert Pavior, a number of other boys had been missed from their homes, and were not afterwards heard of.

During the trial, and after it, boys continued to be missed.

In consequence of certain information given, a watch was kept upon certain places, as parents continued to come to the courts in terrible grief at the loss of their boys, to whom no clue could be obtained.

Till the information given parents, though disconsolate for their loss, had indulged in the hope they had gone to sea.

Warrants, however, were issued for certain men of rank, but they escaped to the Continent.

TRYING TO CHEAT THE GALLOWS.

Captain Henry Nicoll, a retired officer from the 14th Regiment of Infantry, who also belonged to the same gang as Captain Beauclerc, and to the same gang as some of those who had fled to the Continent, was afterwards arrested on a similar charge.

He was found guilty at the Croydon Assizes, and sentenced to death.

He was brought to Horsemonger-lane Gaol for execution, when Elmes, the chief warder, thinking he might endeavour to avoid the gallows, as Captain Beauclerc had done, searched him, and on doing so found a long nail upon him, ground almost as sharp as a lancet.

On it being discovered, the culprit admitted that he had provided it for the purpose of committing suicide with it.

Just before Calcraft pinioned him, the culprit made a full confession of his guilt, and admitted that he truly deserved death.

When he appeared on the platform he was received with most horrid groans, and on Calcraft withdrawing the bolt, he at once fell, but struggled for several minutes. He was executed in August, 1833.

SAVED FROM THE GALLOWS BY THE DEAD ALIVE.

A remarkable instance, showing the caution with which persons should swear to the identity of the dead, occurred at an inquest held on the 16th of August, 1833

The body of a young girl about seventeen was taken out of the water, and an inquest was held upon it in Christ Church Workhouse, Blackfriars-road.

The body was identified by various persons as that of Eliza Baker, aged seventeen, who had formerly been a servant to Mr. Peter Wood, an eating-house keeper, of the Bermondsey New-road.

There were marks of violence on the body, as though she had been murdered and thrown into the Thames.

Mr. Wood, her master, was also called, and identified the body as that of his late servant, whom his wife had discharged from their service because she was jealous of her.

He, however, knew nothing, he said, of the marks of violence upon her, nor how she came by her death.

Matters now began to look very serious for him, for it was shown that he and his wife had serious quarrels over her.

The jury were about taking further evidence to try and connect the marks of violence and her death with some alleged intimacy on his part, when a drayman, in the employ of Messrs. Whitbread and Co., who had heard of the finding of the body of Eliza Baker under such mysterious and dreadful circumstances, hurried into the jury-room, and interrupting the proceedings, said he had come to tell the jury that the young female upon whom they were holding an inquest was then alive and in good health.

The coroner and jury were struck with amazement, and treating his declaration as absurd ordered the man to be quiet and not interrupt the proceedings in that manner.

"Oh," said the man, "I can prove what I say is correct, for I can produce the young woman, for I have just seen her and know where she is."

At this moment the young woman stepped into the jury-room and stood before her master.

He was so amazed that for a time he was both motionless and speechless.

The young woman then, taking him by the hand, said—"Why, Mr. Wood, how could you make such a blunder as to take another body for mine? Do you think I would commit such an act?"

Mr. Wood, who could not reply, fell senseless in a fit, and had to be carried away.

The jury returned to look at the body again, and then declared they had never seen two persons more alike.

There was no evidence to show who the deceased was, and after a very long investigation, a verdict of found drowned was returned.

SERIOUS MISTAKE OF THE RECORDER IN SIGNING A DEATH WARRANT.

In June, 1833, Calcraft was nearly hanging a man through a very serious mistake on the part of the Recorder of London in signing the death warrant of a postman whose sentence had been commuted.

It appears that Job Cox, a letter-carrier, had been convicted at the Old Bailey of stealing from a letter a £5 note.

He had been led to understand that he would only receive the milder punishment.

In the usual course of time, however, the recorder sent the warrant to Newgate in the usual form, sealed with the black seal, and signed Newman Knollys, ordering "Job Cox for execution next Tuesday."

The chaplain lost no time in informing the prisoner of the melancholy tidings.

He received the awful news as through he had been stuck with lightning, and for a time became quite speechless, as he had been led to believe the sentence would be commuted.

Calcraft had received notice to carry the execution out, and everything was in readiness.

Meantime when everything was prepared, the Chief Justice on Monday happened to be reading a newspaper which contained the recorder's report, and, seeing that Job Cox was marked for execution, he thought there must be some mistake.

He immediately sent for the under-sheriff, who went at once to the recorder, and asked him if he was not mistaken.

The recorder said no; he could be under no misapprehension, for the man was to be executed, and he firmly maintained this assertion till late at night.

In this unsatisfactory and uncertain state of affairs the sheriffs communicated with Lord Melbourne, the Home Secretary.

It was then ascertained that the man's sentence had been commuted, and that the recorder was wrong, having signed the warrant after his dinner entirely in mistake.

The man was then informed that his life was still to be spared, and he then became overjoyed.

RESIGNATION OF THE RECORDER.

On the following Monday a special meeting of the common Hall was held to take the recorder's conduct into consideration.

Mr. Stevens, in strongly condemning the conduct of the recorder, deprecated an infirm, imbecile, old man being continued in such an important office.

He had held it forty-seven years, and was too old to perform its duties. Had the unfortunate man's life been sacrificed the case would have, he said, amounted to murder.

The general indignation was so strong that the recorder at once sent in his resignation.

The Court of Aldermen held a special meeting expressing their sorrow that ill-health and infirmity had compelled the recorder to take the step after forty-seven years of faithful service.

MYSTERIOUS MURDER OF MISS ELMES.

In the month of May, 1833, another mysterious murder, in which the assassin escaped undetected, was perpetrated at Chelsea.

The victim in this instance was Miss Catherine Elmes, a maiden lady, about sixty years of age.

She resided at 17, Wellesley-street, Chelsea, near the new church.

The house in which she resided had been noticed shut up several days, and the neighbours, not having seen her about, gave information to the police.

On Saturday, the 4th of May, one of the officers entered the house, and then found the unfortunate old lady lying on the floor in her bedroom, with five fearful cuts about the head and face, and her head nearly severed from her body.

An inquest was held upon the body before Mr. Stirling, coroner, at the "Wellesley Arms," Robert-street, when the evidence given showed that the house was also found ransacked from top to bottom, as though robbery had been the motive.

A young woman, who went by the name of Mrs. Mortimer, was in the habit of lodging at the house, but had been away several days.

At the inquest, however, she gave the name of Maryann Eastman, aged twenty-six, and stated that on the previous Tuesday she left the deceased at home quite well.

It was shown that the old lady on Tuesday night went into the "Wellesley Arms" for her supper beer.

About this time two men were seen loitering about the house, and one of the theories was that in her absence they entered, and then murdering her on her return, proceeded to search for plunder.

Mr. Henry Elmes, of Lancing, near Worthing, brother of the deceased, identified the body as that of his sister; and it was shown that so far from the deceased being in affluent circumstances, she was really indigent.

The jury returned a verdict of wilful murder against some person or persons unknown, and the government offered a reward of £100 to anyone who would give such information as would lead to the murderer's detection.

CONTINUATION OF POLITICAL EXCITEMENT AND MURDER.

The political excitement which continued throughout the year 1833, and the growing opposition to anything like despotism in the Government, was greatly aggravated by the general conduct of the new police, and the hatred they incurred through the unwarrantable officiousness and brutal violence of some indiscreet members of the force.

The early ranks of the police were largely filled by men of the most disreputable, unreliable, and worthless characters.

There were numerous cases recorded of them meeting and abusing respectable women in the streets in a shameful manner, and if any resistance or indignation was shown, then the women were dragged in a violent way to the station and scandalous charges concocted against them.

In other instances, many of the men were found absent from their beats, and comfortably located with servant girls while daring robberies were penetrated.

Many others received bribes from publicans and the keepers of disreputable houses, so that they might openly set the law at defiance, whilst others actually fraternised with thieves, assisted in their robberies, and shared their booty.

So numerous were the complaints that some of the magistrates sometimes made nightly observations, and they openly admitted that the abuses in the police force were so great that they would not have credited them had they not seen for themselves.

In addition there were in the force many of the lower orders of Irishmen, who, having been invested with wooden truncheons and a little brief authority, and being naturally prone to whiskey and fighting, they constantly used their truncheons in every little street squabble as they would have used their shillelaghs at Donnybrook fair, seeming under the impression they had full licence to break the people's heads with impunity.

For these irregularities and mistakes a great many of them were dismissed the force, and sent back to the ranks from which they came.

It was at this period when a political meeting, called for the purpose of forming a National Convention, was largely advertised to be held in Calthorpe-street, Coldbath-fields.

The Home Office, in opposition to it, issued a proclamation prohibiting it as being illegal.

This prohibition exasperated the leaders still more, and the people, looking upon the proclamation as an attempt on the part of the Government to interfere with the freedom of speech, and the right of political discussion, they determined that the meeting should be held.

The meeting was fixed to take place on the 13th of May, and at two o'clock, the hour appointed, the populace began to assemble in various parts of London for the purpose of marching to the place of rendezvous.

Shortly after twelve large detachments of the metropolitan police marched to Coldbath-fields, and took up their quarters in the Riding School.

Colonel Rowan and Mr. Mayne, the two commissioners, had already arrived, and were accommodated at a house in the neighbourhood, attended by two clerks for the purpose of marking the ringleaders, and of keeping observation on the proceedings.

In addition, there were several magistrates there, and some officers of the 1st regiment of Life Guards, ready to call their regiment out, a detachment of which was under arms and ready at a moment's notice.

The people began to assemble, and soon there were between 3000 and 4000 persons there.

The members of the Union, consisting of about 150 persons, then made their appearance, carrying flags and banners, with the mottoes "Liberty or Death," with a skull and cross bones on a black ground and red border, "Holy Alliance of the Working Classes," "Equal Rights and Equal Justice." Then there were a tri-coloured flag, the Republican flag of America, and a pole with the cap of liberty.

They had scarcely got upon the ground, before a detachment of the A Division, supported by some other divisions, marched into Calthorpe-street with great order and precision.

Their promptitude and formidable appearance seemed to make a momentary impression on the mob, but a man, pointing to the banner, "Liberty or Death," shouted "Men be firm."

This at once roused the spirit of the people.

They called out, "Down with them—liberty or death!" and appeared determined to resist to the utmost.

"Go on, go on," now resounded from all sides to the speaker.

The division of police halted in the middle of the street, having received orders to act with calmness and forbearance.

They then walked forward with their staves in their hands clearing their way through the crowd to the man who still continued to address the people.

The police were then instantly attacked by the people.

The sound of the blows and the shrieks of the women were loud, and the conflict all at once was severe.

When a little clearance was effected at least twenty men were on the ground with blood streaming from their heads.

Sergeant Harrison, of the D division, seized a banner, but received a violent blow on the arm.

Policeman Robert Cully, C 95, and his brother made up to another, when, in the midst of the fight, Cully received a wound in the abdomen from a stiletto, and instantly expired.

Sergeant Brooks was also wounded, besides others who received blows.

The people rallied in the open space by the prison and made a vigorous attack on the police, which was repelled, though not till they had attempted to rescue the banner, "Liberty or Death."

The police were then formed into lines extending across the different streets.

They then arrested the ringleaders, and in the course of the night the street was cleared.

Among the prisoners arrested there were three men charged at Bow-street with having been concerned in stabbing some of the police.

The first prisoner put to the bar was Robert Tilley, charged with being concerned in the murder of the policeman Cully. George Fursey and Thomas Tilley with stabbing other police.

George Fursey was committed to take his trial for stabbing two of the police, Brookes and Redmond.

THE INQUEST.

An inquest was held on the body of the policeman, Cully, before Mr. Stirling, the coroner.

There was a great deal of respectable evidence given to show that when once the police were let loose they beat the people and broke the heads of men, women, and even beat children in the most merciless manner.

The inquest was continued for some days, but owing to the political state of the country, and the irregular proceedings taken in the attempted prohibition of the meeting, the jury seemed determined to justify the loss of the policeman's life.

The proclamation prohibiting the meeting was not signed, but merely ended with the words "By Order of the Secretary of State," and it was contended that, for aught the people knew, it might have been a forgery.

The jury, therefore, returned a verdict of justifiable homicide on these grounds:—"That no Riot Act was read, nor any proclamation advising the people to disperse; that the Government did not take the proper precautions to prevent the people from assembling, and that the conduct of the police was ferocious, brutal, and unprovoked by the people; and we, moreover, express our anxious hope that the Government will in future take better precautions to prevent the recurrence of such disgraceful transactions in the metropolis."

The coroner said that the verdict only traduced the police and the Government, and that they were not borne out by the evidence in justifying the death of that man.

Were those people innocent who had used the murderous weapons they had seen—such as stilettoes, bludgeons, and lances?

The foreman then said that they had stated in their verdict the grounds on which they had justified the homicide.

The people were peaceable till they were attacked by the police.

They, therefore, would not alter one word of their verdict, and he must either record that verdict or dismiss them.

The coroner said that he considered their verdict a disgrace to them. The people then shouted, "Bravo! jurors; you have done your duty!"

The Solicitor-General then carried the case to the King's Bench, and got the verdict quashed.

The proceedings now caused greater excitement. Robert Fursey was tried at the Old Bailey, and every attempt was made to gain a conviction. The jury, however, found him not guilty.

Great meetings were afterwards held, addressed by Mr. O'Connell, M.P., and others, and a determined stand was made against the efforts of the Government to suppress free speech, and the brutal conduct of the police.

CHAPTER XL.

ASSASSINATION OF MR. THOMAS ASHTON BY TRADE UNIONISTS AT MANCHESTER—EXTRAORDINARY CASE.

AMONG the many outrages which occurred during the trade riots of 1831 few cases created more sympathy and interest than the murder of Mr. Thomas Ashton, one of the principal cotton-spinners at Hyde, in the neighbourhood of Manchester.

The deceased gentleman, who was a son of Mr. Samuel Ashton, a very large proprietor, one evening in January undertook to superintend the work at his brother James's manufactory at Apethorne.

He had not long left his house at tea-time before a messenger came to state that as he was going along the lane back to the factory he had been met and shot, and in less than ten minutes he was brought back to the house quite dead.

At the inquest, which was afterwards held, it was shown, by the book-keeper, that about six weeks previously three men named Ralph Stopford, Thomas Platt, and Matthew Both, had, for certain irregularities, been discharged from the mill, and it was at first thought that this might have had something to do with the prompting of the murder.

Martha Percival, a girl nine years of age, stated that just before the murder was committed she met three men in the road carrying, what she called, a gun.

There, however, being no direct evidence against the prisoners the jury returned a verdict of wilful murder against some person or persons unknown.

The father of the deceased offered a reward of £500 for the discovery of the offenders, the other relatives offered another £500, and the Home Secretary offered a reward of £1000, making a total of £2000, with pardon to any accomplice, excepting the one who actually fired the pistol—the weapon which the girl wrongly described as a gun.

As there had been general wages disputes throughout the locality, there was a wide-spread belief that the crime was a trades union outrage, and there was the greater desire to bring the offenders to justice, in consequence of the extreme secrecy of the trades unionists, and the oaths taken by them. The following was

THE OATH.

I, ———, do before Almighty God and this loyal lodge, most solemnly swear that I will not work for any master that is not in the union, neither will I work with any illegal man or men, but will do my best for the support of wages, and most solemnly swear to keep inviolate all the secrets of this order; nor will I ever consent to have any money for any purpose but for the use of the lodge, and the support of the trade;

nor will I write, or cause to be written, print, mark, either on stone, marble, brass, paper, or sand, anything connected with this order. So help me, God, and keep me steadfast to this my present obligation. And I further promise to do my best to bring all legal men that I am connected with into this order, and if I ever reveal any of the rules, may what is before me plunge me into eternity.

CONFESSION OF THE MURDER.

More than three years elapsed before there was any direct clue to the murder, and, probably, it would never have been discovered had not one of the culprits been tempted to give certain information in the hope of obtaining the large reward offered.

This was a man named William Garside who, in April, 1834, was a prisoner in Derby Gaol for felony.

While there he sent for the governor, Mr. John Sims, and asked him whether he thought he would receive a full pardon and a remission of his sentence if he gave information in reference to a murder.

The governor replied that he could not tell him, but what murder did he allude to?

Garside then said he would rather not say unless he was sure of a free pardon of his present sentence of eighteen months and a full exoneration from any proceedings consequent upon what information he might give; then what he had to say he would like to say before a magistrate.

As the governor thought, from the manner of the prisoner, that he had something to reveal, he told him he had better see a magistrate.

Dr. Forrester, J.P., a local magistrate, saw him and the prisoner then put the same query to him.

The magistrate informed him that he had better read the advertisements in reference to the murder he alluded to.

Mr. William Jeffrey Locket, the Mayor of Derby, also saw the prisoner, but for some time he refused to say anything further unless he had a guarantee that nothing would be done to him.

The magistrate ascertained from the prisoner that the murder to which he alluded was the murder of Mr. Ashton, in 1831.

From the inquiries which the magistrates set going, they arrested two other men, brothers, named William Moseley and Joseph Moseley.

Wm. Moseley then desired to become approver, and give king's evidence.

Upon this Garside also gave evidence, and William Moseley then made a full statement to the following effect:—

He said that he had been a boatman, but at the time of the murder he was out of employment.

While he was looking out for some work, the two prisoners, Joseph Moseley and William Garside, stopped him and asked him if he had anything to do.

He replied that he was looking out for something.

They then told him that they had just seen two men, one of whom was named Scholfield, who belonged to a trades union, who wanted them to undertake to do something, and if he liked to wait a bit for a day or two, they could put him in the way of getting a little money.

He then agreed to meet them again, and then they told him that what the man wanted them to do was to shoot one of the Mr. Ashton's; it did not matter which—either of them would do. They agreed to do it, and then Garside and Joseph Moseley were provided with pistols by the men.

Garside had a large horse pistol, and Joseph Moseley had a small one with a bright barrel.

On the night when the murder was arranged to take place, they hid themselves in the lane through which it was known one of the Mr. Ashtons would pass.

He, William Moseley, and Garside then changed shoes and caps. Garside put his heavy hob-nailed boots on, and his furry cap, and he put Garside's boots and high hat on.

While they were waiting in the lane to commit the murder they saw a man and a little girl pass down.

Then Mr. Ashton came along, and the other two shot him.

After that, the next day, they met the man who had agreed with them to do it, at the "Bull's Head," Marple. He then came out. The man then said to him that he had given Joseph Moseley and Garside their share of the money, and then he offered him, witness, three sovereigns.

He witness, however, would not take the three. He only took two sovereigns, as he told the man that would be enough for him.

They then all signed a book, and put their marks as receipts for the money. The man then asked them to go down on their knees and swear secrecy.

They all four then went down on their knees, and took a solemn oath never to reveal the murder.

As they took the oath a knife was held over the head of each, and they each one then said, "I wish God may strike me dead if ever I tell."

The man who paid the money knelt down and took the oath first, and Garside next, and then he (witness) and his brother.

The prisoners were several times confronted with each other in Chester Gaol, and on the 18th of July, when they were again brought face to face in the gaol, and William Moseley's statement read, Joseph Moseley turned to Garside, and looking him full in the face said—

"Thou seest what thou hast done for us both. Now we will have it all out."

Captain Clarke then cautioned the prisoners not to say anything to criminate themselves, as what they said would be taken down, and might be given in evidence against them.

The prisoner Garside then turned to William Moseley, and said—

"Well, Will, don't thee say any more, and then they cannot hurt us."

Joseph Moseley, however, would not be deterred. He now put in a written statement, in which he charged Garside and his brother William with a number of offences, and also with being the principals in the present murder. He further said that Garside was a man that would do anything, or swear any man's life away for money.

THE TRIAL.

The prisoners, William Garside and Joseph Moseley, were then brought up at the ensuing Chester Assizes, when, after the whole of the evidence had been given, the two prisoners were sentenced to death.

REFUSAL OF THE SHERIFFS TO EXECUTE.

The day was appointed for the execution of both prisoners, and the time fixed was a few days after the trial.

When the time, however, came, the sheriffs, both of the county and of the city, refused to execute them.

Several orders were made, but, as the sheriffs claimed to be exempt from such orders by the repealing of certain orders and laws appertaining to Chester, they would not carry it out, and the men were respited from time to time.

THE LIFE OF WILLIAM CALCRAFT, THE HANGMAN.

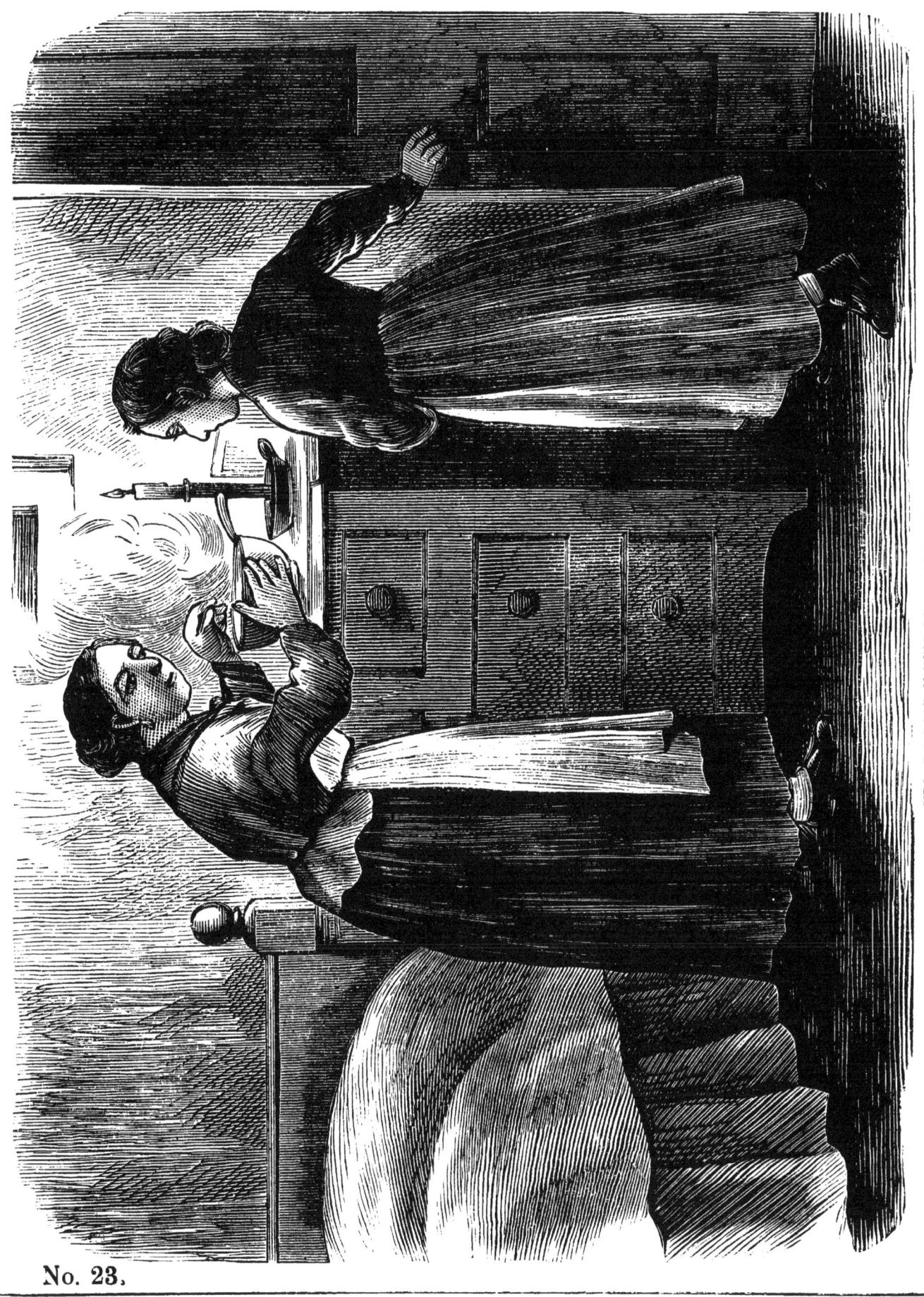

MRS. BURDOCK MIXING THE POISON WITH THE GRUEL.

No. 23.
177

SINGULAR PROCEEDINGS IN THE COURT OF KING'S BENCH.

As the case was exciting intense interest, and as the conduct of the sheriffs of the city and county of Chester was looked upon by many as only a legal quibble, there was a general cry for justice to be done upon the miscreants already sentenced.

On the 6th of November, 1834, the Attorney-General in the Court of King's Bench moved for a writ of certiorari to remove into this court the conviction in this case, and for a writ of habeas corpus to bring up the bodies of the prisoners to the bar of the court.

He believed that he was entitled as a matter of right to these writs, but from respect to the court he preferred also stating the circumstances which had given rise to the application.

The two men whom it was now sought to bring before the court had been tried at Chester before Mr. Justice Park, for the murder of Mr. Thomas Ashton, a magistrate of Chester, and they were convicted and sentenced to death.

In the usual course, their execution would have taken place on the following Friday, but they had been respited from time to time by order of the Secretary of State; the time for the expiration of the last reprieve being on the 18th of the present month.

The cause of this delay had been a dispute between the sheriffs of the county and the city of Chester, as to upon whom fell the obligation to put into execution the sentence of death; the sheriff of the county declaring that the obligation fell upon the sheriff of the city, and the latter claiming exemption under the 11th Geo. IV.

Previously to the passing of this Act all complaints in the county palatine of Chester had been tried by the Chief Justice of Chester, when rules of court were made for the execution of such prisoners as were condemned to death, which orders were carried into effect by the sheriff of the city of Chester.

But by the Act in question this court was abolished, and in its stead assizes, under commissions of oyer and terminer, were to be held there, as in the other counties of the kingdom.

By the 16th section of this Act, however, it was provided that nothing therein contained should affect the duties and obligations of the magistrates and citizens.

In the present case the sheriff of the city of Chester refused to execute the prisoners, alleging as a reason that his obligation to do so only extended to the Palatine Court, which had been abolished, and also that if there were any obligation it lay upon the mayor and citizens, and not upon the sheriff.

Under these circumstances the learned judge had been under the necessity of respiting the prisoners, who up to the present time had not been executed.

Bills of indictment had been preferred against the sheriffs of the county and city, but they had been thrown out by the grand jury, and he (the attorney-general) had deemed it his duty to file informations against the sheriff.

As much time, however, would necessarily elapse before the question to be raised by them could be decided, and as in the meantime it was necessary and most important that the sentence of the law should be carried out upon the prisoners, he (the learned counsel) after much thought had deemed it right to make the present application to the court, that their lordships might exercise the power he should be able to show was invested in them of ordering the execution of the prisoners, either by the above-mentioned county or city sheriffs, or by the sheriff of Middlesex or Surrey, or by the marshal of the court.

The learned counsel then cited a vast number of cases, and of authorities for the proceeding which he wished the court to adopt.

After mentioning a case in the reign of James II., in which one Thomas Middleton was executed by order of this court, the learned counsel adverted to the well-known case of Sir Walter Raleigh, who had been condemned to death for high treason, but had been confined in the Tower and elsewhere, after sentence, for several years, until ultimately he was executed by order of this court under the original sentence.

The learned counsel then adduced several similar cases, wherein this court had interfered to order the time and place of execution, particularly in the cases of three of the regicides, who, after having been sentenced for high treason passed upon them, were ordered by the court to be executed at Tyburn.

In Hales's "Pleas of the Crown" it was laid down that when judgment of death had been given in the Court of King's Bench execution is to be made by the marshal of the court, the prisoner being supposed to be in the custody of the court, which doctrine was acted upon in the reign of Charles II. in the case of Brown, executed in Surrey, for an offence committed in Middlesex, the marshal being the officer of the Court of King's Bench in all counties.

The learned counsel then referred to the case of Mr. Charles Ratcliffe, brother of Lord Derwentwater, who had been convicted of high treason in joining the rebellion of 1715, and who having made his escape, and after residing in France for many years, was again (in 1745) taken on the high seas on his way to join the rebellion in that year, when his execution was ordered by this court under the original conviction, which execution was performed by the sheriff of Middlesex on Tower-hill.

In the case of Earl Ferrers, who had been convicted of murder before a competent tribunal, the judges replied to a question put to them, that should the day named for execution pass over without such execution taking place then, that a new day could be appointed by the House of Lords, or by the Court of Queen's Bench, the record being removed.

The learned counsel then cited a number of other subsequent cases in support of his declaration that the court had power to order execution, and in particular adverted to the case of the King v. Thomas, wherein it had been decided that the attorney-general was entitled to the *certiorari*, and to the *habeas corpus* as now moved for.

Sir James Scarlett mentioned a case within his own recollection, where a man sentenced to death for sheep-stealing, and who had escaped, was subsequently brought up and ordered for execution.

The Attorney-General further remarked that if the writs were granted it would bring the case before the court, and then it would be decided whether or not they had the power to order the execution.

The court then granted the rules.

On the following Monday the two prisoners were brought from Chester gaol, heavily ironed and strongly guarded, and lodged in Newgate.

THE CULPRITS IN THE COURT OF KING'S BENCH.

On the following Tuesday they were brought up at the Court of King's Bench.

Every available place was crowded, and great interest appeared to be taken in the proceedings, especially by the members of the learned profession.

The Attorney-General said it was now his duty to pray that the sentence of the court might be passed upon the prisoners.

Their lordships, after consulting a short time, retired, and on returning—

Lord Denman said that the court had been desirous of considering for a short time the novel circumstances under which the proceedings came before them.

Although the court could not hold out any hope to the prisoners that the sentence would not be carried out, yet their lordships wished a little longer time to consider all the bearings of the case.

The prisoners were then again removed in custody to Newgate.

On the following Thursday the prisoners were brought up again, when, at a very early hour, all the avenues of the court were entirely filled by persons anxious to hear the proceedings.

The Attorney-General said he had now to move that the prisoners be asked if they had anything to say why execution should not be awarded against them.

Mr. J. Dunn, on behalf of the prisoner Garside, moved that the return to the writ of *habeas corpus* and the record of conviction be first read.

The documents were then read by the officer of the court.

Mr. Dunn said it was his duty to submit to their lordships that they could not award sentence of execution against the prisoner Garside, because by virtue of the king's proclamation he was entitled by legal right to his pardon. He also contended that the prisoner was entitled to make this plea *ore tenus*, and not by a written plea.

Lord Denman: It is for the prisoners to plead that if they think fit.

Mr. Dunn: I plead it for them. The learned gentleman then read the proclamation, dated at Whitehall the 6th of January, 1831, declaring that his Majesty was graciously pleased to grant a free pardon to any person (except the individual who had actually fired the shot) who would give such evidence as would lead to the conviction of the parties concerned in the murder of Mr. Ashton. That information had been given by the prisoner Garside, who avers that he was not the person who actually fired the shot, and that in consequence William and Joseph Moseley were apprehended, and the latter convicted.

The Attorney-General urged that the facts stated by the learned counsel would be of no avail now. Had these facts been proved, most indubitably the prosecution of Garside would have been improper; and those who advised it would have incurred great responsibility and blame.

Lord Denman: Do you demur to the plea?

The Attorney-General: I do, my lord. If the prisoner has been pardoned by Act of Parliament, it must be pleaded. If he is pardoned under the Great Seal, it must be pleaded. But I contend a promise of pardon is of no avail in bar to the indictment. The law laid down in "Blackstone's Commentaries," 4th volume, as to the mode of pardoning, provides that it must be under the sign manual, and that a warrant under the Great Seal is not a complete and irrevocable pardon. The king's charter of pardon must be specially pleaded, and that at the time of the arraignment; for if a man is indicted and has the king's pardon in his pocket, and afterwards pleads the general issues and puts himself upon his trial, he has waived his right. But the question was submitted to the jury at the trial as to whether Garside had actually fired the pistol; and the verdict was "Both guilty; the blow inflicted by James Garside." The plea therefore could have been of no avail, as it was by his hand that the murder was committed.

Lord Denman then referred to the record of the conviction, and observed that the verdict was guilty, and that the record was endorsed in the special terms stated by the Attorney-General that Garside's hand committed the murder.

Mr. Dunn contended that if a promise of pardon by his Majesty was not considered a free pardon, the consequences would be most dreadful, for no man would be so silly as to give information of a murder if the king could turn round on him and say, "You have done what you ought, but I don't mean to pardon you." He urged nothing in favour of a merciful consideration of Garside's case, for he feared the circumstances did not warrant him in so doing; but he contended that in strict point of law he was entitled to plead the king's pardon. In the case of the King v. Hunt and Thurtell, it had been urged by Mr. Thesiger in bar of the indictment in that court, that Hunt had given evidence which led to the finding of the body, and the answer was that the time for such a plea had not arrived. When the proper time did arrive the prisoner's life was spared on such terms as the Crown thought fit. He submitted, therefore, that execution should not be awarded until the Crown could take the circumstances into its consideration, and he now left the matter in the hands of the court.

Lord Denman then said: The two prisoners, James Garside and Joseph Mosely, had been brought up on a writ of habeas corpus accompanied by a record of their conviction for murder. They had been called upon to say why execution should not be recorded against them, and Garside pleads the king's pardon, which, he says, he is entitled to by legal right. But it is quite clear that such a plea can furnish no defence against an indictment, nor no reason why execution should not be awarded. They were not to presume that the King would not perform his promise; there was no doubt that he would perform most strictly and faithfully everything that had been guaranteed to the meanest and most criminal of his subjects. As the application had been made in the present instance, time enough would be granted to renew and consider that application, although he (Lord Denman) was bound to state candidly that any hope of their lives being spared would only lead to the most dreadful disappointment. The court would now proceed to award execution in the usual course.

The Attorney-General said it was now his painful duty to pray that execution might be awarded.

Mr. Hill, after apologising for interrupting the proceedings of the court, said he had to submit, on behalf of the Sheriff of Middlesex, that the award of execution should not be directed to him. He was prepared with authorities if the court thought fit to hear him.

Lord Denman said that the court had power to order any sheriff in England to do execution, and the Court did not think it was competent to hear any argument against the exercise of its jurisdiction.

The prisoners were then asked whether they had anything to say whether death should not be executed upon them.

Moseley then lifted his hands up as far as the irons would permit, for he was very heavily ironed, and said:

"I swear I am innocent of the murder. It was my brother, William Moseley, who was admitted as King's evidence, who had more to do with it than I had."

Garside trusted to the defence made by his counsel.

Mr. Justice Taunton then proceeded to pronounce the order of the court in pursuance of the conviction and judgment already passed upon the prisoners. He said that the order of the court was that execution be done upon both prisoners on the following Tuesday by the marshal of that court, and that the Sheriff of the county of Surrey do assist in execution of the said judgment.

PETITION TO THE KING.

The prisoner Garside then, through his solicitor, sent a petition to the King, setting forth that he, having seen an advertisement offering a large reward to any one who would give information of the murder, and a free pardon also, providing such person was not the one who actually fired the pistol, begged most humbly to submit that he, having given the first information which led to the arrest of the two other prisoners and the conviction of one of them, therefore he was legally entitled to his Majesty's pardon, and he therefore further prayed that the pardon might be granted to him accordingly.

The petition was duly taken into consideration, and the prisoner then received a reply signed by the Duke of Wellington, stating that the King saw no reason to interfere with the course of justice and the carrying out of the sentence.

THE EXECUTION.

The prisoners, who up to that time had been confined in the King's Bench Prison, were now conveyed to Horsemonger-lane Gaol for execution.

On the Tuesday morning appointed the gallows was erected as usual on the top of the gaol, and one of the greatest crowds ever met together assembled to witness the carrying out of the sentence.

Calcraft was engaged as the executioner, and when he was introduced to the culprits all hope then seemed to leave them.

After their irons were knocked off and they were pinioned they seemed scarcely able to ascend to the scaffold.

Garside, to the very last moment, seemed disappointed at the pardon being refused him, and he frequently gave details of the manner in which the the crime was committed, and the part each one took in the work of the dreadful assassination.

His plausible concoctions at times had such an air of truth that to the last moment many believed him, and looked upon him as a man who, for the confession he had made, was really entitled to a pardon, and to the £2000 offered as a reward.

The culprits were attended on the scaffold by two clergymen, who exhorted them to repentance.

Calcraft then finally adjusted the fatal ropes, and was proceeding to draw the caps over their faces, which would shut from their view the sight of this world for ever, when Garside shouted out, "I have something more to say. All that I have previously said is utterly false."

Calcraft then slipped behind the scaffold, and drew the bolt, and the drop fell.

Moseley died comparatively easy, but Garside struggled fearfully, and plunged about in a most terrible manner. He was several minutes dying, and the sight was shocking to see.

So ended the lives of two out of three men who, for a paltry sum of £3 7s., each undertook to be assassins, and to murder in the most deliberate manner a gentleman, a large employer of labour, and one who was a magistrate, too, at the bidding of a set of dastardly cowards, with whose quarrel the culprits had really nothing to do.

For the sake of obtaining the reward the man Garside broke through the terrible oath they all had taken with the knife over their heads. He betrayed his companions in crime.

He also betrayed the men who prompted them to the commission of it. Then he sought to fix the actual guilt upon the man who was most innocent, whilst he himself was the most guilty.

He persisted in a series of lying statements till the halter was actually round his neck, playing the hypocrite with the clergymen, and it was only at the very last moment that he shouted out, "All that I have previously said is utterly false."

The case, in itself, is one more remarkable instance of the pertinacity with which criminals will attempt to fix their own guilt upon other people, and, in the delusive hope of thereby escaping justice themselves, will cling even upon the gallows drop to the most lying and fearful statements.

This case is also a very remarkable one in another point of view. There are some who, in reference to great crimes, hold their opinion very strongly that murder is such a fearful crime that it is generally done by one person alone, and that it is seldom that more than one person is in the dreadful secret. Here we have a case in which the murder was first resolved upon in council.

Then there was an officer deputed to find willing assassins, and treat with them as to the price to be paid for the murder.

After two assassins had been stipulated with they then took a third into the dreadful secret and the commission of the dreadful crime.

From this and many other cases which might be cited, it is clear that there are often cases in which more than one person is concerned in a murder, and when there are reasons to suspect that such may be the case, the officers of justice should certainly apply themselves to the unravelling of the whole mystery, and not merely confine themselves to an endeavour to fix the guilt upon any particular person alone—a course which sometimes ends in the total defeat of justice itself.

One of the singular points in this extraordinary case was, that the police for three years had been suspecting three men, who had once been discharged from one of the Messrs. Ashton's employment, and by this wrong conjecture they had for three years been on an entirely false track.

CHAPTER XLI.

TRIAL OF THE SHERIFF OF THE COUNTY OF CHESTER

Mr. GIBBS CRAWFORD ANTROBUS, the Sheriff of the county of Chester, was then tried in the Court of King's Bench, on the 13th of February, 1835, for having refused to execute Garside and Moseley.

There were many legal arguments on both sides, and among other information which came out was the expense of executions.

It was shown that in one instance the charge of the Sheriff of Chester for executing and putting a man in chains on Stockport Moor was no less than £69 15s.

Lord Denman, at the close of the case, decided against the Attorney-General, and held that under the various enactments which had taken place the Sheriff of Chester could not be called upon to execute criminals.

DEATH OF MR. JOHN WONTNER, THE FORMER GOVERNOR OF NEWGATE.

Mr. Wontner, the former Governor of Newgate, died at his residence in the Old Bailey at twelve o'clock, on the 6th of November, 1833, of brain fever. He had only been indisposed two days.

On the previous Monday he had been to Chatham, and on his return complained of a cold.

He had been some years in the service of the Corporation; first as one of the City Marshals. While filling that office he was thrown from his horse and fractured his leg, which was afterwards amputated.

He was much esteemed for his humanity during the whole of the time he filled the office of governor, and frequently received letters from convicts thanking him for his kindness.

EXECUTION OF A NOTORIOUS INCENDIARY.

On the 7th of December, 1833, John Staliain, the notorious incendiary, was executed by Calcraft, at Cambridge.

This criminal at a time when bread was dear and wheat was scarce was charged with wilfully setting fire to a barn. There had been many fires in the district, and great loss of property, and some of the agricultural labourers were suspected.

It happened, however, in many instances that the culprit gave information of the various fires as soon as they were breaking out. He was at length suspected and watched, and being caught he was found guilty and sentenced to death.

Before his execution he made a full confession of having wilfully fired eleven stacks for the purpose of getting the 6s. 6d. which the fire offices allowed for the first information.

The property which he thus ruthlessly destroyed, for the purpose of getting rewards amounting to only £3 11s. 6d., was estimated at considerably more than £60,000.

THE TRIAL OF MRS. BURDOCK.

The following case is about one of the most extraordinary cases on record, and illustrates many phases of social life.

It created very great interest at the time, and no doubt will be read with interest even now.

LIFE IN LODGINGS IN GREAT CITIES—MRS. WADE'S LODGINGS.

Most people who live in great towns know what a difficult thing it is to get good lodgings.

Yet there are plenty of places vacant, for cards of "apartments to let" and "lodgings for single gentlemen" attract our attention in some localities in almost every window we see.

The difficulty lies in knowing how to choose the best among so many.

It would be out of place here to depict all the sorts of landladies and landlords that are to be met with among that very large fraternity known as lodging-house keepers, but to cite a few of them we may mention that first there is the landlady who, when you go to inquire about her apartments, puts her spectacles up on her forehead, and, resting her two broad fat hands on her hips, takes a full survey of you from head to foot, and then, inquiring "what might be your pwerfession," tells you that she is wery perticker in the pussons she takes in, and eventually concludes by asking you whether you can give her a reference or a satisfactory "karackter from your last place."

But, as history shows us, whilst there are many landladies who are very "pertickler" whom they take in, yet there are also a very large number who are very particular whom they let out. Again, it seems rather strange that applicants for lodgings do not more frequently retort that they also are very particular where they go, and then ask her in turn whether she can give a reference and character too; and also whether she can satisfactorily account for all the lodgers she has previously had.

To those who are unacquainted with the records of crime this may seem an unnecessary caution, and appear like an exaggeration of the dangers of social life.

But it is not so. There is no doubt that the great majority of people who let lodgings are honest, kind-hearted, industrious people, who treat their lodgers with every consideration, and with as much kindness as they would members of their own family.

But there are some exceptions to the rule, for there are not a few lodging-house keepers into whose lodgings it is positively dangerous to enter, as they are nothing less than systematic thieves and murderers, into which a lodger having once entered neither his goods, character, nor life are safe.

People then, looking out for lodgings, especially aged lonely people with money, or young men or young women who may have a little property about them, cannot be too careful into whose houses they enter as lodgers, seeing the thousands of persons who are missed every year, and are never again heard of.

Mrs. Wade, as she was called, was a fine stout, tall, and good-looking woman, with a healthy rosy complexion. At the period of which we write, the year 1833, she kept a lodging house in Trinity-street, Bristol, where in the window was displayed the usual notice "lodgings to let."

She had not much difficulty in letting her apartments, for she was a clean-looking woman, and, as a rule, particular lodgers like a clean-looking landlady.

Mrs. Wade, whose maiden name was Mary Ann Williams, was born at Ross, but at the age of nineteen she came to Bristol to look out for a place of service, and she succeeded in obtaining a situation in the family of Mr. Plumley, of Nicholas-street.

She, however, in the course of time, obtained sufficient money to commence keeping a lodging-house, and thus began her course in life. When she lived in Trinity-street she was about thirty-four years of age.

Mrs. Wade, having young children, kept a servant, named Mary Evans, to assist her in her house duties, and at the period of which we are writing she had been in Mrs. Wade's service nearly twelve years.

Among Mrs. Wade's lodgers there was an old lady named Mrs. Clara Ann Smith, a widow, who occupied one of the upper rooms in Mrs. Wade's house.

It may be as well here to state at once that though Mrs. Wade lived with Mr. Wade as his wife, and to all outward appearances was a very respectable woman, she was not really married to him.

In fact, before living with Mr. Wade, she had lived with a man named Agar, a tailor, who, having a wife living at the time, could not marry her.

Then she resided with a man named Thomas, a gentleman's servant, by whom she had a son; and afterwards she lived with Wade, who kept a clothes shop on the quay at Bristol.

He also kept lodging-houses, and as he was steward to a steam packet as well, he was frequently away on a voyage.

In the meantime his reputed wife, or rather Mary Ann Williams, for she had never yet been married, looked after her own and his lodging-house business. Everyone seemed to like Mrs. Wade, for in various ways she appeared to be of a very obliging disposition.

Her old lady lodger, Mrs. Clara Ann Smith, looked upon her as a treasure of a landlady, for when she was at all chilly she would make her a good fire, and she would always make her some nice gruel if she had the slightest cold.

It is not surprising, then, that when Mrs. Smith was taken very ill, in 1833, she had great faith in the kindness, and little niceties made for her by Mrs. Wade, and her confidence in her was still further increased when she went and engaged a very excellent young girl, named Mary Ann Allen, specially to wait upon her and attend to her.

But in October, 1833, after Mrs. Smith had been with Mrs. Wade some weeks, after being unwell for several days, she died.

Mrs. Wade appeared in trouble. She could not bear the idea of seeing the "poor old soul" buried by the parish she said, and as the old lady had left nothing to be buried with, excepting a few articles almost worthless, she determined to sell what few there were towards the expense, and make up the deficiency herself.

So she sent for Mr. James Thomas, an undertaker, of 52, Castle-street, and agreed with him to make a respectable coffin, for which she, Mrs. Wade, would pay.

She also agreed with the sexton to put a few flowers to mark the grave where "the poor old soul" was buried, which might be recognised if any relations, if she had any, should ever be found.

The old lady was accordingly buried, one or two gowns and other small things were offered to the servants, and so in the course of a few weeks the name and memory of the deceased were forgotten.

In life she had not troubled much after her relations, and her relations apparently had not troubled much after her.

In the course of a little time Mrs. Wade began to furnish her house in a more superior style to that in which it had formerly been, and both she and Mr. Wade gave extensive orders for other goods, and they appeared in really prosperous circumstances.

They both, however, explained that they had had a considerable sum of money left them; in fact, that they had enough to keep them through life.

Some time afterwards, while they appeared in the height of their prosperity, Mr. Wade died, and he, having been respectably interred, Mrs. Wade was to all appearance a deeply distressed, disconsolate, but a fine well-to-do buxom widow.

No doubt, with such a costly house of furniture, and with so much money invested, she was looked upon by many as a very desirable prize.

She had offers of marriage, and among those who sought her hand, was a gentleman named Burdock, a clothier, from America, lodging in her house.

He proposed to her that by a marriage they could go over to America and set up a large establishment there, where they would both be sure to do well.

She seemed to like the idea—she consented to the arrangement, and they were duly married.

STRANGE RUMOURS.

While, however, they were making arrangements, a sudden difficulty sprang up, which seemed likely to throw an impediment in the way.

Soon after the marriage was completed, and Mrs. Wade had become Mrs. Burdock, her husband, Mr. Burdock, was greatly surprised by people calling at the house to see if Mrs. Burdock could give them any information of an old lady, named Mrs. Smith, who formerly lived in the house.

Mr. Burdock at first could not understand what all these inquiries were about, but his wife generally answered the people by replying "Yes," that she had had an old lady, named Mrs. Smith, who formerly lived with her, but who died in her house so poor that she had to defray nearly the whole cost of her funeral.

The friends were not satisfied with these explanations, and as time went on some strange rumours began to get about.

At last a nephew came over from Wales, who, having heard of her death, began to make inquiries about her property.

Mrs. Burdock still maintained that if the old lady had property she did not bring it to her house, and therefore she did not know anything about it.

As Mrs Burdock was apparently so sincere in her protestations, some then thought that perhaps her servant, Mary Evans, knew something about her property, and Mary Evans was at one time questioned strongly upon the matter.

Eventually, in 1835, nearly fifteen months after the death of the deceased, the relatives became so concerned and so importunate that at last they petitioned the Government for a full inquiry into the matter.

After considerable trouble and delay, at length an order for an inquest was granted, and the body was exhumed from the grave.

THE EXHUMATION.

Great excitement was caused when it became known that an order for the exhumation had been obtained, and large crowds assembled outside St. Augustine's churchyard, where the body was buried, when it became known.

When it was opened it was found that in consequence of the grave being deep the coffin was nearly full of water with which the body was partly covered.

The coffin was then opened in the presence of Drs. Riley, Symonds, and Dick; and Messrs. N. Smith, E. E. Day, J. J. Evans, surgeons, and Mr. Herapath, the analytical chemist.

Though the body had so long been buried in a wet grave the medical gentlemen did not despair of being able to make a satisfactory analysis.

THE INQUEST

Was then opened before the coroner at the "Ship Inn" on the Butts.

Mr. Payne, solicitor, attended to watch the proceedings on the part of Mrs. Burdock, the former landlady of the deceased.

Several of the surgeons having given evidence as to the state in which they found the body,

Mr. W. Herapath, lecturer on chemistry and chemical toxicology at the Bristol medical school, was next called.

He said he had made a very careful and complete examination, and found that the body was partly converted into adipocire, which he attributed to some antiseptic substance.

He first took the stomach and spread it flat on a board. He then slit it open and found a large quantity of yellow powder.

He took a small portion and put it on blotting paper to absorb the moisture. He then dried it on a hot plate.

He ground some of it up with carbonate of soda and some charcoal. He introduced it into a reducing tube, and then found a volatile metallic body, which he knew to be metallic arsenic.

He then oxidised it, and it sublimed into a white crust, which was arsenious acid.

He then made a solution of it, and put a small portion of ammoniacal nitrate of silver, and there was the yellow precipitate of arsenite of silver.

He put into another drop a minute portion of ammonia sulphate of copper, and immediately found the green precipitate of Scheele, or arsenite of copper. He next reduced a larger quantity, and passed through it a stream of sulphuretted hydrogen gas, and reproduced the original orpiment.

He repeated the experiment five or six times, and invariably found the same results.

No other substance would produce the same results. He was perfectly satisfied it was arsenic.

He next washed the stomach in water, and allowed the substance to precipitate, and then dried it and weighed it, and found it to contain seventeen grains.

He destroyed the animal matter, dissolved the arsenic, and turned the sulphur into sulphuric acid, and precipitated the whole by sulphuretted hydrogen, that reproduced sulphuret of arsenic.

There were still more portions adherent to the stomach, which he could not wash off.

All the medical gentlemen gave it as their positive conviction that without doubt the deceased had been poisoned by arsenic.

The difficulty of the case now lay in being able to prove by whose hand the poison had been administered.

Mary Evans, the servant, was called, and after being duly cautioned that she need not answer any question likely to criminate herself, was then sworn, and said that she had lived as a servant with Mrs. Burdock twelve years before she was married to Mr. Burdock.

She used at one time to go by the name of Mrs. Wade, but Mr. Wade died in 1834. He used to live with her mistress.

She recollected the old lady, Mrs. Smith, coming to lodge at her house. She lived there about a month before she died.

Before Mrs. Smith's death she had taken things to pledge for her mistress.

Mrs. Smith had a large and a small trunk with her when she came, and also a carpet bag, all of which were very heavy. The deceased lady also had a watch. There were not any rats in the house, and never heard her mistress say that there were.

She remembered the old lady getting ill one day, and her mistress, Mrs. Wade, went and got a young girl, named Mary Allen, to come and wait upon her. The day before Mrs. Smith died her mistress told her that the old lady was worse.

While Mary Allen went home to her tea, her mistress told her that Mrs. Smith wanted some whey, which she told her to get, and to turn it with a little vinegar. Witness made it, and her mistress took it upstairs.

She took her some tea, some whey twice, and then some milk twice. Mary Ann Allen was upstairs when she took her the first milk.

I went to bed, leaving some of the milk in the saucepan. Mrs. Burdock gave me directions to make up the fire—Mary Ann Allen was present.

Mr. Wade was very unwell, and I made him some gruel. I left half a packet of groats in the kitchen—I put some water in the kettle before I went to bed.

I was called up in the night by Mrs. Burdock telling me Mrs. Smith was dead.

I said, "That can't be," and Mary Ann Allen said she was, and begged me to get up.

Mrs. Burdock told me to get some water and lay her out. After I had laid out the body, Mrs. Burdock gave me the things to put on it. She took them from a chest of drawers.

Mrs. Burdock then opened the cupboard and took out different things. She took out several bits of sugar and said, "How covetous she must be to save up such bits as those!" and that the sugar must have been taken from her.

She then said "What a drunkard the old woman must have been to have so many bottles," and she called her an old devil.

She then laughed, and said with a smile, "Ah, Mrs. Smith was very poor."

By the court: There was a slop bucket kept by Mrs. Burdock's door, and it was Mary Ann Allen's duty to take the slops from Mrs. Smith's room. There was a basin, and soap and water in Mrs. Smith's room on the day of her death. She occasionally used a nail brush. I have said that Mrs. Smith came to her death unfairly, but that I had no hand in it, but I did not understand the question; I cannot believe she died unfairly.

Mary Anne Allen, a very respectable girl, having been sworn, said she was nearly sixteen and lived with her mother in Horse-street.

Mrs. Burdock came to their house in October, 1833, and engaged her to wait upon an old lady, who, she said, was ill at her house.

After she had engaged her Mrs. Burdock told her she was to be sure and not touch anything that the old woman ate or drank out of, for she was a very dirty old woman.

Her mother then said to Mrs. Burdock that she hoped there was nothing that was catching, and Mrs. Burdock replied, "Oh, no, but the old woman had got a sore mouth." Witness was to have three shillings a week and go home to her meals.

When she left her home to go with Mrs. Burdock to her house, Mrs. Burdock crossed the bridge, and went into a druggist's shop, while she waited outside.

She then accompanied her to her house.

It was about six in the evening, and on arriving they went up to Mrs. Smith's bedroom, and found her ill in bed.

Mrs. Burdock told her that, if Mrs. Smith asked her where she came from, she was to say that she came from Trenchard-street, or Sheep-street, and not from Horse-street, because Mrs. Smith did not like to take any one from Horse-street.

When she got there Mrs. Smith asked her what her name was, and she told her.

When she went down at night for a candle Mrs. Burdock asked her what Mrs. Smith had been saying to her, and she replied, "Nothing particular."

She then again cautioned her not to take anything after the old woman, for she was a dirty old woman, and spat in everything, and she added, "Now mind, my dear child, what I say to you."

Mrs. Burdock's servant came upstairs to assist her to make Mrs. Smith's bed, and Mrs. Smith got out of bed herself.

She did not appear very weak. She did not complain of illness. Witness slept at night at the foot of Mrs. Smith's bed.

Mrs. Smith was very quiet at night, except asking once for water. Witness got up next morning, and asked Mrs. Smith how she was, and she said "better," and she hoped to be down by Sunday, for it was only a bit of a cold she had.

Mrs. Burdock came upstairs, and asked her how she got on, and witness replied, "very well," and then she went home to her breakfast.

When she came back Mrs. Burdock again repeated her caution to her not to touch anything the old woman had to eat, and she also told her that if Mrs. Smith asked her whether she knew of any other lodgings, that she was to say, "No; I do not."

After some further evidence the jury then returned a verdict, "That the deceased, Clara Ann Smith, died from the effects of arsenic administered to her by the hand of Mary Ann Burdock," and she was therefore committed to take her trial for wilful murder.

THE TRIAL.

The prisoner was brought to trial at the ensuing Bristol Assizes, before the Recorder, Sir C. Wetherell.

The case excited great interest throughout the country, and a vast concourse of persons assembled at the Guildhall to hear the trial.

The prisoner stood at the bar with great firmness, and the indictment having been read, she pleaded, in a clear tone of voice, not guilty.

She was accommodated with a chair, and throughout the proceedings was perfectly composed.

Her general appearance seemed to make a favourable impression. Her figure was good — she was inclining to be portly.

Her countenance was handsome, of a florid complexion, with a clear skin, dark hair, large dark eyes, and aquiline nose, and she was altogether of a very pleasing appearance.

Mr. Smith, Mr. Rogers, and Mr. Cooke conducted the prosecution. Mr. Payne and Mr. Stone appeared for the prisoner.

Mr. Smith opened the case by stating the circumstances to the jury.

In the course of his observations he said that the deceased lady was formerly a Miss Lumley, but was subsequently married to Mr. Smith, who carried on business in the old market.

She became a widow about five years before her death, and from the time of the death of her husband she resided at different places in lodgings, until at length she died about the 26th of October, 1833, at the house of the prisoner.

She died and was buried, no pains having been taken to inform her relatives, who remained ignorant of the circumstances for nearly fourteen months.

At the expiration of that time, a nephew of the deceased happening accidentally to hear of her death, he was induced to make some inquiries about her property, the result of which was the present investigation.

The evidence given at the coroner's inquest was then given at the trial, together with other very important information which one of the witnesses through fear had kept back.

Mary Allen, the mother of the young girl engaged by the prisoner to wait upon the deceased, said she recollected Mrs. Burdock coming to her house and engaging her daughter in October, 1833, to wait upon Mrs. Smith.

She stated that Mrs. Smith was a very dirty old woman, and that her daughter must not, on any account, touch anything after her, as she was in the habit of spitting in everything. She said the old woman was a foreigner and came from the East Indies.

Witness's daughter had been at home with her for some time. She was not sixteen yet; she had been religiously educated, regularly attended divine service, and was altogether of a religious, steady, conscientious turn of mind.

Mary Ann Allen called, said that she did not say all she knew before the coroner.

She then omitted the strongest parts of her evidence against the prisoner, because she was afraid to give it. She was afraid, that if she stated all, she would be the cause of the prisoner's death.

She had only lately mentioned other facts, because she had thought that, if she did not state them, she would be guilty of telling an untruth.

The part she had kept back was that she had seen the prisoner put a yellow powder into the deceased's gruel. The gruel was given to the deceased by the prisoner on the second evening that she went into her service.

She had not observed any alteration in Mrs. Smith's appearance in the early part of the day, but after she came back from tea that evening Mrs. Smith said she was poorly.

Mrs. Burdock came upstairs after tea and asked Mrs. Smith how she was, and Mrs. Smith replied, "Very poorly."

Mrs. Burdock then asked her if she would take anything, and she replied, "No."

Mrs. Burdock said, "Have some gruel." Mrs. Smith said, "No, my mouth is so sore."

Mrs. Burdock then said, "Do take it, there's a good soul; I will go and make you a nice drop of gruel," and Mrs. Burdock then left the room and went downstairs.

In about a quarter of an hour Mrs. Burdock came upstairs again and walked into her own bedroom.

From where she was witness could see the door. Mrs. Burdock had a candlestick in her hand with a dessert spoon in the candlestick, and in the other hand a blue half-pint basin with gruel, and a blue paper in the same hand, done up as a powder.

Witness did not notice whether it was tied. She followed Mrs. Burdock into the room, and Mrs. Burdock asked her what she wanted, and witness replied, "Nothing."

Mrs. Burdock then placed the basin, candlestick, powder, and spoon, on the chest of drawers. She opened the paper, and pinched up a small bit of powder out of it, and put it into the gruel.

There was a white paper inside the blue paper. The powder was yellow. Witness asked her what it was, and Mrs. Burdock replied, "Oh, it is nothing—it is only something to ease her, she is so griped."

Mrs. Burdock put two pinches of powder into the gruel in witness's presence. She then went to the wash-hand basin and washed her hands, and threw the water into the slop pail outside the door.

Mrs. Burdock then washed her hands a second time, and scrubbed the nails of one of her hands with a nail brush. She wiped her hands, and then stirred the gruel with a spoon.

Witness said to her, "What a curious way to give a powder! Would it not be better to mix it up with a drop of water in a tea-cup?" Mrs. Burdock then said, "Mrs. Smith would not take it, for she would think we were going to kill her."

She told me to go into the bedroom, as Mrs. Smith would be wanting me. The gruel was of a red colour before she put the powder in.

Mrs. Burdock then said to me, "Don't tell Mrs. Smith that I am in the bedroom, but say that I shall be up directly, and don't tell her that you saw me put anything in the gruel, she is so deep."

I then went into Mrs. Smith's room, and Mrs Burdock followed me in about five minutes with the gruel and took it to the bedside, and gave it to Mrs. Smith, who drank about half of it.

Mrs. Burdock immediately took the basin and went out of the room with it. Mrs. Smith then lay down, and in about half an hour she became very ill indeed.

She rolled about the bed in great agony and pain. She said she was poorly in five minutes after she had taken the gruel.

Mrs. Burdock came up again and went to her bedside, and asked how she felt, and Mrs. Smith then said, "Go along and leave me alone."

THE LIFE OF WILLIAM CALCRAFT, THE HANGMAN.

THE MURDER OF LORD WILLIAM RUSSELL.

Mrs. Burdock then turned to me and laughed. Mrs. Smith rolled on the bed and moaned, but did not say anything.

I then said to Mrs. Burdock, "Had you not better fetch a doctor?"

Mrs. Burdock then pretended to ask Mrs. Smith whether she would have one.

She then said to me in a whisper, Mrs. Smith says, "What! have a doctor to kill me? No."

These words were uttered in a whisper.

Mrs. Burdock never asked Mrs. Smith in my presence to have a doctor.

Mrs. Burdock then sat down, and Mrs. Smith during that time was very ill, moaning and rolling about the bed.

Mrs. Burdock and I sat some time, but did not say anything.

Mrs. Burdock then opened the table drawer, and took out some bits of candle and rushlight, and said, Only think of the old woman having these things."

Mrs. Smith, as she was rolling about in agony, raised her head up, and struck it against the head board.

After this she was quiet, and I did not hear her moan or move afterwards. This was about two hours from the time she had taken the gruel.

Mrs. Burdock took no notice of the sound of her head knocking against the bed.

In about half an hour Mrs. Burdock looked at her and said, "She is asleep, and I hope she is going to be quiet for a time."

CHAPTER XLII.
THE STILLNESS OF DEATH.

It would perhaps be impossible to have a more graphic description of a deliberate, relentless murder than this young girl gave.

It is not often that there are records of such direct testimony by an actual eye witness.

Convictions for murder are generally brought about by a chain of unbroken details, forming in the end a chain of circumstantial evidence so strong that it can neither be broken nor gainsaid.

The gaps of the fearful details have to be supplied by the imagination.

But here we get, what is not often given in evidence, all the horrid details of the murder.

On the bed a poor lonely woman, aged, lay dead.

A young girl, not sixteen, who had been religiously brought up, ignorant of the nature of the deadly ingredient given to the "poor old soul," in her youthful innocence thought the poison was a soothing powder.

She had, as she thought, been engaged to attend upon the poor old lady, and to tenderly nurse her till she got better.

When she saw the now helpless sufferer she wanted a doctor to be fetched.

Who can fully estimate the anxiety and sympathy of that young girl's heart, when she saw the tortured body rolling and heaving, and moaning in the throes of death, racked in fearful agony?

She would have flown for a doctor if she could. But there, by the bed-side, sat the mistress of the house. She a kindly-looking and a handsome woman.

She had appeared to have been doing all she could for the lonely old lady in her lodgings. She was gifted with a fair exterior, and, assuming the mask of the hypocrite, she pretended to be anxious for the little ailment of a cold the old lady was suffering from. She said she would make her some gruel.

In her own room in secret she put into it the deadly poison. With an assumed air of kindness and sympathy she brought it to the old lady. She said, "It is so nice. Do take it—there's a good soul," and the old woman, beguiled with the charm of her soft and tender tone, unsuspectingly drank the deadly poisoned potion, whilst the fiend who administered it, the mercenary embodiment of covetousness, hypocrisy, and unrelenting cruelty, the demon in the fair shape of a woman, sat coolly down by her bedside to watch unmoved, and untouched by any remorse or sympathy, the death throes and agonies of her poisoned victim.

There is scarcely such another case on record; but the witness, Mary Allen, proceeded to give the court a further detail of what occurred.

She said: In a short time afterwards, when all was still, I went to the bedside and looked at her, and then I said to Mrs. Burdock I think she is asleep. We will let her sleep, as she has had no sleep to-day. I then believed she was asleep.

I shortly afterwards went again, and touched her on the cheek, and, feeling that her face was cold, I said to Mrs. Burdock, "La! she's dead."

Mrs. Burdock said, "Come and sit down. Don't make thyself a fool."

I went and sat down again, and Mrs. Burdock then said to me, "If thee do'st go there again she'll grab hold of thee."

In a short time afterwards I lifted her up, and I found she was dead.

I said, "Mrs. Burdock, she is dead. Why don't you come? Why do you sit there?"

Mrs. Burdock then came to the bedside, put up her hands, and said, "Lord, my God, she is dead! What shall I do to bury her?"

She only looked at her, but did not touch her.

CHAPTER XLIII.
THE SLANDER AND THE PLUNDER.

Scarcely was the breath out of the body when the designing fiend began the work of defaming the character of the dead, and of plundering everything she possessed.

The hour had now come when she might fearlessly ransack her boxes, and lay claim to the coveted treasure.

So Mary Ann Allen in her evidence next proceeded to state to the court how deliberately Mrs. Burdock went to work.

She said the first thing she did was to go to a corner of the room where there were two or three parasols.

She then took them up and said, "Those are mine," and went out of the room.

Proceeding, the witness said: I went with her down to Mary Evans's room, and told her that Mrs. Smith was dead.

Mrs. Burdock then gave her orders to go and lay the old woman out.

Mary Evans dressed herself and went upstairs.

Mary Evans then got warm water, and they both then laid her out.

While they were doing this, Mrs. Burdock got Mrs. Smith's keys, and opened a sort of cupboard in the wall, and looked at the things.

She saw some bits of sugar, and said, "Only think of the drunken old thing having this. I used to blame my poor boy of taking this."

Mrs. Burdock then ordered me to take the earrings out of the deceaseds' ears, and I did so, and gave them to her, and she said, "Those would help to bury her."

Mary Evans and I afterwards went into Mrs. Burdock's parlour, and took tea.

The night Mrs. Smith died Mr. Wade came into the

room and looked at her. When it was daylight I told Mrs. Burdock I was going home.

She told me to ask my mother what I was to have for my short attendance.

I called in the day and told her three shillings. She said that was a good deal out of her pocket, she having to bury her; she then paid me.

She told me never to tell anything of Mrs. Smith, who she was, or what she was, nor that I had ever lived with her, and if anyone asked, that I was to say that she was a stranger, and a foreigner from far away in the East Indies, and she said, "Don't you ever tell anyone that you saw me put anything into the gruel, for people might think it was curious."

I then left her. I was examined before the coroner, but I did not then state that I had seen her put anything into the gruel. The question was not asked me.

When I had heard that arsenic was a yellow powder, and that I had seen it put into the gruel, I was afraid to tell of it. I did not know it was arsenic, for I had never seen arsenic before. I was afraid if I told of it I should be the cause of Mrs. Burdock's death.

I afterwards felt unhappy in my mind that I had not told of it, as I was afraid I should tell an untruth if I did not tell.

The witness was so completely overcome with exhaustion, after having been cross-examined for a long time, that she had to be taken out of court, but nothing was elicited in any way to shake her evidence.

After she was recalled, she said that the deceased moaned a little quietly before she took the gruel, which she saw her have.

She had not told the coroner's jury that she rolled and moaned before she had it; she did not roll before she had it.

Several solicitors and other witnesses were next called, who proved that the deceased lady was a person of considerable wealth, and that shortly before her death she was in possession of at least £1000 in cash.

Mr. Paul, a banker's clerk, next proved that about three months after the death of the deceased—namely, on the 30th of January, 1834, £400 was paid into the bank, at which he was engaged, in the maiden name of the prisoner—namely, Mary Williams.

Mr. Norman, another clerk in the same bank, proved that another £100 was paid in on the 20th of May, 1834, in the names of Messrs. Collins and Blathyn, as trustees for the prisoner.

Several other witnesses, former landladies and other persons, who had recently known the deceased, were called, all of whom swore that she was a person of particularly clean and tidy habits, and that in addition to large sums of money she always had by her, she had valuable gold watches, and costly jewellery.

Another witness was called, who stated that she called upon the prisoner, and told her that she had heard the deceased lady had died in her house, and she wished to know what had become of her property, to which the prisoner replied that the deceased had died very poor, and had left nothing. She had had to bury her at her own expense, and she should give no further information to her friends unless they first refunded her the £15 it had cost to bury her.

Elizabeth Hayman stated that later on the prisoner had told her that the deceased was a rich old lady, and that she had left her property to Wade.

Mr. Thomas Blathyn, a solicitor, stated that he was a witness to Wade's will. Wade died in April, 1834. The prisoner applied to him for advice as to proving the will, and also in reference to her money becoming settled upon her before she married Mr. Burdock.

It was also shown that Wade was in debt before he lived with the prisoner.

Edward Evans, a seaman, sworn, deposed that at the time of the deceased's death he was also a lodger in the prisoner's house at the time she went by the name of Mrs. Wade. The prisoner asked him about six days before the deceased's death to purchase two pennyworth of arsenic for her, as there were rats under her husband's bed. She gave him the twopence, and he went and had a can of Burton with it. When he went home at night the prisoner asked him if he had bought the arsenic, and he said he had not. He then went and borrowed twopence off Mr. Bussell, and as the druggist wanted a witness he took him as a witness as well as a man named John Johnson.

Mr. Hobbs, a druggist, said he recollected the man Evans coming for two pennyworth of arsenic. He would not sell it to him alone, and then he brought Bussell and Johnson.

The two witnesses, Bussell and Johnson, were called and corroborated the evidence.

Charlotte Thomas deposed that she lived with Mrs. Smith as servant for nine days. Mrs. Smith was ill in bed. Witness left because she herself was taken ill. Mrs. Burdock used to appear kind to Mrs. Smith, and used to ask her whether she would have anything.

Cross-examined: Mrs. Burdock used to send her every night for half a pint of brandy for the deceased. The deceased used to spit blood, and Mrs. Burdock used to ask her whether she should get a doctor for her. Mrs. Smith used to reply that she did not want a doctor to murder her. A week after she had left Mrs. Smith's service she called on the Sunday night to see how she was. Mrs. Burdock answered her, and told her that Mrs. Smith had left, and she supposed she had gone to Bath. Witness did not know she was dead till the day of the inquest, but deceased must have been lying dead in the house when she called.

Police-constable Thomas Griffith deposed that when the inquiry commenced he called at Mrs. Burdock's house, and asked for Mary Evans, as he had to take her to the Council-house. Prisoner said to Mary Evans, "Mind, Mary, you know nothing about it." She followed Mary Evans to the door, and repeated the caution more than six times.

Police-constable F. N. Watkins said he called with the solicitor and administratrix of the deceased to ask for the property to be given up, and the prisoner said deceased had no property. The deceased did not die worth 30s. She said there was a bill of £28 due from the deceased to her. She also said she had paid £1 to a medical man for examining the body. Witness then said, "You have paid a medical man £1 for examining the body?" Prisoner then said, "Well, I shall have to pay it. I have not paid it yet."

The Recorder then proceeded to sum up the case, and in the course of a long review of the evidence he said, that if the jury came to the conclusion that the deceased died by the administration of arsenic, the next question was by whom was that administered.

Unless they thought that Evans, the seaman who purchased it, administered it, there were but three other persons who had access to her. In reference to Evans, the seaman who purchased the poison six days before, there was nothing to show he was in the house that night.

Then there was Mary Evans, the servant. It was shown that she was in bed. There was no proof that Wade was upstairs before her death, or that he had anything to do with the deceased's food, so far as they had seen.

Well, then, did the girl Mary Ann Allen administer it? They had heard that she had been sworn to tell the truth, and the whole truth, before the coroner, and she had since admitted that she did not.

But she now had stated that she was afraid, since the powder she saw used was poison, that her evidence might be the means of bringing Mrs. Burdock to death. Then she said that feeling unhappy in her mind at not having told the truth she had determined to say what she knew.

She had been cross-examined upon every point, and though she had given what took place with such minuteness, her evidence had not been shaken in the least. It had been corroborated in many ways, and, therefore, he saw no reason to disbelieve her last statement, or the explanation she had given for not telling it all before the coroner.

The learned judge minutely dwelt upon the other parts of the evidence, and then left the case in the hands of the jury.

The jury retired for rather more than a quarter of an hour, and then returned into court with a verdict of guilty.

The prisoner then stood up, and, addressing the judge said: My lord, I am innocent—I am innocent. Standing at this bar I call upon the Almighty to put his judgment upon me if what I am now saying is not true. I know nothing of it, I am innocent—and the Almighty, I hope, will put his judgment upon me if what I am now saying is not true. I know nothing of it—I am innocent, and the Almighty, I hope, will put his judgment upon me at this moment if I am not innocent.

The Recorder then assuming the black cap, said: You, Mary Burdock, stand at that bar convicted of murdering, by poison, a lady, an inmate and a sojourner in your house. After a patient and laborious investigation, which has lasted three whole days, no man of any sound sense who has heard the evidence can come to any other conclusion than that you are rightly convicted of the crime laid to your charge. You have had a fair, a full, and a righteous trial, and it now only devolves upon me to pass upon you the sentence of the law. He then sentenced her to death in the usual form, and she was then removed to

THE CONDEMNED CELL.

The conduct of prisoners in the condemned cell has been very varied, but in many instances the inherent passions and tendencies of the criminal's mind have been strongly displayed.

When this culprit was conveyed to her cell she gave way to violent passion, and after rating in strong terms her solicitor and counsel, the witnesses, the jury, and the court, she declared that she had not had a fair trial; and that through the manner in which the case had been mismanaged she was nothing less than a murdered woman.

She then flung herself violently down on her pallet, and said to her attendant:

"Well, what's best to be done now?" as though she was strongly under the impression that something could still be done to save her life.

Shortly afterwards she was visited by the chaplain, who tried to induce her to prepare for her final end.

To these entreaties, however, she only replied that she did not want any advice of that kind.

What she wanted was something to be done to save her life. When some of her friends came to see her they too tried to prevail upon her to look the fact calmly in the face, that she had to die, for the public feeling was against her, and it was evident that there would be no attempt to obtain a reprieve.

To them she replied that if they could not talk to her in her trouble about something better than preparing for death, and thus making her feel more low-spirited still, that they had better keep away.

Towards the evening of the next day, when her brother visited her, she said to the attendant:

"Well, if I am to die I had better get ready. Who makes the coffins? Because I would like to see that mine is big enough. I would like to have mine brought into the cell on the over night."

When the matron informed her who made the gaol coffins she turned to her brother and said: "Well, Jim, see that I have a good plain coffin made, and let it be well lined with flannel, and mind I have a good warm shroud. But mind, Jim, don't you give more than two pounds for the coffin, and see that it's a full size, and broad in the shoulders, and don't have it screwed down too tight. And now let's get to the other business. Mind, Jim, you get the lawyer's bill taxed. Don't let them have all the money. About the £500 in the bank, her relations can't claim it; that's all stuff."

Her solicitor informed her that he thought they would.

"Oh, no, they can't," said she. "What would there be left for my children when all the bills are paid?"

She then insisted on making a will, leaving all her property to be divided between her two children, a boy fifteen years of age and a girl between eight and nine.

It appears that she grounded this right to make a will on the fact that it was left to her by Wade, who it was believed in his lifetime was accessory to the murder.

The chaplain then again visited her, and also some religious ladies, who tried to make an impression upon her mind, but it appeared of little avail, for the hardness of her heart and the general callousness of her demeanour were the subject of general observation.

THE MORNING OF EXECUTION.

When the morning of execution, the 15th of April, 1835, came, there was a special service held in the chapel of the gaol, at which all the prisoners were present.

The condemned woman sat in the centre, immediately below the pulpit, but she appeared to take no part in the service, for she neither rose when the Psalms were repeated nor knelt during the prayers.

Her conduct was different even from the worst of the other prisoners, for they did evince some decorum and interest in the solemnity of the service.

The service was conducted by the Rev. Mr. Jennings, who chose for reading the 39th and 90th Psalms. In going through the Commandments he laid particular stress upon the one, "Thou shalt do no murder."

He took for his text the 31st verse of the 35th chapter of Numbers:—"Moreover ye shall take no satisfaction for the life of a murderer, which is guilty of death, for he shall surely be put to death."

He then depicted the terrible sin of murder as the greatest crime against both God and man, and showed that God by his laws had required that the murderer should, for the crime of murder, pay the penalty with his own life.

Passing on he proceeded next to dwell upon the terrible sin of lying, and he publicly urged the culprit not to go to her death with a lie on her lips.

He dwelt also upon the sin of "covetousness, and the love of money as being the root of all evil," and concluded with an earnest exhortation to the prisoner to become fully penitent before it was too late, and with an earnest wish that the prayers of all present might go up to Heaven for mercy on her behalf.

The service, which began at ten, was over by half-past eleven, and the culprit then proceeded back to her cell, where shortly afterwards she was brought out to the pinioning-room and introduced to Calcraft.

At the sight of the hangman and the warders who were to assist him, she became much unnerved.

The stolid firmness with which she had stood everything before, unnerved, now seemed to leave her.

The colour went from her cheeks, and her face assumed a pallid, ghastly, waxy hue.

As she stood up, Calcraft first pinioned her arms with straps, which met and buckled behind.

Then he tied her hands with some good thin but strong cord.

After that he put the rope round her neck, and the white cap on her head, and all being now ready the chaplain commenced reading the burial service, and the procession proceeded to the scaffold erected over the gaol.

As soon as the culprit appeared in sight she was received with groans and hisses from the indignant crowd.

As she cast her eyes round and surveyed for a moment the surging crush of the assemblage, which numbered over 50,000 persons, her courage and nerve seemed to fail her.

She hurriedly said to those around her, "Give my love to my husband—will you?"

Calcraft by this time had applied the other end of the rope to the fatal beam.

At the last she said, "Lord, have mercy upon me—Christ, have mercy upon me!" and immediately the drop fell, and she swung in the air, amidst the general execration of the crowd.

THE CONFESSION.

As she made no confession either to the governor of the gaol, the chaplain, or the matron, it was feared that she died without making any confession at all, for to them she persisted in her innocence even to the last moment.

She, however, did make a confession to one of the women warders attendant upon her.

The attendant made the following declaration:—

"On Tuesday morning, the day after trial, Mrs. Burdock appeared very low in spirits. There was another female in the room, named Margaret Hibbert, who assisted me in attending upon her.

"On Margaret leaving the room, Mrs. Burdock said she would tell me the secret if I would swear not to name it to any person till after her death.

"I said, 'Upon my soul I would not.' She was not satisfied with that promise, but made me swear and call upon God to witness.

"I did so, and Mrs. Burdock then told me that she gave Evans two penny pieces to buy the arsenic, but that he did not know what it was for; that she kept it in her pocket for five days, and then gave it to Wade, and he put a little of it in some milk on the following evening. He put it in with a mustard spoon.

"She (Mrs. Burdock) did not think he had put enough in, and the next night he put in some more in some thickened milk with the same spoon, and then broke the spoon and put it in the fire.

"She then took the milk upstairs into her own bedroom, set it down on a bureau bedstead, which looks like a chest of drawers, and then stirred it in the milk with a dessert spoon.

"Then she went to a trunk, took a clean pocket-handkerchief, and on turning round saw the girl Allen standing at the door.

"She asked her what she wanted, and wondered at her impudence in following her.

"She then took it and gave it to Mrs. Smith, who drank it.

"She said no more to me concerning the murder, but expressed great desire to know what the lawyers had done with the money they had had, and what the counsellors had been paid.

"She said she was very glad she was not tried for thieving the money, as then it would have been taken from them, and now the £500 would do for her children.

"The declaration of ANN BAYNTON, 17th April, 1835."

The deceased measured 5 feet 7 inches, and was a fine woman. The body was placed in a plain elm coffin, and buried within the precincts of the gaol.

The following is the inscription on a large stone which marks the place where this extraordinary criminal lay:—

Beneath this stone lie the remains of Mary Ann Burdock, who was executed in this gaol
April 15th, 1835,
in her thirty-eighth year,
FOR THE WILFUL MURDER (BY POISON) OF
CLARA ANN SMITH,
OF THIS CITY.

Before burial a cast was taken of her head for phrenological purposes. It was stated by phrenologists that the organs of firmness, secretiveness, and cunning were largely developed. The love of offspring was indistinct and small.

The organs of reverence, benevolence, and conscientiousness too were unusually small.

The culprit was also suspected of having committed one or more murders.

It appears that a youth, named Clarke, at one time lodged in her house, that he suddenly disappeared, and though every search was made for him no trace of him could be discovered.

His friends, after the trial of Mrs. Burdock, obtained leave to see if any of his clothes or property was left in the house.

They found the inside paper of his watch containing its number, but nothing more.

The case excited great interest throughout the country, and is one of the most remarkable cases on record.

CHAPTER XLIV.

THE MYSTERIOUS MURDER OF LORD WILLIAM RUSSELL.

AMONG the many murders of Calcraft's time no case excited greater sympathy among the aristocracy than that of the murder of Lord William Russell, uncle to the celebrated reformer, Lord John Russell, so widely known among all classes.

The atrocious crime was perpetrated about midnight on the 5th of May, 1840, after the unfortunate nobleman had retired to bed.

Early on the morning of the 6th the inhabitants of the metropolis were thrown into a state of the greatest alarm by a report that his residence at No. 14, Norfolk-street, Park-lane, was found ransacked, as though thieves had entered, and that on the housemaid calling up the valet, Lord William Russell was found with his throat cut, and dead in his bed.

His head was almost separated from his body, and so great had the flow of blood been that the bed and mattresses were saturated with his gore.

No sooner was the dreadful deed known than many of the nobility hastened to tender their sympathy with the various branches of the illustrious family, and also their assistance in anything that could be done to track the assassin, and duly bring him to justice.

It had happened that for years a number of mysterious murders had been perpetrated, and the *Times*, the *Observer*, and other newspapers were loud in their denunciations against what they considered the shortcomings of the police in elucidating those mysteries, and bringing murderers to justice.

The *Times* advocated the establishment of a *special detective* police force, and various other papers, whilst giving an account of the numerous terrible mysterious murders, in which the murderers had not been detected, pointed out that scarcely anyone could feel safe in their homes unless something could be done for the better detection of such fearful assassins.

The whole case was shrouded in mystery; and so great was the interest which his late Royal Highness Prince Albert and other members of the Royal family took in the case, that there were constant inquiries at the chief police-offices as to the progress of the case, and the possibility the police thought they had of detecting the murderer.

In fact the whole kingdom was thoroughly aroused and excited from one end to the other, and the cases of mysterious murder had been so numerous, in which the murderers escaped undetected, that there was a general public cry for more earnest attention on the part of the Government, and to the necessity of some course of action for the detection of such criminals.

The little value set upon human life was truly appalling. The records of mysterious murders seemed to prove that there were many persons in existence who thought no more of committing a murder than they would think of committing a petty robbery.

As they escaped entirely undetected, it was painful to reflect that they were actually mixing in society unsuspected and unknown, and ready at any time to kill and rob again when society and circumstances afforded them a chance.

In addition, however, to the danger from the evil tendencies of some, this danger was still further increased by the lax manner in which some of the trials and inquiries were made.

Some cases were brought to light entirely by the acuteness of the officers engaged, whilst others were still more darkened and shrouded in mystery by the bungling of the officers engaged. There were then, as now, all sorts of oversights and omissions.

Officers engaged then showed their utter incapacity for their office by not making the necessary inquiries at the proper time and places when the most important information was to be had.

The same want of perception is even seen now, and requires remedying.

There are, and always have been, good men in the force, but, on the other hand, there are lamentable failures from the bungling of others.

Whilst, however, some cases have either wholly or partly failed through the incapacity of the officers employed, some have failed through the hurried unsystematic manner in which coroners' inquests have been conducted.

From time immemorial the ancient court of the coroner has been instrumental in bringing many intricate cases to light, and murderers to justice.

When an inquest is properly held it is one of the most useful institutions we have for investigating and elucidating great mysteries.

Though there are some who carp at a coroner's functions and quibble over his duties, it cannot be denied that many years have established the principle that it is their prerogative and duty to inquire by what means a person dying from unknown causes came to his death.

Some assert that the law does not require it, and that it only requires to know the cause of death.

The interpretation put upon the words as carried out for centuries shows that it does require that a jury shall ascertain how, when, and where, and by what means a person comes to his death; the precedent for years shows also that coroners have deemed it their duty, if possible, in the case of murder to ascertain also by whom the death was caused.

There are, however, a variety of causes why coroners' inquests are loosely conducted, but among the chief there are two of constant occurrence. The one is, that in many cases the jurymen cannot really afford the time required in a long mysterious case, as they are unpaid; and the other principal cause is, that the coroner's officer is not sufficiently paid, even if he were sufficiently qualified to get up the necessary evidence.

Owing then to these repeated miscarriages of justice the press for upwards of one hundred years has been calling attention to the matter, and even so late as June 13th, 1880, the press is still raising its voice, and among others we find the edition of *Lloyd's Newspaper* of that date in a leading article on the subject of the Harley-street mystery asserting that—

"It is becoming a national disgrace that murder after murder committed in the populous centres of London should baffle the power of the police, and so encourage miscreants to the commission of crime.

"The undetected tragedies of modern London are a national scandal; and they constitute a fresh danger to life, since they are proofs of the ease with which life may be taken without risk to the assassin."

In reference, however, to the murder of Lord William Russell the inquest was held the same day, and, considering the importance of the case, it was, like many others of later times, very badly and unsatisfactorily conducted.

There was scarcely an important question asked, and scarcely any important facts elicited. We give the report in the main to show what a meagre inquiry it was.

THE INQUEST

Was held before Mr. Higgs, deputy coroner, at the "City of Norwich" public-house.

The Right Hon. George Dawson was foreman, and the room was filled with various representatives of the Treasury, police-officers under Sir Richard Mayne, and gentlemen anxious to assist in the inquiry.

Mr. Henry Elsewood, surgeon, of 91, Park-street, Grosvenor-square, said he was sent for at half-past seven in the morning, and he found the deceased gentleman with his throat cut from ear to ear, and the wound appeared to him to have been inflicted with a knife or some sharp instrument.

The wound was such that the deceased could not have inflicted it himself.

He had also been informed that, when found, he had a towel over his face, which the deceased could not have put there had the wound been self-inflicted.

Mr. John Nursey, a surgeon, who said he had been the medical adviser of the deceased for several years, also corroborated that view. The deceased, whom he had recently seen, was well in health, and was seventy-three years of age.

Sarah Mancell, housemaid to the deceased, stated

that when she got up in the morning she went into his lordship's drawing-room and there found his papers all lying about, his writing-desk broken open, various drawers broken open, and different silver articles lying thrown about. There were three servants in the house; the cook, the valet, and herself.

She immediately went upstairs to the cook, and asked her whether she had heard anything during the night, and the cook said she had not.

She told her that the silver was lying all about, and the cook said she had better go and call the valet, and she did so. When she went up to his room she found him dressed, excepting his coat.

She asked him what he had been doing to the silver downstairs, and he said he had not been doing anything with it.

He then came down with her to the pantry, and there they found all the drawers open.

The valet then said, "Some one has been robbing us. He was then going upstairs again, and she then said to him, "For God's sake go and see where his lordship is."

He went and opened the shutter, and she then went after him, and saw his lordship lying on the bed, dead.

She then ran upstairs and told the cook that his lordship was murdered.

They ran over the way to No. 23, rang the bell, and fetched the butler from there to assist them. He came, and they got a policeman directly.

John Stedman, inspector of police, examined, said he was called to Lord William Russell's house about half-past seven in the morning, and in the course of his evidence he continued:—

The first part of the house that I examined was the bottom part. When I went into the house I found the valet sitting in the room adjoining the kitchen. The two women servants were close by. I asked them what way it was likely that anyone could get into the house.

One of the women servants, whose name, I believe, is Arnold, showed me the door leading to the area at the back of the house.

I found this door as if some one had been trying to open it with some blunt instrument. There were some bruises and marks on the door and door-posts. It was difficult to say whether they were done inside or out.

I looked round the walls of the area, but could not see any marks of anyone having come in that way. I then requested the servants to accompany me upstairs, and to show me where the body lay.

We all went to the room, where I found the curtain about half drawn. One of the shutters of the window was broken.

I opened them, and then pulled a cloth from the face of the deceased.

I asked the valet to assist me a little, and he fell back in a chair, and said:

"This is a shocking job! I shall lose my place and character."

On examining the house I found almost every drawer in all the rooms partly open, and the papers disturbed.

I asked the man servant how he found the door, and he said he found the chain down, and the bolt drawn. He said he had fastened it. The key was inside. The latch kept the door to.

I have since searched the whole of the servants' rooms, and found in the valet's box this purse, containing a £5 note marked, and six sovereigns.

I asked the valet where he got the note from, and he said he gave five sovereigns to Lord William Russell for it some time ago.

I asked the valet if Lord William Russell used to keep much money about him, and he said he saw a £5 and a £10 note with him yesterday.

He said they should be in their usual place at the head of the bed in a little box.

He looked in the box and said, "No, it's gone, and his gold watch is gone also." I also saw in the bedroom a dressing-case, which had been broken open from behind.

The valet looked at it and said that some of the rings had gone. The valet has appeared very much concerned during the day, and has been drinking water every ten minutes.

My opinion is that the marks on the back door were done from the inside. Anyone wanting to force it could have done so with a good push.

I searched very carefully to see if we could find any instrument by which it was done, but we found nothing.

We had the water-closets taken up by direction of Mr. Commissioner Mayne, but found nothing.

Henry Beresford, inspector of police from No. 6 division, said—

I went over the house of the deceased with the last witness, and found the body as it has been described.

I took a list from the valet of the articles he said were gone.

The dressing-case upstairs was broken open, but nothing gone. The list of articles is: Two plain gold rings, one ring set with turquoise, one gold repeating watch with three gold seals, one of stone, with the Russell arms on.

Afterwards he told me that there were three pins, but he could not give any description of them, but that they were stones, and that one was a blue stone.

This was all that was missing at that time.

Then from his own pantry the articles used for dinner the night before were gone—five tablespoons, three dessert ditto, four silver forks, and two teaspoons.

I searched all the three servants' boxes, and found in the valet's box a middling-sized chisel.

I fitted it to the marks in his own pantry, and it had every appearance of fitting exactly.

A juror: Were not those drawers under his own care?
—They were.

A juror: Then what necessity for using a chisel to force them open?

Inspector Beresford: There might be various reasons why they would not be opened with the key in the ordinary way.

Although the drawers were open, the locks were still shot. I have examined the back door, where the marks of violence appeared, and I am quite certain that these marks of violence were not the means by which the door had been opened.

There were marks of a blunt instrument, but some of these were from the inside, evidently after the door had been opened.

The marks have been recently made. I infer that the marks were made after the door was opened, because some of the marks were pushed out from the inside; and where the marks are on the door-post, there are no corresponding marks on the door where it touches the post.

I cannot come to any other conclusion than that the marks were made when the door was open.

The socket of the top bolt was forced off. I examined the bolt, and some instrument seems to have been put in to force it off.

The instrument was black, for it left a mark on the

door. In my opinion the socket of the bolt was forced off when the door was open.

Mr. Pearce and myself searched for any instrument which might have made these marks, and we found the pantry poker actually bent, and recently broken.

In fitting the marks where the point of the poker was offered, it certainly fitted the marks on the door and the post.

Inspector Pearce, of the A Division, here produced the chisel and the poker, and stated that he had compared the chisel and the poker with the marks that had been made, and they seemed to correspond.

Francis Benjamin Courvoisier, the valet, was here introduced into the room.

He was a young man, apparently about twenty-five years of age, having very dark hair and eyes, brown complexion, regular handsome features, a black intelligent eye, but downcast, and exhibiting in his bearing neither the look nor the demeanour of a foreigner.

He did not evince in the jury-room any of that agitation which, by some of the police, had been previously noticed.

He appeared to feel that he was suspected, and concentrated all his energies to maintain a sufficient firmness of demeanour to dispel the suspicion.

He was evidently a man of great natural ability, and being a Swiss from one of the French cantons, spoke English remarkably well.

When asked to spell his name he dictated the manner of spelling it with great precision to the coroner's clerk.

He, in reply to the coroner, having been cautioned in the usual manner that he need not say anything to criminate himself, said—

Last night his lordship came home from his club, and gave me a letter to take to the post-office; that was at twenty minutes before six, or before dinner.

His lordship went out for a little while after that, and returned about half-past six to dress for dinner.

He sent me with a letter to the stable, to give to the groom for him to take it to the post-office.

His lordship dined at home, and stayed at home all the evening. The servants went to bed between ten and eleven. I fastened the door after the cook came in.

I did not unfasten the door afterwards or go out. The housemaid went to bed first, and the cook afterwards.

About ten minutes before twelve Lord William rang his bell to undress. I went upstairs to his bedroom, and helped to undress him as usual.

I saw nothing unusual in his manner—he was the same as usual.

I came downstairs again, waiting to hear him ring his bell to have his bed warmed.

He generally washed after he undressed, and then he had his bed warmed.

When Lord William rang the bell again it was about a quarter-past twelve.

Lord William used generally to have a rushlight all night in his room, and I got it ready.

He asked for his candlestick and a book, and I left him a lighted candle. Shortly afterwards I went to bed, and heard nothing during the night, until the housemaid came in the morning and knocked at my door.

I began to dress then, and about five minutes afterwards, when I was putting on my waistcoat, the housemaid knocked at the door again, and asked what was the matter with Lord William last night. I said, "Nothing more than usual."

She said everything was upset in the dining-room, and the plate was all about the room.

When I came down and saw the drawing-room in that state I went to the pantry, and found that the plate had gone from there.

I had a friend who visited me the day before at three o'clock. I cannot say exactly where he lives, but I believe it is somewhere in South-street.

His name is Henry Carr, and when I lived with Mr. Fector he was a coachman there. We lived very nearly two years together.

He came to see me about five o'clock, took tea with me, and left at about a quarter to six.

A juror: Where is he to be found?—I don't know where he lives exactly, but he is to be found to-night at the Royal Exchange, Adam's-mews.

Have you been into Lord William's room?—Yes, I went in this morning.

Did you see the body?—Yes, I did; it had a cloth over the head. His arm was crooked, and there was blood on each of his shoulders.

Is that all you know?—That is all I know.

Are you quite sure that after the cook came in you did not go out again?—Yes, quite sure.

Is there an area door?—Yes, it was bolted when I went to bed.

Are you quite certain you bolted the door?—Yes, I am quite certain I bolted the door. I am as certain as I can be.

Did the police officers search your box?—Yes, I believe the police officers searched all my boxes. They found a little chisel in one of my boxes, and my purse.

What had you the chisel for?—I have had it these two or three years.

The Coroner: It is my duty to caution you as to what you say, as it will be taken down. Not that I wish to say that suspicion attaches to you, but I wish to caution you. What have you to say to the chisel?—The chisel was given to me in Dover. I often used it, as I was fond of cutting things in wood—that is, of making different things with wood.

Who had charge of the pantry?—I had.

Did you go and fetch the cook some beer last night?—I did not; yes, I did—now I recollect. I did go and fetch a pint of beer.

Were the things last night all put in their places?—Yes.

When you went out for the beer did you go out by the front door?—Yes, I went out by the front door. After a pause, No, I went by the area door—now I recollect, because I told the cook that the front door was fastened, and that I should go by this door.

Where did you get the £5 note?—I gave the change for it to Lord William Russell more than a week ago.

Did you write anything on the back of it?—No, I did not.

Did he give you that for wages?—No, it was for change. His lordship did not keep much money in the house. He had a £10 note and a £5 note some days ago, but I have not seen them these three days. I do not think he kept much money in the house. I have lived with his lordship five weeks. The change I gave for the £5 note was four sovereigns, and the rest in shillings. The things that were lost were three gold pins, and his watch, five or six table spoons, four large silver forks, small silver spoons, and a salt spoon.

How long has Carr been out of a situation?—He has been out of a situation about ten or twelve months.

THE LIFE OF WILLIAM CALCRAFT, THE HANGMAN.

COURVOISIER MAKING HIS CONFESSION IN THE CONDEMNED CELL.

How long has he been out of a situation now since he left his last place?—About three months. Before that he had a place for three months.

Was this man in distressed circumstances?—No, sir; he did not want anything from me.

Why did he come to you?—He came for a gun.

Whose gun was it?—It was his own gun.

Juror: I suppose he wished to get some money on it? The valet made no answer.

The coroner then asked him if he had any objection to write the word "Canterbury?" The witness replied that he had not, and having asked how it was to be spelt, immediately wrote the name.

On comparing it with the same name written on the note found in his box there was plainly no similarity between them.

The coroner then stated that he had that day seen Mr. Fector, who gave Courvoisier a most excellent character, he having lived with him for three years.

The coroner then inquired whether it was the wish of the jury that the proceedings should be adjourned, or whether they had made up their minds to return a verdict at once.

Mr. Dawson, the foreman, said he did not see the least occasion for an adjournment. He, for one, was prepared to say that the deceased had been murdered, but as there was no evidence as to who the person or persons were, the verdict must be that he was murdered by some person or persons unknown. It would be keeping alive a vast deal of excitement in the public mind by adjourning from day to day, while it would deprive the family of the deceased of the satisfaction which a verdict would give them. If there was any doubt upon his mind that the deceased had not been murdered, he should have no objection to delay; but returning a verdict now would not frustrate the ends of justice, whereas adjourning would only be casting suspicion upon individuals, when the matter might be more properly left in the hands of the police for investigation. He hoped that the perpetrator of the horrid deed would be ultimately discovered, but he for one was now prepared to record a verdict.

The jury then returned a verdict of wilful murder against some person or persons unknown.

Some of the newspapers commented on the inquest being so soon closed, and the result being so unsatisfactory.

We cannot do better than give one leading article, which appeared at the time, from the *Examiner*, which said:—

No crime within our recollection has filled the public with such horror and alarm as the murder of Lord William Russell, and no crime within our recollection has been so ill-investigated. Indeed the word investigation is hardly applicable to the proceedings, in which investigation has been so astoundingly wanting.

From first to last the omission of a close and searching inquiry is lamentably remarkable.

To begin with the inquest, if its object had been to avoid the discovery of the assassin its proceedings would have been most skilfully conducted for that purpose.

Questions the most necessary were unasked, and no attempt was made to clear up discrepancies in the evidence; indeed, though glaring enough, they seemed to escape notice.

For example, the housemaid, Sarah Mancel, stated positively that there was no cloth over the face of the murdered nobleman when she saw the body, which was the first time that it was seen, she and the valet having entered the room together.

The valet stated that there was a cloth over the head.

Stedman, the inspector of police, stated the same, and that he removed it; he being the third person who saw the deceased.

The discrepancy between the housemaid's evidence and that of the other witnesses does not seem to have struck the jury, for no cross questions were put upon the point.

A discrepancy in the evidence on such a point is not immaterial, nor insignificant; it may not raise any presumption against the truth of any of the witnesses—it may be accounted for by the confusion of alarm, but it has its import in that case as indicative of the state of the mind and faculties of perception at the moment.

In these cases every fact has its value, and every circumstance on which a doubt hangs that can be cleared up should be cleared up.

Nothing can be said to be immaterial. If a fact appear to be intrinsically insignificant, the truth or untruth of it, as stated in evidence, is material.

The housemaid, Sarah Mancel, stated that, upon the discovery of the robbery, the valet, Courvoisier, at her suggestion, went into the room and opened the shutter, when she saw his lordship dead.

She was not asked whether they rapped at the door, nor why she followed Courvoisier into the room, and he in his examination was not asked any questions as to his manner of entering the room, or going straight to open the shutter instead of going, as might be more natural, to the bedside; the point to be ascertained being whether they acted as though they thought Lord William Russell living or dead.

The valet's examination was surprisingly meagre. He was not asked whether the area door was fastened after him when he went out the last time for beer, nor whether any one of the female servants, or who, followed him to the door to secure it, on that occasion, nor how he got in again.

When a question was asked about the purposes for which the valet had a chisel in his possession, the coroner (Mr. Higgs), interposed: 'It is my duty to caution you as to what you say, as it will be taken down—not that I mean to say that suspicion attaches to you, but I wish to caution you.'

Was this inquest? Was this inquiry? A witness, not a prisoner accused, was before the coroner, and the business of the court was to obtain from him the fullest disclosures, and not to close his lips by advice to consult his own safety in the statements he might make.

Another point omitted was the question whether any knife was missing; the knives having been disturbed.

The murderer must have had his hands deluged with blood, but there was no inquiry as to the state of the washing apparatus in the different parts of the house.

The housemaid might have given evidence as to the quantity of water she left in the ewers, and as to the towels, whether they were in their places, and what was their state, but no question relating to these points was asked.

The state of the candles, as found next morning, was a point for remark. The murderer must have had a light for the robbery downstairs, and he had extinguished Lord William's rushlight.

Carr, the valet's visitor, had a latch-key to let himself into his lodgings. His statement that he was at home at the time when the murder must have been committed could not be questioned, and he was not detained.

It might be quite right not to detain the man on suspicion, but the search of his lodgings was a step due both to his character and to public justice, and this was not done.

Omission characterises these proceedings throughout. There is nothing else to remark upon in them. Even the surgeon of the murdered nobleman so carelessly examined the body that he confidently declared there was no wound upon it except that in the throat, though, in fact, the ball of the thumb was nearly cut off.

The inadvertence is curious in connection with such a tissue of imperfect investigation.

It was not so that Mr. Greenwood examined the body of Greenacre's victim.

The only man who seemed to have his wits about him, and to exercise any acuteness of observation, was the inspector, Beresford, and his intelligence was an unknown tongue to the jury.

As to the chisel in the possession of the valet, he said—

I fitted it to the marks in his own pantry, and it had every appearance of fitting exactly—the chisel goes into the marks exactly.

By a juror: Were not those drawers under his care?—They were.

Then what necessity for using a chisel to force them open?—There might be various reasons why they would not be opened with the key in the ordinary way. Although the drawers were opened, the locks were still shot. I have examined the back door, where the marks of violence appeared, and I am quite certain that these marks of violence were not the means by which the door had been opened.

Beresford saw that studied and false appearance of housebreaking violence had been attempted in one place, and he thought that the same intention might account for the use of the chisel instead of the keys in the other instances.

It is not that a man's character or life is to be taken away upon such a coincidence as the correspondence between the marks of violence and the size of a chisel in his possession; but circumstances of this nature are neither to be made too much of nor slighted altogether, as the sapient person who interrupted Beresford would have slighted it.

The juror mistook the improbability. It was not improbable that the man who had the keys would have used a chisel instead of them, supposing him for the instant capable of the crime, but it was highly improbable that, having so used the chisel, he would have deposited it in his trunk, the search of which he must have anticipated.

Lastly, we ask why Lord Ashley's evidence, as to some suspicious circumstances, was not had?

Throughout the proceedings in this horrible case the search for clues has been wanting, and clues will never be found unless they are sought for with the minutest attention.

Many circumstances, slight and insignificant in themselves, must be investigated in order to get on the traces of crime.

Indeed, much that does not bear upon the crime must be inquired into to get at what does bear upon the crime.

Many crimes enveloped in the deepest mystery have been brought to light by investigations, proceeding on the principle of attaching importance to every fact and circumstance, including the most minute and apparently insignificant; but widely different from such inquiries has been the conduct of recent investigations.

It seems to us that the fear of raising suspicion against persons who may be innocent is carried to an extreme incompatible with the vigorous pursuit of the truth.

In defence of the conduct of the inquest we see it argued in the *Globe* that the business of inquests is confined to the question how the deceased was destroyed, whether by his own hand or that of another.

Does the *Globe* then mean to say that inquests in finding verdicts of wilful murder against individuals have exceeded their functions?

And further, how are verdicts of manslaughter, and justifiable homicide arrived at, but by as searching an investigation of all the circumstances as a criminal court could effect?

Moreover, in the cause of death, the agency is generally so involved that it is impossible, were it desirable, to separate the one from the other.

What other opportunity than that of a coroner's inquest is there for obtaining evidence and clues to guilt, in cases in which suspicion is not strong enough to justify a charge against any one, and an examination of him by the magistracy.

Coroners are not the functionaries they ought to be, but their juries, with occasional exceptions, bring to the investigation intellects sharpened by the intense interest they feel in the detection of a great crime.

With all the faults of coroners' inquests—and the faults lie for the most part with the president—as apathetic as the jurors are earnest (the business being the trade of the coroner and generally a new and exciting duty to the jurors), many murders would have been undiscovered but for the active and searching inquiries of coroners' inquests.

A better tribunal for preliminary investigation might perhaps be devised, but until that be done it would be imprudent to limit the inquiry of inquests to the question how, and not by whom, the deceased was destroyed; or in such cases it would be necessary to take the *Standard's* advice, and to furnish every bedchamber with arms for the defence of its occupant.

Such, then, was the opinion expressed forty years ago by the press in reference to the inquest upon the body of Lord William Russell.

We would ask our readers who are acquainted with the manner in which very important inquests are held by some of our present coroners, whether they have at all improved in the manner of holding such important inquiries.

We could, if space permitted, point to a long list of signal failures and miscarriages of justice through the want of that information which the various coroners through their juries might have obtained.

There are numerous cases on record of inquests hurried through in the most discreditable manner, where valuable information that was wanting, and might have been had, was actually excluded by the indecent haste which has marked some of the proceedings at coroners' inquiries.

To return, however, to the murder of Lord William Russell.

The man, Henry Carr, was for some time suspected, and he was under the surveillance of the police.

There was a difference in the minds of some of the officers. Some inclined to the opinion that it might be one of the female servants.

Others thought that it might possibly be the Swiss valet, Courvoisier, and that the marks on the door, as though a jemmy had been used, had been purposely done by him to give the appearance of the house having been broken into and the murder committed by burglars.

Some of the police even went so far as to openly say to him that those marks on the doorposts had been done for an express purpose of leading the police off the track, and that they had no doubt that the murder had really been committed by some one in the house.

Courvoisier was firm in his protestations of his innocence, and in the most positive and solemn manner he assured everyone that he knew nothing of the crime.

The officers, however, on searching the house, and taking up the wainscoting and some portion of the floor, discovered some of Lord William Russell's valuables hidden away, and then they were strengthened in their opinion that the robbery and murder had been perpetrated by one of the servants in the house, as no one outside could have so hidden them away.

Though there were slight circumstances which looked suspicious against some of the other servants, the more serious circumstances all pointed to Courvoisier, and he was ultimately arrested and taken to Bow-street, and there charged with the murder before Mr. Hall, the presiding magistrate.

A great deal of evidence was given against him, and eventually he was committed to take his trial at the Central Criminal Court.

CHAPTER XLV.
THE TRIAL OF COURVOISIER.

The trial commenced at the Old Bailey on the 18th of June, 1840, the judges being Lord Chief Justice Tindal and Baron Parke.

The counsel for the Crown were Mr. Adolphus, Mr. Bodkin, and Mr. Chambers; the prisoner was defended by Mr. Charles Phillips and Mr. Clarkson.

The prisoner pleaded "Not guilty," and preferred an English jury to a jury composed of half Englishmen and half foreigners.

The court was densely crowded, many of the nobility being present, there scarcely ever being a trial known in which the aristocracy seemed to take so much interest.

Mr. Adolphus, in opening the case, laid at great length the facts before the jury.

In the course of his observations he said they might be told for the defence that there was no motive which the prisoner could have had for the committal of such a crime.

No man could assign a motive for such a crime, but they had the fact before them that it was done.

But with respect to the prisoner, he must maintain that there was not such an absence of motive as some might think.

The prisoner was a foreigner, having no connection with this country, no wife, no relative to attach him to the soil.

He left the service of a very worthy individual to go to the service of the noble lord. In reference to payment, he had once said "I changed a sovereign, and have only got seventeen shillings in return."

On another occasion he had been heard to say, "I know old Billy has a great deal of money, and if I only had a third of it I need not be long here, but should return to my own country."

He may have fallen into the notion which many foreigners possess that English noblemen always carry large sums of money about with them in gold, and the *rouleaux* which he had seen might have led him to this conclusion.

His lordship kept the box containing these *rouleaux* himself; he always opened it himself, it was always kept in his possession. The ivory boxes had been kept sealed up, and it was natural to suppose they were full of money, and so, gentlemen, you may account for this crime.

We Englishmen are not apt to suppose that murder must always precede plunder.

Foreigners in many instances think the reverse, and that to put the person robbed out of the way of giving evidence is to secure their own safety.

The learned counsel then detailed how the property had been scattered about his lordship's rooms, and after assigning a probable motive for every act proceeded to call the witnesses.

There were numerous witnesses, and the evidence was very voluminous.

Every witness that came up for the prosecution was cross-examined with great ability by the counsel for the defence, and in some instances it seemed as though a doubt was thrown upon the value of their testimony.

The proceedings lasted several days, and, at the close of each day's proceedings there was intense excitement, many people and many of the counsel present even strongly maintaining that though circumstances were suspicious against the prisoner, yet that there was not legal evidence sufficient to convict him.

THE VALUE OF THE PRESS.

Mr. Phillips, the prisoner's counsel, expressed himself confident of being able to obtain the prisoner an acquittal.

He argued that with such little direct evidence against the prisoner no jury could possibly find him guilty.

While the excitement, however, was at its highest, and public opinion was vibrating between the two opinions, as to whether he would be convicted or acquitted, some further important evidence was brought to the court in the very midst of the trial, through the instrumentality of the press, and whilst even the counsel for the prisoner was ably supporting, by cross-examination of the witnesses, the possibility of the prisoner's innocence.

Some of the plate which had been stolen from Lord William Russell's house, it appears, was still missing, and, in spite of all the private inquiries of the police, it could not be traced.

One of the reporters, however, obtained a description of this plate, and one of the papers in publishing it in a small paragraph expressed an opinion that as the prisoner was a foreigner he would doubtless be acquainted with some of the foreign hotel-keepers in London, and further suggested that he had possibly deposited the missing plate with some of them for safety.

But it was further added that, as many of these hotel-keepers did not read the English newspapers, but read the French, a paragraph in one of the French newspapers might be of service.

One of the French newspapers accordingly copied this paragraph, and at the very time that this trial was going on at the Central Criminal Court, when the life of Courvoisier was vibrating in the balance, this paragraph was read by some French people who kept a house called "l'Hotel de Dieppe," in Leicester-place, Leicester-square, where Courvoisier had formerly been a waiter, and where he actually had taken the stolen plate, wrapped up in a parcel, sealed, and left it there with a request that they would keep it for him till he should call again for it.

As soon as the people in the house read that paragraph in the French paper, they then recollected that Courvoisier had left a parcel there. They then thought to open it, but up till that time they had not noticed that the property was missing, and, further, they had scarcely paid any attention to the murder.

When the parcel was opened it was found to contain the plate of Lord William Russell, with the coat of arms, and it was brought down in a cab to the Central Criminal Court and produced in evidence against him.

Mrs. Charlotte Piolane was then called, and said she was the wife of Louis Piolane, a Frenchman, who kept a house of entertainment called l'Hotel de Dieppe, in Leicester-place, Leicester-square.

She knew the prisoner at the bar. He was formerly a waiter in their hotel. A few Sundays ago he came to the hotel and asked her whether she would take care of a parcel for him.

She said, "Certainly I will." He then left it and went away, and she then put the parcel in the cupboard, and thought no more about it.

Her cousin, Joseph Vincent, read a paragraph in a French newspaper, which he showed her, and then she thought of the parcel left.

She sent for some persons as witnesses—they opened the parcel, and then found the property produced.

Courvoisier turned pale in the dock at this startling and unexpected evidence.

Those who had hitherto held the conviction that he must be acquitted, now altered their opinion, and the belief was now general that there was not the slightest hope for the prisoner.

The evidence, however, for the defence was proceeded with, and Mr. Phillips made a most able and eloquent appeal on the part of the prisoner.

In doing so, he said that after twenty years' experience in Criminal Courts he had seldom risen to address a jury under more painful or anxious feelings.

The horrid nature of the crime itself, the rank of the deceased, the numerous connections mourning their bereavement, all filled him with apprehension.

But when he turned to the dock and saw this isolated helpless foreigner, far from his native land, far from the friends that loved, and the associates that in the hour of danger would have crowded around him, he felt his spirits sink within him when he contemplated the public indignation which was manifested against the unhappy man before them.

He thought he had reason too to complain of the opening address of the counsel for the prosecution, for Mr. Adolphus was an historian, and history ought to have taught him that there was no nation so free from crime as Switzerland, of which country the prisoner was a native.

In reference to one observation said to have been made by the prisoner, that, "If I had the wealth of such an one, I would not be long away from my own country," why, ambition's visions, glory's baubles, wealth, reality, were all nothing as compared with his native land.

Not all the enchantments of creation, not all the splendour of scenery, not all that gratification of any kind could produce, could make the Swiss forget his native land.

> Dear is that shed to which his soul conforms,
> And dear that hill which lifts him to the storms,
> And as a child by jarring sounds oppressed
> Clings close and closer to its mother's breast,
> So the loud torrent, and the whirlwind's roar,
> But binds him to his native mountains more.

The learned gentleman then went on and contested every disputable point of evidence, contending that there was great doubt as to the guilt of the prisoner, and in conclusion he besought the jury to give the prisoner the benefit of that doubt, which he felt they must have.

The judge then summed up, and the jury afterwards retired to consider their verdict.

After a long absence, however, they returned into court with a verdict of guilty, and, amidst general satisfaction, the prisoner was sentenced to death in the usual form.

He was then removed from the court, and taken to the condemned cell.

When he arrived here he acknowledged the justness of his trial and sentence, and then, seeing that all hope was banished from him for ever, he made the following confession:—

COURVOISIER'S CONFESSION.

The following is a copy of the confession made by Courvoisier, and sent to the Home Office from Newgate on the same day:—

Newgate, June 22nd, 1840.

On the Friday before the murder was committed I began two or three times not to like my place.

I did not know what to do. I thought if I gave warning none of my friends would take notice of me again, and I thought by making it appear a kind of robbery he would discharge me; so on the Saturday before I took this plate to Leicester-place.

I had a mind to rob the house on Monday, and after I had forced the door downstairs I thought it was not right and went to bed; nothing further happened on the Monday.

On Tuesday night when his lordship went to bed (he had been rather cross with me before about the carriage) he gave me two letters, one for the post, and told me, rather angrily, that he was obliged to write those letters in consequence of my forgetting the carriage; this was in the drawing-room, about eleven o'clock at night.

I then went downstairs into the kitchen and stood reading a book for some time.

About twelve o'clock he rang the bell. I went up to him, and took the lamp out.

After that I thought he had gone upstairs to his bedroom, and when he rang his bedroom bell I thought it was to warm his bed, and I took the warming-pan up with coals in it just as usual, and he began to grumble because I did not go up to see what he wanted instead of taking the warming-pan.

I told him he always used to ring the bell for the warming-pan, and that I thought it was for that purpose that he had rung, and he said I always ought to go up and answer the bell first to see what he wanted.

He took off his clothes, and I came downstairs again with the warming-pan, and I waited there till about twenty minutes past twelve o'clock.

He rang again for me to warm his bed. He told me rather crossly that I should take more notice of what I was doing and what he was telling me, and pay him more attention.

I did not answer at all as I was very cross. I went downstairs and put everything in the state it was found in the morning.

As I was in the dining-room with a light he came downstairs to the water-closet; he had his wax-light.

I was in the dining-room, but as he had his slippers on I did not hear him come down.

He opened the dining-room door and saw me.

I could not escape his sight. He was quite struck, and said—

"What are you doing here? You have no good intentions in doing this. You must quit my service to-morrow morning, and I shall acquaint your friends with it."

I made him no answer. He went to the water-closet, and I went out of the dining-room downstairs.

He was about ten minutes in the water-closet, and I waited to see what he would do after he came out.

While he was in the water-closet I put some of the things to rights again in the dining-room.

When he left the water-closet he went straight into the dining-room, where he stayed about a minute or two.

I was on the corner of the stairs that go from the dining-room to the kitchen. I watched him up stairs. I stopped perhaps an hour in the kitchen, not knowing what I should do.

As I was coming upstairs from the kitchen I thought it was all up with me, my character was gone, and I thought it was the only way of covering my faults by murdering him.

This was the first moment of any idea of the sort entering my head.

I went into the dining-room and took a knife from the sideboard.

I don't remember whether it was a carving-knife or not. I then went upstairs.

I opened his bedroom-door, and heard him snoring in his sleep. There was a rushlight in his room burning at this time.

I went near the bed by the side of the window, and then I murdered him.

He just moved his arm a little, and never spoke a word.

I took a towel, which was on the back of the chair, and wiped my hand and the knife; after that I took his key, and opened the Russian leather box, and put it in the state it was found in in the morning, and I took all the things that were found downstairs; the towel I put over his face; I took a purse; I also took a £10 note from a note-case, which I put in the purse, and I put them in a basket in the back scullery; the day after I thought it would be better to put it behind the skirting board.

I had before I went to Richmond lost a shilling behind the skirting, so I thought that would be a good place to put it.

While at Richmond Lord William's locket dropped from his coat while I was brushing it.

I picked it up, and put it in my trousers pocket, but had not the least idea of taking it.

I intended to have returned it to his lordship while I dressed him in the morning.

I put my hand in my pocket at that time, but I found I had changed my trousers. This was on the morning we left Richmond for Campden-hill. I did not put the trousers on again while we were at Campden-hill.

I did not recollect the trousers being different, and thought I had lost the locket.

I then thought it best to say nothing about it. On the Friday morning I was looking at some of my old clothes, the policeman who had cut his chin was watching me, and in taking the trousers out of the drawer, in the pantry the locket fell out of the pocket; it was wrapped up in a piece of brown paper, the policeman opened the paper and looked at it and said, "What's that?"

I said to him it was a locket, but, in the position in which I was, I did not like to say it was Lord William's locket, as if I told the truth I should not be believed. The policeman then returned it to me, and I put it in my trousers pocket.

The watch and seal was in my jacket pocket, which I had on until the Friday morning, and then I undid the riband, and took the seal off. It was the day the sweeps were in the house, which would be either Thursday or Friday.

Having the watch in my pocket, the glass came out. I did not know what to do with it; the police were watching me, so I took the watch from my pocket, and put it between the lining of my jacket, and twisted the pocket until I smashed the glass. After that I dropped some of the pieces about the dining-room, and at different times put the large pieces in my mouth, and afterwards, having broken them with my teeth, spat them in the fire-place.

The watch I had by me until Friday morning. I then burned the riband, and put the watch under the lead in the sink.

I kept the seal in my pocket until they came into the dining-room to show me the ring they had found behind the skirting board.

When I was called to go down into the pantry I let the seal fall, and put my foot upon it, and afterwards put it behind the water-pipe in the scullery.

Beresford and Cronin and two masons were there at the time, taking the drain up, but did not see me do it.

The watch, the seal, and the locket, together with two sovereigns, I had about me until Friday, and if they had searched me they must have found them; but they did not do so until Friday, after I was taken into custody in my bedroom.

The two sovereigns I afterwards (on the Friday when I slipped the locket under the hearthstone) also slipped down near the wall under the flooring.

There is no truth in saying I put anything in the ale or beer, for all that time I had no idea of committing the deed.

I had scarcely had any beer all the week, and the ale that I had drunk that night, together with the wine and some more I took after the cook went to bed, affected me.

The gloves were never placed in the shirt by me, nor to my knowledge.

When I left Mr. Fector's I gave all my white gloves to the coachman.

The handkerchiefs that were found in my portmanteau were never put there by me.

They were in my drawer, where I used to keep my dirty linen, or in my bag with my dirty linen, in the pantry. If there is blood on them it must have been from my nose, as it sometimes bled.

I know nothing whatever of the shirt front. I turned up my coat and shirt sleeve of my right hand when I committed the murder. I did not use the pillow at all.

After I had committed the murder I undressed and went to bed as usual. I made the marks on the door on the outside, none of them from the inside, for the purpose of having it believed that thieves had broken in.

I never made use of the chisel or the fire-irons.

I placed the things about the house to give the appearance of robbery. It is not true that the bottom bolt was never used to secure the door; it was bolted that night.

I took the jewellery after I had committed the deed. All the marks on the door were made from the outside on the Monday night, for I got out of the pantry window and broke in at the door, and while getting out of the pantry window made a little mark on the wall outside near the water pipe, which the witness Young saw, and mentioned in his evidence.

I went to bed about two o'clock. I burnt nothing. I did not wash my hands or the knife in the bidet in his lordship's bedroom. Sarah Mancel knew nothing about it. Neither did the cook or any of the other servants. I am the only person who is at all guilty.—
FRANCIS BENJAMIN COURVOISIER.

Witnesses:—J. FLOWER, W. W. COPE.
June 22, 1840.

COURVOISIER IN THE CONDEMNED CELL.

After his condemnation he was removed to the cell generally reserved for notorious murderers, closely watched. This was a very necessary precaution, as it was afterwards ascertained by the governor that he intended taking his own life.

It was discovered that from the time of his being first arrested, he had meditated suicide in the event of being convicted, and for this purpose he had secreted a piece of wood about him, which he had previously cut to a very sharp point.

His intention was, he said, to have cut a vein open in his arm, and thus to have bled himself to death.

He, however, had not the slightest chance of carrying his design of cheating the law into effect, and when he saw this he seemed to settle down more resignedly, and listened to the ministration of the prison chaplain, the Rev. Mr. Carver, and a Swiss clergyman who also visited him.

He appeared to feel his position acutely, and continually paced his cell denouncing himself for being so wicked and saying "Oh, how could I have been so bad! How came I to do such a wicked act!"

He received several very affectionate letters from his sister in Switzerland, and he also wrote her several in return.

She begged him to be penitent, if he had really committed the crime, and to atone for it as much as he could by making a full confession if he was guilty.

In answer he wrote to say that he was guilty, and that no one but himself knew the remorse he felt at having brought so much disgrace on his family and his country.

He trusted that Switzerland would forgive him, for he would do anything if he could only once again wipe the foul stain of murder from his hands.

THE EXECUTION.

When the morning of execution came he was fully prepared to meet his fate.

On Calcraft being introduced to him, he at once submitted to be pinioned with perfect resignation, and when everything was all prepared and ready, he joined the mournful procession with a heart ready for his fate.

He mounted the scaffold with great firmness, and at once placed himself beneath the drop.

The crowd around was very great, and he was received with marks of general abhorrence and indignation.

Calcraft quickly fastened the end of the rope to the beam, whilst the ill-fated man stood with the noose round his neck. In another moment the drop fell and Courvoisier paid the penalty of the law.

After hanging the usual time the body was cut down and taken within the precincts of the gaol.

Thus ended the career of a man who, as a foreigner in this country, might have done well.

His first great sin, however, was covetousness.

He had the greed for gain, and to possess, as he thought, wealth, he hesitated not to take the life of his master, a nobleman whose family have been an honour to the country.

There was something remarkable in the craftiness he showed in taking the steps he did to avert suspicion, and make the act appear the deed of burglars.

But with all his adroitness he failed in his scheme.

It is not a little remarkable that the very steps he took to hide his guilt were the very means which led to his condemnation.

The property hidden in various parts of the house, even the things hidden behind the wainscoting, all spoke against him, and even the property he carried from the house, and left at the hotel in Leicester-place came from its secret cupboard just at the very moment of time, and completed the evidence of his guilt.

Had it not been for that being brought forward it was very doubtful whether he would have been convicted.

The general impression was that he must have been acquitted, but the publicity and aid given by the press led to his condemnation in a most remarkable manner.

Considering the number of undetected murderers there are at large, and the many miscarriages of justice which take place through the lack of evidence, it seems rather astonishing that the police oftentimes act with so much reticence, when the press by giving publicity could render them such valuable assistance.

This case, too, like some hundreds of others which could be quoted, shows the danger people run when they recklessly engage unprincipled servants.

A MODEL LADY'S MAID.

I could, if space permitted (said Calcraft), give you many remarkable accounts of the curiosities of crime through servants, and though I do not propose to go into any of those cases at length, I may mention one to prove to you that all persons are not exactly what they seem to be, and as an illustration of this, I need only refer to one case which I recollect, and which caused a great deal of merriment at the time.

I have known many robberies and murders committed through masters and mistresses not being particular in having good characters with their servants.

Some people, when they are going to get married, say, "Property, property—there's nothing like property;" but I say, when a master or mistress is going to engage a servant, "character, character." There's nothing like looking after the character.

Some people, you know, have very fair faces and fascinating ways, and they can get round people and into good berths, where people, who haven't such a pretty face, but have better hearts, don't stand a chance.

There was a noble lord, who, with his family, resided in Hertfordshire in the year 1835, who had a good many servants.

They had a magnificent mansion, and a splendid estate.

The wife of the noble lord, Lady ——, from time to time missed a large amount of valuable jewellery, and as there was a very large retinue of servants each one in turn was suspected.

Eventually, so many articles went that it became absolutely necessary to communicate with the police upon the matter.

When the police arrived they, seeing from the circumstances of the case that the robberies must be committed by some of the servants, proposed that Lord and Lady —— should insist upon a general search, not only of the boxes, but also of the persons of the whole of the servants in the house.

Lady ——, on the proposition being made to her, said she thought it would be a very good plan, but she added that there would be no need to search her maid, as she was very respectable, and, as she was quite sure she was above suspicion, she did not wish to hurt her feelings by casting any slur upon her.

The police replied that if they searched one servant they ought to complete their work by searching all, and they were not quite sure that the lady's maid, however fair and honest she might appear, was any more above suspicion than the rest.

Lady —— replied that she was quite sure her maid had not committed the robberies, for she was a very superior person, and one that would not be likely to commit a robbery at all.

The officer replied that however much her ladyship might suspect some of the inferior servants yet their experience led them to oftentimes suspect those the most who are generally the least suspected.

Her ladyship then very reluctantly gave her consent for her own private maid to be questioned and searched.

The bell was then rung, and the lady's maid obeyed the summons.

She was apparently a handsome, modest-looking young lady about twenty-three years of age.

The officers then informed her that, though they had no ground for suspecting her, yet they were going to request all the servants to submit to be searched, and they hoped that they might be allowed to commence with her first.

Her ladyship then retired from the room, and on the police proceeding with their work they found a large quantity of Lady ——'s jewellery upon the maid in question, and they made also a still further discovery —namely, that the lady's maid was a man dressed up in women's clothes; in fact, a convict escaped from gaol, for whom they had been looking a considerable time.

When the discovery was made known to Lady ——, she was utterly astonished, and could scarcely credit the revelation made.

The fellow had been in her ladyship's service some months as her maid without the slightest doubt or suspicion as to his sex.

The startling discovery, however, caused her ladyship great uneasiness and annoyance, as the affair was generally talked of, and greatly discussed among the aristocratic circles.

It was generally admitted, however, that though the man had outraged decency in taking such a situation, yet by all in the house it was shown that in other respects he had conducted himself with strict propriety, and this to such an extent as to amount almost to prudery.

The prevailing opinion was that he had adopted the disguise, and taken the situation with the motive of concealing himself as an escaped convict from the officers of justice, and that, being in that situation, he soon saw the facilities there were for him to practise his thievish operations, for which he had a natural tendency.

PREVALENCE OF MURDER BY POISON.

In the early years of Calcraft's professional career, after a stop had been put by the passing of the Anatomy Act to the horrible work of the burkers and resurrection men, the fearful crime of murder by secret poisoning became terribly on the increase.

In many instances private individuals who were possessed of wealth, and who had made wills bequeathing their property to those who were near and dear to them, and from whom they thought they had a right to expect filial affection, fell victims to the deadly-poisoned draughts.

In proportion as the feeling of repugnance against capital punishment increased, and the deterrent effects of the certainty of its being carried out became very uncertain, the detestable sin of murder extended itself into almost every rank of society.

Cases of poisoning, not only of single individuals, but frequently of whole families followed rapidly one after the other.

Nothing seemed to be thought of the sacredness of human life, and the number of cases in the annals of crime is truly appalling.

In some instances, it was the ancient sire of a family, who, having amassed a fortune by his frugality and industry in his early days, fell a sacrifice to the covetous rapacity of his own descendants.

The greater the number of dependents upon the old man's will, the greater the danger seemed to be of his being removed by one or the other of those anxiously awaiting his end.

In some instance where a man was known to be worth £30,000 or £80,000, the unfortunate possessor of worldly wealth was found to have been wilfully poisoned, but by whom the poison was administered the jury were unable to say.

Sometimes the guilt of the crime lay between his own son, or his grandson, whilst in some instances not only was the founder and holder of the wealth himself cut off, but some of the expectants too were similarly deprived of their life.

But whilst many murders have been perpetrated in the hope of gain, there is something dreadful in the further fact that so many others also have been committed with apparently scarcely any object whatever.

Even for the sake of the most trivial paltry plunder valuable human life has been taken.

The Sale of Poisons Act, by which the sale of poison was restricted in this country, was an absolute necessity, forced upon the attention of the legislature by the fearful proneness to evil inherent in the hearts of some.

It has been said by some of the writers upon crime "that the philosopher is often startled at the phenomena of nature," and when we ponder over the constant relentless sacrifice of life we almost daily witness, it is certainly time for the Government to do even more than it has done to aid in the repression of murder.

The old sins of infanticide, baby farming, murders, wilful starvation of infants, deaths of little helpless innocents by unnatural mothers, or pretended mothers, lying upon them and purposely smothering them, are crimes craftily carried out, and are well known to be constantly put in practice.

We do not like to dwell upon the perpetration of crime.

But the long black pages of its history, so full of revolting details, make us feel that in the interest of humanity, in the interest of poor little helpless babies, in the interest of helpless orphans, frequently done to death by terrible cruelty and starvation, in the interests of agonised mothers and broken-hearted fathers, who mourn the loss of misguided, unsuspecting daughters, who have fallen victims, first to the wiles of the seducer, and then to the murderer's hammer or the assassin's knife—in the interests of those thousands of

THE EAST-END MURDER—PEGSWORTH STABBING MR. READY.

people who mourn the loss of loved ones, of whom no tidings can be heard, but whose bodies may be yet lying hidden in some of the cellars under the London pavements—that it is quite time the nation was roused from one end of the land to the other in indignation at the apparent apathy with which the sin of murder seems to be investigated by our legislative system, and passed over as though murder was over as only a small offence, scarcely worth the trouble of inquiring about, and treated as a lesser offence than boys playing at pitch and toss, or a starving woman stealing bread.

No city in the world can appear fairer and brighter and more prosperous on the surface than the great metropolis of England.

No civil courts in the world appear to be conducted with greater decorum and care where money is plentiful and civil rights are at stake; but let a foreigner go into the by-ways, into the squalid alleys, into the slums in close contiguity to the mansions of the rich, where the poor herd together in a manner at which decency is shocked, where crime, profligacy, infanticide, are rampant, and he will find much that wants remedying in the vaunted land of England.

Where there are great mixed communities of people of all nations as we have, there will no doubt be always repeated acts of profligacy and crime.

But we maintain that of late years there has been too much a tendency by our legislature, by our detective and criminal investigation departments, to hide crimes away; to do as some of the murderers do with the bodies of their victims—namely, hide them away in roofs or in pavement cellars till such time as the odour becomes unbearable, and even the putrifying corpse demands by its very corruption to be removed from its hiding, so that the foulness of its murder shall be brought to light.

In the light of history we see these terrible deeds constantly recurring. We stand aghast at the perpetration of crimes which set all human calculation at defiance as transgressing the limits to which the criminality of human nature has previously been carried.

Many efforts have been made by philanthropists to benefit their fellow-men and to stem the torrent of crime; but, in spite of all, deeds are perpetrated which bring despair over the heart, and seem to incline us to believe that it will yet be a long time before we can hope to arrest the progress of crime.

We believe that general society, and even philanthropists, know very little of the extent of the crime and the number of murders committed in this country.

People who only mix with respectable people are too apt to believe that there is no more crime than what they see, and that human nature is much alike.

Keenly alive as the human mind is to everything that is extraordinary and wonderful, yet in the cases of the murders committed by the burkers the crime appeared to be too great to be believed.

It was treated by many as an idle tale, framed to feed the vulgar appetite for the marvellous, and too horrible for any credibility to be attached to it; nor need we wonder that the most credulous should have been startled by the recital of such atrocious cruelty, which far surpasses anything that is usually found in the records of crime.

The offence of murder, dreadful as it is, is unhappily familiar in our criminal proceedings, but such a systematic traffic of blood as was disclosed on the trials of Bishop, Williams, and May, of Calkin, and of Mrs. Cook, other burkers, were certainly never before heard of in this country.

It was a new passage in our domestic history—it was entirely out of the ordinary range of iniquity, and stands by itself a solitary monument of villainy, such as would seem almost to mark an extinction in the heart of all those social sympathies which bind man to his fellow-men, and even of that light of conscience which awes the most hardened by the fear of final retribution.

In works of fiction no doubt, where the writer to produce effect borrows the aid of his imagination, we have accounts of such deeds perpetrated, perhaps, in the secret chambers of some secluded castle, or in the deep recesses of some lone and sequestered haunt.

But the awful and striking peculiarity of the cases which we saw there exhibited lies not in the high-wrought scenes of romance, but in the sober records of judicial inquiry. A den of murderers in the very bosom of civilised society, in the heart of our populous city, amid the haunts of business, and the bustle of ordinary life, who have been, if we may so speak, living on their fellow-creatures as their natural prey. Words would fail to convey an idea of the sensation that was excited in the court, as in the progress of the trial the horrid details of the murders were gradually unfolded, independently of the novel and extraordinary scene which was exhibited of the guilt of the perpetrators. At every view of this unhappy story it assumed a deeper dye.

What a fearful character does murder in its various forms then present of cunning and violence, the true ingredients of villainy!

From first to last we see the same spirit of iniquity at work to contrive and to execute. We witness no doubt, no wavering, no compunctious visiting of the conscience, nor any soft relenting, but a stern deliberation of purpose in all murders that is truly diabolical, and it is fearful to reflect that persons capable of such crimes should often escape and be still haunting our streets, mixing in society, and coolly selecting subjects for their sanguinary work.

We fear that many of those who have once committed murder, and escaped undetected, are still wandering about, mixing unknown in society, ready for other acts of violence.

The cases of deaths from violent attacks in lonely places, supposed to have been done by tramps are numerous, and thus the number as well as the variety of murders in which the mystery still remains unsolved all go to prove that what is imperatively demanded is some legislative action to bring about a more active system of detection, and a more searching investigation at coroners' inquiries.

CHAPTER XLVI.
CONTINENTAL CRIME.

It must not be supposed, however, that other nations have not the same amount of terrible crime.

We find, on the contrary, that all countries have had to contend, more or less, with fearful deeds committed through the inherent depravity of the human heart, and the want of a more kindly Christian culture.

Instances of crime as foul and numerous as those which have been perpetrated in England are found to have been committed in Continental cities, towns, and villages, and some of them almost too terrible to relate.

France, Germany, Italy, Spain, and America, have all their terrible annals, and, in support of our assertion, we will only quote one or two trials—one, first, which took place before the Court of Assizes at Mayence, in Germany, in March, 1835.

The trial caused great interest, and shows that even women, who are supposed to be tender in their sympathies, can be, and have been, guilty of the most diabolical acts.

POISONING OF EIGHT PERSONS.—ALLEGED APPEARANCE OF A SPECTRE.

Maria Jaeger, a widow, and servant to Mrs. S. K. Reutora, also a widow, both about thirty-eight years of age, were accused before the court at Mayence, the first of having killed by poison eight persons, all of whom, except one, were her near relatives.

The latter prisoner was charged with having poisoned her husband at the instigation of her servant, the aforesaid Maria Jaeger.

According to the indictment, Maria Jaeger, in May, 1825, poisoned her uncle; in June, 1826, she poisoned her mother, sixty-eight years of age; in December, 1830, she poisoned her father, seventy years old; in August, 1831, she poisoned her husband; in December the same year she poisoned her three daughters, two, five, and ten years old; and lastly, in August, 1833, she poisoned the husband of her mistress with her assistance.

She had perpetrated all these terrible deeds with so much caution that no suspicion, whatever, was caused by the deaths of the seven persons.

It is probable that even the death of the eighth person would not have led to any detection, but from the fact, as the indictment stated that the horried work of this monster of a woman had been cut short by the interference of a supernatural agency, which had led the woman to confess the whole of the murders she had committed during the previous eight years.

It appeared from the details of the statement that after the commission of the eighth murder the woman, Maria Jaeger, was haunted by the attendance at night of an awful spectre.

She tried to close her eyes against the sight of the terrible appearance, but she could not.

Though she tried to calm her mind with the assurance that the fearful sight was only the conjuring up of her own fears it was of no avail.

As soon as she opened her eyes again there was the terrible spectre before her, attending her whereever she went.

The sight so terrified her that at last she could endure the haunting spirit no longer, and she at length made a full confession of her crimes.

The evidence adduced was considered conclusive, and on the 27th of March, 1835, the jury found both prisoners guilty of murder, and they were both sentenced to death.

POISONING OF FIFTEEN PERSONS.

Lest, however, it might be considered that the above case is but an exceptional one, we will quote one more from the foreign records of terrible crimes.

They are very numerous, and the case will only strengthen our assertion, that in large communities there are often great crimes committed under circumstances so devoid of suspicion as to render it imperative in the interests of society, that very strict and public investigations should take place when cases of suspicion arise.

What we assert here applies not only to England, but from our perusal of crime in foreign parts. We say it applies to America and to every nation.

Another widow, named Gottfried, at Bremen, was charged with poisoning fifteen persons, and also with administering poison to a very large number of other persons, from which they also received great injury.

The court, after a long and patient hearing, found her guilty, and she was also further found guilty, by her own confession, of having killed by poison: 1 and 2, her father and mother; 3, 4, and 5, her three children; 6 and 7, her first and second husbands; 8, her own brother; 9, her bridegroom; 10, Paul Thomas Zimmerman; 11, John Moses; 12, the wife of Mr. J. C. Rumpff; 13, the wife of Mr. F. Schmidt; 14, Mr. F. Klein, of Hanover; and 15, with having caused the death of Eliza, daughter of Mr. Schmidt.

The prisoner fully confessed her guilt, and the court, on October 11th. 1830, ordered—

"That the accused, widow of Michael Christopher Gottfried, for her own well-merited punishment, and as a warning to others, be publicly beheaded, and that all the costs of the trial and proceedings be defrayed out of her personal estate."

The execution was duly carried out, and witnessed by a large concourse of persons.

In some instances counsel at the English bar have alluded to the proneness of some foreigners to accompany the act of robbery with the violence of murder, and there are many cases that could be cited to justify the observation.

CHAPTER XLVII.
CRUELTY AND CRIME.

COMING back now to English crime, there are unhappily many records of long-existing wanton cruelties from which many deaths have ensued, but which have been hushed up by parochial or other official interference, instead of being brought to light and punished by those having the cognisance and conduct of our law.

In a former chapter we have alluded to the very little watchful care which has been exercised by our legislature over youthful life, as seen in the laxity and carelessness with which children at early ages have been apprenticed to masters and mistresses utterly devoid of kindness, sympathy, or feeling.

Certainly there have been attempts at legislative interference and provisions; but these efforts have been slow and ineffectual.

The old cruelties to children are not yet arrested, and the indifference of their parents is not yet combated with.

When we reflect upon the many existing social abuses and the amount of human suffering there still exists in the lower strata of society it is painful to see how much valuable time is frittered away in Parliament by obstructionists and other men who are very anxious to talk, but who have neither knowledge nor interest in any subject worth talking about, while so many of these abuses are still allowed to exist.

If we turn over the cases of cruelties of the past we see many instances related of terrible deaths, by the most fiendish tortures which have been passed over in some instances without the slightest punishment as though the acts were almost necessary evils.

What could exceed in fiendish atrocity the acts recorded of some of the old master sweeps towards the unfortunate helpless children they obtained as apprentices?

The extent of the horrible cruelties towards these children almost baffles description.

It is only by considering the miles of houses in London, and the many thousands of houses the chimneys of which required sweeping that we can calculate the extent of the trade, and the magnitude of the terrible horrors that had to be undergone by those former hapless children of England known as the climbing boys.

But it was not only in the metropolis, it was all over the kingdom that these children were subjected to these terrible atrocities.

The number so employed was very great.

They were obtained in various ways.

Some at the very early age of seven years were sold to the sweeps for a certain amount—a few pounds paid down—it was called apprenticing the children, but it was, in fact, selling them into the most fearful slavery.

The conditions frequently were, that the parents were never to hear of them, nor trouble after them again, and, as they were often bought by sweeps who tramped from town to town, the parents had little opportunity of looking after their welfare even if they had been so well disposed.

Numbers of other children, in the recollections of Calcraft's early professional years, were stolen—kidnapped from their homes.

Instances are reported of children well and tenderly brought up, the offspring of well-to-do parents having thus been stolen away.

The mode of procedure was for two or three of these scoundrels to go round the country in a horse and cart.

When they saw a little boy about six or seven years of age, unprotected, playing somewhere near his parents' grounds, they would invite him for a ride in the cart.

The unsuspecting little fellow would generally accept the offer, and get into the vehicle.

If he was seen by his parents, then the fellows would make the excuse "that they didn't mean any harm, and that they were only going to give him a ride," whilst if they were not seen then, they invariably drove off with him to some town miles away, where they would strip him of his clothes, sell them, and then, dressing him in common apparel, they would either put him to work for themselves, or sell him to other sweeps that would take him still further away.

There are some well-authenticated cases showing that almost as soon as a child was stolen, and dressed and disguised so that he would not be known the cruelties began.

In some instances when he was being taken from town to town he was not even allowed to ride in the cart, but he was tied by a rope to the hind part of the cart, and made to run behind.

This was said to be done for the purpose of hardening the feet.

The poor little sufferer would be dragged in this manner for miles till his feet were so blistered and bleeding, and he was so out of breath, that he was almost physically incapable of proceeding further.

In one of these instances the miscreants were seen by some farmers. They rescued the child, and took him into the house.

The sweeps claimed him as their apprentice, and proceeded in a most threatening and violent manner to search the premises for him.

The wife of the farmer, however, succeeded in secretly conveying him to another neighbouring farmer, while the men on the premises defended themselves from the gang of sweeps.

It was ultimately found that the poor little fellow belonged to very respectable parents, and in this manner, by repeated journeys, had been conveyed more than one hundred miles from his home.

A gentleman in the neighbourhood, ascertaining where he had been brought from, paid his coach fare home, and he was thus, after nearly a fortnight's absence, during which time he had received shocking treatment, restored to his disconsolate parents.

In the days of the climbing-sweep boys, the supply was not equal to the demand, and we find cases on record where even little girls were also dragged through the streets in all weathers, early and late, in winter and summer, and put to the trade of climbing sweeps.

Doubtless, however, it was the parochial authorities who were in those days greatly to blame, in supplying the great demand from the ranks of the poor unfortunate workhouse boys.

The revolting tortures some of those boys underwent were so dreadful, that it is a standing disgrace to this country that such a system should have been permitted to have been carried on for the number of years it was.

Not only were the children kicked, unmercifully flogged, and oftentimes kept for hours without food, to compel them to ascend chimneys, but other tortures were ruthlessly applied.

Numbers of cases are related where it was shown to be the practice of some masters to force the terrified boys up high chimneys, by beating them till they went up a certain height, and then when they were so terrified that they dare not ascend higher, then they in the most inhuman manner applied lighted torches to their feet, so that in many cases the children were frightfully burned.

Another very common way was to force them up higher and higher by sticking pins or needles into their feet.

If a small boy found the flues so small that he could scarcely get up, then another boy was sent up after him to prick his feet still more, and thus forced him to the top.

Instances are on record where the poor child's cries and screams have been heard getting fainter and fainter; till at last his dying words have been "Oh! master, master, I can't get up any higher."

Then all has been still; a lighted paper has been put up in the hope that the suffocating fumes would compel him to struggle through; but no, the last spark of life had vanished; the little sufferer, whose parents had gone before, had been released from his early life of suffering; he was now no more, and all that remained of the little orphan child was now to be looked for amidst the clogs of soot in the narrow chimney shaft of a gentleman's house.

We could cite many cases of terrible cruelty, but we will only give one more instance, which occurred also in this metropolis, so full in some places of thoughtlessness and cruelty, and yet in others so full of sympathy and kindness.

In one case one of these sooty monsters took his little apprentice to sweep a chimney in the city.

There was a large fire burning in the grate when he went, but the master, knowing it was a very difficult chimney to ascend, got to the top of the house through a skylight with the boy.

As he knew it was very narrow, he made the boy nearly strip, and then forced him down from the top of the chimney.

The great fire had only just been extinguished, and the suffocating smoke was still ascending.

When the master put the boy down the chimney, he soon began to cry out with the heat of the bricks.

In the most piteous manner he begged to be allowed to come up till the chimney got cold, but his inhuman master still compelled and forced him down.

Soon afterwards the boy began to shriek in the most terrible manner that he was being burnt to death.

Still the master dared him to come up.

In a short time all, too, was silent here. The boy's spirit had also fled. His life was gone.

There was no response to the brutal enquiry, "Now, then, what are you doing? Why don't you go down?"

All was still, and then, after the lapse of some time, the master began to fear that the boy was dead.

The bricklayers were fetched, and the chimney was taken down.

It was then seen that the unfortunate little fellow was dead; but before they could get him out the chimney had to be further opened, and then it was found that a great iron girder had been built in across the flues, and the space between was so small that no boy could have got through.

The examination showed that the boy had been forced upon it while it was red hot, and when they got him his flesh was scorched to the bar.

These cases of cruelty were frequently and generally passed over as almost matters of necessity.

In some instances they were passed over even without the slightest observation.

These cases, to some readers, may appear foreign to this work. We maintain they are not.

They were cases of downright deliberate wanton horrible cruelty.

Some may say, "Well, what have they to do with Calcraft?"

Our answer is, that they were downright actual murders, and that though the perpetrators were not tried for murder, they ought to have been, and though Calcraft did not hang them, he ought to have done.

But we go further. We have another object in writing these cases.

We know, as a positive fact, from years of acquaintance with almost every phase of life, that cruelty to orphan and other helpless children is not yet extinct.

There were many cases in Calcraft's time, that ought to have been treated as murder, that were not.

Many crimes, the perpetrators of which deserved the gallows, escaped with their characters unscathed.

One of the great crimes of his time was that of wilfully wrecking vessels by putting up false lights, and thus decoying homebound vessels amidst the rocks upon a dangerous shore, so that the ship might go to pieces, the passengers looking joyfully at the sight of land be drowned in the very view of home, so that murderous miscreants might share the spoil of the plunder of the wreck.

And yet how few of those who engaged in that fearful trade have been brought to justice in comparison with the monstrous crimes committed!

Our object in writing a record of some of the crimes of the past is to call attention to some of the remaining crimes of the present time.

Though Calcraft is gone, there are many that Marwood ought to hang that he does not.

Is it not a crime amounting to wilful murder to deliberately freight unseaworthy vessels, and to insure them, and send sailors in them, with the full knowledge that they will be drowned, their wives left widows, and their children orphans, so that the men who commit these atrocities may make large fortunes by the heavy insurances they secure.

Do not the abuses against which Mr. Plimsoll has so nobly raised his voice require a stern and immediate remedy?

The philanthropists of the past had to labour incessantly against some of the bygone evils against which we have written, and the philanthropists of the present, such men as Mr. Plimsoll, Joseph Arch, and many others we could mention, will yet have to labour unceasingly till they can get the cumbrous, slow stagecoach of parliamentary progress to move other present existing abuses away.

With reference to the present sufferings of little children, we have only to look into some of our squalid courts and slums, and see the neglect there.

If we go to the fields, look at the sufferings some of them undergo in their daily toil among the agricultural gangs.

Pass on to our river population and see the ignorance, the dirt, the immorality, and frequently the terrible cruelty towards children among the canal boat population.

It may be said, "Oh! but the School Board is working all these improvements."

Our answer is, that it is not.

The School Board officers, as a rule, look pretty closely after the children of those who can afford to pay for their children's schooling, while the little homeless Arabs still run the gutters, and the canal and gipsy populations are still almost neglected.

The existence of all these evils will then justify us in our assertion that we have in our midst even now a great deal of actual crime which is not looked upon as crime, and we have still many murders committed that are not looked upon as murders, at the very number of which, including the numerous cases of infanticide, coroners close their eyes, and say they must all be left to the police. The juries bow assent—the case closes—the newspapers are all silent, and the public generally all in the dark.

MYSTERIOUS MURDER OF JOHN BRILL NEAR UXBRIDGE.

Another of those mysterious murders which baffled the ingenuity of the police occurred in Feb., 1837, at Uxbridge.

The unfortunate victim, John Brill, was but fourteen years of age.

He was in the employ of Mr. Charles Churchill, an extensive farmer of that place.

He had been sent to repair a gap in the hedge, and as he did not return to his work on the following day, his master sent to inquire for him.

His parents said they had seen nothing of him, and then a number of villagers joined in the search.

It went on for several days without him being discovered.

On the Sunday morning following, a man named James Bray discovered the body of the boy fearfully mutilated in the wood.

A bill-hook which he had been using was found very near him.

An inquest was held before Mr. Stirling, the coroner, when the medical evidence showed that the poor boy had been beaten to death probably with a thick stick or bludgeon.

It appears that the unfortunate boy had two months previously given evidence against two men, named Thomas Lavender and James Bray, for poaching.

Some threats of violence were afterwards used towards him by some of those men and their friends.

Three men named Charles Lamb, Thomas Lavender,

and James Bray were arrested on suspicion of committing the murder, and at the inquest it was shewn that on the supposed evening of the murder the prisoner Charles Lamb was seen to come from the direction of the wood in a state of great perspiration.

As usual in this class of cases there seems to have been very little evidence given at the coroner's inquest. Very few witnesses called and scarcely any questions asked.

The jury returned a verdict of wilful murder against some person or persons unknown, and the three men in custody were discharged.

EXECUTION OF JOHN PEGSWORTH FOR THE MURDER OF MR. JOHN HOLLIDAY READY.

In reading the history of Calcraft it is very remarkable to note the very small offences which have from time to time led up to the crime of murder.

On the ninth of January, 1837, a terrible murder was committed in Ratcliff Highway.

The victim, Mr. John Holliday Ready, carried on business as a tailor and draper, at 125, Ratcliff-highway, and had made a coat for the son of John Pegsworth, a little boy eight years of age.

The father of the boy kept a small tobacconist's shop, and was also a messenger in the tea department of St. Katherine's Docks.

He thought the charge for the coat was too much, and disputed payment.

Mr. Ready then sued the man, John Pegsworth, in the Court of Requests, and obtained judgment against him.

After this Pegsworth called on Mr. Ready, in an apparently friendly manner, and was asked into the sitting room.

He then asked Mr. Ready whether he intended to still enforce his claim, as he was yet unable to pay.

Mr. Ready replied that if he did not pay he should be obliged to take out the judgment summons.

Pegsworth then drew out a long-bladed knife, which he had bought for the purpose, and stabbed him.

He was tried, found guilty, and sentenced to death.

On March the 9th the gallows was erected in front of Newgate, and great crowds assembled to witness the execution.

He met Calcraft with fortitude, and submitted to be pinioned with resignation.

On arriving on the drop he placed himself underneath the beam, and Calcraft, with great celerity, withdrew the bolt, and the unfortunate man died with scarcely a struggle.

EXTRAORDINARY CRIMINALS.

We must still further pass over a very large number of the criminals of the ordinary class whom Calcraft executed for murders committed in fits of violent passion, or for the purpose of robbery, in which the cases were clearly proved and the criminals duly punished. The number would be large even to record in his long eventful career, and further, there would be a great sameness in the details of many, which would render the work uninteresting.

We shall, therefore, now confine ourselves strictly to the most notorious and interesting cases by giving an account of the chief extraordinary criminals, and shall therefore commence this series of cases with

THE MURDER BY GREENACRE.

On Wednesday, December 28th, 1836, the whole of the metropolis was shocked by the announcement that the trunk part of the body of a woman had been found in a horribly mutilated state in the Edgeware-road.

Great excitement especially prevailed at Paddington, and large crowds gathered to gain what information could be got.

It appears that shortly after two o'clock in the afternoon, as a labouring man named Robert Bond, residing at No. 45, Edward-street, Dorset-place, Dorset-square, Marylebone, was proceeding along the Edgeware-road, in the direction of Kilburn, he discovered, behind a large flag-stone on the side of the road near the toll-gate, a package enveloped in a coarse sack or bag tied with cord, which contained the trunk of the body of a female, the head and legs having been severed therefrom.

The body was carried to Paddington poor-house. The spot where the discovery was made was situated about a mile and-a-half from Cumberland-gate, at the end of Oxford-street, and on the high road to Edgeware.

In addition to the human trunk the wrapper contained a child's frock made of the commonest printed cotton, and in a very tattered condition from much wearing.

There was also an old huckaback towel much patched, and marked J. C. B. 2, in red marking cotton, and a square piece of an old white cotton shawl with a narrow blue border.

Both were very dirty. The blood found oozing from the canvas had a fresh appearance.

Mr. Girdwood, of 3, Devonshire-place, Edgware-road, the parish surgeon, who examined the body, said he could not say exactly when death occurred.

It was possible that life had not been extinct more than twenty-four hours; on the other hand the body might have lain three or four days where it was found, the severity of the frost and the snow preserving the fresh appearance which it exhibited.

He considered the deceased to have been a middle-aged female, of about the middle stature, and believed her to have been married, from the marks of a wedding-ring being distinctly on her finger.

The arms were long, and the hands large, and exhibited every appearance of the ill-fated woman having been used to hard work from the dirt being grimed into the skin.

He also considered that the mutilation has been committed subsequently to death.

The head had been severed close from the shoulders, and the thighs within about three inches of their sockets.

The bones had been sawn through in a very clumsy manner, and apparently with a common carpenter's saw.

He was further of opinion that it had not been done for the purpose of an anatomical lecture, the body presenting no appearance of disease, but, on the contrary, of the deceased having been remarkably healthy.

He was therefore fully of opinion that she had come by her death by unfair means.

During the day Policeman Pegler, of the S Division, searched the whole of the unfinished buildings near the spot, but found nothing likely to afford a clue as to who the deceased woman was.

He stated that about eight o'clock on Saturday evening he observed a cart, covered with mud, drawn up with the horse's head towards town, close against the footpath where the stone was placed.

Thinking it was placed there for the purpose of robbing the unfinished houses he walked on to the toll gate and watched it for about twenty minutes, when, finding it drive off without his suspicion being confirmed, he thought no more of the matter.

He now firmly believed the package to have been then deposited behind the stone, and that opinion was strengthened by the fact that although the snow had drifted in at each end of the stone there was none underneath the package, and it did not commence snowing until Sunday morning.

THE INQUEST.

On the following Saturday an inquest was opened before the coroner, at the White Lion Inn, Paddington.

Charles Bond called, said: About two o'clock on Wednesday afternoon last, I was at work in cleaning away the snow from the front of some new buildings on the left hand side of the Edgware-road, near the Pine Apple-gate, when I observed a sack near the wall under a large flagstone, that was in a reclining position against the wall, over the sack.

It struck me that it was tied up in a very singular manner with a number of ropes. On passing my hand over the sack I felt something like a human body.

I opened the mouth of the sack, when at first sight I thought it contained a piece of raw beef, but on closer inspection I was horror-struck at finding that it was a human body, without head, legs, or thighs.

I called a man named John White, who was working with me, and I then gave information of the discovery to the police, and the trunk was removed to the workhouse.

Samuel Pegler, police-constable of the S division, No. 104, being sworn, said: At the hour and day named by the last witness, I received information of the mutilated body of the present inquiry being found. At the workhouse I made a minute examination of the trunk.

The head was off as also the legs, and part of the thighs. The latter appeared to have been severed by a saw.

The arms were tied across the belly by a quantity of twine. I did not observe any marks of violence on the trunk, with the exception of a pressure upon the loins, apparently done by lying on a rusty bolt.

The body was tied up in a coarse sack, sewn up at the edges, and round which was twisted a quantity of rope twine and tape; the former appeared to be the remnants of a sack line.

The whole of these things were wet with clotted blood; there was also fastened round the trunk with tape and twine, a piece of a dark coloured shawl, a child's frock patched with nankeen, and a coarse towel; to the latter some remnants of sacking are affixed with with pins, whole of which were besmeared more or less the clotted gore; the letters "J. B. C. 2," were on the towel; in the sack was also a quantity of mahogany shavings damp with moist blood.

On Saturday evening last I was on duty, and about eight o'clock I observed a heavy cart such as is used in the butcher's markets behind a large heap of earth, within a few feet of the stone where the body was found.

A boy was in the cart, and by the light of the gas-lamp on the readside I could observe that he wore a fustian jacket and cap.

I had some notion that the cart was there for the purpose of robbing building materials, and I watched it until it drove away, which was in about a quarter of an hour after I had first observed it.

The coroner observed that the business about the butcher's cart was very mysterious and suspicious.

Mr. Gilbert Finley Girdwood examined said: I am surgeon of the parish, and examined the body of the deceased at the workhouse.

The head was severed from the body just above the shoulder joints.

The thighs and legs were divided below the hips, the arms and hands were tied tightly across the abdomen.

There were some slight bruises about the posteriors, but of a superficial nature. His opinion was that the mutilated body was that of a female between thirty and forty years of age, of a fair complexion, and in stature about 5 feet 6 inches, and unquestionably she had never been a mother.

In continuation, he added that on the middle finger of the left hand there appeared a mark, showing that the deceased had, during life, worn a ring.

In a post-mortem examination, made by him and three other medical gentlemen, the whole of the organs of life were found in a perfectly healthy state, and one remarkable fact struck him most forcibly in the examination, which was the entire absence of blood from the whole of the vessels of the body. Such fully demonstrated that the deceased died suddenly, and, as a matter of decided opinion, he should say by having her throat cut, by which means the vital fluid escaped rapidly.

Had she, on the contrary, died a sudden death by natural causes, and been subsequently mutilated, the blood would have been retained in the viscera and heart.

By the jury: The separation of the head and limbs was done in rather a clever manner, but I am not prepared to say that such was done by a medical practitioner; as a matter of opinion I should say not. The analysation has been performed by Dr. Lane, and the result of such is that there are just grounds to suppose that a monstrous and bloody act has been perpetrated.

Dr. Hunter Lane, of No. 37, Euston-square, New-road, lecturer on medical jurisprudence, sworn, said: I have examined the contents of the deceased's stomach. It contained meat, vegetables, and pastry, in an undigested state, which proves that such sustenance was taken a short time before death. I could not detect any poisonous matter in the stomach; the organs of life were healthy.

This concluded the evidence.

The jury retired for about ten minutes, and then brought in a verdict of wilful murder against some person or persons unknown.

In consequence of the excitement which existed at Paddington and the neighbourhood, the parochial authorities of Paddington resolved to do everything in their power to bring to justice the perpetrator of the barbarous and revolting deed.

With this view a meeting was convened at the vestry-room, the Rev. Mr. Campbell, the rector, presiding, when it was unanimously agreed to offer a reward of £50 for the apprehension of the guilty party, and large bills giving a description of the multilated corpse, with the announcement of the above reward, were extensively posted about the parish.

It was also further resolved by the meeting that a communication should be immediately made to the Secretary of State, urging upon the Government the necessity and propriety of the Government offering a still further reward, with a free pardon to any accomplice giving such information as would lead to a conviction, such accomplice not being the actual murderer.

The funeral took place on the following Thursday, when the horribly mutilated remains of the woman were interred in the burial ground of St. Mary's, Paddington.

In consequence of the large concourse of persons

ich, it was expected, would have assembled had the time of the funeral been known, it was deemed expedient to keep the time as secret as possible.

Only very few persons were therefore present when in the stillness and darkness of the evening the remains of the body were lowered into the grave by the light of a lantern dimly burning.

As there was little in the mutilated trunk to lead to any identification, the police seemed to have had but little hope of unravelling the mystery.

The amazing publicity, however, given to all the circumstances of the case by the aid of the press caused the matter to be generally talked of in all circles of society, and there seemed to be a constant watch for every little incident that might turn up to aid in bringing the crime to light.

Every day, not only London, but all England, was excited by the discussion of the terrible act, and reports of missing individuals came from every quarter of the kingdom.

FINDING OF THE HEAD.

On the 6th of January, 1837, another discovery was made at a distance of at least six miles from where the trunk was found, which renewed again the energies of those employed in the case.

It appears that about half-past eight o'clock a barge belonging to Mr. Tomlin, a lighterman, was coming up the canal, and had got into the inside lock in Stepney-fields.

Many of those best acquainted with London know but little of Stepney.

It was a sort of *terra incognita*—it was then a district scarcely known.

The holder of the spot (called Ben Jonson's fields) was a member of the Society of Friends, well known in the vicinity as Quaker Johnson.

At the corner of the place where the canal runs was a public-house, called the "Ben Jonson's Head," and tradition tells that the rare Ben was wont to study or get rid of the fumes of his over-night canary at that place, the time he was an actor and dramatist at Bankside.

This lock was situated in a lonely spot between two bridges—one on Stepney-road, past the "World's End," an old public-house, alluded to by some of the best writers of the last century, and the other higher up, northwards.

The lock-house and a miserable hovel between it and the brow of the bridge were the only dwellings close to the spot.

The bridge in question would be known to the holiday-makers as near the tavern, entitled the "Edinburgh Castle," within view of the Limehouse Church. a more desolate or solitary spot it would be difficult to find in the vicinity of London.

In the winter, especially, the place was quite deserted, and it was rare to find anyone about in the evening.

The bargeman, who was known by the name of "Berkham Bob," was about to close the flood-gates at the back of the lock, when he was prevented from doing so by some obstacle at the bottom of the gates.

He called to Mathias Ralph, the lockman, who ordered him to ease the gate back and procure a long boat-hook, observing he had no doubt it was the carcase of a dead dog.

While Ralph held back the gate the bargeman put down the boat-hook and brought up a human head, which appeared quite fresh. He was so terrified that he dropped it, and exclaimed "I'm done."

Ralph then took the hitcher and brought up the head, and, proceeding with it to the Mile-end Police-station, gave information to the police.

The discovery of the mutilated head caused immense excitement in Stepney, and on Sunday it was sent to Paddington for the purpose of having the doctor's opinion as to whether it belonged to the mutilated trunk.

The following is an abstract from Mr. Girdwood, the surgeon's, report:—

"The head is that of a female, and of a middling size; the skin is fair; the hair is brown, with a trace of grey here and there in it; the longest tresses are two feet long.

"The eyebrows are well marked, and, with the eyelashes which are not very long, are of a dark brown colour.

The eye is grey, with a shade of hazel in it; the nose is at the upper part flat, and a short way above the point is depressed; the tip itself has a slight twist to the right side, occasioning the right nostril to be somewhat more dilated than the left.

The mouth is middle-sized, the lips large, more especially the upper and prominent, the front teeth are good, the chin is small and round, but it's exact shape cannot be well ascertained on account of its mutilated state, and the fracture of the lower jaw on the left side.

The profile struck all of them as being much like that of the lower order of Irish, the ears are flat, and there is the mark of pressure on the upper part of the concia.

Both ears are pierced for rings.

The left ear for that purpose has been pierced the second time, the original hole having given away from having apparently been bored too near the end of the lobe.

This circumstances we are satisfied has not been recent, the notch being completely skinned over.

The face is very much bruised and wounded, and the upper jaw is fractured.

Section made throughout the cerebellum presented no abnormal peculiarity.

The wound of the right ear had not injured the orbitary plate.

The body without head and legs, on which an inquest had been held, was exhumed.

The head now under examination was placed with the two cut surfaces in opposition.

They were found in every way to correspond, even to the superficial cut noticed at the inquest as existing on the right side of the neck.

The excitement occasioned by the finding of the head had scarcely subsided when the interest of the public was again aroused by the finding of two legs in an osier ground in Cold Harbour-lane, Camberwell, by some men who were cutting osiers on the spot.

Cold Harbour-lane ran from Camberwell into the Brixton-road.

Fourteen years previously this then open road was a green lane, with hanging wood on either side, and it has been the scene of many robberies.

At the time we allude to only one farm-house existed in it, that belonging to Mr. Tempenny, the back of which is towards the lane.

Nearly opposite, upon the ground belonging to Mr. Tempenny, the two limbs were found deposited.

The osier field was a mere strip of land, with a ditch on the south, and a fence on the north side, and a meadow immediately in front, so that the place itself was about fifty yards from the lane.

HANNAH BROWN MURDERED BY GREENACRE.

On Saturday afternoon an inquest was held at the "Royal Veteran" beer-shop, Cold Harbour-lane, Brixton, so as to make it a legal record of what human body the two thighs and legs found in the osier bed had formed part.

James Page, labourer, living at 10, Wood's-buildings, Cold Harbour-lane, deposed that on Thursday morning, about a quarter-past eleven o'clock, he was cutting osiers, in company with Edward Brook, in a field of Mr. Tempenny's.

He was round the bushes to see if he could find any osiers, when he saw a sack.

He called his mate, at whose suggestion he pulled the sack out to a distance of seven or eight yards to an open spot.

On looking in they saw the knee and leg of a human being protruding. They then gave information to the police.

Inspector John Bass, of the P division, deposed that he received information of the finding of the sack. On going to the spot he could see two legs through the hole in the sack.

He sent for Mr. Hammond, surgeon, of Brixton-place. The cord of the sack was then cut, and the sack ripped open so as to expose the contents.

It was not a complete sack, but only the bottom part of one. The cord was such as was used for sash lines.

Mr. Hammond examined the legs on the spot, and they were afterwards conveyed to the station.

The limbs had a white appearance, and were very little decayed, but they had since undergone great changes.

He examined the sack and found it marked in large Roman capitals, in red paint with part of an "E," and the letters "R W E L L."

In another place in capitals were the letters "E L E Y," with what appeared to be part of an S before.

It had been suggested that it might have belonged to Mr. Moseley of Camberwell, and witness called on him, but he said though the sack might be his, he had no knowledge of losing such property.

Mr. Hammond, surgeon, of Upper Brixton-place, deposed that the sack, which was tied round with a cord, was opened in his presence, and there were then exposed to view two legs and thighs which he judged to have belonged to a female, and to have lain there five or six weeks.

They were much soddened with wet, particularly the soles of the feet, but were very little decayed. He made a cursory examination, and found they had been sawed partly through at the upper extremity, and then broken off.

The sawing was from the inside of the leg towards the outside. The next day he made a more minute examination in company with Mr. Girdwood. On the skin of the left leg, below the knee, was a bruise. The upper part of the left thigh had been gnawed and destroyed by some animal.

He had no doubt that the limbs belonged to a female body. The limbs were bent at an acute angle so as to occupy the least possible space.

The saw used seemed to have been a fine edged one, which had caused very little loss of substance.

Mr. G. Girdwood, surgeon, of the Edgware-road, deposed that he had examined the legs and thighs in question, and had made a comparison with the upper part of the sockets found in the trunk of the female found in the Edgware-road. They were found to correspond in all the irregularities both of the half sawn and the unbroken surfaces. There were also some marks on the left leg.

The sack had been turned inside out, and what was formerly the inside was smeared with white paint. There were a few shavings of wood in the corner of the sack.

The wrapper that enclosed the trunk was made of two carpenters' aprons, and there was inside a piece of cloth, which had evidently been used for wiping tools, and also some shavings.

From the similarity of the circumstances he was led to infer that the agent who deposited both the trunk and the limbs was engaged in some kind of carpentering business. The feet and legs were stained with purple dye such as is usual with persons who wear black stockings.

Mr. Edward Mosely, brewer, and coal and corn merchant, of Camberwell, deposed that he had examined the piece of sacking in which the legs were found, and had no doubt it formed part of one out of a number of forty which he had purchased in 1834 of Messrs. Edgington.

At that time witness dealt largely in potatoes, for which trade the sacks were bought.

He had lost all these sacks except one. It was impossible to say who may have had them, as they were dispersed all over London.

A small portion of a sack found inside the wrapper at Paddington evidently belonged to the sack in which the limbs were found.

The jury returned a verdict that the pair of legs found in this parish are those of a female, and belong to the trunk of the female lately found in Paddington, but how the legs came where they were found the jury have no evidence to show.

CLUE TO THE MYSTERY, AND ARREST OF JAMES GREENACRE AND SARAH GALE.

On Monday, March 25th, an extraordinary degree of excitement prevailed throughout the parishes of Paddington and Marylebone, in consequence of the apprehension of a man and woman on suspicion of having been concerned in the late horrid murder of the female whose shockingly mutilated trunk had been discovered the previous month.

The names of the prisoners were James Greenacre, a cabinet-maker, and Sarah Gale, with whom the former cohabited.

Greenacre was a man about fifty years of age, of middle height, and rather stout.

He was wrapped up in a brown great coat, and without appearing to betray much emotion gazed at all around.

It appears that the first clue to the unravelment of the mystery connected with the horrible tragedy, was obtained by the police through Mr. Gay, a broker, residing in Goodge-street, Tottenham Court-road, brother of the deceased, calling on Mr. Thornton, of the Harrow-road, one of the churchwardens of Paddington, whom he informed of the removal of his sister from her lodgings at Mr. Corney's, No. 45, Union-street, Middlesex Hospital, accompanied by Greenacre, on the afternoon of Christmas Eve last, and that from that time no person either connected with the family or acquainted with the deceased, had heard of her since that period.

Strong suspicions had been entertained by her relations that she had been unfairly dealt with.

JAMES GREENACRE AND SARAH GALE BEFORE THE MAGISTRATES.

When it became known that the two prisoners, James Greenacre and Sarah Gale, would be brought up before the magistrates at Marylebone Police-court, a great portion of High-street, and every avenue leading to Marylebone office, were thronged by dense crowds anxious to catch a glimpse of the prisoners.

On this occasion, when they were brought before the sitting magistrate, Mr. Rawlinson, Greenacre, still wrapped up in the brown great coat in which he was arrested, appeared very weak from having made a most determined attempt to strangle himself while locked up during the night in the station at Hermitage-street, Paddington.

As soon as they entered the court all eyes were directed towards them.

Greenacre, who was a man about fifty, and rather stout, of middle height, and dark complexion, gazed around at the crowded court, and then, leaning on the iron railing of the dock, placed his cheek on his left hand, and continued in that position throughout the first long investigation.

He seemed throughout the day to feel the effects of his attempted suicide, for when he was discovered by Sergeant Brown he was black in the face, and appeared lifeless.

Mr. Girdwood, the surgeon, however, by promptly bleeding him, and other means, succeded in restoring him to animation.

Sarah Gale was also rather a dark and a good-looking woman.

She had a child with her when arrested, which remained with her in the cell, and during the examination.

The two prisoners were then charged with murdering Mrs. Hannah Brown, on or about the evening of the 24th of December, 1836, to whose body the mutilated remains found were supposed to belong.

During the first examination Greenacre made a full statement confessing that the remains found were those of the missing Mrs. Hannah Brown, in which he alleged that he was going to marry her, but that a quarrel ensued between them, and he, in a moment of passion threw a rolling pin at her while she was at his house, which striking her on the head killed her.

He positively declared that he had no intention of taking her life, but finding her dead through the blow, he resorted to the means of mutilating and throwing the body away to avoid detection.

He throughout every examination asserted in the most positive manner that Sarah Gale knew nothing either of the murder or of the disposal of the body.

After several adjournments had taken place, and voluminous evidence had been taken, the magistrates committed both prisoners to the Central Criminal Court, to take their trial for wilful murder.

THE TRIAL.

The trial of James Greenacre and Sarah Gale, on the charge of murdering Hannah Brown, commenced at the Central Criminal Court on Monday morning, the 10th of April, 1837.

At a very early hour crowds began to assemble, in the hope of gaining admission. Many seats were allotted to the personal friends of the authorities, but all the remaining places were soon filled by persons who paid 10s. 6d. each for admission.

The court was densely crowded by half-past eight.

At ten o'clock precisely Lord Chief Justice Tindal, who came to try the case by special appointment, entered the court, followed by Mr. Justice Coleridge, Mr. Justice Coltman, and the Recorder.

Mr. Adolphus, Mr. Clarkson, and Mr. Bodkin were engaged for the prosecution; Mr. Price and Mr. Payne were for the prisoners.

Mr. Adolphus stated the case to the jury.

He commenced by stating that on the 28th of December, 1836, the trunk of a woman was found in the Edgware-road, without legs or head.

On the 6th of January, 1837, the head of a woman was found in a canal lock at Stepney.

Several days later two legs were found in an osier bed at Camberwell. Inquests were held on the remains, but as no clue could be got to the identity of the woman, a verdict of wilful murder was returned against some person or persons unknown.

Nearly three months elapsed before there was, in fact, the slightest clue to the mystery.

It appeared that in the month of March of the present year, 1837, information was given to the police that a Mrs. Hannah Brown, who used to lodge at Mr. John Corney's, at 45, Union-street, Middlesex Hospital, and who used to get her living by washing and mangling, had been missing since the afternoon of the 24th of December of the previous year.

She then left in a coach with the prisoner, James Greenacre, to whom she said she was going to be married, taking all her things with her, and it was also said that they were both going to America.

As none of her relations or friends had heard from her since, they had their suspicions aroused, and at last some of them went to see the head that was found in the canal at Stepney, and then, to their great horror and dismay, they found that the head discovered nearly three months previously was the head of the missing woman, Hannah Brown.

From the evidence which would be adduced it would be seen that on the afternoon of the 24th of December Greenacre took the woman, Hannah Brown, to his house, at No. 6, Carpenter's-buildings, Windmill-lane, near the Wyndham-road, Camberwell, where tea was got, and he then murdered her.

After disposing of the body as described, Greenacre and the woman, Sarah Gale, left there, and they went to live at No. 1, St. Alban's-place, where they were traced by the police and both apprehended.

When before the magistrates Greenacre made a statement professing to give an account of how the death of Hannah Brown occurred.

In that statement he said that the prisoner, Sarah Gale, was not present at the time of the murder, and knew nothing at all about it.

He thought that the evidence that he should call would prove that Greenacre's statements were not true. The following was

GREENACRE'S STATEMENT.

I have to say that a great many falsehoods have been stated about me. I will now state the facts.

It is true that I was to be married to Mrs. Brown, and there are circumstances about it which may cost me my life, but this female by my side is in no way implicated in the affair.

When I courted Mrs. Brown she told me that she could at any time command from £300 to £400, and I told her that I was possessed of property to some amount, which was not the case, so that there was duplicity on both sides.

On Christmas Eve Mrs. Brown came to my lodgings in Carpenter's-buildings; she was the worse for liquor.

We had tea together, about eight o'clock, and Mrs. Brown sent out for some rum, which she drank in her tea, which made her worse.

I thought this a favourable opportunity to press her regarding her property, when she confessed she had none.

I expressed my displeasure at being deceived, when

she made a laugh of the matter, and said that I was as bad as she was, as I had deceived her regarding my property.

She then began to sneer and laugh, at the same time rocking herself backwards and forwards in her chair; when I gave it a kick and she fell backwards to the floor.

Her head came with great violence against a lump of wood behind her which I had just been using.

I found out that she was not a suitable companion for me, which may be fairly concluded from her conduct towards her brothers and sisters.

I adhere strictly to the truth in what I am saying, although there are many circumstances in the evidence combining together against me, and which, perhaps, may cost me my life.

One of the witnesses has said that I helped to move her boxes on the Saturday; that is true, but I will precede that remark by stating that I had this female (the other prisoner) in a room at the time where we were lodging, and she did my cooking for me.

I gave her notice to leave previous to Mrs. Brown coming home, and she had left accordingly on the Saturday night before Christmas Day.

Mrs. Brown came down to my house rather fresh from drinking, having, in the course of the morning, treated a coachman, and insisted upon having rum, a quantity of which she had had for her tea.

When I pressed upon her to give me a true state of her circumstance, she was very reluctant to give me an answer, as she had often, in my hearing, dropped insinuations about her having property enough to enable her to go into business.

I then told her I had made some inquiry about her character, and had ascertained that she had been to Smith's tally-shop in Long-acre, and tried to procure silk gowns in my name; she then put on a feigned laugh, and retaliated on me by saying that I had been deceiving her with respect to my property.

It was at this time that she was rocking backwards and forwards in her chair.

I then put my foot to the chair, and she fell back with great violence.

This alarmed me very much, and I went round the table, and took her by the hand, and kept shaking her, and she appeared to be entirely gone.

It is impossible to give a description of my feelings at the time, and in the state of excitement I was in I, unfortunately, determined to put her away. I deliberated for a little while, and then made up my mind to conceal her death in the manner already gone forth to the world.

I thought it might be more safe that way than if I gave an alarm of what had occurred.

No one individual, up to the present moment, had the least knowlege of what I have stated here.

This female I perfectly exonerate from having any more knowledge of it than any other person, as she was away from the house.

Some days after, when I had put away the body, I called upon this woman, and solicited her to return to the apartments.

As regards the trunk and other things I told this female that as Mrs. Brown had left them there we would pledge all we could, and the whole of the articles pawned fetched only £3.

That is all I have to say. Mrs. Brown had eleven sovereigns by her, and a few shillings in silver, and that is a true statement of facts.

The learned counsel then continued to say :—The female prisoner Sarah Gale had also made a statement, a copy of which I have here, and which is as follows :—

SARAH GALE'S STATEMENT.

I know nothing about it. I was not at Camberwell. These rings taken from me are mine.

One I gave 5s. 6d. for in the City twelve months ago, and the other my little boy found in the garden while digging, together with half a sovereign, two half-crowns, a five shilling piece, and sixpence in coppers.

The ear-drops I have had seven or eight years, and with respect to the shoes a Mrs. Andrews gave me one of the tickets, the other I picked up in the street near my own house.

Mr. Greenacre told me I was to leave his house a fortnight before Christmas, but I did not then leave, as I could not then suit myself with lodgings, and I went away on the following Thursday.

On the Monday week after that I returned to the house. He told me that the correspondence between him and Mrs. Brown was broken off.

That is all I have to state.

GREENACRE'S SECOND STATEMENT

Greenacre also made a further detailed statement as follows :—

He said: Having lost a considerable part of my property, I conceived the idea of having a companion, who might have a small pecuniary means to join with me as my wife and go with me to America.

I was introduced to the family of Mr. Ward, of Chenies Mews, who were going to America. I took the opportunity of making an offer to Mrs. Brown, who was at Ward's house, and who, in my hearing, had been expressing a wish to go with Mr. and Mrs. Ward.

I had previously asked Mr. Ward if he thought Mrs. Brown had any property.

He stated his opinion that she had, but that he knew nothing of her, only that she had purchased the mangle of them twelve or fifteen months before.

I corresponded with Mrs. Brown, she sometimes coming to my house in Carpenter's-buildings, and I sometimes calling upon her, Mrs. Brown still keeping up the deception of her circumstances.

The time was fixed for our wedding, and I helped to remove her three boxes, a small feather bed, and a bag containing kettles, saucepan, and a frying-pan, which things would be wanting on our voyage to cook with. On the Saturday I went to help Mrs. Brown to move to my house.

I called upon Mrs. Bishop, of No. 1, Windsor-place, Tottenham-court-road, to whom I had once introduced Mrs. Brown.

Mrs. Bishop then told me to be upon my guard, for that she thought Mrs. Brown was an artful woman, that she did not believe that she had any property, and that Mrs. Brown had called upon her and had been to a shop with Mrs. Bishop and had asked Mrs. Bishop to help her to get a silk dress upon credit.

This was on the Saturday that I moved Mrs. Brown's goods, a few hours afterwards, to my house.

In the evening, when Mrs. Brown was at my house to tea, I told her what I had heard that morning, and that my suspicions were excited, and that I believed she was deceiving me, and playing the coquette.

Mrs. Brown replied that she was not going to buy a man by stating what she had; but if after marriage I was not satisfied, I could go to America, and she would remain in England and keep possession of the house.

I then felt that I was deceived, and I was also angry

that Mr. and Mrs. Davis should have been directed to prepare a dinner and meet us at the church.

Under this angry feeling I threw the rolling pin at her, when, alas, it struck her on the face, and she fell, never to rise again; striking her head on the block, which I at first said her chair hit against.

She was standing up at the time on the opposite side of the table, going to wash the tea-things.

Finding that I had killed the woman, terror seized upon my mind.

I then decided to go to Mr. and Mrs. Davis's house at once to stop them from preparing to receive us on the morrow, by telling them that the wedding had been put off.

I started to go, but thinking it best to conceal the murder, I returned back, cut off the head, wrapped it up, and took it with me to their house.

I continued in the house alone all that night, and called upon Mrs. Gale the next day, and told her likewise that the wedding was broken off.

On the Monday early I attempted to remove the remainder of the body, but could not.

I therefore took off the legs and removed them to the place where they were found.

I returned and removed the trunk in a cab to where it was found. I went in the afternoon to Mrs. Gale's and asked her to come to my house to make a giblet pie.

This she did, and stayed that night. Mrs. Gale observed the boxes under the table by the window and made some remark.

I told her that Mrs. Brown had hired a porter, and took away what goods she wanted, and had left these boxes to call or send for another time.

The next day, Tuesday or Wednesday, I was at Mrs. Gale's, and the report of the Edgeware-road murder was in the paper, and very exactly described to me Mrs. Brown, or it appeared to be so to me.

Mrs. Gale expressed her fears that I should be suspected of the murder, and that if her goods were found upon me it would be a most shocking thing for me.

I encouraged the suggestion, and thus did I account to her for my most obvious state of fear and anxiety, which she, poor innocent woman, endeavoured to assuage by assisting me to put away the goods, and although Mrs. Gale might feel convinced in her mind that the female, whose parts had been found, was Mrs. Brown, yet she always supposed that it had been done by some other hand.

She never knew or suspected that the fatal tragedy had originated from me.

Greenacre made several other statements, all varying, as if purposely altered to meet the medical evidence.

In another statement he said: The first thing I did was to take the money out of her pocket, which was eleven sovereigns, and then cut her throat. I afterwards separated the head from the body, which I had great difficulty in effecting, and I used a knife, which has not been produced, and which is not now to be found.

I caught the blood from the throat in a pail, and sopped up what was spilled on the floor with flannel, and threw it down the closet.

I cleaned the head from blood, folded it up in canvas, and then tied it in a handkerchief, and went with it into the Camberwell-road, where I got into an omnibus, carrying the head on my knee.

On reaching London, I went to Leadenhall-street, and got into a Mile-end omnibus to the Regent's Canal, where I got out, walked about a hundred yards from the road, and then dropped the head into the canal.

I returned to London, and called upon Mr. Davis to tell him and his family that the marriage was not to take place.

I remained the greater part of Sunday with the body, and at night I cut off the legs.

The next morning at a quarter before five I took the legs and placed them in the osier bed.

A great number of witnesses were then called, and in addition to the prisoner Greenacre's confession the crime was clearly brought home to him by independent testimony.

It was also sworn by several witnesses that the prisoner Sarah Gale was absent from her own lodgings on the night of the murder, and that she was seen by various people at Greenacre's house on that night.

In opposition to Greenacre's assertion that the deceased, Hannah Brown, had sent out for rum, and that she, in great measure, aggravated him while she was partly intoxicated, the medical analysis proved that she had had no rum, but that only a very small quantity of gin with other food was found in the stomach.

Lord Chief Justice Tindal then summed up the case, and the jury retired.

After a quarter of an hour's absence they returned into court with a verdict of guilty of wilful murder against both prisoners.

On the prisoners being brought to the bar to receive the sentence, Greenacre, in a husky but firm voice said:—

My lord, my unhappy condition in this unfortunate affair has given rise to abundance of evidence against me, such as might be collected in any pot-house or gin-shop, owing to the reports set abroad to my prejudice on which the jurymen have acted.

It is contrary to reason and common sense to suppose that I should have meditated the death of the woman, much less that I should effect it in the manner described, because of the property she had.

If that had been my object I could have done it all on the next morning, when our marriage was to have taken place, and then it would have been mine.

What then was my motive for murdering her? In the next place, my lord, I wish to say that this woman is innocent, and that she was utterly ignorant of the whole affair up to the time of my being taken to the police-office.

This I say as I am going into my grave that she is innocent. I invited her back to the house after the body was removed, and she never knew anything of it. I deem it a religious duty to exculpate her from having any concern in this unfortunate affair.

The usual proclamation for silence was then made. The prisoner Gale was then led to a chair at the back of the dock.

The Recorder, in a solemn and impressive tone, said—

James Greenacre, after a protracted trial, which endured for two entire days, a jury of your country have found you guilty of the crime of wilful murder.

The appalling details of your dreadful case must be fresh in the recollection of all who now hear my voice, and the remembrance of it will long live in the memory and in the execration of mankind, and generations yet to come will shudder at your guilt.

You have acquired for yourself an odious notoriety in the annals of cruelty and crime.

The means to which you were prompted to resort, in order to conceal the mangled and dismembered portions of your victim, were for a time attended with partial success.

You disposed of her remains as you thought in places secure from discovery, but that course availed you not, for after a short interval accumulated evidence and irrefragable proofs of your guilty contrivance became apparent.

The amputated limbs and severed body were united to the bloodless head of the murdered woman, and every injury inflicted by you after death afforded the means of proving by comparison beyond doubt that the wound on the eye was inflicted by you while your victim was in life and strength and health.

Horrible and revolting to humanity as was the spectacle presented by the mutilated trunk and mangled remains fresh discoveries and details showed both the means and the manner by which you accomplished the destruction of the deceased.

Both surgical still and medical science came to the assistance of common observation, and it was proved that, while the blood was in a fluid state and circulating through the veins and arteries, you accomplished your horrible object by severing the head from the body.

Stupor of the senses and suspended animation were the effect of your blows, and then you embrued your hands in the gushing life's blood of the wretched and unhappy being who was stretched senseless and unconscious at your feet.

The still warm corpse was then barbarously mutilated and mangled by you in the hope that the eye of man would not detect your guilt.

But the eye of God was upon you, and the circumstances of this case show how the hand of Providence points out the guilty, and provides both the means of detection, and the certainty of punishment.

The certain but unseen agency of Providence is exhibited in the development of the peculiar and complicated circumstances of your case, and lead to the inevitable conclusion that neither cunning nor ferocity can shield a murderer; for although the crime may be hidden for a time—although delays may occur, and the mystery of the transaction almost preclude the hope of its discovery, yet the all-seeing eye of God is cognizant of the deed, and man becomes the agent of its discovery.

It is plain, from the attention which I perceive you are listening to what I say, that I am addressing an individual not devoid of education, reasoning faculties, and strength of mind.

I will not draw arguments, therefore, from my own feeble sources alone, but I will call your attention to the observations of others, in order to endevour to induce you and implore you to repent before it is too late.

His lordship then read to him an extract from a book called "The Analogy of Religion, Natural and Revealed," for the purpose of trying to bring him to a sense of the dreadful position he stood in, almost on the brink of eternity.

He then concluded by passing the sentence of death upon him in the usual form.

Sarah Gale was then brought to the front to receive sentence. She was then sentenced to be transported beyond the seas for the full term of her natural life.

Both prisoners received the sentence with comparative indifference.

Thousands of persons were waiting outside the court to hear the first announcement of the verdict, and as soon as it was known there were general shouts of satisfaction and loud hurras.

GREENACRE IN THE CONDEMNED CELL.

After his removal to the condemned cell set apart for his use, and which has ever since, in Newgate, been known as the "Greenacre cell," he became as calm as though he had not been sentenced, but reprieved.

He was evidently a man of very strong nerve, and spoke of the approach of death as though there was nothing terrible in it.

He was very communicative as to the manner in which he alleged the deceased, Mrs. Brown, met her death.

Among the various statements he made was one that he flung the rolling-pin at her without intending to kill her, and that the rolling-pin he afterwards burnt.

He then repeated a former statement, that, after he had cut off the head, he actually took it with him in a canvas bag to the house of Mr. Davis.

Mr. Cope, the governor of the gaol, from a variety of circumstances under his knowledge was convinced that the culprit intended committing suicide if he had the chance, and he, therefore, had everything removed that was likely to afford him an opportunity.

Two turnkeys were constantly kept with him, and in addition to this the precaution of putting a straight waistcoat on him was taken every night when he went to bed.

He seemed particularly anxious that it should be thought that he was naturally a kind-hearted man, and that he had always been respected by all who knew him.

He endeavoured at times to explain, and put a good colouring on certain actions of his past life, and there were many incidents which transpired which went to show that the words of the learned judge who tried him were quite true when he said that the prisoner was evidently a man of education and intelligence.

His general conversation showed that he was a man of quick perception, who had studied the various phases of human life and character.

The following letters to his children and brother and sisters will also corroborate the opinion:—

GREENACRE'S FINAL LETTER TO HIS CHILDREN.

Chapel-yard, Newgate, May 1st, 1837.

DEAR CHILDREN,—It grieves me to inform you that the die of your father is cast. His hours are numbered, and all his fond hopes of seeing you in manhood and prosperity have departed from him. And as I shall never see your faces again in this world, I have penned this letter for your future guidance.

But as it regards the untimely fate of your father no precaution can be of any avail, for that which has happened to me may prove the fate of any man.

To detail the catastrophe I conceive to be unnecessary, for that is now universally known, but never was there a more decided accident in the moment of anger in the world; it was, alas, the subsequent proceedings into which I was propelled by an aberration of mind; this it was that involved the accident in mystery, and has terminated the life of your father on the odious charge of "wilful murder."

To avoid such a fate I may admonish you never to throw at any person nor to yield to passion.

But in case of an accident with a gun or otherwise (as that of your uncle, Samuel Greenacre, killing your grandmother and shooting off your aunt Mary's hand), in cases of death if terror should seize the mind and suspended reason ensue, no charge can be laid to any act under such a state of mind.

Such, however, was my state of mind, as that God is just and true before whom I must soon appear.

Now, my sons, in directing your minds to your

future interests, I would have you blend in your hearts' study your worldly as well as your spiritual welfare, for be you assured that upon your temporal circumstances depends your happiness or your wretchedness in this life, as much as the fate of your soul depends upon the moral rectitude of your character.

This conclusion is most obvious to me by much experience, and by my recent observations upon the wretched and woe-worn countenances of those who form the assembled congregation in the chapel of Newgate.

There I beheld an index of the heart, which excited my sympathy and pity, as delineated in the faces of men and children of all ages, which more than proclaimed necessity to be the source of their crime.

I would call your attention to a text which I have no doubt you have many times repeated, "From our enemies defend us, O Christ."

There are many ways to dilate and expound almost every passage of Scripture as seen in the various and clashing opinions of vain and voluminous commentators; but, my sons, exercise upon these and all other matters, where it is demanded, that best gift of God to man, your own reason and reflections, "From our enemies defend us, O Christ."

Be you assured, my dear boys, that there is no enemy to man equal to that of poverty. It is poverty that fills the country with sin and crime—poverty fills the gaols, the workhouses, and the streets with the forlorn, the wretched, and distressed.

Poverty, it is true, is too often the consequences of those snares and traps of our personal enemies as spoken of in the text. But be you assured that God never assists those who bury in the earth, or lay up their talent in a napkin—that is, those who do not exercise their reason and discretion to help themselves. And herein is the chief use of those talents to distinguish your enemies from your friends.

God has made man the head of the creation, and by his peculiar understanding for art and cunning he is thereby enabled to render all animate and inanimate nature subservient to his will; so also are those faculties for art and cunning in daily practice by man against man.

The chief danger is not the petty thief, the highwayman, or housebreaker; these, though bad enough, are under the vigilant constraint of the law.

The danger against which I would caution you, my sons, is that of falling into the society of designing knaves, who, under the garb of sanctity or friendship, will spare neither time, pains, nor expense to ingratiate themselves so as to accomplish the swindling and ruin of their fellow-man.

I speak this advisedly, having sustained great losses by the same means.

You have each an ample legacy to start you in business, and to carry you through life in ease and comfort with attention and care.

The painful vices of drunkenness and senseless pleasure I beseech you to shun.

And let your books be miscellaneous, not all religious, lest enthusiasm usurp the power of reason, and you become like some infatuated creatures whose minds are absorbed by an ardent thought upon one thing. Wishing you health, happiness, and prosperity through life.—I remain, your affectionate father, JAMES GREENACRE.

GREENACRE'S LETTER TO HIS BROTHER AND SISTER.

In addition to the letter to his children, Greenacre also wrote the following letter to his brother and sister:—

Chapel-yard, Newgate, May 1st, 1837.

DEAR BROTHER AND SISTER,—I very much regret that I have brought disgrace upon the family to which I belong, as it is an extensive family, and the only one in England that bears the name of Greenacre.

It grieves me to think that I have brought such disgrace by a fatal accident. Sobriety, industry, integrity, humanity, and a quiet demeanour have been the careful study of my life.

It is with pride that I feel that I have enjoyed the esteem and confidence of my neighbours during my long residence in Southwark.

Had not character been more to me than gold, I might have made a purse at the expense of my creditors, as I was made a bankrupt for only £40, and I could have obtained credit for a much larger amount.

My untimely end is an awful proof of the vicissitudes of life, and shows that no care or prudence can protect us from the decrees of fate.

But, my dear brother and sister, I solemnly declare to you that I no more contemplated the death of that unfortunate woman, Brown, than did our brother Samuel contemplate the death of our mother, and the loss of Mary's hand by the accident of his gun; and may my most precious soul never enter the presence of Almighty God if mine were not as decided an accident in the moment of anger as ever occurred in the world.

It is the subsequent act into which I was propelled by the aberration of mind, and the unavoidable mystery that this act produced, which has given rise to conjectures and surmises that are by many considered to be facts.

It is, my dear relations, indeed that state of mind which led me to put away the body out of my sight that has terminated my fate, and blasted my reputation as a wilful murderer. In concluding this long letter I deem it my duty to declare the perfect innocence of all knowledge of the fatal accident on the part of Mrs. Gale, so help me God. Wishing you all health and happiness, and that you may not sorrow nor experience any evil consequences from the fate of your unfortunate brother.—JAMES GREENACRE."

GREENACRE'S ANTECEDENTS.

It is sometimes curious to notice the difference of opinion some persons form of their own character to that which other people form of them.

Greenacre throughout life always had a good opinion of himself. On the contrary, other people had a very bad opinion of him throughout the whole of his life.

The early days of his youth seem to have been anything but satisfactory.

His early manhood appears stamped with the blackest infamy. One of the earliest charges against him was of having endeavoured to commit a rape on a very estimable young lady named Miss Emma Watson.

Greenacre had obtained an introduction to the family, and the young lady was not only celebrated for her accomplishments, but for her beauty and integrity.

She was engaged to be married, and Greenacre, with the cunning of a villain, formed the design of effecting her ruin. He was so often a visitor to their house that he knew her habits and engagements.

Being aware that she went frequently out on a visit to a lady's house over Moreton Common, and through a wood, he conceived the project of meeting her one evening on her return home through the wood, for the purpose of accomplishing his design.

It so happened, however, that one of her father's ploughmen was generally sent to meet her.

Greenacre first waylaid this man, and made him helplessly drunk, and then, disguising himself in a smock frock, and putting crape over his face, he awaited the young lady's return through the wood.

As her father's ploughman, who had been made intoxicated, did not meet her she came alone.

Greenacre then, in a most lonely part, when the darkness of the night was coming over the thickness of the wood, pounced upon her, and throwing her down on the ground, struggled hard with her to effect his purpose.

Her screams fortunately were heard just in time, and assistance came, and her assailant fled. She was then, when found, quite prostrate with exertion and fright.

As it was afterwards ascertained that Greenacre had been drinking with her father's ploughman, and had made him drunk, he was suspected and arrested on suspicion.

She, however, described the man as having been dressed in a smock-frock.

This did not accord with Greenacre's dress, and he was acquitted. Though many things were against him the magistrates gave him the benefit of the doubt.

Some time afterwards the whole thing came to light. Some sportsmen found the smock-frock which he wore concealed under a bush, with the name of Greenacre upon it.

When he came to London he was a great visitor at Astley's Theatre, and he led a very gay and dissipated life.

It was at Astley's Theatre that he first met Sarah Gale.

Her mother held an office in the wardrobe there, and Sarah Gale was then one of the most beautiful young girls just growing into life that were ever seen.

Greenacre pretended to court her, and in the innocence and virtue of her youth she implicitly believed him, but before marriage unfortunately fell a victim to his seductions.

Greenacre's friends, thinking to restrain his voluptuous passions, set him up in housekeeping, thinking that if he had a good housekeeper, and the attractions of a good home, the gaieties of the city would have less allurement for him.

But the housekeepers that Greenacre's friends wished him to choose from did not suit Greenacre's taste—so he sought for a respectable young lady.

One was obtained, but in consequence of Greenacre attempting her chastity one night after she had retired to her bedroom, her friends took her away, and other after incidents clearly proved that no woman would be safe in his house.

In connection with some of his adventures we will just quote one letter—namely, the following, which will tell its own tale:—

SIR,—From the conviction that you were the individual who secreted himself under my bed, the purpose of which cannot be misunderstood, I consider that you are no longer worthy of that confidence which I was disposed to place in you.

I have, therefore, lost not a moment in removing myself from under your roof, and I shall return immediately to my parents.

Your servant Hannah has determined to leave your house upon the same principles.—I remain, yours, &c.,

To Mr. Greenacre.　　　　ELIZABETH TOWLER.

When Greenacre rose the next morning, thinking to find his breakfast ready as usual, he was surprised to find instead the note above.

The two girls had called a coach early in the morning, and had taken their boxes and gone. This is but one reported instance of similar attempts.

GREENACRE'S MARRIED LIFE.

Having now glanced at his early manhood, we shall take a short survey of his married life, and then we shall next proceed briefly to touch upon the leading features of Greenacre's life, until the commission of the horrid deed for which he forfeited his life.

By a deep and cunningly-laid stratagem he procured as a wife Miss Mary Ann Ware, an amiable woman of eighteen years of age, daughter of Mr. Ware, of the "Crown and Anchor Tavern," Woolwich, and then took the house No. 12, London-road, in the rules of the King's Bench.

He opened it as a grocer's. About this time he became a violent Atheist, was indefatigable at his studies, openly professed his disbelief of revelation, and was connected with Thistlewood and Preston.

It is reported that he was closely connected with the gang who were engaged in the Cato-street plot for the purpose of assassinating the Ministry of that day, on whose detection the unfortunate Smithers, the Bow-street officer, was mortally wounded by Thistlewood.

It has been stated by a person, who professes to be acquainted with the subject, that he was actually in the loft with the conspirators on the night before the explosion took place.

His wife died after experiencing gross ill-treatment from him.

She denounced him in her last moments as the cause of her death. She left a son, and it is this son that Greenacre has been accused of destroying.

A few months after the death of the above unfortunate woman, Greenacre married a Miss Ann Mumford, the daughter of a farmer in Essex.

With this lady Greenacre obtained a considerable sum of money; but he behaved very badly to her, and she did not long survive, but left a son, who has been taken care of by his mother's relations.

Greenacre was well versed in the trickery of assignments, compositions, bankruptcies, and fraudulent dealing, and would do anything for money.

About the year 1827 Greenacre left the London-road, and went to reside in the Kent-road as a grocer.

Here his third wife, who was a Miss Simmons, was confined, and it was remarked, to his discredit, by the neighbours, that no medical man was called in until long after she was delivered—an instance of neglect which excited very strong feelings of disapprobation from all who knew the circumstances.

Mrs. Greenacre had been unkindly treated before her confinement, and the child was in convulsions—the presumed result of such ill-treatment—for the first six weeks of its life.

The mother was confined to her room for ten weeks. The case of the apprentice has been mentioned several times in the London papers. The facts are these. Greenacre, entering the shop of his neighbour, said, "My apprentice has robbed me of half-a-crown, and I wish you to speak to him."

On going back with him Greenacre said in his presence, "He has robbed me of half-a-crown."

The apprentice admitted it, and said he had never done anything of the kind before, and never would again.

The neighbour added his solicitation that Greenacre would forgive the lad.

THE LIFE OF WILLIAM CALCRAFT, THE HANGMAN. 217

GREENACRE, DISGUISED, AWAITING MISS WATSON IN THE WOOD.

No. 28.

He said that he would, but he immediately went to Union Hall, where he accused the apprentice of the theft, and cited his neighbour as a witness that the boy had made a voluntary confession of it.

The magistrates, seeing the youth of the lad, adjourned the case, and allowed Greenacre to make it up with the boy's parents.

The result was that Greenacre was allowed to keep the £100 premium he had received with his apprentice, who was permitted to go off, Greenacre then declining to follow up the charge against him.

Greenacre was very fond of boasting that he was deep in the councils of the Cato-street conspiracy, and that by good luck he escaped whilst the others were taken. He was quite a parish politician; violent, yet very cautious, rarely committing himself, but frequently involving others in unpleasant circumstances.

He was fond of exciting people to make violent and inflammatory speeches at the Rotunda, in the Blackfriars-road, when Hunt and Taylor, the old Atheist lecturer, who was tried for blasphemy, were there.

At the time of the London riots, when the Reform Bill agitation was going on, he went about with a pistol, threatening to shoot the Duke of Wellington.

GREENACRE'S OPINION OF HIMSELF.

Having now glanced at the opinion people held of Greenacre, it is a little refreshing to turn from that part of the subject, and see the opinion he held of himself. While in the condemned cell he said:

From the moment I became a landlord I never distrained upon any tenant for rent.

When my claims for rent have been met by an apology through sickness, the times of accouchement, and other causes of distress, I have felt all the sympathy of a near relative for my tenants.

Now, as regards my domestic history, I will just refer to my disposition and general character as a husband, a father, a master, and a friend.

I have been a man of affliction in losing three amiable companions with whom I always lived in the most perfect harmony.

As a father I always sought after the prospects of my issue by forming an alliance where my children might reap the advantages of their mothers' dower on the death of their parents, and I have much consolation in finding that my children, by each of my wives, are amply provided for by legacies.

Before I pass over this trait of my character, as a husband and a father, the scandalous reports of my enemies make it necessary to refer to the deaths of my wives.

He then refers in detail to the deaths of all his wives, and he says that though they died from highly contagious diseases he not only had a competent nurse, but he waited upon them till he nearly lost his own life in personally attending upon them.

He adds, my old housekeeper always attended as nurse to all my wives and upon all occasions of sickness, making a period of nearly thirteen years.

As a sober and affectionate husband no man living can deny but this has uniformly been my character.

I have always abhorred a public-house, and the babble of drunken men. The society of my books and wife and children have always been to me the greatest source of delight that my mind could possibly enjoy.

No servant or inmate of my house can say that I ever lifted my hand against my wife, or caused a tear by harsh treatment.

As a master and friend I have always encouraged my servants and apprentices by very many indulgences and kind treatment, and as my apprentices have always been the sons of respectable persons with whom I always had a good premium, I always found them obliging and assiduous in business.

I have continued in the business twenty years in the parish of St. George, in the Borough, and I have always lived under the same firm or landlord.

To show the esteem of the parishioners I was elected to the office of overseer on Easter Tuesday, 1832, by the largest vestry that ever assembled in the parish church of St. George.

A poll was demanded, and never before or since have there been so many parishioners polled.

Greenacre next alludes to the circumstances of his bankruptcy. It appears that while he resided in the Kent-road a seizure of sloe leaves was made upon his premises, which it was supposed he was going to mix with the tea for adulteration.

To avoid the penalty he temporarily fled to America, when his creditors, finding that he had gone, made him a bankrupt, for the purpose of recovering their accounts.

Before absconding he wrote a pamphlet, exposing the subject of the adulteration of tea by a mixture of sloe leaves, in which he set forth that his was pure genuine tea.

This pamphlet had the effect of greatly increasing his trade in the tea business, and so led the people astray, till it became publicly known, by the seizure of sloe leaves on his own premises, that he was one of the greatest adulterators himself.

When he returned from America and found that his property had been seized by the Bankruptcy Court, he then wrote "an appeal to the generous public," asking them for subscriptions to enable him to pay off his just debts, supersede his outlawry, and proceed with his case to recover back his children and property left to them, and which had been taken out of his hands by their relations.

Though he professed to be a very upright man, it appears that before his departure to America he was fined £5 for short weights.

While he was in America his other wife fell ill and died.

Finding that he could not recover possession of the property he previously held in trust for his children, and the other property, which he said he had got by his own industry, amounting to £1000, he went to one of the houses where his daughter was sheltered to see if they would come to some arrangement and allow him one-tenth of the property.

In a statement which he afterwards published he says that instead of some of his deceased wife's friends meeting him amicably, one of them met him at the door with a loaded bludgeon, and nearly killed him by beating him about the head.

Greenacre, however, issued another able appeal to the generous public, and some charitable lady, it seems, felt disposed to assist him; but before doing so she wrote to the Mendicity Society asking that before she did so they would make some inquiry into his character.

Greenacre finished his long begging petition to the generous public in the following words:—Any lady or gentleman who will aid the cause of the oppressed by giving the reference of one or more of their humane and kind-hearted acquaintances that they may be called upon such course will greatly promote the cause of justice, and will meet with the strictest honour and indelible gratitude of

JAMES GREENACRE.

The applications stated that the smallest subscriptions would be thankfully received, and subscribers would please kindly say whether their amounts were free donations, or loans only advanced to be returned.

The following was the reply of the Mendicity officer to the lady who wrote for the character of the begging applicant Greenacre.

MADAM.—I find that the applicant has absconded from his lodgings indebted £3 to his landlord. He told him he had left a portmanteau containing a gold chain and a musical snuff-box as security for his rent, which he would shortly redeem.

On examining the portmanteau it was found to contain the duplicate of a chain, and a great quantity of printed papers, but no musical snuff-box.

The landlord states that the applicant often boasted of sums of money he received from various persons who had interested themselves in his situation, amounting in some instances to £7 and £8.

The visitor feels justified in adding that he appeared to be a rogue as well as a madman.—Dated, August, 1835.

We have now had before us a pretty good review of Greenacre's life from his youth till about sixteen months previous to his commission of the dreadful murder of Hannah Brown.

He was then, as he had often been before, wife-seeking, and money-hunting.

He appears to have been led into a correspondence with the unfortunate woman by his belief that she had property, but when he found she had not, and that she only laughed at him, then he became so enraged and chagrined that he killed her.

Whether he premeditated her murder for the sake of possessing the trifling amount of cash she had our readers must judge for themselves.

Whether he was a greatly maligned, unfortunate injured man—whether he was a virtuous man, a good husband, a good father, and a sincere friend, or whether he was a libertine, an unscrupulous villain, a designing knave, a fawning hypocrite, as well as a murderer, our readers will now be able to judge.

We have given both versions of his character up to the time of the murder, and we will close the history of his character by one more narrative of him after the confession of the murder.

CHAPTER XLVIII.
WANTED A WIFE AS A COMPANION TO A MURDERER.

THE above announcement no doubt would read very strangely if inserted among the business advertisements of any morning newspaper. Now, if Greenacre had been really the candid man he professed be, instead of the whining hypocrite he really was, he would have been honest enough to have issued an advertisement with the above heading, instead of the one he did.

Nothing could more forcibly show his villainous character than his actions immediately after the murder.

Scarcely was the blood of his victim cold before he contemplated forming another matrimonial alliance.

Just about a month after the murder and mutilation of the unfortunate Mrs. Hannah Brown, we find that on the 23rd of January, 1837, he inserted in the *Times* newspaper the following advertisement :—

"Wanted a partner, who can command £300, to join the advertiser in a patent to bring forward a new invented machine of great public benefit, that is certain of realising an ample reward. Applications by letter only (post paid), for J. G., at Mrs. Bishop's, No. 1, Tudor-place, Tottenham Court-road."

Among the answers to that advertisement was one from a female of great respectability, who, having a little money at her command, indiscreetly wrote to him on the subject, and afterwards had two or three interviews with him, without, however, coming to any arrangement.

Greenacre, with that tact for which, throughout the proceedings, he was so remarkable, clearly saw that it would be more advantageous to him if he could form an alliance with the lady in question, and he accordingly determined, without delay, to make an offer of his hand, which he did in a very characteristic letter, written on Saturday, the 4th of February, the very day on which the inquest was held on the limbs of his murdered victim, and probably at the very moment while it was sitting.

The following is an authentic copy of his letter—

February 4th, 1837.

DEAR MADAM,—Having had several letters in answer to my advertisement, yours is the third to which I have applied for an interview, and is the last one I shall answer.

I advertised in the *Times* newspaper, of the 23rd of January, for a partner with £300 to join me in a patent to bring forward a new invented machine, of which I have enclosed a printed specification from scientific gentlemen of property, each anxious to co-operate with me in it.

But upon mature consideration, and by the advice of my friends, I have determined not to throw away the half of this important discovery for the trifling sum of £300, as it is certainly worth as many thousands.

It is, therefore, my wish to meet with a female companion with a small capital, one with whom a mutual and tender attachment might be formed, who would share with me in those advantageous pecuniary prospects which are now before me, and thereby secure the advantages of my own production.

No man can have a greater aversion than myself to advertising for a wife. Nevertheless, this advertisement was intended to give an opportunity by which I might make propositions of an honourable nature to one I might prefer as a companion for life.

It may be, however, that the first impression from our short interviews has left very different feelings towards me than those by which I am influenced to write this letter to you; I hope, however, otherwise; or at least that you will not yield to any unfavourable conjectures relative to the moderation of my views as regards the sum of money I named in my advertisement.

It is, I think, sufficient to convince you, or any of your advisers or friends, that property forms but a small share of my hopes and object in turning my attention towards a partner for life.

I am a widower, thirty-eight years of age, without any incumbrance, and am in possession of a small income arising from the rent of some houses.

I was sixteen years in a large way of business, which I relinquished about three years ago, and have lost much of my property by assisting others, and confiding too strongly in the professions of pretended friends.

Under these circumstances I am induced to seek a partner or a companion with a small sum to co-operate with me in securing the advantages of this machine, which will be a great public benefit, and which has long been attempted by many scientific persons, and is certain of realising a competency.

Having given you this plain statement of my situation I beg leave to add that my mind is thoroughly fixed upon making you the future object of my affections and constant regard.

If you should feel disposed to favour my sincere and honourable intentions I shall take the liberty of calling upon you, and hope that you will divest your mind of any idea beyond that of the utmost sacred candour and honourable intentions on my part.

Should you feel disposed to communicate any remarks on the subject by letter I hope that you will do so.

Excuse the dissimulation by which I have obtained an introduction to you, and believe that my present proposal is dictated by every honourable and affectionate feeling towards you.

I am, dear madam, yours most sincerely,
JAMES GREENACRE.

Nothing could more clearly show the character of Greenacre than the fact that at the very moment he wrote the above letter not only was he cohabiting with Sarah Gale, but that he was also at that time a married man, having left his fourth wife, a young woman of considerable personal attractions, behind him in America.

It appears that he parted from her and his son, by his first wife, at the corner of a street in New York, where he left them both in great distress, without giving them the slightest idea that he was coming to England.

A printed circular, afterwards issued, by him also shows the versatility of his mind, and his various methods of gaining money.

The circular is headed " England and America. An Important Discovery. Notice to the Public. James Greenacre while in America discovered a herb the juice of which, when combined with the English coltsfoot, forms an amalgamated candy most efficacious in the removal and prevention of colds, coughs, sore throats, hoarseness, asthma, and shortness of breath. As some difficulty has been experienced in obtaining a regular supply of a well-selected quality of the coltsfoot, in order to meet the increasing demand of the public, and to obviate this inconvenience, J. G. has returned to England where he intends to manufacture his amalgamated candy, and supply his own family in America with it wholesale, who will transmit the American exotic to him in London."

Having now reviewed Greenacre's life in the world we will return to him in Newgate, and see him as he appeared in the prison chapel listening to the condemned sermon.

On the Sunday morning previous to his execution the sermon to the condemned was preached in the chapel of Newgate, by the Reverend Dr. Cotton, the ordinary.

Every available seat was filled by those who had obtained the necessary order of admission, and were anxious to see how this extraordinary criminal would conduct himself as his last hours in this world were fast drawing to a close.

A little before eleven the chapel bell began to ring the last call to the house of prayer that would ring upon the prisoner's ear. A sort of unvoluntary shudder was noticed among the gallery visitants.

This was a signal that the various classes and groups of prisoners should proceed to the chapel, which they did in becoming order, and, lastly, Greenacre made his appearance, accompanied by Mr. Sergeant, a senior and also a junior turnkey, who also took their seats in the centre or condemned pew.

The convict fell on his knees, and remained for a minute in a prostrate situation, when he rose and glanced for once round the chapel.

He was dressed as at the time of his trial, and appeared remarkably clean. To one who had not seen him since the day of sentence a very marked alteration was apparent.

He had evidently become more spare, but his features had relaxed the rigidity by which they at that time were frequently marked.

The morning hymn having been sung, the reverend ordinary read the formula of the Church of England in his usual sonorous and impressive manner, and many parts of the lessons and psalms appointed for the day were applicable for the solemn occasion.

Greenacre joined with becoming attention in the service, and repeated the responses with a solemn intonation.

When the ordinary got to the part of the litany where the mercy of God is implored "for all prisoners and captives," he adds on these occasions: "and especially for him who awaits the awful execution of the law."

The persons in the gallery not being aware of this commenced the response too early, which created a little confusion and a pause, which produced a momentary shudder in the frame of Greenacre.

The conduct of the criminal was such as became his dreadful situation, but he looked sternly once more at the turnkey when he offered to point out to him some of the service, as much as to say I know how to find it myself.

During the Communion service when the clergyman said "Thou shalt do no murder," every eye was directed to the condemned pew but none could discern the least change in the prisoner's countenance.

The greatest awe and solemnity prevailed during the solemn preliminary service, and the auditory seemed surprised at the excellent singing of the females who chanted many of the responses which are usually read in the churches. " The Lamentation of a Sinner " having been sung, the reverend ordinary delivered a discourse replete with the anxiety of a pastor, the eloquence of an orator, and the persuasion of a Christian minister, from the following passage, Psalm xxv., 5th and 11th verses—" For Thy name's sake, O Lord, pardon my iniquity, for it is great."

In the course of his sermon Dr. Cotton referred, in a solemn and pointed manner, to the case of Greenacre, and he most impressively enforced upon him the necessity, if he hoped for mercy hereafter, of making a true and complete confession.

He observed that the evidence adduced in this dreadful case had fully brought home to the prisoner the crime of murder, and he said that there could be no doubt of his guilt.

No human eye beheld the deed; it was long concealed, and for a considerable time it baffled the searching inquiries of the officers of justice.

But the vengeance of the Almighty, though slow, was sure.

Gradually was the mystery developed, and from week to week link by link was discovered, till at length the whole formed a chain of evidence, convincing and conclusive, which no legal ingenuity could rebut, which nothing could withstand.

Call not this chance or accident, but call it what it was—the Providence of God working out his behest:— " Whoso sheddeth man's blood by man shall his blood be shed."

The reverend divine discoursed upon the nature of

repentance, confession, and faith; and then turning to Greenacre, said:

And you, my brother, will be saved, not for all that you can do; not for all you must suffer, but you can be saved by the redemption of Christ.

Alas! my brother, this is probably the last discourse you will ever hear. Are you really convinced of the real necessity of true confession of sin; of sincere repentance, and a firm reliance on the mercy of God, and the intercession of Christ alone for forgiveness?

Is it so with you, my brother, in deed and in truth? Then let your conduct be clear and decided. Beware of self-deceit; only reflect how deceitful the heart of man is by nature, and how desperately wicked.

Make, therefore, a clear conscience; lay your heart bare and naked before the Throne of Mercy; and because the number of your sins are like the hair on your head, or the sands upon the sea-shore, confession must need be a very extensive duty, and calls for the strictest care and severe self-examination, for who can tell how oft it offendeth? It ought, therefore, to be sincere, minute, and as particular as possible, as the more circumstantial the confession is the more genuine and safe will be the repentance.

But not alone to God, but to man is a criminal confession due, for we are expressly commanded to confess our faults one to another.

Accordingly we find that the Jews and Gentiles commenced the work of repentance by confession.

But it frequently happens that persons doomed to suffer may have gone on in a long course of wickedness therefore it were well if the whole sins of an evil life were laid open to his religious friends.

The penitent has no option as to the acknowledgment of the crime when convicted by a jury of his country, and for which he is about to die; and in this case, my poor dear soul, this is a duty which I should say is highly requisite.

Before you depart out of this life it is most desirable that you should disclose the particulars of that lamentable transaction for which you are about to suffer death.

The only reparation you can now make is to leave behind you a plain and distinct statement of the melancholy catastrophe.

You owe it also as a proper tribute of respect to the administration of justice upon which we all rely under God for the protection of our persons and property, and also those to whose decisions we are taught to look with confidence and veneration, and may God grant you a disposition to declare the truth, the whole truth, and nothing but the truth.

This, I hope and trust, you have already done to your Maker.

Be not ashamed then to bear witness, though it may be against yourself, before man, even should the truth vary from any account you may have already given.

For why should you attempt to conceal the truth now, when in a very short time it must be proclaimed before angels and men, yea even the assembled world, at the great judgment day?

Besides, you will thereby quiet men's minds, which are now fermenting and busied in rumours and surmises, positively much worse than the actual case would warrant.

By so doing you will not only make a clear breast, but you will leave a clear proof behind you that, however you may have lived, you die an altered man; an Israelite, indeed, in whom there is no guile; a converted sinner; a confessing Christian; a subject of hope and of commiseration. Finally, sir, I pray you to pardon my earnestness on this subject, and to take it as it is meant in Christian charity, and from intense anxiety for your soul's health, and to hasten your thoughts on this suggestion when retired into the solitude of your cell; and may He, to whom all hearts are open, all desires known, and from whom no secrets are hid, bless the admonition and give you grace to follow it!

It is customary for the condemned to leave the chapel before any other person, then their keepers. After the service had concluded, and Greenacre had remained on his knees for a short time, he rose, and, with a placid countenance, addressed the auditory in the following words:—

I beg leave, and I feel it my duty, to thank the congregation for the prayers they have put up in my behalf.

At the same time I feel called upon to state this publicly before God and man that the unfortunate woman, Mrs. Gale, knew no more of this affair, either before or after the transaction, than any person breathing.

With respect to the death of the unfortunate person deceased, I solemnly declare that I never committed a premeditated murder.

I have to complain that I have been much stigmatised and injured by the public press, and I hope (looking steadfastly at a person whom he recognised as having taken the whole evidence of his trial) that when I am gone the press will do me justice.

As for myself I wish not to avoid death; I fear it not. My anxiety is that others should not be involved as well as myself.

CHAPTER XLIX.
GREENACRE'S LAST HOURS IN THE CONDEMNED CELL.

IMMEDIATELY after the conclusion of the service Dr. Cotton visited the culprit in his cell, and he was then received by the convict with great coolness.

Greenacre, however, was the first to speak, so he addressed the reverend ordinary, as follows: Sir,—I do not know whether it was your duty to make the allusions you did in your sermon to-day, but, whether your duty or not, you treated me as though I was a murderer.

Dr. Cotton replied: Whether you approve of what I said or not, I am bound to tell you that my duty to the public, but more especially the duty which I owe to you, prompted me to say what I did. My dear sir, you stand a convicted murderer by the verdict of a jury of your country, and as such I must speak of you, as you have laid no evidence before the Secretary of State to disprove the charge.

Greenacre: But you said a good deal of the necessity of a confession. Why need you have done that? You know I have already confessed. What can I say more?

Dr. Cotton: I am aware you have made statements more than once. All that is required is that there should be no mental reservation.

A rather sharp remonstrance then took place between the two, Greenacre still persisting that he was not a murderer, as death resulted from the accident of a blow, and that he did not premeditate the woman's death; but, as the law demanded his life for an accident, he was willing to resign it.

During the Sunday and Monday he was calm and firm, and he remained so till the time of the execution.

On Monday night the area of Newgate was more

crowded at nine o'clock than it had been in former times at the actual hour of execution.

Many persons remained round the prison all night.

At about four on Tuesday morning the ponderous gallows was wheeled out of the yard and put in position in front of the debtors' door amidst the huzzas and exultations of the mob assembled.

As the morning advanced thousands kept arriving upon horses and carts, and every kind of vehicle. The preparation of the gallows and the shouting of the populace, had the effect of arousing Greenacre from a deep sleep, and he then got up and dressed himself, and wrote several letters to his friends.

Meanwhile, a scene of the most savage description was going on round the prison walls.

Every house which commanded a view of the gaol, was filled by people, who paid from 5s. to 10s. for a seat at the windows, or for standing room on the tops of the houses.

The police, though in large force, had plenty of work to do, in consequence of the numerous pickpockets among the crowd, and the various broils and pugilistic encounters which took place. Many windows were broken, and many heads felt the force of a constable's truncheon.

At one period of the night the mob bid open defiance to the whole body of watchmen and police, and not only rescued thieves, but broke the watch-house windows.

So little sympathy was there for the criminal that the whole assembly seemed glad that the world was going to be rid of such a character, though doubtless there were many among the crowd whose characters, had the opportunities offered, would not have been much better.

Thieves there were in great number, and two prizefighters actually sparred with boxing gloves under the gallows, and the spectators around seemed lighly delighted at the brutal exhibition.

At length the pressure on many points became so irresistible that screams and groans from fainting persons, and others, who were being trampled on, came from every direction.

When Dr. Cotton visited Greenacre on the morning of his execution Greenacre received him with politeness, but not with his usual fervour.

Dr. Cotton, as the time for the culprit's execution was fast approaching, once more earnestly endeavoured to make some sort of religious impression upon him.

Greenacre then said:

"I would give worlds if I could undo what I have done, and bring Hannah Brown to life."

He then knelt down, and offered up the following prayer:

"O God, be merciful to me, and let not the sins of her whom I have been the unhappy instrument of sending into eternity be laid to my charge, who am already sinking under the load of my transgressions; but vouchsafe O merciful God to wash them all away In the blood of the Redeemer through whose merits, and for whose sake alone, I dare to hope for pardon."

About seven o'clock on the morning of his execution he partook of a cup of tea, and a piece of bread and butter.

While he was eating it he was observed to shed tears, being the first that had fallen from him since he had been in Newgate.

He then said:

" Ah, I am very differently situated now to what I was some years ago, for I was then highly respected, and was returned as one of the overseers of the parish of St. George's by one of the largest majorities ever known."

It was then about a quarter to eight, and Greenacre was informed that Calcraft, the executioner, was then waiting for him, and that he had not much time left.

Greenacre became pale and agitated, but rose, and at once prepared to meet the hangman.

Before leaving his cell, he turned to one of the sheriffs, and said he had one favour to ask, and that was that they would not allow him to be long exposed on the gallows to the gaze of the crowd.

He gave a small parcel, which contained his spectacles, to Mr. Sheriff Duke, and begged him to give them to Sarah Gale.

He then at once proceeded to the press-room, to surrender himself to Calcraft.

During the time that Calcraft was pinioning him he seemed pale and anxious, but the hangman very adroitly performed the operation. About five minutes before eight the procession was formed, and began to move towards the gallows.

First went the two sheriffs and the under sheriffs with their staves, then followed the ordinary in his white gown, reading the burial service, then the criminal bringing up the rear.

"I am the resurrection and the life, saith the Lord," commenced the voice of Dr. Cotton, and then immediately upon that the dismal tolling of the prison bell fell upon the culprit's ear, as the procession moved along the winding corridors of the gaol towards the debtors' door.

It was a solemn and melancholy sight to behold the culprit now passing up the steps of the gallows to death.

On his appearance outside on the gallows he was greeted with a storm of terrific yells and hisses, mingled with groans, cheers, and other expressions of reproach, revenge, hatred, and contumely, but he answered nothing to the questions put to him, nor did he seem in any way moved.

He said not one word of hope, of repentance, or of reconcilement, nor did he make a speech as it was expected he would do.

Calcraft, who had already placed the noose round the culprit's neck, and fixed the end of the halter to the fatal beam, now placed him in position upon the drop.

Greenacre then said to Calcraft, " Don't leave me long in sight of this concourse."

Calcraft shook hands with him, and went down the steps behind the drop to await the usual signal of death.

The ordinary, meantime, was proceeding with the solemn service, and at length came to the words : " In the midst of life we are in death; of whom may we seek for succour but of thee, O Lord, who for our sins are justly displeased? Yet, O Lord, most mighty, O holy and most merciful Saviour, deliver us not into the bitter pains of eternal death;" then the plank on which the murderer stood gave way, and Greenacre, who at once fell, passed into the presence of Him whose decree it is, " That whoso sheddeth man's blood, by man should his blood be shed."

As the body hung quivering in mortal agonies the eyes of the assembled thousands were rivetted upon the swaying corpse with a kind of satisfaction, and all seemed pleased at the removal of such a bloodstained murderer from the land.

So loud was the shout which hailed the exit of the culprit from the world that it was distinctly heard at the distance of several streets, and penetrated to the innermost recesses of the prison.

On hearing it the woman Sarah Gale fainted away in her cell, and although restoratives were immediately applied, it was long before she recovered from her death-like swoon.

The body having hung the usual time was now cut down, and the immense crowds dispersed.

CHAPTER L.
THE MYSTERIOUS MURDER OF ELIZA GRIMWOOD.

In the month of May, 1838, another of those strange mysterious murders, which have from time to time shocked the metropolis, was discovered.

From the report of the proceedings it appears that on the 28th of May, of the above year, an inquest was held before the coroner at the "York Hotel," in the Waterloo-road, on the body of Eliza Grimwood, a young woman twenty-five years of age, who resided at No. 12, Wellington-terrace, in the Waterloo-road, and who was found in her bedroom murdered on the Saturday morning previous.

The deceased lived with George Hubbard, a bricklayer, and a married man, but separated from his wife. According to the evidence of the surgeon who examined the body, she had been wounded in several places—in the abdomen and under the left breast—with a sharp-pointed instrument, about half an inch wide in the deepest part.

But the chief wound, and that which must have caused instant death, was in the neck, extending nearly from ear to ear, and nearly severing the windpipe.

Her left thumb was also cut, as if done in struggling with her destroyer.

It appears that the deceased was in the habit of taking persons home with her from theatres; and that on Friday night at the Strand Theatre she met with an acquaintance who had the look of a foreigner, and was said to be tall, pale, with large whiskers, and who wore the garb of a gentleman.

With this person she entered a cab and went home about twelve o'clock.

The man was not seen afterwards, and how or when he left the house could not be ascertained.

The man Hubbard slept in another apartment.

He stated that early on Saturday morning, as he was going out to his work, he discovered the corpse lying steeped in blood, and partly undressed, near the door of the half-opened bedroom on the ground floor.

He immediately awakened a commercial traveller who slept in the house with another woman, and then alarmed the police.

Suspicion fell upon Hubbard, partly in consequence of his razor not being found; but it was afterwards found, and, moreover, according to the evidence of the surgeon the wounds could not have been inflicted with a razor.

It was at first thought unaccountable that neither the persons in two rooms overhead, nor the female servant, who slept below, heard the slightest noise, but this was partly ascribed to the instantaneous death from the principal wound.

The deceased had a purse with ten or eleven sovereigns, which were missing, also about £20 in a savings bank, as appeared in a bank book found in her room, and a gold watch.

She was about twenty-five years of age, good-looking and of sober habits. Some evidence given at the inquest gave rise to the suspicion that her murderer was the man who accompanied her home from the Strand Theatre.

The principal witness was Catherine Edwin, who was present when that person engaged to meet Grimwood at the theatre. She stated that she had frequently seen them together.

The cabman, who drove them home, also corroborated the general appearance of the man.

Catherine Edwin further expressed her belief that the man was an Italian, but that he could speak English fluently, and that he had been acquainted with deceased for months.

She knew that the man was in the habit of going to see deceased, as she had often seen them together, and she had heard the deceased say, "Here comes my tormentor."

She had often met them in the street together, and she had once heard the man ask Grimwood to marry him.

This was in a confectioner's shop in Piccadilly.

Witness, deceased, and the Italian were in a private room.

The man threw off his cloak, and also his coat, and as he did so something dropped out of his pocket on to the floor, which witness picked up.

She then saw that it was a large clasp knife, and on drawing down a spring the blade flew open, which was of the width of a thumb nail.

Here the witness gave a minute description of the knife.

Grimwood's stays were produced, and shown to the witness, and she said that she thought the cut could have been produced with such a knife that she saw drop from the Italian's pocket.

She noticed that the point had been recently sharpened after apparently having been broken at the point.

Eliza Grimwood often used to speak to her of this man, and say that he was a man of depraved habits.

He frequented the neighbourhood of the "Spread Eagle" in the Regent Circus, and wore a ring, on one side of which were the words "Semper fidelis" engraved. The deceased gave the man that ring.

He was not a gentleman, but looked like a thief.

She again heard him offer to marry the deceased, and on her refusing him she heard him declare that he would throw her over the bridge.

Maria Glover, a witness who lived in the same house with Grimwood, said she knew the deceased's affairs better than anybody else, but never heard of her acquaintance with the Italian or of her having had an offer of marriage from an Italian, or of her having been tormented by one.

She did not believe that anyone could have gone down the stairs and committed a murder without her hearing them.

The deceased never complained of ill-usage from Hubbard.

Harriett Chaplin, another witness and niece to the murdered woman, said that the deceased had told her that Hubbard had declared that he would not mind shooting her, and that she had herself seen him strike her when angry.

John Owen, a cooper, living in Cottage-place, Waterloo-road, was examined in reference to a statement he had made to one of the jurors on the inquest.

The substance of this man's story was, that early on Saturday morning he saw a person standing at the door of the house on Wellington-terrace in light drawers, his shirt sleeves tucked up to the elbows, and blood on his hands.

He heard him say, "Oh—oh! I have done the deed; now, how must I escape from it?"

Hubbard was produced, but Owen did not recognise him as the person he saw in his shirt sleeves. He pointed out another person in the room as most like him.

Owen had been to the house where the murder was committed, to try, as he said, to raise a little money upon some security.

This man's appearance was thought to denote insanity, though he said he could produce respectable reference who would speak to his being in his competent senses.

He was very reluctant to take the oath, and said it was his objection to do so which had prevented him from coming forward at first.

On further examination Owen was proved to be unworthy of credit.

Many other witnesses were examined, and several adjournments took place, but no progress was made towards the discovery of the murderer.

A policeman stated that he had been with the witness, Catherine Edwin, to Regent's Circus, and to the pastrycook's shop in Piccadilly, but that he could obtain no clue to the person described by the witness.

Charlotte Rosedale, who kept the shop, recollected that a person answering the description of the supposed murderer went into a back room with two females; she did not hear the conversation, or the knife drop, but her shop was full of people, and she did not pay much attention to the persons in the back room.

The girl Catherine Edwin re-stated her evidence again with perfect coolness and accuracy. Many particulars of no interest were detailed.

The coroner then summed up the case to the jury, and after some deliberation the jury returned a verdict of "wilful murder against some person or persons unknown."

CHAPTER LI.
HOAXING LETTERS.

Some time afterwards several letters of a hoaxing character were received by the police which gave them a great deal of trouble.

It is very difficult to account for the motive which induces some people so constantly to indulge in these foolish freaks.

But in nearly every murder case the police have these senseless productions transmitted to them.

Not only does it take up the valuable time of the officers engaged in these complicated and difficult cases, but it frequently is the cause of them being sent, when tired and overtaxed, for miles away, altogether on a wrong track.

No punishment could be too severe for persons who, if in possession of their faculties, can act so idiotic.

Of course when the letters come from insane persons the nature of their malady is some excuse.

But persons who do such things cannot seriously reflect upon the terrible crime of murder, and the suffering it oftentimes causes to bereaved friends; neither can they have any respect for justice, or the senseless witlings would cease their silly pranks.

But when, as is sometimes the case, anonymous letters are sent to the police for the purpose of so misleading the police as to cast suspicion upon innocent persons, then such conduct is nothing short of a terrible crime, which ought to be heavily punished, and no trouble or expense should be spared to bring such offenders to justice.

CHAPTER LII.
ARREST, ON SUSPICION, OF WILLIAM HUBBARD.

William Hubbard, the man who lived with the woman, Eliza Grimwood, was arrested in consequence of a letter sent to the police, and signed with the name of "John Walter Cavendish."

The writer professed that he was the person who accompanied Eliza Grimwood from the Strand Theatre on the night in question—the night of the murder—and that while he was with the woman Hubbard came downstairs, broke in upon them, and in a storm of rage, particularly directed against the unhappy woman, turned him out of the house.

The police made a diligent search for the writer of this letter in Goswell-street, and the adjoining districts.

At last, finding that it was post-marked at Highbury, by the help of the person who kept the post-office there, they traced the authorship, as they believed, to Mr. M'Millan, junior, who was in consequence ordered to attend on the following Tuesday, when Hubbard was again examined.

In the meantime two other letters were received by the magistrates, in both of which the writers (of different names) declared themselves the true murderers, and demanded the release of Hubbard.

All these letters appear to have been hoaxes, though the object of the writers in thus endeavouring to mislead the magistrates and the police it is difficult to understand.

The letter signed "John Walter Cavendish" was characterised by the magistrates as a malicious fabrication.

Mr. M'Millan, of Highbury, positively denied being the author of it, and there seems to have been no sufficient reason for suspecting him.

A foreigner was taken up and kept in custody a short time, in consequence of a resemblance to the whiskered Italian mentioned by the girl, Eliza Edwin.

The only evidence against him, however, was founded on his whiskers.

After remaining a week in custody, Hubbard, who had been arrested on account of the letter, was released, there being no evidence to fix upon him the guilt of the murder.

A public meeting was afterwards held in the parish of Lambeth, when it was agreed to offer a reward for the apprehension of the murderer.

No further evidence was obtained, and thus the murder of the unfortunate girl Eliza Grimwood, like many other cases, remains a mystery of the past.

There were other mysterious murders in the neighbourhood of Manchester and other places, about this time, which would be too numerous to mention.

CHAPTER LIII.
INHUMAN MURDER AT SEA OF BENJAMIN DRISCOLL.

Few cases perhaps show more the love of torture which seems to exist in some uncultivated minds.

As a rule it is frequently seen that those who are the greatest cowards—the men who shrink from every threatened punishment with the greatest awe—are, however, the greatest tyrants, and the most brutish when in power.

In August, 1838, a trial for a barbarous murder came on for hearing at the Central Criminal Court, which certainly shows the brutality of the hearts of some people, and should be a caution to those who would put youths to sea, as to the captains or mates under whose care they might trust their sons.

It appears that a man named Benjamin Driscoll was employed among the crew of the ship "Eleanor," and he was kept so many hours at work that exhausted nature gave way, and he could scarcely by any means keep awake at his post.

THE LIFE OF WILLIAM CALCRAFT, THE HANGMAN.

MURDER BY TORTURE ON BOARD A VESSEL.

The mate of the vessel, who was named Clarke, seemed to delight in the torture of forcing the unfortunate man to go on working without cessation or sleep.

When it was the man's turn to go down to his hammock the mate detained him again and again on deck, and made him walk about with a handspike on his shoulder, as a punishment.

The mate said that if Driscoll would sing a song he would let him go below to his berth.

This the man did, but the mate then only laughed at him, and then kept him to work again.

Ultimately the man said: If I have done anything wrong I would sooner receive any other punishment at once than be kept, without sleep, to the cruel torture of work. As I cannot longer stand without sleep, I would sooner submit to be flogged. He did not care what it was with providing they would allow him one half hour's sleep.

The mate then said: Very well then, you shall have a rope's-ending with your clothes off, and then I will let you go for half an hour.

The man consented, and the mate sent the boy Jack for "a point" (a strong rope tarred at the end).

With this the unhappy man was fearfully flogged; but after that the mate only laughed at him, and then set him to work again.

The man again prayed for even twenty minutes' sleep, and the mate then said he should have it if he would submit to a flogging with a cat made of eight or nine twisted lines.

This the man submitted to.

After this the man fell senseless on the deck, and they filed his mouth with horrible filth.

He begged for something to drink, and the mate then ordered some brine to be fetched from the "stink tub."

They rubbed him with this, and then threw water over him.

The evidence showed that the mate, when the man's muscles were drawn up with the pain, only laughed, and said he had nothing the matter with him but cramp.

After being kept a long time in this manner he was carried down, helpless and senseless, to his hammock.

The particulars are too terrible and revolting to fully relate, but the man begged that they would read prayers over him, sew him up in canvas and throw him overboard rather than prolong his torture.

He said he now knew he was dying, and he implored them to let him have a prayer-book to read a few prayers.

This also was refused him.

The man at length died in the most terrible agony; and when examined it was said his body in appearance looked like a bullock's liver.

In the course of the trial it was asked where the captain was all this time.

It was then shown that he was the father of the mate, Clarke.

When the ship arrived home, Clarke the mate, and Mitchell, the cook of the vessel, were indicted for the wilful murder of the deceased.

The jury acquitted Mitchell, and returned a verdict of manslaughter against the mate Clarke, and he was sentenced to three months' imprisonment in Brixton gaol.

The sentence and case generally caused intense excitement and dissatisfaction.

The case, however, is one showing very strongly the vagaries and the absurd uncertainties in the administration of the law.

CHAPTER LIV.

THE CHARTIST RIOTS.

The tide of revolution which threatened to sweep over the country in 1829 and 1830, after receding for a time, returned again with greater violence and force in 1839 and 1840.

The determination to obtain greater Parliamentary reforms, or to involve the country in the civil war of a revolution seemed to have fermented almost the entire working classes.

Scarcely ever before was there such a widespread and determined organisation, and the movement was all the more formidable because it was led in many instances by men of intelligence and education.

Some of them no doubt were inspired by feelings of true patriotism, whilst others were violent and unscrupulous

An agitation had been going on to obtain what was considered to be the rights of the people—namely, the People's Charter, or the "five points."

These were—"the vote by ballot," "universal suffrage," "annual Parliaments," "payment of members," and "the abolition of a property qualification."

The national petition for this object was signed by 1,200,000 persons, and was presented to the House of Commons by Mr. Thomas Attwood, on the 14th of June, 1839.

During the whole of that year the country was greatly agitated, and various arrests were made.

One of the most notable was a Mr. Stephens, a Wesleyan local preacher, who was carried to Manchester under strong escort for advising the people to get pikes, guns, pistols, and any other weapons they could obtain, and, if they had not those, then to get their knives and forks and apply them to the tyrants' throats.

He further added that they need not fear the military or police, for they in heart were with the people.

Among some of the prominent leaders in the cause were the late lecturer, Henry Vincent, Arthur O Neil, and many others, who, by their voice and pen, in more temperate language, have done much to aid the cause of reform, though in their younger days they suffered in reputation, and some of them endured imprisonment too.

Henry Vincent, with Mr. W. Edmonds, W. A. Townsend, and John Dickinson, all Chartist leaders, were tried at Monmouth for sedition.

All the prisoners were found guilty.

Vincent was sentenced to one year's imprisonment, Edwards to nine months, and Dickenson and Townsend to six months each.

The work of agitation, however, went on, and movements of a threatening and alarming character were made throughout the land.

The Chartists were in the habit of going round from house to house with two books, and saying that those persons who subscribed should be put down in one book, while the non-subscribers were entered in the other.

The non-subscribers were informed that a time would come when the refusal to subscribe would be remembered.

Those who put down their names paid a small contribution, and received in return a ticket, which they were told would be a security to the person who held it when the day of revolution came.

Simultaneously with the Chartist agitation there was also going on at the same time the movement for the repeal of the corn laws.

The Government became anxious for the safety of the country, especially as the Chartist organization so rapidly spread.

Serious conflicts with the police occurred in many places—Devizes, Llanidloes in Wales, Sheffield, Bolton, Newcastle, and the district of the Potteries, but in the month of July, 1839, the town of Birmingham became the scene of the most alarming disturbances.

While the National Convention was holding its sittings in that town the Chartists assembled every evening on the open ground called the Bull-ring.

On the 5th of July the Chartists met as usual.

The borough magistrates, however, who had for some time been in communication with the Home Office, had bespoken a picked body of sixty policemen from London.

They were brought by train that evening to Birmingham, and, without even waiting for the co-operation of the military, they proceeded immediately to the scene of confusion.

They began by ordering the people to disperse, but when this injunction was seen to take no effect, the police filed off four abreast, and made for the monument of Lord Nelson, which stood in the Bull-ring, and which was set round with the flags of the convention.

These they succeeded in capturing, but the Chartists, who had been at first disconcerted by the impetuosity of the charge, when they beheld their ensigns, one of which bore a death's head, in the hands of the enemy, made a desperate return, recovered the contested banners, and then, in turn, made a terrible onslaught on the police.

At this time the 4th Dragoons arrived on the spot. Riding up every avenue which led to the place, they completely enclosed the Bull-ring, and the appearance of the military caused a great many of the people to disperse.

The cavalry pursued the people down Digbeth, and up Bromsgrove-street to St. Thomas's Church.

Here, however, some of the Chartists made a stand, tore up the palisades, and for a time a general fight ensued.

Some of the Chartist leaders were arrested, and the others for the night dispersed.

A large force of military remained in the Bull-ring, and almost the whole of the loyal inhabitants who were sworn in as special constables, paraded the various districts of the town during the night.

The next day the riots were partially resumed, and for some days the town was in great excitement.

On the 15th of July a number of houses were attacked, and some were fired.

The police-station in Moor-street was also partly destroyed by the rioters, and in the general battle which then ensued, no sort of weapon came amiss; broken flagstaves, heavy bludgeons, old scythes, and the loosened pavements were brought into use as weapons wherewith to fight.

A number of houses were attacked, and damage to property done.

PROPOSED GENERAL RISING THROUGHOUT THE COUNTRY.

The movement began in England, and rapidly spread to Wales, and in the same year great preparations were made for a general rising throughout the country.

People who supported the Chartist movement marched by thousands over the country, armed with guns, pikes, and pistols, and headed by their various leaders.

Before the day of battle came, however, some of their leaders were arrested and brought to trial.

The news of their arrest caused great consternation among the supporters of the movement.

CHAPTER LV.

FROST, WILLIAMS, AND JONES SENTENCED TO DEATH.

ON the 1st January, 1840, a special commission was opened at Monmouth to try some of the Chartist leaders who had been arrested.

The judges were Lord Chief Justice N. Tindal, Mr. Baron Parke, and Mr. Justice Williams.

The prisoners, John Frost, Zephaniah Williams, and William Jones were then placed at the bar charged with high treason in levying war against her Majesty, in endeavouring to compass the deposition of the Queen from her throne, and also with levying war against the Queen, with the intent to compel her to change her measures.

The Attorney-General, in stating the case for the prosecution, first described the geography of the country, in which he said that it was wild and mountainous, and abounded with mines of coal and iron.

Fifty years since there was scarcely any inhabitants save a few shepherds scattered in huts—now there was a dense population of upwards of 40,000.

The disposition of these people was not peaceable, owing to the influence the Chartist leaders had obtained over them.

In order to press on the Chartist movement it had been arranged that the members of the association should assemble on the night of the 3rd of November, 1839, being the evening immediately preceding the day appointed for a general insurrection.

They were to assemble in three principal divisions. The first division was to be under the command of the prisoner, John Frost, who was to assemble his men at Blackwood.

The second division was to be under the command of the prisoner, Zephaniah Williams, who was the keeper of a beer-shop much higher up the country, at a place called Coalbrook-vale; and the third division was to be under the command of the prisoner, William Jones, who was a watchmaker, residing at Pontypool.

All the divisions were to meet at Risca about midnight on Sunday, and then they were all to march upon the town of Newport, at which it was intended they should arrive about two o'clock on the morning of Monday, the 14th—a time when it was supposed that no suspicions would be aroused, no preparations for defence made, at the dead hour of the night when the peaceful inhabitants, buried in sleep, would be unprepared to offer the slightest resistance to their treasonable designs.

On their arrival at Newport it was arranged that the Chartists should attack the troops, break down the bridge which crosses the splendid river Usk, and thus stopping her Majesty's mail, signal rockets were to be thrown up upon the hills; and the stopping of the mail was to be a signal, by its non-arrival for an hour and a half over its usual time at Birmingham, to those who, it was said, were there connected with these treasonable designs, for a rising at Birmingham, and a general rising throughout the North of England, and the law of the Charter was at once to be proclaimed throughout the land.

The Attorney-General then proceeded to narrate the various orders in which the vast assembly of Chartists moved.

The prisoner, John Frost, remained with this body under his command until daylight, waiting the arrival of other bodies. There were then with him at least 5000 men, most of whom were armed, some with guns, others with swords, a large number with pikes, and some with mandrels—a sort of instrument with which they cut coal, a kind of pickaxe, and others were armed with scythes fixed on sticks, while others were provided with bludgeons of various sizes.

He then described the march towards Newport, and the manner in which Frost acted, while waiting for the other divisions, who were late coming up.

As they were late Frost marched towards the town, and gave the command to "Fire."

The Attorney-General next stated the means taken to defend the town, and the manner in which the Government having received information of the general rising, and the threatened revolution throughout the country, arrested the leaders and brought the present prisoners to trial.

A vast number of witnesses were then called, and many interesting facts were laid before the jury.

Some of the witnesses gave evidence of the hundreds of volleys fired by the Chartists; how the windows were broken by staves, and how, in the early morn, the dead were lying about.

Other witnesses stated how the town was saved from further slaughter and devastation by the prompt action of the military, and the case for the prosecution then closed.

Mr. Fitzroy Kelly then addressed the jury in a most able speech on behalf of the prisoners.

The jury found the prisoners guilty.

Proclamation having been made for all persons to keep silence while sentence of death was being passed upon the prisoners.

The three learned judges put on their black caps, and the greatest solemnity prevailed.

The Lord Chief Justice, addressing the prisoners, said that they who by armed numbers, or violence, or by terror, endeavour to put down established institutions, and to introduce in their stead a new order of things, open wide the flood-gates of rapine and bloodshed, destroy all security of property and life, and do their utmost to involve a whole nation in anarchy and ruin.

It had been proved that they had combined together to lead from the hills, at the dead hour of midnight, into the town of Newport, many thousands of men armed with weapons of a dangerous description, in order that they might take possession of the town, and supersede the lawful authority of the Queen.

It was entirely owing to the interposition of Providence alone that their wicked designs were frustrated by the greater number of the band not arriving till daylight, or the consequences would have been worse perhaps than a foreign invasion.

By the penalty they were about to suffer they would be held up as a warning to their fellow-men.

The sentence of the Court upon each of you is, therefore, that you John Frost, Zephaniah Williams, and William Jones be taken from hence to the place from whence you came, and be thence drawn on a hurdle to the place of execution, and that each of you be there hanged by the neck until you be dead, and that afterwards the head of each of you shall be severed from his body, and the body of each, divided into four quarters, shall be disposed of as her Majesty shall think fit, and may the Lord have mercy on your souls.

Sentence of death was also recorded against other prisoners, for participation in the Chartist movement.

For various reasons, however, the sentence was commuted.

There was a strong feeling at that time set in against capital punishment, and this was urged as one reason why the dreadful sentence was not carried out.

It was further urged that if the lives of the leaders were spared it would tend to appease the people, whilst on the other hand, if the executions were carried out there might be further outrages.

Another reason set forth with great force was, that as the young Queen was just on the point of marriage with Prince Albert, it would be a fitting act of grace which would cause her Majesty to be honoured and revered, and her person and life held sacred by the general body of the people. These arguments had great weight, and the sentences were commuted to transportation for life.

CHAPTER LVI.
ATTEMPTED ASSASSINATION OF THE QUEEN AND PRINCE ALBERT BY EDWARD OXFORD.

THE year 1840 was also a very remarkable year in the social history of the country, and it was also characterised by many dastardly outrages of a violent description.

Shortly after the assassination of Lord William Russell, London—in fact, the whole civilised world—on the 10th of June, 1840, was startled and agitated by a report of a dastardly attempted assassination of her Majesty Queen Victoria, and the late deeply-lamented Royal Consort of the Queen, H.R.H. Prince Albert.

It appears that at a quarter-past six on Wednesday evening, the day in question, the young Queen, accompanied by her revered husband, Prince Albert, left Buckingham Palace in a very low open phaeton, drawn by four bays, to take their usual drive in Hyde Park before dinner.

It happened that the Queen sat that evening on the left, and not on the right side of Prince Albert, where she usually sat, so that as they went up Constitution-hill, the road leading from Buckingham Palace to Hyde Park Corner, her Majesty was next to the long brick wall on the left side of the road, instead of the open railings of the Green Park on the right.

The carriage had proceeded a short distance up the road when a young man, who had been standing with his back to the Green Park fence, advanced to within a few yards of the carriage, and then deliberately fired, pointing towards the Queen.

The ball, happily, did not take effect, and her Majesty rose from her seat, but she was instantly pulled down again by Prince Albert.

As might be expected in a moment of such terrible peril, she turned pale, and appeared excessively alarmed, but made no exclamation.

The supreme calmness and presence of mind of Prince Albert doubtless tended to save her life, by his thus preventing her from rising up, and thus offering the assassin a better aim.

The postillions paused for an instant, but Prince Albert in a loud voice ordered them to drive on.

The assassin immediately said, "I have got another," and he then discharged a second pistol at her Majesty, which also proved harmless.

The miscreant was at once secured, and gave his real name as Edward Oxford.

It was ascertained that he had lodged at 6, West-street, West-square, Lambeth, and that his last employment was that of a barman at a public-house, the

"Hog in the Pond," Oxford-street, at the corner of South Molton-street.

The miraculous preservation of her Majesty and Prince Albert was the cause of general rejoicing, as the death of either would have been a national calamity.

The prisoner, Edward Oxford, who was then about eighteen years of age, was afterwards tried at the Central Criminal Court for high treason, before Lord Denman, Baron Alderson, and Mr. Justice Patteson.

A great deal of evidence was given, and the jury found the following special verdict:—

"We find the prisoner, Edward Oxford, guilty of discharging the contents of two pistols, but whether or not they were loaded with ball has not been satisfactorily proved to us, he being of unsound state of mind at the time."

A great deal of legal discussion ensued, and the verdict was amended.

He was then found guilty of high treason, but the jury also found that he was insane at the time.

He was ordered to be detained during her Majesty's pleasure.

There appeared to be some doubt as to whether there were any balls in either of the pistols; but, if so, the life of her Majesty and that of Prince Albert seem to have been preserved in a most providential manner, and the nation has since enjoyed the fruits of the great encouragement which Prince Albert gave to the study of the arts and sciences, and the country has greatly profited and advanced under the long and peaceful reign of her Majesty the Queen.

CHAPTER LVII.
UNAVENGED MURDER OF MR. TEMPLEMAN.

On the 23rd of March, 1840, Mr. John Templeman, an elderly man, of small property, who resided in a cottage in Pocock's Fields, Islington, was found murdered.

His hands were tied together with a cord, a gory stocking was found fastened over his eyes, and his head was smashed and bleeding.

Suspicion fell upon a man, named Richard Gould, and John and Mary Jarvis, and they were arrested.

The prisoners were all about twenty-four years of age.

The chief witness against Gould was a Mrs. Mary Allen, the landlady, with whom he lodged, who stated that he was out on the night in question.

He was also seen washing blood from his clothes.

A stocking containing £4 19s. was also found secreted in the roof of his lodgings.

The other two prisoners were acquitted, but he was committed for trial.

He was tried at the Central Criminal Court, for the murder, before Mr. Justice Littledale and Baron Alderson.

A very great deal of circumstantial evidence was given.

The judge, in summing up, told the jury that, however suspicious the case might be, if they felt any doubt, they must give the prisoner the benefit of it.

Eventually they found him not guilty.

It appears that the law officers of the Crown felt justified in offering a reward for such evidence as would lead to a conviction, and a reward of £200 was offered for the apprehension of the murderer.

At the conclusion of the trial Gould took a passage on board a vessel for Sydney, but the ship was followed by some of the detectives as far as Gravesend, and the bill offering the reward was shown to Gould.

He was asked if he could tell anything about the case, and he then said that if they would give him £100 and a free passage to Sydney he would tell all about it, and who committed the murder.

He was then re-arrested on the charge of burglary, by breaking into Mr. Templeton's house, and stealing therefrom.

While in the cell he made a statement, in which he said that the robbery was planned by Jarvis, Mrs. Jarvis, and himself; that Jarvis and he went to the cottage on the night of the murder, whilst Mrs. Jarvis kept watch outside, and that Jarvis then murdered the deceased with a stick which he brought with him.

Jarvis and his wife were then re-apprehended and brought to Bow-street.

He then, when taken before the magistrates, said that his story against Jarvis and his wife was a mere fabrication to get the £200 reward.

Jarvis and his wife were then discharged, and the prisoner Gould was committed to take his trial for burglary.

On the trial he told the judge that he knew nothing of the robbery or murder, and that his only reason for saying that the Jarvises were implicated was because Sergeant Otway pressed him to disclose all the facts, and had said to him that as he was leaving the country £200 would be of use to him, and nothing more could be done to him.

The case created great excitement at the time, shows the various subterfuges prisoners will put forth, and the utter unreliability of some of the statements they make.

He was found guilty of the burglary, and sentenced to transportation.

MURDER OF MR. BURDON IN EASTCHEAP.

On the night of the 21st of September, 1841, a shocking murder was committed at the "King's Head" public-house, Eastcheap.

It appears that on the evening in question a man man named Robert Blakesley accosted Sergeant Bradley of the City police, and asked him which was the best way to get his wife out of the "King's Head."

It appears that his wife was sister to Mrs. Burdon, the landlady of the public-house, and she used to be engaged serving there.

The officer told him he had better go quietly and ask her to come away.

About ten o'clock, however, Blakesley ran into the house in an excited state, and seeing his wife sitting down, he ran behind the bar. He pulled a butcher's knife out of his pocket, and stabbed her in a fearful manner.

Mr. Burdon got up to the rescue, and he stabbed him.

He next stabbed Mrs. Burdon, who ran upstairs bleeding from her wounds.

Mr. Burdon died in the course of a very little time, but the wife of Mr. Burdon, and Mrs. Blakesley, the wife of the murderer, recovered.

The prisoner made his escape for some time, but was ultimately arrested, and tried before Mr. Justice Abinger.

Evidence was given showing that the prisoner had remonstrated at various times against his wife being there, and that he had demanded her return home. The jury found him guilty, and he was executed by Calcraft on the 15th of November, 1841.

EXECUTION OF DANIEL GOOD.

This extraordinary criminal was executed by Calcraft in the front of Newgate on the 23rd of May, 1842, for the wilful murder of Jane Jones, otherwise Jane Good.

The discovery of the murder, and the circumstances which led to the conviction of this most notorious murderer are about the most remarkable on record.

Daniel Good was a middle-aged Irishman in the employment as coachman of Mr. Shiell, an East India merchant, residing at Granard-lodge, Roehampton.

On the 6th of April, 1842, Good called in a chaise at the shop of Mr. Collingbourn, a pawnbroker, in Wandsworth, and bought a pair of black-knee breeches, which he took on credit.

The shop-boy saw him at the same time put a pair of trousers under his coat skirt, and place them with the breeches in the chaise.

Mr. Collingbourn followed him out, and charged him with the theft, but he denied it, and hurriedly drove off.

The pawnbroker sent a policeman, William Gardner, after the thief, and with the officer went the shop-boy and Robert Speed, a neighbour.

Good lived at the stables, about a quarter of a mile from Mr. Shiell's house, and the boy went and rang the bell, whilst Gardner, the policeman, kept in the back ground.

Good answered the bell, and the policeman stepped forward and told him that he had orders to arrest him for stealing a pair of trousers.

Good positively denied having done so, but the policeman said he must come in and search the place. He then pushed his way in, and the boy and Mr. Speed followed.

Having searched some portion of the place, they proceeded to search the stable, but Good put his back against the door, and tried hard to hinder them.

While searching one of the stalls, they pulled out some hay, and then found what they at first thought was part of the carcase of a pig.

The boy, who was the first to see exactly what it was, said, "Why, it's part of the body of a woman!"

When they got it into the light they discovered that it really was the trunk of a female, with the head, legs, and arms chopped off.

As soon as the discovery was made Good, though under arrest for the robbery of the trousers, slipped out of the stable door, the key of which, by the policeman, had thoughtlessly been left in the lock outside.

Having thus got them safe inside Good shut the door, and locked Mr. Speed and the boy and the policeman inside.

He then took the key and made good his escape.

As it was a strong door, and the stable was a considerable distance from the house, they were some time trying with a stable fork to open it, during which time Good got miles away.

On examing another of the stalls they discovered a large quantity of blood, and also a heavy axe, and a saw all covered with gore.

In fact, the place looked like a slaughter-house, and it was very apparant that a dreadful murder had only recently been committed.

They next went to the coach-house, attracted by the dreadful smell emanating from the place.

Here they found a large fire laid, and on the ground a quantity of charred bones, the remains of which led to the supposition that the head, legs, feet, hands, and arms of the unfortunate victim had already been burnt.

Information in the meantime had been conveyed to the police at Wandsworth, and an immediate search for Good was commenced.

All efforts, however, to find him were for some time fruitless.

The next chief obstacle in the case was the difficulty of identification as no one could recognise the body, and for some time no one knew who she was.

From inquiries made, however, it was ascertained that Good had been renting a kitchen at 18, Southampton-street, Manchester-square, where he formerly had in keeping a woman named Jane Jones, whom he at one time professed to be courting, but to whom afterwards he was said to be married, and who had recently passed as Mrs. Good.

There was also living with her an intelligent boy about ten years of age, who was said to be a son of Good by a former wife.

This boy was always instructed to call her mother, and in his evidence at the inquest he stated that he had always been told that she was his own mother's sister, who had died about seven years previously.

The medical evidence showed that the doctors believed the remains to be those of a finely developed young woman, about twenty-four years of age, who had never borne a child, but who would have given birth to one in about five months.

It was also shown that Jane Jones, alias the reputed wife of Good, had on the previous Saturday afternoon gone out to meet her supposed husband.

She and Good were seen together at Barnes, and they were finally traced together to the stable, where, on the Sunday night, she evidently went to sleep with Good.

She was said to be thought forty years of age.

The motive for the murder was supposed to lie in the fact that Good had recently been keeping company with a young woman named Lydia Susannah Butcher, who had formerly been in respectable service at Wimbledon, but who, at the time of the murder, was living with her father at 13, Charlotte place, Woolwich.

Though over fifty years of age, Good was accepted, and engaged to be married to this girl, and he was looked upon as her future husband.

He had told her that his wife was dead, and that there was a good deal of clothing, and a mangle of hers which the girl, Lydia Susannah Butcher, could have.

The coroner's jury found a verdict that the remains found were those of Jane Jones, alias Mrs. Good, and that she was wilfully murdered by her reputed husband, Daniel Good.

A reward was offered for his apprehension, and another wife of Good was found residing at Flower and Dean-street, Spitalfields.

She was an old woman who kept a stall, and was known by the name of "old Molly Good."

After his escape from the stable, it would appear that Good immediately went to the old woman, and told her that he was sorry he had been such a bad husband, and that he wished to come back and live with her.

He, however, had previously been and fetched away all the things belonging to Jane Jones from Southampton-street, and also the boy, and had told the landlady that she was not coming back again.

The police having ascertained that old Molly Good was Daniel Good's wife, kept a watch on the place, but instead of going in plain clothes, they went making inquiries about him in uniform.

Good, who was in the house, was watching for their coming, and as soon as he saw them he again made off, and got clear away.

The whole of the police who managed this part of the business in such a bungling manner got discharged.

It was now some time before Good was heard of

again, and perhaps he would never have been discovered had not the reward offered for his apprehension caused the people throughout the country to keep a sharp look-out.

On the 16th of April he was at length recognised at Tunbridge Wells, by a man who had formerly known him, and at which place he had obtained employment as a labourer.

When he was first accosted as Daniel Good he denied in the most positive manner that that was his name.

He was then passing in the name of Connor, and to all persons who came to see him he declared that Connor was his name.

The police were further communicated with, and he was eventually identified beyond a doubt.

He was brought to London and tried at the Central Criminal Court, before Lord Denman, Baron Alderson, and Mr. Justice Coltman.

The Attorney-General, Mr. Waddington, Mr. Adolphus, and Mr. Russell Gurney, the late Recorder of London, were for the prosecution, and Mr. Deane was for the prisoner.

The jury found him guilty.

When asked in the usual way whether he had anything to say why sentence of death should not be passed upon him he said that he was entirely innocent, that he did not take the life of the deceased, but that she committed suicide herself, by cutting her throat with a knife, because she had found out that he was keeping company with Lydia Susannah Butcher, and she was jealous of her.

He added that when he found her dead he consulted a man who used to come round with matches, and asked him what he had best do with the body.

The match man said he had better burn it, and he offered for the sum of one sovereign to cut the body up, and burn some, and carry the rest away.

He gave the man a sovereign to do this, and the match man did part of it, and left the rest.

The learned judges then assumed their black caps, and sentence of death was passed upon him in the usual form.

In the condemned cell Good adhered to this statement, but no one appeared to give it the slightest evidence.

On the morning of the execution Calcraft arrived at Newgate about half past seven. Shortly before eight Good was introduced to him, and Calcraft pinioned him.

The procession to the gallows was then formed.

Up to the last moment Good kept saying, "I have never taken a life."

Dr. Carver, the chaplain, endeavoured to prevail upon him not to go to his death with a lie on his lips, but the culprit seemed to cling to the hope that his protestations of innocence might save his life.

When Calcraft had pulled the white cap over his face and adjusted the noose, the culprit at the last moment seemed as though he wished to say something more, and cried out, "Stop, stop!"

Calcraft, however, gave him no more time.

As soon as the Ordinary came to the fatal words, "In the midst of life we are in death," Calcraft pulled the bolt, and the culprit fell.

The crowd who witnessed the execution was one of the largest that had ever assembled in front of Newgate.

DISCOVERY OF AN UNKNOWN MURDER AT BLACKHEATH.

On the 24th of January, 1844, as a labourer was digging about thirty yards from the high road leading to Shooter's-hill, Blackheath, he came upon some bones.

He proceeded very cautiously, and then discovered the entire skeleton of a young female.

She had hair of great length, of a light gold colour, beautifully braided.

On examination by medical men, a deep, distinct fracture at the back of the head was found; and the skull being completely beaten in, it was evident that a foul and mysterious murder had been committed.

EXECUTION OF WILLIAM SAVILLE.
AWFUL CATASTROPHE.

Among the many frightful scenes which from time to time occurred at Calcraft's executions, one particularly lamentable occurred on the 7th of August, 1844, at Nottingham, at the execution of William Saville, for the murder of his wife and three children at Colwick.

On the trial, the unfortunate man was found guilty of the whole of the murders.

It appears that he lived very unhappily with his wife, with whom he had been intimate before marriage.

Before his execution he made a statement which he said was a narrative of his life.

He said that he had been compelled to marry the woman against his will, by two of her friends who threatened to murder him if he did not.

They put up the banns in church without his knowledge, and then, when the day arrived, they made him intoxicated early in the day, and took him to the church and got him married without him knowing what he was about.

Though he had not known his wife long, she gave birth to a child shortly after marriage, which he said could not be his.

They lived so unhappily that he determined to drown them, and he took them one night out for a walk for that purpose. He, however, did not do so.

On the following day the woman and her three children, it appears, were found in a wood at Colwick with their throats cut, and the razor was so placed in the woman's hand as to try and make it appear that she had murdered the children, and afterwards committed suicide.

The medical evidence, however, showed that the razor was in her hand in such a position that she could not have inflicted the wound on herself.

In his confession he admitted that he had murdered his wife, and placed the razor, as described, in her hand, but he positively declared that he had not murdered the children.

He asserted that his wife had often threatened to murder the children, and that while he left her in the wood a little time she did so.

He came back and saw her with one child on her knee cutting its throat.

He was so put out that he said that he would serve her the same, and he then did so.

The gallows was erected in front of the county hall, and one of the largest concourses of people ever known assembled.

When Calcraft arrived, Saville submitted to be pinioned with great firmness.

A great party of roughs of the worst description assembled in front of the drop, and amongst the dense crowd were many well-dressed people and young girls.

While the awful preparations were going on inside the gaol, the most shocking outrages were going on outside.

Women and girls were literally stripped of their

clothes by the gangs of vagabonds assembled, and as the crowd was so dense none could make their escape.

Numerous pockets were picked, and the thieves obtained a great booty.

When the culprit appeared a yell was set up.

Calcraft performed his work expeditiously, the drop fell, and the wretched man was launched into eternity.

TERRIBLE LOSS OF LIFE.

As soon as the drop had fallen the roughs began to scatter in gangs in all directions, and to crush among the people for the purposes of robbery.

They were in such numbers that it is said the swaying and crushing of the crowd was like the surging of mighty waves.

There was no standing up against the onward onslaught of the roughs.

Women, boys, and girls in numbers were thrown down, trampled upon, and marched over.

The shrieking of the people being trodden to death was fearful.

Eventually the pressure from the outside was loosened, and twelve persons were then brought out dead from among the crowd.

Their names were Mary Stevenson, aged thirty-three, of Daybrook; Mary Percival, aged thirteen, Convent-street; Milicent Shaw, aged nineteen; Eliza Smithurst, nineteen; James Marshall, fourteen; Mary Easthope, fourteen; Thomas Easthope, her brother, aged nine; Eliza Shuttleworth, twelve; James Fisher, twenty-two; John Bednell, fourteen; Hannah Smedley, sixteen; and Thomas Watson, fourteen.

In addition to the above killed there were twenty-one so dangerously wounded that in some instances their arms and legs were obliged to be amputated, and others were not expected to survive.

An inquest was held on the bodies, and a verdict of accidental death returned.

CHAPTER LVIII.
EXECUTION OF JOHN TAWELL.

This remarkable criminal was executed at Aylesbury Gaol by Calcraft on the 28th of March, 1845.

From early life he had been a member of the Society of Friends, but the love of women brought him, as it has many other men, to the gallows in the end.

In his youth he was dissipated, and in his younger days he committed forgery.

Owing to his religious connections with the Quakers, great efforts were made to save his life, and for the crime of forgery he was sent into transportation.

By his good conduct he obtained a ticket-of-leave, and while in Australia he commenced business as a chemist and druggist.

He had a good trade, amassed a considerable sum of money, but losing his wife he came to England.

After the death of his wife, whose death, it is said, was not very satisfactorily accounted for, it being supposed she was poisoned, he took into his service a fine young woman, about thirty years of age, named Sarah Hart.

She, however, became *enceinte* by him, and, in order to avoid the disgrace, it was arranged that she should leave his house.

He used to visit her at her lodgings at Crawford-street, Paddington-green, and afterwards he took a small cottage for her at Bath-place, Salt-hill, Slough.

Here she resided for some time with the two children she had by him.

Tawell then got married again to a highly-respectable young lady, also a member of the Society of Friends, and he lived with her in apparent affluence at Berkhampstead.

He built schools, established savings banks, and contributed to several institutions.

His means, however, were really not equal to this outward show. Though he still adhered to the usual garb of dress worn by the Quakers, also to the simplicity of their language, and their usual quiet demeanour, he was not recognised by them, but was excluded from their association.

He was known to be a libertine, considered by them to be a hypocrite, and to be a disgrace to the cloth he wore.

His wife, who, though at one time she was greatly respected, was also excluded from their fellowship by marrying him, and in spite of all his outward professions the society would not recognise him.

Twenty-five years had now passed away since his conviction and transportation for forgery, when on the night of the 1st of January, 1845, a terrible moaning and groaning was heard in Sarah Hart's cottage.

A neighbour named Mrs. Ashlee hearing her moan so, went across the garden to see what was the matter, and she found the unfortunate woman lying on the floor in the agonies of death.

Dr. Champney was immediately sent for, but when he arrived the woman was dying.

As Mrs. Ashlee, however, a few moments before was just going down the garden, she noticed a quiet elderly-looking man, who appeared like a Quaker, going away.

A person was sent after him to watch him, and the police were immediately communicated with. He was overtaken on his way as he went towards Eton, where he took train to London.

A telegram was immediately sent to the London police, asking particularly that a man might be watched who was expected to arrive in London, dressed like a Quaker.

A detective was accordingly sent to the station to watch him. On his arrival in London he took an omnibus and rode to the Jerusalem Coffee-house in Cornhill.

From here he fetched a coat that he had left there before starting. He asked to be allowed to leave it there for a short time while he went to the West-end.

This was no doubt done for the express purpose of setting up an alibi should he be suspected of the woman's death.

The detective, however, followed him there, and from thence to a coffee-house, kept by a Quaker in the Borough. where he stayed the whole of that night.

In the meantime the poor woman, Sarah Hart, had died from poisoning by prussic acid.

Tawell had chosen an evening in the very depth of winter to go quietly down to her house. He then sent her out for a bottle of porter.

Two glasses were found on the table, with a little porter in them.

One had the remains of prussic acid in it; the other had not.

On the police going to arrest him at the coffee-house in the Borough, he denied all knowledge of the deceased woman.

He said the police must be mistaken; he had not been to Slough at all, and his social standing and circumstance would place him above suspicion.

He was taken to Slough, where he was identified as the man seen to leave the cottage. His intimacy with the woman was proved.

He was shown to have overdrawn his banker's account, and it was proved that the woman was a burthen to him.

Evidence was also given of his having bought the poison in Bishopsgate-street before he started; and on being tried before Baron Parke, the jury found him guilty.

He acknowledged the justice of his sentence, and met his death firmly.

CHAPTER LIX.
MYSTERIOUS MURDER OF A POLICEMAN AT DAGENHAM.

On the 4th of July, 1846, a murder of a very atrocious character, the circumstances of which were left enveloped in deep mystery, came to light at Dagenham.

Owing to the evil deeds of the desperate gangs which at that time infested the shores of the river, a body of rural police was established.

They proved of great service in deterring the commission of some of the frightful outrages which took place on the river side.

Among the men of the force was a young man named George Clarke, who, on the night of Monday, the 29th of June, was ordered on the beat at the "Four Wants."

On the following morning he was not found on his beat, and a search was next day commenced in the numerous ponds of the vicinity.

After a lapse of five days the body of the unfortunate man was found in an adjoining field, with his head terribly beaten in.

His staff was also found, much cut and chopped about, and the throat of the deceased was fearfully cut.

Though an inquiry was held, no clue to the mystery was obtained.

It was shown, however, that the sergeant of that division, together with some of the other police, gave wrong statements as to their proceedings on the night, and they were arrested.

There was a strong suspicion against the sergeant, but whether the unfortunate man fell a victim to some of the desperate thieves of the locality, or whether he fell by the hands of some of his comrades through malice or revenge, was not proved, and the murder remained a mystery.

CHAPTER LX.
EXECUTION OF MANNING AND HIS WIFE.

THESE extraordinary criminals suffered the last penalty of the law in front of Horsemonger-lane Gaol, in the Borough, on the 13th Nov., 1849.

They were executed both together by Calcraft, and an immense concourse of about 10,000 persons assembled on the occasion.

The crime for which they suffered was for the murder of Mr. Patrick O'Connor, an officer of the Customs, and a man of reserved and selfish habits.

The man O'Connor was possessed of considerable property, and was unmarried, and in addition to the pay which he received from the Custom-house, he greatly increased his income as a usurer, by lending at exorbitant interest loans to petty tradesmen.

Mrs. Manning was a native of Switzerland, whose maiden name was Maria De Roux, and she was formerly lady's maid in the household of the Duchess of Sutherland.

She had considerable personal attractions, was a very vain, dressy woman, with a strong unscrupulous mind, and a determined will.

She was married to a man named Frederick George Manning, formerly a guard in the service of the Great Western Railway Company, from which he had been discharged owing to his having been suspected of participation in the great robberies which, prior to that time, had been committed on that line.

The man, Patrick O'Connor, formed an improper connection with Manning's wife, and for the sake of gain, Manning was the willing accomplice in his wife's immorality.

After Manning's discharge from the Great Western Railway Company's service, he and his wife kept an inn at Sainton, but they suddenly abandoned that, and took up their residence at No. 3, Miniver-place, Bermondsey.

On the 9th of August, 1849, Patrick O'Connor went out from his lodgings in Greenwood-street, Mile-end-road, and was afterwards not seen alive. Some days having elapsed without his returning, handbills were circulated offering a reward for his discovery.

He was known to keep a sort of illicit companionship with a Swiss lady, who frequently visited his house, and had access to his boxes and drawers.

On the night that he was missing, it was ascertained that she had been to his lodgings, and that she had been to his drawers and boxes, as she had done before.

On examining them, however, after she had gone, they were found to be rifled of their contents, and these circumstances gave rise to a suspicion that O'Connor had not been fairly dealt with, and that the two Mannings knew something both of him and his property.

Two officers, therefore, named Barnes and Barton, on the 17th of August proceeded to Manning's house, but found it empty.

Manning and his wife had sold their furniture and effects, and had hastily gone away.

The kitchen was left scrupulously clean, and the flags with which it was floored were carefully bathstoned.

One of the officers, while looking at the kitchen floor, observed that some of the joints of the flag-stones appeared to be damp, and that the cement between seemed scarcely to be dry.

Tools were procured, the flags raised, and after removing a few inches of soil the police discovered the projecting hand of the murdered man.

They dug a little further, and then they found his entire body, which was lying on the face, with the legs doubled up and tied to the haunches.

In order to hasten the process of decomposition and render identification impossible a quantity of lime had been thrown upon the body, and a great portion was burnt or corroded away.

A bullet was found near the temple, which led to the belief that O'Connor had been shot, but no report of any firearm had been heard.

In addition to the pistol shot, eighteen wounds were found inflicted upon the head.

Suspicion now, therefore, fixed itself exclusively on the Mannings, and the atrocious ingenuity with which they had carried out their design against the victim, and the knowledge that they had already a good start of the officers of justice, who were quite in the dark as to the track they had taken gave quite an edge to the eager anxiety of the public, whose desire for intelligence had never been exceeded in any case before.

The general solicitude was not kept long in suspense.

Tidings respecting the female fugitive soon reached the metropolis.

She was traced to Edinburgh, whither she had gone by railway by way of Newcastle.

On her way to the Euston-square terminus she had stopped at the South Eastern Railway station at London Bridge, where she deposited some of her largest boxes, having previously affixed cards to them, with the direction "Mrs. Smith, passenger, Paris—To be left till called for."

This she is believed to have done for the purpose of evading detection, or of setting her pursuers upon a wrong track.

On her arrival at Edinburgh she took lodgings at Haddington-place, Leith-walk, whence she soon after proceeded to the office of a sharebroker at the Royal Exchange, to whom she offered shares in the Amiens and Boulogne Railway, which she said she wished to dispose of if she could do so to advantage.

She was arrested and taken to the Southwark Police-station, where the charge was recorded.

She did not appear to be flurried in the least degree, or to be discomposed by the interrogatories addressed to her. In height she was rather above the middle stature, and her figure was large without being clumsy.

Her hair and eyes were dark, and her features, though they were neither regular nor feminine, were rather pleasing than otherwise, and she had evidently been a comely woman.

Her manners and appearance were just what might be expected in a domestic in one of the town establishments of the nobility.

Her age was entered on the charge-sheet as twenty-eight, but she looked at least five or six years older.

At length on the 30th of August Manning was arrested at Jersey, at half-past nine o'clock at night, in bed at a cottage kept by an aged peasant, near Beaumont, in the parish of St. Peter's.

He confessed the murder, adding that he was instigated to the act by his wife, and that she had shot O'Connor with a pistol as he was going downstairs to the kitchen for the purpose of washing his hands.

Manning, after the murder, had sold his furniture to a broker residing in Bermondsey-square, where he engaged apartments for himself and his wife; but on finding that she had absconded, he, two days after, proceeded in a cab by a circuitous route to the South-Western Railway, and thence to Southampton, where he embarked in a steam-boat for Jersey.

When Manning was arrested he voluntarily entered into particulars respecting the murder, which he said had been originally planned and wholly perpetrated by his wife.

He said that the hole in the kitchen floor in which the body was found had been dug many days before the murder; that it had been covered over with boards, and that the wretched victim had several times walked over it, and had inquired for what purpose it had been dug.

Manning added that his wife replied to O'Connor's inquiry by saying that the excavation had been made for the purpose of repairing a drain.

CHAPTER XLI.

EXAMINATION OF MANNING AT SOUTHWARK POLICE-COURT.

ON the 1st of September, 1849, both prisoners were brought up before the magistrate at Southwark Police-court, but were remanded for a week.

On the day appointed the two prisoners stood at the bar side by side.

The female prisoner conducted herself with the same apparent unconcern which she had exhibited on the previous occasion.

Manning appeared to feel his position. His appearance was altogether repulsive.

He was a bull-headed, thick-necked man, with a half-effeminate expression of countenance arising from a very fair complexion and light hair. Once seen he could not easily be forgotten.

The size of his face and the flabby appearance of the lower portion of it were particularly striking, the lower under jaw being clothed all round with folds of fat, which terminated in a huge double chin in front, and extended beneath the ear in lumps of flesh more like swellings than natural formations.

The mouth was unusually small, the lips were thin, and frequently compressed in a manner indicative of great obstinacy of character.

He seemed very nervous, and only once or twice raised his eyes from the ground.

The two prisoners were tried at the Old Bailey Sessions on the 5th of October, 1849, before Chief Baron Pollock, of the Court of Exchequer; Mr. Justice Maule, and Mr. Justice Cresswell, of the Court of Common Pleas. Sir John Jervis, the Attorney-General, with Mr. Clarkson, Mr. Bodkin, and Mr. Clerk, appeared for the Crown; Mr. Sergeant Wilkins, and Mr. Charnock for Manning; Mr. Ballantine and Mr. Parry for the female prisoner.

At the conclusion of the case the jury returned a verdict of guilty against both prisoners.

The Judge then assumed the black cap, and was beginning to pass sentence, when the female prisoner exclaimed—

"I want to say a few words. I have been convicted very unjustly by a jury of Englishmen. There is no law for me; no right. If I had been tried, as I demanded, by a jury half of foreigners, the result would have been different. I have had no protection either from the judge, or from the prosecutors, or from my husband. I am quite innocent of killing Mr. O'Connor. He was very good to me; he was more to me than my husband. If I had wished to have committed murder, how much more likely it would have been that I should have murdered that man (pointing to her husband), who has made my life like a hell on earth ever since I have known him. If I had been a widow, O'Connor would have married me the next month."

Manning eyed his wife intently, but said nothing.

The judge then proceeded to pass sentence on both, but Mrs. Manning, several times interrupting the judge, said, "No—no; I won't stand it. You ought to be ashamed of yourselves. There is neither law nor justice here."

She then tried to leave the dock, but the warders held her there till the sentence was passed.

She then took up some of the rue which it is usual to place on the front of criminals in the dock, and throwing it into the body of the court said, "Base England, I have had no justice here."

Manning received his sentence more coolly, and after sentence of death on both had been pronounced they both left the dock.

THE MANNINGS IN THE CONDEMNED CELL.

After his condemnation Manning retired to the condemned cell set apart for his use, and began to prepare his mind for his approaching end.

Though at times he was to a certain extent buoyed up with the hope that the efforts being made to save his life would be successful, yet he paid particular attention to his religious duties and the ministrations of the chaplain.

He wrote a letter to his wife, begging her also to make a full confession of her guilt and prepare for death, and also to grant him a personal interview.

This, however, she positively refused; and she appeared to hold towards him the most bitter feelings, partly from natural dislike, and partly from a feeling of revenge in consequence of his confession of their guilt.

In a letter to him she at one time tried to induce him to speak the truth, as she called it, and say "that it was that young man from Jersey, an acquaintance of his, who committed the murder in their absence."

This, however, he refused to do, and he made to the chaplain a very long statement, in which he alleged "that his wife shot O'Connor; that he helped to finish him by beating him about the head, and that he also assisted in burying him in the grave which his wife had dug for the man a fortnight before the murder."

He also made a statement of many other particulars—the names she called him in her charges of cowardice against him when he protested against the proposals of murder which she made.

He alleged that she used to say that she did not believe there was either God or devil, and that she oftentimes used to speak with approbation of some of the atrocities committed in the French Revolution.

He further averred his belief that much of her wickedness and the hardness of her heart was caused by the improper views she took of some of those terrible blood-stained acts.

Her general demeanour in the condemned cell appeared to support these assertions, for she remained callous to the last.

She paid little attention to the condemned sermon, and when they went into the chapel for a short service just before their execution she acted with comparative indifference.

At the conclusion Manning asked one of the warders to ask her whether she was going to death in that manner, and whether she would not kiss him and say "farewell" before they parted for ever.

The warder asked her, and at last she kissed him, and wished him good-bye, just before she left the chapel.

EXECUTION OF THE MANNINGS AT HORSEMONGER-LANE GOAL.

The hour of execution, on the 13th of November, had come, and Calcraft had already arrived at the gaol.

All efforts to make any good impression on the mind of Mrs. Manning were of little avail, and she was then given into the hands of Calcraft.

To the last her study seemed to be dress, and the last request she made was that she might be permitted to go to the gallows with a black silk bandage over her eyes.

This was granted, and she was then pinioned.

When all was ready the mournful procession was formed, and the chaplain and the warders led the way. The execution took place on the top of the gaol, and the culprits had a good distance to walk to the drop.

Manning was the first to ascend.

Then his wife with her eyes bandaged was also led on, and placed alongside him.

One of the warders took their hands and placed them together, and they finally shook hands together on the scaffold as well as the straps round their arms would permit.

Calcraft hastily shook hands with each, and then quickly running behind the scaffold, pulled the bolt, and the drop falling, the bodies of both heaved and vibrated before the vast concourse assembled.

SENSITIVENESS OF THE HANGMAN.

They both went down with a heavy thud, and Calcraft, all at once, turned deadly pale.

He at once ran down into one of the warders' rooms, asking a warder to accompany him, and give him some water.

Calcraft was nearly fainting, and some water having been given him, he asked to be taken into the yard.

One of the warders took him by the arm, and led him round the yard for fresh air.

After some time Calcraft was restored, and on the warder asking him what it was that affected him, he replied "That he always disliked the idea of hanging a man and his wife."

It may be here observed that Calcraft is said always to have lived happily with his own wife and family, and it is not at all improbable that his marital feeling caused him to sicken and shudder at the dreadful work he had had to carry out as the "finisher of the law."

After the bodies had hung an hour, however, he returned and cut the bodies down, and after casts of their heads had been taken they were buried within the precincts of the gaol.

The late Mr. Charles Dickens, who was present at the execution and during the preparations, describes the conduct of the pickpockets and roughs, and the execution generally, as one of the most appalling sights that could be witnessed.

CHAPTER LXII.
EXECUTION OF JAMES BLOMFIELD RUSH.

THIS extraordinary assassin was another of the notorious criminals executed by Calcraft.

He was hanged in front of Norwich Castle on the 21st of April, 1849.

This man had been a libertine, and many a heart and family were saddened by his criminal atrocities.

The crime, however, for which he suffered death was for the murder of Mr. Isaac Jermy, the Recorder of Norwich, and also for the murder of Mr. Jermy Jermy, his son, at their residence, Stanford Hall, Norfolk.

Having had a dispute with the father about a farm, Rush, on the evening of the 28th of November, 1848, went to Stanford Hall, and shot them with a pistol.

He was found guilty, and sentenced to death.

When the time for execution came he was conducted to the room of one of the turnkeys, where Calcraft, the executioner, was waiting to receive him.

On observing him, Rush said, "Is that the man that is to perform this duty?" to which the governor replied that it was.

Calcraft then desired him to sit down, and on his doing so he pinioned him.

He was then conducted to the gallows during the reading of the usual burial service, and he then suffered the extreme penalty of the law.

So ended the life of another of the most heartless scoundrels of this age. And here it may be stated, on the authority of a person yet alive, that Thurtell, executed in 1824, for the murder of Mr. Ware, James Greenacre, and Benjamin Blomfield Rush, had been all schoolfellows at Norwich.

CHAPTER LXIII.
EXECUTION OF WILLIAM PALMER FOR THE POISONINGS AT RUGELY.

OF all the cold deliberate murders perpetrated in Calcraft's time perhaps none exceeded in atrocity, the poisonings of William Palmer, of Rugely, Staffordshire.

Palmer was a surgeon residing in that town, and he had married an educated lady of considerable property.

He, however, was what is termed "a fast man;" he owned horses, and betted.

If ever there was one case worse than another which illustrates the evils of gambling, that one is Palmer's.

Owing to his gambling speculations and the fast life he led he became frequently involved.

He had also a circle of racing and betting friends, and among them was Mr. John Parsons Cook, who owned a horse named "Pole Star," which won a large stake.

In 1853 and 1854 Palmer, however, had got into great difficulties, and he sought to raise money on bills, and some of these were accepted by Cook.

Palmer became more and more involved, and then

he resorted to the practice of insuring the lives of his relatives and friends.

He insured the life of his wife to the amount of £13,000.

Though Palmer was frequently drawing money from Cook, yet he was fascinated with Palmer's company, and in any ailment employed him as his doctor.

Such was his leaning towards Palmer, that though while dying with poison, he said he thought that Palmer was dosing him, he yet took his medicines.

Ultimately Cook, aged twenty-eight, died, and on poison being found in his stomach Palmer was suspected and arrested.

It was then ascertained that Palmer had poisoned his wife, his own brother, and about thirteen other persons, and that as in most cases, as their lives had been insured for large amounts, Palmer had largely profited by their deaths.

By a special Act he was brought to the Central Criminal Court for hearing, and after a trial which lasted twelve days before the Lord Chief Justice Alderson and Mr. Justice Cresswell, he was found guilty of the death of Cook, and sentenced to death.

The Attorney-General, Mr. Edwin James, Q.C., Mr. Bodkin, Mr. Welsby, and Mr. Huddlestone, appeared for the Crown.

The prisoner was defended by Mr. Sergeant Shee, Mr. Grove, Q.C., Mr. Gray, and Mr. Kenealy.

He was hanged in front of Stafford Gaol in June, 1856, before one of the greatest crowds that ever assembled.

He died, protesting his innocence to the last.

The hangman in this case was George Smith, of Dudley, and not William Calcraft.

The London executioner, who had now been long in office and had performed executions nearly all over the kingdom, could not always attend, and, further than that, he had performed some of his operations in rather a clumsy manner.

Smith and one or two others had therefore taken work from his hands.

DEATH OF GEORGE SMITH, THE HANGMAN.

GEORGE SMITH, the executioner of Palmer, died on Friday, the 3rd of July, 1874, at his residence, Oakham, near Dudley.

The old man, who formerly had been a cow doctor, was seventy years of age, and retained his faculties until a day before his death.

Smith met Palmer in Stafford Gaol several years before Palmer was hung, Smith being a prisoner there for neglecting to maintain his wife.

It was during one of these imprisonments that he volunteered to hang one or two men condemned for a brutal murder while they were in the employment of Messrs. Pickford and Co.

In the course of his life Smith executed nearly sixty people, three of whom were females.

SHOCKING SCENE ON THE GALLOWS — EXECUTION OF WILLIAM BOUSFIELD.

DURING Calcraft's long career he had many terrible struggles with some of his unfortunate victims, and, in addition to his repulsive work of hanging, he was also an eye-witness of many shocking scenes on and around the gallows.

One of these occurred at the execution of William Bousfield, generally known as the Soho murderer.

He was thirty-seven years of age, a very tall man, a French polisher by trade, and lived with his wife and three children at 4, Portland-street, Soho.

He was an idle sort of man, passing much of his time in doing nothing.

His wife was a clean, hard-working, industrious woman, but there were sometimes words between him and his father-in-law, owing to his not providing better for his family.

The father, who resided in the same house, set his daughter up in a small stationery and sweetstuff shop. Early in February, 1856, William Bousfield went to the Bow-street police station, and gave himself up for murdering his wife and three children.

On the police going to the house, his statement was found to be true; he had cut the throats of all four, and had slightly attempted, by the same means, to kill himself.

He was tried at the Central Criminal Court, and on being found guilty was sentenced to death.

The evidence showed that he was greatly jealous of his wife, and that he did not like the civilities paid to her by the young men who came for tobacco and cigars, which they also kept.

A most shocking scene took place at the execution.

While he was in the condemned cell, the culprit pretended to be insane, in the hope of thereby getting a reprieve.

He threw himself on the fire, refused to take food, and did other similar stupid things.

The doctors were, however, of opinion that he was shamming, and the execution was ordered to proceed.

The execution took place at the latter end of March in front of Newgate.

Many thousands assembled, and the brutality and ribaldry round the gallows were truly shocking.

At that period the pickpockets and roughs were frequently a terror to respectable people, and there were often acts of violence perpetrated upon the police and others engaged in the administration of the law.

CALCRAFT'S LIFE THREATENED.

A few days before the execution of Bousfield, Calcraft received a letter stating that he had better provide himself with a helmet and a breastplate like those worn by the Horse Guards, for at the next execution he would most assuredly be shot.

Calcraft was greatly terrified, and for some time lived in constant terror of his life being taken.

There were various pamphlets published at the time against capital punishment, in which the executioner was spoken of as "that hideous, hard-hearted, old wretch, Calcraft, who could mount the scaffold and strangle, without remorse, man, woman, or child."

In some of these pamphlets some of the shocking scenes in the executions by Calcraft were graphically described and discussed.

They seem to have been written in a bitter and factious spirit, like many letters which have from time to time appeared.

When the time for Bousfield's execution came a series of shocking scenes were witnessed.

Calcraft, who was fearful of the outrages of the mob, stole secretly to Newgate.

When the time to pinion Bousfield came the culprit would not get up.

He lay down on the pallet of his cell with his head on his breast, as if unconscious of all around.

As he would not get up Calcraft pinioned him, lying down, and as he would not, or could not, either walk or stand, four stalwart warders were sent for, who put him in an armchair, and carrying him in it, placed him sitting in the chair underneath the drop.

Calcraft, who believed that the time was now also come when an attempt would be made upon his own life, scarcely dared to show himself on the scaffold.

At last he summoned courage to come stealthily on, and was received with yells and groans.

He put the rope round the culprit's neck, and then going behind pulled the bolt, and the drop fell.

As it went down, however, the culprit, who had been sitting on the chair, managed to get his feet on the drop, and he commenced, in the most violent manner, to try and free himself from the halter.

The sight of the man struggling with death was horrible to witness.

There were renewed hisses, and groans, and cries of "The man is being butchered! He is being murdered!"

While this fearful scene was going on, Calcraft had run away, and for some time was nowhere to be found.

At last he was discovered, and fetched back.

The yelling of the excited crowd was now terrific, and the executioner was positively afraid to face the crowd.

He, however, came on to the scaffold again, and pushed the culprit off into the drop beneath and then ran again.

Bousfield kicked and plunged fearfully, and actually succeeded in getting his legs on to the sides of the drop again, and another fearful struggle with death took place.

The hooting and execrations of the crowd were now redoubled, and came like the mighty roaring of fearful thunder.

Calcraft dreaded to come on the scaffold again, and the wretched man was once more pushed off the sides of the drop again.

Calcraft now seized the legs of the wretched man, and swung upon him, but even this was not sufficient to cause his death.

Several warders had to take hold of the body and also weight it down till at last the culprit was fairly strangled.

A special meeting of the Court of Aldermen was afterwards held, when the above facts were stated by the sheriffs, and Calcraft's conduct, especially his running away, and his dread of assassination were severely censured.

By some of the aldermen it was considered that he had held office long enough, and it was argued that, as he had been more than a quarter of a century in office, he had no longer nerve for the dreadful work, and that it was quite time he was pensioned off.

PAINFUL SCENE AT THE EXECUTION OF JOHN WIGGINS.

Eleven years later, a similar shocking scene to that at the execution of William Bousfield occurred at the same place at the hanging of John Wiggins.

This man was sentenced to death for the murder of a woman with whom he lived.

He protested his innocence all along, and when on the 15th of October, 1867, he appeared on the drop, the scene was most painful.

On the drop he again and again reiterated his innocence, and for some time struggled hard to prevent Calcraft from putting the rope round his neck.

He kept crying out, "Don't hang me, don't hang me! Cut my head off, if you like; but don't hang me. I'm innocent, I'm innocent!"

Calcraft at length got the rope round his neck, but by some means or other the culprit, after the drop had fallen, got hold of the halter with his hands, and, raising himself up, for some time prevented his strangulation.

Calcraft, however, and some of the warders got old of his legs, and then hung on him till life was extinct.

The indignation of the populace was very great, and there was another general cry-out for the dismissal of Calcraft, and the abolition of the hangman's office.

There were many similar cases of hard struggles in which the culprit fought hard with death and the hangman, but these two will suffice as illustrations of the shocking sights which oftentimes used to be witnessed at execution scenes.

DECLINE OF CALCRAFT'S POPULARITY.

From this time Calcraft's popularity as a skilful hangman began to decline, and his want of strength and nerve was very often commented on.

The advocates of the abolition of capital punishment were loud in their denunciations, and a great many of the mishaps, which arose really from the terror or obstinacy of the culprits, were put down to Calcraft's bungling.

We have not space to go into the details of all the terrible crimes perpetrated by the notorious criminals Calcraft executed in his long career of office.

We must pass over hundreds of them, but among some of the other notorious heartless monsters he put out of existence were William Dove, who, coming under the baneful influence of the notorious Leeds wizard, sold his soul to the devil, and who was afterwards executed at York, in 1856, for the murder of his wife.

Then there was Catherine Wilson, one of the most wicked hypocrites and cruel poisoners that ever disgraced humanity, whom he hung at Newgate in 1862.

Another was Franz Müller, a German, whom he executed at Newgate on November 14th, 1864, for the murder of Mr. Briggs in a railway carriage.

His escape to America, and capture after an exciting chase by the late Chief-Inspector Clarke of Scotland-yard will ever be remembered as one of the most exciting pursuits and trials on record.

Among some of the other classes of criminals were pirates and scuttlers of ships.

Of the most notorious of these were five of the "Flowery Land" pirates, whom he executed all together at Newgate in November, 1864, for the murder of the captain, the mate, the steward, his brother, and several others.

Another was Walter Miller, for the murder at Chelsea of the Rev. Elias Huelin and his aged housekeeper, Mrs. Ann Bass. He was executed at Newgate on the 1st of August, 1870.

After that he executed that ferocious monster, John Owen, for the murder of the Marshall family, seven in number.

The murder of these unfortunate people took place at their house near Uxbridge.

The sight was truly terrible and the circumstances appalling.

This brutal criminal was executed by Calcraft at Aylesbury, on August 8th, 1870.

Another was Margaret Walters, the notorious baby-farmer, of Camberwell, who cruelly murdered a large number of innocent babes at her house by systematic starvation and neglect.

There was also Michael Campbell for the murder of Mr. Galloway at Stratford, whom Calcraft executed at Chelmsford, on the 24th of April, 1871.

The last criminal that he executed was John Godwin, whom he hung at Newgate on the 25th of May, 1874.

Calcraft then resigned, after having held office exactly forty-five years.

He was then succeeded by Marwood, who, having performed several executions, hung his first victim at

Newgate—namely, the woman, Frances Stewart—on the 29th of June, 1874.

We have now given specimens of mostly all kinds of murderers, and we shall bring the work to a close by a brief review of

EXECUTIONERS SINCE THE SIXTEENTH CENTURY.

Formerly, when hanging was the punishment for nearly every offence, almost every county had its own hangman—known as the common hangman.

The chief executioner of England, however, was the headsman of the Tower, who was chiefly employed in the work of beheading for high treason.

In the case of Frost, Williams, and Jones, Calcraft, as the common executioner of England, would probably have been called upon to use the axe, had not the sentence been commuted. Though there was a headsman of the Tower then living, he probably would not have been called upon to perform any duty of that kind beyond the Tower precincts.

The last headsman of the Tower died in 1861, and as it had for some time been a sinecure, the office has not since been filled up.

The characters of the London executioners have been very various, but the work they were called upon to perform was such, no doubt, as tended to deaden their sense of feeling.

Gregory Brandon, the London executioner in the time of James I., aimed at dignity in his office, and procured an armorial coat of arms from the College of Heralds.

Some time after Brandon Mr. John Ketch filled the office of executioner, and as he was nicknamed Jack Ketch, the name of Jack Ketch was applied to nearly all the hangmen afterwards.

Some of the London hangmen, as well as some of the provincial executioners, have been scoundrels of the worst type,

John Price, one of the former London executioners, was hung on a gallows erected in Bunhill-fields, for rape, robbery, and murder of an old woman, who near to Bunhill-fields used to keep a small stall.

This man was actually arrested for the murder as he was accompanying a criminal for execution at Tyburn.

On the 24th of May, 1736, another of the London executioners was arrested for picking the pocket of a woman after hanging five felons at Tyburn.

In 1682 we find that Alexander Cockburn, the hangman of Edinburgh, was executed for the murder of a mendicant friar. In the eighteenth century the executioner of Edinburgh was John Dalgleish, who acted at the execution of Wilson, the smuggler in 1736.

This was also the same man who officiated at the execution of the celebrated Maggie Dickson, a woman condemned in 1738 for infanticide, but who came to life again, after enduring the sentence of the law, and lived unmolested for years after, as a hawker of salt in the streets of Edinburgh, and was always known afterwards as "Half-hanged Maggie."

John High, or Heisch, afterwards accepted the office of executioner at Edinburgh, in order to escape punishment for stealing poultry; he died in 1817.

The emoluments of the Edinburgh executioners were at one time very curious; they consisted of a double handful of meal from every sack in the market.

These emoluments were afterwards commuted into a regular salary of 12s. per week, besides a free house, and a special fee of £1 11s. 6d. for each execution.

The last of the Edinburgh executioners was John Scott, whom it was customary to confine in gaol for eight days previous to an execution, in order to insure his attendance; in addition, his expenses in the gaol were discharged by the city.

He, however, was set upon and killed, and since his time Edinburgh has had no regular hangman.

After Scott was killed Edinburgh had to depend upon the services of the London executioner, the well-known William Calcraft.

For an execution at Edinburgh Calcraft's fees and expenses amounted to £33 14s., and in addition his assistant received £5 5s. at each execution.

The Glasgow executioners, however, were paid a far less sum.

In 1815 the magistrates of Glasgow entered into an agreement with Thomas Young to act as executioner for the sum of £1 per week, a free house, with coal and candles, a pair of shoes and stockings once a year, and a fee of one guinea at each execution.

At Young's death, in 1837, John Murdock was appointed.

He was paid £1 per month by way of retainer, and £10 for each execution.

At his death Calcraft also became the general executioner for Glasgow, so that we see Calcraft in his younger days had a great portion of the work of the kingdom.

With reference to the Continental executions they form no subject in the present history.

They have been numerous, and the tortures under the Russian and Austrian knout, by which men and women have been flogged to death are truly dreadful to read.

The most noted executioner of Paris was the late M. Sanson, who officiated at the death-scene of Louis XVI. and Marie Antoinette.

He was afterwards assisted by his son, the late Henri Sanson. No regular executioner is employed at the executions in America.

Having now so far reviewed Calcraft's career we may state that, when he retired in 1874, he was just seventy-four years of age.

Up to that advanced age he personally carried out nearly all the executions in the country. Whatever hard things may have been written or said of him, we cannot find much fault with him.

He took office in times of strong excitement and great social danger, when knaves and murderers abounded and, owing to the previous scandalous neglect of social legislation, there was very little protection for either property or life.

Work, too, was scarce. Trade was in a depressed state, the workhouses were filled to overflowing, and, as we have shown, the children of the poor were sold into a servitude worse than Turkish or African slavery, where, in thousands of instances, they wore taken, for the sake of the £5 parish premium, to be literally starved and beaten to death.

In addition there was gross immorality, and a gigantic organised system of international procuration of young females for prostitution. There were murders by wholesale for various purposes.

Some to make money, by selling the bodies for dissection, others to gain insurance money, wholesale poisonings for the sake of obtaining property, and other murders for a great variety of other reasons.

It is a long black list, which shows how desperately cruel and insensible to the feelings of others some men and women can be.

The punishment, according to the law of the land, is death for such terrible crimes, and as long as it is the law some one must carry it out.

Whatever may be the feelings of some persons who

advocate the abolition of capital punishment, there are others who believe that the punishment of death is merited and deterrent, and that such brutal monsters we sometimes read of as the perpetrators of such crimes are not fit to live.

We have, in the course of a long experience, seen whole families stricken down in grief, and some die of broken a heart, mourning for the loss of loved ones cut down in the bloom of life by the ruthless murderer's hand.

We have seen many of these terrible criminals overtaken by the officers of justice, and then, when sentenced to a righteous doom, whine like cowards that their lives may be spared, and beg for that mercy which to their helpless victims they never showed.

But one of the most unaccountable anomalies in respectable society is to see the number of friends these monsters have.

Why, every time one is condemned a host of crotchety people come to the front, and cry aloud that a national murder is about to be perpetrated, and a gross injustice done.

They are silent while the seducer traps unsuspecting girls, and, after robbing them of their honour, hacks them down in the bloom of life.

The grief of loving fathers, or the anguish of affectionate and bereaved mothers, who mourn the loss of their children through murder, is nothing to them. They are mute then over such crimes as these.

They do not lift their voices against the wholsale farming and murder of innocent helpless babes. No! All these social curses may go on unrebuked by them, but only let a murderer be condemned, and then see how they will come to the front, and what a noise they will make!

Women even may be cruelly tortured to death by slow starvation, but though the poor victims or their friends have no sympathy from them, they are loud in their denunciations against the punishment of the offenders, and to the world would even proclaim them as injured innocents.

They will even suggest that murder by slow starvation is only death by meningitis, and they will rake the vocabulary of the English language to find a harmless term for murder wherewith to bamboozle and puzzle a jury.

Why even some persons are not satisfied when the lives of some culprits are spared; they even clamour for their absolute freedom.

There is no knowing the extent of the vagaries into which the idiosyncrasies of some people will lead them.

Well, only let us suppose that these people could have their way, and that they could re-introduce into society all the murderers of the past, what excellent company we should have!

Fortunately they cannot do so. In most instances they have suffered the penalty of their fearful crimes, and in executing them Calcraft only carried out the law, which is administered in most instances by painstaking and righteous judges, who, in the performance of their duty, award, in strict justice, that law which is believed to be for the welfare and protection of the community at large.

In the carrying out of these painful sentences of death we believe that Calcraft was not the brutal hardened man he has sometimes been represented to be. He was doubtless one of the best of his class.

He is spoken of as having been a good husband, a kind father, and a quiet respectable neighbour.

He deeply lamented the decease of his wife, which took place nine years before his death.

After that he lost his granddaughter, the offspring of his own daughter, of whom he was exceedingly fond.

Her death in early womanhood was a great blow to him, from which he never recovered.

His spirits drooped, and about a year before his death he went to Margate for the benefit of his health.

Here he met an old friend from Birmingham, who induced him to have his photograph taken, who also procured a copy for us.

We believe it is the only portrait of him, but having obtained it we are enabled to present our readers with a very faithful likeness of one of the most celebrated executioners of England.

CALCRAFT'S DEATH.

He died peacefully at his residence in Poole-street, Hoxton, on Saturday, the 13th of December, 1879, in the eightieth year of his age, having resided in the same house over twenty-five years.

He used to be a regular attendant at the Church of England, and prior to his death he was constantly visited by the clergyman of Hoxton Church.

He was buried at Abney Park Cemetery, and leaves behind him one daughter and two sons.

Calcraft was never known to have committed any crime, and he left the world respected by all his personal friends.

Having now brought his life to a close, we trust that the perusal of the fate of so many criminals will tend to deter others from the commission of such crimes.

Having read the reports of all the great cases in his eventful career, we have this fact forced upon our minds, that there is no rest for a man after the sin of murder.

The testimony of many murderers is that the remembrance of their guilt continually haunted them.

In addition to the crime of depriving a fellow-creature of life there is also to be remembered the suffering that is caused to bereaved friends.

The great lesson, then, to be learnt is, "Do no murder;" and never raise the hand in passion lest murder should unintentionally ensue.

THE END.